Honor Among Enemies

BAEN BOOKS by DAVID WEBER

Honor Harrington:
On Basilisk Station
The Honor of the Queen
The Short Victorious War
Field of Dishonor
Flag in Exile
Honor Among Enemies

Mutineers' Moon
The Armageddon Inheritance
Heirs of Empire

Path of the Fury

Oath of Swords

with Steve White:
Insurrection
Crusade

DAVID WEBER

Honor Among Enemies

HONOR AMONG ENEMIES

Copyright © 1996 by David M. Weber

A Baen Books Original

Baen Publishing Enterprises
P.O. Box 1403
Riverdale, NY 10471

ISBN: 0-671-87723-2

Cover art and illustrations by David Mattingly

First printing, June 1996

Distributed by Simon & Schuster
1230 Avenue of the Americas
New York, NY 10020

Library of Congress Cataloging-in-Publication Data

Weber, David, 1952—
      Honor among enemies / by David Weber
          p.   cm.
      "Honor Harrington"
      "A Baen Books Original"
      ISBN 0-671-87723-2 (HC)
      I. Title
    PS3573.E217F57   1996
    813'.54—dc20   96-11391
                                                               CIP

Typeset by Windhaven Press: Editorial Services, Auburn, NH
Printed in the United States of America

FOR BOMBUR
If cats had hands, he would have been Nimitz.

SILESIAN CONFEDERACY

Willis

Hendrikson

Jarmon

Sarah

Carlton

Terrance

Tumult

Brinkman

Breslau   Hume

Silesia

Gosset

Telmach

Tyler's Star

Hillman

Libau

Walther

Arendscheldt

Posnan

Sigma

Zoraster

Lutrell

Sachsen

Schiller   Sharon's Star

Marsh

Trellis   Magyar   Creswell   Hera

Saginaw

Slocum

Psyche

15 LY

• PROLOGUE

"Got a problem here, Skipper."

"What is it, Chris?" Captain Harold Sukowski, master of the Hauptman Lines freighter *Bonaventure*, looked up quickly at his executive officer's taut announcement, for "problems" had a way of turning deadly with very little warning in the Silesian Confederacy. That had always been true, but the situation had become even more dangerous in the past year, and he felt the rest of *Bonaventure*'s bridge watch freeze about him even as his own heart began to pump hard and fast. To have come so close to their destination without problems only made the sudden, adrenaline-bitter tension worse, for *Bonaventure* had completed her translation back into n-space barely ten minutes before, and the Telmach System's G0 primary lay just twenty-two light-minutes ahead. But that was also twenty-two minutes's *com* time, and the Silesian Navy's Telmach detachment was a joke. For that matter, the Confederacy's entire *navy* was a joke, and even if Sukowski could have contacted the detachment commander in time, it was virtually certain there was nothing in position to intervene.

"We've got somebody coming up fast from astern, Skip." Commander Hurlman never looked up from her display. "Looks fairly small—maybe seventy, eighty k-tons—but whoever it is has a military-grade compensator. He's eighteen-point-three light-seconds back, but he's got an overtake of two thousand KPS and he's pulling about five-ten gees."

The captain nodded, and his expression was grim.

Harold Sukowski had earned his master's certificate over thirty T-years before. He was also a commander in the Royal Manticoran Naval Reserve, and he didn't need Chris to paint him any pictures. At six million tons and with commercial-grade impellers and inertial compensator, *Bonaventure* was a sitting duck for any warship. Her maximum possible acceleration was scarcely 201 g, and her commercial particle screening held her max velocity to only .7 c. If her pursuer had military-grade particle shields to match the rest of his drive, he could not only out-accelerate her but pull a sustained velocity of *eighty* percent light-speed.

Which meant, of course, that there was no possible way for Sukowski to outrun him.

"How long to overhaul?" he asked.

"I make it roughly twenty-two and a half minutes to a zero-range intercept even if we go to max accel," Hurlman said flatly. "We'll be up to roughly twelve thousand seven hundred KPS, but *he'll* be hitting almost nineteen thousand. Whoever he is, we aren't going to shake him."

Sukowski gave a choppy nod. Chris Hurlman was less than half his age, but like him, she was one of *Bonaventure*'s keel plate owners. She'd been the freighter's original fourth officer, and while he would never have admitted it, Sukowski and his wife regarded her very much as one of the daughters they'd never had. Deep inside he'd always hoped she and his second oldest son would someday settle down together, but however young she might be for her rank, she was very good at her job, and her appraisal of the situation matched his own perfectly.

Of course, her estimate was for a least-time intercept, and the bogey wouldn't go for that. He was almost certain to decelerate in order to kill his overtake velocity once he was certain he had *Bonaventure* nailed, but that wouldn't make any difference to the fate of Sukowski's ship. All it would do was delay the inevitable . . . slightly.

He tried desperately to think of a way—*any* way—to

save his ship, but there wasn't one. On the face of things, the possibility of piracy as a paying occupation shouldn't have existed. Even the hugest freighter was less than a dust mote on the scale of interstellar space, but like the ancient ocean-borne vessels of Old Earth, the ships which plied the stars followed predictable routes. They had to, for the grav waves which twisted through hyper space dictated those routes much as Old Terra's prevailing winds had dictated the square-riggers'. No pirate could predict exactly where any given starship would make her alpha translation back into n-space, but he knew the general volume in which *all* ships would do so. If he lurked long enough, some poor, unlucky son-of-a-bitch would sail right into his clutches, and this time it was Sukowski's turn.

The captain swore with silent venom. If only the Silesian Navy was worth a fart in a vac suit, it wouldn't matter. Two or three cruisers—hell, even a single destroyer!—deployed to cover the same volume would cause any pirate to seek safer pastures. But the Silesian Confederacy was more of a perpetually ongoing meltdown than a star nation. The feeble central government—such as it was—was forever plagued by breakaway secessionist movements. What ships it had were always desperately needed somewhere, and the raiders who infested its space always knew where that somewhere was and took themselves somewhere *else*. That had always been true; what had changed was that the Royal Manticoran Navy units which had traditionally protected the Star Kingdom's commerce in Silesia had been withdrawn for Manticore's war against the People's Republic of Haven, and there was no one at all to whom Harold Sukowski could turn for help.

"Challenge him, Jack," he said. "Demand his identity and intentions."

"Yes, Sir." His com officer keyed his mike and spoke clearly. "Unknown starship, this is the Manticoran merchant vessel *Bonaventure*. State your identity and intentions." Forty endless seconds ticked past while the red blip in Hurlman's display closed with ever increasing speed, and the com officer shrugged. "No reply, Skipper."

"I didn't really expect one," Sukowski sighed. He sat staring at the star he'd almost reached for another moment, then shrugged. "All right, people. You know the drill. Genda," he looked at his chief engineer, "slave your department to my console before you clear out. Chris, you're in charge of the bail out. I want a headcount, and I want it confirmed before you undock."

"But, Skip—" Hurlman began, and Sukowski shook his head fiercely.

"I said you know the drill! Now get the hell out of here while we're still beyond effective missile range!"

Hurlman hesitated, face torn with indecision. She'd served with Sukowski for over eight T-years, almost a quarter of her entire life. *Bonaventure* was the only true home she'd known in all those years, and abandoning her skipper and her ship went hard with her. Sukowski knew that, and because he did, he gave her a cold, savage glare.

"The people are *your* job now, so get your ass in gear, goddamn it!"

Still Hurlman hesitated, and then she gave a choppy nod and whirled for the bridge lift.

"You heard the Skipper!" Her voice was harsh, harrowed by grief and guilt. "*Move*, damn it!"

Sukowski watched them go, then turned back to his console. Lieutenant Kuriko had already slaved Engineering to his panel; now Sukowski punched in more commands, taking over the helm, as well. He felt the sick, hollow emptiness in his belly and longed desperately to follow Chris and the others. But *Bonaventure* was his ship, his responsibility, and so was her cargo. The chance that he could do anything to preserve that cargo was vanishingly small, but it did exist, especially if the raider was a privateer and not an outright pirate. And if there was any chance at all, it was Harold Sukowski's job to do what he could. That was one of the duties which came with his rank, and—

A tone beeped, and he pressed a com key.

"Talk to me," he said shortly.

"Headcount confirmed, Skip," Hurlman's voice replied. "I've got 'em all in Bay Seven."

"Then get them out of here, Chris . . . and good luck." Sukowski's voice was much softer.

"Aye, aye, Skipper." He heard the hesitation in her voice, tasted her need to say something more, but there was nothing she *could* say, and the circuit clicked as she cut the link.

Sukowski watched his display and let a long sigh of relief ooze from his lungs as a small, green dot appeared upon it. The shuttle was one of *Bonaventure's* big, primary cargo haulers, with a drive as powerful as most light attack craft's. Unlike a LAC, it was totally unarmed, but it shot away at over four hundred gravities, slower than its pursuer but twice as fast as its mother ship. The pirates must be pissed to see the crew they'd hoped to make man their prize for them escaping, but *Bonaventure* and her shuttle were still outside their powered missile envelope, and there was no way they'd go chasing after a mere shuttle with a six-million-ton freighter to snap up. Besides, Sukowski thought bitterly, they'd no doubt planned for exactly this contingency. They'd have their own engineers aboard to manage *Bonaventure's* systems.

He let himself lean back in the comfortable command chair which would be his for another half hour or so and hoped these people were ready to believe Mr. Hauptman's offer to ransom any of his people who fell into pirates' hands. It wasn't much, and Sukowski knew Hauptman had hated making it, but it was all he could do with the Navy withdrawn from Silesian space. And however arrogant and hard the old bastard was, Sukowski knew better than most that Klaus Hauptman stood by the people in his employ. It was a Hauptman tradition to—

Sukowski's thoughts broke off with a snap as the lift

doors hissed open. He whirled his command chair in shock, and then his eyes lit with fury as Chris Hurlman stepped onto the bridge.

"What the *hell* are *you* doing here?" he barked. "I gave you an order, Hurlman!"

"Oh, screw your orders!" She matched him glare for glare, then stalked across the bridge to her own station. "This isn't the frigging Navy, and you aren't Edward Saganami!"

"I'm still master of this ship, damn it, and I want you the hell off her right now!"

"Well isn't that just too bad," Hurlman said much more mildly as she sank back into her own bridge chair and adjusted the com set over her black hair. "The only problem with what you *want*, Skipper, is that I fight lots dirtier than you. You try to throw me off *my* ship, and it might just happen that *you* get tossed off instead."

"And what about our people?" Sukowski countered. "You were in charge of them, and you're responsible for them."

"Genda and I flipped a coin, and he lost." Hurlman shrugged. "Don't worry. He'll get them to Telmach in one piece."

"Damn it, Chris, I don't *want* you here," Sukowski's voice was much softer. "There's no *need* for you to risk getting yourself killed—or worse."

Hurlman looked down at her console for a moment, then turned to meet his eyes squarely.

"There's just as much need for me to risk it as there is for you, Skip," she said quietly, "and I will be damned to Hell before I let you face these bastards alone. Besides," she smiled with true affection, "an old fart like you needs someone younger and nastier to look out for him. Jane would kick my butt if I went off and left you out here on your own."

Sukowski opened his mouth, then closed it. A fist of anguish seemed to be locked about his heart, but he recognized the total intransigence behind that smile. She wouldn't go, and she was right; she *was* a dirtier fighter

than he was. A part of him was desperately glad to see her, to know he
wouldn't face whatever happened alone,
but it was a selfish part he loathed. He
wanted to argue, plead—*beg*, if that was what it took—
yet he knew she wouldn't go without him, and he couldn't
turn his own back on a lifetime of responsibility and
obligation.

"All right, goddamn it," he muttered instead. "You're
an idiot and a mutineer, and if we get out of this alive
I'll see to it you never find a billet again. But if you're
determined to defy your lawful superior, I don't see how
I can stop you."

"Now you're being reasonable," Hurlman said almost
cheerfully. She studied her display a moment longer, then
rose and crossed to the coffee dispenser against the after
bulkhead. She poured herself a cup and dropped in her
normal two sugars, then raised an eyebrow at the man
whose orders she'd just ignored.

"Like a cup, Skip?" she asked gently.

• CHAPTER ONE

"Mr. Hauptman, Sir Thomas."

Sir Thomas Caparelli, First Space Lord of the Royal Manticoran Navy, rose with his very best effort at a smile of welcome as his yeoman ushered his guest into his huge office. He suspected it wasn't very convincing, but, then, Klaus Hauptman wasn't one of his favorite people.

"Sir Thomas." The dark-haired man with the dramatically white sideburns and bulldog jaw gave him a curt nod. He wasn't being especially rude; that was how he greeted almost everyone, and he held out his hand as if to soften his brusqueness. "Thank you for seeing me." He did not add "at last," but Sir Thomas heard it anyway and felt his smile become just a bit more fixed.

"Please have a seat." The burly admiral in whom one could still see the bruising soccer player who'd led the Academy to three system championships waved his guest politely into the comfortable chair facing his desk, then sat himself and nodded dismissal to the yeoman.

"Thank you," Hauptman repeated. He sat in the indicated chair—like, Caparelli thought, an emperor taking his throne—and cleared his throat. "I know you have many charges on your time, Sir Thomas, so I'll come straight to the point. And the *point* is that conditions in the Confederacy are becoming intolerable."

"I realize it's a bad situation, Mr. Hauptman," Caparelli began, "but the war front is—"

"Excuse me, Sir Thomas," Hauptman interrupted, "but I understand the situation at the front. Indeed, Admiral Cortez and Admiral Givens have—as I'm certain you

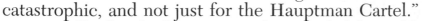

instructed them to—explained it to me at considerable length. I realize you and the Navy are under tremendous pressure, but losses in Silesia are becoming catastrophic, and not just for the Hauptman Cartel."

Caparelli clenched his jaw and reminded himself to move carefully. Klaus Hauptman was arrogant, opinionated, and ruthless . . . and the wealthiest single individual in the entire Star Kingdom of Manticore. Which was saying quite a bit. Despite its limitation to a single star system, the Star Kingdom was the third wealthiest star nation in a five-hundred-light-year sphere in absolute terms. In per capita terms, not even the Solarian League matched Manticore. A great deal of that was fortuitous, the result of the Manticore Worm Hole Junction which made the Manticore Binary System the crossroads of eighty percent of the long-haul commerce of its sector. But almost as much of its wealth stemmed from what the Star Kingdom had done with the opportunity that presented, for generations of monarchs and parliaments had reinvested the Junction's wealth with care. Outside the Solarian League, no one in the known galaxy could match the Manticoran tech base or output per man-hour, and Manticore's universities challenged those of Old Earth herself. And, Caparelli admitted, Klaus Hauptman and his father and grandfather had had a great deal to do with building the infrastructure which made that possible.

Unfortunately, Hauptman knew it, and he sometimes—often, in Caparelli's view—acted as if the Star Kingdom belonged to him as a consequence.

"Mr. Hauptman," the admiral said after a moment, "I'm very sorry about the losses you and the other cartels are suffering. But your request, however reasonable it may seem, is simply impossible to grant at this time."

"With all due respect, Sir Thomas, the Navy had better *make* it possible." Hauptman's flat tone was just short of insulting, but he stopped himself, then drew a deep breath. "Excuse me," he said in the voice of one clearly unaccustomed to apologizing. "That was rude and confrontational. Nonetheless, there's also a kernel of truth in it. The war effort depends upon the strength of our economy. The shipping duties, transfer fees, and inventory taxes my colleagues and I pay are already three times what they were at the start of the war, and—" Caparelli opened his mouth, but Hauptman held up a hand. "Please. I'm not complaining about duties and taxes. We're at war with the second largest empire in known space, and *someone* has to pay the freight. My colleagues and I realize that. But *you* must realize that if losses continue climbing, we'll have no choice but to cut back or even entirely eliminate our shipping to Silesia. I leave it to you to estimate what that will mean for the Star Kingdom's revenues and war effort."

Caparelli's eyes narrowed, and Hauptman shook his head.

"That's not a threat; it's simply a fact of life. Insurance rates have already reached an all-time high, and they're still climbing; if they rise another twenty percent, we'll lose money on cargos which *reach* their destinations. And in addition to our financial losses, there's also the loss of life involved. Our people—*my* people, people who've worked for me for decades—are being *killed*, Sir Thomas."

Caparelli sat back with an unwilling sense of agreement, for Hauptman was right. The Confederacy's weak central government had always made it a risky place, but its worlds were huge markets for the Star Kingdom's industrial products, machinery, and civilian technology transfers, not to mention an important source of raw materials. And however much Caparelli might personally dislike Hauptman, the magnate had every right to demand the Navy's help. It was, after all, one of the Navy's primary missions to protect Manticoran commerce and citizens, and prior to the present war, the Royal Manticoran Navy had done just that in Silesia.

Unfortunately, it had required a major fleet presence. Not of battle squadrons—using ships of the wall against pirates would have been like swatting flies with a

sledgehammer—but of light combatants. And the critical needs of the RMN's war against the People's Republic of Haven had drawn those lighter units off. They were desperately needed to screen the heavy squadrons and for the countless patrols and scouting and convoy escorts the Fleet required for its very survival. There were never enough cruisers and destroyers to go around, and the overriding need for capital ships diverted yard space from building them in the necessary numbers.

The admiral sighed and rubbed his forehead. He wasn't the RMN's most brilliant flag officer. He knew his strengths—courage, integrity, and enough bullheaded stubbornness for any three people—but he also admitted his weaknesses. Officers like the Earl of White Haven or Lady Sonja Hemphill always made him uncomfortable, for he knew as well as they that they were his intellectual superiors. And White Haven, Caparelli admitted, had the infuriating gall to be not only a better strategist, but a better tactician, as well. Nonetheless, it was Sir Thomas Caparelli who'd been named First Space Lord just in time for the war to explode in his face. That made it his job to win the thing, and he was determined to do just that. Yet it was *also* his job to protect Manticoran civilians in the course of their legitimate commercial activities, and he was desperately conscious of how thin his Navy was stretched.

"I understand your concerns," he said finally, "and I can't disagree with anything you've said. The problem is that we're stretched right to the very limit. I can't—not won't, but literally *cannot*—withdraw additional warships from the front to reinforce our convoy escorts in Silesia."

"Well we have to do *something*." Hauptman spoke quietly, and Caparelli sensed the arrogant magnate's very real effort to match his own reasonable tone. "The convoy system helps during transits between sectors, of course. We haven't lost a single ship that was under escort, and, believe me, my colleagues and I all appreciate that. But the raiders realize as well as we do that they can't attack the convoys. They also know simple astrographics require us to route over two-thirds of our vessels independently after they reach their destination sectors . . . and that the available escorts simply can't cover us when we do."

Caparelli nodded somberly. No one was losing any ships in the convoys covering transit between Silesia's nodal sector administration centers, but the pirates more than made up for that by snapping up merchantmen after they had to *leave* the convoys to proceed to the individual worlds of the Confederacy.

"I'm not certain how much more we can do, Sir," the admiral said after a long, silent moment. "Admiral White Haven's returning to Manticore sometime next week. I'll confer with him then, see if there's *any* way we can reorganize and pry a few more escorts loose, but, frankly, until we can somehow take Trevor's Star, I'm not optimistic. In the meantime, I'll put my staff to work on an immediate study of anything—and I do mean *anything*, Mr. Hauptman—we can do to ease the situation. I assure you that this matter has the second highest priority, after Trevor's Star itself. I'll do everything possible to reduce your losses. You have my personal word on that."

Hauptman sat back in his chair, studying the admiral's face, then grunted. The sound was weary, irate, and just a little desperate, but he nodded grudgingly.

"I can ask no more than that, Sir Thomas," he said heavily. "I won't insult you by trying to insist on miracles, but the situation is very, very grave. I'm not certain we have another month . . . but I *am* certain we have no more than four, five at the most, before the cartels will be forced to suspend operations in Silesia."

"I understand," Caparelli repeated, rising to extend his hand. "I'll do what I can—and as quickly as I can—and I promise I'll personally brief you on the situation as soon as I've had a chance to confer with Admiral White Haven. With your permission, I'll have my yeoman set up another meeting with you for that purpose. Perhaps we can think of something at that time. Until then, please stay in touch.

You and your colleagues may actually have a better feel for the situation than we do at the Admiralty, and any input you can offer my analysts and planning people will be greatly appreciated."

"Very well," Hauptman sighed, standing in turn, and gripped the admiral's hand, then surprised Caparelli with a wry smile. "I realize I'm not the easiest man in the universe to get along with, Sir Thomas. I'm trying very hard not to be the proverbial bull in the china shop, and I genuinely appreciate both the difficulties you face and the efforts you're making on our behalf. I only hope that there's an answer somewhere."

"So do I, Mr. Hauptman," Caparelli said quietly, escorting his guest to the door. "So do I."

Admiral of the Green Hamish Alexander, Thirteenth Earl of White Haven, wondered if he looked as weary as he felt. The earl was ninety T-years old, though in a pre-prolong society he would have been taken for no more than a very well-preserved forty, and even that would have been only because of the white stranded through his black hair. But there were new lines around his ice-blue eyes, and he was only too well aware of his own fatigue.

He watched space's ebon black give way to deep indigo beyond the view port as his pinnace dropped towards the city of Landing and felt that weariness aching in his bones. The Star Kingdom—or, at least, the realistic part of it—had dreaded the inevitable war with the People's Republic for over fifty T-years, and the Navy (and Hamish Alexander) had spent those years preparing for it. Now that war was almost three years old . . . and proving just as brutal as he'd feared.

It wasn't that the Peeps were that good; it was just that they were so damned *big*. Despite the internal wounds the People's Republic had inflicted upon itself since Hereditary President Harris' assassination, despite its ramshackle economy and the pogroms which had cost the People's Navy its most experienced officers, despite even the indolence of the Republic's Dolists, it remained a juggernaut. Had its industrial plant been even half as efficient as the Star Kingdom's, the situation would have been hopeless. As it was, a combination of skill, determination, and more luck than any competent strategist would dare count on had allowed the RMN to hold its own so far.

But holding its own wasn't enough.

White Haven sighed and massaged his aching eyes. He hated leaving the front, but at least he'd been able to leave Admiral Theodosia Kuzak in command. He could count on Theodosia to hold things together in his absence. White Haven snorted at the thought. Hell, maybe she could actually take Trevor's Star. God knew *he* hadn't had much success in that department!

He lowered his hand from his eyes and gazed back out the view port while he took himself to task for that last thought. The truth was that he'd had a very "good" war to date. In the first year of operations, his Sixth Fleet had cut deep into the Republic, inflicting what would have been fatal losses for any smaller navy along the way. He and his fellow admirals had actually managed to equalize the daunting odds they'd faced at the start of the war, and taken no less than twenty-four star systems. But the second and third years had been different. The Peeps were back on balance, and Rob Pierre's Committee of Public Safety had initiated a reign of terror guaranteed to stiffen the spine of any Peep admiral. And if the destruction of the Legislaturalist dynasties which had ruled the old People's Republic had cost the PN its most experienced admirals, it had also destroyed the patronage system which had kept other officers from rising to the seniority their capabilities deserved. Now that the Legislaturalists were out of the way, some of those new admirals were proving very tough customers. Like Admiral Esther McQueen, the senior Peep officer at Trevor's Star.

White Haven grimaced at the view port. According to

ONI, the people's commissioners the Committee of Public Safety had appointed to keep the People's Navy in line were the ones who really called the shots. If that was so, if political commissars truly were degrading the performance of officers like McQueen, White Haven could only be grateful. He'd begun getting a feel for the woman over the last few months, and he suspected he was a better strategist than she. But his edge, if in fact he had one, was far thinner than he would have liked, and she had ice water in her veins. She understood the strengths and weaknesses of her forces, knew her technology was more primitive and her officer corps less experienced, but she also knew sufficient numbers and an unflinching refusal to be bullied into mistakes could offset that. When one added the way Manticore's need to take Trevor's Star simplified the strategic equation for her, she was giving as good as she got. Losses had been very nearly even since she took over, and Manticore simply couldn't afford that. Not in a war that looked like it might well last for decades. And not, White Haven admitted, when every month increased the threat that the Republic would begin to figure out how to redress its technological and industrial disadvantages. If the Peeps ever reached a point where they could face the RMN from a position of qualitative equality, as well as quantitative superiority, the consequences would be disastrous.

He heard the pinnace's air-breathing turbines whine as it began its final approach to Landing and shook himself. Between them, he and Kuzak had finally evolved a plan which might—*might*—let them take Trevor's Star, and that was something they had to do. The system contained the only terminus of the Manticore Worm Hole Junction which Manticore did not already control, which made it a deadly potential threat to the Star Kingdom. But it was a two-edged sword for the Peeps. Its capture would not only eliminate the threat of direct invasion but give the RMN a secure bridgehead deep inside the

Republic. Ships—warships, as well as supply vessels—could move between the RMN's most powerful fleet bases and the battle front virtually instantaneously, with no threat of interception. Capture of Trevor's Star—*if* it was ever captured—would both ease the Navy's logistics enormously and open a whole new range of strategic options, which made it the most valuable prize short of the Haven System itself. But even if White Haven's plan worked, it would take at least four more months, minimum, and from Caparelli's dispatches, maintaining the momentum that long wasn't going to be easy.

"So that's the situation," White Haven said quietly. "Theodosia and I think we can do it, but the preliminary operations are going to take time."

"Um." Admiral Caparelli nodded slowly, eyes still on the holographic star chart above his desk. White Haven's plan was no daring lightning stroke—except, perhaps, in its final stage—but the last ten months had been ample proof a lightning stroke wasn't going to work. In essence, the earl proposed to abandon the messy, inconclusive fighting of a direct approach and work around the perimeter of Trevor's Star. His plan called for crushing the systems which supported it one by one, simultaneously isolating his true objective and positioning himself to launch converging attacks upon it, and then bringing up Home Fleet itself in support. That part of the proposed operation *was* more than a bit daring—and risky. Three and a half full battle squadrons of Sir James Webster's Home Fleet could reach Trevor's Star from Manticore almost instantly via the Junction, despite the huge distance between the two systems. But the passage of that much tonnage would destabilize the Junction for over seventeen hours. If Home Fleet launched an attack and failed to achieve rapid and complete victory, half its total superdreadnought strength would be trapped, unable to retreat the way it had come.

The First Space Lord rubbed his lip and frowned. If

the plan worked, it would be decisive; if it failed, Home Fleet—which was also the RMN's primary strategic reserve— would be crippled in an afternoon. In an odd way, that potential for disaster was one of the things which might make it work. No sane admiral would try it unless he was absolutely certain of success or had no other choice, so it was unlikely the Peeps would expect it. Oh, no doubt they'd drawn up contingency plans against such an attempt, but Caparelli had to agree with White Haven and Kuzak. Contingency plans or no, the PN would never really *expect* an attack like this, especially if White Haven's preparatory operations were such as to give him a realistic chance of victory without using the Junction. If he could draw their covering fleet out of position, convince them *Sixth* Fleet was the real threat, before he tried it . . .

"Coordination," Caparelli murmured. "That's the real problem. How do we coordinate an operation like this over such distances?"

"Absolutely," White Haven agreed. "Theodosia and I have wracked our brains—and our staffs' brains—over that one, and we've been able to come up with only one possibility. We'll keep you as closely informed as we can by dispatch boat, but the transit delay's going to make actual coordination impossible. For it to work at all, we have to agree ahead of time when we'll make our move, and then Home Fleet is going to have to send a scout through to see if we've pulled it off."

"And if you *haven't* 'pulled it off,'" Caparelli said frostily, "it's going to be a bit rough on whoever we send through from Manticore."

"Agreed." White Haven's voice didn't flinch, but his nod acknowledged Caparelli's point. The mass of a single vessel would destabilize the Junction for mere seconds, and if the Peep defenders had, in fact, been diverted as planned, a scout would be able to transit, make its scans, and turn and run back down the Junction before it could be engaged. But if the Peeps *hadn't* been diverted, Home Fleet would never even know what had killed its scout.

"I agree it's a risk," the earl said. "Unfortunately, I don't see an alternative. And if we're cold about it, risking a single ship is nothing beside the risk of letting operations continue to drag on. If I had to, I'd send an entire squadron through, even knowing I'd lose them all, if it let us pull this off. I don't like it, but compared to what we've already lost—what we're going to go *on* losing if we keep pounding away frontally—I think it's our best option. And if it does work, we'll catch the defenders between two fires, with a real possibility of taking them *all* out. Certainly it's chancy, but the potential prize is enormous."

"Um," Caparelli grunted again, and tipped his chair back while he pondered. It was ironic that White Haven should propose something like this, for it sounded much more like something *Caparelli* would have come up with—if, he conceded, he'd had the nerve to consider it in the first place. White Haven was a master of the indirect approach, with a sense for choosing the right moment to make an unexpected pounce or carve another few squadrons out of an enemy's fleet that amounted to near-genius, and his hatred for "all or nothing" battle plans was legendary. The notion of risking the entire war on the turn of a single card, with all the subtlety of a sledge-hammer, must be anathema to him.

Which, Caparelli admitted, was another reason it might just work. After all, the Peeps had studied the RMN's officer corps as closely as Manticore had studied the PN's. They knew something like this was completely atypical of White Haven's normal thinking, and they also knew it was White Haven who'd shaped the RMN's overall strategy to this point. Given that, they'd almost have to be looking the other way when he launched his sucker punch . . . assuming the timing worked.

"All right, My Lord," the First Lord said finally. "There are still quite a few questions I'll want answered before I commit myself either way, but I'll turn it over to Pat

Givens, the War College, and my staff for evaluation. You're certainly right that we can't go on bleeding ourselves forever, and I don't like how effective McQueen is proving. If we take Trevor's Star away from her, maybe the Committee of Public Safety will shoot her *pour encourager les autres.*"

"Maybe," White Haven agreed with a grimace Caparelli understood only too well. *He* didn't much like the notion that someone was willing to execute good officers who'd done their utmost simply because their best efforts failed to stop the enemy either, but the Star Kingdom was fighting for its life. If the People's Republic was obliging enough to eliminate its best commanders for him, Thomas Caparelli would accept the favor.

"The one thing about your plan which bothers me most—aside, of course," he couldn't quite resist the dig at the earl, "from the possibility of crippling Home Fleet—is the delay. For you to pull this off, we'll actually have to strengthen your light forces, not weaken them, and with the situation in Silesia—" He shrugged, and White Haven nodded in understanding.

"How badly will it really hurt us?" he asked, and Caparelli frowned.

"In absolute terms, we could survive even if we completely halted trade to Silesia," he said. "It wouldn't be pleasant, and Hauptman and the other cartels would scream bloody murder. Worse, they'd be justified. The disruption could literally ruin some of the smaller ones, and it wouldn't do the big fish like Hauptman and Dempsey any good, either. And I'm not sure what the political ramifications might be. I had a long talk with the First Lord yesterday, and she's already catching a lot of flak over this. You know her better than I do, but I got the impression she's under extreme pressure."

White Haven nodded thoughtfully. He *did* know Francine Maurier, Baroness Morncreek and First Lord of the Admiralty, better than Caparelli. And as the Crown minister with overall responsibility for the Navy,

Morncreek was undoubtedly under just as much pressure as Caparelli suggested. Indeed, if she was letting it show, it was probably even worse than Caparelli thought.

"Add the fact that Hauptman's in bed with the Liberals *and* the Conservative Association, not to mention the Progressives, and we've really got a problem," the First Space Lord continued grimly. "If the Opposition decides to make a fight over the Navy's 'disinterest' in his problems, things could get messy. And that doesn't even consider the direct losses in import duties and transfer fees . . . or lives."

"There's another point," White Haven said unwillingly, and Caparelli raised an eyebrow. "It's only a matter of time until someone like McQueen sees the possibilities," the earl explained. "If a bunch of pirates can hurt us this badly, think what would happen if the Peeps sent in a few squadrons of battlecruisers to help out. So far, we've kept them too far off balance to try anything like that, but frankly, they're better able to cut light forces loose, given all those battleships they still have in reserve. And Silesia isn't the only place they could hurt us if they decided to get into commerce warfare in a big way."

White Haven, Caparelli thought sourly, *did* have a way of thinking up unpleasant scenarios.

"But if we can't free up the escorts we need," the First Space Lord began, "then how—"

He paused suddenly, eyes narrowing. White Haven cocked his head, but Caparelli ignored him and tapped a query into his terminal. He studied the data on his display for several seconds, then tugged at an earlobe.

"Q-ships," he said, almost to himself. "By God, maybe *that's* the answer."

"Q-ships?" White Haven repeated. Caparelli didn't seem to hear for a moment, then he shook himself.

"What if we were to send some of the Trojans to Silesia?" he asked, and it was White Haven's turn to frown in thought.

Project Trojan Horse had been Sonja Hemphill's idea,

and that, the earl admitted, tended to prejudice him against it. He and Hemphill were old and bitter philosophical foes, and he distrusted her material-based strategic doctrine. But Trojan Horse hadn't involved any major diversion from the fighting, and it had offered enough possible benefits even if it failed in its main purpose to win his grudging support.

In essence, Hemphill proposed turning some of the RMN's standard *Caravan*-class freighters into armed merchant cruisers. The *Caravans* were big ships, over seven million tons, but they were slow and unarmored, with civilian-grade drives. Under normal circumstances, they'd be helpless against any proper warship, but Hemphill wanted to outfit them with the heaviest possible firepower and seed them into the Fleet Train convoys laboring to keep Sixth Fleet supplied. The idea was for them to look just like any other freighter until some unwary raider got close, at which point they were supposed to blow him out of space.

Personally, White Haven doubted the concept was workable in the long term. The Peeps had used Q-ships of their own to some effect against previous enemies, but the fundamental weakness of the tactic was that it was unlikely to work against a proper navy more than once or twice. Once an enemy figured out you were using them, he'd simply start blowing away anything that *might* be a Q-ship from the maximum possible range. Besides, the Peep Q-ships had been purpose built from the keel out. They'd been fitted with military-grade drives which had made them as fast as any warship their size, and their designs had incorporated internal armor, compartmentalization, and systems redundancy the *Caravans* completely lacked.

Now, however, Caparelli might have a point, because the raiders who plagued Silesian space didn't *have* proper warships . . . and they were no part of any proper navy. Most were independents, disposing of their plunder to "merchants"—fences, really—who bankrolled their operations and asked no embarrassing questions. Their ships tended to be lightly armed, and they normally operated in singletons, certainly not in groups of more than two or three. The normal unrest of the Confederacy, where star systems routinely attempted to secede from the central government, complicated things a bit, since the "liberation governments" were fond of issuing letters of marque and authorizing "privateers" to hit other people's commerce in the name of independence. Some of the privateers were heavily armed for their displacement, and a few were commanded by genuine patriots, willing to work together in small squadrons for their home system's cause. Even they, however, would tend to run from a properly handled Q-ship, and unlike operations against the Peeps, the strategy might become more effective, not less, once word of it got out. Pirates, after all, were in it for the money, and they were unlikely to risk losing the ships which represented their capital or settle for destroying potential prizes from stand-off ranges. Where a Peep commerce raider might be willing to accept the risk of encountering a Q-ship in order to simply *destroy* Manticoran shipping, a pirate would be looking to *capture* his victims and would be unlikely to hazard his ship against a merchant cruiser unless he anticipated a particularly luscious prize.

"It might help," the earl said after considering the notion carefully. "Unless we have an awful lot of them, they won't be able to *destroy* many raiders, of course. I'd have to say the effect would be more cosmetic than real in those terms, but the psychological impact could be worthwhile—both in Silesia and Parliament. But do we have any of them ready to commit? I thought we were still at least several months short of the target date."

"We are," Caparelli agreed. "According to this"—he tapped his terminal—"the first four ships could be ready sometime next month, but most of them are still a minimum of five months from completion. We haven't assigned any crews yet, either, and frankly, our manpower's stretched tight enough to make that a problem, too. But

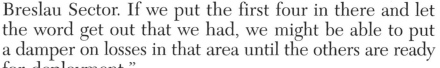

we could at least make a start. And as you say, My Lord, a lot of the benefit will stem from purely psychological factors. The situation's worst in the Breslau Sector. If we put the first four in there and let the word get out that we had, we might be able to put a damper on losses in that area until the others are ready for deployment."

"We might." White Haven rubbed his chin, then shrugged. "It won't be more than a sop—not until the other ships are ready. And whoever you give it to will have a hell of a job on his hands with only four ships. But, as you say, at least we'll be able to tell Hauptman and his cronies we're doing something." *And*, he thought, *doing it without diverting the ships* I *need in the process.*

"True." Caparelli drummed on his desktop for two or three seconds. "It's only a thought at the moment. I'll run it by Pat this afternoon and see what BuPlan has to say about it." He considered a moment longer, then tossed his head. "In the meantime, let's look a bit closer at the nuts and bolts of this plan of yours. You say you'll need another two battle squadrons at Nightingale?" White Haven nodded. "Well, suppose we draw them from—"

• CHAPTER TWO

Soft classical music made a fitting background to the elegantly attired men and women in the huge room. A sumptuous meal lay in ruins behind them, and they clustered in small groups, glasses in hand, while the seaside murmur of their voices competed with the music. It was a scene of relaxed wealth and power, but there was little relaxation in Klaus Hauptman's voice.

The trillionaire stood with a woman who was only marginally his inferior in terms of wealth and power and a man who wasn't even in the running. Not that the Houseman clan was *poor*, but its wealth was "old money," and most of its members disdained anything so crass as actual commerce. Of course, one had to have managers, hired hands to see to the maintenance of one's family fortune, but it was hardly the sort of thing *gentlemen* did. In his own way, Reginald Houseman shared that prejudice against the *nouveau riche*—and by Houseman standards, even the Hauptman fortune was very *nouveau* indeed— but he was widely acknowledged as one of the half-dozen top economists of the Star Kingdom.

He was not, however, so recognized by Klaus Hauptman, who regarded him with virtually unmitigated contempt. Despite Houseman's innumerable academic credentials, Hauptman considered him a dilettante who personified the ancient cliché that "Those who can, do; those who can't, teach," and Houseman's sublime self-importance was immensely irritating to a man who'd proven his own competence in the one way no one could question: by succeeding. Not that Houseman was a *total*

24

idiot. For all his intellectual bigotry, he'd proven a facile and often effective advocate of using private sector incentives to power public economic strategies. Hauptman considered it unfortunate that the man was so firmly wedded to the notion that governments were equipped—as they manifestly were not—to tell private enterprise how to do its job, but even he had to admit Houseman had paid his dues as a policy analyst.

Up until six years before, he'd also been a rising star in the diplomatic service, and he was still called in as an occasional outside consultant. But when Queen Elizabeth III took a personal dislike to a man, only the hardiest politico would propose actually employing him in the Crown's service. Nor had the Houseman family's powerful connections within the Liberal Party been an asset since the war began. The Liberals' longstanding opposition to the Star Kingdom's military expenditures as "alarmist and provocative" had dealt their entire platform a body blow when the People's Republic launched its sneak attack. Worse, the Liberals had joined the Conservative Association and Progressives in opposition to the Cromarty Government following the bungled coup which had destroyed the Republic's old leadership. They'd attempted to block a formal declaration of war in a bid to prevent active operations because they'd believed the regime arising from the chaos of the coup offered an opportunity for a negotiated settlement. Indeed, many of them, including Reginald Houseman, still felt a priceless opportunity had been squandered.

Neither Her Majesty nor the Duke of Cromarty, her Prime Minister, agreed. Nor, for that matter, did the electorate. The Liberals had taken a pounding in the last general election, with crippling consequences in the House of Commons. They remained a force to be reckoned with in the Lords, but even there they'd suffered defections to Cromarty's Centrists. The party faithful regarded those defecting opportunists with all the scorn such ideological traitors merited, but their loss was an inescapable reality, and the erosion of their power base had forced the Liberal leadership into even closer alliance with the Conservatives—a profoundly unnatural state of affairs made tolerable only because both parties, for their own reasons, remained bitterly and personally opposed to the current Government and all its minions.

Their alliance had, however, proved of considerable value to Klaus Hauptman. Always a shrewd investor, he'd spent years cementing personal (and, via judicious campaign contributions, financial) ties all across the political spectrum. Now that the Liberals and Conservatives had been driven together and regarded themselves as a beleaguered minority, his patronage was even more important to both parties. And while the Opposition was mainly aware of the clout it had *lost*, Hauptman knew Cromarty's crowd remained nervous about their thin majority in the Lords, and he'd learned to use his influence with the Liberals and Conservatives to considerable effect.

As he was using it tonight.

"So that's the best they'll do," he said grimly. "No additional task forces. Not even a single destroyer squadron. All they're prepared to offer us is four ships—just *four!* And 'armed merchant cruisers,' at that!"

"Oh, calm down, Klaus!" Erika Dempsey replied wryly. "I agree it's hardly likely to make much difference, but they *are* trying. Given the pressure they're under, I'm surprised they've managed even this much so quickly. And they're certainly right to concentrate on Breslau. Why, my cartel's lost nine ships in that sector in the last eight months alone. If they can make any sort of hole in the pirates there, surely that's worth *something*."

Hauptman snorted. Privately, he was inclined to agree, not that he intended to say any such thing until he'd trolled the bait before Houseman properly, and he wished Erika hadn't joined the conversation. The Dempsey Cartel was second only to the Hauptman Cartel, and Erika, who'd headed it for sixty T-years, was as sharp as she was attractive. Hauptman, who respected very few people, most assuredly *did* respect her, but the last thing he needed just now was the voice of sweet reason. Fortunately, Houseman didn't seem particularly susceptible to her logic.

"I'm afraid Klaus is right, Ms. Dempsey," he said regretfully. "Four armed merchantmen won't accomplish much, if only because of sheer scale. They can only be in so many places at once, and they're hardly ships of the wall. Any competent raider squadron could swarm one of them under, and there are at least three secessionist governments in Breslau and Posnan at the moment. All of them are recruiting privateers who won't take kindly to any imperialist adventures on our part."

Erika Dempsey rolled her eyes. She had little use for the Liberals, and Houseman's last sentence was straight out of their ideological bible. Worse, Houseman, for all his opposition to the current war, regarded himself as a military expert. He considered any use of force proof of failed diplomacy and stupidity, but that didn't keep him from being fascinated—though always, of course, from a safe distance—with the subject. He was quick to proclaim that his interest stemmed solely from the fact that, like a physician, any peace-loving diplomat must study the disease against which he fought, but Hauptman doubted the claim fooled anyone but his fellow idealogues. The truth was that Reginald Houseman was firmly convinced that had *he* been one of those evil, militarist conquerors like Napoleon Bonaparte or Gustav Anderman—which, thank God, he was not, of course—he would have been far better at it than *they* had. As it was, his study of the military not only allowed him to enjoy the vicarious thrill of indulging in something evil and decadent out of the highest motives but also gave him a certain standing as one of the Liberal Party's "military experts," and the fact that most Queen's officers, whatever their branch of service, regarded him as an arrant coward didn't faze him in the least. Indeed, he interpreted their contempt as fear-based hostility spawned by how close to home his trenchant criticisms of the military establishment hit.

"At this point, Mr. Houseman," Dempsey said in a chill voice, "I'm prepared to settle for any 'imperialist adventure' I can get if it means men and women in my employ won't be killed."

"I quite understand your viewpoint," Houseman assured her, apparently oblivious to her contempt. "The problem is that it won't work. I doubt even Edward Saganami—or any other admiral I can think of offhand, for that matter—could accomplish anything with such weak forces. In fact, the most probable outcome is that whoever the Admiralty sends out will lose all his *own* ships." He shook his head sadly. "The Navy's done a lot of shortsighted things in the last three T-years. I'm very much afraid this is just one more of them."

Dempsey looked at him for a moment, then sniffed and stalked away. Hauptman watched her go with a sense of relief and returned his own attention to Houseman.

"I'm afraid you're right, Reginald," he said. "Nonetheless, this is all we're going to get. Under the circumstances, I'd like to maximize whatever chance of success it has."

"If the Admiralty insists on doing something this stupid, I don't see a lot we *can* do. They're sending a grossly inadequate force straight into the lion's den. Any competent student of history could tell them they're simply going to lose those ships."

For just a moment, and despite his own plans, Hauptman felt an overpowering urge to slap some sense into the younger man. It wouldn't be the first time someone had tried it; unfortunately, it didn't seem to have done much good the last time, and Hauptman's designs didn't allow him to show his contempt as openly as Erika had.

"I understand that," he said instead, "and no doubt you're right. But I'd like to get the most good we can out of them *before* they're destroyed."

"Cold-blooded, but probably realistic, I'm afraid," Houseman sighed, and Hauptman hid a mental grin.

For all his pious opposition to "militarism," Houseman, like many theorists, was less moved by the thought of casualties than the "militarists" he scorned. After all, the people who died had all volunteered to be Myrmidons, and one couldn't make an omelette without cracking a few eggs. Hauptman's own observation was that people who actually had to send others to die tended to consider their options far more carefully than armchair "experts." He himself rather regretted the fact that he shared Houseman's estimate of the Q-ships' probable fate, but at least Houseman's response told him we was reaching the buttons he'd wanted to punch.

"Absolutely," he said. "But the problem is that without a capable officer in command, the chance they'll do any good before they're lost is minimal. At the same time, I hardly think we can expect the Admiralty to *send* a capable officer to command a forlorn hope like this— especially if it's no more than a sop to ease political pressure on them. We're more likely to see them shuffling it off on some incompetent they'll be just as happy to be rid of when the shooting's over."

"Of course we are," Houseman agreed instantly, ready, as always, to ascribe the most Machiavellian motives to the militarists.

"Well, in that case, I think we should make it our business to exert every possible pressure to keep them from doing just that," Hauptman said persuasively. "If this is all the support they're going to give us, we have every right to demand that they make it as effective as possible."

"I can see that," Houseman replied in a thoughtful tone. He was obviously running through a mental file of possible COs, but it was no part of Hauptman's plan to let Houseman make his own suggestion. Not, at least, until he'd gotten his own nominee into the running. The trick was to do it in a way which wouldn't let Houseman instantly reject Hauptman's candidate.

"The problem," the magnate said with a finely blended mix of casualness and thoughtful consideration, "is finding an officer who might be able to do some good and who they'd also be willing to risk losing. It wouldn't do to push for someone who's too much of a thinker, either." Houseman raised an eyebrow, and Hauptman shrugged. "I mean, what we need is someone who's a good *fighter*. We need a tactician, someone who knows how to employ his ships effectively but isn't likely to recognize the ultimate futility of his mission. Anyone with the judgment to consider things realistically is likely to recognize that the whole operation's no more than a gesture, and that means he'd be unlikely to operate aggressively enough to do us much good."

He held his mental breath as Houseman considered that. What he'd *really* just said was that they needed someone who would charge into battle and get himself and several thousand other people killed, and he was honest enough—with himself, at any rate—to admit that saying so was fairly sordid. Still, it was the business of people in uniform to fight, and people who did things like that often got killed. If they managed to help salvage his battered position in Silesia in the process, he was willing to live with that. Houseman, on the other hand, *had* no direct interest in Silesia. In his case, the entire affair was little more than an intellectual consideration, and even now Hauptman wasn't certain the other was cold blooded enough to sentence men and women to probable death when the casualties would be real and not simply numbers in a simulation.

"I see what you mean," Houseman murmured, gazing down into his wineglass. He rubbed an eyebrow, then shrugged. "I'd hate to see anyone killed unnecessarily, of course, but if the Admiralty's set on this, you're right about the ideal sort of officer to send." He smiled thinly. "What you're saying is that we need someone with more balls than brains but with the tactical ability to make his stupidity count."

"That's exactly what I'm saying." Despite his own

careful maneuvering, Hauptman was repelled by Houseman's amused contempt for someone prepared to die in the performance of his duty. Not that he intended to say so. "And I also think I may have just the officer in mind," he said instead, with an answering smile.

"Oh?" Something in his tone made Houseman look up. Vague suspicion showed in his brown eyes, but there was a flicker of anticipation, as well. He loved the sensation of being on the "inside" of high-level machinations, and Hauptman knew it. Just as he knew it was a sensation he'd been denied ever since that unfortunate incident on the planet Grayson.

"Harrington," the magnate said softly, and saw the instant fury that flashed through Houseman at the mere mention of the name.

"*Harrington?* You must be joking! The woman's an absolute lunatic!"

"Of course she is. But didn't we just agree a lunatic is what we need?" Hauptman countered. "I've had my own problems with her, as I'm sure you realize, but lunatic or not, she's compiled a hell of a record in combat. I'd never suggest her for any assignment that required someone who could actually see the big picture or *think*, but she'd be perfect for a job like this."

Houseman's nostrils flared, and a bright patch of red burned on either cheekbone. Of all the people in the universe, he hated Honor Harrington most . . . as Hauptman was perfectly well aware. And little though he might agree with Houseman on any other subject, Hauptman found himself in accord with the economist where Harrington was concerned.

Unlike Houseman, he refused to underestimate her— again—but that didn't mean he *liked* her. She'd caused him profound embarrassment and not a little financial loss eight T-years ago when she'd uncovered his cartel's involvement in a Peep plot to seize control of the Basilisk System. Not that Hauptman had known anything about his employees' activities. He'd managed, fortunately, to prove that in a court of law, yet his personal innocence hadn't saved him from massive fines—or prevented the blackening of his cartel's good name and, by extension, his own.

Klaus Hauptman was not a man who tolerated interference well. He knew that, and he admitted, intellectually, that it was a weakness. But it was also a part of his strength, the driving energy that propelled him to one triumph after another, and so he was willing to endure the occasional instances in which his choleric disposition betrayed him into error.

Usually. Oh, yes, he thought. Usually. But not in Harrington's case. She hadn't simply embarrassed him; she'd *threatened* him.

He clenched his jaw, memory replaying the incident while he let Houseman grapple with his own rage. Hauptman had gone out to Basilisk Station personally when Harrington's officious interference had become intolerable. He hadn't known at the time about any Peep plots or where it was all going to lead, but the woman had been costing him money, and her seizure of one of his vessels for carrying contraband had been exactly the sort of slap in the face he was least able to handle. And because it was, he'd gone out to smack her down. But it hadn't worked out that way. She'd actually *defied* him, as if she didn't even realize—or care—that he was *Klaus Hauptman*. She'd been careful to phrase it in officialese, hiding behind her precious uniform and her status as the station's acting commander, but she'd all but accused him of direct complicity in *smuggling*.

She'd punched his buttons. He admitted it, just as he admitted he really ought to have kept a closer eye on his factors' operations. But, damn it, how *could* he monitor something as vast as the Hauptman Cartel in that kind of detail? That was why he *had* factors, to see to the details he couldn't possibly deal with. And even if she'd been totally justified—she hadn't been, but even if she had—where did the daughter of a mere yeoman get off talking to *him* that way? She'd been a two-for-a-dollar commander, CO of a mere light cruiser he could have bought out of pocket change, so how *dared* she use that cold, cutting tone to him?

But she had dared, and in his rage he'd taken the gloves off. She hadn't known his cartel held a majority interest in her physician parents' medical partnership on Sphinx. All it should have required was an offhand mention of the possible consequences to her family if she forced him to defend himself and his good name through unofficial channels, but she'd not only refused to back down, she'd trumped his threat with a far more deadly one.

No one else had heard it. That was the sole redeeming facet of the entire affair, for it meant no one else knew she'd actually threatened to *kill* him if he ever dared to move against her parents in any way.

Despite his own deep, burning fury, Hauptman felt a chill even now at the memory of her ice-cold almond eyes, for she'd meant it. He'd known it then, and three years ago she'd proven just how real the threat had been when she killed not one but two men, one a professional duelist, on the field of honor. If anything had been needed to tell him it would be advisable to move very cautiously against her, those two duels had done it.

Yet his hatred for her was one of the very few things he and Houseman truly had in common, for she was also the one who'd ruined Houseman's diplomatic career. It was Harrington who hadn't simply refused his order to pull her squadron out of the Yeltsin System, abandoning the planet Grayson to conquest by a Peep proxy, but actually struck him when he tried to intimidate her into accepting it. She'd knocked him clear off his feet in front of witnesses, and the searing contempt with which she'd spoken to him had simply been too good to be kept quiet. By now, everyone who mattered knew *precisely* what she'd said, the cold, vicious accuracy with which she'd laid bare his cowardice, and the official reprimand she'd caught for striking a Crown envoy had been more than offset by the knighthood which came with it—not to mention all the honors the people of Grayson had heaped upon their planet's savior.

"I can't believe you're serious." Houseman's cold, stiff voice pulled Hauptman back to the present. "My God, man! The woman's no better than a common murderer! You know how she hounded North Hollow into that duel. She actually had the sheer effrontery to challenge him on the floor of the House of Lords, then shot him down like an animal after *his* gun was empty! You can't seriously suggest her for *any* command after we finally got her out of uniform."

"Of course I can." Hauptman gave the younger man a cold, thin smile. "Just because she's a fool—even a dangerous fool—is no reason not to use her to our own advantage. Think about it, Reginald. Whatever else she is, she's an effective combat commander. Oh, I agree she should be kept on a leash between battles. She's arrogant as sin, and I doubt she's ever even tried to control her temper. Hell, let's be honest and admit she's got the makings of a homicidal maniac! But she *does* know how to fight. It may be the *only* thing she's good for, but if anyone's likely to really hurt the pirates before they kill her, she is."

He let his voice go silky soft with the last sentence, coming down just a bit harder on the word "kill," and something ugly flared in Houseman's eyes. Neither of them would ever say so, but the message had been passed, and he watched the younger man draw a deep breath.

"Even if I assumed you're right—and I'm not saying I do—I don't see how it would be possible," Houseman said finally. "She's on half-pay, and Cromarty would never propose recalling her to active duty. After the way she challenged North Hollow on the floor, the entire House would rise up in revolt at the mere suggestion."

"Maybe," Hauptman replied, though he had his doubts

on that point. Two years ago, Houseman would undoubtedly have been correct; now Hauptman was less certain. Harrington had retreated to Grayson to take up her role as Steadholder Harrington, the direct feudal ruler of the Steading of Harrington which the Graysons had created after her defense of their planet. Given Houseman's ignoble role in that same defense, it was hardly surprising that he denigrated the importance of such foreign titles, but the Hauptman Cartel was deeply involved in the vast industrial and military programs underway in the Yeltsin System since Grayson had joined the Manticoran Alliance. Given his own experience with her, Hauptman had made a careful study of Harrington's position on Grayson, and he knew she wielded a greater power and influence there than anyone short of the Duke of Cromarty himself wielded in the Star Kingdom.

Just for starters, she was probably, whether the Graysons realized it or not, the wealthiest person on their planet, especially since her Sky Domes Ltd. had begun turning a profit. When the Manticoran interests Willard Neufsteiler oversaw for her were added in, she was almost certainly a billionaire in her own right by now, which wasn't bad for someone whose initial capital had come solely from prize money awards. But her wealth hardly mattered to the Graysons. She'd not only saved them from foreign conquest, but also become one of the eighty-odd great nobles who ruled their world, not to mention the second ranking officer in their navy. Despite the lingering repugnance the more conservative of Grayson's theocratic people might feel for her, most Graysons regarded her with near idolatry.

More than that, she'd actually saved the system a second time early last year. Whatever the House of Lords might think, the newsfaxes' accounts of the Fourth Battle of Yeltsin had made her almost as much a hero to the Star Kingdom's population as she was on Grayson itself. If the Cromarty Government ever felt confident enough of its majority in the Lords to try bringing her back into

Manticoran uniform, Hauptman felt certain the attempt would succeed.

Unfortunately, Cromarty and the Admiralty seemed unwilling to risk the inevitable nasty floor fight. And even if they'd been willing to, it was extremely unlikely they would even consider wasting someone like her on the command of four armed merchantmen so far from the front. But if the proposal came from somewhere else . . .

"Look, Reginald," he said persuasively. "We're agreed Harrington's a loose warhead, but I think we're also agreed that if we could get her sent to Silesia she might at least do some damage to the pirates when she went off, right?"

Houseman nodded, his obvious unwillingness to admit even that much clearly tempered by the appeal of sending someone he hated off to an assignment with an excellent chance of getting her killed.

"All right. At the same time, let's admit that she's still very popular with the Navy. The Admiralty would *love* to get her back in Manticoran uniform, wouldn't they?"

Again Houseman nodded, and Hauptman shrugged.

"Well, what do you think would happen if *we* suggested assigning her to Silesia? Think about it for a minute. If the *Opposition* supports her for the command, don't you think the Admiralty would jump at the chance to 'rehabilitate' her?"

"I suppose they would," Houseman agreed sourly. "But what makes you think she'd accept even if they offered it to her? She's off playing tin god in Yeltsin. Why should she give up her position as the number two officer in their piddling little navy to accept something like *this*?"

"Because it *is* 'a piddling little navy,' " Hauptman said. It wasn't, and only Houseman's bitter hatred for anything to do with the Yeltsin System could lead even him to suggest it was. The Grayson Space Navy had grown into a very respectable fleet, with a core of ten ex-Peep superdreadnoughts and its first three home-built ships of the wall. From the perspective of personal ambition,

Harrington would be insane to resign her position as second-in-command of the explosively expanding GSN to resume her rank as a mere captain in the Manticoran Navy. But for all his own hatred of her, Hauptman understood her far better than Houseman did. Whatever else she might have become, Honor Harrington had been born a Manticoran, and she'd spent three decades building her career and reputation in the service of her Queen. She had both personal courage and an undeniable, deeply ingrained sense of duty, he admitted grudgingly, and that sense of duty could only be reinforced by her inevitable desire to justify herself by reclaiming a place in the Navy from which she'd been banished by her enemies. Oh no. If she was offered the job, she'd take it, though it would never do to tell Houseman the *real* reasons she would.

"She may be queen frog in the Grayson Navy," he said instead, "but that's a pretty small puddle compared to *our* Navy. Their whole fleet wouldn't make two full strength squadrons of the wall, Reginald—you know that even better than I do. If she ever expects to exercise *real* fleet command, there's only one place she can do it, and that's right here."

Houseman grunted and threw back a long swallow of wine, then lowered the empty glass and stared down into it once more. Hauptman felt the conflicting emotions ripping through the younger man and laid a hand on his shoulder.

"I know I'm asking a lot, Reginald," he said compassionately. "It would take a big man to even consider putting someone who'd assaulted him back into the Queen's uniform. But I can't think of anyone who fits the profile this mission requires better than she does. And while it would be a great pity to see any officer killed in the line of duty, you have to admit that someone as unstable as Harrington would be less of a loss than some other people you can think of."

With anyone else, that last barb would have been too

blatant, but the fresh flicker in Houseman's eye was intensely satisfying.

"Why are you discussing it with *me*?" he asked after a moment, and Hauptman shrugged.

"Your family has a lot of influence in the Liberal Party. That means it has influence with the Opposition generally, and given your own in-depth military knowledge and, ah, experience with her, any recommendation from you would have to carry a lot of weight with other people who have doubts about her. If you were to suggest her to Countess New Kiev for the assignment, the party leadership would almost have to take it seriously."

"You really are asking a lot of me, Klaus," Houseman said heavily.

"I know," Hauptman repeated. "But if the Opposition nominates her, Cromarty, Morncreek, and Caparelli will jump at the chance."

"What about the Conservatives and the Progressives?" Houseman countered. "Their peers aren't going to like the idea any more than Countess New Kiev will."

"I've already spoken to Baron High Ridge," Hauptman admitted. "He's not happy about it, and he refuses to commit the Conservatives to officially support Harrington for the slot, but he *has* agreed to release them to vote their own consciences." Houseman's eyes narrowed, and then he nodded slowly, for both of them knew "releasing them to vote their consciences" was no more than a diplomatic fiction to allow High Ridge to maintain his official opposition while effectively instructing his followers to support the move. "As for the Progressives," Hauptman went on, "Earl Gray Hill and Lady Descroix have agreed to abstain in any vote. But none of them will actually put Harrington forward. That's why it's so important that you and your family speak to New Kiev about it."

"I see." Houseman plucked at his lower lip for an endless moment, then sighed heavily. "All right, Klaus. I'll speak to her. It goes against the grain, mind you, but I'll defer to your judgment and do what I can to support you."

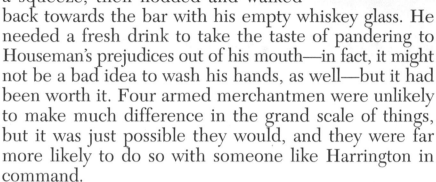

"Thank you, Reginald. I appreciate it," Hauptman said with quiet sincerity.

He gave the younger man's shoulder a squeeze, then nodded and walked back towards the bar with his empty whiskey glass. He needed a fresh drink to take the taste of pandering to Houseman's prejudices out of his mouth—in fact, it might not be a bad idea to wash his hands, as well—but it had been worth it. Four armed merchantmen were unlikely to make much difference in the grand scale of things, but it was just possible they would, and they were far more likely to do so with someone like Harrington in command.

Of course, as he'd been at some pains to point out to Houseman, it was even more likely that she'd get herself killed before she could accomplish anything. That would be a pity, but there was at least a chance that she'd do some good.

And the bottom line, he told himself as he handed his glass to the barkeep with a smile, was that whether she managed to stop the pirates or the pirates managed to kill her, *he* still came out ahead.

• CHAPTER THREE

Any semiautomatic pistol was a technological antique, but this one was more so than most. In point of fact, its design was over two thousand T-years old, for it was an exact replica of what had once been known as a "Model 1911A1" firing a ".45 ACP" cartridge. It was quite a handful, with an unloaded weight of just under 1.3 kilograms in Grayson's 1.17 standard gravities, and the recoil was formidable. Its antiquity didn't make it any less noisy, either, and despite their ear protectors, more than one of the armsmen on the neighboring firing lanes winced as the 11.43-millimeter slug rumbled down range at a mere 275 MPS. That was a paltry velocity, even beside the auto-loaders to which the Grayson tech base had been limited before the Yeltsin System joined the Alliance, much less the 2,000-plus MPS at which a modern pulser punched out its darts, but the massive fifteen-gram bullet still reached the end of its twenty-five-meter journey with formidable kinetic energy. The jacketed slug exploded through the equally anachronistic paper target's "X" ring in a shower of small white fragments, then vanished in a fiery flash as it plowed into the focused grav wall "backstop" and vaporized.

The deep, rolling *Boom!* of the archaic handgun cut through the high-pitched whine of the pulsers again, then a third time, a fourth. Seven echoing shots thundered with precise, elegant timing, and the center of the target disappeared, replaced by a single gaping hole.

Admiral Lady Dame Honor Harrington, Countess and Steadholder Harrington, lowered the pistol from her

preferred two-hand shooting stance, checked to be certain the slide had locked open on an empty magazine, and laid the weapon on the counter in front of her before taking off her shooting glasses and acoustic earmuffs. Major Andrew LaFollet, her personal armsman and chief bodyguard, stood behind her, wearing his own eye and ear protection, and shook his head as she pressed a button and the target hummed back towards her. Lady Harrington's hand cannon had been a gift from High Admiral Wesley Matthews, and LaFollet wondered how the GSN's military commander-in-chief had discovered she would like such an *outré* present. However he'd figured it out, he'd certainly been right. Lady Harrington took the noisy, propellant-spewing, eardrum-shattering monster to the range, whether aboard her superdreadnought flagship or here at the Harrington Guard's outdoor small arms range, at least once a week, and she seemed to draw almost as much pleasure from the ritual of cleaning it after each firing session as she did from battering everyone else's ears with the thing.

She took the target down and put her pocket rule on it, measuring the three-centimeter group with evident satisfaction. Despite his own reservations about the thunderous archaic weapon, LaFollet found her accuracy with it both impressive and reassuring. Anyone who'd seen her on the Landing City dueling grounds knew she hit what she shot at, but as the man charged with keeping her alive, he was always glad to see her demonstrate her ability to look after herself.

He snorted in wry amusement at the thought. She hardly looked it, standing there like a slim green-and-white flame in her ankle-length gown and hip-length vest, silky brown hair falling loose over her shoulders, but she was probably the most dangerous person on the range . . . including Andrew LaFollet. She continued to work out regularly with her armsmen, and though they'd improved markedly in their own mastery of her favored *coup de vitesse*, she still threw them around the mat with absurd ease.

Of course, at just over a hundred and ninety centimeters she was taller than any of them, and her birth world's gravity well, almost fifteen percent deeper than Grayson's, had given her impressive strength and reflexes. She might be slim, but that sinewy slimness was all firm, hard-trained muscle. Yet that wasn't the real reason she made it seem so easy. The *real* reason was that although the third-generation prolong treatments she'd received as a child might make her *look* like someone's barely postadolescent sister, she was actually thirteen T-years older than LaFollet himself, and she'd spent over thirty-six years training in the *coup*. That meant she'd been practicing for as long as LaFollet had been alive, though even he sometimes had trouble believing that was possible when he looked at her youthful, exotically beautiful face.

She finished examining the target and drew a stylus from her pocket to note the date on it, then placed it with a dozen other perforated sheets of paper and slipped the handgun into its carrying case. She put both extra magazines in with it and sealed the case, tucked it under her arm, slid her shooting glasses into a pocket, and gathered up her ear protectors, and the almond eyes she'd inherited from her Chinese mother twinkled as LaFollet tried not to sigh in relief.

"All done, Andrew," she said, and the two of them walked away from the range towards Harrington House's rear entrance. A sleek, six-limbed, cream-and-gray Sphinx treecat rose from his peaceful repose in a patch of sunlight, stretched lazily, and padded to meet them as LaFollet pulled off his earmuffs, and she laughed.

"Nimitz seems to share your opinion of the noise level," she observed, bending to scoop the 'cat up. He bleeked a cheerful agreement with her comment, and she laughed again as she set him on her shoulder. He took his normal position—mid-limbs' hand-paws sinking centimeter-long claws into her vest's shoulder while his true-feet dug in just below her shoulder blade—and flirted his fluffy tail as LaFollet smiled back at her.

"It's not just the noise, My Lady. It's the energy level. That's a brute-force weapon if I ever saw one."

"True, but it's more fun than a pulser, too," Honor replied. "I'd prefer something more modern in a fight myself, to be perfectly honest, but it *does* speak with authority, doesn't it?"

"I can't argue with you there, My Lady," LaFollet admitted, eyes sweeping their surroundings in the automatic threat search of his calling even here, on Harrington House's immaculate grounds. "And I'm not so sure it would be all that useless in a fight, either. If nothing else, the sheer *racket* ought to give you the advantage of surprise."

"You're probably right," she agreed. The artificial nerves in the rebuilt left side of her face pulled her smile just a bit off center, but her eyes danced. "Maybe I should take away the Guard's pulsers and see if the High Admiral can't get me enough for all of you, too."

"Thank you, My Lady, but I'm quite satisfied with my pulser," LaFollet replied with exquisite politeness. "I carried a chemical-burner of my own, if not one quite that, ah, *formidable*, for ten years before you upgraded us. Now I'm spoiled."

"Don't say I never offered," she teased, and nodded to the sentry who opened Harrington House's back door for them.

"I won't," LaFollet assured her as the closing door cut off the sounds from the range behind them. "You know, My Lady, there's something I've wanted to ask you," he added. She quirked an eyebrow and nodded for him to go on. "Back on Manticore, before your duel with Summervale, Colonel Ramirez was a lot more nervous than he tried to show. I told him I'd seen you practicing and that you were no slouch with a handgun, but I've always wondered just how you got so good with one myself."

"I grew up on Sphinx," Honor replied, and it was his turn to crook an eyebrow. "Sphinx has been settled for almost six hundred T-years," she explained, "but a third of the planet's still Crown land, which means virgin wilderness, and the Harrington homestead backs smack up to the Copper Wall Nature Preserve. Lots of things on Sphinx wouldn't mind finding out how people taste, and most adults and older children pack guns in the Outback as a matter of course."

"But not antiques like that one, I'll bet," LaFollet returned, gesturing at the pistol case under her left arm.

"No," she admitted. "That's my Uncle Jacques' fault."

"Uncle Jacques?"

"My mom's older brother. He came out from Beowulf to visit us for about a year when I was, oh, twelve T-years old, and he belongs to the Society for Creative Anachronism. They're a weird group that enjoys recreating the past the way it *ought* to have been. Uncle Jacques' own favorite period was the second-century Ante Diaspora— uh, that would be the twentieth-century," she added, since Grayson still used the ancient Gregorian calendar, "—and he was Planetary Reserve Grand Pistol Champion that year. He's just as handsome as Mother is beautiful, too, and I adored him." She rolled her eyes with a grin. "I followed him around like a love-struck puppy, which must have been maddening, but he never showed it. Instead, he taught me to shoot what he called *real* guns, and—" she chuckled "—Nimitz didn't like the muzzle blast *then*, either."

"That's because Nimitz is a cultured and discerning individual, My Lady."

"Ha! Anyway, I kept it up pretty regularly till I went off to the Academy, and I considered going out for the pistol team then. But I was already pretty good with small arms and I'd only started studying the *coup* about four years before I passed the entrance exams, so I decided to stick with the martial arts and wound up on the unarmed combat team, instead."

"I see." LaFollet took two or three more strides, then

grinned wryly. "In case I've never mentioned it before, My Lady, you're not very much like a typical Grayson lady. Guns, unarmed combat . . . Maybe *I* should hide behind *you* the next time it hits the fan."

"Why, Andrew! What a shocking thing to say to your Steadholder!"

LaFollet chuckled in reply, yet he couldn't help thinking she was quite right. Normally, no properly brought up Grayson male would even have considered discussing such violent subjects with a properly brought up female. But Lady Harrington hadn't *been* brought up as a Grayson, and the local rules defining proper behavior were changing, anyway. The changes must seem slow to an outsider, but to a Grayson, whose life was built on tradition, they'd come with bewildering speed over the past six T-years, and the woman Andrew LaFollet guarded with his life was the reason they had.

It was odd, but she was probably less aware of those changes than anyone else on the planet, for she came from a society which would have greeted the very notion that men and women might be considered unequal with incomprehension. But Grayson's deeply traditional, patriarchal society and religion had evolved in a thousand years of isolation on a world whose lethal concentrations of heavy metals made it its own people's worst enemy. The bedrock strength of those traditions meant any change was bound to be incremental, not something that happened overnight, but LaFollet was constantly aware of the small, subtle adjustments taking place around him. For the most part, he thought they were good changes—not always comfortable ones, as the group of religious zealots who'd tried to destroy his Steadholder little more than a year ago had demonstrated, but good ones. Yet he was virtually certain Lady Harrington still didn't realize the extent to which younger Grayson women were beginning to reshape their own lives around the pattern she and the other Manticoran women serving in Grayson's naval forces provided. Not that Grayson showed any particular signs of turning into a mirror image of the Star Kingdom. Instead, its people were evolving a new pattern all their own, and he often wondered where it would end.

They reached the end of the short passage and took the lift to Harrington House's second floor, where Honor's private quarters were located. An older man with thinning sandy hair and gray eyes was waiting when the lift doors opened, and she cocked her head.

"Hello, Mac. What can I do for you?" she asked.

"We've just received a message from the space facility, Ma'am." Like Honor, James MacGuiness wore civilian clothes, as befitted his role as Harrington House's major-domo, but he was the only member of her personal staff who ever addressed her as anything other than "My Lady." There was a very simple reason for that; Master Chief Steward MacGuiness had been her personal steward and—as she was fond of saying—chief keeper for over eight years, and that made him the only member of her household who'd known her even before she'd been knighted, far less become a countess and steadholder. He normally addressed her as "Milady" in front of visitors, but in private he had a tendency to revert to the older military courtesy.

"What sort of message?" she asked, and he smiled broadly.

"It's from Captain Henke, Ma'am. *Agni* made her alpha translation three hours ago."

"Mike's here?" Honor said delightedly. "That's wonderful! When do we expect her?"

"She'll be landing in about another hour, Ma'am." Something about MacGuiness' tone was a bit odd, and Honor looked a question at him. "She's not alone, Ma'am," the steward said. "Admiral White Haven is with her, and he's asked if it would be convenient for him to accompany her to Harrington House."

"Earl White Haven? Here?" Honor blinked, and MacGuiness nodded. "Did he say anything about the reason for his visit?"

"No, Ma'am. He just asked if you could see him."

"Of course I can!" She stood in thought for another moment, then shook herself and handed the gun case to MacGuiness. "I suppose I should get tidied up, under the circumstances. Would you see about cleaning this for me, Mac?"

"Of course, Ma'am."

"Thank you. And I suppose you'd better tell Miranda I need her, too."

"I already have, Ma'am. She said she'd meet you in your dressing room."

"Then I shouldn't keep her waiting." Honor nodded and swept off down the corridor to her waiting maid, and her mind whirred as she tried to guess why White Haven wanted to see her.

A knock on the frame of the open door alerted Honor, and she looked up with a smile as MacGuiness ushered her visitors into her spacious, sunny office. Aside from Nimitz and LaFollet, whose constant presence was required under Grayson law, she was alone, for Howard Clinkscales, her regent and administrative executive, was in Austin City for the day, conferring with Chancellor Prestwick, and she rose and walked around her desk, holding out her hand to the slim woman whose skin was barely a shade lighter than her space-black RMN uniform.

"Mike! Why didn't you warn me you were coming?" she demanded as the other woman clasped her hand firmly.

"Because I didn't know I was." Captain (JG) the Honorable Michelle Henke's husky, soft-textured contralto was wry, and she grinned at her host. Mike Henke was a first cousin of Queen Elizabeth, with the unmistakable features of the House of Winton, but she'd also been Honor's roommate and social mentor at the Academy's Saganami Island campus. Despite the vast social gulf between them, she'd become Honor's closest friend, and her eyes were warm. "*Agni*'s just been reassigned to Sixth Fleet, and Admiral White Haven nabbed us for a taxi."

"I see." Honor gave Henke's hand another squeeze,

then turned to the tall, broad-shouldered admiral who'd accompanied her. "My Lord," she said more formally, extending her hand once more. "I'm delighted to see you again."

"And I to see you, Milady," he replied, equally formally, and her cheekbones heated as he bent to kiss her hand instead of shaking it. It was the proper way to greet a woman on Grayson, and she'd become accustomed to it under most circumstances. But she felt uncomfortable when White Haven did it. She knew, intellectually, that her steadholder's rank actually took precedence over his, but her title was barely six years old while the Earldom of White Haven dated from the very founding of the Star Kingdom, and he was also one of the two or three most respected flag officers of the navy in which she'd served for over thirty years.

He straightened, and his blue eyes twinkled, as if he understood exactly what she felt and was chiding her for it. She hadn't seen him in almost three T-years—since, in fact, the day she'd gone into exile on half-pay—and she was privately shocked by the fresh deep lines around those twinkling eyes, but she only smiled.

"Please, sit down," she invited, gesturing to the chairs clustered around a coffee table. Nimitz hopped down from his wall-mounted perch as they obeyed her invitation, and Henke laughed as he padded across the table to hold out one strong, wiry true-hand to her.

"It's good to see you, too, Stinker," the captain said, shaking the proffered hand. "Raided any good celery patches lately?"

Nimitz sniffed his opinion of her idea of humor, but Honor felt his own pleasure over their empathic link. Even people from Manticore and Gryphon, the other two inhabited planets of the Star Kingdom's home system, were distinctly prone to underestimate the intelligence of Sphinx's treecats, but Mike and Nimitz were old friends. She knew as well as Honor that he was brighter than most two-footed people and, despite his inability to form the sounds required to speak it, understood more Standard English than most Manticoran adolescents.

She also knew about the addiction every 'cat shared, and she grinned again as she fished a stalk of celery from the pocket of her tunic and passed it over. Nimitz grabbed it happily and started chewing before his person had time to say a word, far less object, and Honor sighed.

"Not here five minutes, and already you're encouraging him! You're an evil person, Mike Henke."

"Comes from the friends I associate with," Henke replied cheerfully, and it was Honor's turn to laugh.

Hamish Alexander leaned back in his chair and watched the others with unobtrusive intensity. The last time he'd seen Honor Harrington had been after the duel in which she'd killed Pavel Young, the Earl of North Hollow. The duel which had cost her her career had come very close to costing her her life, as well, when North Hollow turned early and shot her in the back, and her left arm and surgically rebuilt shoulder had still been immobilized at their last meeting. Yet her physical wound had been nothing beside the ones which had cut deep into her heart.

His own eyes darkened as he remembered her pain. Killing North Hollow might have avenged the paid-for murder of the man she loved, but it couldn't bring Paul Tankersley back to life. It had made it possible for her to survive his loss, perhaps, yet it had done nothing to lessen her anguish. White Haven had tried to prevent that duel, for he'd known what it would mean for her career, but he'd been wrong to try. It had been something she'd *had* to do, an act of justice whose inevitability had stemmed from the very things which made her what she was. He'd accepted that, in the end, however much he regretted the consequences, and he wondered if she realized how completely he'd come to understand her motives—or how much he knew about grief and loss. His own wife had been a total invalid for over fifty T-years. Before the freak air car accident, Emily Alexander had been the Star Kingdom's most beloved HD actress, and the anguish he still felt at seeing her dauntless will and courage locked into a frail, useless prison of the flesh had taught Hamish Alexander all about the pain love could inflict.

But this woman wasn't the grief-haunted, white-faced officer he remembered from that day aboard the battle-cruiser *Nike*. It was also the first time he'd ever seen her out of uniform, and he was amazed by how comfortable she looked in her Grayson attire. And how regal. Did she even realize how much she'd changed? How much she'd grown? She'd always been a superb officer, but she'd gained something else here on Grayson. She was half his own age, yet he was acutely conscious of the understated power of her presence as she laughed with Captain Henke. He sensed an underlying melancholy behind the laughter, where the awareness of how much loss could hurt cut deep, yet that background sorrow only seemed to hone her strength, as if the anguish she'd survived had tempered the steel within her, and he was glad. Glad for her and for the Royal Manticoran Navy. There were far too few Queen's officers of her caliber, and he wanted her back in Manticoran uniform . . . even if it meant accepting the Breslau command.

She finished laughing with Henke and looked up.

"Excuse me, My Lord. Captain Henke and Nimitz are old cronies, but I shouldn't have let that distract me. How can I help you, Sir?"

"I'm here as a messenger, Dame Honor," he replied. "Her Majesty asked me to see you."

"Her Majesty?" Honor sat up straighter as the earl nodded.

"I've been deputized to ask you to accept recall to active duty, Milady," he said quietly, and the sudden, brilliant light in her chocolate-dark eyes stunned him. She started to speak, then closed her mouth and made herself inhale deeply, and he saw the light dim. It didn't fade; rather it was as if it had been banked by an awareness of all the permutations of who and what she had become, and he felt a fresh sense of respect for the ways she'd grown.

"Active duty?" she repeated after a moment. "I'm

honored, of course, My Lord, but I'm sure you and Her Majesty are both aware of the other obligations I'm now under?"

"We are, and so is the Admiralty," White Haven replied in that same, quiet voice. "What you've done here, not merely as Steadholder Harrington but as an officer of the Grayson Navy, has been a tremendous accomplishment, and that's why Her Majesty has asked me to *request* that you accept recall. She's also charged me to inform you that she will not—now or ever—attempt to command you to do so. The Star Kingdom has treated you very badly—"

Honor started to speak, but he raised his hand. "Please, Milady. It has, and you know it. Specifically, the House of Lords has treated you with a contempt which is a slur upon you, your uniform and personal honor, and the honor of the Star Kingdom. Her Majesty knows it, Duke Cromarty knows it, the Navy knows it, and so do most of our citizens, and no one could possibly blame you for remaining here, where you've been shown the respect you deserve, instead."

Honor's face blazed, but her link to Nimitz carried the earl's sincerity to her. The 'cats had always been able to sense human emotions, but as far as she knew, she was the first human who'd ever been able to sense a 'cat's emotions—or, through Nimitz, other *humans'* emotions—in return. It was an ability she'd developed only over the last five and a half T-years, and in some ways, she was still dealing with its ramifications. Though she'd come to accept the extension of her senses, there were still times she wished she *couldn't* feel others' emotions, and this was one of them. She knew it was a one-way link. White Haven couldn't possibly feel her own reaction to his emotions, but the deep, sympathetic respect welling into her from him was horribly embarrassing. Whatever anyone else might think of her, she was too well aware of her faults and weaknesses to believe for one moment that she deserved to be regarded so.

"That wasn't what I meant, My Lord," she said after

a moment. Her soprano came out just a little husky, and she cleared her throat. "I understand why the Lords reacted the way they did. I may not *agree* with them, but I understand, and I was fairly certain at the time what their response would be. What I meant was that I've accepted my duties and position as a steadholder, not to mention my commission in the GSN. I have obligations I can't simply ignore, however much I'd love to get back into active service for the Star Kingdom again."

She glanced over her shoulder at Andrew LaFollet, standing silent and expressionless in his position behind her chair, and she felt his emotions, too. They were more confused than White Haven's, a blend of fierce approval at the notion that she would be allowed to vindicate herself in Manticoran service mixed with a cold agreement with White Haven's assessment of how the Star Kingdom had treated her and an uneasy fear over what a return to active service with the RMN might mean for the safety of the woman he was charged to protect. But she sensed no pressure either way from him. He was a Grayson armsman. His duty was to guard his Steadholder, not to tell her what to do. That prevented him neither from trying, with exquisitely polite, mulish obstinacy, to manipulate her if he thought she was in danger nor from taking action against anyone who offered her insult, but he would never attempt to dictate to her conscience. Yet this went deeper than that, just as his devotion to her did. What he wanted was for her to do what *she* felt was right, and she drew a subtle strength from that as she turned back to White Haven.

"I understand exactly what you're saying, Milady, and I respect it," the earl said. "As I say, Her Majesty is simply asking you to consider it, and she's instructed the Admiralty to abide by your decision. If you choose not to return to active duty, you'll be free to remain on half-pay status for as long as you wish—until you *do* decide to return."

"Just what, exactly, is it that the Admiralty wants me to do?"

"I wish I could say they have a job commensurate

with your accomplishments, Milady, but I can't," he replied frankly. "We're assembling a small Q-ship squadron for deployment to Silesia. I assume you're at least generally aware of conditions there?" Honor nodded, and he shrugged. "We can't commit the forces the situation truly requires, but the pressure is growing to do *something*, and this is the best the Admiralty can manage. But if they can't send adequate forces, they'd prefer to send the best officer they can in hopes that she can accomplish something despite her limited resources."

Honor regarded him thoughtfully, tasting the emotions behind the words through Nimitz. Then she smiled one of her crooked smiles, and this time there was no humor in it.

"I don't think that's the only reason they want me, My Lord," she said shrewdly, and he nodded without surprise. He'd always known she was sharp.

"Frankly, Milady, you're right. If Admiral Caparelli were free to do so, he would prefer to promote you to the flag rank you've proved you deserve and give you a squadron of the wall, or at least your own battlecruiser squadron. But he can't do that. The same political factors which forced him to put you on half-pay are still present, though they've weakened somewhat."

"Then why should I accept *this* offer?" Anger edged her voice, White Haven noted with approval, and her almond eyes flashed. "Forgive me, My Lord, but it sounds like what you're really offering me is a chance to be shuffled off to another Basilisk Station—with the same sort of inadequate resources I had there!"

"In a sense, I am," he admitted. "But looked at another way, it's a window of opportunity to get back into Manticoran uniform at all. And much as it angers me to say so, that window is the best we're likely to see for quite some time. Believe me, the Admiralty considered very carefully before offering you the command. Neither Baroness Morncreek nor the First Space Lord told me so in so many words, but they *wouldn't* have offered it to you if not for other considerations."

"Which are?" she asked tightly.

"Milady, you're one of the Navy's finest officers," White Haven said flatly. "If not for political enemies—enemies you made in no small part because you did your duty so well—you'd already be at least a commodore, and the Fleet is well aware of why you aren't. But in this instance, some of those very enemies nominated you for the slot."

Honor's nostrils flared in surprise, and he nodded slowly. She sat back in her chair, reaching out to Nimitz as he flowed into her lap. The 'cat cocked his head, turning his grass-green gaze on the admiral, and she lifted him in her arms. She held him to her breasts, one hand rubbing his chest, and her eyes commanded White Haven to continue.

"We can't be sure of all her reasons, but Countess New Kiev suggested you," the earl said. "I'm quite certain someone else put her up to it, but the rest of the Opposition either went along or made no comment. The current Earl North Hollow was the only peer who actively opposed the idea, and after what happened to his brother, he almost had to—either that or openly admit what sort of scum Pavel Young really was.

"As I say, we're not certain why they did it. Partly, I suppose, it's because however much they hate you, they have to realize how good you are. Another factor may be what happened in the last general election. They took a real beating at the polls, and the way they've treated you was one of the hot-button emotional issues, so perhaps they see this as a way to recover some lost ground without giving you the kind of command you truly deserve. And they may have even less savory motives. Let's be honest; the odds against your achieving much with only four Q-ships are high, however good you are, so they may see this as a chance to set you up for a failure they can use to justify the way they've treated you in the past."

Honor nodded slowly, following his logic, and an icy

core of anger burned within her pleasure at the thought of getting back into
Manticoran uniform again at last.

"Under most circumstances," White
Haven said levelly, "I'd advise against accepting, because
if they are counting on the odds against you, they've got
a point. But these aren't most circumstances, and whoever's orchestrating their strategy is a shrewd customer.
Since the Opposition itself has suggested you, the
Admiralty has almost no choice but to offer you the slot.
If it doesn't, or if you turn it down, the Opposition will
be able to say you had your chance and rejected it. In
the long run, that probably wouldn't be enough to keep
you from returning to the Queen's service *eventually*, but
it would probably delay your recall for at least another
full T-year, possibly longer, and it would certainly make
your final return much more difficult.

"On the other hand, if you *do* accept the command, you
probably won't have to hold it for more than six to eight
months. By that time, the war situation will probably have
changed enough to free up the light forces we need for
Silesia. Even if it hasn't, enough additional Q-ships will
be available to make a real dent in our problems there.
In either case, once you're back on active duty for *any*
reason, the Admiralty will be free to assign you to other
duties, as it sees fit, after a suitable interval. Given the
fact that the Lords have to confirm promotions out of the
zone, it will probably still be impossible to jump you to
the rank you've demonstrated you're ready to handle, but
that won't keep the Admiralty from giving you the *acting* authority you deserve."

"So what you're saying, My Lord, is that you think I
should accept it," Honor said. White Haven hesitated
briefly, then nodded.

"I suppose I am," he sighed. "It goes against the grain—
I'd far rather have you commanding one of my squadrons in Sixth Fleet—but given the situation, it's almost
a case of paying your dues. It's not fair. In fact, it's damned
*un*fair. But it's also the way it is." He twitched his

shoulders unhappily. "As I say, no one could blame you if you decided to stay here, and I'm sure Protector Benjamin and High Admiral Matthews, to say nothing of the people of Harrington Steading, will want you to do just that. But I'll be honest, Milady. *We* need you as badly as Grayson does, if in a different way. We're up against the most powerful navy in space, in terms of sheer tonnage, in a fight for our very survival. Chasing pirates in Silesia may not seem of life or death importance to the Sky Kingdom, because it isn't. But if sending you off to do that for a few months is the only way we can get you back for the things we *do* need you for, it's a price the Admiralty is prepared to pay. The question is whether or not *you're* prepared to pay it."

Honor frowned thoughtfully at him, fingers stroking gently through Nimitz's soft fur, and the 'cat's subsonic purr rumbled as she held him against her. That cold anger at the prospect of accepting what was in many ways a calculated insult still burned within her, yet she knew White Haven was right. He was asking her to give up her own superdreadnought squadron and her position as the second ranking officer of an entire navy to accept command of an inadequate squadron of converted merchantmen in a strategic backwater, yet he was right. The Opposition *did* have the power to demand that from her as the price of regaining her place in the navy of her birth kingdom and the vindication of her professional abilities.

She sat silent for almost three full minutes, then sighed.

"I won't say yes or no, My Lord. Not right now. But I *will* discuss it with Protector Benjamin and the High Admiral. I realize you have to get back to your command, but if you could possibly see your way to remaining here as my guest for a day or so, I'd appreciate it. I'd like to discuss the matter with you again after I've spoken to the Protector and Admiral Matthews."

"Of course, Milady," he said.

"Thank you. And now," she stood, "if you and Captain Henke would join me for supper, my chef would love to introduce you both to authentic Grayson cuisine."

• CHAPTER FOUR

The Grayson light cruiser *Nathan* twitched as the powerful tractor locked onto her, and her helmsman cut the reaction thrusters he'd been using for the last eighteen minutes and rolled his ship on her gyros as Her Majesty's Space Station *Vulcan* drew *Nathan's* hammerhead bow steadily into the cavernous docking bay. *Nathan's* captain sat silent in his command chair, refusing to jostle his helmsman's elbow, but he'd watched the entire operation with more than normal anxiety. Not only was his ship maneuvering under the eyes of one of the galaxy's premiere navies, but he also had a steadholder on board, and that was enough to make any skipper nervous.

Honor understood what Commander Tinsdale was feeling, which was why she'd declined his respectful invitation to share his bridge for the final approach, much as she would have loved to accept. Despite the length of her own naval career, or perhaps because of it, she felt an almost sensual delight in watching any well-executed maneuver, however routine, yet Tinsdale didn't need a great feudal lady who also happened to be an admiral breathing down his neck.

That was why she sat before her cabin view screen, instead. She watched *Nathan's* bow settle into place with smooth precision, but for all her concentration, she wasn't as focused on the operation as she normally would have been, and she tried to analyze her own feelings.

The space-black-and-gold of the RMN's uniform felt alien after eighteen T-months in the blue-on-blue of Grayson, and she was surprised by how much she missed

the broad gold stripes and collar stars of her Grayson rank.
It was . . . odd to be a "mere" senior-grade captain once
more, and she felt vaguely undressed without the heavy
gold chain of the Harrington Key about her neck. She
did wear the blood-red ribbon of the Star of Grayson,
just as she wore the golden Manticoran Cross, the Order
of Gallantry, and half a dozen other medals. She felt a
bit like a jewelers' advertisement, but she was in mess
dress, and actual medals—including foreign awards—and
not simply ribbons were required in mess dress. But the
Key *wasn't* a decoration. It marked her status as Steadholder Harrington, a head of government and arguably
an actual head of state, and RMN dress regulations made
no provision for the regalia of foreign rulers.

Honor knew she could have insisted upon wearing the
Key, yet she had no intention of doing so, for she found
herself very much in two minds over the reason she could
have. To her immense embarrassment, Protector Benjamin had insisted upon an amplification of the Queen's
Bench writ which had recognized that Captain Harrington
and Steadholder Lady Harrington were two distinct
people who happened to live in the same body. He'd been
unwilling to settle for a mere extension of the original
writ authorizing the presence of Honor's armsmen and
granting them diplomatic immunity. Instead, he'd insisted
on—*demanded*, really—a formal, permanent recognition
of Honor's split legal personality. Captain Harrington
would, of course, be subject to all the rules and regulations of the Articles of War, but *Steadholder* Harrington
was a visiting head of government who, like her bodyguards, enjoyed diplomatic immunity. Honor had wanted
to let that writ, and all its potential complications, quietly lapse, but Benjamin had been adamant. He'd flatly
refused to release her from her duties in Harrington
unless the writ was both continued and extended in scope,
and that was the way it was.

Officially, his insistence stemmed from the Grayson
requirement that any steadholder *must* be accompanied
by his (or, in Honor's case, her) armsmen. Since the

Articles of War forbade armed foreign nationals in a Queen's ship, satisfying Grayson law had required a modification of *Manticoran* law to permit Andrew LaFollet and his subordinates to retain their weapons. That was the official reason; in fact, most of Benjamin's stubborn intransigence had come from his determination to rub the House of Lords' collective nose in Honor's status. For all the diplomats involved in negotiating the conditions Benjamin had specified, she thought, it was hardly a diplomatic move. Whether the Star Kingdom's peerage chose to admit it or not, a steadholder wielded a direct, personal authority the most autocratic Manticoran noble had never dreamed of possessing. Within her steading, Honor's word, quite literally, was law, so long as none of her decrees violated the planetary constitution. More than that, she held the power of High, Middle, and Low Justice—a power she'd executed a T-year before as Protector Benjamin's champion when she killed the treasonous Steadholder Burdette in single combat.

No doubt her enemies privately wrote that all off as the barbaric posturing of a backward planet, but Benjamin's stubbornness had seen to it that they couldn't do so publicly. They might have expelled Countess Harrington from the House of Lords, but they would have no choice but to treat *Steadholder* Harrington with dignity and respect. And, to top it off, her steadholdership gave her precedence over every one of the nobles who'd voted to boot her out. Of the House of Lords' entire membership, only the Grand Duke of Manticore, Grand Duchess of Sphinx, and Grand Duke of Gryphon outranked Steadholder Harrington, and they'd all supported her.

Honor shuddered every time she thought of how the rest of the peerage was going to react to *that*. Benjamin's insistence had all the subtlety of a kick in the belly, yet she'd been powerless to talk him out of it. Benjamin IX was a well-educated, cosmopolitan, and sophisticated man, but he was also a stubborn one who remained coldly furious at how the Opposition had treated her. And, as a sovereign ally of the Star Kingdom, he had the clout to do something about it.

Yet the change in uniform and her concern over the Opposition's potential reactions were only a part of Honor's own ambiguous feelings. HMSS *Vulcan* orbited Sphinx, Manticore-A IV, the world of her birth, and she was eager to see her parents once more and smell the air of the planet which would always be her true home. But the starscape against which that world floated seemed somehow distant, like something out of a history tape. Too much had happened to her in Yeltsin, and she'd changed in too many ways. In some obscure fashion she couldn't quite define, she'd become almost a stranger here, someone whose existence was poised between two wildly different "home worlds," and she felt a bittersweet pang as she realized she truly had.

She drew a deep breath and stood. Her mess dress uniform seemed horridly pretentious to her, but she'd been given no choice about *that* either. She was only a captain here to assume a rather modest command, but the protocolists had decreed that until she formally resumed active duty with the RMN, Admiral Georgides, *Vulcan's* commander, must receive her as Steadholder Harrington, and that meant a full state dinner. She made a mental note to wring Benjamin IX's neck the next time she saw him, then sighed in resignation and turned to face MacGuiness.

Her steward was back in RMN uniform as well, and looked insufferably pleased about it. He'd never said so, but she knew how bitter he'd been over what the Navy had done to her, and, unlike her, he looked forward to the state dinner as a moment of vindication. She considered speaking sternly to him about it, but not for long. MacGuiness was more than old enough to be her father, and there were times he chose to regard her with fond indulgence rather than the instant obedience her rank should have imposed. No doubt he'd listen with perfect attentiveness and respect to anything she had to say . . . and then go right on gloating.

He met her eyes blandly, and she raised her arms to let him buckle her sword belt. Mess dress required the archaic sidearm, which she'd always thought rather ridiculous, but this was one point on which she found herself in agreement with MacGuiness and the Protector. Instead of the light, useless dress sword most Manticoran officers wore, the blade MacGuiness had just belted about her waist was lethally functional. Up until fourteen months ago, it had been the Burdette Sword; now the eight-hundred-year-old weapon was the *Harrington* Sword, and she settled it on her left hip as MacGuiness stood back.

She turned to the mirror and placed a black beret carefully on her head. The white beret which denoted a starship's commander was still packed away, waiting until she officially assumed command of her new ship, and she brushed the four gold stars on the left breast of her uniform. Each of them represented command of a hyper-capable vessel of the Queen's Navy, and despite all her ambiguity, she felt bone-deep satisfaction at the thought that she would shortly add a fifth.

She examined herself in the mirror, more carefully than she had in weeks, and the person she saw was *almost* familiar. The strong, triangular face was the same, as were the firm mouth, high cheekbones, and determined chin, but the braided hair was far longer than it had been the last time Captain Harrington had looked out of a mirror at her, and the eyes . . . The huge, almond eyes were different, too. Darker and deeper, with just a hint of sadness behind their determination.

She would do, she decided, and nodded to MacGuiness.

"I imagine I'll be returning aboard *Nathan* for tonight, at least, Mac. If there are any changes, I'll let you know."

"Yes, Ma'am."

She turned to glance at Andrew LaFollet, immaculate in his green-on-green Harrington uniform. "Are Jamie and Eddy ready?" she asked.

"Yes, My Lady. They're waiting in the boat bay."

"I trust you had that little *discussion* with them?"

"Yes, My Lady. I promise we won't embarrass you."

Honor regarded him sternly for a moment, and he returned her gaze with level gray eyes. She didn't need her link to Nimitz to tell her LaFollet actually believed that. He was perfectly sincere in his promise of good behavior, but she also knew her armsmen were just as pleased—and disinclined to put up with any foolishness— as MacGuiness. *Wonderful*, she thought dryly. *My entire staff is ready to start its own private war if anyone even* looks *like he's offering me* lèse-majesté! *I hope this "state dinner" is less memorable than it has the potential to be.*

Well, there was nothing more she could do to see that it wasn't, she told herself, and reached out to Nimitz. The 'cat leapt into her arms and swarmed up onto her shoulder, radiating his own pleasure at her rehabilitation, and she sighed once more.

"All right, Andrew. In that case, let's be about it," she said.

So far, Honor thought as Admiral Georgides' steward refilled her wineglass, things had gone much better than she'd feared. The diplomatic corps was present in strength, determined to prove it could take even a bizarre situation like this in stride, yet for all their determination, the diplomats still seemed just a bit off balance. They were like dancers who weren't quite certain of the steps, as if her uniform's visual proof that she was Captain Harrington interfered with their mental image of her as Steadholder Harrington.

Admiral Georgides, on the other hand, seemed perfectly comfortable. Honor had never met the admiral before—the last time she'd been aboard *Vulcan* Admiral Thayer had held the command—but Georgides was a fellow Sphinxian. He was also one of the rare serving officers who, like Honor, had been adopted by a treecat.

As a rule, 'cats adopted humans who were already nearly or fully adult. Child adoptions, like Honor's (or,

for that matter, Queen Elizabeth's), were extremely rare. No one was quite certain why, though the leading theory held that a 'cat needed an unusually powerful personality and empathic ability to handle a link with a child. All 'cats loved the uncomplicated emotions of children, yet that very lack of complication—of a personality still in the process of formation—seemed to make it hard for them to anchor themselves in a child's emotions. And, as Honor could personally attest, the hormonal and emotional stress a human experienced on her way through puberty and adolescence could have tried a saint's patience, far less that of an empath permanently linked to her!

Because they'd followed the more normal pattern, Aristophones Georgides and his companion Odysseus hadn't gone through Saganami Island together, for Georgides had been a senior-grade lieutenant before Odysseus turned up in his life. That had been over fifty T-years ago, however, and Odysseus was several Sphinx years older than Nimitz. He and his person were a comfortable and (though Honor wouldn't have cared to admit it) a comforting presence as she and Georgides sat at the head of the table together.

"Thank you," she said as the steward finished pouring. The man nodded and withdrew, and she sipped appreciatively. Grayson wines always seemed a bit too sweet for her taste, and she rolled the rich, strong Gryphon burgundy over her tongue with pleasure.

"That's a very nice vintage, Sir," she said, and Georgides chuckled.

"My father is a traditionalist, Milady," he replied. "He's also a romantic, and he insists the only proper drink for a Greek is retsina. Now, I respect my father. I admire his accomplishments, and he's always *seemed* reasonably sane, but how anyone could willingly drink retsina is something I've never understood. I keep a few bottles in my cellar for him, but I like to think my own palate's become a bit more civilized over the years."

"If this is from your cellar, it certainly has," Honor said with a smile. "You ought to get together with *my* father sometime. I like a good wine myself, but Daddy's quite a wine snob."

"Please, Milady, not 'wine snob'! We prefer to consider ourselves connoisseurs."

"I know you do," Honor said dryly, and he laughed.

She turned her head and glanced at the two highchairs at the table. She sat at Georgides' right as his guest of honor, and, normally, Nimitz would have been placed at her own right. Tonight the seating had been arranged to put the two 'cats side by side to the admiral's left, and Nimitz faced her across the table. Both he and Odysseus had displayed impeccable manners throughout the meal, but now they sat back comfortably, each of them chewing on a celery stalk, and she was faintly aware of a complex interplay between them. It surprised her, somehow. Not because she felt it, but because it went so deep she could sense it only imperfectly.

This was the first time she and Nimitz had met another 'cat in over three T-years, and she knew her own sensitivity to their link had grown steadily over that period. She'd never explicitly mentioned its existence to anyone, though she suspected MacGuiness, her mother, Mike Henke, and Andrew LaFollet, at least, had all guessed it was there, and she wasn't really certain why she hadn't. She could think of several reasons why she *ought* to conceal it, starting with the uneasiness her ability to read emotions might evoke in other people if they knew of it. But those reasons, however rational, had occurred to her only after the fact. She'd never made a conscious decision to conceal it; she just had, then decided later why she should have.

Yet so far as she knew, no other human had shared the same ability, and she suddenly wondered if what she was feeling now might be confirmation of some of the wilder theories about the 'cats. Although their empathic ability had been accepted as a given for centuries, no one had ever been able to explain how it worked or how that

same sense might interface with another treecat rather than a human. The 'cats obviously shared a much more complex linkage among themselves, but the conventional wisdom held that it was only an intensification of what they shared with humans. Yet that theory had always seemed suspect to Honor. Very little was known, even now, about treecat clans' social organization "in the wild," and few non-Sphinxians even realized that the 'cats were tool users, but Honor knew. She had also, as a child, accompanied Nimitz back to his home clan. Not even her parents knew about that—they'd have had three kinds of fits at the thought of an eleven-year-old Honor traipsing off into the wilds of the Copper Wall Mountains accompanied only by a treecat!—but she'd always been glad she'd made the trip, and it had given her a far better insight into 'cat society. She probably, she mused, actually knew more about the 'cats than ninety-nine percent of her fellow Sphinixians, much less off-worlders, and she'd always wondered how creatures with only the most limited spoken language, even among themselves, had built a society as complex as the one Nimitz had introduced her to.

Unless, of course, the wilder theories were right and they didn't *need* a spoken language because they were telepaths.

The thought was disturbing, despite all her years with Nimitz. In spite of millennia of effort, no one had ever managed to demonstrate reliable telepathy among humans—or, for that matter, any of the few dozen non-human sentients humanity had encountered. Personally, Honor had always assumed simple physics would preclude anything of the sort, but what if the 'cats *were* telepaths? What if their "empathic sense" was no more than an echo, the resonance of a single, small facet of their intraspecies abilities with humanity?

She frowned, rubbing a finger up and down the stem of her wineglass as she considered the implications. What sort of range would they have? she wondered. How sensitive to one another were they? How deeply did their personalities, their thoughts, interlink? And if they *were* telepaths, then how could someone like Nimitz endure spending years on end separate from others of his kind? She knew Nimitz loved her with a fierce, protective devotion, just as she loved him, yet could being with her *truly* be worth losing the deep, complex communion he was sharing with Odysseus at this very moment?

Nimitz looked up, meeting her gaze across the table, and his grass-green eyes were soft. He stared at her, and she felt the reassurance, the love, flowing from him, as if he sensed her sudden fear that their bond had somehow robbed him of something precious. Odysseus paused in chewing his own celery and gazed speculatively at Nimitz for a moment, then turned his own eyes to Honor, and she sensed a sort of interested surprise from the older 'cat through her link to Nimitz. He cocked his head, gazing at her intently, and another strand of emotion joined Nimitz's reassurance. It "tasted" quite different, burnished with tart amusement and friendly welcome, and she blinked as she realized the two 'cats were deliberately relaying it to her. It was the first time anyone had knowingly used her link with Nimitz to communicate with her, and she felt deeply touched by it.

She wasn't certain how long it lasted—certainly no more than three or four seconds—but then Nimitz and Odysseus flipped their ears in obvious amusement and turned to look at one another like old friends sharing some secret joke, and she blinked again.

"I wonder what all *that* was about?" Georgides murmured, and Honor glanced at the admiral to find him gazing intently at the 'cats. He studied them a moment longer, then shrugged and smiled at Honor. "Every time I think I've finally gotten the little devil completely figured out, he goes and does something to prove I haven't," he observed wryly.

"A trait they *all* share, I think," she agreed feelingly.

"Indeed. Tell me, Milady, is there any truth to the story

that the very first human ever adopted was one of your ancestors?"

"Well," Honor glanced around to reassure herself that only LaFollet, in his proper position behind her chair, was close enough to overhear, for this was something one shared only with trusted friends or someone else who'd been adopted, "according to my family's traditions there is, anyway. Good thing, too. If the family stories are right, it was the only thing that saved her life. It may be selfish of me, but I'm just as glad she survived."

"I'm glad she did, too," Georgides said quietly, reaching out to run his fingers gently down Odysseus' spine. The 'cat pressed back against the caress, green eyes gleaming at his person, and the admiral smiled. "The reason I asked, Milady, was because if the legend *is* true, I wanted to express my thanks."

"On behalf of my family, you're welcome," she replied with a grin.

"And while we're on the subject of thanking people," Georgides went on a bit more solemnly, "I'd also like to thank you for accepting this assignment. I know what you sacrificed in Yeltsin to do it, and your willingness to give all that up only confirms all the good things I've heard about you." Honor blushed, but the admiral ignored it and went on quietly. "If there's anything *Vulcan* can do to get your command ready—anything at all—please let me know."

"Thank you, Sir. I will," she assured him equally quietly, and reached for her wine once more.

• CHAPTER FIVE

Honor's cutter drifted through the enormous hatch of HMS *Wayfarer*'s Number One Hold. The small craft was a tiny minnow against the vast, star-speckled maw of cargo doors which could easily have admitted a destroyer, and the hold they served was built to the same gargantuan scale. Work lights created pockets of glaring brilliance where parties of yard dogs labored on the final modifications, but there was no atmosphere to diffuse the light, and most of the stupendous alloy cavern was even blacker than the space beyond the hatch.

A final puff of thrusters killed the cutter's last momentum. It hovered in the hold's zero-gee, and Honor rolled Nimitz over in her lap to get a clear view of his skinsuit's environmental panel. After three years of practice, the 'cat had become completely comfortable with the small suit Paul Tankersley had designed for him, but that didn't mean she intended to take any chances with him, and she made a quick but thorough check of his suit's seals and illuminated telltales.

Nimitz endured the scrutiny with patience, for he was as well aware as she that a mistake could have fatal consequences, but all lights were green. Honor stood against the cutter's internal gravity, lifted him to her shoulder, and sealed her own helmet. LaFollet had already sealed his, and he stood waiting beside the hatch as his Steadholder nodded to the flight engineer.

"We're ready, PO."

"Aye, aye, Ma'am," the petty officer replied, but she made a quick visual check of Honor's own readouts before

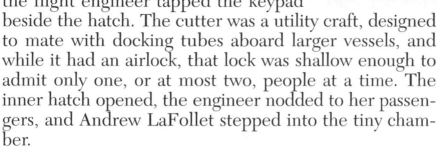

she spoke to the flight deck. "Flight, we're cracking the hatch."

"Understood," the pilot replied, and the flight engineer tapped the keypad beside the hatch. The cutter was a utility craft, designed to mate with docking tubes aboard larger vessels, and while it had an airlock, that lock was shallow enough to admit only one, or at most two, people at a time. The inner hatch opened, the engineer nodded to her passengers, and Andrew LaFollet stepped into the tiny chamber.

Strict protocol called for Honor, as the senior officer aboard, to disembark first, and under normal circumstances, LaFollet would have deferred to custom. But the black, forbidding vastness of the hold awoke an instinct-level wariness that overrode his deference, and Honor chose not to protest as he closed the hatch behind him and the lock cycled. The outer hatch opened, and he stepped out, thirty meters above the hold deck, and flicked his suit thrusters. The impetus carried him gently to the deck plates and his boot soles' tractor pads clicked as they made contact. He stood there a moment, looking about him, then nodded.

"Come ahead, My Lady," he said over his com, and Honor and Nimitz stepped into the lock with Commander Frank Schubert, the officer in charge of *Wayfarer's* overhaul. She held the 'cat in her arms while Schubert cycled the lock, then released him as the outer hatch opened once more. She and Schubert landed almost simultaneously beside LaFollet, but Nimitz disliked the sticky resistance of his own "boots" and chose to stop a meter above her head. He drifted there easily, in total control of his muscle feedback-activated thrusters, and Honor heard his cheerful bleek. Nimitz always had loved free-fall, and she sensed his delight as he hovered effortlessly.

"Just don't get lost, Stinker. It's a big hold," she cautioned over her com, and felt his silent reassurance. A gentle impetus from his thrusters sent him drifting downward, and he reached out, gloved true-hands catching the grab loop on her suit's shoulder to anchor him in place. She configured her artificial left eye to low-light mode and gazed about the hold, noting the gaunt, gantry-like rail work which festooned its bulkheads, then turned her head to grin at the 'cat. He wrinkled his whiskers back at her, and she sent him a gently admonishing thought to stay close before she turned her attention to Schubert. Admiral Georgides had assured Honor that despite his relatively junior rank, Schubert was one of his best people, and everything she'd seen so far confirmed Georgides' high opinion of the commander.

"Welcome aboard, Milady." Schubert's voice was a resonant tenor, and he smiled as he waved an arm at the gaping hold like a king displaying his kingdom.

"Thank you," Honor replied. Schubert's welcome wasn't the polite nothing a civilian might have thought it, for until *Wayfarer*'s overhaul was complete, she belonged to *Vulcan*, not Honor. That meant she was Schubert's ship, in so far as a powered-down, motionless hunk of alloy could be considered a "ship," and that Honor was a guest aboard her.

"If you'll follow me, please?" Schubert continued, and Honor nodded, then hit her own thrusters as Schubert sailed gracefully away. LaFollet followed, holding station on her as precisely as if he'd spent half a lifetime in a Manticoran skinsuit, and she gazed about with sharp interest, left eye still in low-light mode, as Schubert continued speaking over the com.

"As you can see, Milady," he said, "one thing we've got is *lots* of cubage. When they drew the plans for the conversion, they figured they might as well take advantage of it. In fact, the main reason we're running behind on the original target date is the extent of the changes BuShips made after the initial concept was approved."

The three humans and the treecat arrowed through the vacuum towards one of the islands of light, and Schubert pulled up in a gentle, momentum-braking arc. Honor and LaFollet followed suit, and she switched her eye back to normal light levels as the yard dog gestured to the hardsuited work party before them.

"This is one of the main rails, Milady," he said, his voice now completely serious. "There are six of them, equally spaced around the circumference of the hold, and we've incorporated cross rails every two hundred meters. You'll be able to launch six pods in each salvo, and if you lose a section of any rail, you'll be able to route the pods up or down to the next cross link and still have access to that rail's load out."

"Understood, Commander," Honor murmured, watching the work party. They'd finished the final welds; now they were testing the power train, and she felt an almost unwilling stir of admiration for the basic design. Admiral White Haven's lack of involvement with Project Trojan Horse had left him able to give her only the most general notion of what BuShips intended, but she'd had time to do some research of her own, and, almost despite herself, she was impressed.

Honor had her own reasons to dislike Admiral of the Red Lady Sonja Hemphill. "Horrible Hemphill," as she was known to certain segments of the Fleet, was the leading spokesperson of the *jeune ecole*, the Navy faction which rejected the "traditionalist" views of officers like Earl White Haven. Or, for that matter, of Lady Honor Harrington. Hemphill was willing to admit the study of classic strategy and tactics had something to offer, but she argued—vehemently—that doctrine had petrified. The weapons of modern ships of the wall were the product of incremental improvements on a theme which had been established T-centuries earlier, and in consequence, the tactics for their employment had been thoroughly explored. In Hemphill's view, that exploration equated to stultification, and the *jeune ecole* proposed to shatter the "log jam of outdated concepts" by introducing new weapons. Their idea was to introduce technologies which were so radical that no navy which failed to adopt them could hope to survive against one which did.

To a considerable extent, Honor agreed with both their

analysis and their ambition. She didn't believe in magic bullets, but the tactician in her hated the formalism which had become the norm, and the strategist in her hungered for some way to fight battles which would be *decisive*, not attritional affairs from which the weaker force was free to disengage.

Given the distances involved in interstellar warfare, launching some sort of lightning thrust to an enemy's vital nerve center—like the Haven System—usually meant uncovering your *own* strategic center. If you had sufficiently overwhelming strength, you might be able to protect your own critical areas while simultaneously attacking his, but in a serious war that was seldom the case. Armchair strategists forgot that when they demanded to know why a navy bothered to fight for intervening systems. Ships could move freely through the immensity of space and, with judicious routing, avoid interception short of their target, so why not simply do it? The People's Republic, after all, had carried out dozens of such strokes in its fifty-odd years of conquest.

But the Peeps had been able to do that only because their opponents' navies had been too small to mount serious defenses. The RMN, however, was large enough to give even the People's Navy pause, and in a war between serious opponents both sides knew their fleets could strike straight for the other's core systems. Because of that, neither was willing to uncover its own vitals. Instead, they maintained fleets and fortifications they hoped were capable of protecting those areas and con-ducted offensive operations only with what was left over—which meant their own offensive forces were seldom powerful enough to execute the daring stroke the ama-teurs thirsted for. That was why they wound up fighting for star systems between their home systems and the enemy's. The systems targeted were normally chosen for their own inherent value, but the true object was to com-pel the enemy to fight to hold them . . . and give your-self the chance to whittle away at his strength until he could no longer simultaneously protect himself and attack

your own strategic center. That was precisely why Admiral White Haven and Sixth Fleet were so intent on taking Trevor's Star. Not only would it eliminate a threat to the Manticore System and greatly simplify the Alliance's logistic problems, but fighting as far forward as possible in Havenite space would keep the Peeps on the defensive which, hopefully, would force them to fight on the Alliance's terms . . . and preclude any temptation they might feel to attempt a "daring stroke" of their own. They'd already tried that twice, once in the war's opening phases, and again in Yeltsin barely a year ago, and no one in the Alliance wanted them to feel tempted to try a third time.

It wasn't the fastest way to win a war, and Honor would have loved to launch the sort of attack the armchair warriors advocated. Unfortunately, you could only get away with that against an opponent who *let* you, and whatever else one might say about the Peeps, they'd been in the conquering business too long to let that happen. That meant the destruction of their fleet—and thus their ability to sustain offensive or defensive operations—was the only workable strategic goal. The more quickly and decisively the Manticoran Alliance could achieve that destruction, the fewer of its own people it would lose along the way, and Honor was in favor of anything—even if it was suggested by Horrible Hemphill—which could speed that process up.

Some of the traditionalists, however, were—exactly as the *jeune ecole* argued—simply afraid of change. They *understood* the present rules, and they had no desire to face a radically different combat environment in which their advantages in experience became irrelevant. Honor understood that, and she disagreed with *them* at least as strongly as she did with the *jeune ecole*, just as she knew White Haven did. The problem was that Hemphill had fought so hard for changes that she seemed to see *any* new concept as desirable simply because it *was* new. Worse, for all her talk of new weapons, she was firmly

wedded to the concept of material warfare . . . which was
simply another term for the very sort of attrition Honor
wanted to break free of. Hemphill's ideal was to wade
straight into the enemy, hopefully equipped with superior weapons, and simply keep smashing until something
gave. Sometimes that was the only option, but officers
like Honor and White Haven were appalled by the body
counts the *jeune ecole* was prepared to accept.

What was really needed, Honor often thought, was
someone who could fuse the tenets of the competing phi-
losophies. Admiral White Haven had accomplished some
of that with his insistence that there was room for new
weapons but that those weapons must be carefully evalu-
ated and fitted into classic concepts. He and a handful
of other senior officers—like Sir James Webster, Mark
Sarnow, Theodosia Kuzak, and Sebastian D'Orville—had
made a start in that direction, but every time they gave
a centimeter, Hemphill and her fellows thought they saw
the opposition crumbling and charged to the attack,
demanding still more and quicker change.

None of which was to say that Hemphill hadn't accomplished a lot that was worthwhile. The RMN's short-range
FTL communication capability stemmed directly from
one of her pet projects, and so had the new, improved
missile pods. There were rumors of other projects sim-
mering away on various back burners which might produce equally valuable innovations, and if only Hemphill
were less . . . vociferous, Honor would have had no reservations. Unfortunately, then-Commander Harrington
had been on the receiving end of one of Horrible
Hemphill's efforts to force a radical (and radically *flawed*)
concept into general deployment. She'd been compelled
to take the resultant experimental armament into a fight
to the death—against a *Peep* Q-ship—which had killed
half her crew and battered her ship into scrap, and that
was enough to make her take any Hemphill-authored
suggestion with a very large grain of salt.

In this instance, however, Hemphill's brainchild was
impressive, particularly in light of Honor's personal

experience of how dangerous a well-handled Q-ship could be.

She floated in zero-gee, and the surface of her brain listened attentively to everything Schubert said. She knew she'd be able to replay the entire conversation verbatim later, but for now her inner thoughts were busy with what she'd already learned about Project Trojan Horse.

The Peep Q-ships like the one Honor had tangled with had been purpose built from the keel out. In effect, they were warships disguised as merchantmen, with military-grade impellers, sidewalls, and compensators to match their armament. Under normal circumstances, they could expect to hold their own against even a battlecruiser, because they'd been built with the toughness to absorb heavy damage and remain in action.

That was the biggest weakness of Trojan Horse, for the *Caravan* class were true merchantmen—big, slow, bumbling freighters, without armor, without military-grade drives, without internal compartmentalization or a warship's sophisticated damage control remotes. Their hulls were the flattened, double-ended spindles of any impeller drive vessel, but they'd been laid out to maximize cargo-handling efficiency, without a warship's "hammerhead" ends, where the hull flared back out to mount powerful chase armaments. They'd also been built with only one power plant apiece which, like many of their vital systems, was deliberately placed close to the skins of their hulls to facilitate access for maintenance and repair. Unfortunately, that also exposed it to hostile fire, and though *Vulcan* had added a second fusion plant deep inside *Wayfarer*'s hull, no one in her right mind would ever consider her a "proper" warship.

But the undeniably fertile imagination of Hemphill's allies in BuShips had given her Q-ships some advantages the Peeps had never thought of. For one thing, their energy batteries would come as a major surprise to anyone unfortunate enough to enter their range. The Peeps' Q-ships had settled for projectors heavy enough to deal with cruisers and battlecruisers, but Hemphill had taken advantage of a bottleneck in the super-dreadnought building schedule. Weapons production had gotten well ahead of hull construction, so Hemphill had convinced the Admiralty to skim off some of the completed lasers and grasers sitting around in storage. *Wayfarer* had barely half the energy mounts of her Peep counterparts, but the ones she did have were at least three times as powerful. If she ever got close enough to shoot anyone with those massive beams, her target was going to know it had been kissed.

Nor would any raider enjoy taking her on in missile combat. Since the Trojans were intended as armed cruisers, Hemphill had convinced the Admiralty to go whole hog and delete *all* cargo carrying capacity, aside from a generous allowance for spares and other maintenance items. Even after cramming in all the additional life support *Wayfarer*'s Marines and weapons crews would require, that left the designers an enormous cubage—after all, a *Caravan* massed 7.35 megatons—and they'd shown a devious inventiveness. They'd provided magazine space for a stupendous ammunition supply for her twenty broadside missile tubes, which, like her energy weapons, were as heavy as one would normally find in a *Gryphon*-class SD. It made sense to give a vessel which might be called upon to operate outside the logistic pipeline for extended periods as much ammunition stowage as possible, but that was an almost secondary consideration where her broadside armament was involved, for the Trojans' real long-range punch was a totally new departure which Honor found herself totally and unequivocally in favor of.

Wayfarer's Number One Hold had been reconfigured solely to carry missile pods. Its size gave her room for literally hundreds of them, and judicious modification to her stern meant she could do something no regular warship could. A superdreadnought might tractor as many as ten or twelve pods inside her impeller wedge to deploy when she needed them. Smaller warships, with tighter,

less powerful wedges, were forced to tow them astern, where they degraded acceleration rates and were also vulnerable to proximity "soft kills," since they were outside the towing ship's sidewalls. *Wayfarer*, however, lacked the traditional stern chasers which normally crammed the aft section of a warship to capacity. Her limited after beam, compared to a warship, had created some problems, but a little ingenuity on Schubert's part had allowed *Vulcan* to extend Number One Hold almost to the stern plate. That meant her repositioned cargo doors could be used to dump cargo directly out the after aspect of her impeller wedge—which couldn't be closed with a sidewall anyway—and her ejector rails would allow her to launch salvos of six ten-missile pods at the rate of one salvo every twelve seconds. In effect, she could put an additional three hundred missiles per minute into space.

Nor had the designers stopped there. Since they had all that space available, they'd outfitted holds Three and Four as LAC bays. Traditional light attack craft were considerably inferior to hyper-capable warships for many reasons. Their small size left no room for hyper generators, so they couldn't translate into or out of h-space. Nor could they mount Warshawski sails, which meant they couldn't be employed inside the grav waves starships normally rode even if they could somehow be gotten into hyper in the first place. Their relatively weaker impeller wedges and sidewalls also made them more fragile than larger warships, and they were too small to pack in worthwhile amounts of armor or sufficient armament for sustained combat. They were eggshells armed with hammers, equipped with heavy missile loads for their displacement, usually in low-mass, single-shot box launchers, and against most opponents about the best they could hope for was to get their missiles off before they were annihilated.

But the new LACs the Star Kingdom had been laying down over the last four T-years (also, Honor admitted, as one of Hemphill's brainstorms) were a whole new breed. BuShips had made enormous strides in inertial compensator design, building on the original research Grayson had undertaken when no one would tell them how compensators worked. Denied the advantage of everyone else's knowledge—or the limitations of everyone else's assumptions—Grayson's Office of Shipbuilding had innocently followed up a concept everyone else "knew" wouldn't work and opened the door to an entirely new level of compensator efficiency. BuShips hadn't thought of it first, but the Star Kingdom's shipbuilders had an immense store of technical expertise, and they were improving upon Grayson's groundwork steadily. Honor's last Manticoran ship, the battlecruiser *Nike*, was barely four years old, and she'd been fitted with what was then the newest and best Manticoran compensator, based on the original Grayson research. Ships now on the drawing board would be equipped with compensators which increased *Nike*'s level of efficiency by an additional twenty-five percent . . . and *Wayfarer*'s LACs already had them. Fitted with more powerful impellers to match, they could pull over six hundred gravities of acceleration, and that made them the fastest sublight ships in space—for the moment.

They also mounted much heavier sidewalls and semi-decent energy armaments to back up their missile cells. They'd given up something in terms of total throw weight to squeeze all that in, but they were faster, tougher, and far more dangerous within the energy envelope, and even at long range, their new launchers—using the same technology as the missile pods—let them throw missiles which were individually much heavier and more capable.

More to the point, perhaps, most pirates weren't proper warships, either. A single one of the new LACs was as heavily armed as a typical raider, and *Wayfarer* had been reconfigured to carry six of them in each of her modified cargo holds. Anywhere *except* in a grav wave, she could multiply her force level by dropping no less than twelve modern and, for their size, powerful parasite warships into the engagement.

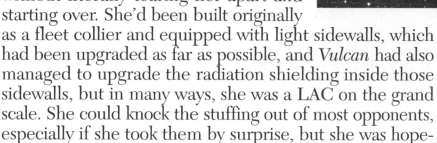

Her biggest weakness was that it had been impossible to upgrade her drive without literally tearing her apart and starting over. She'd been built originally as a fleet collier and equipped with light sidewalls, which had been upgraded as far as possible, and *Vulcan* had also managed to upgrade the radiation shielding inside those sidewalls, but in many ways, she was a LAC on the grand scale. She could knock the stuffing out of most opponents, especially if she took them by surprise, but she was hopelessly incapable of absorbing much damage of her own.

All in all, Honor thought as Schubert finished his explanation and soared off to show her the next point of interest, *Wayfarer* and her sisters might just prove more effective in the Breslau Sector than even the Admiralty was willing to believe. Honor had once spent most of a two-year commission in Silesian space, chasing pirates in the heavy cruiser *Fearless*. She knew the area at least as well as most Manticoran officers, and she'd never met the pirate who could stand up to what *Wayfarer* could hand out. Some of the "privateers" who also plagued the Confederacy might be another story—some of them could nearly match a battlecruiser's offensive power—but they were few and far between and, for the most part, careful to avoid Manticoran shipping. That could have changed with so much of the Fleet diverted to the battle front, but privateers had to worry about the "liberation governments" they nominally represented. No breakaway star system wanted to irritate the Star Kingdom unduly, and at least one "privateer" had found itself seized by its own government, its entire crew handed over to the Manticoran courts, when that government had been informed of what would happen to it if the offending crew *wasn't* surrendered.

No, she mused thoughtfully, with a decent ship's company behind her, she wouldn't be unduly worried about taking on any pirate or privateer *she'd* ever heard of, and she realized she was actually beginning to look forward to the assignment after all.

• CHAPTER SIX

Admiral of the Green Sir Lucien Cortez, Fifth Space Lord of the Manticoran Navy, stood behind his desk as his yeoman ushered Honor Harrington into his office.

The last three days had been a whirlwind for her. She'd managed to steal a few hours to visit her parents, but every other available instant had been spent crawling around her new ship's gizzards and discussing her modifications with *Vulcan's* experts. There was no time for any major changes in the original plans, but she'd been able to suggest a couple of improvements which could still be incorporated. One was an additional lift cross-connecting the two LAC holds, which would allow service personnel to move much more easily under normal conditions and cut the time required for the LAC crews to man their ships in a "scramble" situation by twenty-five percent. That was the more fundamental and labor intensive of the two, and BuShips had hemmed and hawed for thirty-six hours before authorizing it.

Her other suggestion had been much simpler and more subtle. When she'd gone after the Peep Q-ship *Sirius* in Basilisk, her first warning that her opponent was armed had come when the Peeps jettisoned the false plating concealing their weapons bays and her radar picked up the separating debris. Partly in response to that portion of her own after-action report, *Vulcan* had provided the Trojans with powered hatch covers rather than false plating and gone to some lengths to make the covers look like standard cargo hatches. It had been a laudable idea,

but by the time they provided for the LAC launch bays, as well, there were far too many "cargo hatches" along *Wayfarer's* flanks to fool anyone who got a decent optical on her.

Unless, of course, the hatches were invisible, which was why Honor had proposed covering them with plastic patches formed and painted to blend perfectly with the surrounding hull. The patches, she'd pointed out, would be invisible to radar. They could be jettisoned for action without any betraying radar detection, they'd be cheap, they could be fabricated in mere days, and her ships could stow hundreds of them away for replacement after each action.

Commander Schubert had loved the idea, and even BuShips had offered no quibbles, which made it one of the easiest sells Honor had ever proposed. Yet even as she immersed herself in the hardware details, she'd been nigglingly aware of two things no one had yet discussed with her: personnel, and the specifics of her mission brief.

She knew, in general terms, what the Admiralty expected her to do in Breslau, but no one had made it official so far . . . just as no one had said a thing to her about her ships' companies. There could be a lot of reasons for that—after all, it would be over three weeks before *Vulcan* released *Wayfarer* for post-refit trials— but it did seem odd. She didn't even know who her exec was going to be, or who was slated to command the other three ships of her small squadron. In some ways, she was just as happy not to have to worry about that yet, but she knew she shouldn't be. Much as she might prefer concentrating on one thing at a time, it was important to start gaining a feel for her command team quickly, and she'd wondered what was causing the delay.

Now, as she crossed the Fifth Space Lord's office and reached out to take the hand he offered in greeting, she knew she was about to find out. And as she sampled Cortez's emotions through Nimitz, she also knew she wasn't going to like the reason.

"Please, Milady, be seated," Cortez offered, gesturing at the chair before his desk.

Honor sank into it, and the sharp-faced, slightly balding admiral sat back down, propped his elbows on his desk, and laced his fingers together to lean his chin on them while he regarded her. They'd met only twice before, both times more or less in passing. But he'd followed her career, and he'd wondered what she would feel like in person, for Lucien Cortez was a man who'd learned to trust his instincts. Now he absorbed her level eyes, calm and composed even though she must realize there had to be a special reason for the Fifth Space Lord to summon a mere captain to a face-to-face meeting, and gave a mental node of approval.

Of course, he reminded himself, she wasn't actually a "mere" captain. For the past T-year and a half, she'd been a full admiral—in a relatively new navy, perhaps, but an admiral. And though she hadn't mentioned it to anyone, Cortez also knew the Grayson Space Navy had simply detached her for "temporary duty" with the RMN. As far as the Graysons were concerned, she was still on active service with *their* fleet, and her GSN seniority would continue to accrue. How many officers, he wondered wryly, knew that by resigning from one navy they could instantly be promoted four full ranks in another? It must give her a rather unusual perspective, but she seemed totally unaware of it as she waited, with all the respect of any captain for a flag officer.

Honor felt the intense scrutiny his mild brown eyes hid so well. She couldn't tell what he was thinking behind it, but she *could* feel his strange combination of amusement, curiosity, anger, frustration, and apprehension. She was reasonably certain the last three emotions weren't directed at her, yet she knew she—or her squadron—were at the bottom of them, and she waited patiently for him to explain.

"Thank you for coming, Milady," the man in charge of managing the RMN's manpower said finally. "I'm sorry we couldn't meet sooner than this, but I've been beating the bushes for the personnel to man your ships."

Honor's mental antennae twanged at his half-acid, half-apologetic tone, and she sat up straighter, hands buried in Nimitz's fluffy coat, and eyed him sharply. Cortez saw it and grimaced, then leaned back in his chair and raised his hands in a throwing-away gesture.

"We've got a problem, Milady," he sighed. "Specifically, the pressure to expedite your deployment is playing merry hell with my manning plans."

"In what way, Sir?" Honor asked carefully.

"Essentially," Cortez replied, "we've been asked to deploy your ships six months ahead of schedule, and we hadn't allowed for it in our personnel assignments. No doubt you're aware of how tightly stretched we are just now?"

"In a general way, Sir, but I *have* been out of the Star Kingdom—and the Queen's uniform—for three T-years." She managed, with difficulty, to keep a residual edge of resentment out of her voice.

"I'll summarize briefly, then." Cortez braced his elbows on the arms of his chair and steepled his fingers across his middle. "As I'm sure you *do* know, we have something like fifty thousand RMN officers and ratings currently on loan to the GSN, not including the purely technical support personnel we've assigned to their Office of Shipbuilding and R&D sections. Given their own critical shortage of trained manpower, that's barely enough for them to fully man their fleet, and the situation's gotten worse since they started commissioning home-built SDs.

"I mention the situation in Yeltsin only as an example—one of many, I'm afraid, though certainly the largest single one—of the personnel we've been forced to loan out to our allies. All told, we've got a hundred and fifty thousand Manticorans in other people's uniforms right now. Add in all the technical support staffs, and the number comes to about a quarter million."

He regarded Honor intently, and she nodded slowly.

"In addition to that, we have our own manpower needs. We've got roughly three hundred of the wall in commission, with an average crew of fifty-two hundred. That uses up another million and a half men and women. After that, we've got a hundred and twenty-four forts covering the Junction, with another million plus people aboard them. Then there's all the *rest* of the Fleet, which uses up another two and a half million, our own shipyards, fleet bases on foreign stations like Grendelsbane, R&D, ONI, and so on and so on. Add in all the people we need for routine personnel rotations, and we've got something on the order of eleven million people in Navy and Marine uniforms. That's only a bit over three-tenths of a percent of our total population, but it comes out of our most *productive* population segments, and our projections call for the figure to double over the next two T-years. And, of course, we have to worry about manning both the Army and the merchant marine, as well."

Honor nodded again, even more slowly, as she began to see where Cortez was headed. The Royal Manticoran Marines were specialists who held shipboard duty assignments as well as providing boarding parties and emergency ground combat components. Heavy planetary combat was the role of the Royal Army, which, undistracted by the need to master shipboard systems, could concentrate solely on planetary combat hardware and techniques. In peacetime, the Army was usually severely downsized, since the Marines could handle most peacekeeping roles, but in time of war, it had to be recruited back up to strength for garrison duty, if nothing else. The Marine Corps, for example, had handed the planet Masada over to an Army commander just a T-year earlier, with a profound sigh of relief, and the Army was also currently responsible for garrisoning no less than eighteen Peep worlds. In fact, for Manticore actually to win this war, the Star Kingdom was going to have to take—and garrison—a *lot* of Peep planets, and that meant the Army's appetite for personnel was going to grow in direct proportion to the Navy's successes.

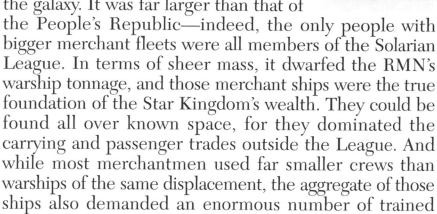

That was a serious enough diversion of manpower, but the Manticoran merchant marine was the fourth largest in the galaxy. It was far larger than that of the People's Republic—indeed, the only people with bigger merchant fleets were all members of the Solarian League. In terms of sheer mass, it dwarfed the RMN's warship tonnage, and those merchant ships were the true foundation of the Star Kingdom's wealth. They could be found all over known space, for they dominated the carrying and passenger trades outside the League. And while most merchantmen used far smaller crews than warships of the same displacement, the aggregate of those ships also demanded an enormous number of trained spacers.

"The reason I've gone into this, Milady," Cortez said, "is so that you can understand what sort of numbers BuPers has to juggle. You may not be aware that we've doubled class sizes at the Academy because of our need for trained officers. Even so, we've been forced to recall a much larger percentage of reservists from the merchant fleet than we'd like, and in the not too distant future we're going to have to set up OCS programs to turn merchant spacers without previous military experience into Queen's officers, as well. Despite that, we're keeping up with demand, however barely, and our new training programs have been planned to keep pace with the requirements of our new construction. But our entire manpower management plan is a very carefully orchestrated—and fragile—edifice.

"Now, we incorporated Trojan Horse into our schedules, but we anticipated six more months of lead time. As you know, your own ship—and her LACs—require twenty-five hundred officers and ratings and another five hundred Marines, and the total unit strength for Trojan Horse is projected at fifteen. That's forty-five thousand more people, Milady, almost as many as we have on loan for GSN fleet duty, and we don't have them. In six months we will; right now, we don't."

He raised his hands again, and Honor bit her lip. This was an aspect of the manning problem she hadn't considered, and she kicked herself for it. She darned well *should* have thought about it, and she wondered if some subconscious part of her had deliberately avoided doing so.

"Just how bad is it, Sir Lucien?" she asked finally, and he shrugged unhappily.

"Your four ships shouldn't be that much of a problem. We're only talking about twelve thousand people for all of them, after all. Unfortunately, it *is* a problem. To make up the numbers, we're going to have to draft people from existing ships' companies. I estimate something like a third of your total strength will have to come from there, and you know no captain voluntarily gives up his better people. We'll do our best for you, but the majority of your crews will consist of totally inexperienced newbies fresh from training or old sweats whose current skippers are delighted to be rid of them. Your Marine complements should be solid, and we'll do the best we can to weed real troublemakers out of the drafts from other ships, but I'd be lying if I said you'll have the sort of crews *I'd* want to take into action."

Honor nodded once more. She understood Cortez's emotions now. The Fifth Space Lord was an experienced combat commander. He understood the implications of what he was telling her, and he felt personally responsible for them. He wasn't, but that didn't change the way he felt.

Her brain ticked with a curious detachment as she considered the news. No captain wanted to take an ill-prepared crew into combat, and, in a way, that was more true of a Q-ship's CO than any other. Q-ships normally operated solitaire. There wouldn't be anyone else to bail them out if it hit the fan, and they would live or die by how well their own people did their jobs. Worse, the rush to deploy her squadron meant there would be next to no time for the drilling misfit crews required. She felt confident of her ability to convince even the worst troublemaker to do things her way, but she'd need time to do it, and people whose sole shortcoming was lack of experience would need even more careful handling. If she didn't *have* that time . . .

"I'm sorry, Milady," Cortez said quietly. "I assure you my staff and I will do the best we can, and, frankly, I delayed this meeting as long as I could in hopes that one of my people would come up with some brilliant solution. Unfortunately, no one did, and, under the circumstances, I felt it was my duty to explain the situation to you personally."

"I understand, Sir." Honor gazed down at Nimitz for a moment, stroking his spine, then looked back up at the admiral. "All you can do is the best you can do, Sir Lucien, and every captain knows it's up to her to kick her crew into shape, if that's what it takes. We'll manage."

She heard the false confidence in her own voice, but it was the only possible response, for it *was* a captain's responsibility to turn whatever manpower she was given into an effective fighting force. It was also a job she'd done before—but not, a small inner voice said coldly, under quite this severe a handicap.

"Well," Cortez looked away for a moment, then met her eyes once more, "I can offer you one thing, Milady. Short as we are on experienced personnel, I've managed to scrape together a core of solid officers and NCOs. Frankly, most of them are a bit junior for the posts we'll be assigning them to, but their records are excellent, and I believe you'll find several have served with you before." He took a data chip from his desk drawer and leaned over the desk to hand it to her. "I've listed them on the chip here, and if there are any other officers or ratings you'd care to specifically request, I'll do my utmost to get them. I'm afraid it'll be a case of whether or not they're available, but we'll certainly try. As far as the newbies are concerned, your squadron has first call. They may still be wet behind the ears, but at least we'll give you the ones with the highest efficiency ratings."

"I appreciate that, Sir," Honor said, and she did.

"I have managed one other thing I think you'll pleased to hear," Cortez said after a moment. "Well, two, actually. Alice Truman's just made list, and we've assigned her to command *Parnassus* as your second-in-command."

Honor's eyes lit at that, but there was an edge of concern under her delight. Despite the anticipation she'd begun to feel over the past three days, she remembered how *she'd* first seen her command. An officer of Truman's caliber, especially one who'd just made the senior captain's list, which virtually assured her of future flag rank, might well regard assignment to a Q-ship as a slap in the face. Honor wouldn't blame her, but if she held Honor responsible for it—

"I think I should mention," Cortez added, as if he could read her mind, "that we explained the situation fully to her and she volunteered for the slot. She was slated to assume command of *Lord Elton*, but *Elton's* in for a five-month overhaul. When we asked her if she'd consider a transfer to *Parnassus* instead and explained she'd be serving with you, she accepted immediately."

"Thank you for telling me that, Sir," Honor said with a smile of mingled gratitude and pleasure. "Captain Truman is one of the finest officers I've ever known." And, she reflected, the fact that Alice had volunteered even knowing the immense task they faced warmed her heart.

"I thought you'd be pleased," Cortez replied with a small smile of his own. "And, in addition, I think I've found you an executive officer you'll like."

He pressed a button on his com panel and leaned back in his chair again. A few moments later, the door opened once more and a tall, dark-haired commander walked through it. He was built on long and lean lines, with a hawk-like nose and a ready smile. The breast of his tunic bore the white-barred blue ribbon of the Order of Gallantry and the red-and-white ribbon of the Saganami Cross, and, like Honor herself, the blood-red stripe of the Monarch's Thanks marked his right sleeve. He looked decidedly on the young side, even for a prolong recipient,

to have acquired two of the Star Kingdom's four top medals for valor, and
even as Honor rose in pure delight, her
mind's eye could still see the awkward
puppy of a junior-grade lieutenant she'd taken to Basilisk Station with her just eight years before.

"Rafe!" she cried, cradling Nimitz in the crook of her
left arm to extend her right hand.

"I believe you two have met, Milady," Cortez murmured with a small smile as Commander Cardones
gripped her hand fiercely.

"I didn't get the chance to serve with you very long
in *Nike*, Skipper," he said. "Maybe this time will work
out better."

"I'm sure it will, Rafe," she said warmly, and turned
to look at Cortez. "Thank you, Sir. Thank you very much."

"He was due for a stint as *someone's* exec, Milady," the
Fifth Space Lord said, waving off her thanks. "Besides,
you seem to be making something of a career out of
completing his training. It would be a pity to break up
the team when you clearly still have so far to go."

Cardones grinned at the comment which, eight years
before, would have reduced him instantly to red-faced,
mumbling incoherence, and Honor smiled back at him.
For all his youth, Rafael Cardones was one of the best
tactical officers she'd ever seen, and he'd clearly gone
right on maturing in the time she'd spent in Yeltsin.

Cortez watched her evident pleasure and Cardones'
matching happiness—and respect for his new CO—and
wondered if Lady Harrington realized how deliberately
the younger officer had modeled himself on her. Cortez
had gone to some lengths to find her the right executive officer, and a simple comparison of Cardones' record
before and after first serving under her showed that his
own teasing comment wasn't far off the mark. In fact,
Cortez had run similar comparisons on several officers
who'd served under her, and he'd been impressed by what
he'd found. Some of the RMN's most effective combat
commanders had never been good teachers; Honor

Harrington was. In addition to her sterling battle record, she'd shown an almost mystic ability to pass her own dedication and professionalism on to subordinates, and to the officer commanding the Bureau of Personnel, that was almost more precious than her own combat skills.

Now he cleared his throat, recapturing their attention, and nodded to Cardones.

"The Commander has a partial roster of *Wayfarer*'s company, Milady. It's very rough so far, but at least it may serve as a beginning. He's already suggested a few other officers and petty officers to help flesh it out, and my staff is currently running a records search to see how many, if any, of them are available. I understand Admiral Georgides estimates another three weeks before you can power up and begin moving personnel aboard?"

"Approximately, Sir," Honor replied. "I think he's being pessimistic, but I doubt he'll be able to shave more than a few days off his estimate. *Parnassus* and *Scheherazade* will complete about the same time, but it looks like *Gudrid* will need at least another ten days."

"All right." Cortez pursed his lips, then nodded to himself. "I'll have at least a captain and an exec for all four of them by Thursday. By the time you can actually start putting people aboard, we should have all your commissioned personnel either on hand or designated and en route. We'll try to have your warrant and petty officers all lined up by then, too, and General Vonderhoff assures me your Marine complements won't present any problem. As far as your enlisted personnel are concerned, however, it's going to be catch as catch can. I have no idea how quickly, or in what order, we'll be able to assemble them, though we'll do our best."

"I'm sure you will, My Lord, and I appreciate it," Honor said sincerely, well aware of how unusual it was for Cortez to personally discuss the manning problems of a single squadron with the officer designated to command it.

"It's the least we can do, Milady," Cortez replied, then grimaced again. "It's never a good thing when partisan politics interfere in military operations, Milady, especially when it costs us the services of an officer with your record, and I regret that your return to Manticoran uniform has to take place under such circum-stances. But in case no one else has told you, we're all delighted to have you back."

"Thank you, Sir." Honor felt her cheekbones heating once more, but she met his gaze steadily and saw the approval in his eyes.

"In that case, Milady, I'll let you and Commander Cardones get started." Cortez held out his hand once more. "You've got a big job ahead of you, Captain, and you're facing some constraints you shouldn't have to. But if anyone can get it done, I feel certain you're the one. In case we don't see one another again before you ship out, good luck and good hunting."

"Thank you, Sir," Honor repeated, squeezing his hand hard. "We'll do our best."

• CHAPTER SEVEN

Honor leaned back in her chair to massage her aching eyes.

She'd been quartered in *Vulcan's* "Captains' Row" until she could move aboard *Wayfarer*, and her cabin was spacious enough. Smaller than the one she would occupy aboard her Q-ship and *much* smaller than the one she'd given up aboard the superdreadnought *Terrible*, but large by Navy standards and ample for comfort. Unfortunately, she was finding little opportunity to enjoy that comfort— or, for that matter, even the time to work out in *Vulcan's* senior officers' gym. The paperwork always piled a light-year deep when a new captain assumed command of a ship, and it was worse when that ship came straight from yard hands. Add the sea of documents—electronic and hardcopy—involved in assembling any squadron, then put it all under the pressure of a rushed deployment date, and there was hardly time to breathe, much less exercise . . . or sleep.

She grinned wryly, for if *she* had reams of paper to deal with, Rafe Cardones had more. A captain *commanded* a ship and held ultimate responsibility for every aspect of its operation and safety, but the exec *managed* that ship. It was her job to organize its crew, stores, maintenance, training schedules, and every other aspect of its operations so smoothly her captain hardly noticed all she was doing. It was a tall order, but a necessary one . . . and it was also why a stint as exec was usually the Navy's final test of an officer's ability to command her own ship. That would have been enough to keep any officer busy, but the Admiralty hadn't assigned Honor a staff. It made sense, she conceded, given that her "squadron" would almost certainly be split up into divisions or individual units rather than operate as a whole, yet it meant Rafe also had to shoulder the burden of an acting flag captain's role in addition to all the duties his post as *Wayfarer*'s exec imposed.

But even though the pressure-cooker urgency of getting the squadron ready for deployment added measurably to Rafe's arduous schedule, he was doing an exemplary job. He'd taken over full responsibility for coordinating with the yard dogs, and he and Chief Archer, her yeoman, were intercepting everything they could, whether specific to *Wayfarer* or to the squadron as a whole, before it reached her plate. She recognized and appreciated their efforts, but she was ultimately responsible for all of it. The best they could do was to get it so organized and arranged that all she had to do was sign off on the decisions they'd already made, and, frankly, they were proving very, very good at it.

Which wasn't going to save her from the report on her display.

She finished rubbing her eyes, took a sip of cocoa from the mug MacGuiness had left at her elbow, and returned doggedly to her duty. Archer had highlighted the summaries for each section, and it was really more Cardones' job than Honor's to deal with most of the items. He'd entered his own solutions at most of the decision points, and though one or two weren't quite the answers Honor would have chosen, she made herself consider each dispassionately. So far, they all looked workable, even if she might have done them differently, and some were actually better than her own first reaction would have been. What mattered most, though, was that they were Rafe's decisions to make. She had to sign off on them, but he had a right to do things his way as long as he handed her a ship that was an efficient, functional weapon when she

needed it. Under the circumstances, she had no intention of overriding him unless he screwed up in some
major way, and the chance of that happening was virtually nonexistent.

She reached the bottom of the endless report at last
and sighed again, this time with satisfaction. The entire
half-meg document had required only six decisions from
her, and that was far better than most captains could
have anticipated. She dashed a signature across the scan
pad, entered the command to save her own modifications, and dumped the entire document back into
Archer's queue.

One down, she thought, and punched for the next. A
document header appeared, and she groaned. Hydroponics. She *hated* hydroponic inventories! Of course they
were vital, but they always went on and on and on and
on. She took another sip of cocoa and cast an envious
glance up at Nimitz, snoring gently on his perch above
her desk, then gritted her teeth to dive back in.

But her dive was interrupted as the admittance chime
sounded. Her eyes—natural and cybernetic alike—lit with
pleasure at the thought of a reprieve, however temporary, from nutrients, fertilizers, seed banks, and filtration
systems, and she pressed the stud on her desk.

"Yes?"

"A visitor, My Lady," LaFollet's voice said. "Your Flight
Ops officer wants to pay his respects."

"Ah?" Honor rubbed her nose in surprise. Flight Ops
was one slot she and Rafe had been unable to fill, and
it was one of the more important ones. So if Rafe had
picked her visitor for the duty without even speaking to
her, the officer in question must have excellent credentials.

"Ask him to come in, Andrew," she said, and rose
behind her desk as the hatch slid open. To her surprise,
LaFollet didn't precede the newcomer through it. She
was quite certain she was safe from assassins aboard
Vulcan, yet for Andrew to let *anyone* into her presence
unescorted unless she specifically instructed him to

constituted a shocking breach in his professional paranoia. But then she saw the
young lieutenant who stepped through
the hatch, and she smiled hugely.

"Lieutenant Tremaine, reporting for duty, Ma'am,"
Scotty Tremaine said, and braced to attention with
Saganami Island precision. A burly, battered looking man
in the uniform of a senior chief petty officer followed
him and came to attention to his right and a half pace
behind him.

"Senior Chief Gunner's Mate Harkness, reporting for
duty, Ma'am," the petty officer rumbled, and Honor's
smile became a grin.

"If it isn't the dreadful duo!" she chuckled, moving
quickly around her desk and reaching out to grasp
Tremaine's hand. "Who agreed to let you two aboard my
ship?"

"Well, Commander Cardones said he was getting desperate, Ma'am," Tremaine replied with an irrepressible
twinkle. "Since he couldn't find any *qualified* personnel,
he figured he'd just have to make do with us."

"What *is* the Navy coming to?" Honor gave Tremaine's
hand a final squeeze and released it to offer her own hand
to Harkness in turn. The SCPO with the prizefighter's
face looked acutely embarrassed for a moment, then took
it in a powerful grip.

"Actually, Ma'am," Tremaine said more seriously, "I was
overdue for reassignment from *Prince Adrian*, anyway.
We were in Gryphon at the time, and Captain McKeon
was under orders to ship directly out to Sixth Fleet or
he'd have come by in person. But when BuPers told him
he had to come up with fifteen people, including an
officer, for your squadron, he decided he could spare my
services. As a matter of fact, he said something about
getting me out of his sight and into the hands of someone he knew could 'restrain my impetuosity.'" The lieutenant wrinkled his brow. "I don't have any idea what he
meant," he added innocently.

"Of course not," Honor agreed with another smile.

Ensign Prescott Tremaine had made his very first cruise
out of the Academy with her. In fact, he'd been with
her in Basilisk when it all came apart . . . and again in
Yeltsin, she thought, smile fading. He'd been there when
she learned what the Masadan butchers had done to
the crew of HMS *Madrigal*, and though they'd never
discussed it—and never would—he'd saved her career.
Not many junior-grade lieutenants would have had the
guts to physically restrain their squadron CO from an
act of madness.

"Well," she said, giving herself a mental shake and turning her attention to Harkness. "I see you've managed to
keep the extra rocker, Senior Chief."

Harkness blushed, for his had been a checkered
career. He was far too good at his job for the Navy to
dispense with his services, but he'd been up for chief
petty officer over twenty times before he made it and
kept it. His encounters with customs officers—and any
Marine he met in a bar off-duty—were legendary, but
he seemed to have reformed since entering Tremaine's
orbit. Honor didn't understand exactly how the makeover
had worked, but wherever Tremaine went, Harkness
was sure to turn up shortly. He was a good thirty years
older than the lieutenant, yet the two of them seemed
to constitute a natural pair not even BuPers could break
up. Which, she reflected, might be because BuPers recognized what a *formidable* pair they made.

"Uh, yes, Ma'am—I mean, Milady," Harkness said.

"I'd like to see you go on keeping it," she said a bit
repressively. "I don't anticipate any problems with customs"— Harkness' blush deepened—"but we *will* have
a full battalion of Marines on board. I'd appreciate your
not trying to reduce their numbers if we manage to find
someplace for liberty."

"Oh, the Senior Chief doesn't do that anymore,
Ma'am," Tremaine assured her. "His wife wouldn't like
it."

"His *wife?*" Honor blinked and looked back at Harkness, and her eyebrows rose as the petty officer turned

a truly alarming shade of crimson. "You're married now, Chief?"

"Uh, yes, Milady," Harkness mumbled. "Eight months now."

"Really? Congratulations! Who is she?"

"Sergeant Major Babcock," Tremaine supplied while Harkness positively squirmed, and Honor giggled. She couldn't help it. She *hated* it when she giggled, because she sounded like an escapee from high school, but she simply couldn't stop herself. *Harkness* had married *Babcock?* Impossible! But she saw the confirmation on the senior chief's face and fought her giggles sternly into silence. She had to hold her breath a moment to be certain they were vanquished, and her voice wasn't quite steady when she spoke again.

"T-that's wonderful news, Senior Chief!"

"Thank you, Milady." Harkness stole a sideways look at Tremaine, then grinned almost sheepishly. "Actually, it *is* good news. I never thought I'd meet a Marine I even *liked*, but, well—" He shrugged, and Honor felt her levity ease at the glow in his blue eyes.

"I'm glad for you, Senior Chief. Really," she said softly, squeezing his shoulder, and she was. Iris Babcock was the last person in the world she would have expected to marry Harkness, but now that she thought about it, she could see the possibilities. Babcock's career had been as exemplary as Harkness' had been . . . colorful, and she was one of the best combat soldiers—and practitioners of *coup de vitesse*—Honor had ever encountered. Honor would never even have considered Babcock and Harkness as a pair, but the sergeant major was precisely the sort of woman who would make certain the senior chief stayed on the straight and narrow. And, Honor thought, she was also a woman who'd obviously been wise enough to look past Harkness' exterior and realize what a truly good man he was.

"Thank you, Milady," the petty officer repeated, and she nodded briskly to them both.

"Well! I see why the Exec plugged you into Flight Ops,

Scotty. Have you had a chance to look over your new boat bay?"

"No, Ma'am. Not yet."

"Then why don't you go do that—and take the Senior Chief with you. I think you'll like what the yard dogs have done for you. You'll be working with Major Hibson—I'm sure you remember her—for the boarding parties, and Commander Harmon, our senior LAC commander, but neither of them have reported in yet. Sergeant Major Hallowell is around somewhere, though. Page him and get him to go with you. We've still got a few days before the yard turns us loose, so if you see any minor changes you want, let me or the Exec know about them by supper."

"Yes, Ma'am." Tremaine braced to attention once more, returning to the attentive officer he always was on duty, and Harkness followed suit.

"Dismissed, gentlemen," Honor said, and smiled fondly as they left. She was glad she'd been able to meet them here, where she could relax the formality which would be the rule aboard ship without seeming to play favorites, and she was *delighted* to have them. The squadron's crew lists were beginning to fill up, and while the officers and senior ratings looked just as solid as Admiral Cortez had promised, the junior petty officers and enlisted personnel looked just as green—or problematical—as the admiral had feared. It was good to pick up a few unanticipated bright spots along the way.

She shook her head with another chuckle. Iris Babcock! Lord, that must have been an *interesting* courtship! She considered it for another moment, then sighed, squared her shoulders, and marched back around her desk to the hydroponics report.

The waiting officers rose as Honor entered the briefing room aboard *Vulcan*. Cardones and LaFollet flanked her, and Jamie Candless, the number two armsman of her normal travel detachment, took up his position outside the hatch as it closed. She crossed to the data terminal

at the head of the long conference table and sank into her chair. The other officers waited until she'd been seated, then sat back down themselves, and she let her eyes sweep over them.

The squadron's personnel were still coming in, but the core of her senior officers was now in place, and Captain of the List Alice Truman faced her from the far end of the table, golden blonde and green-eyed, still the same sturdily built woman who'd been her second-in-command in Yeltsin six years before. Commander Angela Thurgood, *Parnassus'* exec, sat beside Alice, and Honor suppressed a small smile, for Thurgood was just as golden-haired as Alice. Blondes weren't all that rare in the Star Kingdom, but they weren't especially common, either. Yet it seemed to be a tradition that whenever Honor saw Truman, her senior subordinate—male or female—would be one of them.

Captain Junior-Grade Allen MacGuire, *Gudrid's* CO and the squadron's third in command, sat to Alice's left. MacGuire was a small man, twenty-five centimeters shorter than Honor, and another blond. He was the only one of her captains she hadn't known previously, but she'd already discovered he had a lively sense of humor, which would probably stand a Q-ship's commander in good stead. He was also sharply intelligent, and he'd worked closely with Commander Schubert since his arrival. cBetween them, they'd managed to shave three more days off *Gudrid's* projected completion date, which would have been enough to endear him to Honor even if she hadn't been aware of what an asset he would be in other ways.

Like Honor herself, Commander Courtney Stillman, MacGuire's exec, was considerably taller than he was. She might be ten or twelve centimeters short of Honor's height, but that still made her seem to tower over her CO. They were an odd-looking pair, and not just because of the altitude differential. Stillman was dark-skinned, with eyes an even darker brown than Honor's, and she wore her close-cropped black hair at least as short as Honor had worn hers up until four years ago. She also seemed to have absolutely *no* sense of humor, yet she and MacGuire obviously got along together well.

And then there was Captain (JG) Samuel Houston Webster, *Scheherazade's* CO. He was another officer who'd served with her in Basilisk, and he'd very nearly died of his wounds there. They'd served together again on Hancock Station at the start of the present war, when she'd commanded Admiral Mark Sarnow's flagship. Webster had been on Sarnow's staff, and it was good to see he'd gotten the promotion he deserved since. Not that the tall, gangling redhead had ever been likely *not* to be promoted. He had the distinctive "Webster chin" that marked him as a scion of one of the RMN's more powerful naval dynasties; fortunately, he also had the ability to deserve the advantages that chin brought with it.

Commander Augustus DeWitt, Webster's exec, completed the gathering. DeWitt was another officer Honor didn't know, but he looked competent and confident. He was brown-haired and brown-eyed, but his skin was as dark as Stillman's, with the weathered look that seemed to mark all natives of Gryphon—otherwise known as Manticore-B V. Gryphon had the smallest population of any of the Manticore System's inhabited planets (which, inhabitants of Sphinx and Manticore declared, was because only lunatics would live on a world with Gryphon's climate), but it seemed to produce a disproportionate number of good officers and NCOs . . . most of whom seemed to feel a moral obligation to keep the sissies who lived on their sister worlds in line.

It was a good team, Honor thought. No doubt it was early to be making such judgments, yet she trusted her instincts. None of them thought it was going to be a picnic, but none of them seemed to see their assignment as some sort of exile, either. That was good. In fact, that was *very* good, and she smiled at them.

"I've just received an update from BuPers," she said. "Another draft of five hundred personnel will be coming aboard *Vulcan* for us at zero-five-thirty. We don't have complete packages on them, but it looks like we'll at least be able to make a start on bringing your engineering section up to strength, Allen." She paused, and MacGuire nodded.

"That's good news, Milady. Commander Schubert's ready to test Fusion Two tomorrow, and I'd like to have a full crew section available when he does."

"It looks like you will," Honor said, then looked at Truman. "I've *also* just received our official mission brief," she said more soberly, "and it's going to be as tough as we thought."

She tapped a command into her terminal, and a star chart blinked into existence above the conference table. The rough sphere of the Silesian Confederacy glowed amber, its nearest edge a hundred and thirty-five light-years to galactic northwest of Manticore. The slightly larger sphere of the Anderman Empire glowed green, a bit further away from Manticore and below and to the southwest of Silesia, but connected to the Star Kingdom by the thin, crimson line that indicated a branch of the Manticore Wormhole Junction. One scarlet edge of the enormous, bloated sphere of the People's Republic was just visible a hundred and twenty light-years northeast of Manticore and a hundred and twenty-seven light-years from Silesia at its closest approach, and the golden icon of the Basilisk System terminus of the Wormhole Junction glowed squarely between Haven and the Confederacy. One look at that chart was enough to make all the advantages—and dangers—of the Star Kingdom's astrographic position painfully clear, Honor thought, studying it for a moment, then cleared her throat.

"First," she said, "we've finally received our unit designation. As of zero-three-thirty today, we're on the list as Task Group Ten-Thirty-Seven." She smiled wryly. "'Task group' may be a bit grand for the likes of us, but I thought you'd like to know we have a name now."

Several of her officers chuckled, and she nodded to
the star chart as she went on in a more serious voice.

"As you all know, our destination is the Breslau Sector, here." She highlighted a section near the Confederacy's western edge in darker amber. "The shortest
route for us would be to use the Junction's Basilisk terminus, then head west across the Confederacy, but the
Admiralty's decided to send us out through Gregor, down
here in Andermani space." The green dot at the end of
the crimson line blinked, and a broken green line
extended itself from Gregor to the Breslau Sector. "Our
total voyage time will be about twenty-five percent longer,
which is regrettable, but it offers certain offsetting
advantages."

She leaned back in her chair, watching their faces as
they studied the chart.

"From the perspective of readiness, it won't hurt to
extend the trip by thirty or forty light-years, since it
will give us that much longer to shake down, but that's
not the main reason the Admiralty wants us to use this
routing. Traffic over the Triangle Route"—she pressed
another key, and a green line extended itself from
Manticore, down the scarlet line to Gregor, up to the
heart of the Confederacy, across to the Basilisk System, and down its terminus link to return to Manticore—"is way down. In fact, commerce through Basilisk
in general has declined since the war began. There's
still a lot of it, but a large percentage of merchant lines
are diverting from their normal routes—including the
Triangle—to stay well clear of the war zone. The
Basilisk Station picket is powerful enough to handle
most Peep raiding squadrons, and Home Fleet is only
a Junction transit away, but merchies don't get paid to
risk their cargos.

"Because of that, most of our own commerce is passing through Gregor, then looping up to Silesia from the
south. Of course, that's been a normal pattern for us for
years, since it lets us call at Andermani ports first. The
big change is that our shipping comes back down to

Gregor rather than continuing on to Basilisk to complete the Triangle. But since that's where most of our shipping is, and since the Admiralty wants us to look like any other merchant ships until we've gotten our teeth into a few pirates, we'll be following the same pattern." Captain Truman raised two fingers, and Honor nodded to her. "Yes, Alice?"

"What about the Andies, Milady?" Truman asked. "Do they know we're coming?"

"They know four merchies are coming."

"Their navy's always been a bit on the proddy side about Gregor, Milady," MacGuire observed, "and we're going to have to cross a lot of their sphere, as well."

"I understand your point, Allen," Honor said, "but it shouldn't be a problem. The Empire recognized our preexisting treaty with the Gregor Republic when it, ah, *acquired* Gregor-B forty years ago. They may not exactly be delighted about it, but for all intents and purposes, Gregor-A belongs to *us*, and they've always acknowledged our legitimate concern over the security of the Junction terminus there. They also know what kind of trouble we've been having in Silesia. I don't say they're shedding any tears over it, since anything that decreases our presence there *increases* theirs, but they've been generous about granting our convoy escorts free passage. As far as they'll know, we'll just be one more convoy, and since we won't be landing cargo on any imperial worlds along the way, customs inspection will be a moot point. They should never realize we're armed at all."

"Until we start killing pirates, Milady," Truman pointed out. "They'll know then, and they'll know where we came from and how we got to Breslau. I'd think there could be repercussions about that after the fact."

"If there are, they'll be the Foreign Secretary's concern. I suspect the Andermani will let it pass. There won't be anything they can do about it, after all, without risking an incident with us, and they won't want that."

Heads nodded soberly. All of them knew the Anderman

Empire had cast covetous eyes on the Silesian Confederacy for over seventy years. It was hard to blame the Empire, really. The chronic weakness of the Silesian government and the chaotic conditions it spawned were bad for business. They also tended to be more than a little hard on Silesian citizens, who found themselves in the way of one armed faction or another with dreary regularity, and the Andermani had been faced with several incidents along their northern frontier. Some of those incidents had been ugly, and one or two had resulted in punitive expeditions by the Imperial Andermani Navy. But the IAN had always walked carefully in Silesia, and that was the RMN's fault.

More than one Manticoran prime minister had looked as longingly at Silesia as his or her imperial counterparts. Economically, Silesia was second only to the Empire itself as a market for the Star Kingdom, and chaos there could have painful repercussions on the Landing Stock Exchange. That was an important consideration for Her Majesty's Government, and so—though only, Honor was prepared to admit, in a lesser way—was the continual loss of life in Silesia. Eventually, unless there was a major change in the Confederacy's central government's ability to govern, something was going to have to be done, and Honor suspected Duke Cromarty would have preferred to take care of the problem years ago. That, unfortunately, would have involved one of those "aggressive, imperialist adventures" which *all* the current Opposition parties decried for one reason or another. So instead of cleaning up the snakes' nest once and for all, the RMN had spent over a century policing the Silesian trade lanes and letting the Confederacy's citizens slaughter one another to their homicidal hearts' content.

That same fleet presence was all that had deterred the last five Andermani Emperors from grabbing off large chunks of Silesian territory. At first, the deterrence had stemmed solely from the fact that the RMN was a third again the size of the IAN, but since the Peeps had turned expansionist, the Empire had discovered an additional

reason to exercise restraint. The Emperor must be tempted to try a little smash and grab while Manticore was distracted, but he couldn't be certain what would happen if he did. The Star Kingdom *might* let it pass, under the circumstances, but he could also find himself in a shooting war with the RMN, and he didn't want that. For sixty years, the Star Kingdom had been the roadblock between his own empire and Peep conquistadors, and he wasn't about to weaken that barricade now that the shooting had started.

Or that, at least, was the Foreign Ministry's analysis, Honor reminded herself. The Office of Naval Intelligence shared it, and she tended to agree herself. Yet Alice and MacGuire had a point, and given the independent nature of the squadron's operations, it was going to be up to Honor to handle any diplomatic tiffs that arose. It wasn't a thought calculated to make her sleep well, but it came with the territory.

"At any rate," she went on, "the real job starts once we get to Breslau. The Admiralty's agreed to leave our operational patterns up to us, and I haven't decided yet whether I want to operate completely solo or in pairs. There are arguments both ways, of course, and we'll run some sims to see how it looks. I hope we'll have time for some actual maneuvers once we've completed our trials, as well, but I don't advise anyone to hold her breath. As I see it now, however, the strongest point in favor of splitting up is the greater volume it would let us cover, and as long as we're dealing only with the normal, run-of-the-mill scum, we should have the individual firepower to deal with anything we're likely to meet."

Head nodded once more. Aside from Webster, all of Honor's captains had personal command experience in Silesia. Policing Silesian space had been the main shooting occupation of the RMN for a hundred T-years, and the Admiralty had developed the habit of blooding its more promising officers there. Rafe Cardones had amassed two years' experience in the Confederacy as Honor's tactical officer aboard the heavy cruiser *Fearless*, and Webster, DeWitt, and Stillman had all served there in subordinate capacities, as well. Between them, Honor's senior officers, despite their relatively junior ranks, had spent almost twenty years on the station . . . which no doubt had something to do with their selection for their current mission.

"All right," she said more briskly. "None of us has ever commanded a Q-ship before, nor has *any* Navy officer ever commanded a vessel with the armament mix we'll have. We're going to be learning as we go, and our operations will form the basis the Admiralty uses to formulate doctrine for the rest of the Trojans. In view of that, I'd like to begin our skull sessions right now, and I thought we'd start by considering how best to employ the LACs."

Most of her subordinates produced memo pads and plugged them into the terminals at their places, and she tipped her chair further back.

"It seems to me that the biggest concern is going to be getting them into space soon enough without doing it *too* soon," she went on. "We'll need to get some idea of how fast we can manage a crash launch, and I'm going to try to get us enough time to practice it against some of our own warships. That should give us a meterstick for how easy our parasites are to detect and whether or not we can conceal them by deploying them on the far side of our own impeller wedges. After that, we need to take a good look at tying them into our main fire control, and given our own lack of proper sidewalls or armor, our point defense net.

"Alice, I'd like you to take charge of setting up a series of sims to—"

Fingers tapped notes into memo pads as Captain Lady Dame Honor Harrington marshaled her thoughts, and she felt her mind reaching out to the challenge to come.

• CHAPTER EIGHT

Electronics Technician First Class Aubrey Wanderman was almost as young as prolong made him look. He was brown-haired and slim, with the wiry, half-finished look of his youth, and he'd dropped out of Mannheim University's physics program half-way through his freshman form to enlist. His engineer father had opposed the decision, but he'd been unable to change Aubrey's mind. And though James Wanderman still bemoaned his son's "excessive burst of patriotic fervor," Aubrey knew he'd developed a hidden pride in him. And, he thought sardonically, not even his father could complain about the schooling the Navy had subjected him to. Any major university would grant him a minimum of three years' credit for the intensive courses, and the fact that he'd completed them with a 3.93 rating explained the first-class stripe on his sleeve.

But gratifying as his rate was, he'd taken the better part of two years to earn it. He knew a modern navy needed trained personnel, not unskilled cannon fodder, yet acquiring that training seemed to have taken *forever*, and he'd felt vaguely guilty as combat reports from Nightingale and Trevor's Star filtered back to Manticore. He'd been looking forward to shipboard duty—not without fear, for he didn't consider himself a particularly brave person, but with a sort of frightened eagerness—and he'd actually been slated for assignment to a ship of the wall. He knew he had, for Chief Garner had let him have a peek at the initial paperwork.

Only now he wasn't. In fact, he wasn't assigned to *any*

proper warship. Instead, he'd been yanked out of the regular personnel pipeline and assigned to an armed *merchant* ship.

The disappointment was crushing. Everyone knew merchant "cruisers" were jokes. They spent their time on long, boring, useless patrols too unimportant to waste real warships on, or trudged from system to system playing convoy escort in sectors where real escorts weren't needed while other people got on with the war. Aubrey Wanderman hadn't put his civilian life on hold and joined the Queen's Navy just to be shuffled off to oblivion!

But one thing Aubrey had learned was that when the Navy gave an order, it expected to be obeyed. He felt a wistful envy for the old sweats who'd been around long enough to figure out how to bend the system subtly to their wills, but he was still too wet behind the ears for that. Chief Garner had been sympathetic, but he hadn't offered any encouragement to Aubrey's half-hearted hints that there must be some way to change his orders, and he'd known he had no choice but to accept his disappointment.

He'd gone through the next two days of endless bureaucratic processing in a state of resigned depression, and his sense of betrayal had grown with every hour. He'd busted his butt to graduate number two in his class—surely that should have bought him *some* consideration! But it hadn't, and he'd packed his locker with glum, mechanical neatness and joined the rest of the school draft detailed to the same duty.

And that was when he'd begun to hope that perhaps, just perhaps, it wasn't a banishment to total obscurity after all. He'd been sitting in the school concourse, contemplating his unappetizing assignment while he waited for his shuttle, when Ginger Lewis plunked herself down on the bench beside him.

Ginger was a gravitics specialist like Aubrey. The trim redhead had graduated nineteenth in their class of a hundred to his second-place spot, but she was twelve years older than he was, and he'd always secretly felt a

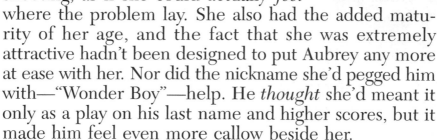

little in awe of her. She wasn't anywhere near as strong as he on theory, yet she had an uncanny instinct for trouble-shooting, as if she could actually *feel* where the problem lay. She also had the added maturity of her age, and the fact that she was extremely attractive hadn't been designed to put Aubrey any more at ease with her. Nor did the nickname she'd pegged him with—"Wonder Boy"—help. He *thought* she'd meant it only as a play on his last name and higher scores, but it made him feel even more callow beside her.

"Hey there, Wonder Boy!" she said cheerfully. "You assigned to Draft Sixty, too?"

"Yeah," he agreed glumly, and she raised her fox-red eyebrows at him.

"Well, don't let me keep you from your funeral or anything!" He had to grin at her tone, but her gibe hadn't been that far off the mark.

"Sorry," he muttered, and looked away. "I had an assignment to *Bellerophon*," he sighed. "Chief Garner showed me the paperwork. Then they pulled me for a *merchant cruiser*."

His lip curled with the last two words, and he was totally unprepared for Ginger's reaction. She didn't sympathize. She didn't even commiserate with him as any properly sensitive fellow sufferer should have done. She *laughed*.

His head snapped back around, and she laughed again, harder, at his expression. She shook her head and patted him on the shoulder the same way his mother had done when a ten-year-old Aubrey had piled up his grav-scooter.

"Wonder Boy, I see you are *far* behind on the scuttle-butt. Sure, they're sending you off to a merchant cruiser, but aren't you just a little curious about whose merchant cruiser it *is*?"

"Why should I be?" he snorted. "It's either some doddering old reservist or a total ass they can't trust a *real* warship to!"

"Oh, my! You *are* out of the loop, aren't you? Listen, Wonder Boy, your 'doddering old reservist' is Honor Harrington."

"*Harrington?*" She nodded, and he stared at her, jaw hanging, for almost fifteen seconds before he could make his voice work again. "You mean *the* Harrington? *Lady* Harrington?"

"The one and only."

"But . . . but she's still in Yeltsin!"

"You really ought to read the 'faxes occasionally," Ginger replied. "She's been back for over a week. And a certain well-placed informant of mine who's *always* been reliable, for obvious reasons," she batted her eyes sexily at him, "informs me that she's been tapped for senior officer of our new little squadron."

"My God," Aubrey murmured. He warned himself not to get too excited. After all, Lady Harrington had been all but forcibly banished after her scandalous duels. It was entirely possible she was being shuffled off to exactly the sort of oblivion Aubrey had assumed this assignment must be, but he couldn't believe it. The woman the newsies had dubbed "the Salamander" from her habit of always being where the fire was hottest was too good a combat commander for that. And it hadn't exactly been the Navy's idea to put her on half-pay to begin with. If the Fleet had her back again, *surely* they'd want to make the best use they could of her!

"Thought that might cheer you up a bit, Wonder Boy," Ginger said. "You always did want a shot at the glory, didn't you?" He blushed fiery red, but she only chuckled and patted him on the shoulder again. "I'm sure that as soon as Lady Harrington realizes what a sterling soul you are, she'll put you to work on her own command deck."

"Oh, give me a break, Ginger!" he said, laughing almost against his will, and she grinned.

"That's better! And—" she paused and cocked her head "—I do believe they're announcing our shuttle."

*   *   *

That had been fourteen hours ago, and now Aubrey sighed gratefully as he towed his locker into his assigned temporary berthing bay on its counter-grav. He'd seen entirely too many berthing bays since joining the Navy, but at least he shouldn't have to put up with this one for long. The second-class petty officer who'd rounded up his draft on *Vulcan's* concourse had warned them they'd be moving aboard ship in no more than six days, and despite his earlier despondency, Aubrey realized he was actually looking forward to it.

The bay assignments had been made on an alphabetical basis, and Aubrey had been the lone overflow from the rest of his draft. He was used to finding himself at the end of any Navy list of names, but aside from himself, the bay was empty at the moment, and he missed his fellow students as he peered around the compartment. He towed his locker across to check the bulkhead chart, and his eyes brightened. There were still two bottom bunks left, and he shoved his ID chip into the slot and painted one of them for his own use. He heard feet behind him as a small knot of uniforms entered the bay, and he plucked his chip free and stepped back to clear the chart for the newcomers. He towed his locker across to his freshly assigned bunk, shoved it into the space under it, and sat on the bunk, grateful to get off his weary feet.

"You hear who's in command of this shit squadron?" someone asked, and Aubrey glanced at the men clustered around the chart, surprised by the surly tone of the question.

"Yeah," someone else said with profound disgust. "Harrington."

"Oh, Christ!" the first voice groaned. "We're all gonna die," it went on with a sort of morbid satisfaction. "You seen the kinds'a casualty lists she comes up with?"

"Yep," the second voice agreed. "They're gonna dump us right in the crapper, and she's gonna win another medal by flushing our asses down it."

"Not if *I* can help it," a third voice muttered. "She

wants to play hero, that's fine, but I got better things to do than—"

Aubrey's concentration on the grumbling conversation was abruptly interrupted when someone kicked the frame of his bunk.

"Hey, Snotnose!" a deep voice said. "Get your ass off my rack."

Aubrey looked up in astonishment, and the speaker glared at him. The hulking, dark-haired man was much older than Aubrey, with a tough face and scarred knuckles. There were five golden hash marks on his cuff, each indicating three Manticoran years—almost five T-years—of service, but he was only a second-class power tech. That meant Aubrey was actually senior to him, yet he felt anything but senior as cold brown eyes sneered at him.

"I think you've made a mistake," he said as calmly as he could. "This is my bunk."

"Oh no it isn't, Snotnose," the older man said unpleasantly.

"Check the chart," Aubrey said shortly.

"I don't give a flying fuck what the *chart* says. Now get your ass off my rack while you can still walk, *Snotnose*."

Aubrey blinked, then paled as the other clenched a large, dangerous-looking fist and buffed its knuckles on his sleeve with an ugly grin. The younger man darted a look around the bay, but aside from the small knot of six or seven who'd accompanied his tormentor, there was no one else present—and none of the others looked inclined to take his side. They were all older than him, he realized, and none seemed to hold the rates men their age should have. At least half of them were grinning as unpleasantly as the power tech in front of him, and aside from one stocky, fidgety SBA whose nervous eyes kept flitting away from the confrontation, the ones who weren't smiling seemed totally indifferent to the scene.

So far in his Navy career, Aubrey had managed to avoid anything like this, but he wasn't stupid. He knew he was in trouble, yet instinct told him that if he caved in now the consequences would haunt him long after this episode was over. But instinct was matched by fear, for he'd never had a violent confrontation, much less an actual fight, and the grinning power tech out-massed him by at least fifty percent.

"Look," he said, still trying to sound calm, "I'm sorry, but I got here first."

"You're right—you *are* sorry," the power tech sneered. "In fact, you're just about the sorriest piece of shit I've laid eyes on in months, Snotnose. And you're gonna look a hell of a lot *sorrier* if I have to tell you to move your pink little ass again."

"I'm not moving," Aubrey said flatly. "Pick another bunk."

Something ugly flashed in those brown eyes. It was almost a light of vicious joy, and the power tech licked his lips as if in anticipation of a special treat.

"You just made a *big* mistake, Snotnose," he whispered, and his left hand flashed out. It locked in the neck of Aubrey's undress coverall, and the younger man felt a stab of pure terror as it yanked him off the bunk. He caught the other's wrist in both hands, trying to pull it away from his collar, but it was like wrestling with a tree. "Say good night, Snotnose," the power tech crooned, and his right fist drew clear back beside his ear.

"*Freeze!*" The single word cracked like a gunshot, and the power tech's head whipped around. His lips drew back, but there was something else in his eyes now, and Aubrey turned his own head, fighting for breath as the hand twisted in his coverall choked him.

A woman stood in the berthing bay hatch, hands on hips, and her level eyes were every bit as cold as the power tech's. But that was the only similarity between them, for the woman looked as if she'd just stepped out of a recruiting poster. There were seven gold hash marks on her cuff, her shoulder carried three chevrons and rockers centered on the ancient golden anchor of a boatswain's mate instead of the star other branches used to indicate a senior master chief petty officer, and her eyes swept the frozen bay like a subzero wind.

"Get your hands off him, Steilman," she said flatly, with a pronounced Gryphon accent. The power tech looked at her for another moment, then opened his hand with a scornful flick. Aubrey half fell back across the bunk, then struggled back to his feet, pale cheeks blotched with red. He was grateful for the senior master chief's intervention and knew it had just saved him from a brutal beating, but he was also young enough to feel the shame of *needing* to be saved.

"Anyone want to tell me what's going on here?" she asked with deadly calm. No one spoke, and her lip curled contemptuously. "Talk to me, Steilman," she said softly.

"It was just a misunderstanding," the power tech said in the tone of a man who didn't particularly care that his audience knew he was lying. "This snotnose took my bunk."

"Did he, now?" The woman stepped into the bay, and the onlookers drifted out of her way as if by magic. She glanced at the chart, then looked at Aubrey. "Your name Wanderman?" she asked in a much less threatening tone, and he nodded.

"Y-yes, Senior Master Chief," he managed, and flushed darker as his voice broke.

"Just 'Bosun' will do, Wanderman," she replied, and Aubrey inhaled in surprise. Only one person was called "Bosun" by the crew of a Queen's ship. That person was the senior noncom in its complement, and the bosun, as his instructors had made very clear to him, stood directly at the right hand of God.

"Yes, Bosun," he managed, and she nodded, then looked back at Steilman.

"According to this"—her head jerked at the chart— "that's *his* bunk. And in case you hadn't noticed, Wanderman's a first-class. Unless my memory betrays me, that makes him senior to a career fuck-up like you, doesn't it, Steilman?"

The power tech's lips tightened and his eyes flickered, but he didn't speak, and she smiled.

"I asked you a question, Steilman," she said, and he clenched his teeth.

"Yeah, I guess it does," he said in an ugly tone. She cocked her head, and he added a surly "Bosun" to his reply.

"Yes, it does," she confirmed. She looked back at the chart again, then tapped one of the unclaimed upper bunks—the one furthest from both the hatch and the head. "I think this would be an ideal place for you, Steilman. Log in."

The power tech's shoulders were tight, but his eyes fell from her cold, level gaze and he stamped across to the chart. He fed in his chip and painted the indicated bunk, and she nodded.

"There, you see? A little guidance, and even you can find your bunk." Aubrey watched the entire proceeding with an icy worm gnawing at his belly. He was delighted to see Steilman get his comeuppance, yet he dreaded what the power tech would do to him once the Bosun left.

"All right, all of you fall in," she said, pointing to the green stripe across the decksole, and Aubrey stood. The others shuffled resentfully into a line as he crossed to join them, and the Bosun folded her hands behind her and surveyed them expressionlessly.

"My name is MacBride," she said flatly. "Some of you—like Steilman—already know me, and *I* know all about *you*. You, for example, Coulter." She pointed at another power tech, a tall, narrow-built man with pitted cheeks and eyes that refused to meet hers. "I'm sure your captain was *delighted* to see your thieving backside. And you, Tatsumi." She gave the fidgety sick berth attendant a stern glare. "If I catch you sniffing any Sphinx green in *my* ship, you're going to wish I'd only stuffed you out an airlock."

She paused, as if inviting comment. No one spoke, but Aubrey felt resentment and hatred welling up about him like poison, and his nerves crawled. He'd never imagined anything like *this* in a modern navy, yet he knew he should have. Any force the size of the RMN had to have its share of thieves and bullies and God alone knew what else, and his heart sank as he realized the other men in this berthing bay were among the worst the Navy had to offer. What in the name of God was *he* doing here?

"There's not one of you—except Wanderman—who isn't here because your last skipper could hardly *wait* to get rid of you," MacBride went on. "I'm happy to say that most of the rest of your crewmates are like him, not you, but I thought we'd just have a little welcoming chat. You see, if any of you *gentlemen* step out of line in *my* ship, you're going to think a planet fell on you. And you'd better pray to *God* I deal with you myself, because if you ever wind up in front of Lady Harrington, you'll find yourself in hack so fast your worthless ass won't catch up with you till you land in the stockade. And you'll *stay* in hack so long you'll be old and gray even with prolong before you see daylight again. Trust me. I've served with her before, and the Old Lady will eat the whole candy-ass lot of you so-called hard cases for breakfast—without salt."

She spoke calmly, without passion, and somehow that gave her words even greater weight. She wasn't making threats; she was stating facts, and Aubrey felt a sort of animal fear superimposing itself on the others' resentment and hostility.

"You remember what happened the last time you and I locked up, Steilman?" MacBride asked softly, and the power tech's nostrils flared. He said nothing, and she smiled thinly. "Well, don't worry. You go right ahead and try me again if you want. *Wayfarer* has a *fine* doctor."

Muscles lumped along Steilman's jaw, and MacBride's thin smile grew. Although she was a sturdily built woman, Aubrey couldn't quite believe what she seemed to be saying—until he glanced sideways at Steilman and saw the fear in the burly power tech's eyes.

"Now this is the way it's going to be," MacBride said,

sweeping them all with her eyes once more. "You worthless screw-ups are *not* going to screw up in my ship. You are going to do your jobs, and you're going to keep your noses clean, and the first one of you who doesn't *will* regret it—deeply. Is that clear?" No one answered and she raised her voice. "I said *is that clear?*"

A ragged chorus of assents answered, and she nodded.

"Good." She turned as if to leave, then paused. "There's just one more thing," she said calmly. "Wanderman's assigned to this bay because I didn't have anyplace else to put him. You'll find a half-dozen Marines joining you shortly, and I'd advise you to behave yourselves. I'd especially advise you to be very sure that nothing, ah, *unfortunate* happens to Wanderman. If he should as much as stub his toe, I personally promise you that every single one of you will wish you'd never been born. I don't care what you got away with in your last ship. I don't care what you'd *like* to get away with in mine. Because, people, what you *will* get away with is nothing."

Her voice was like ice, and she smiled again, then turned and strode from the compartment. Aubrey Wanderman wanted, more than he'd ever wanted anything else in his life, to run after her, but he knew he couldn't, and he swallowed hard as he turned to face the others.

Steilman glared at him with naked, undisguised hatred, lips working. It took every ounce of Aubrey's courage not to back away from the power tech, but he stood his ground, trying to look unintimidated, and Steilman spat on the deck.

"It ain't over, Snotnose," he promised softly. "We're gonna be in the same ship a long time, and snotnoses have *accidents*." He bared his teeth. "Even *bosuns* can have accidents."

He turned away, towing his battered locker towards the bunk MacBride had assigned him, and Aubrey sank back onto his own bunk and tried to hide the muscle tremors of reaction racing through him. He'd never heard such ugly, venomous hatred in a voice before—certainly never directed at him. It wasn't fair! *He* hadn't done anything to Steilman, but the power tech had smeared his own dream of what Navy service was supposed to be like with something sticky and evil. It was as if Steilman soiled the very air he breathed, and the dark, ugly streak inside him reached out to Aubrey like a sick hunger.

Aubrey Wanderman shivered on his bunk, trying to pretend he wasn't afraid, and hoped desperately that some of those Marines MacBride had mentioned turned up soon.

• <u>CHAPTER NINE</u>

Honor Harrington sat in her command chair, one hand caressing the treecat in her lap, as HMS *Wayfarer* decelerated towards the central terminus of the Manticore Wormhole Junction at the eighty-percent power setting the Navy allowed as its normal maximum. *Vulcan* had completely stripped the freighter's original bridge and refitted it with what could have passed for a regular warship's command stations, but one look at Lieutenant Kanehama's power settings gave the lie to *that* illusion, Honor thought dryly, for *Wayfarer's* "maximum power" was only 153.6 g.

An impeller drive vessel's nodes generated a pair of inclined, plate-like gravity waves which trapped a pocket of normal space in their wedge-shaped grasp. The ship floated in that pocket, like a surfer poised in the curl of a comber which, in theory, could have been accelerated instantaneously to light-speed, taking the vessel with them. But minor practical considerations—like the fact that it would have turned the ship's crew into paste—mitigated against it, and the fact that the physics of the drive required the bow and stern aspects of the wedge to be open limited the maximum speed of any starship, as well. Whatever its possible acceleration, the open throat of a ship's wedge meant it had to worry about particle densities and the rare but not unknown micro-meteorite. A warship's particle and antiradiation fields let her pull a maximum normal-space velocity of .8 light-speed in the conditions which obtained within the average star system (max speeds were twenty-five percent lower in h-space, where particle densities were higher, and somewhat higher in areas of particularly low densities), but merchant designers wouldn't accept the expense and mass penalties of generators that powerful. As a consequence, merchantmen were limited to a maximum n-space velocity of about .7 c and a max h-space velocity of no more than .5 c . . . and *Wayfarer* was a merchant design.

The fact that an impeller wedge's throat was almost three times as "deep" as its stern aspect also explained why every tactician's dream was to cross an opponent's "T," since the wedge itself was impenetrable by any known weapon and its sides were protected by weaker but still extremely powerful gravity sidewalls. Energy weapons could burn through a sidewall at close enough range, but a raking shot down the wedge's throat both exposed one to far less return fire and also gave one an unobstructed shot at one's target. But Honor's greatest concern was her ships' sluggishness, for they were going to be slower in sustained flight than any warship they met . . . and they were also going to be slower to accelerate.

A ship's maximum acceleration rate depended upon three factors: its impeller strength, its inertial compensator's efficiency, and its mass. Like impellers, military-grade compensators were more powerful than the far cheaper installations merchantmen mounted, and the *Caravan*-class were the size of many superdreadnoughts. Given equal compensator efficiency, a smaller ship could dump a higher proportion of the inertial forces of its acceleration into the "inertial sump" of its wedge, which explained why lighter warships could run away from heavier ones despite the fact that their maximum velocities were equal. The smaller ship couldn't go any *faster*, but it could reach maximum speed more *quickly*, and unless its heavier opponent was able to close the range before it did so, it could never be forced into action. The situation was even worse for *Wayfarer* than it would have been for a ship of the wall, however, for an SD her size could have pulled over twice her acceleration.

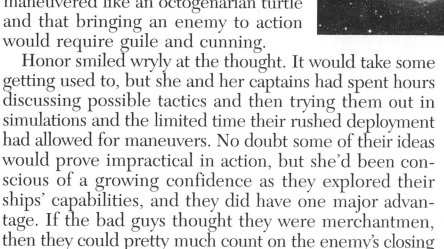

All of which meant that *Wayfarer* maneuvered like an octogenarian turtle and that bringing an enemy to action would require guile and cunning.

Honor smiled wryly at the thought. It would take some getting used to, but she and her captains had spent hours discussing possible tactics and then trying them out in simulations and the limited time their rushed deployment had allowed for maneuvers. No doubt some of their ideas would prove impractical in action, but she'd been conscious of a growing confidence as they explored their ships' capabilities, and they did have one major advantage. If the bad guys thought they were merchantmen, then they could pretty much count on the enemy's closing the range *for* them. Which was where the cunning and guile came in, for it would be up to her to convince the enemy *Wayfarer* truly was a fat, juicy, defenseless prize until it was too late for him to avoid her.

Honor let her eyes run over the displays deployed about her command chair with a sense of satisfaction. *Parnassus* and *Scheherazade* hung neatly off *Wayfarer*'s port and starboard quarters, holding station clear of her hundred-kilometer-wide wedge, while *Gudrid* brought up the rear of their diamond-shaped formation. Their intervals were professionally tight, and given the time constraints, Honor was pleased with how well their working up had gone. Not that she wouldn't dearly have loved just a little more time. *Wayfarer* had completed her acceptance trials with flying colors three weeks before, closely followed by *Parnassus* and *Scheherazade*, but *Gudrid* had been allowed less than two weeks from trials to deployment. Captain MacGuire had done wonders, and he and Commander Stillman projected a confident attitude, but Honor knew both of them were concerned over the potential weaknesses—human and hardware—which they might simply have had too little time to find. For that matter, Honor shared their concerns. She'd deliberately had the old sweats with the worst records assigned to *Wayfarer* and *Parnassus*, where she and Alice could ride herd on them, yet she was acutely aware of the potential weakness of her mix of newbies and embittered rejects. Virtually all her departments were still shaking down, and she would have given two fingers off her left hand for even one more week to drill and train her people. But the Admiralty had been emphatic about the need to get TG 1037 into Breslau space, and, given her own intelligence briefings, she couldn't disagree.

Worse, other sectors were beginning to report alarming loss rates as well, and the latest assessment of Silesian conditions from Second Space Lord Givens Office of Naval Intelligence had been blunt: the RMN's failure to respond to the Star Kingdom's rising losses was emboldening even raiders who'd previously steered clear of Manticoran vessels. Under the circumstances, the Admiralty had decided it was almost as important for the squadron to make its presence known to the Confederacy's spaceborne vermin as it was for Honor to actually start killing pirates. They hadn't ordered any changes in her mission profile, but Admiral Caparelli had made it quite clear that he needed Honor and her ships in Breslau at the earliest possible moment.

It was odd, she thought as the icon marking the invisible portal of the Junction grew in her maneuvering display. She'd never before been involved in a project with this much urgency, even when she'd helped organize the Fifth Battlecruiser Squadron on the eve of the war. The unremitting time pressure had driven her to take shortcuts she'd never taken before, and she'd never felt quite so anxious about the quality of her own crew. She'd been so busy organizing the *squadron* that she'd had virtually no opportunity to get to know any of her non-bridge personnel, nor had they had an opportunity to come to know her. Still, they'd performed fairly creditably in the limited maneuvers she'd been able to carry out. There were still far too many rough edges, and she harbored no illusion that she and Cardones wouldn't come up against more that they simply didn't know about yet, but despite Admiral Cortez's

worries and her own concern over one or two specific personnel files, the raw material of her crews seemed fundamentally sound.

"We'll cross the fortress perimeter in eighteen minutes, Milady," Lieutenant Kanehama announced from Astrogation, and Honor nodded.

"Very good, Mr. Kanehama. Mr. Cousins, contact Junction Central and request transit clearance and priority."

"Aye, aye, Ma'am." The black-skinned communications officer spoke briefly into his boom mike, then looked back at Honor. "We're cleared to transit, Ma'am. *Wayfarer* is number twelve in the Gregor queue. Priorities for the rest of the squadron are at your discretion."

"Thank you. Inform the squadron that we'll transit in descending order of seniority, please."

"Yes, Ma'am." The lieutenant turned back to his panel, and Honor glanced at her helmsman.

"Slip us into the queue, Chief O'Halley."

"Aye, aye, Ma'am. Coming into the approach lane now."

Honor nodded. A Junction transit wasn't a battle maneuver, yet neither was it as simple as the casual observer might believe, and her bridge crew had had only a few weeks to drill, even in sims. But they moved with a quiet efficiency that was vastly reassuring, and she sat back, stroking Nimitz while she watched the green beads of her squadron track steadily through the Junction's protective fortresses.

The smallest of those mammoth forts massed over sixteen million tons; the space between them was thickly seeded with mines; and a quarter of them were always at full general quarters readiness. They changed off every five and a half hours, cycling through their readiness states once per Manticoran day, and the cost in wear and tear on their equipment was sobering.

Unfortunately, it was also necessary . . . at least until Trevor's Star was taken, and that underscored the absolute priority Sixth Fleet's operations held.

Those fortresses were individually more powerful than

any superdreadnought, but not even Manticore Astro Control's traffic managers could know a ship was about to use the Junction inbound until it actually arrived. That meant a hostile mass transit would *always* take the forts by surprise, and losses among them would be heavy. The *attacker's* losses would probably be total, yet the new Peep regime had amply demonstrated its ruthlessness, and no one could afford to ignore the possibility that it might launch what amounted to a suicide attack.

Honor had once participated in a Fleet maneuver built around the assumption that the PN might employ some of the enormous number of battleships it had built for area defense to do just that. Everyone knew BBs were too weak to engage superdreadnoughts or dreadnoughts—as Honor had demonstrated once again in the Fourth Battle of Yeltsin—which was why Manticore had none. The RMN could afford to build and crew only ships that *could* lie in the wall of battle, but if a navy had them, BBs were ideal for covering rear areas against raiding squadrons of cruisers or battlecruisers. They were also potent tools for keeping restive systems from asserting their independence—a major reason the old regime had built them and a task upon which the new one was currently employing something like two-thirds of them.

But the maneuver's authors had assumed that since battleships were useless in fleet actions, the PN might throw them at the Junction from Trevor's Star for the sole purpose of whittling down the fortresses, instead. The umpires had calculated that the Peeps could have put roughly fifty through the Junction in a single transit. That was little more than thirteen percent of their total battleship strength, which meant—in theory—that they could do the same thing more than once if it worked . . . and for their sacrifice, the "Peep CO" in the war games "destroyed" thirty-one fortresses, or a quarter of the entire Junction Defense Force. In purely material terms, that was a sacrifice of roughly two hundred million tons of shipping and, assuming no survivors from any of their ships, 150,000 men and women in return for destroying

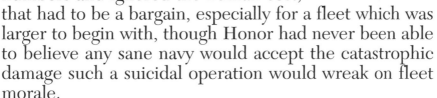

four hundred and eighty million tons of fortresses and killing over 270,000 Manticorans. If one simply looked at the numbers and ignored the human cost, that had to be a bargain, especially for a fleet which was larger to begin with, though Honor had never been able to believe any sane navy would accept the catastrophic damage such a suicidal operation would wreak on fleet morale.

Unfortunately, no one could rely on an enemy's rationality when the risk was the crippling of your capital system's defenses. Especially when, unlike the People's Republic, that system was also the only one you had. The need for the Junction forts had eaten so deeply into the RMN's budget for decades that the Star Kingdom had started the war with a marked inferiority in ships of the wall, and their ongoing cost and manpower demands continued to suck resources away from the front. The ability to stand down even half of the Junction forts would have released the trained personnel to man twenty-four *squadrons* of SDs and added over fifty percent to the RMN's strength in that class—a thought, given her own experience of BuPers' manning problems, which was more than enough to boggle Honor's mind.

Yet none of that could be done until Admiral White Haven captured Trevor's Star, which meant the Peeps were going to fight desperately to stop him . . . and explained why her ships were all the Admiralty could spare for Breslau.

Wayfarer's light bead came neatly to a halt, motionless relative to the Junction, and a red number "12" glowed under it in the display. The number changed quickly to "11" as the ship at the head of her queue made transit, and Honor punched a stud on her command chair's arm. The small screen at her right knee blinked alight with the face of a red-haired, green-eyed man, and the right corner of her mouth twitched in amusement as Nimitz sat up straighter in her lap and pricked his ears. The slim, six-limbed shape on the other human's shoulder also sat up straighter, and once again Honor felt the very edge of a deep, complex exchange as the two treecats' eyes met.

"Engineering, Commander Tschu," the deep-voiced man said, and Honor smiled.

"Stand by to reconfigure to Warshawski sail, Mr. Tschu."

"Aye, aye, Ma'am. Standing by," Tschu replied.

Like Admiral Georgides, Harold Tschu was a fellow Sphinxian, but his companion was an even more unusual off-Sphinx sight than Nimitz or Odysseus, for she was female. Most 'cats who adopted humans were male. Honor, who knew more adoptees than most humans, could think of only half a dozen females who'd established the bond, and all of them had adopted Forestry Service rangers who never left Sphinx. Yet Tschu's companion was not only female, but she'd adopted him when he was only ten years older than Honor had been. In fact, he'd been just half-way through his third form at the Academy when he came home on leave and met Samantha, and Honor shuddered to think how adjusting to *that* must have complicated the balance of his time on Saganami Island. No doubt it would have been far more convenient if his companion had waited, but as a long line of Sphinxians had discovered before him, 'cats had minds of their own.

Physically, Samantha was a bit smaller than Nimitz, with a coat of dappled brown and white that would have been even harder to see in her native environment than his solid cream and gray. She was also younger than him, and by treecat standards, an extremely handsome young lady. A point, Honor thought wryly, which wasn't lost on Nimitz. 'Cats paired up in the spring, which was what most Sphinxians meant when they spoke of treecat "mating season," but like humans, they were sexually active year 'round . . . and it had been something like three T-years since Nimitz had last seen a female of his own kind. Honor wasn't certain she wanted to think about just where *that* might lead, but given the disproportionate adoption rates of male and female 'cats, it was probably a situation

Tschu had dealt with before. She hoped so, at any rate.

Nimitz turned his head, looking away from the screen to gaze up at her with twinkling green eyes, and she grinned and tugged on one of his ears. It might complicate her life if he chose to dally with the companion of one of her subordinates, but nothing in regulations prohibited it. Besides, she would never dream of trying to stand in the way of any arrangement Nimitz and Samantha might decide suited them, and Nimitz knew it.

"Coming up on transit, Milady," Kanehama announced, and Honor roused from her thoughts to discover that the number under *Wayfarer*'s icon had worked its way down to "3."

"Thank you, Mr. Kanehama. Put us in the transit lane, Chief O'Halley."

"Aye, aye, Ma'am. Entering transit lane now."

The helmsman sent *Wayfarer* creeping forward once more, following sedately behind the two ships still in front of her, and Honor felt herself tense inwardly, ever so slightly. Although it was called a "wormhole" by spacers and the public, astrophysicists decried the misuse of that term. It wasn't *totally* inappropriate, but in effect the Junction was a crack in the universe where a grav wave even more powerful than one of the "Roaring Deeps" had breached the wall between hyper-space and normal space. For all intents and purposes, it was a frozen funnel of h-space, and not a calm one, for the grav wave twisting endlessly through it was extremely potent. Impellers couldn't be used for the actual transit, and proper alignment required exquisitely accurate astrogation. One of Honor's Academy instructors had described it as "shooting a tsunami in a kayak," and she'd never encountered a better analogy.

But the right support could make even that routine, and Lieutenant Kanehama sat relaxed and calm before his panel as Central's traffic control computers projected his exact track into the Junction's heart. Chief Coxswain

O'Halley took *Wayfarer* down that track with the polished competence of fifteen years of naval service, and Honor looked back at Tschu.

"Reconfigure foresail now."

"Aye, aye, Ma'am. Reconfiguring to foresail—now. Hyper generator standing by for transit mode."

"Very good," Honor replied, and turned her attention to her engineering repeaters.

Engineering had more than its share of rough spots, but Tschu had put his best people on the duty roster for the transit, and *Wayfarer's* impeller wedge dropped to half strength as her forward nodes reconfigured smoothly. They no longer produced their portion of the wedge's total strength; instead, their beta nodes were out of the circuit entirely while their alpha nodes generated the all but invisible, three-hundred-kilometer-wide disk of a Warshawski sail, and Honor watched red numerals dance as her ship continued creeping forward under the power of her after nodes alone and the sail edged deeper into the Junction.

"Stand by for aftersail," she murmured to Tschu, never looking away from her repeaters.

"Standing by," the engineer replied

At this velocity there was a safety margin of almost fifteen seconds either way before the grav wave's interference would blow *Wayfarer's* after nodes, but a poorly executed transit could produce nausea and violent dizziness in a crew. Besides, no captain wanted to look sloppy, and Honor watched the numbers for the foresail spin upwards with steadily mounting speed until, suddenly, they crossed the threshold. The sail was now drawing enough power to provide movement independent of the wedge, and she nodded sharply.

"Rig aftersail now!"

"Rigging aftersail, aye," Tschu replied instantly, and *Wayfarer* twitched gently as her wedge disappeared entirely. She moved forward more quickly, gathering way under Warshawski sail alone even though she was still technically in normal space, and a time-to-transit icon flashed brightly, ticking downward in the corner of Honor's display.

"Stand by for hyper," she said. Then—"Hyper now!"

"Aye, aye, Ma'am."

Tschu threw power to the generator at precisely the right instant, and HMS *Wayfarer* vanished. For a fleeting instant no chronometer or human sense could measure, she simply ceased to exist, and then, suddenly, she was no longer in Manticore but seven hundred light-minutes from the F9 furnace known as Gregor-A, one hundred and eighty light-years distant from Manticore in Einsteinian space. The disks of her sails were blazing blue mirrors as they bled transit energy, and her hyper generator kicked back off at the conclusion of its programed burst of power. The ship slid forward once more, this time riding out of the terminus instead of into it, and Honor nodded in pleasure at how smoothly it had gone.

"Transit complete," Chief O'Halley announced, and Honor nodded again.

"Thank you, Chief. And you, Mr. Kanehama. That was well executed." She saw the astrogator's pleasure at her complement and looked back at Tschu.

"Reconfigure to impeller, Mr. Tschu."

"Aye, aye, Ma'am. Reconfiguring to impeller now."

Wayfarer folded her wings as she slid free of the grav wave, and Chief O'Halley needed no instruction to bring her wedge up quickly. The ship accelerated clear of the transit threshold, clearing the way for *Parnassus* to follow her as she headed down the Gregor arrival lane, and Honor checked her plot once more.

The Gregor terminus had its own fortresses, although they were far smaller and less numerous than those in Manticore, and Lieutenant Cousins cleared his throat.

"Gregor Defense Command is challenging, Milady."

"Send our number," Honor replied. Every ship was subject to the same challenge, even though it was largely a formality. Ships could move to or from Manticore via any of the Junction's termini, but it was impossible to move directly from one secondary terminus to another, so any arrival here must have been cleared by Junction Central. But Gregor Defense had its own responsibilities, and Honor approved of how promptly the challenge had come.

"We're cleared, Milady," Cousins reported. "Rear Admiral Freisner welcomes you to Gregor and regrets the fact that you won't be able to dine with him," he added, and Honor smiled.

"My compliments to the Admiral. Thank him for the thought and tell him I'll look forward to dining with him on the way home."

"Yes, Milady."

Honor watched her plot as *Parnassus* flicked into existence behind her, accelerating down *Wayfarer*'s wake, and wished she could have accepted Freisner's hospitality. Unfortunately, as far as anyone outside Gregor Defense Command knew, the squadron was simply a small, four-ship convoy, and it would have been totally outside the profile for Gregor's CO to invite a passing merchant skipper to dine with him. Besides, the rest of the convoy TG 1037 was slated to join for the trip to Sachsen, the closest nodal system of the Confederacy, was waiting for her. The senior officer of the convoy's two-destroyer escort knew what Honor's ships truly were, but she was the only person in the convoy who did, and Honor hoped Commander Elliot would remember to treat her with the sort of brusquely impatient courtesy she would show to any other merchie.

"Do you have the convoy beacon, Ms. Hughes?"

"Yes, Milady," Lieutenant Commander Jennifer Hughes, *Wayfarer*'s tactical officer, replied. "Beacon bears zero-one-three by one-zero-one. Range two-point-three million klicks."

"Thank you. Take us to join the neighbors, Mr. Kanehama."

"Aye, aye, Ma'am. Helm, come to zero-one-three one-zero-one at fifty gravities."

"Coming to zero-one-three one-zero-one at fifty

gravities, aye," Chief O'Halley responded, and Honor Harrington crossed her legs while anticipation hummed in the back of her brain. Despite all the rush, all the thousands of details, all the still unanswered questions about the quality of her crew or the exact nature of the threats she must face and overcome, she was on her way, once more in the Queen's uniform, and she allowed herself to luxuriate in the feeling of homecoming as her ship moved to meet whatever lay ahead.

• CHAPTER TEN

"They're coming around again!" Lieutenant Commander Hughes snapped as a fresh salvo of missiles ripped down on *Gudrid*. "Get those gravitics back *now!*"

ET/1c Wanderman felt sweat dripping down his face as he crouched over his diagnostic probe, and the harsh flow of combat chatter washed over him as the surviving LAC skippers maneuvered hard to intercept the raiders' latest pounce. The attack had come as a complete surprise, and it was obvious they were up against an entire squadron of privateers, not run-of-the-mill pirates. Hughes' tac team's first warning had been the missile salvo which blew one of their escorting destroyers to splinters, and then the enemy had come charging down his missiles' wake.

"I *know* they're out there," Lieutenant Wolcott, *Wayfarer*'s assistant tac officer, snarled, and Aubrey felt a stab of inadequacy. Whoever these people were, they had excellent electronic warfare systems of their own, and that EW was playing merry hell with *Wayfarer*'s active sensors. They also had at least one heavy missile platform, which was engaging the convoy escorts from beyond Wolcott's active detection envelope. Sensor range was always degraded in hyper-space, and Wolcott needed her gravitics to pick her enemies' impeller signatures out of the background hash of charged particles, jamming, and the EMP of detonating laser heads. But the entire gravitational detection system was down, and he couldn't get it back.

"We've lost *Thomas!*" someone announced, and this

132

time Hughes swore out loud. Three raiders were already dead, but that was the *fourth* LAC the enemy had picked off, and Captain MacGuire's *Gudrid* had taken a beating, as well.

"Targeting change! Stand by port!" the tac officer snapped, punching keys at her console, and *Wayfarer's* massive energy batteries quested hungrily as someone finally entered their range.

"Breakdown on Graser Five!" someone barked, and Aubrey heard terminal keys rattle. "Damn, damn, *damn!* It's operator failure!"

"Crap!" Hughes bent over her terminal. *Wayfarer's* people were still too raw, and it was showing. She input a query and spat a silent curse. "Override Five! Try to slave it to central!"

"Slaving," the first voice announced. "Coming in—now! Back on-line in central control!"

"Tracking!" Hughes' chief yeoman said. "Tracking . . . tracking . . . *lock!*"

"Fire!"

Eight grasers, each as heavy as any ship of the wall might mount, fired as one, blazing away through the "gun ports" in *Wayfarer's* sidewall, and a battlecruiser-sized raider vanished in the brilliant flash of a failing fusion bottle.

"That's *one!*" someone snarled.

"Yeah, but now they know what *we're* armed with," someone else said grimly.

"Permission to deploy pods?" Wolcott called, but Hughes shook her head violently.

"Negative. We still haven't found *their* missile plat-forms."

Wolcott nodded unhappily. *Gudrid* had lost her after cargo doors to a freak hit early in the attack, crippling her missile pod system. That meant *Wayfarer* had the only heavy missile capacity left to Hughes, but if she revealed it against the targets she could see, the ones she *couldn't* see would concentrate all their fire on her. Given

Wayfarer's fragility, that would be disastrous, and Aubrey swore under his breath as the panel of his diagnostic flickered. Numbers and schematics cascaded across it as it interrogated the gravitic system's software and test programs examined the hardware. He needed Ginger and her instinct for troubleshooting, but Ginger was a casualty down in Gravitic One, and—

A red light flashed, and his display froze. His eyes darted across the schematic, and he swore again. The hit which had destroyed Gravitic One had spiked the main array. The fail-safes had protected the array itself, but the spike had bled back through the data transmission chain and burned out the primary data coupling from Gravitic Two. Fixing the problem was going to require complete replacement, and that would take *hours*.

"There goes *Linnet*!" a plotting rating announced as the convoy's last regular escort blew apart.

"They're coming in on *us* now, Ma'am!" Wolcott said suddenly. "Bogies Seven and Eight coming up from astern and low, two-four-zero by two-three-six." Her voice was already taut; now it went even harsher as she completed her report. "Thirteen and Fourteen are swinging in from starboard and high, too, Ma'am. One-one-niner by zero-three-three. Looks like they're trying to overtake and cross our T!"

"Show me!" Hughes snapped, and Wolcott dumped her data onto the main tactical plot. The lieutenant commander studied the icons for an instant, then nodded. "Roll port and come to three-three-zero, same plane!"

"Rolling port, coming to three-three-zero, same plane, aye," Chief O'Halley acknowledged, and *Wayfarer* began a ponderous swerve.

"*John* and *Andrew* just nailed Bogie Nine," Hughes' yeoman reported, but the tac officer said nothing. Her eyes were glued to her display as the lumbering converted merchantman rolled up on her port side, presenting her belly to the threat from starboard, and turned back across the convoy's track. The maneuver brought her port side down toward the two cruiser-range raiders coming in from "below" her, and Hughes' fingers flew over her panel.

"Radar lock on Bogies Seven and Eight," her yeoman announced.

"Fire as you bear," Hughes replied grimly.

"There goes *Gudrid*," someone groaned. "She's breaking up!"

"Carol, find me those missile ships!" Hughes said, and Aubrey closed his eyes while his mind raced.

The raiders had caught the convoy at its most vulnerable moment, as it transited between grav waves in the depths of hyper-space. The two waves were over a half-light-day apart at this, their closest approach. At the convoy's best h-space speed it would take thirty hours to make the transition, and by catching the convoy here, the raiders had been able to come in under impellers. They'd not only intercepted when the merchantmen were slowest and least maneuverable but done so under conditions which let them use their own sidewalls and missiles. Worse, no one had spotted them because of the poor sensor conditions and their unexpectedly good EW until their opening salvos had savaged both destroyers and crippled *Gudrid's* pods. The fact that they weren't currently in a grav wave had at least let Hughes get her LACs away, and their unanticipated appearance—and power—had given the enemy pause, but it hadn't driven them off. Apparently they'd decided anything this heavily defended had to be worth capturing, and despite their own losses, they were still driving in hard. Without their missile support, *Wayfarer* and her remaining LACs could still take all of them, but doing anything about their missile platforms required the ability to at least *see* them, and with the coupling down, how the *hell* did Aubrey—

Wait! His eyes popped open, and he punched a query into his probe, then grinned fiercely. It was completely against The Book, and it would be cumbersome as hell, but if he took down Radar Six and routed the input from Grav Two through Six's systems to Auxiliary Radar at

Junction Three-Sixty-One, then ran a hardwired shunt from AuxRad—

"Port battery firing—now!" Hughes' yeoman snapped, and fresh energy howled from *Wayfarer's* grasers as they came to bear. Two more raiders blew up, but one of them lasted long enough to fire back. Her weaker lasers blew right through the Q-ship's underpowered sidewall and nonexistent armor to rip Graser Three, Graser Five, and Missile Seven and Nine apart, with near total casualties on both energy mounts.

Aubrey's fingers flew, setting up the required commands. He was working as much by feel as training, for no one had ever tried anything like this before, so far as he knew, but there wasn't time to work it all out properly. His execution files were quick and dirty, but they *ought* to do the trick, and he dropped his control box and ripped open his tool kit.

"Keep an eye on those suckers to starboard," Hughes ordered.

"Enemy missile fire shifting to us from *Gudrid*," Lieutenant Jansen reported from Missile Defense.

"Do your best," Hughes said grimly, and Aubrey hurled himself under the radar display, burrowing into the limited space so quickly Jansen didn't have time to get out of the way. The lieutenant gave a chopped off, surprised cry, then snatched his feet out of Aubrey's path, and the tech ripped the front off the main panel. He forced himself to take a moment, making sure of his identification, then clamped the heavy alligator clips to the input terminals. He rolled onto his back, sat up, grabbed the edge of the console, and sent himself slithering across the decksole on the seat of his trousers, then rolled under Wolcott's panel.

Unlike Jansen, the assistant tac officer had seen him coming, and she turned her chair sideways to give him room to work even as she continued driving her sensors.

"*Paul* reports loss of her wedge, and *Galactic Traveler's* taken two hits in her after impeller ring. Her accel's dropping."

"Put us on a least-time for *Traveler*, Helm!" Hughes snapped. "Starboard batteries, stand by. Eleven and Thirteen are pulling ahead of us!"

"Incoming birds in acquisition!" Jansen sang out, then swore as Aubrey reached out, clamped his cable to the terminals under Wolcott's console, and brought his improvised software on-line. "We've lost Radar Six! Going to emergency override Baker-Three!"

"*Gravitics up!*" Wolcott shouted in sudden triumph. "Enemy missile platforms bear zero-one-niner two-zero-three, range one-point-five million klicks! Designate them Bogies Fourteen and Fifteen! They look like a couple of converted freighters, Ma'am!"

"Got 'em!" Hughes barked back. "Stand by to roll pods!"

"Programming fire control," Wolcott replied. A handful of seconds ticked past, and then. "Solution accepted and locked! Pods ready!"

"Roll them!" Hughes snapped, and six missile pods spilled from *Wayfarer's* stern. Their sudden appearance took the raiders by surprise, and no one even tried to fire on them before attitude thrusters kicked them to the right bearing and they launched. Sixty missiles, far heavier than anything the raiders had, shrieked towards their targets, and Aubrey rolled up on his knees, panting, to watch their tracks cross the main plot. The laser heads reached attack range and detonated, and scores of X-ray lasers ripped at the missile ships. Their defenses were even weaker than *Wayfarer's*; they never had a chance, and both of them blew apart under the terrible pounding.

"*All right!*" someone screamed.

"Watch starboard!" Hughes barked. The two raiders still sweeping up and around *Wayfarer's* starboard bow could still have killed them, but the privateers had already lost half their squadron, and the sudden revelation of *Wayfarer's* missile power, coupled with the loss of their own missile platforms, took the heart out of them. They

broke off, accelerating hard and rolling to cover themselves with their own wedges, and Hughes' lips drew back
to bare her teeth. "Keep rolling pods, Carol! I want those
bastards!"

"Aye, Ma'am. New solution locked. Launching now."

A fresh stream of pods rolled from *Wayfarer's* after
cargo doors. The fleeing raiders were much harder targets than the missile ships, but not hard enough to resist
that sort of fire. It took only five more salvos to kill them
both, and Hughes sat back with a sigh as the raiders on
the far side of the convoy's track also spun away and fled
madly.

Aubrey sank down to sit on his heels and dragged a
forearm across his sweaty forehead as the displays suddenly blanked. Then they came up again, this time showing the untouched ships of the convoy still plowing
serenely along down grav wave MSY-002-91, and Hughes
ran a hand through her hair before she turned to her
tactical crew.

"Not too shabby, people," she said as the tone announcing the simulation's end sounded. "We were late picking them up, but once the shooting actually started you
did good."

"Indeed they did," a soprano voice said, and Aubrey
scrambled to his feet with a start. Captain Harrington
stood in the open hatch between Alpha Simulator and
Beta, where Commander Cardones had been running the
"raiders." Her treecat was cradled in her arms while she
rubbed his ears, and Aubrey had no idea how long she'd
been standing there. From the look on Lieutenant Commander Hughes' face, he wasn't the only one who
wondered.

Everyone else rose as the Captain stepped into the
compartment, but she shook her head.

"As you were, people. You've earned a chance to sit
down."

Smiles of pleasure greeted her compliment, and she
walked across to Hughes' panel and tapped in a command. The moment at which the missile platforms had

suddenly appeared on the plot replayed itself and froze, and she nodded.

"I thought Rafe had you with that hit on Grav One, Guns," she observed.

"Yes, Ma'am. So did I," Hughes agreed feelingly, and Lady Harrington chuckled.

"Well, if *he* couldn't get you, I guess the bad guys are going to have a few problems, too, aren't they?" she said, and her 'cat bleeked a soft laugh of agreement.

"He *would've* had us without Carol," Hughes replied, but Wolcott shook her head.

"Not me, Skipper," she told the Captain. "It was Wanderman." She nodded her chestnut-haired head at Aubrey and grinned. "I don't know what he did, but it certainly worked!"

"So I noticed," Lady Harrington murmured, and turned her own attention to Aubrey. The electronics tech felt his face go crimson, but he came to attention and met her gaze as steadily as he could. "What *did* you do?" she asked curiously.

"I, uh, I rerouted the data, Ma'am—I mean, Milady," Aubrey said, flushing darker than ever as he corrected himself, but she only shook her head gently.

"'Ma'am' is fine. Where'd you reroute to?"

"Uh, well, the array itself was still up, Ma'am. It was only the coupling. But the data from all the arrays runs through Junction Three-Sixty-One. It's a preprocessing node, and the blown sector was downstream." He swallowed. "So I, uh, I overrode the main computers to reprogram the data buses and dumped it through Radar Six."

"So *that's* what happened," Lieutenant Jansen said. "You know you cut half my starboard point defense radar out of the circuit when you did it?"

"I—" Aubrey looked at the missile defense officer, then swallowed again, harder. "I didn't think about that, Sir. It was just, well, it was the only thing I could think of, and—"

"And there wasn't time to discuss it," Lady Harrington

finished for him. "Well done, Wanderman. Very well done. That was quick thinking—and it showed initiative, too." She studied Aubrey thoughtfully, and her 'cat turned his head to bend his own green eyes upon the electronics tech. "I don't believe I ever saw that particular trick pulled before."

"That's because it shouldn't work," Hughes pointed out. She punched up something on her own terminal and studied it for a moment, then whistled. "There *is* a cross-link at Three-Sixty-One, but I still don't see how he forced data compatibility. For that matter, he had to convince battle comp to bring three independent buses into it."

She shook her head in disbelief, and all eyes turned to Aubrey, who wished he could sink through the deck-sole. But the Captain only smiled and cocked an eyebrow at him.

"Where'd you get the software for it?" she asked, and Aubrey shrugged uncomfortably.

"I, uh, sort of made it up as I went along . . . Ma'am," he admitted, and she laughed.

"You made it up as you went along?" She looked back at Hughes with a twinkle. "We still have a few problems on the weapons decks, but you seem to have quite a team here, Ms. Hughes. My compliments to all of you."

Aubrey could actually feel the pleasure which filled the simulator, and the Captain lifted her 'cat to her right shoulder. She turned for the main hatch, then paused and looked back.

"I'll want to review the chips with you and the Exec this evening, Ms. Hughes. Can you and Ms. Wolcott join us for supper?"

"Of course, Milady."

"Good. And be sure you bring along a copy of Wanderman's improvisation. Let's see if we can't clean it up a bit and store it permanently just in case we need it again."

"Yes, Ma'am."

"Made it up as you went along," Lady Harrington

repeated softly, smiling at Aubrey, then shook her head, chuckled, and walked out of the simulator.

Honor leaned back in her command chair as *Wayfarer* and the rest of the convoy decelerated at a steady four hundred gravities, riding grav wave MSY-002-91 toward the beta wall and a return to normal space. That kind of decel would have killed her entire crew under impeller drive, but even the weakest of hyper space's grav waves were enormously more powerful than anything man could generate, and their "inertial sumps" were proportionately deeper. Not that it was strictly necessary to decelerate. A ship bled over ninety percent of its velocity as it broke each hyper-space wall in a downward translation, which could be a handy tactical maneuver. But crash translations were rough on personnel and systems, and merchant skippers preferred the gentler, safer stress of a low velocity translation. It not only allowed their crews to avoid the violent nausea crash translations induced but also reduced alpha node wear by a measurable percentage, and that made their employers' bookkeepers happy with them, too.

The convoy was coming up on the New Berlin System, capital of the Anderman Empire, roughly forty-nine light-years from Gregor. Left to themselves, Commander Elliot's escorting destroyers could have made the trip in seven days by the universe's clocks (or just over five by their own, given the time dilation effect), but they would have had to move well up into the eta bands to do it. Given the elderly nature of some of her charges, Elliot had held the convoy to the lower delta bands, where their maximum apparent velocity was only a little over 912 *c*, so the trip had taken almost twenty days objective, or seventeen days subjective. The commander had checked her decision with Honor who, whether anyone else knew it or not, was the convoy's true senior officer, but Honor hadn't even considered overriding her. It might have looked suspicious if Elliot had piled on too much speed. Besides, it had given Honor more time for simulations, like the one in which Jennifer Hughes had pinned Rafe's ears back.

She smiled at the thought and glanced across the bridge at her exec as he examined a yeoman's message board and dashed a signature across the scan plate. Despite his own skill as a tac officer, Rafe had gotten just a bit too eager when he realized *Wayfarer's* gravitics were down and *Gudrid* had lost her missile doors. The rules of the sim had precluded him from acting on his knowledge of the Q-ships' armament until it was revealed to him, and he'd done his best to obey them, but he'd *known* something had to have happened to Hughes' fire control when she didn't kill his missile platforms. He'd crowded in on her then, going for the quick kill, and ET Wanderman's improvisation had cost him the engagement.

Some officers might have been ticked off with the electronics tech, but Cardones had been delighted. With Honor's approval, he'd transferred the youngster from his original duty station and, despite his lack of seniority, assigned him as Carolyn Wolcott's permanent gravitics chief as an acting third-class petty officer. Wanderman seemed unable to believe his good fortune, and Honor hadn't needed Nimitz to know the young man had a serious case of hero worship where she herself was concerned. She felt a certain amusement over it, but Wanderman seemed to have it under control, so she hadn't spoken to him about it. *After all,* she told herself, *he'll only be this young and on his first deployment once. There's no point embarrassing him—let him enjoy it.*

She let her eyes drift from Cardones to Wolcott with a small smile. Carolyn Wolcott had come a long way from her own first deployment aboard the heavy cruiser *Fearless.* She'd always had poise; now, as a senior-grade lieutenant, she radiated an unmistakable aura of confidence. She wasn't all that much older than Wanderman—there were only nine T-years between them, which wasn't much in a society with prolong—but the acting petty officer was clearly in awe of her.

The convoy crossed the alpha wall, breaking back into

normal space a conservative twenty-five light-minutes from New Berlin's G4 primary, and the swirling patterns of hyper space vanished from the visual display. The Empire's capital sun was tiny from this range, but Honor's repeater plot was suddenly speckled with scores of impeller signatures. The closest were barely a couple of light-minutes away, and one of them headed towards the convoy under a leisurely two hundred gravities as it picked up the freighters' FTL hyper footprints.

Seconds ticked past, and then Lieutenant Cousins cleared his throat.

"Commander Elliot is being challenged by an Andy destroyer, Milady."

"Understood." Honor pressed a stud to drop her own earbug into the circuit and listened to the routine transmissions between the Andermani and Elliot's *Linnet*. The picket ship continued closing until its own sensors had confirmed Elliot's description of her charges, then swung back towards its original station with a courteous welcome. It all seemed dreadfully blasé to Honor, but no doubt that was because her own kingdom was at war.

The convoy continued inward, bound for the orbital warehouses and cargo platforms around the capital planet of Potsdam. There were scores of warships out there, including what looked like three full battle squadrons on some sort of maneuvers, and Honor felt a wistful longing. The IAN was smaller than the RMN, but its hardware came closer than most to matching Manticore's, and she wished Duke Cromarty had managed to bring the Andies into the war. After all, if Manticore went down, the Empire had to be next on the Peeps' list, and the support of those well-trained warships would have been of immeasurable value.

But the House of Anderman didn't think that way. Or, rather, the current Emperor, Gustav XI, had no intention of coming into the war until there was something in it for him, which seemed to be an Anderman genetic trait. Generations of emperors had extended their borders in slow, steady expansion by the time-honored tradition of fishing in troubled waters, and Gustav XI clearly intended to do the same thing. So far, Manticore had more than held its own, but Gustav obviously hoped the time would come when the Star Kingdom's need for an ally was so pressing it would make concessions in Silesia to buy the services of his navy. Honor found that rather shortsighted, but it would have been unrealistic to expect anything else of an Anderman. And at least once the Empire came in on someone's side it had a record of staying the distance.

Perhaps it was only natural, she mused. After all, Gustav Anderman had been a mercenary—and one of the best in the business—before he decided to "retire" to his own empire, and his descendants seemed to have inherited his mindset. The surprising thing was how well the Empire had held together. Dozens of warlords had built vest-pocket realms over the last six or seven centuries, but only the Anderman dynasty had made it stick, because whatever its other faults, it seemed to produce extremely competent rulers. Of course, some of them had been a little on the strange side, starting with its founder.

Gustav Anderman had been convinced he was the reincarnation of Frederick the Great of Prussia. In fact, he'd been *so* convinced that he'd run around in period costume from the Fifth Century Ante Diaspora. No one had laughed—when you were as good a military commander as he'd been you could get away with that sort of thing—but one could hardly call such behavior *normal*. Then there'd been Gustav VI. His subjects had been willing to put up with him even when he started talking to his prize rose bush, but things had gotten a bit out of hand when he tried to make it chancellor. That had been too much even for the Andermani, and he'd been quietly deposed. Removing him had created problems of its own, since the Imperial Charter specified that the Crown passed through the *male* line. Gustav VI had been a childless only son, but he'd had half a dozen male cousins, and a nasty dynastic war had been in the making

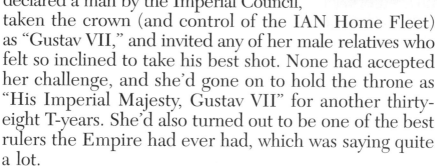

until the oldest of his three sisters put an end to the foolishness by embracing a legal fiction. She'd had herself declared a man by the Imperial Council, taken the crown (and control of the IAN Home Fleet) as "Gustav VII," and invited any of her male relatives who felt so inclined to take his best shot. None had accepted her challenge, and she'd gone on to hold the throne as "His Imperial Majesty, Gustav VII" for another thirty-eight T-years. She'd also turned out to be one of the best rulers the Empire had ever had, which was saying quite a lot.

The Empire was not, Honor thought wryly, your run-of-the-mill monarchy, but despite the occasional quirks in its gallop, the House of Anderman had, by and large, done well by its people. For one thing, its members were wise enough to grant an enormous degree of local autonomy to their various conquests, and they'd shown a positive knack for picking up systems which were already in trouble for one reason or another. Like the Gregor Republic in Gregor-B. The entire system had fallen apart in a particularly messy civil war before the IAN moved in and declared peace, and like so much else about the Empire, that tendency to "rescue" their conquests went back to Gustav I and Potsdam itself.

Before Gustav Anderman and his fleet moved in on it, Potsdam had been named Kuan Yin, after the Chinese goddess of mercy. Which had been one of the more ironic names anyone ever assigned a planet, for the ethnic Chinese who'd settled it had found themselves in a trap as deadly as the one which had almost killed the Graysons' ancestors.

Like the original Manticoran settlers, Kuan Yin's colonists set out from Old Earth before the Warshawski sail had made hyper space safe enough for colony vessels. They'd made the centuries-long voyage sublight, in cryo, only to discover that the original survey had missed a minor point about their new home's ecosystem. Specifically, about its microbiology. Kuan Yin's soil was rich in all the necessary minerals and most of the required nutrients for Terrestrial plants, but its local microorganisms had shown a voracious appetite for Terran chlorophyll and ravaged every crop the settlers put in. None of them had bothered the colonists or the Terrestrial animals they'd introduced, but no Terrestrial life form could live on the local vegetation, Terran food crops had been all but impossible to raise, and yields had been spectacularly low. The colonists had managed—somehow—to survive by endless, backbreaking labor in the fields, but some staple crops had been completely wiped out, dietary deficiencies had been terrible, and they'd known that for all their desperate efforts, they were waging an ultimately hopeless war against their own planet's microbiology. Eventually, they were bound to lose enough ground to push them over the precipice into extinction, and there'd been nothing they could do about it. All of which explained why they'd greeted Anderman's "conquest" of their home world almost as a relief expedition.

None of Gustav Anderman's peculiarities had kept him from being a gifted administrator, and he'd possessed an outstanding capacity for conceptualizing problems and their solutions. He'd also had a talent, which most of his reasonably sane descendants appeared to share, for recognizing the talents of other individuals and making best use of them. Over the next twenty T-years he'd brought in modern microbiologists and genetic engineers to turn the situation around by creating Terrestrial strains which laughed at the local bugs. Potsdam would never become a garden planet like Darwin's Joke or Maiden Howe, with food surpluses for export, but at least its people were able to feed themselves and their children.

That made him quite acceptable to the natives of Kuan Yin as their new Emperor. His foibles didn't bother them—they would have been prepared to forgive outright lunacy—and they became *very* loyal subjects. He'd started out by raising and exporting the one product he fully understood—competent, skillfully led mercenaries—and then gone into the conquistador business on his own.

By the time of his death, New Berlin had been the capital of a six-system empire, and the Empire had done nothing but grow, sometimes unspectacularly but always steadily, ever since.

"We're being hailed, Ma'am," Lieutenant Cousins said suddenly, and Honor blinked as his voice intruded into her reverie. She looked at him, eyebrows raised, and he shrugged. "It's a tight beam addressed specifically to 'Master, RMMS *Wayfarer,*'" he said, and Honor frowned.

"Who is it?"

"I'm not certain, Ma'am. There's no identifier, but it's coming from about zero-two-two."

"Jennifer?" Honor looked at Hughes, and the tac officer tapped a query into her panel.

"If Fred's bearing is right, it's coming from that Andy superdreadnought squadron," she said after a moment, and Honor's frown deepened, for there was no logical reason for an IAN ship of the wall to hail a single Manticoran merchantman. She drummed on the arm of her command chair for a moment, then shrugged.

"Put it through, Fred, but hold a tight focus on my face."

"Yes, Ma'am," Cousins replied. Tight focus wasn't customary, but neither was it unheard of, and at least it should keep Honor's betraying Manticoran uniform out of the image area. She smiled as the ready light on the pickup by her right knee lit a moment later and a man looked out of the small screen below it.

Like most citizens of New Berlin, he was of predominantly Chinese ancestry, and the skin around his eyes crinkled into a smile as he digested Honor's own appearance. He wore the white uniform of an IAN fleet admiral, but a small, rayed sun of worked gold glittered on the right side of his round, stand-up collar, and it was hard for Honor to keep her face expressionless as she saw it, for that sun was worn only by individuals in the direct line of succession to the imperial crown.

"*Gutten Morgen, Kapitain.*" The official language of

the Empire was German. "I am Chien-lu Anderman, Herzog von Rabenstrange," he went on in slightly guttural Standard English, "and on behalf of my cousin the Emperor, I welcome you to New Berlin."

"That's very kind of you, Sir," Honor said carefully, trying to imagine any conceivable reason for an Andermani duke to extend a personal greeting to the captain of a merchant ship. She couldn't, yet Rabenstrange obviously *had* one, and the fact that she was crossing imperial territory with an armed vessel no one had bothered to mention to the Empire suggested that she be very, *very* careful in anything she said.

"Ah, do you suppose you might extend the focus of your pickup, Lady Harrington?" the admiral murmured, and Honor's eyes narrowed. "It can't be very comfortable to sit so still just to keep me from seeing your uniform, My Lady," he added almost apologetically, and she felt her mouth quirk in a wry smile.

"I suppose not," she said, and nodded to Cousins, then leaned back in her chair.

"Thank you," Rabenstrange said.

"You're welcome, *Herr Herzog*," Honor replied, determined to match his own urbanity, and he smiled. "I must confess," she went on, "that you've taken me at a bit of a disadvantage, Sir."

"Please, My Lady. We *do* have our own intelligence services, you know. What sort of wicked militarists would we be if we didn't keep track of people crossing our space? I'm afraid some of your people were somewhat loose-lipped about your squadron and its purpose. You might want to bring that to Admiral Givens' attention."

"Oh, I will, Sir. I certainly will," Honor assured him, and he smiled again.

"Actually," he went on, "the reason my cousin asked me to contact you was to assure you that the Andermani Empire has no objection to your presence in our space and that we understand your concerns in Silesia. His Majesty *would* consider it a personal favor if Admiral Caparelli would inform us before his next Q-ship

deployment, however. We can see why you would prefer to conceal your deployment from the Confederacy, but it's a bit rude to keep *us* in the dark."

"Point taken, My Lord. Please extend my apologies to His Majesty for our, ah, oversight."

"Not necessary, My Lady. He realizes that any oversight was your superiors', not yours." The admiral was clearly enjoying himself, but his assurance was serious, and Honor nodded. "In the meantime, however, I would be honored if you would be so kind as to dine with me aboard my flagship. I fear your reputation precedes you, and my officers and staff would be delighted to meet you. In addition, the Emperor has instructed me to offer you official IAN logistic support in your operations, and my intelligence officer would like to share our own latest updates and appreciations on conditions in the Confederacy with you."

"Why, thank you, My Lord—both for myself, and on behalf of my Queen." Honor tried to hide her astonishment, but she knew she'd failed, and Rabenstrange shook his head gently.

"My Lady," his voice was deeper and far more serious, "the Empire and the Star Kingdom are at peace, and we fully appreciate the severity of your losses. Pirates are the enemies of all civilized star nations, and we will be pleased to offer any assistance we can against them."

"Thank you," she repeated, and he shrugged.

"Would eighteen-thirty local be convenient for you?" he asked. Honor glanced at the chrono calibrated to local time and nodded.

"Yes, Sir. That would be fine. But there is one thing, My Lord."

"Yes?"

"I see our security screen's leaked like a sieve where imperial intelligence is concerned, but I would be most grateful if we could avoid giving anything away to anyone else."

"Of course, My Lady. Your convoy is scheduled for a

three-day layover. If you'll take a pinnace to Alpha Station, one of *my* pinnaces will pick you up there for delivery to *Derfflinger*. I've taken the liberty of pre-clearing you for an approach to the civilian VIP bay at Alpha Seven-Ten, and station security will see to it that the gallery is unoccupied when you dock."

"Thank you again, My Lord. That was very thoughtful." Honor's wry tone acknowledged defeat. Rabenstrange had not only known she was coming, but anticipated her request for anonymity as well. *Maybe it's just as well we are at peace with these people,* she thought. *God help us if the* Peeps *ever catch us out this way!* But at least he was being a gentleman about it.

"Not at all, My Lady. In that case, I'll look forward to seeing you at eighteen-thirty," the admiral said with yet another charming smile, and cut the circuit.

• CHAPTER ELEVEN

Honor stood and tugged the hem of her dress tunic down as her pinnace docked with Alpha Station, the central node of Potsdam's orbital infrastructure. Approach Control had indicated no awareness of anything special about her pinnace—not that she'd expected it to. She suspected someone as good as Herzog Rabenstrange at finding things out was even better at keeping them secret . . . which was a bit of a mixed blessing at the moment. She wondered what the Empire's real agenda was where her squadron was concerned, yet she was certain she would discover only what Rabenstrange chose to *let* her discover. Still, if the Empire had intended to object there was no need for the admiral to dissemble. That had to be a good sign, and his explicit offer of operational support was another.

The green light lit as the docking tube established a solid seal, and the flight engineer popped the hatch. Honor glanced once at her trio of armsmen, then lifted Nimitz to her shoulder. Unlike her Graysons, the 'cat was completely relaxed, and she decided to take that as another good sign as she reached for the grab bar and swung into the tube's zero-gee.

As promised, the dock gallery was empty but for a single IAN commander. The aiguilette of a staff officer hung from her shoulder, and she came to attention and saluted as Honor swung from the tube. Honor returned the salute, and the Andermani officer held out her hand.

"Commander Tian Schoeninger, My Lady," she said.

"I'm Admiral Rabenstrange's operations officer. Welcome to New Berlin."

"Thank you, Commander." Honor returned her grip carefully, for Potsdam's gravity was only about eighty-five percent of T-standard, less than sixty-five percent of Sphinx's. Like most Andermani, Schoeninger was small, fine-boned, and slender, and eyes as almondine as Honor's own twinkled as the commander smiled up at her towering height.

"My armsmen," Honor said, waving her free hand at LaFollet, Jamie Candless, and Eddy Howard. The commander frowned slightly and started to speak as she saw their holstered pulsers, then closed her mouth and settled for a nod of greeting.

"Gentlemen," she said after the briefest of pauses. "I don't believe I've ever had the pleasure of meeting a Grayson. I understand your world is as, ah, strenuous as Potsdam."

"In its own way, Ma'am," LaFollet acknowledged for his fellows, and she smiled. Then she released Honor's hand and waved at the IAN pinnace docked beside *Wayfarer*'s. "If you'll follow me, My Lady, Admiral Rabenstrange is expecting you."

The IAN pinnace was a VIP model with all the comforts of an expensive civilian passenger shuttle, including a bar with an impressive array of bottles. The decksole was carpeted, the seats were sinfully comfortable, and music played from concealed speakers, and Honor wondered if it was part of *Derfflinger*'s normal parasite complement. It was a fairly useless specimen as military small craft went, but perhaps the IAN considered it appropriate for an admiral—particularly when that admiral was also the Emperor's cousin.

The pilot made an oblique approach to Rabenstrange's flagship to give the passengers a chance to appreciate the superdreadnought, and Honor studied *Derfflinger* with interest. She'd seen quite a few Andermani warships during her previous duty in Silesia, but, like the RMN, the IAN relied primarily upon light units in the Confederacy. This was her first close look at an imperial ship of the wall, and it was impressive.

She knew from her intelligence briefings that the *Seydlitz*-class ships like *Derfflinger* were a half million tons smaller than the RMN's own *Sphinx*-class, which made them a tad over three-quarters of a million tons lighter than the newest *Gryphon*-class ships, but that still brought Rabenstrange's flagship in at well over seven million tons. She shared the double-ended, hammerhead hull of all impeller-drive warships, but she was a haze gray instead of the white both the RMN and PN favored, and instead of a hull number, her name was emblazoned just aft of her forward impeller ring in red-edged golden letters at least five meters tall. Her armament was also arranged differently, the mounts segregated into a single, relatively light graser deck between two *very* heavy missile decks, and Honor pursed her lips in a silent whistle. *Derfflinger* was already smaller than an RMN SD, and the magazine capacity for that many tubes had obviously cut deep into mass which might have been used for energy weapons. But while the ship would be far weaker in energy-range combat than one of her Manticoran counterparts, she also carried half again the missile broad-side of a *Sphinx*. Honor had known that from her brief-ings, but actually seeing it was still something of a shock. She could see several advantages to the armament mix, but *Derfflinger* would find herself in serious trouble if an enemy managed to close with her.

The ship drifted against the stars in her parking orbit, a mountain of alloy and armor jeweled with the green and white lights of a moored starship, and as Honor stud-ied her, she suddenly realized why the IAN had accepted smaller SDs. *Derfflinger*'s lower mass would let her pull a higher acceleration than a *Gryphon*, assuming equal compensator efficiency, and that liveliness was perfectly suited to the missile-heavy doctrine the IAN seemed to have adopted. Of course, she thought with a carefully hidden smile, the Andies might find that less effective against the RMN than they expected. Manticore's missile pods and improved inertial compensators would go a long way towards negating *Derfflinger's* advantages. An RMN SD could more than match her throw weight, at least in the opening broadside, and the Manticoran ship's better compensator would make her at least as maneuverable, despite *Derfflinger's* mass advantage.

On the other hand, she thought, suddenly losing any temptation to smile, *their intelligence types were able to find out about the squadron. I wonder if they're working on getting hold of our* compensator designs, *as well? Now* there's *a happy thought!*

The pinnace swept closer and killed her wedge, coming in beneath the orbiting behemoth on conventional thrusters, and a tractor drew her upward into the glowing cavern of a boat bay. It deposited her neatly in a cradle, and the carpeted deck trembled as mechanical docking arms engaged securely.

A meticulously turned-out lieutenant commander saluted and his side party came to attention as Honor swung herself out of the tube. The intercom omitted the normal announcement of an officer's arrival, but bosun's pipes twittered. They were the old-fashioned, lung-powered kind, not the electronic version the RMN used, and Honor held her return salute until they died.

"Permission to come aboard, Sir?" she asked then.

"Permission granted, My Lady," the lieutenant commander replied, snapping his hand down from the brim of his tall, visored cap. His high-collared uniform had to be uncomfortable, Honor thought, and keeping its pristine whiteness spot-free must be a pain, but it *did* look sharp.

So did the Marines of the honor guard. Like the Grayson Navy, but unlike the RMN, the IAN's Marines were Army units assigned to shipboard duty. Andermani ships also carried fewer of them, since their sole function was to provide a ground combat and boarding force, but their drill was as sharp as anything Honor's own

Marines might have turned out, and they looked both competent and dangerous, even in dress uniform. The breasts of their black tunics were elaborately frogged, which looked decidedly odd to Honor, and the officer at their head actually had a fur-trimmed pelisse thrown over one shoulder and wore a tall, furred cap with a silver skeleton on the front.

Honor's eyebrows rose, for that skeleton marked *Derfflinger*'s "Marines" as a detachment of the *Totenkopf* Hussars, the equivalent of the Queen's Own Regiment of the Royal Manticoran Army. Gustav Anderman had personally designed the *Totenkopfs*' uniform to reflect his "Prussian heritage," and Honor wondered if it could possibly be as uncomfortable as it looked. On the other hand, like the man who'd designed their uniform, the *Totenkopfs*' reputation was such that people seldom felt inclined to laugh at them. But they were rarely seen off Potsdam except in time of war, and their presence here was a sign that Rabenstrange stood high in the Emperor's favor.

Their officer raised his sword in salute as the troopers came to attention, and Honor acknowledged the courtesy as she followed Schoeninger to the lift. The commander punched in a destination code, then gave Honor a rueful smile as the lift began to move.

"Our people are certainly *colorful*, aren't they?" she murmured.

"Yes. Yes, they are," Honor replied in a neutral tone, uncertain of where Schoeninger was headed, but the commander only shook her head.

"I assure you, our work uniforms are much more practical, My Lady. There are times I could wish for a little less deliberate anachronism in our dress uniform tailoring, but I suppose we wouldn't be *us* anymore if we gave it up."

Her tone was so wry Honor smiled, but it also offered an opening.

"Those were *Totenkopf* Hussars, weren't they?" she asked.

"Yes, they were." Schoeninger sounded surprised Honor had recognized them, though there was no surprise in the emotions Honor sensed through her link to Nimitz.

"I was under the impression they left Potsdam only in wartime." Honor made the statement a question, and Schoeninger nodded.

"That's normally true, My Lady. Herzog Rabenstrange, however, is the Emperor's first cousin. They attended the Academy together, and they've always been quite close. His Majesty personally directed that the *Totenkopfs* be assigned to his flagship."

"I see." Honor nodded slowly, and the commander smiled again. It was a faint smile, but Honor felt Schoeninger's satisfaction and realized the commander had deliberately guided the conversation just so she could make that last statement. Honor wondered if it had been simply to make her own boss's importance clear for social reasons. From the little she'd so far seen of Commander Schoeninger, it seemed unlikely. It was far more probable the commander wanted to be certain Honor was fully aware that anything Rabenstrange said could be taken as coming from the Emperor's inner circle. Whatever her intentions, Schoeninger had been smooth about it, and Honor felt an ungrudging admiration. Subtlety wasn't her own strong suit, but that didn't mean she couldn't appreciate it in others.

The lift reached its destination, and the commander led them down a passage to a hatch guarded by two more black-uniformed Marines, who came to attention at her approach.

"Guests to see the Admiral," Schoeninger said. "We're expected."

"Yes, Ma'am." The Marine who responded spoke Standard English, not German—a courtesy which Honor appreciated—then pressed a com key. "*Fregattenkapitänin Schoeninger und Graffin Harrington, Herr Herzog,*" he announced, and a moment later, the hatch slid open.

"If you'll come with me, My Lady," Schoeninger said, and led the way into the most magnificently appointed cabin Honor had ever seen. The dimensions were marginally smaller than her own quarters aboard *Terrible* had been, but the furnishings were on an entirely different scale.

"Ah, Lady Harrington!" Chien-lu von Rabenstrange himself rose to greet her, extending his hand with a smile, and two more officers stood behind him. Both were men—one, stocky for an Andermani, in the uniform of a captain, and the other a commander who, like Schoeninger, wore the aiguilette of a staff officer.

"Herzog Rabenstrange," Honor murmured, shaking his hand. The captain behind him wore a slightly pained expression as he saw her armsmen's sidearms, and his eyes cut sideways to his admiral with an edge of worry, but Rabenstrange himself only nodded to his companions.

"Captain Gunterman, my flag captain, and Commander Hauser, my intelligence officer," he said, and his subordinates came forward to shake hands in turn.

"My armsmen, My Lord," Honor said. "Major LaFollet, Armsman Candless, and Armsman Howard."

"Ah, yes!" Rabenstrange replied. "I read of Major LaFollet in your dossier, My Lady." He extended his hand to the Grayson with absolutely no hesitation to indicate an awareness of his own exalted birth, and this time the smile he gave Honor was far more serious. "You are fortunate to have such devoted and—from the record— competent guardians."

LaFollet blushed, but Honor only nodded.

"Yes, My Lord, I am," she said simply. "I hope their presence isn't a problem?"

"Under the strict letter of protocol, I suppose it could be considered one," Rabenstrange replied. "Given the present circumstances and your own status, however, they're welcome."

Captain Gunterman clearly wanted to dispute that, and Honor sympathized. She knew how *she* would have felt if a foreign officer had wanted to bring armed retainers into the presence of a member of the House of Winton. Rabenstrange sounded entirely sincere, however. Indeed, he appeared genuinely pleased to meet her, and the emotions coloring her link to Nimitz combined welcome, amusement, anticipation, and a certain devilish delight with an undeniable seriousness.

"Thank you, My Lord. I appreciate your understanding," she said, and the admiral shook his head.

"There's no need to thank me, My Lady. I invited you as my guest. As such, I expected you to satisfy the legal requirements of your own position."

Honor felt her eyebrows rise at the fresh indication of how completely briefed he'd been on her. Very few Manticorans realized Grayson law *required* her armsmen's presence, and she was astounded that Rabenstrange did. Her surprise showed, and the admiral smiled once more.

"We have quite a thick dossier on you, My Lady," he said in a tone that was half-amused and half-apologetic. "Your, ah, *achievements* have made you of particular interest to us, you see."

Honor felt her own cheekbones heat, but Rabenstrange only chuckled and waved her to a chair. The other Andermani seated themselves as well, and LaFollet took his position at her shoulder while Candless and Howard parked themselves as unobtrusively as possible against a bulkhead. A steward appeared to offer them wine, then vanished as silently as he'd come. The wine was so dark it was actually black, and Rabenstrange waited while Honor sampled her glass.

"Very nice, My Lord," she said. "I don't believe I've ever tasted anything quite like it."

"No, it's a Potsdam vintage. When the microbiologists redesigned our Terrestrial crops, they accidentally created a strain of grapes which will grow only on Potsdam but which produces a truly remarkable wine. One of their more serendipitous achievements, I believe."

"Indeed, My Lord." Honor sipped again, appreciatively, then sat back and crossed her legs. Nimitz flowed into her lap and draped himself comfortably, and she cocked her head at Raben-strange with a faint smile. "Nonetheless, My Lord, I rather doubt you invited me aboard only to share your cellar with me."

"Of course not," Rabenstrange agreed, leaning back in his own chair. He propped his elbows on its arms, cupping his wineglass comfortably in both hands, and returned her smile. "As I said, I wanted Commander Hauser to have an opportunity to share our own data on the situation in the Confederacy with you—in fact, I've had him prepare a chip folio which summarizes all our reports for the last several T-months. But to be perfectly frank, My Lady, I invited you because I wanted to meet you."

"Meet me, My Lord? May I ask why?"

"Certainly you may." Rabenstrange's smile grew, and she felt a stronger wash of that devilish delight as his eyes twinkled. "I suppose I should first admit that there's still a certain amount of the bad little boy in me," he said disarmingly, "and one of my objectives is to dazzle you with the depth of our intelligence on the Star King-dom generally and on you specifically." Honor cocked a polite eyebrow, and he chuckled. "One thing we Andermani have learned over the years, My Lady, is that it's never wise to leave a potential ally—or enemy—in ignorance of our own intelligence capabilities. It makes life so much simpler if the people you must deal with are aware that you probably know more than they think you do."

Honor had to laugh. Here, she thought, was a man who delighted in playing the game. There was· an indisputable arrogance in his emotions, a sense of his own position within the imperial hierarchy, but there was also a refusal to take himself too seriously. She felt the underlying steel of his personality, knew he was just as devoted to the concept of duty as she herself was, but that didn't mean he couldn't enjoy himself. No doubt he could be an extremely dangerous man, yet he was also one with a zest whose like she'd seldom encountered.

"Consider me dazzled, My Lord," she told him wryly. "I assure you my next report to the Admiralty will emphasize your intelligence capabilities as strongly as you could possibly desire."

"Excellent! You see? Already I've discharged a sizable portion of my mission." Captain Gunterman shook his head like a tutor with a wayward charge, but Rabenstrange paid no heed as he continued. "Next, I very much wanted to meet you because of what you've accomplished for your Queen. You have a remarkable record, My Lady. Our analysts expect to be seeing much of you in years to come, and I think it can never be a bad thing for serving officers to know one another's mettle from personal observation."

There was a faint but distinct edge of warning in that. Rabenstrange's welcome didn't abate in the least, but Honor understood. She wasn't certain she shared his estimate of her own importance within the RMN, but she understood. Whether as allies or enemies, personal knowledge of the person behind an officer's name would be invaluable to any commander.

"And last but far from least, My Lady, you're about to take your squadron into Silesia." Rabenstrange had gone completely serious now, and he leaned forward in his chair. "The Empire fully realizes how critical the situation has become there, and both the reduction in your kingdom's normal force levels and the nature of your own command is a clear indication of how fully committed your fleet is against the People's Republic. My cousin wishes me to make clear to you—and, through you, to your Admiralty—that our diplomats' current views on the Confederacy are fully shared by our military."

"And those views are, My Lord?" Honor asked politely as he paused.

"As your own kingdom, the Empire has powerful interests in Silesia," Rabenstrange replied quietly. "No doubt you've been fully briefed, and I know you've served

in the area before, so I'll make no attempt to conceal the fact that we con-sider much of the Confederacy to be an area vital to our own security. Certain factions within the government and the Fleet have always advocated taking—stronger action, shall we say?—in those areas, and the present upsurge in piratical activity has given added point to their arguments. The fact that the Silesian government is in greater disarray than usual is also a factor in their thinking. Nonetheless, His Majesty has directed that we will take no action there without prior consultation with your government. He's fully aware of the strain your own Navy is under and of the threat the People's Republic poses to Silesia and, by extension, to the Empire. He has no intention of committing himself to any action which might . . . *distract* your fleet from its present concentration against the Peeps."

"I see." Honor did her best to hide her relief. Raben-strange's statements were in accord with both the For-eign Office's and ONI's analysis, but there was a vast difference between analysts' opinions and a direct, for-mal statement. More, Rabenstrange's birth and naval rank made him an extremely senior spokesman, and the Andermani Empire had a reputation for meaning what it said. It might sometimes simply choose to say noth-ing—which could be one of the most effective ways of lying yet invented—but when it *did* say something, it meant it.

Of course, there were some interesting limits to what Rabenstrange had just told her. He hadn't said the Empire had any intention of giving up its long-range goals in Silesia, only that it wouldn't rock the boat while the Star Kingdom fought for its life against the Peeps. There might even be an implication that it expected a certain post-war freedom of action in return for its present restraint, though Rabenstrange hadn't said so. Fortunately, those were considerations which lay far beyond her own level.

"I appreciate your candor, My Lord, and I'll certainly pass your comments to my superiors."

"Thank you, My Lady. In addition to those reassurances, however, His Majesty desires to support your own operations. Our merchant marine is far smaller than yours, and in order to avoid any impression of provocative behavior, we've somewhat reduced our own presence in the Confederacy. At present, we're restricting ourselves to providing escorts for our own shipping and maintaining light forces only in the most important nodal systems. Naturally, your larger merchant fleet is much more exposed than our own, just as your available units are stretched more tightly. His Majesty wishes me to say that in those areas in which we *are* maintaining an IAN fleet presence, our captains have been instructed to provide protection to your vessels, as well as our own. Should your Admiralty wish to redeploy its available strength in light of those instructions, we will watch your back for you when you do so. We also intend to keep a close eye out for any indication that the People's Republic may be considering, ah, stirring the fire. Should that happen, we will be prepared to bring diplomatic pressure to bear upon the current government in an effort to have its units recalled. Naturally, we can't promise to go beyond diplomatic measures until and unless a Peep warship attacks our own commerce, but what we can do, we will."

Honor blinked at the totally unexpected generosity of the offer. It made sense, for the Andermani would have as little use for pirates—or any other raiders—in Silesia as the Star Kingdom, but it amounted almost to an informal offer of alliance.

"I will certainly pass that along, as well, My Lord," she said, and Rabenstrange nodded.

"Finally, My Lady, as regards your own squadron's operations. Am I correct in assuming you've been provided with a wide selection of transponder codes?"

"I have, My Lord," Honor said a bit cautiously. Resetting the transponder beacon of a starship was the equivalent of the old wet-navy trick of flying false colors. It was acknowledged as a legitimate *ruse de guerre* by most star nations and sanctioned by half a dozen

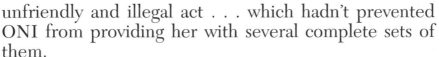

interstellar accords, but the Andermani Empire had never formally accepted it. For the record, the Empire considered the use of its own ID codes an unfriendly and illegal act . . . which hadn't prevented ONI from providing her with several complete sets of them.

"I thought as much," Rabenstrange murmured, "and, of course, a Q-ship operates under rather different constraints from a regular warship." He nodded as if to himself, then went on. "His Majesty wishes me to provide you with an authentication code which will identify your ships to any IAN warship. The same code will also identify you to the commanders of our Silesian naval stations. We have rather fewer of them than you do, but those we have will be alerted to provide you with resupply, intelligence data, and maintenance support. Where possible, they will also offer direct military support against homegrown raiders. In addition, His Majesty has asked me to inform you that, for the moment, our Navy will, ah, look the other way if any of your ships should happen to be employing Andermani transponder codes."

"My Lord," Honor said frankly, "I never anticipated such generous support from your Emperor. You must realize how valuable that kind of assistance can be, especially for a Q-ship. I assure you that *I* recognize its value, and on behalf of myself and my Queen, I would appreciate your extending my kingdom's thanks to His Majesty for his generosity."

"Of course," Rabenstrange replied, then leaned back once more with a sad smile. "The truth is, My Lady, that neither of our nations wants the Silesian situation to boil over. Without doubt, the Confederacy is the largest potential bone of contention between us. Speaking only for myself, I would consider it a disaster for both our nations should that contention ever spill over into outright hostilities. Unfortunately, no one can predict where competing ambition and completely legitimate security concerns will lead interstellar powers, and, as you, I am a servant of the Crown. Yet right now, at this very moment, the sanity of survival against the People's Republic makes it essential that Manticore and the Empire remain friendly powers, and His Majesty has taken the actions I've described as the strongest means at his disposal by which he can make his own commitment to that proposition clear. The fact that it provides me an opportunity to extend support and assistance to an officer whose record and accomplishments I respect is merely a welcome side effect of that commitment."

"Thank you, My Lord," Honor said quietly.

"Yes." Rabenstrange took another sip of wine, then inhaled and stood briskly. "Well! Enough formality, My Lady. I invited you to supper, and my chef has made a special effort on your behalf. If you—and your armsmen, of course—" he added with a flashing smile "—will join Captain Gunterman, Commander Schoeninger, Commander Hauser, and me, perhaps we can enjoy it like civilized beings. There will be time enough for dreary military briefings afterward."

• CHAPTER TWELVE

"Got a minute, Ma'am?"

Honor looked up from her briefing room terminal. Rafe Cardones and Lieutenant Commander Tschu stood in the open hatch. Cardones had a memo board under one arm, and the chief engineer's treecat rode his shoulder, ears pricked and whiskers quivering. As Tschu's weary face suggested, he'd spent virtually all his waking time buried in Engineering, which meant his 'cat had spent little time on the bridge. Now she looked around with bright, green-eyed interest, and Nimitz perked up instantly on the back of his person's chair. Honor waved for the two men to enter, and hid a smile as she felt Nimitz's greeting to Samantha. 'Cats were totally disinterested in human sexuality, and she was relieved to find that even with her unusual link to Nimitz, the 'cat's amatory adventures had no effect on *her* hormones. That didn't mean she wasn't aware of what both he and Samantha were feeling, however, and she wondered if Nimitz had experienced the same thing from her and Paul Tankersley.

She pointed to chairs, then closed the hatch as Cardones and Tschu sank into them. Cardones laid his board on the tabletop, and she smiled faintly as he leaned back with a sigh.

"Why do I have the feeling you two have something on your minds?" she asked, and Cardones twitched a grin.

"Probably because we do," he replied. "I—"

He broke off as Nimitz flowed down from Honor's chair and padded silently across the table. Samantha leapt off Tschu's shoulder to join him, and the two sat neatly, facing each other. They gazed intently into one another's eyes, noses almost touching, only the tips of their fluffy tails flicking, and Cardones gazed at them for a moment, then shook his head.

"Nice to see things are going well for *someone*," he said, then turned and cocked an eyebrow at Tschu. "Does she have a 'cat in every port?"

"No." The engineer's deep voice was amused, despite his obvious weariness. "It's not quite that bad. But she *does* have a way with the men, doesn't she?"

Both 'cats ignored the humans, concentrating on one another, and Honor heard the deep, almost subsonic sound of their purring. The soft rumbles reached out to one another and merged, sweeping together in an oddly intricate harmony, and Tschu shot a startled, almost apologetic glance at Honor, who shrugged helplessly. In their native environment, young treecats often established temporary relationships, but *mature* 'cats were monogamous and mated for life. Those who adopted humans, however, seldom took permanent mates, and she'd often wondered if that was because their adoption bonds took them away from others of their kind or if they adopted humans in the first place because they were somehow different from their fellows. But she'd witnessed 'cat courtships, and this one looked moderately serious, which could have . . . interesting consequences. Unmated 'cats were relatively infertile, but mated pairs were a very different matter.

There was no point discussing it, though. What happened between Samantha and Nimitz was up to them— a point the majority of humans, who persisted in thinking of 'cats as pets, failed to grasp. That misconception probably stemmed from the fact that humans were almost always the alpha partners in their bondings, but that was because treecats who'd adopted had chosen to live in humanity's society and recognized the need to abide by human rules, some of which baffled them. They relied on their people for guidance, and not just socially; they knew they didn't fully understand humanity's technological

marvels, and that those marvels could kill. But anyone who'd ever been adopted knew a treecat was a person, with the same rights and occasional need for space as any human. It was always the 'cat who initiated a bond, and there had been cases in which that bond was repudiated when a human tried to turn it into some sort of ownership. It happened rarely—'cat's seldom made the mistake of choosing someone who could do that—but it *did* happen.

Cardones watched the two 'cats for another moment, smiling and unaware of the full implications of what he was seeing and hearing, then cleared his throat and looked back at Honor. His smile faded, and he laid one hand on his memo board.

"Harry and I have a problem, Ma'am."

"Which is?" Honor asked calmly.

"Crew efficiency, Ma'am," Tschu said. "Specifically, Engineering efficiency. We're still not cutting the mustard down there."

"I see." Honor cocked her chair back and played with a stylus. Their "convoy" was just over a month out of New Berlin and due to reach Sachsen in another week, and the lengthy cruise had given her enough time to get a feel for her crew. She really didn't need Tschu to tell her that his department's efficiency remained marginal. Of course, his wasn't the only one which still had problems—just the one with the biggest gap between target levels and reality. She was relieved that he'd brought it up, however. She'd been willing to let Cardones give Tschu time to try to straighten out the kinks on his own, but she'd also been curious to see how the engineer would respond to the lack of official pressure from above. Some officers would have tried to pretend there *wasn't* a problem until his exec or CO called him on the carpet, and it was good to know Tschu didn't work that way.

"Do you know why you aren't?" she asked after a moment, and Tschu rubbed a hand over his close-cropped hair.

"I think so, Ma'am. The problem is what I do about it."

"Explain to me, Commander," Honor invited, and he frowned.

"Basically, it's a matter of who's got the seniority," he began, then paused and drew a deep breath. "Before I go on, Ma'am, please understand that I'm not making excuses. If you have any advice or suggestions, I'll be delighted to hear them, but I know whose responsibility Engineering is." He met Honor's eyes levelly until she nodded, then went on.

"Having said that, I think I *do* need some advice. This is the first time I've actually run a department, and there are a couple of changes I want to try, but I don't feel comfortable about making them without running them by you first. And if I *do* make them, I'm afraid it'll mean stepping quite a ways outside normal procedures."

Honor nodded again. Nimitz was too preoccupied with Samantha for Honor to sample the engineer's emotions, but she didn't need her link to the 'cat to recognize his frankness. Like many of her officers, he was young for his rank, and, as he'd said, this was the first time he'd held full responsibility for running his own department. He clearly felt his inexperience, and she suspected that what he really wanted was for her to tell him that whatever he had in mind was an acceptable answer, not for her to reach out and solve his problems for him herself.

"All right," he said in a more normal tone. "Like all our departments, I've got a lot of newbies, and the ship's sheer size exacerbates the problem. With Fusion One tucked away at the center of the hull and Fusion Two still in its original position, it takes me almost fifteen minutes just to get from one power plant to the other, and both of them are an awful long way from Main Hyper, the impeller rooms, and Damage Control Central. For the first few weeks, I was spending way too much time trying to shuttle back and forth between widely dispersed work sections, and my assistants were taking their cue from me. I'm pretty sure a big part of that was the fact that I *know* how new most of my people are, and I wanted to be available to them if a problem came up. Unfortunately, all I was really accomplishing was to try to be in too many places at once. I was a moving target, and when trouble *did* crop up, I was almost always in the wrong place."

He shrugged and rubbed one eyebrow with a wry smile.

"That part of it's being taken care of. I've had extra com links run to Fusion One, and we've built complete repeaters of the master control panels from Fusion Two and Hyper in One, as well. That should let me monitor them directly and give me face-to-face capability with every station simultaneously, if I need it."

Honor nodded once more. She'd known Tschu was making modifications, but she hadn't realized they were as extensive as he seemed to be suggesting. She approved, however, and she made another mental check mark by the engineer's name. People who dug right in to solve problems instead of standing around wringing their hands were unfortunately rare.

"My biggest current problem is that I'm not seeing the increased efficiency I anticipated from the new arrangements. Part of it's to be expected, with so many newbies still learning their jobs, I suppose, and it's taking longer to get all the classroom crap out of their brains because we're so thin on experienced people to serve as mentors. But part of it's the nature of those 'experienced' people, too. Frankly, I've got some really bad apples down there, Ma'am."

Honor let her chair swing upright once more and folded her hands on the table. So far—thanks, no doubt, to Sally MacBride—*Wayfarer* had experienced few of the discipline problems Honor had half-expected. The Bosun wasn't the sort to put up with any nonsense, and Honor was reasonably confident she'd settled a few personnel problems with direct intervention of the sort Regs didn't envision. As *Wayfarer*'s captain, Honor could live with that, but it sounded as if Tschu had problems of his own. And, she thought guiltily, *she* was the one who'd deliberately handed *Wayfarer's* officers more than their fair share of potential troublemakers.

"I've got about a dozen genuine hard cases," Tschu said. "Two of them are particular problems. They've got the training and experience for their jobs, but they're trouble-makers, pure and simple. They sit around on their butts if someone doesn't stay on top of them every moment, and they pressure the newbies to do the same. I can't bust them, because there's no place to bust them *to*—they're already at the bottom of the heap."

"Do you want them removed?" Honor asked quietly.

"Ma'am, there's nothing I'd like better," Tschu said frankly, "but I think it would be the wrong move. What I've got to do is get them off their butts and keep them there—and make sure everyone knows I did it."

"I see." Honor nodded in agreement, pleased by Tschu's response.

"The problem is that some of my senior petty offic-ers aren't getting the job done. My problem children are careful not try any crap whenever an officer's around, but the watch logs tell me they're giving plenty of trouble when we're not there. The worst problem's Impeller One—the drive room chief on first watch doesn't have the guts to face the troublemakers down without com-missioned support—but the situation's almost as bad on third watch." The engineer paused, then shook his head. "In a way, I understand why the chiefs in question are running scared," he admitted. "Engineering can be a dangerous place, and to be perfectly honest, I think at least the two I've already mentioned are capable of arranging 'accidents' for someone who ticks them off."

"Anyone who arranges an 'accident' in *my* ship will wish to heaven he or she had never been born," Honor said grimly.

"I know—and you'll only get them after *I'm* through with them," Tschu said. "But until they actually try some-thing, all I can do is warn them, and I don't think they really believe me. Worse, the two senior chiefs who seem to be caving in don't think they believe it, either."

"So what do you want to do about them?"

"Well, Ma'am . . ." Tschu glanced at Cardones, who nodded, then drew a deep breath. "What I want to do, Ma'am, is relieve both senior chiefs I've mentioned. I'll find some crap assignment for them—one that will both keep them out of other people's hair and make it clear to their people that they've been removed for lack of performance. But I'm already one senior chief short of establishment. If I boot them, I'll have to replace 'em with someone with the guts to do the job, and I'm fresh out of people with the seniority and attitude for it."

"I see," Honor repeated, and her mind flickered over options. Given the rush with which her ships had been manned, they were stretched tight for personnel, and Tschu was right about his lack of senior petty officers. Nor did anyone else have equivalent personnel to spare the engineer.

"What about Harkness?" she asked Cardones after a moment.

"I thought about him, Ma'am. One thing I know for sure is that he wouldn't take any crap off anyone, and only a lunatic would push him. The problem is that Scotty needs him. He may technically be a missile tech, but he's also the best small-craft flight engineer we've got. He's not only keeping the pinnaces on-line, but spending a lot of his time on loan to the LAC squadrons, as well. If we pull him from Flight Ops, we're going to leave an awful big hole in that department."

"Point taken," Honor murmured, and looked back at Tschu. "I assume, Harry, that since you're making this proposal you have candidates of your own in mind?"

"Yes, Ma'am, but none of them have the seniority for the jobs. That's my problem. CPO Riley's already holding down a the chief of the watch's slot in Damage Control Central, and I figure I can bump him to senior chief and give him Impeller One on third watch. But that still leaves me needing someone for *first* watch, which is the real hot spot, plus a replacement for Riley in DCC. I've got two people in mind, but they're actually on their first deployments. I know they can handle the responsibility and do the job, but they're both only second-class techs."

"You want to put a second-class tech in a *senior chief's* slot?" Honor asked in a very careful voice, and Tschu nodded.

"I know it sounds crazy, Ma'am, but my watch bills are awful fragile. I've already made a lot of assignments based on capability, not grade, because it was the only way to get the job done, but there's a limit to how much readjusting I can do without actually making the problem worse. If we bump the people I'm thinking about, it'll do the least overall damage to my assignments."

"You don't have anyone senior you think could handle the slots?"

"No, Ma'am. Not really. Oh, I've got some really good people down there—I'm not trying to say they're all, or even most, a problem. But we're spread so thin—and spread out so widely—that, like Chief Riley, the ones with the necessary experience and, ah, intestinal fortitude are already in essential spots. I can't pull one of them without making another hole, and I don't have anyone to replace them with to plug the holes."

"I see. Exactly which second classes are we talking about here?"

"Power Tech Maxwell and Electronics Tech Lewis, Ma'am," Cardones put in, keying his memo board and glancing down at it. "Both have first-rate marks from school, both have performed in exemplary fashion since coming aboard, and both of them are a bit old for their rates. That's because they only enlisted after the war started," he added by way of explanation. "Maxwell's a drive specialist; he was merchant service-trained, a drive room chief with the D&O Line, and he really just needed the Navy course for certification. He's good, Ma'am, really good. Lewis is a gravitics specialist. She doesn't have any prior experience, but I've taken a hard look at her record

since coming aboard. She's solid, and Chief Riley speaks very highly of her, especially as a troubleshooter. Harry wants her to replace Riley in DCC and Maxwell for Impeller One. Frankly, I think they'd do very well in those slots, but neither one of them is anywhere near having the seniority to justify it to BuPers."

"The Exec's right there, Ma'am," Tschu said, "but they're both really good, and they both have backbones. Neither one of them would back down from the bad apples."

Honor rocked her chair back again and glanced at Nimitz and Samantha without really seeing them while she considered. The problem, as neither Cardones nor Tschu needed to tell her, was that she couldn't just take two second-class ratings and make them *acting* senior chiefs. If they were going to discharge their duties, they not only deserved the official grade to go with them, they *needed* it. There would be resentment enough from people they'd been jumped over, whatever happened; if they didn't receive the imprimatur of the rockers which normally went with the job, their moral authority would be suspect. But if Honor gave them those rockers, she'd have to be able to justify her actions.

The captain of a Queen's ship had broad authority to promote in the course of a deployment. Such promotions were "acting" until the deployment's end, as the one she'd given Aubrey Wanderman. But their confirmation by BuPers at deployment's end was almost automatic, with only the most cursory inspection of the individual's record and efficiency ratings, on the theory that a captain was competent to judge her people's suitability for promotion.

Yet if Honor jumped a technician second class clear to senior chief, BuPers was going to ask some very tough questions. Some captains had been known to play the favoritism game, and that sort of sudden elevation was unheard of. She'd have to be able to justify it by the results she obtained, and that justification had better be strong. Worse, the only way BuPers could rectify any mistake on her part would be to reduce Maxwell and Lewis to what it considered appropriate rates, which would equate to demotion for cause. It wouldn't be called that in their personnel jackets, but that demotion would follow them for the remainder of their careers. Any officer who ever read those jackets would be likely to assume they *had* been promoted out of favoritism, and they'd have to work far harder than anyone else to prove they hadn't.

She pulled her eyes back from the 'cats and focused on Tschu once more. He was watching her anxiously, and his anxiety was a sign he fully recognized the implications of his request. But he also seemed confident he was on the right track, and, unlike Honor, he knew the individuals in question.

"You realize," she said, since it had to be said, "that you'll put these people—Maxwell and Lewis—in a very difficult spot?"

"Yes, Ma'am." Tschu nodded without hesitation. "I'd really prefer to simply make it an acting position, but—" He shrugged, indicating his own awareness of what Honor had already considered. "As far as Maxwell is concerned, he knows his stuff A to Z, and my enlisted people know he does. They also know where he got his experience, and he's a big, tough customer. I doubt even Steil—" He paused. "I doubt even the worst troublemaker would want to push anything with him. Lewis isn't all that imposing physically, but I honestly believe she has the greater leadership ability, and she's some kind of magician at troubleshooting. She's weaker on theory, but she's stronger than ninety percent of my other people even there. I wouldn't be surprised to see her go mustang in another ten years and wind up doing *my* job, Ma'am. Maybe sooner, with the quickie OCS programs BuPers is talking about setting up. She's that good."

Honor simply nodded, but she was astonished by Tschu's estimate of Lewis' potential. The RMN had more

"mustangs" who'd started out enlisted and earned their commissions the hard way than most navies with an aristocratic tradition, but it was unheard of for someone to single out a mere second class on her very first deployment as a future officer. A brief suspicion that Tschu might have personal reasons for pushing Lewis flickered across her brain, but she dismissed it instantly. He wasn't the sort to get sexually involved with his enlisted personnel, and even if he had been, she surely would have sensed something from him through Nimitz.

The bottom line was that Harold Tschu was asking her to put her professional judgment on the line for two people she didn't even know. That took guts, since many captains would have delighted in taking vengeance on him if BuPers came down on them over it, but it didn't necessarily mean he was right. On the other hand, it was his department. Unlike Honor, he *did* know the people involved, and *something* had to be done. Every other department in the ship depended upon Engineering, and Damage Control would be absolutely critical in any engagement.

What it all really came down to, she mused, was how much faith she had in *Tschu's* judgment. In a sense, he'd backed her into a corner. She didn't blame him for it, but by proposing his solution, he'd given her only two options: agree with him, or *dis*agree and, in so doing, indicate that she lacked faith in him. No one would ever know except her, Rafe, and Tschu himself . . . but that would be more than enough.

"All right, Harry," she said at last. "If you think this is the solution, we'll try it. Rafe," she looked at Cardones, "have Chief Archer process the paperwork by the turn of the watch."

"Yes, Ma'am."

"Thank you, Ma'am," Tschu said quietly. "I appreciate it."

"Just go back down to Engineering and show me it was

the right move," Honor replied with one of her crooked smiles.

"I will, Ma'am," the lieutenant commander promised.

"Good."

The two officers rose to leave, and Samantha hopped from the table top to Tschu's shoulder. But she didn't swarm all the way up it. She paused, clinging to his upper arm, and looked back at Nimitz—who turned and glanced at Honor with laughing eyes.

"Are you up to carrying *two* 'cats, Mr. Tschu?" she asked dryly.

"I'm a Sphinxian, Ma'am," the engineer replied with a small smile.

"That's probably a good thing," Honor chuckled, and watched Samantha flow the rest of the way to his right shoulder. Nimitz followed a moment later, perching on Tschu's *left* shoulder, and a sense of complacency suffused his link to Honor.

"Just don't stay out late, Stinker," she warned him. "Mac and I won't wait supper—and we're having rabbit."

• CHAPTER THIRTEEN

The freighter shouldn't have been there.

The dead hulk drifted in the outer reaches of the Arendscheldt System, so far from the G3 primary no one should ever have found it. And no one ever would have if the light cruiser had been less busy hiding herself. She'd taken up a position from which her sensors could plot the commerce of the system, evaluating the best locations in which to place other ships when the time came, and she'd detected the wreck only by a fluke. *And,* Citizen Commander Caslet thought coldly, *because my resident tac witch had "a feeling."*

He wondered how he could phrase his report to make it seem he'd had a concrete reason to chase down the faint radar return. The fact that Denis Jourdain, PNS *Vaubon*'s people's commissioner, was a surprisingly good sort would help, but unless he could come up with some specific reason for making the sweep, someone was still going to argue he should have tended to his own knitting. On the other hand, the Committee of Public Safety didn't trust the military to ride herd on its own. That meant the people who passed ultimate judgment upon its actions, by and large, had no naval experience . . . and that most people who *did* have that experience were prepared to keep their mouths shut unless someone screwed up royally. It should be possible to come up with the right double-talk, especially with Jourdain's covert assistance.

Not that it mattered all that much to Caslet right this moment as he watched the secondary display which relayed Citizen Captain Branscombe's video to him. The citizen captain and a squad of his Marines were still sweeping the cold, lightless, airless interior of the ship, but what they'd already found was enough to turn Caslet's stomach.

The ship had once been a Trianon Combine-flag vessel. The Combine was only a single-system protectorate of the Silesian Confederacy. It had no navy—the Confederacy's central government was leery about providing prospective secessionists with warships—and it was unlikely anyone was looking out for its commerce. Which might explain what had happened to the hulk which had once been TCMS *Erewhon*.

He turned his head to glance at the main visual display's image of *Erewhon's* exterior, and his mouth twisted anew as he saw the ugly puncture marks of energy fire. The freighter had been unarmed, but that hadn't stopped whoever had killed her from opening fire. The holes looked tiny against her five-million-ton hull, but Caslet was a naval officer. He was intimately familiar with the carnage modern weapons could wreak, and he hadn't needed Branscombe's video to know how that fire had shattered *Erewhon's* interior systems.

Why? he wondered. *Why in* hell *do that? They had to know they were likely to wreck her drive and make it impossible to take her with them, so why shoot her up that way?*

He didn't have an answer. All he knew was that someone had done it, and from all the evidence, they seemed to have done it simply because they'd *felt* like it. Because it had *amused* them to rape an unarmed vessel.

He winced at his own choice of verb as Branscombe led his Marines back into what had been *Erewhon's* gym and the pitiless lights fell on the twisted bodies. Whoever had hit *Erewhon* had been unlucky in their target selection. According to the manifest in her computers, the ship had been inbound to pick up a cargo from Central, Arendscheldt's sole inhabited world, and she'd been running light, with little in her holds but heavy machinery

for Central's mines. Loot like that was low in value, and the raiders' fire had crippled *Erewhon*'s hyper generator. There'd been no way to take the ship with them, and it seemed they'd had too little cargo capacity to transship such mass-intensive plunder. But they appeared to have found a way to compensate themselves for their loss, he thought with cold savagery, and made himself look at the bodies once more.

Every male member of the crew had been marched into the gym and shot. It looked like several had been tortured, first, but it was hard to be sure, for their bodies lay in ragged rows where they'd been mowed down with pulser fire, and the hyper-velocity darts had turned their corpses into so many kilos of torn and mangled meat. But they'd been luckier than their female crewmates. The forensic teams had already compiled their records of mass rape and brutality, and when their murderers were done with them, they'd shot each woman in the head before they left.

All but one. One woman was untouched, her body still dressed in the uniform of *Erewhon*'s captain. She'd been handcuffed to an exercise machine where she could see every unspeakable thing the raiders did to her crew, and when they were done, they'd simply walked away and left her there . . . then cut the power and dumped the air.

Warner Caslet was an experienced officer. He'd seen combat and lived through the bloody horrors that were part of any war. But this was something else, and he felt a cold, burning hatred for the people behind it.

"We've confirmed it, Citizen Commander," Branscombe reported, and Caslet heard the matching hatred in his voice. "No survivors. We've pulled her roster from the computers and managed to ID all but three of the crew from it. They're all here; those three're simply so torn up by what the bastards did to them that we can't positively identify them."

"Understood, Ray," Caslet sighed, then shook himself. "Did you get their sensor records?"

"Aye, Citizen Commander. We've got them."

"Then there's nothing else you can do," Caslet decided. "Come on home."

"Aye, Citizen Commander." Branscombe switched to his Marine command circuit to order his people back to *Vaubon*, and Caslet turned to Citizen Commissioner Jourdain.

"With your permission, Sir, I'll report the hulk's position to the Arendscheldt authorities."

"Can we do that without revealing our own presence?"

"No." Caslet managed not to add "of course not," and not just out of prudence. Despite his role as the Committee of Public Safety's official spy aboard *Vaubon*, Jourdain was a reasonable man. He had an undeniable edge of priggish revolutionary ardor, but the two and a half T-years he'd spent in *Vaubon* seemed to have dulled it somewhat, and Caslet had come to recognize his fundamental decency. *Vaubon* had been spared the worst excesses of the Committee of Public Safety and Office of State Security, and her pre-coup company had remained virtually intact. Caslet knew how lucky that made him and his people, and he was determined to protect them to the very best of his ability, which made Jourdain's reasonableness a treasure beyond price.

"If we report it, they'll know *someone* was here, Citizen Commissioner," he said now. "But without an ID header they won't know who sent it, and by the time they receive it, we'll already be over the alpha wall and into h-space."

"Into hyper?" Jourdain said a bit more sharply. "What about our scouting mission?"

"With all due respect, Sir, I think we have a more pressing responsibility. Whoever these butchers are, they're still out there, and if they did this once, they'll sure as hell do it again . . . unless we stop them."

"Stop them, Citizen Commander?" Jourdain looked at him with narrowed eyes. "It's not our job to stop them. We're supposed to be scouting for Citizen Admiral Giscard."

"Yes, Sir. But the Citizen Admiral's not scheduled to begin operations here for over two months, and he's got nine other light cruisers he can send to take a look for him before he does."

He held Jourdain's gaze until the citizen commissioner nodded slowly. There was no agreement in his eyes, but neither was there any immediate rejection of what he had to know Caslet was about to suggest, and the citizen commander chose his next words carefully.

"Given Citizen Admiral Giscard's other resources, Sir, I believe he can dispense with our services for the next few weeks. In the meantime, we know there's someone out here who deliberately tortured and butchered an entire crew. I don't know about you, Sir, but I *want* that bastard. I want him dead, and I want him to know who's killing him, and I believe the Citizen Admiral and Commissioner Pritchart would share that ambition."

Jourdain's eyes flickered at that. Eloise Pritchart, Javier Giscard's people's commissioner, was smart, tough-minded, and ambitious. The dark-skinned, platinum-haired woman was also strikingly attractive . . . just as her sister had been. But the Pritcharts had been Dolists, living in DuQuesne Tower, arguably the worst of the Haven System's housing units, and one dark night a youth gang had cornered Estelle Pritchart. It was Estelle's brutal death which had driven Eloise into the action teams of the Citizens' Rights Union and from there into the Committee of Public Safety's service, and Jourdain knew as well as Caslet how *she* would react to an atrocity like this. Yet for all that, what Caslet was suggesting made Jourdain uneasy.

"I'm not certain, Citizen Commander. . . ." He looked away, unwilling to maintain eye contact, and took a quick turn about the command deck. "What you're proposing could actually go against the intent of our orders," he went on in the voice of a man who hated what duty required him to say. "Our whole purpose out here is to make things so much worse the Manties have to divert forces to deal with it. Killing off homegrown pirates is going to *lessen* the pressure on them, at least a little."

"I'm aware of that, Sir," Caslet replied. "At the same time, I think we both know the task force's operations will have the pressure effect we want, and the way they shot *Erewhon* up and deprived themselves of the ability to take her with them, not to mention what they did to her crew, suggests that these . . . people . . . are independents. I can't see any of the major outfits supporting a bunch of loose warheads like this, if only because of the lost prizes their actions must create. If they *are* independents, taking them out won't decrease the Manties' total losses in the Confederacy significantly. More than that, remember our orders concerning *Andermani* shipping."

"What about them?" Jourdain asked, but his tone told Caslet he'd already guessed. If everything went perfectly, Citizen Admiral Giscard's Task Force Twenty-Nine was supposed to remain totally covert, but in a burst of all too rare realism, someone back home had realized that was unlikely to be possible in the long run. It hadn't prevented them from ordering Giscard to do it anyway, but it *had* caused them to consider how the Andermani were likely to react if the Empire realized what was going on. The diplomats and military were divided over how the Andies would respond. The diplomats felt the longstanding Andermani-Manticoran tension over Silesia would keep the Empire from complaining too loudly on the theory that anything which weakened the Star Kingdom gave the Empire a better chance to grab off the entire Confederacy. The military thought that was nonsense. The Andies had to figure they were next on the Republic's list, and as such, were unlikely to passively accept the extension of the war to their doorstep.

Caslet shared the military's view, though the diplomats had triumphed—in no small part, the citizen commander knew, because of the Committee of Public Safety's lingering distrust of its own navy. But the admirals had been tossed one small bone (which Caslet suspected they would have been just as happy *not* to have received), and the task force's orders specifically required it to assist Andermani merchantmen against local pirates. Doing so would, of course, make it *impossible* to remain covert, but the idea, apparently, was that the gesture would convince the Andies the Republic's motives were pure as the snow where they were concerned. Personally, Caslet thought only a severely retarded Andy could think anything of the sort, but the clause about protecting imperial shipping gave him a tiny opening.

"These people took out a Silesian ship here, Sir," he said quietly, "but it's for damned sure they wouldn't turn up their noses at an Andy. For all we know, they've already popped a dozen imperial freighters. Even if they haven't, they will if they get the chance. If we take them out and can prove we did, that gives us some extra ammunition for convincing the Andermani that we're not *their* enemies if they tumble to our presence."

"That's true, I suppose," Jourdain said slowly, but his gaze was shrewd as he looked into Caslet's eyes. "At the same time, Citizen Commander, I can't avoid the suspicion that the Empire isn't really paramount in your own thinking."

"It isn't." Caslet would never have admitted that to another people's commissioner. "What's 'paramount to my thinking,' Sir, is that these people are sadistic bastards, and unless *someone* takes them out, they're going to go right on doing things like this."

The citizen commander gestured at the scene from the gym, still frozen on his small display, and his face was hard.

"I know there's a war on, Sir, and I know we have to do a lot of things we don't like in a war. But this sort of butchery isn't part of it—or it *shouldn't* be. I'm a naval officer. It's my job to prevent things like this if I can, whoever the ship in question belongs to. With your permission, I'd like a chance to do something decent. Something we can feel proud of."

He held his breath as Jourdain's shoulders tightened at his last six words. They could easily be construed as an oblique criticism of the entire war against Manticore, and that was dangerous. But Warner Caslet couldn't let people who did something like this escape unpunished to go on doing it—not if there was any way at all he could stop them.

"Even assuming I agreed with you," Jourdain said after a moment of pregnant silence, "what makes you think you can find them?"

"I'm not certain I can," Caslet admitted, "but I think we've got a fair chance if Citizen Captain Branscombe's people really have gotten us *Erewhon*'s sensor records. The pirates had to be well within her sensor envelope when they fired into her. I don't expect military-grade data from a freighter's sensors, but I'm confident they got enough for us to be able to ID the emissions signature of whoever did it. That means we can recognize them if we ever see them."

"And how will you find them or even know where to look for them?"

"First, we know they're pirates," Caslet said, ticking off his points on his fingers as he made them. "That means we can be confident they're working another system somewhere. Second, we can be fairly certain none of the major outfits are funding them, since not even one of the Confederacy's system governors would be willing to look the other way for people who do this kind of thing. That means they're probably operating from a system no one else is interested in, one where they could move in and set up basing facilities of their own. Third, they seem to have come up dry here in Arendscheldt. We can't be certain they didn't pick someone else off the very next day, but shipping is sparse out here, and Citizen Surgeon Jankowski's best guess is that they hit *Erewhon* less than two weeks ago. To me, that suggests they probably *didn't* get anyone else, in which case they've no doubt moved on to find richer pickings. Fourth, if *I* were a pirate moving from here,

I'd go either to Sharon's Star or Magyar. Those are the next two closest inhabited systems—and of the two,
Sharon's Star is closer. If they did go
there, they may still be there, given how recently we
know they were here. What I propose to do is inform
Arendscheldt of *Erewhon's* location and move immediately to Sharon's Star. With luck, we may catch them
there. If not, we can move on to Magyar, and since
we'll be going straight through without hunting for
prizes, we can probably beat them there."

"A star system is a big area, Citizen Commander,"
Jourdain pointed out. "What makes you think you'll spot
them even if they're there?"

"We won't, Sir. We'll convince *them* to spot *us*."

"Excuse me?" Jourdain looked puzzled, and Caslet
smiled thinly and waved for his tac officer to join them.

Citizen Lieutenant Commander Shannon Foraker was
one of the very few officers who'd actually been promoted
after the disaster of Fourth Yeltsin. It was she who'd
spotted the trap into which Citizen Admiral Thurston's
fleet had strayed, and it wasn't her fault she'd spotted
it too late. Caslet knew Jourdain's report had had a great
deal to do with Shannon's promotion, and the people's
commissioner had come to share the rest of *Vaubon's*
crew's near idolatry of the tac officer. She was one of the
very few Republican officers who refused to feel despair
over her hardware's inferiority to the enemy's. Indeed,
she took it as a personal challenge, and the results she
sometimes obtained verged on outright sorcery. She was
so good, in fact, that Jourdain had decided to overlook
the frequent lapses in her revolutionary vocabulary. Or
perhaps, Caslet thought wryly, he'd finally realized
Shannon was so deeply involved with her computers and
sensors that she had no time to waste on little things like
social nuances.

"Are you up to speed, Shannon?" the citizen commander asked as Foraker stopped beside his chair. She
nodded, and he tipped his own head at Jourdain. "Then

tell the People's Commissioner why we can count on the bad guys finding us."

"No problem, Skip." Foraker gave Jourdain a bright smile, and Jourdain smiled back, almost against his will. "These bastards are on the hunt for merchantmen, Sir. What we do is tune in our EW, take about half our beta nodes out of the wedge to drop it to an energy signature a merchie might have, and come in where they expect to *see* a freighter. If they're out there, they'll have to come to within, oh, four or five light-minutes, minimum, to see through our EW and realize we're a warship. By the time they do, my 'puters and I'll have their emissions dialed in to a fare-thee-well. If they're the people who did this, we'll know it."

"You see, Sir?" Caslet said to Jourdain. "We'll give them a target they can't resist and try to suck them in. At the very least, we should be able to ID them, and with any luck at all, they'll be coming in to match velocities with us before they know what we really are. Without knowing their max accel or our exact vectors ahead of time, I can't promise to overhaul them, but I can damned sure give them a run for their money. In fact, I'd almost prefer *not* to catch them."

"Why not?" Jourdain asked in surprise.

"Because if we can get close enough to chase them into hyper without overhauling, they may just be stupid enough to lead us to their home system," Caslet said grimly. "Independents or not, they may have more than a single ship, Sir, and I want to know where they nest. I've got a feeling Citizen Admiral Giscard will want them just as badly as we do, and unlike *Vaubon*, he's got the firepower to smash any bunch of pirates who ever operated."

Jourdain nodded slowly, not even seeming to notice that Caslet had said "we" and not "I," and the citizen commander hid an inner smile. Jourdain took another turn around the command deck, hands folded behind him, then nodded again and turned back to *Vaubon*'s official CO.

"All right, Citizen Commander. We can take the time to divert to Sharon's Star, at least. If we don't hit them there, I'll have to reconsider before authorizing you to move on to Magyar, but a diversion to Sharon's Star won't put the rest of the squadron behind schedule. And"—he smiled a cold, wintry smile—"you're right. I *do* want these people, too."

"Thank you, Sir," Citizen Commander Warner Caslet said quietly, and looked at Foraker. "Get Branscombe's data downloaded ASAP, Shannon."

• CHAPTER FOURTEEN

"Well? What do you think?"

Honor sat in her briefing room, a month and a half out of New Berlin, while the squadron orbited the planet Sachsen. Sachsen was one of the Confederacy's sector administration centers, which meant a powerful detachment of the Silesian Navy was home-ported here, and the Andermani Empire had acquired a hundred-year lease on the planet's third moon as the HQ of an IAN naval station. As a consequence, the system was a rare island of safety amid the Confederacy's chaos, but Honor's attention wasn't on Sachsen at the moment. Instead, it was on the holo chart glowing above the conference table, and she raised one hand, palm up in question.

"I'm not sure, Milady." Rafael Cardones frowned at the chart. "If the Andies' information is right, this is certainly the major threat zone. But you're talking about branching out into a whole 'nother sector. The Admiralty might not like that . . . and I'm not sure *I* like splitting the squadron up quite that widely. Captain Truman?"

Honor's golden-haired second-in-command shrugged. "Split up is split up, Rafe," she pointed out. "We'll be just as much out of mutual support range covering one system as ten, unless you want to hold us together, and we'd look a little odd lollygagging around in a bunch. Some of these pirates have damned sensitive survival instincts—if they see a batch of merchies holding station on one another in a single star system, they may smell a trap and stay clear. But if we split into single ships, we can cover a lot more systems. I like the rotation idea, too.

It should not only keep presenting any bad guys with fresh faces, but the changing patrol areas should keep our people from getting stale."

"Maybe so," Cardones agreed. "But if the Andies could twig to us, what's to say someone else hasn't? If the bad guys know we've got Q-ships out here, they're either going to stay away or come in carefully . . . maybe in greater numbers." He looked at Honor. "Remember the sim you set up for me and Jennifer, Skipper?"

Honor nodded and quirked an eyebrow at Truman, who shrugged.

"I can't fault either point, but 'staying away' is what we *want* them to do. I mean, killing them all off would be a more permanent solution, but our real job is to reduce losses, isn't it? As for numbers, of course we're going to get hurt if someone decides to swarm one of our ships. But why should a whole squadron of raiders go after a Q-ship in the first place? They're not going to get any worthwhile loot, but they *will* get plenty of hard knocks, even if they take us out. They know that, so why risk it for no return?"

Honor nodded slowly, rubbing Nimitz's ears while the 'cat curled in her lap. Rafe was playing the cautious devil's advocate—a role foreign to his own aggressive nature—because it was his job to shoot holes in his CO's schemes on the theory that it was better for one's exec to shoot up one's plans than for the enemy to shoot up one's ships. And he had a point. If a bunch of bad guys tried to pounce on a single ship, the odds were that that ship would get badly hurt. But Alice had a point, too.

The problem lay in the new data Commander Hauser had provided. Raiding patterns had shifted since ONI put together her own predeployment background brief. Ships *had* been disappearing in ones and twos in Breslau and the neighboring Posnan Sector, and they still were. But where whoever it was had been snapping up single ships and then pulling out, so that the next half-dozen or so got through safely, now as many as three or even four ships in a row were disappearing—all in the same system. Losses were actually higher now in Posnan than in Breslau, which was what had forced Honor to rethink her original deployment plans, but the new pattern of consecutive losses was almost more worrisome than the total numbers. Consecutive losses meant raiders were hanging around to snatch up more targets, and that was wrong. Raiders shouldn't do that . . . or not, at least, if they were operating in the normal singletons.

No raider captain wanted to stooge around with a prize in tow, because two ships together were more likely to be detected and avoided by other potential prizes. Then there was the manpower problem. Very few pirates carried sufficient crew to man more than two or three—at most four—prize ships unless they captured the original ships' companies and made *them* operate their ships' systems.

On the other hand, she thought unhappily, they might just be managing to hang onto those crews. Normally, something like half the ships hit by pirates were able to get their personnel away before the ship was actually taken, and some incidents were still following that pattern. But some *weren't*, and the crews of no less than eighty percent of the Manticoran ships lost in Posnan had vanished with their vessels. That was well above the usual numbers, and it suggested two possibilities, neither pleasant. One, someone was simply blowing away merchant ships, which seemed unlikely, or two, someone had sufficient ships to use one to run down any evading shuttles or pinnaces while another took the prize into custody.

And that, of course, was the reason for Rafe's concern. If the bad guys had multiple ships working single systems, the opposition might be far tougher than the Admiralty had assumed.

"I wish we knew just how the Andies tumbled to us," Truman murmured, and Honor nodded.

"I do, too," she admitted, "but Rabenstrange didn't say, and I can't really blame him. Just telling us they know could jeopardize their intelligence net. We'd be asking a bit much for them to simply tell our own counterintelligence types how they'd done it."

"Agreed, Milady," Cardones said. He rubbed his nose, then shrugged. "I'd also like to know just *why* the pattern's shifted this way. According to Commander Hauser's figures, we're the only ones losing merchies in groups."

"That may be simple probability," Truman said. "We've got more ships out here than anyone else, despite our losses. If anyone's going to take multiple hits, the people with the most targets are the ones who'd get hit most often."

"And when you add our drawdown in light units," Honor pointed out, "we actually turn into more tempting targets than someone like the Andies, who still have warships available to respond. If I were a raider, I'd pick on the people I knew weren't in a position to drop a squadron of destroyers into my cosy little web."

"I know, but I just can't help feeling there's something more to it," Cardones said.

"Maybe there is, but the only way to find out what it might be is to go see for ourselves." Honor tapped another command into her terminal, and bright green lines sprang into existence in the holo chart. They linked ten star systems—six in Breslau and four in Posnan—in an elongated, complex pattern thirty-two light-years across at its widest point, and she gazed at it moodily.

"If we follow this pattern," she said after a moment, "we'll have one ship—and a different one—entering or departing one of these systems every week or so. If anyone *is* lying low and watching for us, they won't see the same ship hanging around for extended periods. That should keep us from looking like trolling warships, and it puts us in the center of the zone of heaviest losses *and* lets us patrol the widest area once we get there."

"Yes, it does," Cardones admitted. "Assuming we don't run into anyone operating in squadron strength, I'd say it's clearly our best approach. But it does move us into

Posnan, and it leaves all these stars in Breslau"—he tapped at his own terminal, and nine more stars blinked— "uncovered. We're taking losses there, too, and Breslau is where we're tasked for operations."

"I know," Honor sighed. "But if we extend the pattern, we also extend times between stars. We spend more time in hyper and less in n-space, where we're most likely to actually find and kill pirates. This seems to me to give us the best mix of deception and time in the zone, Rafe."

"I agree," Cardones said in turn. "I just wish we could cover more area if we're going to split up anyway. However we go at it, you know we won't be there when *some- one* gets hit, and the cartels are going to howl that we're— that *you're*—not doing our job if that happens."

"The cartels are just going to have to accept the best we can do," Honor replied. "Our shipping will still be hit whatever pattern we follow, and without more Q-ships, there's not much we can do about it. I know they're going to complain if we aren't covering a system and they lose a ship there, but the fact is that the pirates have the initiative. They're the ones who decide where they'll raid; all we can do is follow them and hurt them badly enough the survivors decide to go somewhere else. If we clear one area, they'll move to another and we'll follow them, which should at least let us cramp the scale of their operations. And once we pick a few of them off, the Admiralty can point to the kill numbers as proof that we're actually doing some good."

"You know what I wish?" Truman asked. Honor looked at her, and the other captain shrugged. "I wish we knew who was funding and supporting the bastards. You know as well as I do that the average piracy ring can afford to lose and replace vessels—and crews—all year long if as much as a third of them manage to take a decent prize on each cruise. Think about it. These eleven ships"—she tapped her screen, where the names of the most recently missing vessels were displayed—"represent an aggregate value of almost twelve billion just for the hulls. You can

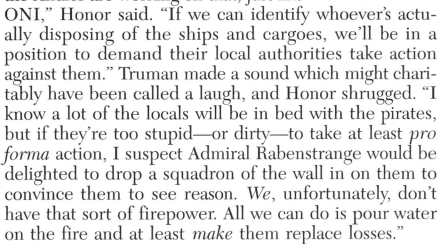

buy a lot of ships heavy enough to kill merchies for that kind of money."

"According to Commander Hauser, the Andies are working on that, just like ONI," Honor said. "If we can identify whoever's actually disposing of the ships and cargoes, we'll be in a position to demand their local authorities take action against them." Truman made a sound which might charitably have been called a laugh, and Honor shrugged. "I know a lot of the locals will be in bed with the pirates, but if they're too stupid—or dirty—to take at least *pro forma* action, I suspect Admiral Rabenstrange would be delighted to drop a squadron of the wall in on them to convince them to see reason. *We*, unfortunately, don't have that sort of firepower. All we can do is pour water on the fire and at least *make* them replace losses."

"I know," Truman sighed, "but I can wish, can't I?"

"I'll wish right along with you," Honor agreed. "In the meantime, this looks to me like the best way to proceed in light of the information and forces available to us."

"Agreed," Truman said, and Cardones nodded, though he still seemed a bit unhappy at the prospect. Honor knew most of his unhappiness was for her sake, since she was the one who was going to catch any criticism that came the squadron's way, and she wondered if he'd worked through the same logic Admiral White Haven had explained to her on Grayson. It seemed likely; Rafe was sharp, and the level of his unease indicated more than a mere sense of tactical exposure.

"All right," she said more briskly, shaking off her own awareness of those same points. "In that case, Alice, we'll go with the pattern you and I discussed. You'll take *Parnassus* to Telmach and Samuel will take *Scheherazade* to Posnan to start your legs. I'll take *Wayfarer* to Libau for the first leg through Walther, and Allen and *Gudrid* will take the first Hume-Gosset leg."

Truman nodded. The patrol pattern Honor had outlined would put her own *Parnassus* and *Wayfarer* in the systems of maximum threat for the first portion of the pattern, while MacGuire's *Gudrid* would have the closest thing to a milk run for her first system.

"All right." Honor said again. She sat up straighter and looked both her subordinates in the eye in turn as Nimitz flowed up over her shoulder to sit on the back of her chair. "There are two more things we should consider. The first is what we do with anyone we capture. Rafe was out here in *Fearless* with me, so he already knows my policy, Alice, but you weren't. Have you had a chance to review my memo on it?"

"I have," Truman replied with a sober nod.

"Do you have any problems with it?" Honor asked quietly.

"No, Ma'am." Truman shook her head. "If anything, you're being too lenient."

"Perhaps so," Honor acknowledged, "but we have to at least pretend the Confederacy has a functional government—until they prove otherwise, at any rate. In the meantime, I'll draft formal orders for you, Allen, and Samuel to cover the situation. Remember that we need any information we can get on operational patterns, though. If anybody wants to deal by turning informer, feel free to use your initiative and judgment as to terms."

Truman nodded, and Honor rubbed her eyes wearily. "And that brings me to my last point—which is the possibility that these new patterns indicate we aren't looking just at normal raiders, or even privateers. The 'liberation governments' in Psyche and Lutrell are the most likely culprits if someone *is* operating in squadron strength, but there's one other possibility."

"Peeps," Truman said flatly, and Honor nodded.

"Exactly. Neither ONI nor the Andies have picked up any signs of it, but the Peeps have their own connections out here. For that matter, their embassies are still open, since they aren't at war with Silesia or the Andies. It wouldn't be too hard for them to make a quiet deal with one of the smaller system's governors for clandestine resupply, and their embassies' intelligence on shipping patterns is probably at least as good as ours. If they *have* managed to slip a raiding squadron in on us, they'd go after *our* shipping, not anyone else's, and they wouldn't want the crews of the ships they hit getting loose to tell us they're here."

"Unless their purpose is to force the Admiralty to cut loose heavier forces to chase them," Truman pointed out. "That's exactly what they tried to do before they hit you at Yeltsin, Honor, and they succeeded. Why not deliberately let our people 'get away'? Wouldn't it make sense to be obvious if their object is to prove to the Admiralty how seriously our shipping here is threatened?"

"A possibility," Honor agreed, "but I don't think they would. Their operations before Fourth Yeltsin were part of a coordinated plan designed to impose a *temporary* change in our deployments to suck forces away from a specific objective for a single offensive strike. They could be trying to draw us into false deployments again, but this far from home there's no way they could coordinate with the front. I suspect that means they'd go for a long-term, general diversion, not a specific, short-term one."

She frowned at the holo, rubbing the tip of her nose, then shrugged.

"On top of that, anything they sent out here would find itself in a world of hurt if we went after it in a big way. Without regular fleet bases of their own—which they don't have—they'd be at a severe disadvantage if we did transfer the forces to go after them. And don't forget the edge our shorter passage times through the Junction give us in information flow and deployment speeds. We'd have an excellent chance of making the transfer, hitting them hard, and getting our light forces back home before the rest of the Peeps even knew we'd made the move. By the same token, I doubt they want to do anything to irritate the Empire. They have to be delighted that the Emperor's sitting things out so far, and open, large-scale fleet operations in the Andies' backyard might just cause him to change his mind. Besides, they don't *have* to operate openly to achieve the same objective. Bottom line, it doesn't matter who's raiding us, just that *someone* is."

"True enough." Truman nodded.

"But the point I'm making is this," Honor went on. "If it *is* the Peeps, they're going to be using real warships, not the lightly armed vessels your typical raider cobbles up. I think it's unlikely we're looking at Peep operations, and it's possible I'm jumping at shadows, but we can't afford to assume anything. So it's important that we all keep our guards up, and for the record, I am instructing all captains to remain covert and avoid action against any Peep warship larger than a heavy cruiser. If we run into a battlecruiser or one of their battleships—which I hope to God we don't—try to avoid action. The loss of a real warship would hurt them more than losing a Q-ship will hurt the Star Kingdom, but it's much more important that we know what we're up against."

"If they *are* operating out here, it's probably with light stuff," Truman said.

"Of course it is, and if we run into any of their light units, we kill them," Honor said. "But I didn't expect to see battleships in Yeltsin last year, either. They've shown they're willing to operate their light battle squadrons aggressively, however inexperienced most of their officer corps was at the start of the war, and if there are any big boys out here, I want to know it. I'm serious, people. No heroics. If you're forced into action, go all out and don't worry about hiding any of your capabilities, but reporting the presence of heavy Peep units is more important than trying to destroy them. Understood?"

Cardones and Truman both nodded, and Honor stood, scooping Nimitz from her chair back and setting him on her shoulder.

"In that case, let's be about it. I want to be headed for our initial stations by zero-three-hundred."

• CHAPTER FIFTEEN

Klaus Hauptman nodded curtly to his driver as she opened the air limo door for him. His expression was thunderous as he climbed out of the palatial vehicle, and the limo's internal atmosphere had been anything but restful during the flight, but Ludmilla Adams took neither the curtness of his nod nor his anger personally. When Klaus Hauptman was upset with an individual, he let that individual know in no uncertain terms. Since he hadn't ripped *her* head off, he must be ticked off with someone else, and she'd learned long ago to view his occasional bursts of anger with much the same equanimity as someone who lived on the slope of an active volcano might view its eruptions. If they happened, they happened, and she was prepared to ride them out. Besides, arrogant and self-centered though he was, he normally did his best to make amends when he realized he'd lashed out at one of his employees for something someone else had done.

Of course, it didn't *always* work that way, and he could be an incredibly vindictive old bastard, but Adams had been with him for over twenty years. She was not only his chauffeur but also his security chief and personal bodyguard, and she had the one quality Klaus Hauptman valued above all others: competence. He respected her, and they'd developed a comfortable relationship over the last two decades. It was a master-employee relationship, of course, not one between equals, but it provided her with a certain insulation against his tiffs.

Now he stepped past her onto the manicured lawn

of the Hauptman estate. The low-growing, sprawled-out mansion appeared to be only two stories tall, but appearances were deceiving. Although the Hauptmans themselves and their small army of servants lived on the upper floors everyone could see, ninety percent of it was buried in the nine basement and subbasement levels which housed its vehicle garages, maintenance areas, data management sections, and the hundreds of other business functions required to manage the Hauptman Cartel.

The architects had created something which resembled a cross between a Roman villa from Old Earth and a rustic hunting lodge. The fusion of styles should have looked ridiculous, yet they merged somehow into a single, coherent whole that was oddly suited to the dense forest surrounding the estate. Of course, the whole thing was an ostentatious affectation in a counter-grav civilization. Towers were far cheaper and more space efficient—it was always easier to build upward than to excavate downward, and servants didn't have to walk half a kilometer from the kitchen to the dining room in a properly designed tower—but Klaus Hauptman's grandfather had decided he wanted a country seat, and a country seat was what he'd built.

"Will we be needing the car again this afternoon, Sir?" Adams asked calmly.

"No," Hauptman snapped, then made himself pause. "Sorry, 'Milla. Didn't mean to bite your head off."

"One of the things I'm here for, Sir," she replied wryly, and he barked a crack of laughter.

"I still shouldn't do it," he admitted, "but—" He shrugged, and she nodded. "At any rate," he continued, "I won't be needing the car again today. In fact, I may be going off-planet soon."

"Off-planet?" Adams. "Should I alert our people to make preparations?"

"No," Hauptman shook his head. "If I go at all, it won't be that sort of trip." Adams' eyebrow rose, and he smiled crookedly. "I don't mean to be cryptic, 'Milla. Believe me,

I'll let you know in plenty of time before we go haring off anywhere."

"Good," Adams said, and pressed a button on the remote on her left wrist. The limo rose behind them and whispered off to the parking entrance, and she followed him into the imposing edifice he modestly called home.

A human butler opened the old-fashioned, unpowered door, and Hauptman nodded to him. The butler took one look at his employer's face and stood aside. He didn't say anything, but he quirked an eyebrow at Adams and shook his head wryly as Hauptman stalked past him. Adams smiled back and trailed the magnate down a long, airy hall embellished with a fortune in art.

"Is Stacey here?" Hauptman grunted, and Adams consulted her wrist remote.

"Yes, Sir. She's out by the pool."

"Good." Hauptman paused and tugged at an ear lobe for a moment, then sighed. "You might as well go on, 'Milla. I'm sure you've got things of your own to take care of, but we'll be staying home tonight. If you're free, I'd appreciate your joining us for supper."

"Of course, Sir." The security chief nodded, then watched Hauptman walk on down the hall without her, and a small smile played about her lips. He was an odd duck, her employer. Curt, self-centered, capable of atrocious rudeness, arrogant, hot-tempered, and totally unaware of the sublime sense of superiority his wealth gave him, yet capable of consideration, kindness, even generosity—as long as he could be those things on his own terms—and imbued with an iron sense of obligation to those in his employ. If he hadn't been the wealthiest man in the Star Kingdom, the only word that would have applied was "spoiled," she thought. As it was, one could only call him "eccentric" and let it go at that.

Klaus Hauptman stalked on down the corridor, unaware of his bodyguard's thoughts. He had other things on his mind, and he wasn't looking forward to them as he stepped out into the estate's central courtyard.

The formal garden's carefully tended Old Earth roses and Manticoran crown blossom formed lanes that splashed the court with color and led the eye to the huge swimming pool at its heart. That pool was half the size of a soccer field, and its center was dominated by an ornate fountain. Vast bronze fish from half a dozen planets spouted water into the pool from their open mouths while mermaids and mermen lounged among them, and the constant, splashing murmur of water was subliminally soothing.

At the moment, however, Hauptman's attention was on the young woman in the pool. Her hair was as dark as his own, but she had her mother's brown eyes. She also had her mother's high cheekbones and oval face to go with those eyes, and her features had their own strength. She wasn't beautiful, but, in its own way, that was a statement of power, for she could have afforded the finest biosculpt in the galaxy and had herself turned into a goddess. Stacey Hauptman had chosen not to, and her willingness to settle for the face genetics had given her when she didn't have to said that this was a woman who was comfortable with who and what she was—and who had no need to prove anything to anyone.

She turned at the end of a lap and paused, treading water, as she caught sight of her father. He waved, and she waved back.

"Hi, Daddy! I didn't expect you home this afternoon."

"Something came up," he replied. "Do you have a minute? We need to talk."

"Of course." She stroked strongly to a ladder, climbed out of the pool, and reached for a towel. She was trim and lithe but richly curved, and Hauptman felt a familiar spurt of irritation at the skimpiness of her suit. He suppressed it with an equally familiar sense of wry self-amusement. His daughter was twenty-nine T-years old, and she'd amply demonstrated her ability to look out for herself. What she did and who she did it with were her affair, but he supposed every father felt the same way.

After all, fathers remembered what *they'd* been like as young men, didn't they?

He chuckled at the thought and walked over to pick up her robe. He held it for her to slip into against the dropping evening temperature, then waved to the chairs around one of the poolside tables. She belted the robe, sat, leaned back, crossed her legs, and looked at him curiously, and his amusement faded as his mind returned to the day's news.

"We've lost another ship," he said abruptly.

Stacey's eyes darkened in understanding, and not just on a personal level. Her father had said "we," and the term was accurate, for Hauptman had learned from his own father's mistakes. Eric Hauptman had belonged to the last pre-prolong generation, and he'd insisted on maintaining direct, personal control of his empire till the day of his death. Klaus had been given some authority, but he'd been only one of many managers, and his father's death had left him woefully unprepared for his responsibilities. Worse, he'd thought he *was* prepared for them, and his first few years in the CEO's suite had been a roller coaster ride for the cartel.

Klaus Hauptman wasn't prepared to repeat that error, especially since, unlike his father, he could anticipate at least another two T-centuries of vigorous activity. He'd married quite late, but he'd be around for a long, long time, and he'd had no intention of letting Stacey turn into an unproductive drone, on the one hand, or of leaving her to feel excluded and shut out—and untrained— on the other. She was already the cartel's operations director for Manticore-B, including the enormous asteroid-mining activity there, and she'd gotten that position because she'd earned it, not just because she was the boss's daughter. She was also, since her mother's death, the one person in the universe Klaus Hauptman totally and unequivocally loved.

"Which ship was it?" she asked now, and he closed his eyes for a moment.

"*Bonaventure*," he sighed, and heard her draw a breath of pain.

"The crew? Captain Harry?" she asked quickly, and he shook his head.

"He got most of his people out, but he stayed behind," he said quietly. "So did his exec."

"Oh, Daddy," Stacey whispered, and he clenched a fist in his lap. Harold Sukowski had been captain of the Hauptman family space yacht when Stacey was a girl. She'd had a terrible crush on him, and it was he who'd taught her basic astrogation and coached her through her extra-atmospheric pilot's license. He and his family had become very important to Stacey, especially after her mother died. Much as he loved her, Hauptman knew he didn't always manage to show it, and her wealth and position had produced a lonely childhood. She'd learned early to be wary of people who wanted to be her "friends," and most of those she'd actually come into contact with had been employees of her father. Sukowski had, too, of course, but he'd also been a rated starship captain, with the glamor that attached to that, and a man who'd treated her not like a princess, not as the heir to the Kingdom's greatest fortune, not even as his future boss, but as a lonely little girl.

She'd adored him. In fact, Hauptman had experienced a deep, unexpected jealousy when he realized how his daughter saw Sukowski. To his credit, he'd exercised self-restraint in the captain's case, and looking back, he was glad he had. He hadn't been the easiest father a motherless daughter could have had, and the Sukowski family had helped fill the void his wife's death had left in Stacey's life. She'd missed Sukowski dreadfully when he turned the yacht over to someone else, but she'd also been delighted when his seniority with the Hauptman Line gave him *Bonaventure* straight from the builders. She'd dragged her father to the commissioning party and presented Sukowski with an antique sextant as a commissioning gift, and he'd responded by listing her as a supernumerary crew member to make her a keel plate owner of his new ship.

"I know." Hauptman opened his eyes and looked out over the pool, and his jaw clenched. *Damn the Admiralty! If they hadn't screwed around, this wouldn't have happened!* Hauptman hated to lose *any* of his people, but he would have cut off his own hand to spare Stacey this. And, he admitted, he felt the loss himself, deeply and personally. There weren't many people he'd ever felt really close to, and he'd never shown Sukowski any favoritism because he made it a policy not to do that, but the captain's loss hurt.

"Have we heard anything?" Stacey asked after a moment.

"Not yet. Our Telmach factor sent off a letter as soon as *Bonaventure's* people reported her loss, but there hasn't been time for anything else to come in yet. Of course, Sukowski had the documentation of our ransom offer in his safe."

"Do you really expect that made any difference?" Stacey asked harshly. Her voice was angry now—not at her father, but at their helplessness. Hauptman knew that, yet hearing her anger only fanned his own, and he clamped his jaw even tighter.

"I don't know," he said finally. "It's all we've got."

"Where was the Navy?" Stacey demanded. "Why didn't they *do* something?"

"You know the answer to that," Hauptman returned. "They're 'stretched too thin meeting other commitments.' Hell, it was all I could do pry four *Q-ships* out of them!"

"Excuses! Those are just *excuses*, Daddy!"

"Maybe." Hauptman looked down at his hands again, then sighed once more. "No, let's be honest, Stace. It probably *was* the best they could do."

"Oh? Then why did they put *Harrington* in command? If they wanted to stop things like this, why didn't they send a *competent* officer to Silesia?"

Hauptman winced internally. Stacey had never met

Honor Harrington. All she knew of her was what she'd read in the 'faxes and seen on HD . . . or what her father had told her. And Hauptman was uncomfortably aware that he hadn't exactly gone out of his way to give his daughter an unbiased account of what had happened in Basilisk. In point of fact, he knew his sense of humiliation had painted Harrington's actions during their confrontation with even darker hues when he described them to Stacey later. He wasn't particularly proud of that, but neither was he about to go back and try to correct the record at this late date. Especially, he told himself fiercely, since Harrington really *was* a loose warhead!

Yet that also meant he couldn't tell her he was the one who'd pushed for Harrington's assignment. Not without making explanations he didn't care to make, at any rate.

"She may be a lunatic," he said instead, "but she's a first-rate combat commander. I don't like the woman— you know that—but she *is* good in a fight. I imagine that's why they chose her. And whatever they've done or not done, or their reasons for it," he went on more strongly, "the fact remains that we've lost *Bonaventure*."

"How much will it hurt us?" Stacey asked, reaching for a less personally painful topic.

"In and of itself, not that badly. She was insured, and I'm confident we'll recover from the insurers. But our rates will be going up—again—and unless Harrington actually does some good, we really may have to look closely at suspending operations in the Confederacy."

"If we pull out, everyone else will," Stacey warned.

"I know." Hauptman rose and jammed his hands into his pockets while he stared out over the pool. "I don't want to do it, Stace—and not just because I don't want to lose *our* revenues. I don't like what a general pull out from Silesia will do to the balance of trade. The Kingdom *needs* that shipping revenue and those markets, especially now. And that doesn't even consider what it might mean for public opinion. If raggedy-assed pirates chase us clear out of the Confederacy, people may see it as a sign that we're not holding our own against the Peeps any longer."

Stacey nodded behind him. Her father's long and stormy history with the Royal Navy stemmed in large part from his role as one of the Star Kingdom's major shipbuilders, which put him in constant conflict with the RMN's accountants, but she knew another part stemmed from the Navy's refusal to bend to his will. In addition, like her father, she was a shrewd political analyst, and she understood how that same rocky relationship, coupled with his wealth, made him so attractive to the Opposition. As one of the Opposition parties' major economic sponsors, he was careful to limit his public support for the war effort to "proper" statements in order to retain their support for his own ends, yet he was fully aware of the implications of the fight against the People's Republic . . . and of what he stood to lose if the Star Kingdom was defeated.

"How many of our people have we lost so far?" she asked.

"Counting Sukowski and his exec, we've got almost three hundred unaccounted for," Hauptman said bitterly, and she winced. Her own sphere of authority didn't bring her into direct contact with their shipping interests very often, and she hadn't realized the number was so high.

"Is there anything more we can do?" Her voice was very quiet, not pushing but dark with the sense of responsibility she'd inherited from her father, and he shrugged.

"I don't know." He stared out over the pool for another moment, then turned back to face her. "I don't know," he repeated, "but I'm thinking about going out there in person."

"Why?" she asked quickly, her tone sharp with sudden alarm. "What can you do from there that you can't do from here?"

"For one thing, I can cut something like three months off the communications lag," he said dryly. "For another, you know as well as I do that nothing can substitute for direct, firsthand observation of a problem."

"But if you poke around out there, *you* could get captured—or killed!" she protested.

"Oh, I doubt that. If I went at all, I'd go in *Artemis* or *Athena*," he assured her, and she paused thoughtfully. *Artemis* and *Athena* were two of the Hauptman Lines' *Atlas*-class passenger liners. The *Atlases* had minimal cargo capacity, but they were equipped with military-grade compensators and impellers, and they were excellent at getting people from place to place quickly. Because *Artemis* and *Athena* had been expressly built for the Silesian run, they'd also been fitted with light missile armaments, and their high speed and ability to defend themselves against run-of-the-mill pirates made them extremely popular with travelers to the Confederacy.

"All right," Stacey said after a moment. "I guess you'd be safe enough. But if you go, then I'm going with you."

"What?" Hauptman blinked at her, then shook his head adamantly. "No way, Stace! One of us has to stay home to mind the store, and I don't want you traipsing around Silesia."

"First," she shot back, not giving a centimeter, "we've got highly paid, highly competent people for the express purpose of 'minding the store,' Daddy. Second, if it's safe enough for *you*, it's safe enough for *me*. And, third, we're talking about Captain Harry."

"Look," her father said persuasively, "I know how you feel about Captain Sukowski, but you can't do anything that I can't. Stay home, Stace. Please. Let me handle this."

"Daddy"—steely brown eyes met blue, and Klaus Hauptman felt a sinking sensation—"I'm going. We can argue about this all you like, but in the end, I'm going."

• CHAPTER SIXTEEN

Honor looked up from her book reader as her com chimed. MacGuiness poked his head into her day cabin and started towards the terminal, but then it chimed again, this time with the two-toned note of an urgent signal, and she thrust her reader aside.

"I'll take it, Mac," she said, standing quickly. Nimitz raised his head from his own position on his perch, and she felt his quick surge of interest, but she had little time to consider it as she punched the acceptance key. She opened her mouth, but Rafe Cardones started speaking with most unusual abruptness almost before his image stabilized.

"I think we've got our first customer, Ma'am. We've got a bogey tracking up from low and astern with an overtake of nine hundred KPS, and he's accelerating hard. Tactical calls it three hundred gees, and he's one-point-seven million klicks back. Assuming constant accelerations, John figures he'll intercept at zero range in about nineteen minutes."

"You just picked him up?"

"Yes, Ma'am." Cardones smiled like a shark. "We don't see any sign of ECM, either. Looks like he was lying doggo and just lit off his drive."

"I see." Honor's smile matched her exec's. "Mass?" she asked.

"From his impeller signature, Jenny figures it at about fifty-five k-tons."

"Well, well." Honor rubbed the tip of her nose for a moment, then nodded sharply. "All right, Rafe. Sound

General Quarters. Have Susan and Scotty assemble their boarding teams, and detail LAC One for launch on my signal. I'll be on the bridge in five minutes."

"Aye, aye, Ma'am."

The GQ alarm began to wail even as Honor cut the circuit, and Nimitz landed on her desk with a thump. She stood and turned to find that MacGuiness had already gotten out her skinsuit, and she flashed him a smile of thanks as she grabbed it and headed for her sleeping cabin. The steward was dragging out the 'cat's skinsuit as the hatch closed behind her, and she began tearing off her uniform. She left it strewn on the carpet—Mac would forgive her this time—and climbed into her suit with painful haste. By the time she was back through the hatch, MacGuiness had Nimitz suited, and she snatched the 'cat up and headed for the private captain's lift at a run.

She punched the destination code and then made herself stand still and consider what she knew. The acuity of merchant-grade sensors varied widely. Any skipper with more than half a brain wanted the best ones he could get if he was going to wander around the Confederacy, but no sensors were any better than the people who manned them, and some merchant spacers tended to be a bit lackadaisical about such things.

Bearing that in mind, whoever was behind *Wayfarer* probably wouldn't be too surprised if she didn't react immediately to his presence, but he was going to be suspicious if she kept on not reacting for very long. Which meant—

The lift door opened, and she strode into the orderly bustle of her bridge. Her weapons crews were still closing up—they still had more rough edges than she liked—but Jennifer Hughes' tac crew was on-line and monitoring the bogey's approach. She glanced at the chrono and allowed herself a small smile. *Wayfarer's* designers had placed her captain's quarters only one deck down from and directly below her bridge, and the private lift was a marvelous luxury. Honor had promised Rafe she'd be here in five minutes, and she'd made it in just over three.

Cardones vacated the chair at the center of the bridge, and she nodded to him as she lowered herself into it. Nimitz swarmed up onto its back while she racked her helmet on the chair arm, and she punched the button that deployed her displays about her.

Wayfarer was twenty-one light-minutes from the G2 primary of the Walther System, just under fifteen light-years from Libau, stooging along at a mere 11,175 KPS with an accel of only seventy-five gravities. That was on the low side, even for a merchie, but not unheard of for a skipper with worn drive nodes, and Honor had chosen it with malice aforethought. She hadn't wanted anyone to miss her, and such a low velocity was the equivalent of blood in the water. And it seemed to have worked. The bogey had closed another two hundred thousand kilometers, and his speed was still building. He already had a velocity advantage of nine hundred and ten KPS, and it was rising steadily, but that was going to change. He wouldn't want too much overtake when he actually overhauled, but he clearly expected *Wayfarer* to bolt when she finally saw him. He wanted a little extra speed in hand if she did, and it would be a pity to disappoint him.

"All right, Rafe. Take us to max accel."

"Aye, aye, Ma'am. Chief O'Halley, bring us to one-point-five KPS squared."

"Coming to one-point-five KPS squared, aye, Sir," the coxswain acknowledged, and *Wayfarer* suddenly bolted ahead at her maximum normal safe acceleration. It was only half that of the ship coming up from astern, but it would be enough to convince him he'd been seen.

"New time to overtake?"

"Make it two-four-point-nine-four minutes, Milady," John Kanehama replied almost instantly, and she nodded.

"Challenge him, Fred. Inform him we're a Manticoran vessel and order him to stand off."

"Aye, aye, Ma'am." Lieutenant Cousins spoke briefly into his pickup, and Honor watched her display narrowly. They were well within the powered envelope for impeller-drive missiles. A pirate wouldn't want to damage his prize, but—

"Missile separation!" Jennifer Hughes sang out. "One bird closing at eight-zero thousand gees!" She watched her display for a moment, then nodded. "Not a hot bird, Ma'am. It'll pass to starboard at over sixty thousand klicks."

"How kind of him," Honor murmured, watching the missile trace tear after her ship. It streaked up on her starboard side and detonated, but not only was it well clear of *Wayfarer*, it was also a standard nuke, not a laser head. Its meaning was clear, however. She considered continuing to run—although the raider had demonstrated he had the range to fire into her ship, he was unlikely to when she couldn't get away anyhow—but there was no guarantee the person behind that missile tube was feeling reasonable.

"Anything on the com?"

"Not yet, Ma'am."

"I see. Very well, Rafe. Bring us hard to port and kill our accel, but keep the wedge up."

"Aye, aye, Ma'am."

Wayfarer stopped accelerating, and Honor punched up LAC Squadron One's flagship. Commander Jacquelyn Harmon, *Wayfarer*'s senior LAC CO, was a dark-haired, dark-eyed woman with a pre-space fighter pilot's ego and a sardonic sense of humor—both of which probably stood the commander of such a frail craft in good stead. It was she who'd insisted on naming the twelve LACs under her command for the twelve apostles, and she rode the cramped command deck of HMLAC *Peter* as her image appeared on Honor's small screen.

"Ready, Jackie?" Honor asked.

"Yes, Ma'am!" Harmon gave her a hungry smile, and Honor shook her head.

"Remember we want them alive if we can get them."

"We'll remember, Ma'am."

"Very well. Launch at your discretion when we drop the sidewall, but stay close."

"Aye, aye, Ma'am."

Honor killed the circuit and looked at Hughes. "Drop the starboard sidewall."

"Aye, aye, Ma'am. Dropping starboard sidewall now."

Wayfarer's starboard sidewall vanished. Seconds later, six small warships spat out of the "cargo bays" on her starboard flank on conventional thrusters. They raced clear of their mother ship's wedge before they brought up their own drives, then hovered there, screened from radar and gravitic detection by her massive shadow, and Honor looked back at her plot.

The bogey was decelerating hard now. Given his current overtake, he'd overfly *Wayfarer* by over a hundred and forty thousand kilometers before coming to rest relative to her, but his velocity would be sufficiently low to make boarding simple. Of course, he might be just a *bit* surprised to discover who was about to be boarded by whom, she thought coldly.

"I've got good passive readouts for Fire Plan Able, Ma'am," Hughes reported. "Solution input and running, and visual tracking has him now. Coming up on your repeater."

Honor glanced down. The decelerating raider was stern-on to the pickup, giving her a good look up the open rear of his wedge. He was smaller than most destroyers, and he couldn't be very heavily armed if he'd shoehorned a hyper drive and Warshawski sails into that hull. He had a conventional warship's hammerhead ends, however, which suggested at least some chase armament, and whatever he mounted was aimed straight at *Wayfarer*. She checked Kanehama's intercept solution and nodded mentally. There was no point letting that ship get close enough to shoot through her sidewall—not when she had a perfect up the kilt shot at *him*.

"On my mark, Jenny," she said quietly, raising her left

hand, then keyed her own com with her right hand. "Unknown vessel," she said crisply, "this is Her Majesty's Armed Merchant Cruiser *Wayfarer*. Cut your drive immediately, or be destroyed!"

She slashed her hand downward as she spoke, and every weapon in *Wayfarer's* broadside fired as one. Eight massive grasers flashed out, the closest missing the bogey by less than thirty kilometers, and ten equally massive missiles followed. As the single shot the bogey had fired, they were standard nukes, not laser heads, but unlike the bogey's, they detonated at a stand-off range of barely a thousand kilometers, completely bracketing him in their pattern.

The message was abundantly clear, and just to give it added point, six LACs suddenly swooped up over their mother ship, locked their own batteries on the bogey, and lashed him with targeting radar and lidar powerful enough to boil his hull paint to be sure he knew they had.

"Acknowledged, *Wayfarer! Acknowledged!*" a voice screamed over the com, and the bogey's drive died instantly. "Don't fire! God, *please* don't fire! We surrender!"

"Prepare to be boarded," Honor said coldly. "Any resistance will result in the instant destruction of your vessel. Is that understood?"

"Yes! *Yes!*"

"Good," she said in that same, icy tone, then cut the circuit and leaned back in her chair to smile at Cardones. "Well," she said far more mildly, "that was exciting, wasn't it?"

"More so for some than for others, Ma'am," Cardones replied with a broad grin.

"I suppose so," Honor agreed, and glanced at Hughes. "Nicely done, Guns—and that goes for all of you," she told the bridge at large. Pleased smiles answered, she turned back to Cardones. "Tell Scotty and Susan they can launch, then match velocities. The LACs can keep an eye on our friend while we maneuver."

"Aye, aye, Ma'am."

Honor stood and stretched, then gathered Nimitz back

up once more. "I imagine you can finish up here, Mr. Exec," she said for the benefit of the rest of her bridge crew, "and you pulled me away from a perfectly good book. I'll be in my quarters. Ask Major Hibson to escort the commander of that object to my cabin after she parks the rest of its people in the brig, please."

"Yes, Ma'am. We can do that," Cardones agreed, still grinning.

"Thank you," Honor said, and headed for the lift while the watch chuckled behind her.

The raider's commander was a squat, chunky man who'd once been muscular but long since gone to fat, and his flabby face was gray with shock as Major Hibson thrust him into Honor's cabin. He wasn't handcuffed, and he outmassed the petite Marine by at least two-to-one, but only a complete fool would have taken liberties with Susan Hibson. Not that the pirate appeared to have anything left inside with which liberties might have been taken.

Nonetheless, Andrew LaFollet stood alertly at Honor's right shoulder, gray eyes cold, and rested one hand on the butt of his pulser as the raider shambled to a halt and tried to square his shoulders. Honor leaned back in her chair, stroking Nimitz's prick ears with one hand, and regarded him with eyes that were just as icy as her armsman's, and his effort to stand erect sagged back into hopelessness. He looked both beaten and pathetic, but she reminded herself of his loathsome trade and let the silence drag out endlessly before she smiled thinly.

"Surprise, surprise." Her voice was cold, and the prisoner flinched. She felt his shock-numbed terror through Nimitz, and the 'cat bared needle fangs contemptuously at him.

"You and your crew were captured in the act of piracy by the Royal Manticoran Navy," she went on after a moment. "As this vessel's captain, I have full authority under interstellar law to execute every one of you. I advise you to spare me any blustering which might *irritate* me."

The prisoner flinched again, and Honor felt a trickle of cold, amused approval of her hard case persona leaking from Susan Hibson. She held the pirate with glacial brown eyes until the man nodded jerkily, then let her chair swing back upright.

"Good. The Major here"—she nodded to Hibson—"is going to have a few questions for you and your crew. I suggest you remember that we took your entire database intact, and we'll be analyzing it as well. If I happen to detect any discrepancies between what it says and what *you* say, I won't like it."

The prisoner nodded again, and Honor sniffed disdainfully.

"Take this out of my sight, Major," she said flatly, and Hibson glared at the pirate and jerked a thumb over her shoulder. The prisoner swallowed and shuffled back out of the cabin, and the hatch closed behind them. Silence lingered for a moment, and then LaFollet cleared his throat.

"May I ask what you're going to do with them, My Lady?"

"Hm?" Honor looked up at him, then smiled briefly. "I'm not going to space them, if that's what you mean— not unless we find something really ugly in their files, anyway."

"I didn't think you would, My Lady. But in that case, what *will* you do with them?"

"Well," Honor turned her chair to face him and waved for him to sit on the couch, "I think I'll turn them over to the local Silesian authorities. There's no real fleet base here in Walther, but they do maintain a small customs station. They'll have the facilities to deal with them."

"And their ship, My Lady?"

"That we'll probably scuttle after we've vacuumed its computers," she said with a shrug. "It's the only way— short of actually executing them—to be sure they don't get it back."

"Get it back, My Lady? I thought you said you'd hand them over to the authorities."

"I will," Honor said dryly, "but that doesn't necessarily mean they'll *stay* turned over." LaFollet looked puzzled, and she sighed. "The Confederacy's a sewer, Andrew. Oh, the ordinary people in it are probably as decent as you'll find most places, but what passes for a government is riddled with corruption. I wouldn't be surprised if our gallant pirate has some sort of arrangement with the Walther System's governor."

"You're joking!" LaFollet sounded shocked.

"I wish I were," she said, and laughed humorlessly at his expression. "I found it almost as hard to believe as you do on my first deployment out here, Andrew. But then I captured the same crew twice . . . and they were a darned sight nastier customers than this fellow. I'd handed them over to the local governor and he'd assured me they'd be dealt with; eleven months later they had a new ship and I caught them looting an Andy freighter in the very same star system."

"Sweet Tester," LaFollet murmured, and shook himself like a dog throwing off water.

"That's one reason I wanted to put the fear of God into that sorry scum." Honor twitched her head at the hatch through which the prisoner had vanished. "If he *does* get turned loose, I want him to sweat bullets every time he even thinks about going after another merchie. And that's also why I'm going to tell him and his entire crew one more thing before I hand them over."

"What's that, My Lady?" LaFollet asked curiously.

"One free pass is all they get," Honor said grimly. "The next time I see them, every one of them will go out the lock with a pulser dart in his or her head."

LaFollet stared at her, and his face paled at the absolute sincerity in her expression.

"Does that shock you, Andrew?" she asked gently. He hesitated a moment, then nodded, and she sighed sadly. "Well, it bothers *me*, too," she admitted, "but don't let that fellow's sad sack look fool you. He's a pirate, and pirates aren't glamorous. They're thieves and killers. That other crew I told you about?" She quirked an eyebrow, and LaFollet nodded. "The second time I captured them, they'd just finished killing nineteen people," she said flatly. "Nineteen people whose only 'offense' was to have something they wanted—and who'd have been alive if I'd executed them the first time I got my hands on them." She shook her head, and her eyes were cold as space. "I'll give the locals one chance to deal with their own garbage, Andrew. Corrupt or not, this is their space, and I owe them that much. But one chance is *all* they get on my watch."

• CHAPTER SEVENTEEN

MacGuiness stacked the dessert dishes on his tray and poured fresh coffee for Honor's guests, then refilled her own cocoa cup.

"Will there be anything else, Milady?" he asked, and she shook her head.

"We can manage, Mac. Just leave the coffee pot where these barbarians can get at it."

"Yes, Milady." The steward's voice was respectful as ever, but he shot his captain a moderately reproving glance, then disappeared into his pantry.

"'Barbarian' may be just a bit strong, Ma'am," Rafe Cardones protested with a grin.

"Nonsense," Honor replied briskly. "Any truly cultivated palate realizes how completely cocoa outclasses *coffee* as a beverage of choice. Anyone *but* a barbarian knows that."

"I see." Cardones glanced at his fellow diners, then smiled sweetly. "Tell me, Ma'am, did you see that article in the *Landing Times* about Her Majesty's favorite coffee blend?"

Honor spluttered into her cocoa, and a soft chorus of laughter went up around the table. She set down her cup and mopped her lips with her napkin, then beetled her eyebrows at her exec.

"Officers who score on their COs have short and grisly careers, Mr. Cardones," she informed him.

"That's all right, Ma'am. At least cocoa drinking isn't as revolting as chewing gum."

"You really *are* riding for a fall, aren't you?" Susan Hibson observed. The exec grinned, and she reached into a tunic pocket to extract a pack of gum. She carefully unwrapped a stick, put it in her mouth, and chewed slowly, sea-green eyes gleaming challengingly. Cardones shuddered but forbore to take up the challenge, and another laugh circled the table.

Honor leaned back and crossed her legs. Tonight's dinner was by way of a celebration of their first victory, and she was glad to see the relaxed atmosphere. With the exception of Harold Tschu and John Kanehama, all her senior officers had assembled in the comfortable dining cabin *Wayfarer's* civilian designers had provided for her captain. Kanehama had the bridge watch, but Tschu had planned to attend until a last-minute problem with Fusion One prevented him from being present. It didn't sound serious, but Tschu, like Honor, believed in getting the jump on problems while they were still minor.

"How did it go dirtside, Ma'am?" Jennifer Hughes asked, and Honor frowned.

"Smoothly enough—on the surface, anyway."

"'On the surface', Ma'am?" Hughes repeated, and Honor shrugged.

"Governor Hagen took the lot of them into custody with thanks, but he seemed just a little eager to see the last of us." Honor toyed with her cocoa cup and glanced at Major Hibson. She and the Marine had delivered their prisoners to the system governor in chains, and she knew Hibson shared her own suspicions. Of course, Susan didn't have the advantage of a treecat. She couldn't have sensed the pirate captain's enormous relief at seeing the governor . . . which wasn't exactly what might have been expected of a man who anticipated being punished.

"He was certainly that, Ma'am," Hibson agreed now. She grimaced. "He seemed a bit put out with your decision to blow up their ship, too. Did you notice?"

"I did, indeed," Honor replied. Governor Hagen had made noises about commissioning the pirate vessel as a customs patrol ship, and "a bit put out" considerably understated his reaction to her refusal to turn it over. She contemplated her cup a moment longer, then shrugged. "Well, it's not the first time, now is it? I'm afraid I can live with the good governor's unhappiness. And at least we're certain we won't see their *ship* again."

"Will you really let me shoot them if we pick them up again, Ma'am?" Honor nodded, her expression momentarily bleak. "Good," the major said quietly.

At less than a hundred sixty centimeters, Susan Hibson was a petite woman, but there was nothing soft in her eyes or finely chiseled features. She was a Marine to her toenails, and Marines didn't like pirates. Honor suspected that had something to do with the fact that Marine boarding parties were so often first to witness the human wreckage raiders left behind.

"Personally," she said after a moment, "I'd just as soon not shoot anyone, Susan. But if it's the only way to really take them out of circulation, I don't see what choice we have. At least we can be sure they have a fair trial before they're executed. And from a pragmatic perspective, it may convince the next batch we pick up that we mean it."

"Like a vaccination, Milady," Surgeon Lieutenant Commander Angela Ryder put in from her place at the foot of the table. Ryder was as dark-haired as Hibson, with a thin, studious face. She was also a bit absentminded and tended to prefer a white smock to proper uniform, but she was a first-class physician. "I don't like killing people, either," she went on, "but if the lesson takes, we may actually have to kill less of them in the long run."

"That's the idea, Angie," Honor replied, "but I'm afraid my own observation is that the sort of people who turn pirate in the first place don't really think it could happen to *them*. They're convinced they're too good, or too smart—or too lucky—to end up dead. And I'm sorry to say a lot of them are right about the luck. The Confederacy's roughly a hundred and five light-years across, with a volume of something like six hundred thousand cubic light-years. Without an effective—and honest—

government to run them out of town, raiders can always find someplace to hole up, and most of them are only hired hands, anyway."

"I've never really understood that, Ma'am," Ryder said.

"Historically, piracy's always been subsidized by 'honest merchants,'" Honor explained. "Even back on pre-space Old Earth, 'respectable' business people fronted for pirates, slave traders, drug smugglers, you name it. There's a lot of money in operations like that, and the front people are always harder to get at than their foot soldiers. They go to considerable lengths to be pillars of the community—quite a few of them have been major philanthropists—because that's their first line of defense. It places them above suspicion and lets them pretend they were dupes if an illegal operation does blow up in their faces. Besides, they never get their own hands bloody, and the courts tend to be more lenient with them if they do get caught." She shrugged. "It's disgusting, but that's the way it is. And when the situation's as confused and chaotic as it normally is in Silesia, the opportunities are just too tempting. There's actually a sort of outlaw glamor to piracy out here in many people's eyes, so why shouldn't someone like Governor Hagen take the money as long as someone else does the actual murdering?"

"You're right, Ma'am; that *is* disgusting," the doctor said after a moment.

"Disgust doesn't invalidate the analysis, though," Hughes put in, "and it's not going to change unless someone *makes* it change. Sort of makes you wish we could just go ahead and turn the Andies loose on them, doesn't it?"

"In the short term, at any rate." Honor sipped cocoa, then lowered her cup with a wry smile. "Of course, in the *long* term an Empire that controlled the entire Confederacy might be an even worse neighbor than pirates. I have a feeling Duke Cromarty would think so, at any rate."

"Hard to blame him," Fred Cousins observed. "We've got enough trouble just dealing with the Peeps."

Honor nodded and started to reply, only to pause as Nimitz rose in his highchair to stretch luxuriously. A lazy yawn bared his needle-sharp fangs, then he looked into her eyes, and she gazed back. They remained incapable of exchanging actual thoughts, but they'd gotten steadily better at sending images to one another, and now she smiled as he sent her a view of the hydroponics section and followed it with another one of Samantha. The female treecat sat primly under one of the tomato trellises used to provide the crew with fresh food, but Honor smiled as she sensed the invitation in Samantha's bright eyes.

"All right, Stinker," she said, but she also raised an admonishing finger in his direction. "Just don't get underfoot—and don't get lost, either!"

Nimitz bleeked cheerfully and hopped to the decksole. Although he normally stuck close to Honor, he'd learned how to open powered doors while she was still a child and how to operate lifts while he and his person were still at the Academy. He couldn't use the lift com to ask central routing for directions, but he was quite capable of punching in memorized destination codes. Now he gave her another laughing look, flirted his tail at her, and flowed out of the cabin, and she looked up to see Cardones regarding her speculatively.

"He wants to stretch his legs a bit."

"I see." Cardones' expression was admirably grave, but Honor didn't need Nimitz to sense his amusement.

"At any rate," she said more briskly, "now that we've got one pirate under our belts, I'd like to go over what Susan and Jenny managed to pull out of their computers. We didn't get much on anyone they might have been coordinating operations with or where they were based, but we know where they've *been* . . . and where they planned to go next, which also happens to be our own next scheduled stop. The question is whether or not we should spend another few days here or go straight on to Schiller. Comments?"

*   *   *

Aubrey Wanderman stepped out of the lift and checked the passage marker on the facing bulkhead.

Wayfarer's civilian designers had provided far too little personnel space for her present, oversized military crew, and the yard dogs had sliced a huge chunk of her Number Two Hold into a rabbit warren of berthing decks which still confused him. The need to sandwich in enough life support for three thousand people hadn't helped, and passages that looked like they ought to go to one place had a maddening habit of ending up someplace else. For most of *Wayfarer's* crew, that was merely irritating, but Aubrey enjoyed exploring the labyrinth—which earned quite a bit of ribbing from the old sweats. Despite their amusement, however, he was finally beginning to learn his way around, thanks to the inboard hull plans he'd loaded into his memo pad. Yet the only way to be sure he had a new route down correctly was to try it out, which was the point of this evening's exercise.

He punched the marker code into his memo pad and studied the display for a moment. So far, so good. If he followed this passage to the next junction forward, he could cut up from Engineering to Number Two LAC Hold and pick up the cross lift to the gym—assuming, of course, that he'd plotted his course correctly to begin with.

He grinned at the thought and set off up the deserted passageway, whistling as he went. He wouldn't have traded his acting PO's grade for Ginger's mightier position on a bet, because his merely acting promotion had put him on the command deck when the Captain snapped up their first pirate, and he'd never felt so excited in his life. He supposed he'd actually gotten more excited than the occasion deserved, given that the raider had massed less than one percent of *Wayfarer's* seven-plus million tons, but he didn't much care. They were out here to catch pirates, and Lady Harrington had managed her first interception perfectly. More than that, he, Aubrey Wanderman, had been right there when she did it. He might have been only one teeny-tiny cog in a huge machine, but he'd been part of it, and he treasured the sense of accomplishment. *Wayfarer* might not be *Bellerophon*, yet he had nothing to be ashamed of in his assignment, and—

The deck came up and slammed him in the face with stunning force. The totally unexpected impact smashed the breath out of him in a gasping whoop of agony, and then something crunched brutally into his ribs.

The impact bounced him off the bulkhead, and instinct tried to curl his body in a protective ball, but he never got the chance. A knee drove into his spine, a powerful hand gripped his hair, and he cried out as it smashed his face into the decksole. He reached up desperately, fighting to grip the hand's wrist, and a cold, ugly laugh cut through his half-stunned brain.

"Well, well, Snotnose!" a voice gloated. "Looks like you *did* have an accident."

Steilman! Aubrey managed to get a hand on the power tech's wrist, but Steilman's free hand slashed it aside, and he drove the younger man's face into the decksole again.

"Gotta watch that running in the passages, Snotnose. Never can tell when a man's gonna trip on his own two feet and *hurt* himself."

Aubrey struck out weakly, and the power tech slammed his face into the deck yet again. He tasted blood and his right cheek felt broken, but he put his full, terrified strength into a single lunge and managed to jerk out of Steilman's grasp. He lurched back against the bulkhead, covering his face with his crossed arms, and the power tech's booted foot shoved his shoulder brutally. He went back down on his side, but his own feet lashed out frantically, and he heard Steilman curse in pain as his heel connected with a shin.

"*Motherfucker!*" the power tech hissed. "I'm gonna—"

"Hey, cool it!" a new voice said urgently, and Aubrey struggled up onto his knees. He blinked, trying to make his blurry vision focus, and recognized the short, stocky sick berth attendant from that first afternoon in the berthing bay aboard *Vulcan*. Tatsumi. That was his name. Yoshiro Tatsumi.

"Stay the fuck out of this, powder head!" Steilman snarled.

"Hey, hey! Calm down!" Tatsumi said with that same, low-voiced urgency. "What you do is up to you, but Commander Tschu's headed this way from Fusion One, man!"

"Shit!" Steilman whirled to look down the passage Tatsumi had just come up, then wiped his mouth with the back of his wrist and glared down at Aubrey. "We ain't done, Snotnose," he promised. "I'll finish your 'accident' later." Aubrey stared up at him in bloody-mouthed terror, and the power tech grinned viciously, then turned his glare on Tatsumi. "As for *you*, powder head, I got three people ready to swear I'm in my rack right now, and you didn't *see* nothing and you didn't *hear* nothing. This fucking snotnose just fell over his own clumsy feet, didn't he?"

"Whatever you say, man," Tatsumi agreed, holding up placating hands.

"And don't forget it," Steilman snarled, and headed down the passage at a trot. Seconds later, one of the maintenance hatchways clanged as he disappeared into the maze of crawlways servicing the ship's internal systems, and Tatsumi bent over Aubrey with a worried expression.

"You don't look so good," the SBA muttered. He crouched beside the younger man, and Aubrey winced in anguish as gentle fingers touched his blood-streaming nose. "Crap. I think the bastard broke it," Tatsumi hissed. He looked up and down the passage, then slid an arm around his shoulders. "Come on, kid. Gotta get you down to sickbay."

"W-what about . . . Commander Tschu?" Aubrey got out. He had to breathe through his mouth, and his voice sounded thick and gluey, but somehow he managed to stagger to his feet with Tatsumi's assistance.

"What about him? Hell, he's still buried up to his elbows in Fusion One!"

"You mean—?" Aubrey got out, and Tatsumi shrugged.

"I had to tell him *something*, Wanderman. That man was gonna kill your ass."

"Yeah." Aubrey tried to wipe blood from his chin, but a fresh, sticky film replaced it instantly. "Yeah, I guess he was. Thanks."

"Don't thank me," Tatsumi said. "I don't like to see anybody hurt, but you're on your own with Steilman. That's one evil son-of-a-bitch, and I don't want anything to do with him."

Aubrey looked sideways at the older man as Tatsumi helped him back towards the lift. He recognized the fear in the SBA's face and voice, and he couldn't blame him.

"You mean you didn't see anything," he said after a moment.

"You got it. I just came along and found you lying there. I didn't see anything, and I didn't hear anything." Tatsumi looked away for a moment, then shook his head apologetically. "Hey, I'm sorry, okay? But I've got problems of my own, and if Steilman decides to put me on his shit list, too—" He shrugged, and Aubrey nodded.

"I understand." Tatsumi got him into the lift and punched the sickbay destination code, and Aubrey patted him weakly on the arm. "Don't blame you," he said muzzily. "Just wish I knew why he hates *me* so much."

"You made him look bad," Tatsumi explained. "I don't think he's right in the head, but the way he sees it, *you* got in *his* face in the berthing bay, and then the Bosun made him back down. Not your fault, but he figures he owes you for that. My guess is that the Exec's deciding to move you to the bridge is the only reason he hasn't gone for you already. Was I you, I'd stay away from Engineering, Wanderman. Far away."

"Can't hide from him forever." Aubrey sagged against Tatsumi's support. "Ship's not big enough. If he wants me, he can find me." He shook his head, then winced as the movement sent fresh stabs of pain through his skull. "I've got to talk to somebody. Figure out what to do."

"Wish I could help, but count me out," the SBA said in a low voice. "You heard what he called me?"

"'Powder head'?"

"Yeah. See, I got messed up with Sphinx green a few years back. Really fucked me up. I'm clean now, but I've got enough black marks on my record to keep me a second class for the next fifty years. You heard the Bosun that first day, and I ain't got any friends in officer country, either. I get Steilman and his crowd on my neck as well, and I'm just likely to disappear out a refuse lock someday."

"How come they didn't bust you out?" Aubrey asked after a moment, and Tatsumi shrugged.

"'Cause whatever else I am, I'm good at my job, I guess. The Surgeon went to bat for me when they caught me sniffing. Didn't keep me out of hack for six months or save me from mandatory counseling, but it kept me in uniform."

Aubrey nodded in comprehension. He understood what Tatsumi was saying, and he didn't blame the SBA for wanting to stay out of his problems. How could he, when Tatsumi had just saved his life? But if Tatsumi wouldn't back up his own version of what had happened, it would be just his word against Steilman's. That might be enough, given the difference in their service records . . . but it might not, too. Besides, if Tatsumi was right and Steilman had a "crowd" to back him up—and the fact that Steilman had known where to ambush Aubrey suggested that he did—even getting the power tech in the brig might not be enough. Everyone on Aubrey's watch knew about his explorations, and he hadn't made any particular effort to keep this evening's plans a secret, but Steilman wasn't *on* his watch. The only way he could have known was if someone else had told him. Aubrey couldn't imagine why anyone would voluntarily associate with an animal like Steilman, but that didn't really matter. What mattered was that somebody apparently did . . . and that Aubrey had no idea who that somebody was.

He raised cupped hands to his battered face, trying to stop the bleeding, and panic throbbed deep inside. He had to find an answer, but how? He could speak privately to the Bosun, but Sally MacBride wasn't the sort to accept half measures. If she believed him, she'd take action, yet without some sort of proof, all she could really do at this point would be to warn Steilman, and she'd already done that. Obviously the power tech thought he could get away with "avenging himself" on Aubrey despite that warning, and Aubrey saw no reason to hope Steilman would change his mind now. Steilman was probably wrong about what he could get away with, but whatever the Bosun might do to the power tech afterward would be little comfort to Aubrey if Steilman put him into sickbay—or worse—first.

"Here we are," Tatsumi sighed relievedly as the lift stopped and the doors hissed open. He helped Aubrey down the short passage, and the younger man closed his eyes. He needed help. He needed to talk to someone who might have enough experience to tell him what to do, but he didn't *know* anyone with that kind of background!

"My God!" someone said. "What happened to *him?*"

"Don't know for sure," Tatsumi said. "I found him in the passage."

"Who is he?" the voice asked.

"Name's Wanderman," Tatsumi replied. "I think it's just his face."

"Let me see him." Hands pushed the SBA aside and cradled Aubrey's head gently, and he blinked as a surgeon lieutenant peered into his eyes. "What happened, Wanderman?" the man asked.

Tell him! an inner voice shouted. *Tell him now!* But if Aubrey told the officer . . .

"I fell," he said thickly.

• CHAPTER EIGHTEEN

The GQ alarm yanked Warner Caslet up from dreamless sleep. He rolled over, sat up, and reached for the com key out of pure spinal reflex even before his eyes were open, and light flared in the darkened cabin as the display came up.

"Captain," he said in a sleep-blurry voice. "Talk to me."

"I think we've got a nibble, Skipper." It was Allison MacMurtree, his executive officer. "I'm not sure it's who we're looking for, but *someone's* coming after us."

"Just one?" Caslet rubbed his eyes, and MacMurtree nodded.

"All we've got so far is a single impeller signature, Skip." Citizen Commissioner Jourdain moved into range of the exec's pickup, looking over her shoulder at Caslet. MacMurtree glanced back at the newcomer, but her face showed no concern, despite the fact that many a people's commissioner considered "Skipper" or "Skip" almost as "disloyally elitist" as daring to call anyone but another commissioner "Sir."

"How far back?"

"Right on nineteen million klicks, Skip. Call it a tad over one light-minute. We're not getting any active—" She broke off and looked away from her pickup. Caslet heard Shannon Foraker's voice, and then MacMurtree looked back out of the display with a chilling smile. "Tactical just confirmed it, Skipper. Active light-speed emissions are coming in now, and they match our boy's signature across the board."

"And he's definitely coming after us?"

228

"Absolutely. We're the only other people out here, and he just lit off his drive two minutes ago," the exec confirmed, and Caslet gave her an equally icy smile.

"I'll be up immediately. You and Shannon know what to do till I get there."

"Aye, Skipper. We'll play fat, dumb, and happy."

"Good." Caslet nodded, killed the circuit, and crossed to his suit locker. One of the many privileges the Republic's officer corps had been required to give up under the new regime was its stewards, but that had never bothered Caslet particularly, and it certainly didn't bother him now. He made a quick visual inspection of his skinsuit telltales before he dragged it out, yet his mind wasn't truly on them. For all the assurance he'd projected for Jourdain's benefit, the chance of finding a single, specific raider was always slim. Now he'd pulled it off, and he wondered if he could manage the next step on his agenda. According to the sensor logs they'd pulled from *Erewhon's* computers, the raider was much lighter than *Vaubon*, and Caslet seriously doubted any batch of pirates could match the efficiency of his well-drilled, veteran crew. He had no doubt that he could *destroy* these people, but what he really wanted was to capture their ship—and its computers—reasonably intact, and that promised to be considerably more difficult.

He climbed into the suit, suppressing a familiar wince as he made the plumbing connections, and sealed it. He wanted that ship, and he was prepared to run a certain degree of risk to capture it, but he was *not* prepared to endanger his own people. If it looked problematical, he was perfectly willing to settle for blowing it away. Indeed, a part of him wanted to do just that, and he bared his teeth as he picked up his helmet and headed for the hatch.

"Looks like we've got him suckered—for now, at least," MacMurtree greeted Caslet as he stepped onto the command deck. She gestured at the main plot and followed him across to it. "He's coming in from almost directly astern—one-seven-seven—but he's high, so all he can see is our roof. No way he can get any kind of radar return or optical on us."

"Good." Caslet handed his helmet to a yeoman, who racked it on his command chair's arm for him, and stood gazing into the plot. The raider had closed to just over eighteen and a half million kilometers, and it was accelerating at almost five hundred gravities. *Vaubon*'s current velocity was 13,800 KPS, and she was accelerating towards the F6 sun called Sharon's Star at a hundred and two gravities, but the raider was already up to 15,230 KPS, an overtake of over fourteen hundred kilometers per second. Caslet considered the vector projections for a moment, then looked at Citizen Lieutenant Simon Houghton.

"Time to intercept?"

"At present accelerations, call it forty-five minutes," the astrogator replied, "but his overtake would be over twelve thousand KPS."

"Understood." Caslet studied the plot a few seconds longer, then walked to his command chair. Jourdain already sat in the matching chair next to it and raised his eyebrows as the citizen commander seated himself.

"You're confident these are the people you want, Citizen Commander?"

"If Shannon says it's them, then it's them, Sir. And so far, they seem to be doing exactly what we want. The problem is to *keep* them doing it."

"And just how will you do that?" Jourdain's question could have been ironic, but it was honestly curious, and Caslet smiled briefly.

"None of their sensors can see through our wedge, Sir. At the moment, all they have to go on are its apparent strength and our active emissions, and Shannon and Engineering have gone to some pains to make both of them look like a merchantman's. We couldn't fool a regular warship for very long if it was suspicious, but these

people *expect* to see a merchie. They should go right on assuming that's what we are until and unless we do something to change their minds or they get a look at our hull. Fortunately, they're well above us, which means they're headed directly towards the roof of our wedge right now. We can't count on that lasting all the way to intercept, but they should give us plenty of excuse to react before then. And if we time it right, the geometry when we finally decide to 'see' them and respond to the threat should keep them from seeing up the rear of our wedge."

"So they won't get that look at our hull," Jourdain said, nodding slowly, and Caslet nodded back.

"That's the idea, Citizen Commissioner. If this is their max acceleration, which seems likely, we've got about a ten-gee edge, but that's not enough unless we can get them in closer. At the moment, their overtake is still so low they could easily evade and get back across the hyper limit before we overhauled if we simply turned and went in pursuit. But if we act like a properly terrified freighter, they should keep coming in—and slowing to board or engage us, as well—until we've got them right where we want them."

"And then we blow them out of space," Jourdain said with undisguised satisfaction. The people's commissioner had spent hours reviewing Citizen Captain Branscombe's visual records of the carnage aboard *Erewhon*, and he'd clearly overcome any lingering reservations about decreasing pressure on the Manties. It was one more indication that he had too much decency to make a proper spy for the Committee of Public Safety, but Caslet had no intention of complaining about *that*. Still, it was time to give Jourdain's thoughts a slightly different direction.

"And then we *can* blow them out of space, Sir," he said. "But satisfying as that would be, I'd rather take them more or less intact."

"Intact?" Jourdain's eyebrows rose again. "Surely that would be far more difficult!"

"Oh, it would, Sir. But if we can get our hands on their database, we'll be in a far better position to tell just how numerous this particular nest of vermin may be. With luck, we may even find enough data to ID some of their other ships if we stumble across them—or find out where they're based. Information is the second most deadly weapon known to man, Sir."

"The second? And what, pray tell, is the first, Citizen Commander?"

"Surprise," Caslet said softly, "and we already *have* that one."

The raider continued to close, and *Vaubon* let it come. The light cruiser forged steadily towards Sharon's Star, plodding along on a routine approach to turnover, and Caslet and Shannon Foraker watched the pirates sweep nearer and nearer. Thirty-four minutes ticked past, and the range fell to just over seven million kilometers.

The raider's overtake velocity was up to almost ten thousand kilometers per second, which seemed excessive to Caslet. Even at the low acceleration *Vaubon* had so far revealed, a sudden reversal of power on her part would force the raider to overrun her at a relative velocity of over six thousand KPS in fourteen and a half minutes. Assuming the "freighter" survived the overrun, the raider would need another twenty-six minutes just to decelerate to zero relative to its target, by which time the range between them would have opened to nine and a half million kilometers once more, and the pirates would have to chase her down all over again. Of course, that would still be an ultimately losing game for the "freighter," given the higher acceleration the raider could pull, but a gutsy merchant skipper might go for it. Useless as it would probably prove in the long run, he *might* be able to spin things out long enough for someone else to turn up, and even in the Confederacy, it was possible that someone else *might* be a warship. The odds against any such happy outcome were literally astronomical, but the fact that the bad guys hadn't allowed for it was one more indication of professional sloppiness.

On the other hand, not even this bunch of yahoos were likely to keep pouring on the accel much longer, particularly since even a merchantman was bound to pick them up in the next million klicks or so. They'd be making their presence known pretty soon, and—

"Missile separation! I've got two birds, Skip, spreading out to port and starboard!"

"All right, Helm," Caslet said calmly. "You know what to do."

"Aye, Sir. Evading now."

Vaubon's nose pitched "down" as the cruiser came perpendicular to the system ecliptic, "diving" frantically, and rolled to starboard. The move snatched her vector away from the missiles and interposed the floor of her impeller wedge against them in the only real evasion maneuver an unarmed ship could execute. Despite the extremely long range, the raider's overtake velocity put *Vaubon* well within his powered missile envelope, and without any active defenses to intercept incoming fire short of target, all a freighter could realistically hope to do was dodge. Of course, the raider had *wanted* her to dodge them, and their conventional nuclear warheads detonated at the end of their run without fuss or bother. But their message had been passed.

"We're being hailed, Skipper," the com officer said. "They're ordering us to resume our original heading."

"Are they?" Caslet murmured, and gave his people's commissioner a smile. "That's convenient. Did they say anything about killing the wedge?"

"No, Citizen Commander. They want us to maintain our original accel while they match velocities."

"That's even more convenient," Caslet observed, and checked the plot. *Vaubon's* "evasion maneuver" had opened the vertical separation a bit further—not a lot, but a little—and he leaned back and rubbed his jaw for a moment. "Ted, hail them—audio only; no visual. Inform them that we're the Andermani merchant ship *Ying Kreuger* and order them to stand clear."

"Aye, Citizen Commander." Citizen Lieutenant Dutton turned back to his pickup, and Jourdain gave Caslet a mildly puzzled look.

"And just what is *this* in aid of, Citizen Commander?" he inquired.

"We're inside their missile envelope, Sir," Caslet replied, "but no sane pirate wants to blow his prize up, and even with laser heads, missiles aren't precision weapons. They're mostly for show; he needs to get in close with his energy mounts to be able to threaten us with the sort of damage that could stop us without destroying us out-right. Merchant skippers know that, and a gutsy captain— or a stupid one—would at least try to talk his way out of it until they managed to bring him into effective range. It wouldn't do to slip out of our role just yet, and more to the point, the more vertical separation I can gener-ate before resuming our original course, the sharper the angle will be when our vectors intercept. They'll have to come in from higher 'above' us, and that should keep our wedge between us and their active systems at least a little longer."

"I see." Jourdain shook his head and smiled faintly. "Remind me not to play poker with you, Citizen Com-mander."

"They're repeating their order to resume course and accel," Dutton announced, and grinned at his captain. "They sound sort of pissed off, Skip."

"What a pity. Repeat the message." Caslet smiled back, then glanced at MacMurtree. "We'll keep protesting till they close to four million, Allison, then obey like a nice little prize."

The chase was winding to a close, and the atmosphere on PNS *Vaubon*'s bridge was far tenser than it had been. The raider's demands that "*Ying Kreuger*" rendezvous with it had become uglier and more threatening, punctuated by increasingly closer near-misses with nuclear warheads,

until Caslet gave in and obeyed. Now the pirate was little more than a quarter million kilometers clear, and Caslet shook his head in wonder. He'd never really expected the idiots to come *this* close without realizing they'd been had, but the raider skipper seemed sublimely confident. The fact that he had yet to get even a single glimpse of his prize's hull meant little to him, since he "knew" from her emissions that she was a merchant ship. No one could see through an active impeller wedge from the outside, anyway, since the effect of a meter-wide band in which local gravity went from zero to almost a hundred thousand MPS^2 twisted photons into pretzels. Someone on the inside, who knew the precise strength of the wedge, could use computer compensation to turn mangled emissions back into something comprehensible, but no one on the outside could manage the same trick. Caslet's maneuvers had kept his wedge between his ship and the raider's sensors for reasons which the pirate saw no cause to question, but the bad guys were well within effective energy weapons range now, and he glanced at Foraker.

"Ready, Shannon?"

"Yes, Sir." The tac officer was so buried in her console she used the pre-coup formality without even thinking, and Jourdain shook his head with wry resignation.

"All right, people. This is where we nail the bastards. Stand by . . . and . . . *execute!*"

PNS *Vaubon* stopped being a freighter. Foraker hadn't been able to use any of her active systems without giving the game away, but her passive systems had run a painstaking track on her opponent for almost two hours. She knew *exactly* where the enemy was, and she also knew that enemy was decelerating towards her at a sharp enough angle to give her an up the kilt shot. Allison MacMurtree rolled *Vaubon* up on her starboard side with sudden, flashing speed, and as the ship rolled, her *port* broadside came to bear on the raider and two powerful laser mounts fired as one. Caslet could have fired a broadside three times as heavy, but he wanted that ship to survive . . . and two clean hits with no sidewall interdiction should be more than enough for his purposes.

Lasers are light-speed weapons, and the raider's first warning was the instant both of Foraker's shots scored direct hits on the stern of his ship. His chase armament vanished in an explosion of shattered plating, and the beams of coherent light blew forward into his after impeller ring like demons. Massive power surges bled through his internal systems, blowing equipment like popcorn as the entire after third of his hull was smashed into rubble, and his fusion plant went into emergency shutdown. His impellers died, and he was suddenly unable to maneuver, stern-on to his would-be victim, with neither wedge nor sidewall to interdict *Vaubon's* fire.

"This is Citizen Commander Warner Caslet," Caslet said coldly into his com. "You are my prisoners. Any attempt at resistance will result in the destruction of your vessel."

There was no reply, and he watched his plot narrowly. Despite the raider's massive damage, at least some of his broadside weapons must have survived, including his missile tubes, and those could still fire at least a few shots on reserve power. But his emissions made it clear that single, devastating rake had completely crippled his vessel. If he *did* choose to fight, it would be one of the shortest engagements in history.

"No reply, Skip," Dutton said. "We may have taken out their transmitters."

Caslet nodded. For that matter, they'd quite possibly taken out the raider's receivers, as well. But whether he'd heard the message or not, whoever was in command over there clearly didn't intend to commit suicide, and Caslet glanced at the small com screen tied into the troop bay of Citizen Captain Branscombe's pinnace.

"All right, Ray. Go get them, but watch your ass. Hold the pinnaces clear and stay out of our line of fire."

"Aye, Sir," Branscombe replied, and two pinnaces packed with battle-armored Marines floated clear of

Vaubon's boat bay. They circled wide to stay out of the play of the light cruiser's broadside weapons, and took up station two kilometers directly astern of the half-wrecked ship. Hatches opened, and individual, armored Marines drifted across the gap to the raider's hull.

Caslet watched on the visual display as the Marines moved forward towards the nearest undamaged personnel hatch. It was possible the pirates would try one final, suicidal gesture of defiance and blow themselves up just to take his Marines with them, but pirates weren't kamikazes . . . and they didn't know that Caslet already knew about *Erewhon*. If they had known, and if they'd suspected what he intended to do with them, they might have suicided anyway, but they didn't, and he relaxed as Branscombe's point men entered the hull and started rounding up the raider crew without resistance.

"Nicely done, Citizen Commander," Denis Jourdain said quietly. "Very nicely done. And under the circumstances," he smiled with an edge of sadness, "I think this really *is* something we can feel proud of."

• CHAPTER NINETEEN

Caslet was waiting in the boat bay gallery when Branscombe's pinnace docked. He folded his hands behind him and stood still, hiding his impatience as the docking tube ran out. The umbilicals engaged, and the tube cycled open. A moment later, Branscombe drifted down it in his battle armor, caught the grab bar, and swung over into *Vaubon's* internal gravity. It wasn't a simple maneuver in battle armor, and more than one Marine's exoskeletal "muscles" had ripped a grab bar completely off its brackets, but Branscombe made it look easy. He landed on the deck, standing a half-meter taller than usual in his massive armor, and raised his visor.

"We ripped hell out of her aft of about frame eighty, Skipper," he said, "and one of our hits blew clear forward to their bridge. It's a mess in there. Everything's down except emergency lighting, and it looks like at least a third of their computer section went up with the hit. But my tech people say they didn't manage to dump their main memory, and Citizen Sergeant Simonson's working on tickling something out of it now."

"Good. Any resistance?"

"None, Sir." Like Shannon Foraker's, Citizen Captain Branscombe's vocabulary had a tendency to backslide, and he smiled evilly. "I figure we killed about half their crew—would you believe only their boarders were even suited?" He shook his head, and it was Caslet's turn to smile.

"Of course they weren't, Ray. We were just a harmless merchie going to the slaughter."

238

"That's what *they* thought, anyway. Some of them seem to feel like we cheated somehow."

"My heart bleeds," Caslet observed, then rubbed his chin. "So Simonson may be able to get something out of their 'puters for us, eh? Well, that's good news."

"She didn't sound real confident, Sir," Branscombe cautioned, "but if anyone can, she can. In the meantime, though, we may have something even better than that."

Caslet looked up sharply, but the citizen captain wasn't looking at him. Battle armor was designed to be nearly indestructible, and the back of Branscombe's helmet was a solid slab of armor. At the moment, he was looking into the small vision display that covered the area directly behind him, and Caslet stepped to the side to see around him. Two more Marines were coming down the tube, with a man and a woman in filthy shipsuits sandwiched between them.

"Is this their senior officers?" Caslet asked coldly.

"No, Sir—I mean, Citizen Commander." The Marine grimaced. "If they're telling the truth, they're not even members of the crew."

"Of course they're not," Caslet said sarcastically.

"As a matter of fact, Skipper, I think they *are* telling the truth." Caslet looked at the Marine again, eyebrows raised, and Branscombe tossed his head in the gesture someone in armor used instead of a shrug. "You'll see why in a minute," he said in a grimmer voice.

Caslet wrinkled his forehead in skepticism but said nothing while the Marines and their prisoners exited the tube. But then he stiffened as the prisoners' appearance registered fully.

Prolong always made it difficult to judge someone's age, but the man had a few streaks of gray in his hair and unkempt beard. His face was haggard, with huge, dark circles under the eyes, and an ugly, recent scar disfigured his right cheek. In fact, Caslet realized, it stretched clear up around the side of his head and his entire right ear was missing.

The woman was probably younger, but it was hard to tell. Once, she must have been quite attractive, and it showed even past her dirty skin and oily hair, but she was even more haggard than her companion, and her eyes were those of a cornered animal. They darted everywhere, watching every shadow, and Caslet fought a sudden desire to step back from her. She radiated a dangerous, half-mad aura of pure murder, and her mouth was a frozen snarl.

"Citizen Commander Caslet," Branscombe said quietly, "allow me to introduce Captain Harold Sukowski and Commander Christina Hurlman." The man's eyes flickered, but he managed a courteous nod. The woman didn't even move, and Caslet watched her tense as the man—Sukowski—slipped an arm around her.

"Citizen Commander," Sukowski said huskily, and Caslet's eyes sharpened at his accent. "I never thought I'd be happy to see the People's Navy, but I am. I certainly am."

"You're Manties," Caslet said softly.

"Yes, Sir." The woman still said nothing. Only her eyes moved, still darting about like trapped animals, and Sukowski drew her closer against his side. "Master of RMMS *Bonaventure*. This—" his voice wavered slightly, and he dragged it back under control "—is my exec."

"What in God's name were you doing over there?" Caslet demanded, waving an arm towards the hulk beyond the gallery bulkhead.

"They took my ship in Telmach four months ago." Sukowski looked around the gallery for a moment, then met Caslet's eyes pleadingly. "Please, Citizen Commander. You must have a doctor on board." Caslet nodded, and Sukowski cleared his throat. "Could I ask you to call him, please. Chris has . . . had a bad time."

Caslet's eyes flickered to the woman, and his stomach clenched as he remembered what these same raiders had done aboard *Erewhon*. A dozen questions chased themselves across his forebrain, but he managed to stop them all before they crossed his lips.

"Of course." He nodded to one of the Marines, who gripped Hurlman's elbow gently to guide her towards the lift. But the instant he touched her, the motionless woman erupted in violence. It was insane—the Marine was in battle armor, with his visor still down—but she went for him with her bare hands and feet, and the total silence of her attack was almost as terrifying as its fury. Had the Marine *not* been armored, any one of the half-dozen blows she landed before anyone could react would have crippled or killed him, and his companion started forward.

"No! Stay back!" Sukowski shouted, and waded into the fray. The first Marine wasn't even trying to defend himself. He was simply trying to back away from his attacker without hurting her, but she wouldn't relent. She leapt from the deck, wrapped her arms around his helmet, and slammed her kneecap into his armored breastplate again and again and again, and Caslet opened his mouth as Sukowski jumped towards her.

"Watch yourself, she'll—!"

But Sukowski ignored the citizen commander. His attention was entirely on Hurlman, and his voice was very gentle.

"Chris. Chris, it's me. It's the Skipper, Chris. It's all right. He's not going to hurt you or me. Chris, they're friends. Listen to me, Chris. Listen to me."

The words poured out like a soft, soothing litany, and the woman's fury wavered. Her attack slowed, then stopped, and she looked over her shoulder as Sukowski touched her.

"It's all right, Chris. We're safe now." A tear trickled down the Manticoran's cheek, but he kept his voice low and gentle. "It's all right. It's all right, Chris."

She made a sound—the first sound Caslet had heard from her. It wasn't a word. It didn't even sound human, but Sukowski nodded.

"That's right, Chris. Come on, now. Come over here with me."

She shook herself and closed her eyes tightly for an instant, and then she released her death grip on the Marine's helmet. She sagged back, crouching on the deck, and Sukowski knelt beside her. He put both arms around her, holding her tightly, but she twisted in his grip, facing away from him. She looked up at the Marines and Caslet, and her lips skinned back to bare her teeth. She was poised to attack yet again, and Caslet licked his own lips as he recognized her body language. The brutality her captors had shown her was agonizingly evident, but she hadn't attacked the Marine to protect herself. It was her *captain* she was defending, and she was ready to take them all on, empty hands against battle armor, if they even looked like threatening him.

"It's over, Chris. We're safe now," Sukowski whispered in her ear, over and over, until, at last, she relaxed ever so slightly. The Manticoran captain closed his own eyes for a moment, then looked back up at Caslet.

"I think I'd better take her to sickbay myself," he said, and his voice was hoarse, without the calm he'd forced into it when speaking to Hurlman.

"Of course," Caslet said quietly. He drew a deep breath and went down on his knees, facing the woman. "No one is going to harm you or your captain, Commander Hurlman," he said in that same, quiet voice. "No one is going to hurt either of you ever again. You have my word."

She glared at him, mouth working soundlessly, but he held her eyes, and something seemed to flicker deep within them. Her mouth stilled, and he nodded, then rose once more, holding his hand out to her.

"Come with me, Commander. I'll take you Doctor Jankowski. She'll get you and your captain cleaned up before we talk again, all right?"

She stared at his hand for a long, tense moment, and then her shoulders sagged. Her head hung for just an instant, and then she reached out. She took his hand as

skittishly as a wild animal might have, and he squeezed gently and drew her to her feet.

Two hours later, Harold Sukowski sat in Caslet's briefing room, facing the citizen commander, Allison MacMurtree, and Denis Jourdain across the table. Christina Hurlman wasn't there. She was sedated in sickbay under Citizen Doctor Jankowski's care, and Caslet prayed Jankowski's prognosis was accurate. Jankowski had been a civilian doctor in DuQuesne Tower before the coup attempt. She'd dealt with rape trauma before, and she seemed almost relieved by Hurlman's homicidal attitude.

"Better someone who's still willing to fight back than someone who's completely beaten, Skipper," the doctor had said. "She's in terrible shape right now, but we've still got something to build on. If she doesn't break up when she realizes she really is safe, I think she's got a good chance to come back. Maybe not all the way, but a lot further than you might believe just now."

Now Caslet shook himself and looked at Sukowski. The Manticoran looked much better now that he'd showered and changed into a clean shipsuit, but the strain in his face hadn't even begun to ease yet, and Caslet wondered if it ever would.

"I think," the citizen commander said, "that we can assume you and Commander Hurlman are who you say you are, Captain Sukowski. I'd still like to know what you were doing aboard that ship, however."

Sukowski gave a small, bitter smile of understanding. Branscombe's Marines had brought all the surviving pirates across to *Vaubon* by now, and Caslet had never seen a more psychopathic crop in his life. He'd never really believed in Attila the Hun in starships. By and large, spacers required a certain degree of intelligence, but these people were something else. No doubt they *were* intelligent, in their own way, but they were also brutal, sadistic scum, and Caslet couldn't imagine how Sukowski and Hurlman had survived as their captives.

"As I said, Citizen Commander, they took my ship in Telmach. I got most of my crew off, but Chris—" His eyes flickered. "Chris wouldn't leave me," he said quietly. "She thought I needed looking after." He managed a shaky smile. "She was right, but *God,* I wish she'd gone!"

He looked down at the tabletop for a moment, then inhaled deeply and raised one hand to where his right ear had been.

"I got this right after they boarded," he said flatly. "They were . . . angry my people got away from them, and three of them held me down while another sawed my ear off. I think they were going to kill me just because they were pissed off, but they wanted to take their *time* about it, and Chris got loose from the one holding her somehow. I wasn't much use, but she crippled the bastard with the knife and took three more of them down before they all piled onto her."

He looked away, and his jaw worked.

"I think she took them by surprise, but they beat the hell out of her once they had her down, and they—" He broke off and drew another deep breath, and MacMurtree handed him a glass of ice water. He sipped deeply, then cleared his throat. "Sorry." The word came out husky, and he cleared his throat again, then set the glass very carefully on the table. "Sorry. It's just that what they did to *her* . . . diverted them from me. They took it out on her, instead." He closed his eyes, and his jaw clenched. "The men were bad enough, but, Jesus, the *women!* They actually gave the sick bastards *advice,* like it was all some kind of—"

His voice chopped off, and his nostrils flared.

"If you need more time—" Jourdain began softly, but Sukowski shook his head sharply.

"No. No, I'm as close to all right as I'll get for a while. Let me go ahead and tell it."

The people's commissioner nodded, though his face was distressed as he sat back in his chair, and Sukowski opened his eyes once more.

"The only reason we're alive is that we're with the

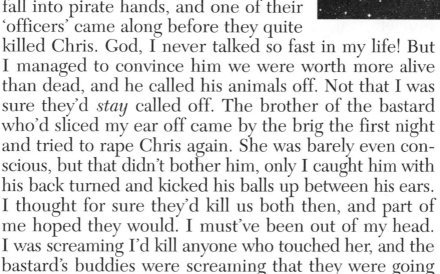

Hauptman Cartel. Mr. Hauptman's agreed to ransom any of his people who fall into pirate hands, and one of their 'officers' came along before they quite killed Chris. God, I never talked so fast in my life! But I managed to convince him we were worth more alive than dead, and he called his animals off. Not that I was sure they'd *stay* called off. The brother of the bastard who'd sliced my ear off came by the brig the first night and tried to rape Chris again. She was barely even conscious, but that didn't bother him, only I caught him with his back turned and kicked his balls up between his ears. I thought for sure they'd kill us both then, and part of me hoped they would. I must've been out of my head. I was screaming I'd kill anyone who touched her, and the bastard's buddies were screaming that they were going to kill *me*, and then Chris was on her feet somehow, trying to get at them, and they butt-stroked her with a pulser and I went for the one with the gun, and—"

He broke off, hands shaking violently, and cleared his throat again.

"That's all I remember for a day or two," he said flatly. "When I started tracking again, their 'captain' told me I'd damned well better be right about that ransom, because if I was lying, he was going to give Chris to the crew and make me watch before they spaced us both. But in the meantime, they left us pretty much alone. I think"—he actually managed a ghastly parody of a smile— "they were afraid that if they tried anything else they'd *have* to kill one or both of their golden geese. At any rate, that's what we were doing in that hell ship, and even a POW camp is going to look like heaven compared to it."

"I think we can avoid that, Captain Sukowski," Jourdain said, and Caslet looked at him in surprise. "You and Commander Hurlman have been through enough. We'll have to hold you for some time, I'm afraid, but I personally assure you that you'll both be handed over to the nearest Manticoran embassy as soon as our own operational posture permits."

"Thank you, Sir," Sukowski said quietly. "Thank you very much."

"In the meantime, however," Caslet said after a moment, "any information you can give us would be extremely useful. We may be at war with your kingdom, Captain Sukowski, but we're not monsters. We want these people—all of them."

"You're going to need more than one ship," Sukowski said grimly. "I never got a chance to look at any of their astrogation data, but they decided I should 'earn my keep' and put me to work in Engineering. They said that since I'd fixed it so they had to man *Bonaventure*, I could help take up the slack in *their* ship. They enjoyed the hell out of giving me all the shit jobs, but frankly, I was glad to have something to do, and they talked in front of me. I kept track of the ship's names they dropped, and as near as I can make out, they've got at least ten of 'em, maybe a few more."

"Ten?" Caslet couldn't keep the surprise out of his voice, and Sukowski smiled bitterly.

"I was surprised, too. I couldn't imagine that anyone would be crazy enough to bankroll maniacs like this, but these aren't 'pirates' at all. What you're dealing with, Citizen Commander, used to be an official squadron of privateers operating out of the Chalice."

"Oh, God," MacMurtree muttered, and Caslet's mouth tightened. Their background brief had covered the Chalice Cluster Uprising and the lunatic who'd launched it. Only a government like the Confederacy's could have let a madman like Andre Warnecke take over a single city, far less an entire cluster with three inhabited planets. Of course, to be fair he'd started out sounding sane enough—until he was in power, anyway. He'd announced his intention to create a republic and hold free and open elections as soon as he'd "provided for the public safety," then put his cronies in charge of internal security and launched a reign of terror which made State Security's purges back home look like a tea party. What had once been NavInt estimated that he'd killed something like three million citizens of the Chalice himself before the inept Confederacy Navy managed to move in and crush his rebellion after over fourteen T-months of trying.

"Exactly," Sukowski said in that same, grim voice. "The Silesians were even more incompetent than usual, and these bastards managed to get out before the roof caved in. Worse, they took Warnecke with them."

"Warnecke's *alive?*" Caslet gasped, and Sukowski nodded. "But they hanged him," Caslet protested. "We've got copies of the imagery in our database!"

"I know," Sukowski grunted. "His people have copies of it, too, and they laugh their asses off over it. The best I could figure it, the Confeds figured he'd died in the fighting but still wanted to make an 'example' of him, so they faked up the imagery of his hanging. But he's alive, Citizen Commander, and he and his murderers've taken over some outback planet lock, stock, and barrel. I'm not sure where it is, but the locals never had a chance when the squadron came in on them. Now Warnecke's using it as a base of operations until he's ready to mount his 'counter offensive' against the Confederacy."

"These people actually believe he can *do* that?" Jourdain asked skeptically, and Sukowski shrugged.

"I can't tell you that. At the moment, they're pirates; Warnecke still has connections somewhere in the Confederacy willing to dispose of loot for him, and they're doing all right for themselves, despite the way they operate. At least some of them *do* seem to think they're building up to take back the Chalice, though others sound more like they're just humoring a lunatic. But for the moment, he's got them in line, and from what one or two of them were saying, his contacts are about ready to start supplying him with additional ships, as well."

"I don't like the sound of *that*," MacMurtree muttered.

"Neither do I," Caslet agreed, and looked at Jourdain. "Nor, I'm certain, will Citizen Admiral Giscard or Citizen Commissioner Pritchart. We thought Warnecke was dead, so I don't have detailed information on him. But

what I do have suggests he's the sort who'd see the chance
to capture a regular warship as a way to add to his 'navy.'"

"Surely you're not suggesting he could threaten *us*,"
Jourdain protested.

"Don't underestimate these people just because they're
animals, Sir. Granted, the Confederacy Navy is incompetent, but Warnecke did hold them off for over a T-year—
and got himself out when it finally fell apart. The ship
we just took was as heavily armed as one of our *Bastogne*-
class destroyers. He may have others even more powerful, and if he swarms us one at a time, he could take
out even a battlecruiser with enough of them."

"The Citizen Commander's right, Sir," MacMurtree put
in. Jourdain looked at her, and she shrugged. "I doubt
Warnecke could capture one of our units in useable
condition, but that doesn't mean he won't try to. And it
won't matter to our people whether their ship is destroyed
or taken. They'll be just as dead either way."

"And none of that even considers what kind of atrocities
these people are going to be committing in the meantime," Caslet added.

"Point taken, Citizen Commander." Jourdain plucked
at his lower lip and looked at Sukowski again. "You don't
have *any* idea where this planet they've taken over is,
Captain?"

"I'm afraid not, Sir," the Manticoran said heavily. "All
I know is that they were working their way back to base."

"That's something," Caslet murmured. "We know where
they were a few weeks ago, and we know where they are
now. That gives us a general direction, anyway." He
scratched his eyebrow. "Were these people operating solo,
Captain?"

"They were the whole time we were aboard, but from
the scuttlebutt, they expected to meet up with at least
two or three other ships fairly soon. I'm not sure where,
but there's supposed to be a convoy coming into Posnan
sometime in the next month or so, and they figure they've
got the muscle to take out the escorts."

"In that case, they probably do have some fairly

powerful units, Skipper," MacMurtree pointed out in a worried voice, and Caslet nodded.

"I assume, Captain Sukowski, that we're talking about a *Manticoran* convoy?" he asked gently. Sukowski said nothing, only looked uncomfortable, and the citizen commander nodded. "Forgive me. I shouldn't have pressed you on that, but I doubt even Warnecke would take on a *heavily* escorted convoy. The only people running escort out here at all are you and the Andies, and you're stretched a lot thinner than the IAN."

He gnawed on his thumbnail for a moment, then nodded again to Sukowski.

"All right, Captain. Thank you very much. You've been of great assistance, and I think I can speak for my superiors when I say we'll do our best to find and destroy the rest of these vermin. For now, why don't you go on back to sickbay and get some rest? Commander Hurlman's going to need you when she wakes up again."

"You're right." Sukowski pushed himself to his feet and looked at the three Peeps, then held out his hand to Caslet. "Thank you," he said simply, crushing the citizen commander's hand, then turned and left. The Marine outside the briefing room took him in tow as the hatch closed behind him, and Caslet turned to the other two.

"It's a damned good thing Sukowski and Hurlman were aboard," he said grimly. "At least we know *something* now."

"Perhaps their computers will tell us more," Jourdain said hopefully, but MacMurtree shook her head.

"Sorry, Sir. I got an update from Simonson just before Captain Sukowski joined us. They did manage a data dump on the main system, but that bridge hit blew their astrogation section to hell. We've got a lot of information on their ship and its operations, and their 'captain's' log tells us where they've been, but it refers to their base simply as 'Base,' with no astro references."

"So we ask the crew," Jourdain said, and smiled coldly.

"I think if we offer not to shoot the one who tells us where 'Base' is, someone will come forward."

"We can try, Sir," Caslet sighed, "but now that Sukowski's told us who's behind this, something that didn't make much sense to me before is starting to seem a lot more believable." Jourdain looked a question at him, and the citizen commander shrugged. "These people are actually working under operational security. I think that's why the log never refers to their base system by name. It may also explain why the noncommissioned crew doesn't seem to have any idea where it is. Most of their officers had already been detached to handle prize ships, and their astrogator, captain, and exec were all killed when the bridge lost pressure. No one among the survivors seems to know, and what they don't know—"

"—they can't tell us, even to save their miserable lives," Jourdain finished disgustedly.

"Exactly." Caslet rubbed his jaw thoughtfully, then punched a command into his terminal, summoning a holographic star map. He tapped additional commands, highlighting certain systems, then leaned back and whistled tunelessly as he studied his handiwork.

"You have an idea, Citizen Commander?" Jourdain asked after a moment.

"A couple of them, actually, Sir," Caslet admitted. "Look. We first picked up their trail here in Arendscheldt, then followed them straight to Sharon's Star, right?" Jourdain nodded, and Caslet gestured to two more stars. "Well, according to their captain's log, the last two places they tried before Arendscheldt were Sigma and Hera. Before that they took a prize in Creswell—that's why they didn't have the personnel to man *Erewhon*; they'd used up their surplus crewmen in Creswell—after failing to hit anything in Slocum. You see? They're coming around in an arc, and Sukowski said they meant to rendezvous before hitting a Posnan-bound convoy. I'd guess that means they were heading for either Magyar or Schiller as their next stop. It may also suggest that their base lies down here to the southwest somewhere, but that's a lot more problematical."

"Um." Jourdain studied the chart in turn for several seconds, then nodded. "All right, I follow your logic so far, Citizen Commander, but where is it taking you?"

"Schiller," Caslet replied with a smile. "Magyar's well below Schiller, which puts it a good twenty light-years closer to us than Schiller. If it weren't for Sukowski, that would make Magyar seem more likely as these people's next objective, but Schiller's elevation places it closer to *Posnan*, and if we head straight there, we may get there soon enough to pick off another singleton who *can* tell us where their base is."

"And if they get there in strength first?" Jourdain asked just a bit frostily.

"I'm not feeling particularly suicidal, Sir," Caslet said mildly. "If they're present in strength, there's no way I'd tangle with them without a very pressing reason. But the other thing that makes Schiller more attractive to me than Magyar is that we have a trade legation there, and the attaché has a dispatch boat. If we pass our information to her, she can use that boat to alert Citizen Admiral Giscard even more quickly than we could."

"True," Jourdain murmured, then nodded. "A very good point, Citizen Commander."

"Then do I have your permission to proceed to Schiller?"

"Yes, I think you do," Jourdain agreed.

"Thank you, Sir." Caslet looked at MacMurtree. "You heard the Citizen Commissioner, Allison. Tell Simonson to finish up as quickly as she can, then get the demolition charges planted. I want to pull out within the next two hours."

• CHAPTER TWENTY

"My God, Aubrey! What *happened* to you?"

Aubrey opened his eyes and peered up at Ginger Lewis. His first wandering thought was to wonder what she was doing in the cabin he shared with three other junior petty officers. His second was to wonder what she seemed so worried about. It was only when he got to number three that he realized he was still in sickbay under observation because of a concussion.

"I fell," he said. The words came out a bit slurred and breathy thanks to his puffy lips and a nose which still refused to admit much air, and he closed his eyes again against a fresh wave of pain. Surgeon Lieutenant Holmes promised quick heal would take care of his more spectacular bruises and contusions within the next couple of days. Unfortunately, it hadn't taken hold just yet, and even when it did, his broken nose and cracked ribs were going to take a bit longer.

"The hell you say," Ginger said flatly, and he opened his eyes once more. "Don't bullshit *me*, Wonder Boy. Somebody beat the crap out of you."

Aubrey blinked at her murderous expression. He felt oddly detached, and he wondered why Ginger was so pissed. She wasn't the one who'd been beaten up, after all.

"I fell," he said again. Even in his disoriented condition, he knew he had to stick to his story. It was important, though he had moments when he couldn't remember precisely why. Then he did remember, and his eyes darkened. "I fell," he repeated a third time. "Just tripped over

252

my own feet. Landed on my face, and—"
He shrugged, and winced as the movement sent a fresh, hot stab through him.

"No way," Ginger contradicted in that same flat, tight voice. "You've got two cracked ribs, and Lieutenant Holmes says your head hit something at least three times, Wonder Boy. Now tell me who did it. I *want* his ass."

Aubrey blinked again. How strange. Ginger was angry because of what had happened to him. He'd always liked her, and even through the icy fear which flowed through him every time he thought of Steilman, he felt warmed by her concern. But he couldn't tell her. If he did, she'd do something about it. That would get her into the middle of it, and he couldn't do that to a friend.

"Forget it, Ginger." He tried, without much success, to make his voice come out stronger and more confident. "It's not your problem."

"Oh, yes it is," she said through gritted teeth. "First, you're a friend. Second, according to Tatsumi, it happened in Engineering, and that's my bailiwick. Third, bastards who go around pounding on people need their assholes reamed out. And, fourth, I'm a senior chief now, and I feel like doing a little reaming. So tell me who did this to you!"

"No." He shook his head weakly. "I can't. Stay out of it, Ginger."

"Goddamn it, I am *ordering* you to tell me!" she snapped, but he only shook his head again. She glared at him, eyes crackling, and started to speak again when Lieutenant Holmes turned up.

"That's enough, Senior Chief," the physician said firmly. "He needs to rest. Come back in ten or twelve hours, and you'll probably be able to get more sense out of him."

Ginger looked at the surgeon for a moment, then drew a deep breath and nodded.

"All right, Sir," she said grudgingly, and gave Aubrey another searing glare. "As for you, Wonder Boy, you get your head straightened out. Whether you tell me or not,

I'm going to find whoever did this, and when I do, he can kiss his ass good-bye."

She turned and stalked out of the sickbay, and Holmes shook his head as he watched her go. Then the doctor looked down at Aubrey and quirked an eyebrow.

"I've seen some ticked-off people in my time," he said mildly, "but I don't believe I can recall anyone recently who was quite *that* ticked. I'd advise you to remember the name of whoever you fell over, because I imagine the Senior Chief's going to make your life pure hell until you do." Aubrey looked up without speaking, and Holmes smiled. "Suit yourself, Wanderman . . . but don't say I didn't warn you."

Ginger stalked down the passage from sickbay, then stopped. She stood for a moment, rubbing one eyebrow, then nodded sharply, turned around, and went back the way she'd come. She found the man she wanted in the dispensary. His back was to her as he ran an inventory, but he turned quickly when she cleared her throat. A worried expression chased itself across his face, and then he put his hand comp on hold and cocked his head at her.

"Can I help you, Senior Chief?"

"I believe you can," she told him. "You're the one who found Wanderman, right?"

"Yes, Senior Chief," he said a bit too carefully, and she gave him a thin smile.

"Good. Then maybe *you* can tell me what I want to know, Tatsumi."

"What would that be, Senior Chief?" he asked warily.

"You know damned well what it is," she said in a voice of steel. "He won't tell me who it was, but you know, don't you?"

"I—" Tatsumi hesitated. "I'm not sure what you're getting at, Senior Chief."

"Then let me spell it out," Ginger said softly, stepping closer to him. "He says he fell, you say you *think* he fell, and all three of us know that's bullshit. I want a name,

Tatsumi. I want to know who did that to him, and I want to know now."

Her blue-gray eyes bored into his, and he swallowed. Tension crackled in the dispensary, twisting his nerves, and it took all his strength to wrench his gaze away from hers.

"Look," he said finally, the edges of his voice hoarse, "*he* says he fell, right? Well, I can't tell you any different. I already did all I can do."

"No, you haven't," she said flatly.

"Yes, I have!" He turned back to her, his expression tight. "I came along in time to save his butt, Senior Chief, and I stuck my own neck out to do it, but I'll be *damned* if I stick my head straight into a meat grinder! I like the kid, but I've got problems of my own. You want to know who did it, you get *him* to tell you."

"I can have you in front of the Bosun or the Exec in five minutes, Tatsumi," she said in that same, flat tone. "With your record, I don't think that's a place you want to be. Especially not when silence could be viewed as complicity."

The SBA glared at her, then squared his shoulders.

"You do whatever you want, Senior Chief," he said, "but as far as I'm concerned, this conversation never happened. You get him to tell you, and maybe—*maybe*—I can back him up, but there is no way I'm gonna start naming any names on my own. I try that, and I'm just likely to turn up dead, you understand? You want to send me back to the stockade, fine. Good. You do that. You do anything you think you have to do. But I am *not* naming names on my own—not to you, not to the Bosun or the Exec, or even to the Captain." His eyes flitted away from hers again, and he shrugged. "I'm sorry," he said in a lower voice. "I really am. But that's the way it is."

Ginger rocked back on her heels. Her initial suspicion that Tatsumi been part of Aubrey's beating had been blown out the lock by the depth of the SBA's obvious fear, and that same fear sent an icy wind through her bones. Something even uglier than she'd first guessed must be going on here, and she bit her lip. Aubrey didn't want her involved, and Tatsumi seemed genuinely frightened for his very life. Somehow she felt certain the SBA would have told her if only one person was involved. After all, if Tatsumi and Aubrey both testified against him, Navy discipline would come down on whoever it was like a hammer. They wouldn't have to worry about him again . . . which meant they were worrying about someone *else*. And that suggested . . .

"All right," she said very softly. "You keep your secrets— for now. But I'm going to get to the bottom of this, and don't think I'm going to be the only one looking. You and Aubrey can say whatever you like, but Lieutenant Holmes knows he didn't fall, and you can bet he's going to write up a full report. That's going to get the Bosun and the Master-at-Arms involved, at the very least, and somehow I don't think the Exec's just going to sit this one out, either. With all that weight looking into it from above, someone's going to figure it out, and if you *were* involved, you better pray someone else finds out about it before I do. Is that clear?"

"Clear, Senior Chief," the SBA half-whispered, and she stalked out of the sickbay.

". . . so that's the story, Bosun. Neither one of them will tell me a thing, but I *know* it wasn't any simple fall."

Sally MacBride tipped back her chair and surveyed the furious young senior chief with level brown eyes. Ginger Lewis had been admitted to the close-knit fraternity of *Wayfarer's* senior petty officers less than a month earlier, but MacBride liked what she'd seen of her so far. Lewis was conscientious, hardworking, and firm with her people, but she'd managed to avoid turning into a little tin god to hide any sense of insecurity in her new position. That was the one thing MacBride had most feared when the Old Lady announced Maxwell's and Lewis' promotions. Now she wondered if she should have worried about something else, for she recognized the outrage in the younger woman's eyes. A petty officer who didn't care what happened to her people was useless, but one who let fury govern her actions was almost worse.

"Sit," she said finally, pointing at the only other chair in her cubbyhole office. She waited until her visitor obeyed, then let her own chair rock back upright. "All right," she said crisply, "you've told me what you think happened." Ginger opened her mouth, but a raised hand stopped her before she could speak. "I didn't say you were wrong, I only said that so far it's a case of what you *think* happened. Is there anything inaccurate about that statement?"

Ginger clamped her teeth together, then inhaled sharply and shook her head.

"That's what I thought. Now, it just happens that Lieutenant Holmes has already spoken to me," MacBride went on, "and that *I've* already spoken to Master-at-Arms Thomas. My own theory—and the Lieutenant's—is the same as yours. Unfortunately, the evidence isn't conclusive. Lieutenant Holmes can tell us that, in his expert opinion, Wanderman's injuries aren't the result of a fall, but he can't prove it. If Wanderman himself won't tell us they aren't, there isn't anything official that we can do."

"But he's *scared*, Bosun," Ginger protested. Her voice was softer, with an edge of pain in it, and she looked at MacBride appealingly. "He's a kid on his first deployment, and he's scared to death of whoever did this. That's why he won't tell me anything."

"Maybe you're right. For that matter, maybe I've got a few suspicions of my own about who might have done this." Ginger's eyes sharpened, but MacBride went on levelly. "Mr. Thomas and I will talk to Wanderman in the morning. We'll try to get him to open up. But if he won't, and if Tatsumi won't, then our hands are tied. And if *our* hands are tied, so are yours."

"What do you mean?" Ginger's question came out just a bit too sharply.

"I mean, Senior Chief Lewis, that you are *not* going

to play vigilante or masked avenger in my ship," MacBride said flatly. "I know you and Wanderman trained together. For that matter, I know you think of him as a kid brother. Well, he's not. He's an acting petty officer, and you're a senior chief. You're not children, and this isn't a game. It's his duty to tell us what happened, and he's a good kid. It may take a while, but I think, eventually, he *will* tell us. In the meantime, however, you *aren't* his older sister—or his nurse—and you will refrain from taking any action outside official channels."

"But—" Ginger began, only to choke herself off as MacBride glared at her.

"I'm not in the habit of repeating myself, Senior Chief," she said coldly. "I approve of your concern and sense of responsibility. Those are good things, and they go with your grade. But there's a time to push, and a time *not* to push. There's also a time to step outside channels and a time to make damned sure you don't. You've brought it to my attention, exactly as you're supposed to. If you can convince Wanderman to tell us something more, good. But aside from that, you will leave this matter in *my* hands. Is that clear, Senior Chief Lewis?"

"Yes, Bosun," Ginger said stiffly.

"Good. Then you'd better be going. I believe you go on watch in forty minutes."

Sally MacBride watched the younger woman stalk out of her office and sighed. As she'd hinted to Ginger, she had a very strong suspicion as to what had happened, and she blamed herself for it. Not that it was *all* her fault, but she should have run Steilman out of *Wayfarer's* company the instant she saw his name on the roster. She hadn't, and she wondered how much of that had been pride. She'd kicked him into line once, after all, and she'd been certain she could do it again. For that matter, she was still certain of it . . . she just hadn't counted on what it was likely to cost someone else, and she should have, especially after his original run-in with Wanderman.

She frowned at her blank terminal. She'd kept an eye

on Steilman, but he seemed to have developed a greater degree of animal cunning since their previous cruise together. Of course, he was ten T-years older, as well, and somehow he'd managed to survive all those years without landing in the stockade. That should have told her something right there, yet she still couldn't understand how he'd gotten to Wanderman without her knowing about it. Unless Ginger Lewis' suspicions were correct, that was. Most of *Wayfarer*'s company was as good as any MacBride had ever served with, but there was a small group of genuine troublemakers. So far, she and Master-at-Arms Thomas had managed to keep them in check—or thought they had. Now she had her doubts, and she pursed her lips as she shuffled through her mental index of names and faces.

Coulter, she thought. He was in on it. He and Steilman were both in Engineering. She and Lieutenant Commander Tschu had split them up as best they could, but they were still on the same watch in different sections. That gave them too much time to get their heads together off duty, and it was probable they'd managed to bring in a few more like-minded souls. Elizabeth Showforth, for example. She was running with Steilman, and she was just as bad, in her own way. Then there were Stennis and Illyushin.

MacBride growled to herself. People like Steilman and Showforth sickened her, but they knew how to generate fear, and the inexperience of most of their crewmates would give them more scope for their efforts. Too many of *Wayfarer*'s company were too damned young, without the grit to stand up for themselves. She'd already been picking up rumors of petty thefts and intimidation, but she'd thought it was being held in check and expected the situation to improve as the newbies found their feet. Given the escalation of what had happened to Wanderman, however, it seemed she'd been wrong. And if the youngster wouldn't come forward and admit what had happened, she couldn't take any official action—which would only increase Steilman's stature with his cronies and make the situation still worse.

Sally MacBride didn't like her own conclusions. She knew she could squash Steilman and his bunch like bugs if she had to, but that would mean a full-scale investigation. It would include a crew-wide crackdown, and the consequences for morale and the sense of solidarity she'd been nurturing might be extreme. Yet if something *wasn't* done, the canker coming up from below would have the same effect.

She pondered for another few moments, then nodded. As she'd told Lewis, there was a time not to push . . . but there was also a time *to* push. Lewis was too new in her grade to do that sort of thing, and MacBride couldn't do it herself without making it too obvious that she was doing so. But there were other people who could make their presence felt.

She punched a code into her com.

"Com Center," a voice said, and she smiled thinly.

"This is the Bosun. I need to see Senior Chief Harkness. Find him and ask him to come to my office, would you?"

• CHAPTER TWENTY-ONE

"What *do* we have here?" Captain (JG) Samuel Webster murmured, as much to himself as to *Scheherazade*'s tac officer.

"Don't know, Skip." Commander Hernando shook his head. "They're coming in on a fairly standard intercept vector, but there's two of them. That's outside the profile for freelancers. And see this?" He tapped a command into his console, and the estimated power figures on the Bogey One's impeller wedge blinked. "That's awful high for his observed accel, Skipper. Puts him in at least the heavy cruiser range—and the same holds true for his buddy."

"Wonderful."

Webster sat back and scratched his craggy chin. It wasn't supposed to be this complicated, he reflected, especially not here. Despite the recent jump in losses in this sector, the real hot spots were still supposed to be at Telmach, Brinkman, and Walther in Breslau, or Schiller and Magyar down in southern Posnan. So what were a pair of heavy cruisers doing flying an obvious pursuit vector on a Manticoran merchantman clear over here at Tyler's Star?

"No possibility they're Silesian?" he asked, and Hernando shook his head.

"Not unless the Confeds' EW systems've gotten an awful lot better than they're supposed to be. If these bozos are holding a constant acceleration, they were inside nine light-minutes before we even saw 'em, and they're harder than hell to hold on passive even now. I doubt your standard merchie would have any idea they were out there."

"Um." Webster scratched his chin again and wished Captain Harrington were here to advise him. He was beginning to have a very unpleasant suspicion about those two bogies, and he suddenly felt entirely too junior for what was about to happen.

He raised a hand and beckoned to his exec. Commander DeWitt crossed the bridge to him, and Webster spoke very quietly.

"What do you say to a pair of Peep heavy cruisers, Gus?"

DeWitt turned to give the plot another look. He rubbed one weathered cheek with the knuckle of his right index finger, then nodded slowly.

"Could be, Sir," he agreed. "But if it is, what the hell do we do about them?"

"It doesn't look like we're going to have a whole lot of choice," Webster said wryly.

Captain Harrington's orders were quite clear. He could take on single Peep heavy cruisers with her blessings; if he ran into a battlecruiser—which, given Hernando's still tentative readings on their impeller strengths, either of these two could yet be—or more than one CA, he was supposed to avoid action if possible. Unfortunately, the bogies, whoever and whatever they truly were, were now only five light-minutes back. *Scheherazade* was up to eleven thousand KPS and accelerating at a hundred and fifty gravities, but the bogies were hitting over forty-three thousand and pulling five hundred gees. That meant they'd overtake in a tad over forty-one minutes, and Webster was much too far inside the hyper limit to escape by translating into h-space. However he sliced it, these people were going to overtake him, and there was nothing he could do about it.

Despite the numerical odds, he figured he had an excellent chance to take both of them on and win, especially if they thought he was only an unarmed freighter until he proved differently. Of course, if they turned out to be battlecruisers, he was going to get badly hurt, but

probably not as badly as *they* would. But what if they split up? If Bogey Two hung back out of missile range—which he might well do, since it was hard to conceive of a Peep CO thinking he'd need two heavy cruisers to swat a single merchie—then Webster would never be able to engage him at all. And that meant he was about to give away an awful lot about his ship's capabilities to the bad guys, whatever happened to the ship which closed. On the other hand . . .

"Probable enemy intentions?" he asked DeWitt.

The exec frowned as he considered. He was five T-years older than his captain, and where Webster had been a com specialist for years, DeWitt had followed a straight Tactical track. Despite that, there was no question which of them was in command, and it was a sign of Webster's self-confidence that he could ask the question he'd just posed.

"If these *are* Peeps," DeWitt said slowly, "they must be here to raid our commerce, which would explain a lot about our losses in this sector." Webster nodded, and the exec's frown deepened. "At the same time, we haven't heard a peep—you should pardon the expression—from anyone to confirm their presence. That means they've managed to grab the crews of every ship they've hit so far, right?"

"Exactly," Webster agreed. "Which is probably the best news we've had yet."

"Agreed." DeWitt nodded vigorously. "Even with first-line Peep EW systems, most merchies would see them coming in time to get their crews away by small craft. That means they must've been working in pairs, at least, all along."

"If I were their senior officer," Webster mused, "I'd come burning in with all the overtake I could generate with both ships. Then I'd hit my com the minute my target's maneuvers showed I'd been spotted and order him to maintain com silence and not to take to his shuttles."

"Absolutely," DeWitt said. "With two of them right on top of us and both with plenty of overtake in hand, we'd never be able to get a shuttle away. And no merchant skipper would break com silence when he was looking straight into a pair of heavy cruisers' broadsides. Not in Silesian space, anyway. Maybe in a Manticoran system he'd take the chance, but the odds of anyone here's passing on his message to us range from slim to none, so why risk his ship and crew?"

"All right," Webster said more briskly. "We can't get away, and they *probably* won't split up. That's the good news. The bad news is that they're at least heavy cruisers, which means they'll have decent point defense, and that they can burn past us at over forty thousand KPS. We won't have long to engage, and they're going to be tough missile targets if they've got time to see our birds coming, so we have to take them both out fast and dirty."

DeWitt nodded once more, and Webster glanced at his tac officer.

"Assume what we have here is a pair of Peep CAs, Oliver. Further assume they'll stay together and maintain present acceleration until we respond to their presence in some way. We won't have any choice but to engage, so cook me up the best way to nail them both on the fly."

"Yes, Sir." Hernando glanced back at his plot, eyes suddenly much more wary. "How close are you willing to let them get before we pop them, Skipper? Clear into energy range?"

"Maybe. Our weapons hatches are hard to spot, but if we let them in close, then they've got a chance to use *their* energy mounts, too. Give me a long-range and a short-range option."

"Yes, Sir," the tac officer repeated, and began to talk very earnestly with his assistant.

"Gus," Webster turned back to his exec, "I want you to get on the com with Commander Chi. If we have to drop his LACs, they're going to have a mighty steep velocity disadvantage. Go over the enemy's approach

profile with him to determine optimum launch time for his people. We probably won't be able to get them out as soon as he'd prefer, but I want his best estimate to crank into Oliver's thinking."

"Can do, Sir," DeWitt agreed, and headed for his own command station while Webster leaned back in his chair once more.

"Coming down on three light-minutes, Citizen Captain."

"Good." Citizen Captain Jerome Waters nodded acknowledgment of the report. His bridge crew—including People's Commissioner Seifert—were relaxed and confident, as well they should be. Tyler's Star was virgin territory, but this would be the fifth overall capture for Waters' cruiser division, and so far the entire operation had gone as smoothly as Citizen Admiral Giscard had predicted. The trickiest part had been keeping any of their prizes' crews from getting away, and so far none of them had shown any particular urge to try.

Waters rather regretted that. He hated the Star Kingdom of Manticore with a white and burning passion. Hated it for what its navy had done to the People's Navy. Hated it for building better ships with better weapons than his own government could provide him. And most of all, the ex-Dolist hated it for having an economy which ignored all the "level field" and "economic rights" truisms upon which the People's Republic had based its very existence . . . and still providing its people the highest standard of living in the known galaxy. That was the insult Waters could not forgive. There'd been a time when the Republic of Haven's citizens were at least as affluent as those of Manticore, and by all the standards Waters had been taught from the cradle, the *People's* Republic's citizens should be even *better* off than Manticore's today. Hadn't the government intervened to force the wealthy to pay their fair share? Hadn't it legislated the Economic Bill of

Rights? Hadn't it compelled private industry to subsidize those put out of work by unfair changes in technology or work-force requirements? Hadn't it guaranteed even its least advantaged citizens free education, free medical care, free housing, and a basic income?

Of course it had. And with all those rights guaranteed to them, its citizens should have been affluent and secure, with a thriving economy. But they weren't, and their economy wasn't, and though he would never have admitted it, the Star Kingdom's successes made Jerome Waters feel small and somehow petty. It wasn't *fair* for such economic heretics to have so much while the faithful had so little, and he longed to smash them into dust as their sins demanded.

And if a few stupid merchant spacers were dumb enough to think he didn't mean his order not to bail out, then he would take immense pleasure in blowing them into very, very tiny pieces.

"Any sign they know we're back here?"

"No, Citizen Captain." No one in Jerome Waters' crew would ever dream of neglecting one iota of the new regime's egalitarian forms of address. "They're holding course all fat and happy. If they knew we were back here, they'd already have responded somehow, if only with a com message."

"How long until they *have* to know we're here?"

"Can't be more than another three or four minutes, Citizen Captain," his tac officer replied. "Even with civilian-grade sensors, our impeller signatures have to burn through pretty quickly now."

"All right." Waters exchanged a glance with People's Commissioner Seifert, then nodded to his com officer. "Stand by to transmit our orders the instant they react, Citizen Lieutenant."

"All right, Skipper," Hernando said. "Even a half-blind merchie would see them by now."

"Agreed." Webster heard the tenseness in his own voice and made himself relax his shoulders as he'd seen Captain

Harrington do in Basilisk and Hancock, and his next words came out in calm and easy tones. "All right, people—I do believe it's time. Helm, execute Alpha One."

"Well, they see us now, Citizen Captain," Waters' exec said as the freighter's acceleration suddenly rose to a hundred and eighty gravities and it swerved wildly to starboard. The citizen captain nodded and swivelled his eyes to his com officer, but the message was already going out.

"Manticoran merchant ship, this is the Republican heavy cruiser *Falchion*! Do not attempt to communicate. Do not attempt to abandon ship. Resume original flight profile and maintain until boarded. Any resistance will be met with deadly force. *Falchion*, out."

The curt voice rattled from the bridge speakers, and Webster glanced at Hernando and DeWitt.

"Exactly according to script," he observed. "Sound like they mean business, too, don't they?" More than one person on the bridge actually smiled, despite their inner tension, and he nodded to his own com officer. "You know what to tell them, Gina."

"Citizen Captain, they claim they're not Manticoran," Waters' com officer said. "They say they're Andermani."

"The hell they do," Waters said grimly. "That's a Manty transponder code. Tell them they have one more chance to resume course before we open fire."

"Manticoran freighter, you are *not*, repeat *not*, an Andermani vessel. I repeat. Resume your original heading and acceleration and maintain further com silence, or we will fire into you. This is your final warning! *Falchion*, out."

"Goodness, they sound testy, don't they?" Webster murmured. "Are they in range, Oliver?"

"Just about, Sir. Missile range in forty-one seconds."

"Then I suppose we shouldn't try his patience too far. Time for Alpha Two."

"Jesus, look at that idiot!" Waters' exec muttered, and the citizen captain shook his head in disgust. Having begun by attempting to run—which was manifestly impossible—and then trying his clumsy bluff, the Manty skipper had obviously panicked. He wasn't simply resuming his original *heading*; he was trying to get back onto his original *vector*, and his second course change was even wilder than the first. He clawed back to port, rolling madly in the process to present the belly of his wedge to *Falchion* and her consort, and Waters snorted.

"Helm, reverse acceleration," he said.

"Here they come," Webster murmured. Both Peep cruisers had made turnover, decelerating hard. They'd still burn past *Scheherazade* at well over thirty thousand KPS, but their deceleration rate was almost three times the best Webster's ship could possibly turn out. There was no way he'd be able to avoid coming right to them once they overflew, and they knew it.

But they didn't know what they were tangling with, he thought grimly. That much was obvious. He'd been careful to present the belly of his wedge to the Peeps while his tactical crews opened the hatches which normally hid their weapons, because opening those hatches had left only the thin plastic patches Captain Harrington had sold *Vulcan* on, and those patches were transparent to radar. A radar hull map would have revealed something very strange about *Scheherazade*'s flanks, and he'd gone to some lengths to be sure the Peeps hadn't gotten one.

But they hadn't even tried to look that closely, and now they were coming in on Webster's ship with sublime confidence. They had their sterns pointed almost directly at her, with only their chase armaments available to them . . . and with the wide-open after aspects of their wedges sitting there in front of God and everybody.

Samuel Webster felt his nerves tingle. Captain Harrington would have loved Hernando's plan and his own refinements to it. But now was no time to be thinking of the Captain. This maneuver was time-critical, with every aspect painstakingly preprogrammed. Either it worked perfectly, or things were going to get very messy indeed, and he looked at his tac officer.

"All right, Oliver. Call the shot," he said quietly, and Hernando nodded.

"Aye, aye, Sir. Helm, stand by to execute Baker One on my command." The tac officer cast another glance over his own panel, checking the firing solution already locked into it, then dropped his eyes to the plot as the range readouts flashed downward.

Samuel Webster sat very still. He'd been tempted to go for Hernando's longer-ranged option, relying on his missile pods to beat the Peeps to death, but there'd been too much chance at least one of them would successfully evade at extreme ranges. A medium-range engagement would have bought *Scheherazade* the worst of both worlds. The Peeps would have been too close to let them break off, yet too far away for his energy weapons to engage, while his birds' flight time would have let them get off at least two and probably three broadsides of their own, and despite her vast size, his ship could take far less damage than either of her opponents.

But if he couldn't fight at long range without letting somebody get away and couldn't fight at medium range without getting badly mangled himself, that left only the short-range option. He needed to cripple both of them in the minimum amount of time, and that meant getting in the first hits with light-speed weapons at the closest possible range. Of course, if he let them get that close and *didn't* cripple them with the first broadside, they were going to rip his ship apart, but not before he smashed both of them into wreckage, as well.

"Stand by," Hernando murmured. "Steady . . . steady . . . *Now!*"

"Citizen Captain! The Manty—!"
Waters jerked up in his chair as the Manticoran freighter swerved suddenly to port. It was insane! If she was trying to evade, she'd picked the worst possible time, for his cruisers would pass on either side of her in less than twelve seconds, and his broadsides would tear her to pieces!
"Stand by to en—" he began, and that was when the universe blew apart.

"Engaging—*now!*" Hernando snapped, and thin plastic hatch shields vanished as eight massive grasers smashed out from *Scheherazade*'s port broadside. The range was barely four hundred thousand kilometers, there was no sidewall to interdict, and seven of the eight beams scored direct hits.
Both heavy cruisers staggered as the kinetic energy transferred into them, and huge, splintered fragments of hull spun away from them. Their flared sterns tore apart like paper, shedding wreckage, weapons, men, and women in a storm front of escaping atmosphere. Their armor meant less than nothing against superdreadnought-scale energy fire, and the grasers blew deep into their hulls, shredding bulkheads and smashing weapons. Both ships lost their after impeller rings almost instantly, and *Falchion*'s emissions signature flickered madly as the power surges bled through her systems.
But *Scheherazade* didn't linger to gloat. Even as Hernando fired, her helm was hard over, completing her hundred-and-eighty-degree turn to port. In the same flashing seconds, she rolled up on her side. The mauled cruisers roared past her, surviving broadside weapons firing frantically in local control over the deep-space equivalent of open sights, but they had no target: only the impenetrable roof and floor of her wedge.
"Baker Two!" Hernando snapped, and the helmsman

threw his helm over yet again. The Q-ship circled still further to port, coming perpendicular to the Peeps' vectors, and rolled back upright, firing as she came. Her broadside flashed once more, spewing missiles as well as grasers this time. Her fire ripped straight down the *fronts* of her enemies' wedges, and even as her port weapons fired, her starboard sidewall dropped and six LACs exploded from their bays to accelerate after the heavy cruisers at six hundred gravities.

The Peeps did their best, but that first, devastating rake had wreaked havoc on their electronics. Central fire control was a shambles, fighting to sort itself out and reestablish a grasp on the situation as secondary systems came on-line. Their surviving weapons were all in emergency local control, dependent on their own on-mount sensors and tracking computers. Most of them didn't even know where *Scheherazade* was, and frantic queries hammered CIC. But CIC needed time to recover from that terrible blow . . . and the cruisers didn't have time. They had only fifteen seconds, and only a single laser smashed into *Scheherazade* in reply to her second, devastating broadside.

Webster's ship shuddered as that solitary hit ripped into her unarmored hull, and damage alarms wailed. Missile Three vanished, and the same hit smashed clear to Boat Bay One and tore two cutters and a pinnace—none, fortunately, manned—to splinters. Seventeen men and women were killed, and eleven more wounded, but for all that, *Scheherazade* got off incredibly lightly.

The Peeps didn't. Hernando's second broadside wasn't as accurate as his first; there were too many variables, changing too rapidly, for him to achieve the same precision. But it was accurate enough against wide open targets, and PNS *Falchion* vanished in a boil of light as one of *Scheherazade's* grasers found her forward fusion room. There were no life pods, and Webster's eyes whipped to the second cruiser just as her bow blew open like a shredded stick. Her forward impellers died instantly, stripping away her wedge and her sidewalls, leaving her only reaction thrusters for maneuver, and Webster bared his teeth.

"Launch the second LAC squadron," he said, and then flicked his hand at his com officer. "Put me on, Gina."

"Hot mike, Skipper," Gina Alveretti replied, and Samuel Houston Webster spoke in cold, precise tones.

"Peep cruiser, this is Her Majesty's Armed Merchant Cruiser *Scheherazade*. Stand by to be boarded. And, as you yourself said—" he smiled ferociously at his pickup "—any resistance to our boarders will be met with deadly force."

"I'm beginning to feel a bit like a father whose children stay out after curfew," Citizen Admiral Javier Giscard observed as he poured fresh wine into People's Commissioner Eloise Pritchart's glass. It was as well for the Committee of Public Safety's peace of mind that neither it nor its minions in StateSec suspected how well Giscard and Pritchart got along. Had they known, they would have been quite shocked, for Giscard and his watchdog were in bed together—literally.

"How so?" Pritchart asked now, sipping her wine. She knew as well as Giscard what would happen if StateSec ever realized the true nature of their relationship. But she also had no intention of letting Giscard get away from her. He was not only a brilliant and insightful officer, he was an outstanding *man*. He'd been trained by one of the People's Navy's finest prewar captains—Alfredo Yu— and, like his mentor, he'd been far better than the old regime had deserved. Pritchart often wondered what would have happened if Yu hadn't been hounded into defecting by his own superiors after that fiasco in Yeltsin. He and Javier together would have made a magnificent combination, but now they were on opposite sides. She hoped the two of them never found themselves directly facing one another, for she knew how deeply Javier respected his old teacher. But Javier had also hated the

Legislaturalists with a passion. He might not care for the new regime—for which Pritchart couldn't blame him as much as she wished she could—but he was loyal. Or would be unless StateSec did something to drive him into being *dis*loyal.

But Eloise Pritchart intended to made very certain nothing like that happened. Javier was too valuable an officer . . . and she loved him too much.

"Hm?" he asked now, nibbling her ear while his hand stroked her hip under the sheet.

"I asked why you feel like a harassed parent?"

"Oh. Well, it's just that some of the children are staying out late to play. I'm not too concerned over *Vaubon*—Caslet's a good officer, and if he's exercised his discretion and gone someplace else, he had a good reason. But I *am* a little concerned over Waters. I should never have given him the option of cruising as far as Tyler's Star before he returned to the rendezvous."

"You don't like Waters, do you?" Pritchart asked, and he shrugged.

"I'm not picking on him for any excess of revolutionary zeal, Citizen Commissioner," he said wryly, tacitly acknowledging the powerful patrons Waters' ideological fervor had bought him. "It's his judgment that worries me. The man hates the Manties too much."

"How can someone hate the enemy 'too much'?" From any other commissioner, that question would have carried ominous overtones, but Pritchart was genuinely curious.

"Determination is a good thing," Giscard explained very seriously, "and sometimes hate can help generate that. I don't like it, because whatever our differences with the Manties, they're still human beings. If we expect them to act professionally and humanely where our people are concerned, we have to act the same way where *their* people are concerned." He paused, and Pritchart nodded before he went on. "The problem with someone like Waters, though, is that hate begins to substitute for good sense. He's a well-trained, competent officer, but he's also young for his rank, and he could have used more experience before he made captain. I don't suppose he's all that different from most of our captains—or admirals," he admitted with a wry grin, "—in that respect, given what happened to the old officer corps. But he's too eager, too fired up. I'm a little worried by how it may affect his judgment, and I wish I'd kept him on a shorter leash."

"I see." Pritchart leaned back, platinum hair spilling over her lover's shoulder, and nodded slowly. "Do you really think he's gotten himself into some sort of trouble?"

"No, not really. I *am* a bit concerned over the reports that the Manties've sent Q-ships out here. If they cruise in company, two or three of them could be a nasty handful for someone who dives right in on them, and Waters had headed out before we got the dispatch alerting us to their presence. But he's under orders to hit only singletons, and I don't see one Q-ship beating up on a pair of *Sword*-class CAs unless the cruisers screw up by the numbers. No, it's more of a feeling that I ought to be looking over his shoulder more closely than anything else, Ellie."

"From what I've seen so far, I'd listen to that 'feeling,' Javier," Pritchart said seriously. "I respect your instincts."

"Among other things, I hope?" he said with a boyish smile as his hand explored under the sheets, and she smacked his bare chest lightly.

"Stop that, you corrupter of civic virtue!"

"I think not, Citizen Commissioner," he replied, and she twitched in pleasure. But then his hand paused. She pushed up on an elbow to demand its return, then stopped with a resigned smile. She did love the man, but *Lord*, he could be exasperating! Inspiration struck him at the damnedest times, and he always had to chase the new idea down before he could set it aside.

"What is it?"

"I was just thinking about the Manty Q-ships," Giscard mused. "I wish we could have confirmed whether or not Harrington is in command of them."

"I thought you just said a Q-ship was no match for a heavy cruiser," Pritchart pointed out. He nodded, and she shrugged. "Well, you've got *twelve* heavy cruisers, and eight *battle*cruisers. That seems like a reassuring amount of overkill to me."

"Oh, agreed. Agreed. But if they're all busy looking *here*, maybe we should go hunting somewhere *else*. Whatever the theoretical odds, there's always room for something to go wrong in an engagement, you know. And a Q-ship *is* likely to beat off one of our units—one of our light cruisers, say—and blow the entire operation by discovering our presence here."

"So?"

"So, Citizen Commissioner," Giscard said, setting his wineglass aside to free both hands and turning to her with the smile she loved, "it's time to adjust our operational patterns. We can leave dispatches for Waters and Caslet at all the approved information drops, but the rest of us are concentrated here right now. Under the circumstances, I think I'll just have a word with my staff about potential new hunting grounds . . . later, of course," he added wickedly, and kissed her.

• CHAPTER TWENTY-TWO

Senior Chief Electronics Mate Lewis tried hard to keep a scowl off her face as she entered Impeller One. This wasn't Ginger's duty station, and she didn't want to be here. Unfortunately, there was a glitch in Impeller One's links to Damage Control Central, and Lieutenant Silvetti, Ginger's boss in DCC, had sent her to supervise the techs looking for the fault. It wasn't, strictly speaking, part of her job as DCC Chief of the Watch to make routine repairs, but Silvetti had already learned to rely on her troubleshooting instincts, and the inexperienced third-class petty officer whose crew had caught the detail was likely to need a little nursemaiding.

Ginger couldn't fault Silvetti's logic, particularly since it let him designate her as a "casualty" and put Chief Sewell into her slot in DCC for the rest of the exercise. Engineering had made strides over the last few weeks, but the department as a whole was still sub-standard and its people needed all the drills they could get. What Ginger *did* object to was that Randy Steilman was assigned to Impeller One, and she'd fully intended to obey Sally MacBride's orders to stay clear of him. Not because she agreed with them, but because they *were* orders.

"Howdy, Ginger." It was Bruce Maxwell, as newly promoted to senior chief as Ginger but ten years older and tough as a well seasoned tree stump. He was chief of the watch for Impeller One, and she didn't envy him a bit. Steilman was on Maxwell's watch, and even with his tough, no-nonsense attitude, that was enough to bring his crew's

276

efficiency rating down a full ten percentage points. Not because Steilman didn't know his job, but because he had a constitutional objection to *doing* that job.

"Hi, Bruce," she replied, standing aside to clear the hatch for PO Jansen and his crew.

"Understand we've got a telemetry problem?" Maxwell raised an eyebrow as Jansen's people clustered around the data links which drove DCC's repeater displays for Impeller One.

"Yeah." Ginger watched Jansen go to work. She had no intention of getting involved until and unless Jansen asked for help, and his people looked good as they set up portable work stands to hold their equipment and got right down to it. "Could just be a bad line plug," she told Maxwell, "but I doubt it. Something took out our readouts on all your odd-numbered nodes."

"Just the odd numbers?"

"Yep. That's the problem. They're all on the same primary link, but there're two separate secondaries, either of which should carry the load alone. Makes me think it's something to do with the monitoring system itself." She shook her head. "I wish *Vulcan*'d had time to do a compete refit on the drive rooms."

"You and me both," Maxwell agreed sourly. Naval designers were great believers in redundancy, and a Navy impeller room would have had two complete *primary* data links, which would have been as widely separated as possible to prevent a single hit from taking both out. Moreover, every line would have served a separate monitoring system, each totally independent of and isolated from all the others. *Wayfarer*'s designers had seen no reason to include battle damage in their consideration of things which might go wrong, however. Her cost-conscious civilian ancestry showed all too clearly in her maintenance links in general, but especially here.

"If we're lucky, it's a minor hardware problem," Ginger

said hopefully, "but if it's in the software—" She shrugged, and Maxwell nodded glumly, then shrugged.

"Well, wherever it is, I'm sure you'll find it," he said encouragingly, and turned back to his own duties.

A part of Ginger's brain watched him move off towards the after end of the huge compartment, vanishing around the far side of a towering bank of generators, but most of her attention was on Jansen and his people. She stood to one side, ready to step in if he screwed up and available for advice if he wanted it, and gave a mental nod of approval as she watched his people. He had two of them checking the physical circuits, but his own focus was on the monitoring system itself, which meant he was thinking the same thing Ginger was.

Several minutes passed, and she drifted closer to watch Jansen's test screen over his shoulder. The third-class glanced up, then gave her a smile of mild triumph.

"Hardware checks out clean, Senior Chief," he reported. "Just one problem: none of these nice, functional systems are doing their jobs."

"And why do you suppose that is?" she asked.

"Well, given that all the hardware on the front end looks good—sensors and interfaces all check out at a hundred percent—and the CPU tests clean, too, it's got to be software-related. I'm interrogating the software now, but if I had to make a bet, I'd put five bucks on corruption of one of the primary execution files. It'd have to be something like that to take the whole system down. Only, if that's what it is, I can't figure out why none of the self-tests twanged back in DCC."

"Where's the self-test software loaded?" Ginger asked.

"It's— Oh." Jansen grinned a bit sheepishly. "I keep forgetting this is a civilian design. It's right here, isn't it?"

"Right." Ginger nodded. "That's why I'm going to take your bet. *My* five bucks says the fault's either in the communications protocols or else that it's a hardware fault after all. If the data link is down, or if the com interface just isn't accepting command input, then the system never got the message to come up and report to DCC in the first place, and—"

"—and if the monitoring system never came up, then the secondaries wouldn't do us a bit of good because they're output only," Jansen finished. "You're right. That would duplicate a dead computer, wouldn't it?"

"Why they pay me the big bucks now," Ginger told him, patting him on the shoulder with a grin. Jansen returned it and started to look back at his display, then jumped in alarm at the sudden, shocking clatter of metal on metal. Ginger's head whipped around, and her blue-gray eyes flashed as she saw the source of the sound. One of Jansen's techs sat on the deck, face clenched with pain while his left hand clutched his right to his chest, and his tool kit's contents had cascaded over the decksole around him, but that wasn't what lit the dangerous glitter in her eyes.

Randy Steilman stood looking down at the tech, shaking his head while an unpleasant smirk twisted his lips. He started to step away, and Ginger took two long strides towards him.

"Hold it right there, Steilman!" her voice cracked across the space between them, and he stopped, then turned with slow, unspoken insolence to face her. His eyes surveyed her with an insolent familiarity all their own, and he cocked an eyebrow.

"Yes, Senior Chief?" he asked with elaborate innocence, but she ignored him to look down at the injured electronics tech. Two of the young man's fingers were bloody, and one of them looked broken to her.

"What happened, Dempsey?"

"I-I don't know," the tech got out through gritted teeth. "I just reached for my kit, and—" He shrugged helplessly, and Ginger looked at the woman who'd been working with him.

"I don't know either, Senior Chief," she said. "I was watching the display. We needed a number-three spanner to get the cover off the next port, and Kirk reached for it, and then I heard it all hit the deck. By the time I looked up, it was all over."

"You still need me?" Steilman put in lazily. Ginger shot him a dangerous look, and he smiled back blandly. She bit down on a sharp remark, mindful of MacBride's orders, and stooped to examine Dempsey's work stand. One look was all it took: both legs at its right end had collapsed, and the locking lever swung loose to her touch.

She straightened slowly, and the fire in her eyes had gone cold as she turned to Steilman.

"I hope you still think this is funny in a few minutes," she told him in an icy voice.

"Me? Think it's funny? Now, why would I think anything like that?" he asked with another of those mocking smiles.

"Because I watched Dempsey and Brancusi set up myself, Steilman. I *saw* Dempsey lock those legs, and they sure as hell didn't unlock themselves on their own."

"What're you saying? You think *I* had something to do with this?" Steilman's smile had changed, and there was an ugly twist to his lips. "You're outa your fucking mind!"

"You're on report, Steilman," Ginger said coldly, and an even uglier light flared in his eyes.

"You're full of shit, *Senior Chief*," he sneered. "You can't prove I did shit to that stand."

"Maybe I can and maybe I can't," Ginger said flatly, "but at the moment, you're on report for insolence."

"*Insolence?*" Steilman said incredulously. "You got delusions of grandeur for a jumped up—"

"Say it and you're dog meat," Ginger snapped, and he paused, mouth gaping open in sheer surprise. Then his right hand clenched into his fist, and he started forward.

Ginger watched him come, not giving an inch. She watched the fist come up and willed it to strike, because the minute it did, Steilman's ass was hers. Striking a petty officer wasn't the capital offense striking an officer was, but it was close enough, and—

"*Right* there, Steilman!" a baritone voice barked, and Steilman froze. He turned his head, and his jaw clenched as he saw Bruce Maxwell bearing down on him. He looked back at Ginger, giving her a look filled with hate, and she swore silently. Why in *hell* had Bruce had to turn up at exactly the wrong moment?

"What the fuck d'you think you're doing?!" Maxwell snarled, and Steilman shrugged.

"Me and the Senior Chief were just having a little difference of opinion."

"Bullshit! Goddamn it, I have had it up to *here* with your crap, Steilman!"

"I didn't do nothing," Steilman insisted sullenly. "I was just standing here, and she jumped my ass over what one of *her* stupid fuckers did."

"Ginger?" Maxwell looked at her, and she looked back levelly.

"Call the Master-at-Arms," she said, the corner of her eye watching Steilman stiffen in the start of true uneasiness at last. "Steilman's on report for insolence—and I want this stand checked for prints."

"Prints?" Maxwell looked puzzled, and she smiled thinly.

"Somebody unlocked its legs to cause it to collapse. Now, it may have been one of my people, but I don't believe it for a minute. I think somebody else did it just for the *fun* of it, and I don't see anyone in this compartment in gloves, do you?"

"But—" Maxwell began, only to be cut off.

"It's not just a prank," Ginger said coldly. "Look at Dempsey's hand. We've got personal injury here. That makes it an Article Fifty, and I want the ass of whoever did it."

Maxwell looked down at the sitting tech, and his face tightened as he took in the impossible angle of his ring finger. When he looked back at Steilman, his expression was bleak and cold, but it was Ginger he spoke to.

"You got it, Ging," he said flatly, and beckoned to another petty officer. "Jeff, go get Commander Tschu, then buzz Mr. Thomas."

*   *   *

"You sent for me, Ma'am?"

"Yes, I did, Rafe. Sit down, please." Honor turned from her contemplation of a bulkhead plaque with the image of a sailplane etched into its heat-warped golden alloy and pointed at the chair facing her desk in her day cabin. She waited until Cardones had seated himself, then folded her hands behind her and regarded him for a long, silent moment.

"What's this I hear about Wanderman?" she asked finally, coming to the point with characteristic bluntness, and Cardones sighed. He'd hoped she wouldn't hear about it until he'd managed to deal with it, but he should have known better. He'd never been able to figure out how she stayed so thoroughly abreast of the most minute happenings aboard her ship. He was certain MacGuiness was part of her network, and no doubt her Grayson armsmen were, as well, now that she had them. Yet he felt certain she would have managed the same thing without any of them.

"I'd intended to take care of it before bringing it to your attention, Ma'am," he said. It was never a good idea for an exec to prevaricate to his CO. At the same time, it was the exec's job to deal with things like this without involving his skipper. The authority of the captain of a Queen's ship was the ultimate sanction against the improper actions of any crew, and it was properly held in reserve until there was no option but to employ it. Once the captain became involved, there was no turning back from the full force of the Articles of War, and Cardones, like Honor, believed it was almost always better to salvage a situation than to call in the heavy artillery.

But sometimes there was no choice but to roll out the big guns, he thought glumly, and the desire to salvage what one could was no excuse for allowing an animal capable of assaulting his own crewmates to go unpunished.

"I appreciate your motives and your position, Rafe,"

Honor said now, seating herself behind her desk and cocking her chair back, "but I'm picking up some rumors I don't much care for . . . including some about an episode in Impeller One." Nimitz dropped from his perch to leap into her lap and sat upright, leaning back against her to regard the exec with his own grass-green gaze, and she rubbed his ears.

"I don't much care for them myself, Ma'am, but at the moment, we're stymied. As far as Wanderman's concerned, he's insisting he fell, and Tatsumi, the SBA who carried him into sickbay, claims he doesn't know anything about it." The exec held up his hands. "I think they're both lying . . . but they're both scared to death, too. Unless something changes, I don't believe either of them will come forward, and unless they do, we don't have an official leg to stand on."

"What does the Master-at-Arms say?"

"Thomas took some of his people and had a very close look at the site of the 'fall.' It wasn't hard to pinpoint—Wanderman bled a good bit. There's nothing in the area for him to have fallen over, and the blood spots are close to the bulkhead, which isn't exactly where someone moving down the middle of the passage would be likely to hit his face in a fall. None of that is conclusive, however, and Wanderman *could* have tripped over his own two feet if he was moving quickly enough."

"And his ribs?" Honor asked quietly.

"Again, unlikely but possible," Cardones sighed. "Angie and I have discussed ways a fall could have inflicted his injuries. We've even run computer models. I'd say it'd take a professional contortionist to manage most of the ways he could have done it, but you know how awkwardly people can land when they're not expecting to fall. My own belief—and that of the medical department, the Bosun, and the Master-at-Arms—is that someone beat him up. Speaking for myself and, I think, the Bosun, we think it was a power tech named Steilman, but we can't prove it. We also believe that whoever was beating on him was interrupted by Tatsumi's arrival. I've considered trying to break Tatsumi down. He's got some serious black marks on his record, and I might be able to sweat the truth out of him, but Angie doesn't want me to. She says he's one of the best SBAs she's ever seen, and whatever his past record may've been like, he's kept his nose clean aboard *Wayfarer* and, apparently, on his last two deployments. If he's really rehabilitated, I don't want to undo what he's managed to put back together."

"And Impeller One?"

"Part of that one is crystal clear, Ma'am. There's no question about Steilman's insolence. There were over twenty witnesses. Some of 'em were slow speaking up— because they're scared of Steilman, I'd say—but they all support Senior Chief Lewis' version of what he said. The other part's not as clear, though. Lewis was smart to try, but Thomas' people couldn't get a clear set of prints off the work stand that collapsed. They managed to pull two partials that definitely don't belong to the people who were using it, but they're too smeared to say more than that. It's pretty clear somebody deliberately unlocked the legs so it fell, but we can't prove it was Steilman."

"But you think it was," Honor said flatly.

"Yes, Ma'am, I do. He's trouble with a capital 'T,' and the fact that Wanderman won't identify him as the one who beat him up is only making him worse. That's one reason I thought so hard about sweating Tatsumi, but, like I say, if he's really put himself back together, we could end up washing out his career right along with Steilman's."

"Um." Honor swiveled her chair slowly back and forth, rubbing the tip of her nose, and frowned. "I don't want to do that either, Rafe . . . but I also won't tolerate this sort of thing. If the only way to get to the truth and put a stop to it is to sweat Tatsumi, we may not have a choice. He's only one person, and we've got an entire ship's company to think about."

"I know that, Ma'am, and if it comes to that, I'll do it. But given what's already happened to Wanderman and how frightened Tatsumi is, I'd also like to proceed cautiously." Cardones scratched an eyebrow, and his hawk-like face was uncharacteristically worried. "The problem is that we don't know everything that's going on. The Bosun and I both *think* Steilman's behind it, but she's also picking up rumbles that he isn't acting alone. Even if we brigged him preemptively, we couldn't be sure one of his cronies wouldn't get to Tatsumi or Wanderman before they talked to us. I suppose we could put both of *them* in protective custody and keep them there until they decide to tell us, but I can't do the same thing with Lewis, and just locking up Wanderman and Tatsumi would constitute an escalation I'd like to avoid. In the short term, it would only point out that Steilman's getting away with it for now."

Honor nodded, still rubbing the tip of her nose, then made herself sit back and folded her hands across Nimitz's soft, fluffy coat. Years of command experience kept her expression calm, but rage boiled deep inside her. She hated bullies, and she despised the sort of scum who could band together to create the kind of fear Cardones was describing. More than that, Steilman's victims were members of *her* crew. She didn't know Kirk Dempsey, but she did know Wanderman, and she liked the youngster. Yet that was almost beside the point. It was the Navy's responsibility—and, aboard *Wayfarer*, that meant *her* responsibility—to see to it that things like this didn't happen and that people who tried to make them happen paid the price. But Cardones was right. As long as Wanderman and Tatsumi refused to name names and they couldn't prove Steilman had caused the "accident" in Impeller One, there were no official grounds for the only sort of action which was likely to call him to heel.

She gazed down at her blotter for two endless minutes of thought, then inhaled sharply.

"Do you want *me* to talk to Wanderman?"

"I don't know, Ma'am," Cardones said slowly. One thing the exec was certain of was that if any officer in *Wayfarer* could get Wanderman to open up, it was the captain.

The kid idolized her, and he trusted her. He might just tell her who'd attacked him. But he might *not*, too. Not only was he scared half out of his mind, but by now he'd insisted on his "fall" in so many interviews that changing his story would be the same as admitting he'd lied, and Wanderman was young enough to feel the humiliation of that deeply.

"There's something else I'd like to try first, Ma'am," the exec said after a few seconds. Honor cocked an eyebrow at him, and he smiled thinly. "The Bosun's decided that what Wanderman may need is a little, ah, *counseling*," he said, "so she's asked Chief Harkness if he'd care to play mentor for the kid."

"Harkness?" Honor pursed her lips, and then she chuckled. There was something evil about the sound, and her almond eyes gleamed with chill delight. "I hadn't considered that," she admitted. "He *would* be a . . . reassuring presence, wouldn't he?"

"Yes, Ma'am. The only thing I'm a little worried about is his tendency to take direct action," Cardones replied, and Honor's eyes flickered as she remembered a conversation in which Admiral White Haven had lectured *her* on the disadvantages of direct action. Still, there were times when that was precisely what a situation called for, and she trusted MacBride's and Harkness' judgment. Every commissioned officer knew who really ran the Queen's Navy, and she was more than willing to give her senior noncoms a little creative freedom of action.

"All right, Rafe," she said at length. "I'll leave that side with you and the Bosun for the moment, but we can hammer Steilman right now for the insolence charge. Captain's Mast tomorrow for Mr. Steilman. We'll see how he likes being a power tech *third*-class, and I want a chance for a little *talk* with him. And I want an eye kept on Wanderman—and Tatsumi, for that matter. I don't want anything else happening to them before we get to the bottom of this. I'll stay out of it to give you—and Chief Harkness—some room to maneuver, but if Wanderman has any more trouble or anyone else 'falls down' or

has an 'accident,' the gloves come off."
She smiled grimly. "All the *way* off," she
added softly.

"Well, well, kid. I see you're up and around again."
Aubrey Wanderman turned quickly, wincing with the
pain in his knitting ribs, at the sound of the deep voice.
The burly, battered looking senior chief in the open hatch
wore the crossed missiles of a gunner's mate. He was a
big man—not as big as Steilman, but five centimeters
taller than Aubrey—and he looked tough. Aubrey had
seen him around, but he had no idea who he was . . .
or, for that matter, why he'd come by sickbay.
"Uh, yes, Senior Chief—?" he said uncertainly.
"Harkness," the senior chief said, tapping the name
patch on the right breast of his utility shipsuit. "I'm in
Flight Ops."
"Oh." Aubrey nodded, but his confusion showed. He
didn't know anyone in Flight Operations, but he knew
the name "Harkness." The senior chief's reputation was
something of a legend, though rumor had it that he'd
reformed of late. Yet Aubrey could think of no possible
reason for Harkness to visit *him*.
"Yeah." Harkness sat on the unoccupied bed opposite
the one Aubrey had spent the last two days in and
grinned. "Understand you had a little accident, kid."
Being called "kid" by Harkness didn't offend Aubrey
the way it did when other old sweats used the term, but
he felt a familiar chill at the word "accident." So that was
it. Harkness was here to try to get him to talk, and Aubrey
felt his face stiffen.
"Yeah," he said, looking away. "I fell."
"Crap." The word came out without heat. In fact,
Harkness sounded almost amused, and Aubrey felt a hot
flush replace his earlier chill. It was hardly *funny*, after
all! His eyes darted back to Harkness, bright with anger,
but the senior chief simply gave him the lazy, confident
grin of a Gryphon kodiak maximus or a Sphinx hexapuma,
and Aubrey flushed.

Harkness let silence linger for several moments, then leaned back on his elbows, half reclining across the bed.

"Look, kid," he rumbled reasonably, "I know that's crap, *you* know it's crap, the Bosun knows it's crap—hell, even the *Old Lady* knows it's crap. You're lying your ass off, aren't you?" He held Aubrey's eyes with that same lazy challenge, then nodded when the younger man said nothing. "Yep, and so is Tatsumi," he went on calmly. "I don't really know as I blame either of you—Steilman can be a nasty SOB—but you don't really think it's going to end here, do you?"

Aubrey felt a fresh, deeper chill as he heard Steilman's name. He hadn't told a soul, and he was sure Tatsumi hadn't, but Harkness knew anyway, and if he went to the Bosun or the Exec, Steilman would never believe *Aubrey* hadn't.

"I—" he began, then closed his mouth and stared at Harkness helplessly.

"Let me explain something." The senior chief's deep voice held an odd note of compassion. "See, I'm not here to ask you to name any names, and I'm not gonna go running to the Bosun or Mr. Thomas with anything you tell me. I happen to think *you* should go to them, but that's up to you. It's not a decision anyone else can make for you, though you might want to think about what you're gonna tell Captain Harrington if *she* decides to ask. Take it from me, kid, when the Old Lady asks questions, she gets answers, and you *don't* want to be the one who pisses her off." Aubrey swallowed, and the senior chief chuckled. "'Course, that's up to you, too, and I'm not gonna tell you what to do about it. Nope," he shook his head, "I'm here for something a little more practical than that."

"Practical?" Aubrey asked hesitantly.

"Yep. What I want to know, Wanderman, isn't what you're gonna *tell* people about it. I want to know what your gonna *do* about it."

"Do?" Aubrey sank onto his own bed, pressing one hand to his ribs, and licked his lips. The quick heal was working, but they were still puffy, and he swallowed again.

"What . . . what do you mean, 'do about it,' Senior Chief?"

"The way I see it," Harkness said calmly, "Steilman beat the crap out of you, and then he probably said something along the lines of 'I've got friends, so keep your mouth shut—or else.'" He shrugged. "The only problem is, if you do keep your mouth shut, then you're gonna have to come up with something to get him off your back yourself, or the end result's gonna be the same. I know assholes like Steilman. They *like* hurting people; it's how they get their kicks. So just how were you planning on handling him next time?"

"I—" Aubrey broke off once more, expression helpless, and Harkness nodded.

"S'what I thought. You haven't thought about that part of it, have you?"

Aubrey shook his head, not even realizing that to do so was to tacitly admit that he had not, in fact, fallen . . . and that Harkness was right about who'd attacked him. His eyes clung to the senior chief's, and Harkness sighed.

"Wanderman, you're a good kid, but *Jesus* are you green. You've got just two choices here. Either you go to the Bosun and tell her what really happened, or you deal with Steilman on your own. One or the other. 'Cause if you don't, you can bet Steilman's gonna deal with *you* as soon as he figures it's safe. So which is it gonna be?"

"I—" Aubrey dropped his eyes to the deck and drew a deep breath, then shook his head. "I can't go to the Bosun, Senior Chief," he admitted hoarsely. "It's not just me—and it's not just Steilman. He's got friends . . . and so do I. If I turn him in, how do I know one of his friends won't go after me or Gin—" He paused and cleared his throat. "Or one of *my* friends?"

"Okay." Harkness shrugged. "I think you're making a mistake, but if that's the way you feel, that's the way you feel, and I ain't your momma. But that only leaves one option. Are you really up for that?"

"No," Aubrey muttered hopelessly. His shoulders

sagged and his face burned with humiliation, but he made himself look up from the deck. "I've never had a fight in my life, Senior Chief," he said with a sort of forlorn dignity. "I don't even know if I'd have the guts to *try* to fight back next time, but even if I did, I wouldn't be very good at it."

"Guts?" Harkness repeated very softly, then laughed. "Kid, you've got a hell of a lot more guts than Steilman!" Aubrey blinked at him, and the senior chief shook his head. "You're scared to death of him, but you're not exactly falling apart in panic," he pointed out. "If you were gonna do that, you'd've been screaming for the Bosun the minute you reached sickbay. Nope, your problem, Wanderman, is that you've got too much guts to panic and not quite enough to do the same thing 'cause you thought it through and realized it was the smart move. You're sort of stuck out there in the middle. But I want you to think about Steilman for a minute. Think about who he decided to beat the crap out of. He outmasses you—what, about two to one? He's more'n twice your age, and he's got ten times your experience. But did he pick a fight with me? Did he stand up to the Bosun? Or Bruce Maxwell? Nope. He went after a green kid he figured for an easy mark, and he was real careful to get you alone. How much guts d'you think *that* took?"

Aubrey blinked. The senior chief was wrong about his own courage—Aubrey knew that—but maybe he had a point about Steilman. Aubrey had never even considered what had happened in that light.

"See, the thing you have to understand about people like Steilman," Harkness said, "is that they're sure thing players. Steilman likes beating people up. He enjoys hurting 'em, and he likes feeling like top dog. And he's a big bastard, too—I'll admit that. He's bigger'n *I* am, and strong, and he fights dirty, and I imagine he likes to think he's a tough, dangerous customer. But he's not really very *smart*, kid. If he were, he'd realize *anybody* can be dangerous. Even you."

"*Me?*" Aubrey stared at the older man and then laughed

a bit wildly. "He could take me apart with one hand, Senior Chief! For that matter, he already *did!*"

"You have hand-to-hand in basic?" Harkness countered.

"Of course I did, but I was never any good at it. You're not going to tell me six weeks of training taught me how to beat up someone like Steilman!"

"Nope. But it did give you the basics—that's why they call it 'basic,'" Harkness said with such total seriousness that Aubrey had to listen to him. "Course, you knew it wasn't for real. It was just training, and you figured—hey, I'm a little, wiry guy, and I've never had a fight, and I'm never *gonna* have a fight, and I don't *want* to have one, even if I could. That about sum it up?"

"It sure does," Aubrey said feelingly, and Harkness chuckled.

"Well, looks to me like you were wrong. You *are* gonna have a fight—the only question is whether or not you're gonna win it or get your fool head busted. And do you know what the secret to *not* getting your head busted is?"

"What?" Aubrey asked, almost against his will.

"It's busting the other guy's head first," Harkness said grimly. "It's making up your mind going in that you're not just gonna try to defend yourself. It's deciding right now, ahead of time, that you're gonna kill the mother-fucker if that's what it takes."

"Me? *Kill* someone like *Steilman?* You're crazy!"

"It's not nice to tell your elders they're crazy, kid," Harkness said with another of those lazy grins. "When I was your age, I wasn't a lot bigger'n you are now. Oh, taller, but I didn't have any more meat on my bones. But what I was, Wanderman, was a hell of a lot *meaner* than you are. And if you want to deal with Steilman and come out in one piece, then you're gonna have to get mean, too."

"Mean? Me?" Aubrey laughed bitterly, and Harkness sighed and sat upright on the other bed again.

"Listen to me," he said flatly. "I already told you you've only got two choices here, and you've already told *me* you aren't gonna do the smart thing. All right, that only leaves the *dumb* thing, and if you're gonna go that route, you've got some things to learn. And that's why I'm here. The one thing in the world that Steilman's never gonna expect is that *you'll* go for *him* next time, and I'll tell you a little secret about Steilman. He doesn't know how to fight. Not for real. He's never had to learn, because he *is* big and strong and mean. So that's why I'm here, kid. If you want to learn how to kick this bastard's ass up between his ears, me and Gunny Hallowell'll show you how it's done. We can't guarantee you'll win, but we can guarantee this much, Wanderman. You give me and the Gunny a few weeks to work with you, and you'll sure as hell be able to make the son-of-a-bitch *work* for it."

• CHAPTER TWENTY-THREE

Aubrey had seldom felt so utterly out of place. His eyes flitted around the Marine gym, and he swallowed nervously as he watched hard, fit men and women throwing one another about with sobering efficiency. It wasn't like the basic unarmed combat courses the Navy taught its recruits. That was almost more of a stylized form of exercise, not the basis for serious mayhem, because Navy types weren't supposed to indulge in such low-brow combat. They threw megaton-range warheads and beams of coherent light or gamma radiation at one another, and, like most of his fellow recruits, Aubrey had considered his rudimentary hand-to-hand training no more than a concession to military tradition.

Marines were different. They were expected to get down in the mud and the blood, and they were entirely serious about learning how to disassemble their fellow humans with bare hands. They were all volunteers, and like most military people from societies with prolong, they'd signed up for long hitches—the minimum was ten T-years—which gave them plenty of time to study their chosen trade. Most of them were working out full contact, in light protective gear, and he winced at the solid, sharp *thud* with which some of those blows and kicks went home as he watched Major Hibson at work.

The major was a little bitty thing, less than half the size of her opponent, but she was built for speed, and for all her small size, she appeared to have been assembled from leftover battle armor parts. Her sparring partner was no slouch, with a formidable advantage in size and reach, and it was obvious they both knew all the attacks and counters. Those moves were so ingrained, came so automatically, that, to the casual eye, he and the major might have been engaged in some elaborately choreographed dance, not trying to take one another's heads off. But they were deadly serious, and for all her smaller size, Hibson was pushing the pace. She was working the perimeter, dodging and feinting with blinding quickness. Even Aubrey understood what she was trying to do, and he was certain her opponent did, yet he had to respond. The major was taking punishment—her partner had gotten in several solid shots—but she seemed to accept that as the price of doing business, and somehow she was always moving away from his best attacks. She blocked them, or rode them to rob them of their force, or simply absorbed them and kept on attacking with a ferocity Aubrey found vaguely chilling, and eventually one of her opponent's punishing jabs went a few bare centimeters too far.

Hibson seemed to sway sideways, eluding the head strike, and this time she was moving in, not away. She was suddenly inside her opponent's reach, and her padded workout shoe flashed up in an impossible-looking back-kick to his jaw as she spun to turn her back on him. He staggered, and her hands darted down while she still balanced on the toes of one foot. She caught his ankle and yanked straight up, and even as he went down, she dropped backwards herself and landed squarely on top of him. He tried to envelop her in a bear hug, but he was half-stunned and just a fraction of a second too slow. She drove a piledriver elbow into his solar plexus, twisted like a freshly landed fish, and ended up kneeling across his chest while her right hand flashed down in a lethal blow that stopped dead just before it crashed into his exposed larynx.

Aubrey shook his head. This was crazy! These people spent years training in this kind of thing, but he was an electronics tech, not a Marine. He supposed it should have been enheartening to see someone Hibson's size take down such a big opponent, but he'd also seen how hard she had to work for it . . . and recognized the degree of skill it had required. *He* didn't have that kind of capability, and the thought that he could somehow acquire it before the next time Steilman tried to cave his head in was ludicrous. He should turn around and—

"Sorry I'm late, kid." Aubrey jumped half out of his skin as a meaty hand clapped him on the shoulder. He spun with a gasp, and Horace Harkness grinned at him. "Seem to be moving pretty good there, Wanderman. Quick heal must of taken hold on those ribs, hey?"

"Uh, yes, Senior Chief," Aubrey muttered.

"Good! Come with me, kid."

Aubrey considered telling Harkness he'd changed his mind, but he couldn't quite get the words out, and he was distantly surprised by how important it seemed that he retain the senior chief's respect. Pride, he thought. How many people over the years had gotten the crap kicked out of them out of a misplaced sense of pride?

His thoughts broke off as Harkness gestured to a giant in a faded sweat suit. The black-haired, dark-eyed man stood at least two meters tall, and heavy eyebrows seemed to meet across the bridge of his nose. His face was darkly weathered, his shoulders were preposterously broad, and his hairy hands looked like cargo grapples, but he moved with a sort of lazy grace which looked out of place in such a big man.

"Harkness." Like the Bosun, the giant had a distinct Gryphon accent, and his voice was even deeper than the senior chief's. It was also soft, almost gentle, as if its owner seldom needed to raise it, and Harkness nodded to him.

"Gunny, this here's Wanderman. He's got a little problem."

"So I hear." The black-haired man surveyed Aubrey thoughtfully, and the younger man felt his shoulders straighten as he realized who the other was. The Royal Manticoran Marines no longer used the rank of gunnery sergeant, but the senior noncom aboard any Queen's ship was still referred to by the ancient title of "Gunny," and that meant this giant was Battalion Sergeant Major Lewis Hallowell—effectively the Bosun's equivalent in Marine Country.

"Oh, ease off, Wanderman," the sergeant major rumbled. Aubrey blinked, and Hallowell grinned. It made his dark, weathered face look suddenly like a mischievous little boy's, and Aubrey felt his own lips quirk, then forced his spine to relax. "Better," Hallowell observed. "You're among friends—even if you *were* introduced by this miserable old vacuum-sucker."

Aubrey blinked again, but Harkness only grinned back at the sergeant major, who snorted before he returned his attention to Aubrey. He pointed at a pile of exercise mats, and Aubrey sank obediently down to sit on them. Hallowell folded himself effortlessly to the deck facing him, planted one fist on each knee, and leaned forward.

"All right, Wanderman," he said more briskly, "the only question I've got for you is how serious you are about this." Aubrey started to glance at Harkness, but Hallowell shook his head sharply. "Don't look at the Senior Chief. I want to know how serious *you* are."

"I'm . . . not sure what you mean, S—Gunny," Aubrey said after a moment.

"It's not hard," Hallowell said patiently. "Harkness here's briefed me on your problem. I know Steilman's type, and I know how deep a hole you're in. What I want to know is if you're really serious about digging your way out, because doing that's going to take work, and it won't be easy. You're going to spend a lot of time sweating, and even more time groaning over bruises, and there're going to be times you wonder if Harkness and I aren't worse enemies than Steilman is. If you're going to fold up on us, I want to know now—and if you tell me you aren't, you'd better be ready to back that up, kid."

Aubrey swallowed hard. This was the moment, he realized. He was still frightened out of his mind and more than half-convinced the entire project was an exercise

in futility, yet he'd come this far. And if he told Gunny Hallowell that he *was* prepared to stick it out, the same sort of pride which had brought him across the gym on Harkness' heels would come into play. If he tried and failed, his already battered sense of self-worth would take crippling damage, and he knew it. But even as those thoughts flickered across his mind, he realized something else: he wanted to do it. He *wanted* to do it, and a slow, lava-like anger began to burn through his fear at last.

He drew a deep breath and looked deep into Hallowell's eyes, then nodded.

"Yeah, Gunny," he said, and the firmness of his voice startled him, "I'm serious."

"Good!" Hallowell leaned closer and smacked him on the shoulder, so hard he almost fell over, and grinned. "There's going to be times you're sorry you said that, Wanderman, but when this worn-out old vacuum-sucker and I get done with you, you'll never have to worry about the Steilmans of the universe again."

Aubrey grinned back, nervously but with feeling, and Hallowell settled himself even more comfortably on the deck.

"Now, the first thing you've got to understand," he began, "is that Harkness and I, we've got different styles. I like finesse and skill; *he* likes brute force and meanness." Harkness made an indignant sound, and Hallowell grinned, but his deep, soft voice was entirely serious as he went on. "The point is, kid, that both styles work, and that's because there aren't any dangerous weapons, and there aren't any dangerous martial arts. There are only dangerous *people*, and if *you* aren't dangerous, it doesn't make a damn bit of difference what you're carrying or how well trained you are. Get that locked in right now, 'cause it's the one thing no one else can really teach you. We can tell you, and we can show you, and we can lecture till we're blue in the face, but until you figure it out for yourself at gut level, it's all just words, right?"

Aubrey licked his lips and nodded, and Hallowell nodded back.

"Now," he went on, "I know what they taught you in basic, and the base course isn't too shabby. At least it teaches you how to move and builds a decent foundation. The way I see it, we don't have time to teach you a lot of new moves, and it's probably been a while since you worked out properly on the ones you already know, so the first thing we're going to do is run you through my own personal brand of refresher course. After that, you'll spend at least three hours in the gym every day, working out with me or Harkness—or maybe both of us. After a week or so, we may get Corporal Slattery involved, too; she's closer to your size and weight. We'll stick pretty much with what you already know and just teach you how to do it for real. Speed, violence, and determination, Wanderman. Those're the keys for now. Of course, if you wind up enjoying it, there's a lot more we can teach you, but for the moment, let's just concentrate on keeping you in one piece and kicking Steilman's worthless ass, right?"

Aubrey nodded again, feeling just a bit giddy and yet suddenly aware that a part of him really believed he might actually be able to do this. At least Senior Chief Harkness and Sergeant Major Hallowell seemed to think he could, and that same part of him told him almost calmly that the two of them were surely better judges of his capabilities than *he* was. It was a surprisingly comforting thought, and he managed to return Hallowell's smile.

"Good! In that case, Wanderman, why don't we start with a little loosening up? Trust me," the sergeant major's smile turned into a lazily wicked grin, "you're gonna need it."

Honor crossed to the main plot and stood gazing down into the display. She considered her options for several seconds, then snorted mentally, for there weren't really all that many available to her. Besides, she'd discovered what she needed to and made her own point, and it was time to go.

Her ship had spent ten days orbiting Walther's single inhabited planet, and the way System Governor Hagen had spun out the paperwork on the pirates had confirmed her suspicions. He intended to delay their "trial" until *Wayfarer* disappeared over the hyper limit, and she knew why. With her out of sight, he could stage manage his hearings to guarantee the pirates walked—or, at worst, received a slap on the wrist— on the basis of some suitable technicality or "ambiguities" in the evidence. But he had no intention of trying that while Honor and her personnel were available to offer testimony to clarify those ambiguities . . . and he knew time was on his side. Every day Honor delayed in Walther was a day she wasn't chasing other pirates, and she found his mask of pious concern over due process and protecting the sovereignty of the Silesian Confederacy more irritating with every conversation.

Well, she'd known what was going to happen from the moment she'd turned the raiders over . . . and she'd warned them, she thought grimly. Of course, she *hadn't* mentioned that the dispatches she'd left with the local Manticoran attaché would provide each ship of the squadron with positive IDs of her erstwhile prisoners as it arrived. If the governor and his raider allies thought hers was the only Q-ship in the sector—or that she was the only RMN captain prepared to carry out her promises to them—they might just discover their error the hard way.

For now, however, it was time to go. Not that the time she'd spent here had been wasted. She'd taken long enough to make the point that she was looking over Hagen's shoulder, on the one hand, and to give the governor some rope, on the other. By now, Hagen knew she was dead serious. He might be laughing at her inability to make him do *his* part, might even consider her an overly officious fool, but he knew she wouldn't have burned ten full days unless she'd meant business. That might help when the next member of the squadron turned up, and, at the very least, it ought to make him a bit more wary where *she* was concerned.

More to the point, every conversation with him was on record, along with his promises that the raiders would be severely punished. When it turned out, as she was certain it would, that nothing of the sort had happened, those recordings would be forwarded to his superiors by Her Majesty's Government. The Star Kingdom seldom involved itself directly in the internal affairs of the Confederacy, but it had done so on occasion, and this was a point she'd discussed in some detail with her superiors before leaving Manticore. Obstructionism by Silesian officials was an old story, and Honor entertained no false hope that it could be eliminated. But the Star Kingdom periodically pruned it back by identifying specific governors whose hands were dirty and going after them with every weapon at its disposal. Even with the current reduction in force levels, Manticore retained more than sufficient nonmilitary clout to squash any given governor. If nothing else, the Board of Trade could simply blacklist Walther for all Manticoran shipping, with devastating consequences for the system's economy. Coupled with official demands for Hagen's recall and prosecution for complicity with the raiders, that was guaranteed to bring his career to a screeching halt. And without his governorship, he had no value to his criminal associates . . . many of whom had a habit of eliminating discarded allies to keep them from turning state's evidence.

Honor hated that sort of roundabout maneuvering, but her options were limited, and the fact that it would be slow didn't mean it would be ineffective. Even if Hagen lived through the experience, other corrupt governors would take note of what had happened to him. It probably wouldn't cause any of them to actually reform, but it *would* make them more circumspect, and anything that put a crimp into the raiders' operations had to be worthwhile.

But she'd assembled all the information she required

for that part of the operation, and there were plenty of other pirate vessels out there. It was time to be about dealing with *them*, she thought, reaching up to rub Nimitz's chest, and glanced at Lieutenant Kanehama.

"Plot a course for Schiller, John," she said. "I want to pull out within the next two hours."

Ginger Lewis watched Electronics Mate Second Class Wilson's section run through the drill. It still felt a bit strange to be supervising, though no one could have guessed it from her expression. Just a few weeks ago, *she'd* been in Wilson's section; now, as chief of the watch, she was the second-class petty officer's boss. But at least she didn't have to put up with the crowd Bruce had down in Impeller One.

She bared her teeth at the thought. Ginger's own people here in DCC were at least civilized, and the fact that she knew her job forward and backward seemed sufficient for most of them. The way Wilson had made it quietly clear he had no problems taking orders from her was an enormous help, as well, and her watch's efficiency was climbing steadily.

That should have been a source of unflawed satisfaction. She had, after all, made something like a fifteen T-year jump in seniority in less than three months, and the fact that Lieutenant Commander Tschu and his officers knew she was pulling her weight in her new slot meant she'd probably get to keep her new grade. And she *was* satisfied in that respect. Yet worry over Aubrey gnawed at her, and her own experience with Steilman only made her even more certain somebody had to jerk the son-of-a-bitch up short and hard.

Of course, it was possible that same experience was making her paranoid, she told herself as Wilson's people completed their drill well within parameters. Wilson looked up, and she nodded her approval, then moved to the central station to call up the duty log. Her watch ended in another twenty minutes, and she busied herself annotating the log entries for her relief, but even as she worked, her brain kept worrying at the problem.

By now, it was an open secret that it was Steilman who'd beaten Aubrey up, and the way the power tech seemed to have gotten away with it had added to his stature. The Captain had come down on him like a hammer over the drive room incident—she'd busted him to third-class and given him five days' brig time, about the maximum punishment for his official offense, and the icy talk which came with it would have terrified any reasonable soul into walking the straight and narrow. But Steilman *wasn't* reasonable. The more Ginger learned about him, the more convinced she became that the man was barely even sane. He'd taken his demotion and brig time not as a warning but as proof that he'd gotten away with arranging Kirk Dempsey's "accident." Worse, his apparent immunity not only won envious respect from the other bad apples but also made those he frightened even more nervous about crossing him. Ginger knew Lieutenant Commander Tschu had delivered his own short, coldly pointed lecture, but the lack of an official follow through for the two acts which should have bought him a crash landing had blunted the chief engineer's warning just as it had the Captain's. Steilman had protested his innocence of all charges—except the insolence, for which he'd actually "apologized" to Ginger—and sworn he was purer than the driven snow, and all the time, Ginger knew, he'd been laughing at what he'd gotten away with. He and his cronies were being circumspect for the moment, yet she was grimly certain they were only biding their time.

She sighed mentally as the formalities of the change of the watch flowed about her. Sooner or later, Steilman and his crowd were going to screw up and the entire universe was going to come down on them. It was as inevitable as entropy, and Ginger knew it. Yet that wasn't going to make whatever damage they did first any less ugly. No, she thought. They needed to be slapped down—

hard—and the sooner the better, but without any official accusation from Aubrey . . .

She watched Lieutenant Silvetti turn over to Lieutenant Klontz and nodded to Senior Chief Jordan, her own relief, then headed down the passage towards her quarters. Somehow, some way, she *had* to get Aubrey to open up, but he'd turned into a clam, and he no longer wandered around the ship, exploring its passages and access ways. She was both relieved and saddened by his obvious wariness, how hard he worked on never being alone anywhere someone else might be lurking. But he wouldn't even *talk* to her, and she'd caught one or two echoes of Steilman's gloating delight at Aubrey's caution. They sickened her, yet there was nothing she could do about it.

At least he was back up and around, but he'd developed a talent for disappearing whenever he had free time. Ginger had tried to figure out where he was vanishing to, but without success . . . which didn't make a lot of sense. *Wayfarer* was a big ship, but her outsized crew packed her life-support spaces. It shouldn't be possible for Aubrey to simply turn invisible this way, and the thought that he might have been so frightened that he'd found some isolated hiding hole and scurried straight into it the instant he went off duty tore at her heart.

But if *she* couldn't find him, Steilman probably couldn't do it either, she told herself. That had to count for something.

Aubrey Wanderman grunted in anguish as the training mat hit him in the face again. He lay there for a second, gasping for breath, then levered himself up on his hands and knees and shook his head. Everything still seemed to be attached in more or less the right places, and he shoved further up to kneel and look up at Gunny Hallowell.

"Doing better there, Wanderman," Hallowell said cheerfully, and Aubrey dragged his exercise suit's sleeve across his sweat-soaked face. Every bone and sinew ached, and he had bruises in places where he hadn't realized he had *places*, but he knew Hallowell was right. He *was* doing better. The combination he'd just attempted had almost gotten through the sergeant major's guard, and he suspected he'd landed so hard because Hallowell had been forced to rush his own counter and thrown him with rather more energy than he'd intended.

Aubrey came back into a set position, still panting, but Hallowell shook his head.

"Take five, kid," he said, and Aubrey collapsed gratefully back onto the mat. The Marine grinned and dropped down cross-legged beside him, and Aubrey suppressed a familiar stab of envy when he realized Hallowell wasn't even breathing hard.

Aubrey rolled onto his back and stared up at the deckhead while *Wayfarer*'s off-watch Marines continued to work out around him. Until he'd started training here, he hadn't realized the degree to which the Marines formed a separate community within the ship's company. Oh, he'd known about the traditional rivalry between the "jarheads" and "vacuum-suckers," but he'd been too immersed in the close-knit world of his own watch section to recognize that *Wayfarer*'s crew actually consisted of an entire series of unique worlds. A man knew the others in *his* branch of the ship's duty structure, and while he might have a few friends scattered in other departments, those friends had their own concerns. In most ways that counted, he had less in common with them than he did even with people he disliked from his own organizational niche.

And if that was true where fellow Navy personnel were concerned, it was ten times as true for Marines. Marines might man weapon stations at GQ, but they had their own mess, their own berths, their own exercise areas, their own officers and noncoms. They had different traditions and rituals which didn't make a lot of sense to a naval rating, and they seemed perfectly content to keep it that way.

All of which left him wondering just why Gunny Hallowell had agreed to help one Aubrey Wanderman, who had absolutely no ambition ever to become a Marine.

He lay there for another moment, then gathered his nerve and shoved up on an elbow.

"Sergeant Major?"

"Yeah?"

"I, uh, I'm grateful for the trouble you're taking, but, well—"

"Spit it out, Wanderman," Hallowell rumbled. "We're not sparring now, so you probably won't get hurt even if you say something really stupid," he added with a grin when the younger man paused, almost wiggling in obvious embarrassment. Aubrey blushed, then grinned back.

"I was just wondering why you're doing it, Gunny."

"I could say it's because *someone* has to," Hallowell replied after a moment. "Or I could say it's because I don't like bastards like Steilman, or even that I just don't want some kid who barely shaves yet on my conscience. And I guess, all things considered, just about any of those reasons would do. But to be honest, the real reason is that Harkness asked me to."

"But I thought—" Aubrey paused, then shrugged. "I appreciate it, Sergeant Major, but I, uh, I thought the Senior Chief didn't exactly get along with Marines, and, well—"

"And vice-versa?" Hallowell finished for him with a subterranean chuckle, then shrugged. "Once upon a time you probably wouldn't have been too far wrong, kid, but that was before he saw the light and married a Marine." Aubrey's eyes opened wide at that, and the sergeant major laughed out loud. "You mean he didn't tell you about that?"

"No," Aubrey said in a shaken voice.

"Well, he did, and she's an old friend of mine; we went through Basic together. But I doubt most of us jarheads ever really held his habits against him. You see, Wanderman, Harkness never meant it personally. He just liked to fight, and picking on Marines was a way to keep it in the family without getting too close to home."

"You mean all those fights, all the times he got himself busted, were for the *fun* of it?"

"I never said he was *smart*, Wanderman," Hallowell replied with another grin, "and the way I hear, about half the times he got busted had to do more with black markets than fights. But, yeah, that just about sums it up." Aubrey stared at him, and the sergeant major shook his head. "Look, kid, by this time you should be starting to grasp how my people go about it when they're serious, and you've worked out almost as much with Harkness as with me. Much as it pains me to admit it, he's pretty damned good himself, for a vacuum-sucker. Not much into science, mind you, but a hell of a brawler. D'you think somebody like him could spend twenty years picking bar fights without getting killed—or killing someone else—if he *wasn't* doing it for the fun of it? I mean, think about it. If he'd meant it seriously, somebody would've gotten medevaced, and aside from the occasional contusion or a few stitches here and there—"

Hallowell shrugged, and Aubrey blinked. The notion of picking fights with big, tough, well-trained strangers for *fun* was more than alien to his own thinking; it was incomprehensible. Yet he knew the sergeant major had put his finger on the truth. Senior Chief Harkness simply *liked* to fight—or had before he reformed. And apparently the Marines had known it all along. In fact, Hallowell sounded obscurely pleased Harkness had chosen to fight Marines rather than fellow Navy types, as if it were some sort of *compliment*.

And as he considered it, Aubrey realized the idea was more understandable than he'd first thought. It wasn't like Steilman. The power tech didn't like to fight; he liked to *hurt* people. And he didn't pick people who were likely to fight back; he picked *victims*. But Harkness

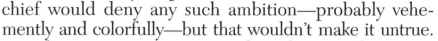

loved the challenge. For him, it was all about competition, a desire to match himself against someone just as tough as *he* was. Aubrey suspected the senior chief would deny any such ambition—probably vehemently and colorfully—but that wouldn't make it untrue.

Perhaps even more surprisingly, Aubrey was beginning to see how someone could feel that way. He'd always been pretty good at team sports, but he'd never contemplated trying anything like the martial arts. Nor would he have now, he admitted, if Steilman hadn't . . . motivated him. Yet now that he was beginning to figure out how it worked, he was more than a little surprised by how much he enjoyed it. For one thing, he was probably fitter than he'd ever been in his life, but it went further than that. There was a sense of discipline, the important kind that came from within, and of competence. Everything he'd learned so far only showed him how much more there was to learn, and it was harder work than anything he'd ever done before, yet that only made his progress even more satisfying. And one thing Gunny Hallowell and Senior Chief Harkness had managed, he thought wryly, was to reteach him that the occasional bruise or sprain wasn't the end of the world. Whereas Hallowell was working with him on technique and attitude, Harkness had an even simpler teaching style, which probably had something to do with the fact that, unlike the sergeant major, he was entirely self-taught. His methodology was to teach Aubrey how to pound on Steilman by pounding on *him* with every trick he'd learned in his colorful career until Aubrey got fast and tough enough to pound back, and it was working.

"The thing you've got to remember here," Hallowell said after a moment, in a different tone, almost as if he'd been reading Aubrey's thoughts, "is that what you and I are doing, or even what you and Harkness are doing, isn't what you're going to have to do when it comes down to you and Steilman."

Aubrey pushed up into a sitting position and nodded,

eyes dark and serious, and the sergeant major smiled thinly.

"You're quicker than he is, but he's bigger and stronger. From his record, he's a brawler, not a fighter. He'll probably try to surprise you and drag you in close, so the first thing you've got to do is stay alert, especially any time you think you're alone. If he *does* get his hands on you, you're in trouble, so if it happens, break fast, back off, and come in again. Whatever you do, *don't* fight his way, because he can take more punishment. What you've got to do is take him out quick and however dirty you have to be. Don't go looking for him, and don't start it—you don't want to get brought up on charges yourself—but the instant he takes a swing, drop his ass, and don't worry too much about how you do it. As long as you don't kill him outright, Doc Ryder should be able to put him back together, and given the difference in your sizes and the fact that *he* started it, I don't think you'll catch any flak for putting him down. But to do it, you've got to remember he *is* tough. You try to match him punch for punch or let him set the limits, and he wins. Go in hard, fast, and like you mean it, and when he goes down, you don't back off. You keep going until you're sure he'll *stay* down, you hear me?"

"Yes, Gunny," Aubrey said very seriously, and if the thought that he might possibly be able to do what Hallowell had just described still seemed unlikely, it no longer seemed absurd.

"Good! Then back on your feet, kid, and this time try not to come at me like my old pacifist aunt."

• CHAPTER TWENTY-FOUR

Margaret Fuchien was not a happy woman as she stood in the gallery of RMMS *Artermis'* Number Two Boat Bay and watched the VIP shuttle dock. As a rule, people aboard *Artemis* went to some lengths to prevent Fuchien from becoming unhappy, for her cuffs carried four gold bands, and she had the no-nonsense, hard-nosed attitude one might have expected from the skipper of one of the Star Kingdom's crack liners. She'd earned every promotion she'd ever had, and she was used to doing things *her* way. It was a privilege she'd earned along with her rank. But the man and woman aboard that shuttle weren't simply two more passengers; they were the ones who wrote—or at least authorized—her paychecks. Worse, they *owned* her ship.

She wasn't at all pleased to see them, for she'd run *Artemis* back and forth on the Silesian run for over five T-years, and she didn't need the latest Admiralty advisories to tell her the situation in the Confederacy was going steadily to Hell. She most emphatically did *not* need to find herself responsible for both members of the Hauptman clan just now . . . not that what *she* needed seemed to be of particular importance to her employers.

The docking tube cycled, and she pasted a smile on her face as Klaus Hauptman walked down it. *Artemis* was a passenger liner; unlike a warship or freighter, her oversized docking tubes generated their own internal gravity to keep ground-grippers' lunches where they belonged, and the magnate stepped easily across the interface into the shipboard gravity. He paused there, waiting until his daughter joined him, then crossed to Fuchien.

"Captain," he held out his hand, and Fuchien gripped it.

"Mr. Hauptman. Ms. Hauptman. Welcome aboard *Artemis*." She got it out without even gritting her teeth.

"Thank you," he replied, and watched another woman step out of the tube. Fuchien and Ludmilla Adams had met on one of the trillionaire's previous voyages, and they exchanged nods and brief smiles. Adams' face was too well trained to say anything she didn't want it to, but Fuchien felt obscurely comforted by the look in the other woman's eyes. Clearly Adams was no happier about this trip than the captain was.

"I've had the owner's suite prepared for you and Ms. Hauptman, Sir," Fuchien said. "At least we've got plenty of room on board."

Hauptman flashed a brief, tight smile at her oblique warning. Her objections had been more explicit when he first informed her of his plans, and despite his equally explicit order to terminate the discussion, she wasn't going to give in without one last try. Not, he admitted, that she didn't have a point. Passenger loads for Silesia had dropped radically in the last five or six months, to a point at which *Artemis* and *Athena* were barely breaking even. Of course, they'd never been exactly cheap to operate, given their out-sized crews and armaments. At barely a million tons, *Artemis* wasn't much bigger than most battlecruisers, but she carried three times the crew of a multimillion-ton freighter like *Bonaventure*, most of them ex-Navy personnel who looked after her weapons systems. She needed to run with almost full passenger loads to show a profit, which wasn't normally a problem, given the security her speed and those same weapons systems offered. Now, however, the situation was so bad that even she was badly underbooked, and the captain's reference to the fact was as close as she would let herself come to suggesting—again—that her boss stay the hell home where it was safe.

Not that he intended to . . . and not that Stacey had

shown any inclination to listen to his arguments that *she* should. He sighed with a mental headshake and wondered if Captain Fuchien had any idea how thoroughly he sympathized with her.

"Well," he said, "at least that means first-class dining won't be too crowded."

"Yes, Sir," Fuchien replied, and waved at the lifts. "If you'd follow me, I'll escort you to your quarters before returning to the bridge."

"You're not serious," Sir Thomas Caparelli said.

"I'm afraid I am," Patricia Givens replied. "I just found out this morning."

"Jesus." Caparelli ran both hands through his hair in a harried gesture he would have let very few people see. ONI's latest update on losses in Silesia had come in just two days ago, and those losses were considerably higher than they'd been when Task Group 1037 was dispatched. One thing the First Space Lord definitely didn't need just now was for the wealthiest man in the Star Kingdom—and his only child—to go haring off into the middle of a mess like that.

"There's no way we can stop them," Givens said quietly, as if she'd read his mind. Which, he reflected, wasn't all that difficult just now. "If private citizens want to take passage through what's for all intents and purposes a war zone, that's up to them. Unless, of course, we want to issue orders to hold *Artemis*."

"We can't," Caparelli sighed. "If we start holding liners, people are going to ask why we're not holding freighters, too. Or, worse, the freighters'll start holding *themselves*. And we can't very well admit we're only worried about two of her passengers, now can we?"

"No, Sir."

"Damn." Caparelli gazed at his blotter for a long moment, then punched a code into his terminal. Less than a minute later, his screen lit with the face of an RMN lieutenant.

"System Command Central, Lieutenant Vale."

"Admiral Caparelli, Lieutenant," the First Space Lord growled. "Let me speak to Captain Helpern, please."

"Yes, Sir." The lieutenant vanished, to be replaced by a chunky, heavyset four-striper.

"What can I do for you, Sir?" he asked politely.

"RMMS *Artemis* is pulling out for the Silesian run in eleven hours," Caparelli said, coming quickly to the point, "and Klaus and Stacey Hauptman are on board." Helpern's eyes widened, and Caparelli nodded grimly. "That's right. We can't stop them, but I don't need to tell you what kind of crap we'll be in if anything happens to them." Helpern shook his head, and Caparelli sighed. "Since we can't stop them, we'd better send along a gunslinger. Can you shake loose a destroyer or a light cruiser?"

"Just a second, Sir." Helpern looked down, and Caparelli heard him punching a query into his own data terminal. Perhaps thirty seconds trickled past, and then Helpern's eyes met the First Space Lord's once more.

"I don't have any cruisers available within that time frame, Sir. If you can hold them for another fourteen hours or so, I could pull *Amaterasu* for the duty, though."

"Um." Caparelli rubbed his jaw, then shook his head. "No. We need this to look casual. If we make a big production out of it, people are going to ask why we can suddenly spare a special escort for this particular ship and not for *all* of them, and one thing I don't want to do is explain that some of Her Majesty's subjects are more important than others."

"Understood, Sir. In that case, though, the best I can do is a tin can. *Hawkwing* is at *Hephaestus* right now, taking on stores. She's due to clear her mooring in thirteen hours for a departure to Basilisk. If I instruct Commander Usher to expedite, he can clear within the window for *Artemis'* scheduled departure."

"Do it," Caparelli decided. "Then have one of your people—someone junior—contact Captain Fuchien. Inform her that *Hawkwing*'s due for routine deployment to Silesia and that she just *happens* to be ready to depart now. Then ask her if *Artemis* would like a little company."

"Yes, Sir. I'll get right on it."

Commander Gene Usher, CO HMS *Hawkwing*, swore softly as he read the message. *Hawkwing* wasn't the RMN's newest destroyer, but she was a most satisfactory billet for a brand new commander, and Usher was proud of her. He hadn't been looking forward to a six-month deployment to Basilisk Station, even if Basilisk was no longer the punishment station it had been, but he'd adjusted to that . . . and he *hated* last-minute order changes.

He reread the dispatch again, and swore a bit louder. *Artemis*. At least playing nursemaid to a single ship was easier than sheepherding an entire convoy, and the *Atlas*-class liners were fast enough to make the passage mercifully short, but Usher had been around. He could read between the lines, and there was only one reason SysCom had appended a copy of her passenger manifest. Two names fairly leapt off the screen at him, and the thought that a vindictive old bastard like Klaus Hauptman had the juice to pull in a desperately needed destroyer just to watch his ass was enough to upset anyone.

He sighed, then handed the board back to the com officer and looked at his astrogator.

"Change of orders, Jimmy. We're going to Silesia."

"Silesia, Sir?" Lieutenant James Sargent frowned in surprise. "Skipper, I don't even have the latest shipping updates on Silesia, and my cartography's all loaded for Basilisk and the Republic."

"Get hold of *Hephaestus* Central, then. Pull the downloads ASAP, then put in a call to RMMS *Artemis*—Com knows where she is. Talk to her astrogator and coordinate with her. We're going to be playing nursemaid."

"All the way to Silesia?"

"All the way to wherever the hell she's going, unless

we can find someone in-sector to hand her off to," Usher sighed, "but don't tell her astrogator that. As far as *Artemis* is concerned, we just happen to be going her way."

"Wonderful," Sargent said dryly. "Okay, Skipper. I'm on it."

Usher nodded and crossed to his command chair. He sat down and gazed moodily at his blank plot for a moment while his brain ticked off the things he had to do. Rewriting a starship's movement orders on less than twelve hours' notice was never easy, but he'd leave it to SysCom to notify the Basilisk Station commander of his impending nonarrival. He had problems of his own to worry about—like expediting the loading of his ship's stores. He nodded to himself and punched an intraship com stud.

"Get me the Bosun," he said.

". . . so if you'd like the company, *Hawkwing* will be happy to tag along as far as Sachsen."

"Why, thank you, Lieutenant," Captain Fuchien told the face on her com screen. She tried very hard to hide a grin which she knew would infuriate the lieutenant, but it wasn't easy. The notion of hauling both Hauptmans into Silesia still didn't appeal to her in the least, but having a destroyer for company couldn't hurt. And she knew how tight stretched the Navy was . . . which also meant she knew which of her passengers had prompted this "coincidental" generosity.

"Of course," the lieutenant added, "you'll be guided by Lieutenant Commander Usher if anything should happen along the way."

"Naturally," Fuchien agreed. It was only fair, after all. The Navy might not want to call it a one-ship convoy, but that was what it would be. *Artemis's* speed meant Fuchien wasn't used to sailing under escort. In fact, she usually tended to take the suggestion that her ship required escorting as something of an insult, but she could stand it just this once.

"Very well, then, Captain. Commander Usher will be in touch with you shortly, I'm sure."

"Thank you again, Lieutenant. We appreciate it," Fuchien said with complete sincerity, then leaned back in her command chair and grinned widely as the screen blanked.

• CHAPTER TWENTY-FIVE

The rippling sound of shuffled cards hovered in the berthing compartment as Randy Steilman's thick fingers manipulated the deck. He'd shed his work uniform for shorts and a T-shirt, and the dense hair on his heavily muscled arms looked like dark fur under the lights. He offered the deck to Ed Illyushin to cut, but the environmental tech—a first-class, which made him the most senior person in the compartment—only rapped it with a knuckle, declining the cut, and coins thumped as the players anted up for the next hand.

"Seven card stud," he announced, and the deck whispered as he dealt the hole cards, then the first face up. "King of diamonds is high," he observed. "What'cha gonna do there, Jackson?"

"Um." Jackson Coulter scratched his jaw, then tossed a five-dollar coin out onto the table.

"Christ, what a big spender!" Steilman's laugh rumbled deep in his belly, and he glanced at Elizabeth Showforth. "How's about you, Sweet Cakes?"

"How'd you like a kick in the ass?" Showforth had the jack of spades showing and tossed out a five-spot of her own. Illyushin, with the ten of diamonds, matched her, and Steilman shook his head.

"Shit, what a bunch of wimps." He himself had an eight of clubs showing, and he tossed ten dollars out without even checking his hole cards, then looked at Al Stennis, the fifth and final player. Stennis had a lowly two of hearts, and he scowled at Steilman.

"Why do you always hafta push so hard, Randy?" he

demanded plaintively, but he matched the dealer's raise. Steilman eyed the other three challengingly, and, one by one, each of them tossed another five dollars into the pot.

"*That's* the spirit!" Steilman encouraged with another laugh. He dealt the next card and cocked an eyebrow as the queen of hearts landed in front of Coulter. "Looking good, there, Jackson! Let's see, possible royal straight to Jackson, nothing much to Sweet Cakes, a possible straight to Ed, jack shit to Al, and—" He dropped the nine of clubs onto his own hand and beamed. "Well, well!" he chortled. "Possible straight flush to the dealer!"

He tossed another ten dollars out, and the others groaned. But they also followed suit, and he started around the table again.

The poker games in Berthing Compartment 256 were its inhabitants' second-most serious occupation—a point which many of their fellow crewmen, who speculated ribaldly on just who did what with whom, would have found difficult to believe.

Traditionally, berthing assignments aboard a Queen's ship were subject to adjustment by mutual consent. Initial assignments were made as personnel reported aboard, but as long as divisional officers were kept informed, the Navy's people were free to swap around as long as the division between ratings, petty officers, and officers was maintained. The Navy had come to that arrangement long ago, though the Marines remained far more formal about the whole thing and required officer approval of changes.

The Navy had also concluded that attempting to enforce celibacy on its mixed crews would not only be a Bad Idea but also doomed to fail, and BuPers had adopted a pragmatic policy over five hundred T-years previously. The only relationships which were absolutely banned were those covered by Article 119: those between officers and or noncoms and any of their own subordinates. Aside from that, personnel were free to make whatever arrangements they chose, and all female personnel received five-year contraceptive implants which could be deactivated upon request. In peacetime, such requests were granted automatically; in wartime, they were granted only if personnel were available to replace the woman making the request. More than that, women who chose to become pregnant were immediately pulled from shipboard duty and assigned to one of the space stations or ground bases, where they could be promptly replaced and transferred to duty without radiation hazards if they did become pregnant. It wasn't fair—women's procreation was more limited, though women could also use a decision to have children to avoid shipboard duty—but biology wasn't fair, either, and the practice of tubing children took a lot of the sting out of it. In fact, BuPers both provided free storage for sperm and ova to its personnel and covered seventy-five percent of the cost for tubed offspring in an effort to even the possibilities still further. Despite periodic complaints, the policy was understood—and, in the main, accepted—as the best compromise a military institution could come up with.

The policy also meant a wise captain and executive officer generally kept their noses out of who was sleeping with whom as long as no one violated Article 119. It was, however, unusual for a single member of one sex to bunk with four members of the *other* sex, which was precisely what Elizabeth Showforth had done. Her choice was all the more remarkable in that Showforth's sexual interests didn't include men . . . but, then, she wasn't bunking with Steilman, Coulter, Illyushin, and Stennis for that particular form of social intercourse. On the other hand, the tradition of not interfering provided a handy cover for the reason she *had* chosen to bunk here.

"I wish to hell you'd slow down a little, Randy," Stennis grumbled as Steilman dealt.

"What, the pot too rich for your blood?"

"I wasn't talking about poker," Stennis said much more quietly, and eyes lifted from cards to meet other eyes all around the table.

"Then what the fuck *were* you talking about, Al?" Steilman asked ominously. Stennis swallowed, but he didn't look away.

"You know what I'm talking about." He did look away then, gaze sweeping the others in an appeal for support. "I know Lewis pissed you off, but you're gonna queer the deal for *all* of us if you keep this shit up."

Randy Steilman set down the deck of cards and pushed his chair back a few centimeters, turning to face Stennis squarely, and his eyes were ugly.

"Listen, you little fuck," he said softly. " 'The deal' you're talkin' about was *my* idea. I'm the one who set it up, and *I'm* the one who's gonna say when we do it. And what I do in the meantime is none of your goddamned business, now is it?"

The sudden silence in the compartment was profound, and sweat beaded Stennis' forehead. He glanced nervously at the closed hatch before he leaned even closer to Steilman, and he chose his words very carefully, but there was a stubborn edge to his tone.

"I'm not trying to say any different. You thought of it and you set it up, and as far as I'm concerned, you're in charge. But, Jesus, Randy! If you keep going after Wanderman or picking fights with POs, you're gonna land us all in the crapper. And then what happens to the whole deal? All I'm saying is that we're all in this together, and if anybody finds out what we're planning, we're all gonna go away for a long, long time. If we're lucky."

Steilman's mouth twisted and his eyes smoldered, but he sensed a certain agreement from the others. They were all more than a little afraid of him—a state which afforded him considerable pleasure—but he needed each of them to make his plan work. And, he conceded, if any of them got scared enough, he—or she—might just blow the whistle on all of them in an effort to buy a little clemency from the court-martial.

But that didn't mean he was going to put up with anyone telling him what he could and couldn't do, and that little prick Wanderman and his girlfriend were going to get everything they had coming. Randy Steilman was used to captain's masts and to being busted. He was no stranger to brig time, for that matter, and, by and large, he accepted it as a condition of his life. But *nobody* got in his face and enjoyed the consequences. That was his one inflexible rule, the mainstay of his existence. He was a man who throve on his own brutality and the fear it evoked in others. It was that fear which gave him his sense of power, and without it he was forced to see himself as he truly was. He'd never reasoned it out, yet that made it no less true, and he could no more have allowed Wanderman and Lewis to get away with *not* being afraid of him than he could have flown without a counter-grav collar.

A part of him knew he'd pushed too far with the business in Impeller One. He'd learned years ago—courtesy of the beating then Chief Petty Officer MacBride had given him one night—that there were limits, even for him. But he'd been bored, and the efficiency Maxwell had been getting out of his people had irritated him, not to mention making him work harder himself. Besides, he'd heard how Lewis was pushing Wanderman . . . and whatever else the incident had produced, he knew he owed the bitch something special for the tongue-lashing her high and mightiness *Lady* Harrington had given him.

Somewhere deep inside, he felt a shiver of fear as he remembered the Captain's icy voice and colder eyes. She hadn't screamed, hadn't ranted like some officers he'd pissed off over the years. She hadn't even sworn at him. She'd simply looked at him with frigid, disdainful loathing, and her tongue had been a precision instrument as she flayed him with her contempt. The shiver of fear grew stronger, and he suppressed it quickly, trying to deny its existence, but it was there, and he hated it. The only other person who'd ever put that fear into him was Sally MacBride, which had been a factor in why he'd finally taken the step from thinking about his plan to putting it into action. He wanted to be as far away from her as he could get, but he knew now that MacBride had been right. Harrington was more dangerous than any bosun. There was a limit to the crap she would put up with, and Steilman felt ominously certain that if it got deep enough, she might choose to forget about procedures and proof. And if she did, he wanted to be even further away from her than from MacBride when the consequences came down.

But Randy Steilman was also convinced he could get away with whatever he chose to do. Perhaps he shouldn't have been, given the number of times he'd been busted or brigged, yet he was. And the reason was simple enough, actually. None of the punishments he'd ever received even approached what *he* liked to do to others, and so some elemental part of him assumed they never would. It wasn't an intellectual assumption. It was deeper than that, where it was never questioned because it was never even considered, and that was what made him so dangerous. He'd never killed anyone yet, but he was convinced he could . . . and this time he intended to.

In point of fact, he looked forward to it. It would be the ultimate proof of his power—and it would also be his valedictory, his final "gift" to the Navy he'd come to hate. He was only four years into his current enlistment, and he never would have reupped if he'd thought a shooting war might actually break out. He wasn't really certain why he'd signed up again, anyway, except that it was the only life he knew, and he hadn't stopped to wonder why the Navy had even allowed him to reenlist. His discipline record had gotten worse, not better, in the preceding ten years, and under normal conditions, the Navy would have declined his services with alacrity. But Steilman didn't think about things like that, and so it had never occurred to him that the only reason he'd squeaked through was that, unlike him, the Navy *had* known war was coming and lowered its screening standards where experienced personnel were concerned because it knew how badly it would soon need them.

What *had* occurred to him was that he might get himself killed. The RMN's casualty lists were far shorter than the Peeps', but they were getting steadily longer, and Randy Steilman saw no reason to get *his* ass shot off for Queen and Kingdom.

Given all that, the decision to desert had come easily, but there was one enormous hitch. The sentence for desertion in peacetime was not less than thirty years in prison; in wartime it was the firing squad, and he didn't particularly want to face *that*, either. Worse, wartime deployment patterns made jumping ship more difficult. Steilman wasn't the sort any captain wanted aboard a destroyer or light cruiser, whose smaller companies meant every individual *had* to pull his weight, but the heavier ships had been pulled from peacetime cruising patterns and concentrated into fleets and task forces. It was only the light combatants which could be spared for convoy escort or antipiracy operations, which meant they were the only ones likely to touch at foreign ports where a man might manage to disappear into the local population.

Until now. He'd been horrified when he first learned he was being assigned to Honor Harrington's ship. The rest of his stupid crewmates could worship the deck "the Salamander" walked on and gas away about what a great combat commander she was. All Randy Steilman cared about was the casualty lists she'd compiled over the years, starting with Basilisk Station. Others could carry on all they liked about how no one else could have done better, about how much worse the casualties *could* have been. They could even point out the amount of prize money her crews—or their heirs—had amassed. Steilman liked money even more than most, but a dead man couldn't spend it, and learning MacBride was *Wayfarer's* bosun had only made a bad situation worse . . . until he'd learned where Task Group 1037 was to be deployed.

Of all the places in the galaxy, Silesia was the best for a man who wanted to disappear. Especially a trained spacer unburdened by anything resembling a scruple.

Randy Steilman was on the wrong side of the war against the pirates. He looked forward to joining the one he belonged on, and sooner or later *Wayfarer* had to touch at a Silesian port.

Steilman had planned carefully for that moment. He'd kept his eyes and ears open to assemble all the information he could on Harrington's ships and their operational patterns. He knew far more about their strengths—and weaknesses—than even the people around this card table suspected. He'd also made bootleg copies of as many tech manuals as he could—it was strictly against regulations, but not that hard for someone with his training, and Showforth's slot in computer maintenance had helped—and he wondered how much a Peep naval attaché would pay him for some of that material. The chips were in his locker, and getting them dirtside when the time came shouldn't pose any problems. Or not, at least, compared to the problem of getting *himself* dirtside in the first place.

But he'd figured that out, too, and that was where Stennis and Illyushin came in. They were in Environmental, and Environmental was responsible for maintaining *Wayfarer*'s escape pods. The number of people who could expect to get out of a ship lost to battle damage would be low, but *someone* almost always made it—unless the damned ship blew up, of course—and ships could be lost to other causes. That was what the pods were for. In deep space, they were little more than life-support bubbles fitted with transponders which both sides were supposedly duty bound to pick up after an engagement, but they were also designed to be capable of independent atmospheric entry if there should happen to be a habitable planet handy when disaster struck.

At Steilman's direction, Showforth had built and Stennis and Illyushin had installed an unobtrusive little box in the circuits which monitored Pod 184. When the time came, that box would be turned on, and it would continue to report that the ten-man pod was exactly where it was supposed to be, with every system at standby, when, in fact, it was somewhere else entirely. The trick would be to create conditions that produced enough confusion to keep everyone too preoccupied to notice any outbound radar traces, and Steilman had worked that out, as well. He and Coulter had already built the bomb for Impeller One. It wasn't a huge thing, but it would be enough to completely cripple two of the alpha node generators. The energy released when the generator capacitors blew would wreak additional havoc, both on the ship and on anyone unfortunate enough to be in Impeller One at the time, and in the ensuing confusion and panic, five people who all happened to be off duty would quietly descend on Pod 184 and depart for greener pastures.

It had taken Steilman weeks to identify the people he needed to make it all work, and the number was higher than he liked. The more people involved, the greater the chance of something going wrong, after all. Nor had he been able to get everything in place in time to put his plan into operation in Walther. But he was ready now. All they needed was to enter orbit around the proper planet—Schiller wouldn't do; its original colonists had come from Old Earth's continent of Africa, and all five of them would stand out like sore thumbs when Harrington demanded the local authorities help track them down—and they were off and free.

But before he left, he was going to square accounts with Wanderman and Lewis. It would be not only his parting gift to the Navy, but to that sanctimonious bitch MacBride, as well. Yes, and to Captain Honor Harrington, damn her!

"Look," he said finally, "I'm willing to lie low for a while. Let the Old Bitch think she's put the fear of God into me—hell, it's no skin off my nose! But don't *any* of you tell me what I can and can't do." He saw the fear in their eyes, and the ugliness at his core basked in its reflection. "I am going to fix Lewis's ass, and I'm gonna kill that fucker Wanderman with my own two hands, and there's nobody gonna stop me, least of all *you*." He bared his teeth and slammed one meaty fist down on the table for emphasis. "I don't want to hear any more shit about it, and if I decide I need one of you to help, then you'd better by God believe you're gonna *give* me that help. 'Cause if you don't, there's gonna be less people in that pod when it lands, you hear me?"

Stennis swallowed and his eyes fell. Then he nodded jerkily, the fear radiating off him in all but visible waves. Steilman let his eyes sweep the others, and, one by one, they nodded as well. All but Coulter, who simply looked back with a thin, cold smile of agreement.

"Good." The single word fell into the background silence like a stone, and then Randy Steilman picked up the deck and began to deal once more.

• CHAPTER TWENTY-SIX

Citizen Commander Caslet heaved a profound sigh of relief as his pinnace docked. His orders to remain covert at all times made sense, he supposed, but they were also an unmitigated pain, especially since not even the Republic's own diplomatic corps knew Citizen Admiral Giscard had been dispatched to the Confederacy. The ambassadors and trade attachés threaded through Silesian space were integral parts of the Republic's intelligence chain, but most were also holdovers from the old regime. The Committee of Public Safety had applied the new broom theory to the diplomats dispatched to places like the Solarian League, but Silesia was a backwater, too far from the critical arenas of diplomatic maneuvering to give the same housekeeping priority. As a result, State Security trusted its own embassy staffs no further than it had to—which, Caslet conceded, was probably wise of the SS. Six senior Legislaturalist ambassadors *had* defected to the Manties . . . after StateSec executed most of the rest of their families for "treason against the people."

That sort of predictable cause and effect was one of the more egregious examples of the lunacies of revolutionary ardor, in Caslet's estimation, and it made his own life difficult. He couldn't tap directly into the diplomatic service's intelligence conduits without revealing his presence and, probably, something about his mission, and that was forbidden, since those very intelligence sources were suspect in the eyes of his superiors. Citizen Admiral Giscard could use any information they turned up, but only after it had been funneled to one of the ambassadors sent out since the coup attempt, and Jasmine Haines, the Schiller System trade attaché, was much too far down the food chain for that. Caslet could use Haines to send encrypted dispatches to Giscard via diplomatic courier, but he could neither tell her what those dispatches said, nor who *he* was, nor even ask her for specific data which might "in any way compromise the operational security of your mission," as his orders succinctly, if unhelpfully, put it.

At least he had the authentication codes to require her assistance, but he'd been forced to skulk into Schiller and hide behind the system's largest gas giant while he sent a mere pinnace in with his dispatches. He'd *hated* that. Hated being stuck at the rendezvous point until his pinnace returned and, even more, hated sending his people into danger when he couldn't go with them. But Allison seemed to have handled the contact as discreetly as he could have hoped, and he watched from the boat bay gallery as the docking tube ran out to the pinnace's lock.

MacMurtree swam the tube, and he felt a twinge of annoyance at the twinkle in her eyes when he returned her salute just that tiny bit too impatiently. She knew him too well, knew he was itchy, eager to get back to trolling for pirates. Of course, he knew *her* pretty well, too. Neither of them had ever said so, but they shared the same contempt for the Committee of Public Safety and its minions—except, perhaps, for the handful like Denis Jourdain. And neither of them really liked the concept of commerce raiding.

Which is pretty silly of us both, Caslet reflected. *The entire purpose of having a navy is to deny the use of space to an enemy while securing it for yourself, isn't it? And how can you deny it to someone else if you're not willing to kill his merchantmen? Besides, merchant tonnage is just as important to the Manties as warships—probably even more so, right?*

He shook off the thought and nodded towards the lifts.

MacMurtree fell in beside him, and he punched the bridge code into the panel.

"How'd it go?" he asked.

"Not too badly," she said with a small shrug. "Their customs patrols really aren't worth a damn. No one even closed to make an eyeball on us."

"Good," Caslet grunted. He'd been unhappy about the "asteroid mining boat" cover his orders specified, since a pinnace didn't look the least bit like a civilian craft. But what had once been NavInt insisted that what passed for a customs patrol out here would settle for a transponder read, and damned if they hadn't been right. *Well, that makes a nice change*, he thought dryly.

"Anyway, we handled it all by tight beam from orbit," MacMurtree went on. "Haines didn't like sending her dispatch boat off, but she accepted her orders. Our dispatches should reach Admiral Giscard"—there were no people's commissioners here to overhear her use of the prerevolutionary rank—"within three weeks." She grimaced. "We could've cut a good ten days off that by sending her straight to the rendezvous, Skipper."

"Security, Allison," Caslet replied, and she snorted with a grumpiness he understood perfectly. To keep StateSec happy, they had to send their dispatches to the Saginaw System, from which *another* dispatch boat (this one under the orders of an ambassador the Committee of Public Safety trusted) would carry them to Giscard. Even at the high FTL velocities dispatch boats routinely turned out, that was going to take time.

"At any rate," he went on, "we can be sure he'll know everything we do—and what we're up to. Which means we can go trolling again with a clear conscience."

"True," MacMurtree agreed. "Anything turn up while I was away?"

"Not really. Of course, we're sort of out of the way here. I figure we'll clear the planetary hyper limit, pop into h-space and move a couple of light-weeks out, then come back in the same way we did for Sharon's Star."

"What if we run into somebody else?"

"You mean a 'regular' pirate instead of Warnecke's happy campers?" Mac-Murtree nodded, and Caslet shrugged. "We've pulled enough out of their com-puters to recognize their emissions. We should be able to ID the ones we want if we see them."

He paused, rubbing an eyebrow, and MacMurtree nodded again. Painstaking analysis had proved that Citizen Sergeant Simonson had gotten more out of the computers of the pirate they'd already knocked out than they'd expected. Which was fortunate, since they'd gotten even less than hoped for out of their prisoners. But that, in its own way, had been highly satisfactory. With no need to make deals, all of the raiders had been given a fair trial before they went out the lock. The People's Navy didn't get its sick kicks the way the prisoners had, how-ever, so Branscombe's Marines had executed each of them *before* he or she hit vacuum.

But among the bits and pieces Simonson had retrieved there was more than enough to confirm Captain Sukow-ski's claims about Andre Warnecke, and some sobering stats on other units of the "privateer squadron." Most were at least as powerful as the one *Vaubon* had destroyed, and they had four ships which looked to be more heavily armed than most of the Republic's heavy cruisers. The good news was that an examination of their capture's weapons systems had shown some glaring defi-ciencies. The Chalice's "revolutionary government" had built its ships to kill merchantmen, which couldn't shoot back, or engage Silesian Navy units, which were hardly up to the standards of major navies, and it showed. They seemed to have insisted in cramming in as heavy an offensive punch as possible, which wasn't an uncommon mistake in the navies of weaker powers. Heavy throw weights were impressive as hell, but it was just as impor-tant to keep the bad guys from scoring on *your* ship, and they were underequipped for that.

Which wasn't to say they wouldn't be dangerous if they were handled properly, but there were no indications of anything that could go toe-to-toe with Giscard's battle-cruisers. Still, if Warnecke's people managed to mass two or three of their ships against *one* of his, things could get iffy. And if that was true for battlecruisers, it was far more true for light cruisers.

That was a sobering thought, but the computers had also coughed up the fact that all of Warnecke's ships had been built in the same yard and fitted with the same derivative of the standard Silesian Navy sensor and EW systems. As far as Foraker had been able to determine, their radar was a unique installation, so all they needed was a good read on it, and they'd know they had the murderous bastards they wanted.

"I guess if we run into somebody else we'll just have to warn them off and send them on their way," he sighed finally. He hated the very thought. Pirates were the natural enemy of any man of war, but he knew he really had no choice. Jourdain was a good sort, but he'd balk at killing off regular pirates who might be expected to help put more pressure on the Manties.

"It's not going to feel right," MacMurtree murmured, and he laughed without humor.

"Just between you and me, Allison, I've felt that way quite a few times in the last three years," he said. She looked at him for a moment, eyes momentarily wide, then smiled and thumped him on the shoulder. Very few officers in the People's Navy would have dared to speak that frankly to anyone, however long they'd served together, and she started to reply, then closed her mouth with another smile as the lift reached its destination. The doors whispered open, and Caslet led the way out onto *Vaubon's* bridge.

"All well, Citizen Exec?" Jourdain asked MacMurtree, and she nodded.

"Yes, Sir," she said crisply. "Citizen Haines has already sent her dispatch boat off."

"Excellent!" Jourdain actually rubbed his hands together in satisfaction. "In that case, Citizen Commander, I think it's time we went looking for these people, don't you?"

"I do, indeed, Sir," Caslet said, and smiled. When Jourdain had first come aboard, Caslet would have wagered five years' pay that he would never be more than a pain in the ass. Now Caslet was only too well aware how fortunate he'd been, and his smile turned genuinely warm for a moment. Then he shook himself and looked at his astrogator.

"All right, Simon. Let's do it."

Harold Sukowski dropped into the chair beside Chris Hurlman's bed and smiled at her. It was easier than it had been, for she no longer looked like a trapped animal. Dr. Jankowski had kept a close eye on Chris, but the surgeon had decided to leave counseling for later and restricted herself to cleaning her up and treating her physical injuries. The fact that Jankowski was a woman had helped, no doubt, but Sukowski suspected it was the sense of safety which had made the real difference. For the first time since *Bonaventure*'s capture, Chris felt genuinely safe, among people who not only didn't threaten her or her skipper but actually wished them well.

The first day or two had been little more than waiting. He'd sat beside her bed virtually every waking hour, and Chris had only lain there, staring at the deckhead. The hysterics hadn't started until the third day, and they'd been mercifully brief. Now she had her good days and her bad ones, but this seemed to be one of the former, and she managed an answering smile as he sat down beside her. It was only a shadow of her previous, infectious grin, and his heart ached at the courage it must take to project even that lopsided effort, but he only patted her hand gently.

"Looks like they do pretty good work here," he observed in a deliberately light tone. Her smile wavered but didn't disappear, and she cleared her throat.

"Yeah," she husked. Her voice sounded rusty and broken, but his aching heart leapt as she spoke, for she hadn't said a single word during their nightmare stay aboard the "privateer." "Maybe I should've obeyed orders," she rasped, and a single tear trickled down her cheek.

"You should've," he agreed, reaching out to wipe the tear with a gentle finger, "but if you had, I'd be dead. Under the circumstances, I've decided not to write you up for mutiny."

"Gee, thanks," she managed, and her shoulders shook with a chuckle that was next door to a sob. She closed both eyes, then licked her lips. "They going to dump us in a POW camp?"

"Nope. They say they'll send us home as soon as they can." Chris turned her head on the pillow, both eyes popping open in disbelief, and Sukowski shrugged. "Nobody's said so, but they've got to be out here to raid our commerce. That's going to give them a heap of merchant spacer POWs. Sooner or later, they'll have to admit they've got them, and the civilian prisoner exchange conventions are pretty straightforward."

"As long as they bother to *take* prisoners," Chris muttered, and Sukowski shook his head.

"I'm no fonder of the Peep government than the next man, but these people seem pretty decent. They've certainly taken good care of us"—he meant "you," and she nodded in agreement—"and they seem as determined to get the bastards who hit us as any of our skippers could be. I've had a chance to look at their visual records from another ship the bastards hit, and I think I understand why they're so hot to get them," he added with a slight shiver, then shrugged again. "Anyway, that's what they're doing right this minute, and that suggests they intend to follow the rules where civilians are concerned."

"Maybe," Chris said dubiously, and Sukowski squeezed the hand he still held. He couldn't blame her for anticipating the worst—not after what she'd been through— yet he was convinced she was doing Caslet and Jourdain a disservice.

"I think—" he began, but he never finished the sentence, for it was chopped off by the sudden howl of *Vaubon's* GQ alarm.

*   *   *

"Talk to me, Shannon!" Caslet said urgently while he watched the ugly picture developing on his plot. A whale-like merchantman wallowed desperately through space on a vector roughly convergent with *Vaubon's* own while no less than three smaller barracudas raced after it. They were all inside Foraker's radar envelope—or would have been, if she'd been able to go active without blowing her "merchantman" disguise, and their impeller signatures burned clear and sharp in the display on vectors which could mean only one thing.

"Just a—" Foraker chopped off in midword. She bent over her readouts, fingers stroking her console like a lover as she worked the contacts, then straightened.

"It's our boys, Skip," she said flatly. "Looks like two a bit smaller than the one we already killed and a third a bit bigger—maybe our size. Hard to say from here without going active, but we're catching some scatter off the merchie, and the radar's right. I'd say it's them . . . and from their maneuvers, they're definitely pirates. Only one hitch, Sir." She turned her chair to look at him, and her smile was grim. "That's a Manty they're chasing."

"Oh, shit." MacMurtree's whispered curse was almost a prayer, so soft only Caslet heard her, and his own face tightened. A Manty. Wonderful—just wonderful! The odds sucked to start with, and the "privateers'" intended victim had to be a *Manticoran* merchantman

He turned his head and looked at Jourdain as the people's commissioner crossed the bridge to him. Jourdain's expression was as troubled as Caslet's own, and the older man leaned over to speak very quietly into the citizen commander's ear.

"What now?"

"Sir, I don't know," Caslet said simply, watching the doomed Manty continue to run at her best, feeble acceleration. The pirates were spread in a cone off her port quarter, on the far side of her base course from *Vaubon,* but they were closing quickly. They'd be into missile range within the next twelve minutes, and it was already impossible for the freighter to evade them.

Caslet bent and punched a query into his own plot, then frowned as the numbers flickered and the various vectors projected themselves across the display. If everyone maintained his or her current heading, the bad guys were going to overtake their prey less than a million kilometers in front of *Vaubon*, which was much too close for comfort. Worse, given the way their courses were folding together and allowing for the raiders' inevitable deceleration to board the freighter, they'd be moving no more than a few hundred KPS faster than *Vaubon* at intercept, which would extend the time on any engagement and make things even dicier.

"Are *we* taking any radar hits?" he asked.

"Negative, Skip. They seem to be concentrating on the Manty." Foraker sniffed in eloquent contempt for the privateers' sloppiness. "Of course, they must have us on gravitics, and they may just not see any reason to look closer our way," she allowed. "We've got *them* on passive, after all. They're probably tracking us the same way, and we look like another merchie. Maybe they're even hoping we haven't seen them yet. If they are, they wouldn't want to knock on the hatch with their radar."

Caslet nodded and frowned down at the display. That freighter was an enemy vessel. Not a warship, no, but still under an enemy flag. And given his mission orders, that made it his duty to attack it. His superiors had certainly never contemplated a situation in which he might even consider *rescuing* it, but he knew too much about the psychopaths manning those raiders. Every instinct cried out to go to the Manty's assistance, yet the odds were daunting. He was prepared to back his people against anything in space ton for ton—always allowing for the Manty tech advantage, he amended sourly—and he doubted the pirates had faced anyone who could shoot back since they set up as independents. More than that, his weapons were better than theirs . . . which made a nice change from being on the short end all the time.

He was confident he could take the two smaller ships; it was the larger vessel that worried him. That, and the fact that if he engaged at all, he could be pretty sure someone up the line would want his head. But, damn it, he couldn't just sit here and watch these barbarians murder another crew!

"I want to engage, Sir." He could hardly believe his own words, and he saw the shock in Jourdain's face as he listened to his own voice go on speaking in calm, level tones which must have belonged to someone else. "They're pirates, and they'll know that even if they take us out, we can hurt them badly first. If we come in openly, they'll probably break off."

"And if they don't?" Jourdain asked flatly.

"If they don't, they *can* take us if we get unlucky. But not until we hammer them so hard they won't be any threat to Citizen Admiral Giscard's operations. And if we don't intervene, they're going to do to this ship exactly what they did to Captain Sukowski and Commander Hurlman—or to *Erewhon*'s crew."

"But it's a Manticoran vessel," Jourdain pointed out quietly. "We're out here to raid their commerce ourselves."

"Well," Caslet felt himself smile, "in that case, we'll have to convince these other people to let us have her, won't we?" Jourdain blinked at him, and Caslet shrugged. "It'll be a bit hard on her crew if we 'rescue' them and then take their ship ourselves, Citizen Commissioner, but once they've had a chance to talk it over with Captain Sukowski, I think they'll agree they're better off with us than with Warnecke's people. And, as you say, we *are* supposed to capture any Manty merchie we run into. It says so right in our orders."

"Somehow," Jourdain said in bone-dry tones, "I doubt the people who drafted those orders expected us to engage pirates at three-to-one odds first."

"Then they should have said so, Sir." Caslet felt his smile grow even broader, felt the reckless surge of adrenaline, and raised one hand in a palm-up gesture. "Given what they *did* tell us, I don't see that we have an option. Our orders aren't discretionary, after all."

"They'll hang us both out to dry if you lose your ship, Citizen Commander."

"If we lose the ship, that will be the least of our worries, Sir. On the other hand, if we pull it off, I think Citizen Admiral Giscard and Citizen Commissioner Pritchart will turn a blind eye to any, ah, *irregularities* in our actions. Success, after all, is still the best justification."

"You're out of your mind," Jourdain said conversationally, then shrugged. "Still, I suppose we might as well be hung for sheep."

"Thank you, Sir," Caslet said quietly, and looked at MacMurtree and Foraker. "All right, people, let's do this smart. Deploy an EW drone, Shannon. Slave it to follow us in about a hundred thousand klicks back and set it to radiate another light cruiser signature. If they're only tracking us on passive, they may figure our 'consort' was hiding her impellers in our shadow until we committed to the attack run."

"Aye, Skip," Foraker replied, and Caslet turned to his astrogator.

"Stand by to bring the wedge to full power, Simon, and plot a direct intercept. Then give me time and velocities at course merge."

"Aye, Skip." Lieutenant Houghton punched numbers that would alter *Vaubon's* course slightly and increase her acceleration radically, then studied his plot for a moment. "Assuming they don't break off, a direct intercept at max accel will cut their base course in eleven minutes and eighteen seconds. We'll come in on a converging vector, range a bit under seven hundred thousand klicks to the nearest bandit, with a relative velocity of plus one-five-niner-six KPS."

"How soon will we enter their missile envelope on that heading, Shannon?"

"Call it eight minutes, Skip."

"All right, people," Warner Caslet decided. "Let's do it."

"We've got a status change on Target Two!"

Commodore Jason Arner stiffened in his command chair on the light cruiser's bridge as his tac officer sang out.

"What kind of change?" he snapped.

"It's— Oh, shit! It's not a merchie at all! It's a god-damned light cruiser, and she's coming in full bore!"

"*A cruiser?*" Arner stabbed a glance at his plot. "Whose?" he demanded. "Is it a Manty?"

"I don't think so." The tac officer brought his active systems and computer support to bear, examining the oncoming ship closely, then shook his head. "Definitely not a Manty. And it's not Andy or Confed, either. Damned if I know *who* it is, but she's coming in loaded for bear, and—" He paused, then spoke flatly. "I'm showing another cruiser astern of her."

"Shit!" Arner glowered at his display, and his mind whirred. His first assumption—that the cruiser was a Manty using the freighter ahead of him to suck in raiders—had just gone out the lock. But if the newcomers weren't Manties or Andies or Silesians, then who in hell *were* they? Another pair of raiders? That happened from time to time, though rarely, but there were rules even for their profession, and poaching on another man's kill was against all of them.

"Where'd the second one come from?"

"I don't know," the tac officer replied frankly. "She's about a hundred-k klicks back, and I suppose she could have been hiding under her EW, but if she was, she's got damned good systems. I've been tracking Target Two on gravitics for over a half hour, and I never even got a sniff of another impeller source. Of course, if they worked it right, they could have kept Target Two between us and them. We wouldn't have been able to see her from here if they came in on exactly the right course."

"Or it might be a drone," Arner pointed out.

"It's possible. I just can't say from here."

"How long before you can confirm or deny?"

"Maybe six minutes."

"Can we still evade at that point if we have to?"

"Tight," the tac officer said. He worked at his console for a moment, then shrugged. "If we hang on that long then go to max accel on our best breakaway vector, they can bring us into missile range and keep us there for maybe twenty minutes, depending on their max accel, but they can't get into energy range unless we let them."

Arner grunted and rubbed his clean shaven chin. Unlike many of his fellows in the squadron, he remembered having been something approaching a regular naval officer, and he kept himself presentable. Some hapless merchant skippers had seen that presentability and hoped it meant they were dealing with a civilized individual. They'd been wrong, but for all his other faults, Jason Arner seldom panicked, and the instincts of the naval officer he'd almost been were at work now. If those were other raiders—or regular warships—and they kept coming, he'd have to fight them. On the other hand, he had three ships to their two, even assuming they were both really ships at all, and his vessels were heavily armed for their tonnage. He was likely to take some nasty knocks, and Admiral Warnecke would be pissed off about that, which was not a cheerful thing to contemplate. But if he took the newcomers as well as the merchantman, he'd not only collect whatever cargo his original victim was carrying but quite possibly add another cruiser to the fleet—maybe even two. That should be enough to keep the Admiral happy, given his plans to return eventually to the Chalice.

"Maintain your pursuit profile," he told his helmsman, and looked back at the tac officer. "Keep on that second ship. Let me know the instant you're certain either way."

"They're not breaking off, Skip," Foraker reported, and

Caslet nodded. A small voice of sanity was screaming somewhere inside him, because despite all he'd said to Jourdain, he knew what he was about to do was incredibly stupid. For that matter, he was sure Jourdain knew that as well as he did. If he had to fight three-to-one odds, *Vaubon* would be hammered into a junk pile even if he won, and if he lost, every man and woman of his crew was probably going to die. Looked at from that perspective, there was no logic at all in risking everything to protect an enemy vessel, yet he knew he was going to do it anyway.

Why? he wondered. Because it was the job of a naval officer to protect civilians from murderers and rapists? Because he truly believed it was his duty to his own navy? That reducing the odds Citizen Admiral Giscard *might* have to face was worth it? Or was it his own insane gesture of defiance to the Committee of Public Safety? His own way of saying, just this once, "Look! I'm still an officer in a navy whose honor *means* something, whatever *you* think"?

He didn't know, and it didn't matter. Whatever drove him, it drove the rest of his officers, as well. He could feel it in them—all of them, even Jourdain—and he smiled grimly at his plot.

Get ready, you bastards, because we're about to rip you a brand new asshole!

"The trailer's a drone," the tac officer said flatly. "Has to be. My radar return from it is lots stronger than from the leader—either it's augmenting its image, or its tac officer just doesn't give a shit how good a lockup I can get for Missile Control."

"Is it, now?" Arner murmured with a wicked smile. The merchantman which had served as the unwitting trigger to the confrontation continued to plug desperately along, but his own ships were decelerating now to match velocity with it. Not that anyone was paying it much heed. The oncoming stranger was hopelessly outgunned, but he *was* armed. That made him the focus of attention. Besides, there'd be plenty of time to scoop up the merchie later.

"You know," the tac officer said slowly, "I think this bird might just be a Peep."

"A Peep?" Arner's tone was an objection. "What would a Peep be doing out here?"

"Damned if I know, but it's not anybody else I can recognize, and I don't think another raider would want to take on all three of us. Besides, most of us don't waste tonnage on EW drones." The tac officer shook his head. "Nope. This is the kind of boneheaded thing a regular Navy officer might try. You know—honor of the Fleet, and all."

"Then we'll just have to show him the error of his ways," Arner said with an evil laugh.

"Entering missile envelope in one minute, Skip," Foraker said tensely. "They're hitting us hard with radar and lidar, but I think they're pretty much ignoring the drone. Doesn't look like they bought it."

"Understood." Caslet locked his shock frame, and a corner of his eye saw the rest of his bridge crew doing the same. He'd never had a lot of hope the drone *would* fool the bastards, he thought distantly, but it had been worth a shot.

He studied the enemy's formation intently, and his upper lip curled. They'd closed up some and turned away a bit, slowing his relative approach speed, but one of their smaller ships was a good half million klicks closer to *Vaubon* than either of her consorts. At their present rate of closure, that would put it inside his powered missile envelope six minutes before its friends could return the favor, and it was about time to start evening the odds.

"Take the near one, Shannon," he said coldly. "Hammer the bastard."

Like the PN's smaller *Breslau*-class destroyers, the

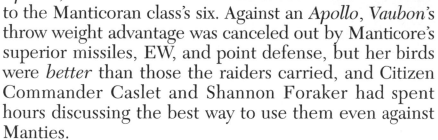

Conqueror-class light cruisers were missile heavy. They were also twenty thousand tons heavier than the RMN's *Apollos*, with a broadside of nine tubes to the Manticoran class's six. Against an *Apollo*, *Vaubon's* throw weight advantage was canceled out by Manticore's superior missiles, EW, and point defense, but her birds were *better* than those the raiders carried, and Citizen Commander Caslet and Shannon Foraker had spent hours discussing the best way to use them even against Manties.

Vaubon came tearing down on her enemies spinning on her central axis like a dervish. The pirates might be forgiven for assuming that was simply a move to gain maximum cover from the roof and floor of her wedge, but it wasn't—as they discovered when Foraker pressed her firing key. Nine missiles spat from her port tubes, but their drives were set for delayed activation. They coasted outward at the velocity imparted by their tubes' mass drivers, and then the cruiser's *starboard* broadside rolled onto the target bearing and fired. It was a complicated evolution, but Foraker had worked it out to perfection, and her careful orders to the first broadside's drives sent all eighteen missiles shrieking down on her target in a single, finely coordinated salvo.

The pirate destroyer had never expected that much fire. Countermissiles raced to meet it, but she didn't have enough missiles—or time—to stop all of them, and five laser heads broke through to attack range. They came in on individual runs, slashing down on her while she rolled frantically to interpose her wedge, and three of them reached attack position. Bomb-pumped X-ray lasers clawed at her sidewalls, and the ship lurched and bucked as they tore into her unarmored hull. Air and debris belched into space, and Warner Caslet's eyes blazed.

"Close us up! *Close us up!*" Arner shouted. God! Where did a single CL *get* that kind of firepower? He glared at his readouts, pounding on one arm of his command chair, and snarled as Tactical gave him the answer. No wonder the bastard was spinning that way! But it wouldn't help the son-of-a-bitch in energy combat.

The follow-up broadsides were already in space, tearing down on the isolated raider even as *Vaubon's* own countermissiles and laser clusters disposed of the incoming fire. The Silesian Navy was a second-rate fleet, and the Chalice's "revolutionary government" had used its ships for models. The raider destroyer had a heavy energy armament for her size, but she mounted only four missile tubes in her broadside, and her point defense was grossly subpar. She lurched again as two more warheads from the second double broadside gouged at her, her impeller wedge fluctuated as drive nodes were wiped away, and shattered hull plating trailed in her wake as she accelerated frantically towards the support of her consorts.

But she'd left it too late, Caslet gloated. He'd take his lumps from the other two, but this bastard wouldn't be around by then. Or if she was, she wasn't going to be good for much.

"Entering the envelope for the rest of them in three minutes, Skip," Foraker warned, and he nodded as yet another salvo of laser heads slashed at his victim. This time they got something important, and her wedge dropped abruptly to half strength as her after ring went into shutdown. There were only two missiles in her next broadside, and her point defense was weaker, as well, and Caslet bared his teeth. Two more broadsides should settle *her* hash, and then it would be time for the main event.

He stole a glance at the merchantman and nodded. The merchie didn't know what the hell was going on—perhaps she'd thought *Vaubon* was simply another pirate coming in to join the attack on her—but her skipper had done the smart thing. She was well within range of all the combatants, any one of which might suddenly decide

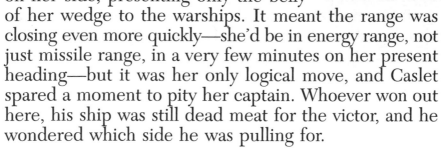

to throw a missile or two her way, so she'd altered her heading by ninety degrees in the same plane and rolled up on her side, presenting only the belly of her wedge to the warships. It meant the range was closing even more quickly—she'd be in energy range, not just missile range, in a very few minutes on her present heading—but it was her only logical move, and Caslet spared a moment to pity her captain. Whoever won out here, his ship was still dead meat for the victor, and he wondered which side he was pulling for.

"In range!" the tac officer shouted, and Arner felt his ship buck as she threw her first broadside at the attacking light cruiser. His face was pale as he watched the missile traces speeding towards his opponent. One of his ships had already taken critical damage, and *Vaubon's* fire only seemed to be intensifying. But he still had twenty tubes to her eighteen, and she *had* to be weak in energy range to pack in that many launchers.

Caslet watched Shannon's fire slash at the incoming missiles. Point defense was doing well, but some of those birds were going to get through, and he gripped the arms of his command chair as *Vaubon* lurched to a direct hit. The laser blasted through her starboard sidewall and deep into her hull, shattering plating and blowing away one of her laser mounts, but her tubes were untouched, and they spat back in maximum rate fire.

One more broadside tore down on the destroyer she'd already mangled, but Shannon had switched to the raider CL without orders, and he nodded in approval. Besides, there was no more need to fire at *Vaubon's* first target. The last salvo took down her entire port sidewall, and then a secondary explosion—not her fusion bottle; the flash wasn't big enough—broke her back just forward of her aft impeller ring. She spun away, whipsawed wildly as her forward impellers ran wild before the fail-safes cut power, and he winced. If her compensator had gone with the explosion, that massive surge of acceleration had just killed everyone in her forward hull.

But he didn't have time to worry about dead men; the living ones required his full attention, and *Vaubon* lurched again as another hit got through. And another. Gravitic One vanished into a chaos of smashed plating and bodies, and Missile Seven and Nine went with it. Another hit breached Number Three Magazine and took it out of the feed queue for her remaining launchers, yet another blew three beta nodes out of her forward ring, and she staggered again as the first shipboard laser smashed at her sidewall. Damage alarms screamed and her drive power dropped, but her own lasers were snarling back and she was getting good hits on the raider CL. The bastard's emissions signature flickered and danced as he took damage, and—

"Jesus Christ!"

Foraker's shocked exclamation burned across the bridge like a buzz saw, and Caslet's mouth fell open as his plot suddenly changed. One instant, his ship was charging into the teeth of two opponents' fire; the next instant, there *were* no opponents. The warships' acceleration had carried them within less than three hundred thousand klicks of the Manty merchantman, which had suddenly rolled back down to present her own broadside to them. Eight incredibly powerful grasers smashed out from the "unarmed freighter" like the wrath of God, and the second raider destroyer simply vanished. A single pair of hits on the light cruiser burned through her sidewall as if it hadn't even existed, and her after third blew apart in a hurricane of splintered and vaporized plating. Three of Shannon's shipboard lasers added their own fury to her damage, chewing huge holes in what was left of her hull, but they were strictly an afterthought, for that ship was already a helpless hulk.

"We're being hailed, Skipper," Lieutenant Dutton said shakenly from Communications. Caslet just looked at him, unable to speak, then looked back down at his plot and swallowed as the unmistakable impeller signatures of a full dozen LACs drifted up from the "freighter's" gravitic shadow and locked their weapons on his ship.

"Speaker," he rasped.

"Unknown cruiser, this is Captain Honor Harrington of Her Majesty's Armed Merchant Cruiser *Wayfarer*," a soprano voice said quietly. "I appreciate your assistance, and I wish I could offer you the reward your gallantry deserves, but I'm afraid I'm going to have to ask you to surrender."

• CHAPTER TWENTY-SEVEN

Honor stood in the boat bay gallery and watched with mixed feelings as the pinnace docked. She'd spent two hours sucking the raiders into going after *Wayfarer*, and she'd been more than a little concerned over how to handle all three of them. She'd had the firepower to take them, but unless they'd come in massed tight, at least one would have had an excellent chance to rip *Wayfarer* up before she or her LACs could nail him. Then a light cruiser—and a *Peep*, at that—had come tearing in out of nowhere to "rescue" her. Despite all the scenarios she and her tac people had gamed out, this one had never occurred to them, and she'd felt both dishonest and guilty as she let the Peep sail straight into her trap and take a hammering in the process. That skipper had lost some of his people—over fifty of them, if Susan Hibson's and Scotty Tremaine's initial reports were accurate—to save an enemy merchantman, and it seemed cruelly ungrateful to "reward" him by taking his ship away from him.

But she had no choice. The mere presence of a Peep CL in Silesia demanded investigation, and that ship *was* an enemy man-of-war. Yet she could at least do everything in her power to assist with the wounded it had taken in its uneven battle, and Angela Ryder, both her assistant surgeons, and a dozen sick berth attendants had gone over in the first pinnace.

Now Honor stood back as grim-faced SBAs swam the tube with the most critical of those wounded. *Wayfarer*'s Marines were very much in evidence in the gallery, but they cleared a path to the lifts, and the SBAs charged down it with Lieutenant Holmes running at their head.

The rush of broken bodies continued for an agonizingly long time, and then Honor drew a deep breath as another group came down the tube. The man at their head wore a Peep skinsuit with a commander's insignia, and she stepped in front of him as he swung into *Wayfarer*'s internal gravity.

"Captain," she said very quietly. The wiry, dark-haired man looked at her for a moment, face white, eyes still shocked, then saluted with painful precision.

"Warner Caslet, Citizen Commander, PNS *Vaubon*." He spoke in the mechanical tones of a nightmare. He cleared his throat, then gestured to the man and women behind him. "People's Commissioner Jourdain; Citizen Lieutenant Commander MacMurtree, my exec; and Citizen Lieutenant Commander Foraker, my tac officer," he said hoarsely.

Honor nodded to each of the others in turn, then held out her hand to Caslet. He looked down at it for several seconds, then squared his shoulders and reached out to take it.

"Commander," she said in that same quiet voice while Nimitz sat very still on her shoulder, "I'm sorry. You showed both courage and compassion in aiding an enemy-flag vessel. The fact that you didn't know we were armed only makes your action in taking on such odds even more remarkable, and I truly believe you would have taken all three of them. I deeply regret the necessity of 'rewarding' you by taking your ship. You deserve better, and I wish I could give it to you. For what it's worth, I can only extend my own and my Queen's thanks."

Caslet's mouth twisted, and he bobbed his head. There was very little else he could do, and she felt his bitter sense of loss through Nimitz. There was a deep, searing anger in that loss—less at Honor than at the universe's ghastly practical joke—and there was also fear. That puzzled her for a moment, and then she kicked herself.

Of course. He wasn't afraid of what *she* might do to him or his people; he was afraid of what his own government would do to them—or their families—and she felt a fresh, bitter anger of her own. This man had taken a dreadful chance to do the honorable thing, and she hated what it was going to cost him.

He stood a moment longer, then drew a deep breath.

"Thank you for your prompt medical assistance, Captain Harrington," he said. "My people—" His voice faded, and she nodded compassionately.

"We'll take care of them, Commander," she promised him. "I guarantee it."

"Thank you," he said again, and cleared his throat once more. "I don't know if you've been told, Captain, but we have two Manticoran nationals on board. We took them off another pirate, and they've had a pretty bad time."

"Manticorans?" Honor's eyebrows rose, and she started to ask more questions, then stopped. Caslet and his companions were on the ragged edge, and the least she could do was give them time to compose themselves. No doubt some hard-boiled ONI type would have argued that catching them while they were still in shock was the best way to get information out of them, but that was too bad. The war between the People's Republic and the Star Kingdom was an ugly one, yet Honor Harrington would treat these people with the respect their actions demanded.

"Commander Cardones, my exec," she said, gesturing Rafe forward, "will escort you to your quarters. I'll have your personal gear brought across as soon as possible so you can get out of those skinnies. We can talk later, over dinner."

"My people—" Caslet began, then stopped. They were no longer "his" people. They were POWs and her responsibility now, not his. But at least he'd already seen that their captors intended to treat them properly, and he nodded. Then he and his companions followed Cardones from the gallery while two Marines fell in behind, and Honor watched them go with a sad smile.

*   *   *

"What do we do with *Vaubon*?" Cardones asked. He and Honor stood on *Wayfarer*'s bridge, gazing at the plot and wondering what the Schiller authorities made of it all. Even Silesian system surveillance sensors must have picked up the emissions of the short, savage battle, but no one was coming out to ask any questions. That might indicate the Schiller governor, like Hagen, had an "understanding" with the local raiders, but it might also be simple prudence, especially if they'd gotten good reads on the weapons employed. According to Honor's intelligence files, Schiller's heaviest unit was a corvette, and nothing that small would want to irritate anything which mounted a ship of the wall's grasers.

"I don't know," she said after a moment. Nimitz chittered softly from the back of her command chair, and she reached out to stroke him without taking her eyes from the plot.

Caslet had followed the proper protocols for surrendering his ship. If a captain had time, she was supposed to take her crew off in her own small craft, then fire her scuttling charges, but the rules of war established different standards if she found herself in a hopeless tactical position. The enemy was supposed to give her a chance to surrender, and she was supposed to take it rather than get her crew killed for nothing. There were, after all, few survivors from a ship destroyed by point-blank fire, and the *quid pro quo* for getting them off alive was that her ship, once surrendered, *stayed* surrendered as the intact prize of the victor.

But before her ship was boarded, she was also supposed to purge her computers and destroy classified equipment, and Caslet had. No doubt ONI would still want to examine the ship in detail, and Honor's search parties would ransack her for any hardcopy documents. Yet there would be precious little data to be recovered, and by now the RMN had taken enough Peep ships to be fully conversant with their technology. Honor expected

no treasure trove from *Vaubon*, but she still had to decide
what to do with her prize . . . and her prisoners.

"The most important thing," she said after a moment,
as much to herself as to Cardones, "is to keep the Peeps
from knowing we've got her. The loss numbers in Posnan
probably explain what she's doing out here, but if she *was*
part of a commerce-raiding operation, she wasn't alone.
So the first thing is to make sure our people know about
this before *their* people realize we do."

"Makes sense, Ma'am. But what about notifying the
Peeps?"

"There's that," Honor agreed unhappily. The Deneb
Accords required combatants to report the names of
prisoners—and KIAs—to the other side, usually through
the Solarian League, since it was almost always the most
powerful neutral around. Though the Peeps were traditionally sloppy about that, the Star Kingdom wasn't, yet
telling the Peeps Caslet and his people were prisoners
would also tell them his ship had been taken.

"We can hold off for a while," she decided. "We're
required to notify their government in 'a reasonable time
period,' not as soon as physically possible. Given our own
operational security requirements, I'm going to interpret
that a bit liberally." Cardones nodded, and she brooded
down at the display for a few more moments, then nodded in decision.

"She's still hyper-capable, so we'll put a prize crew
aboard—Lieutenant Reynolds can take command—and
send her in to Gregor Station for return to Manticore.
On the way, she can call at the Andy naval station in
Sachsen and again at New Berlin. I think this is something we need to pass on to Herzog Rabenstrange, and
we can ask our Sachsen ambassador to relay the information to our stations in the Confederacy. We'll drop
dispatches with our naval attaché here in Schiller for the
rest of the squadron as they rotate through, too. That's
probably the fastest way to get the word out without
blowing security."

"Yes, Ma'am. And the prisoners?"

"We don't have brig space to hang onto them," Honor murmured, rubbing the tip of her nose, "and I'd like to get their wounded into a proper hospital as soon as possible. We owe them that." She scooped Nimitz off her chair and cradled him in her arms while she considered, then nodded once more. "*Vaubon's* sickbay is undamaged, and her life support's in good shape. We'll strip out the officers and send most of her enlisted personnel—and all the wounded—off in her, and I'll have Reynolds ask the IAN to take her casualties off in Sachsen."

Cardones nodded back. He understood the logic in stripping out *Vaubon's* officers; they were the ones most likely to instigate some effort to retake their ship during the voyage ahead. "I'll ask Major Hibson to detail a suitable security detachment," he remarked, and Honor nodded.

"Well!" the exec said more briskly. "That takes care of the Peeps—what about the pirates?"

"They get the standard treatment," Honor replied. There was some risk in turning the handful of raiders who'd survived the engagement over to the system governor. Even if he was an honest man, they might spill the beans about *Vaubon's* capture. On the other hand, there weren't many of them. In fact, there were *none* from the two lighter ships, and no bridge officers from the light cruiser. The survivors knew they'd been shooting at a light cruiser, but it was unlikely they knew it had been a Peep, and they'd had no opportunity to discover that since. Still . . . "It might not be a bad idea to gloat a little over how they fell for 'our' light cruiser's ambush," she added.

"I'll see to it, Ma'am," Cardones agreed. He moved off to pass the necessary orders, and Honor remained where she was, still gazing at the display.

There were unanswered questions here. Those raiders' numbers had come as a surprise, and they'd also been unusually heavily armed. Merchantmen were almost universally *un*armed, and it didn't take a lot of firepower to force them to surrender, but these people had packed in enough weapons to seriously reduce the life support required by the big crews pirates normally carried.

Well, at least she had an excellent chance to find out what it had all been about. There'd been no survivors from *Vaubon's* first victim; total compensator failure and fifty-one seconds of runaway acceleration at over four hundred gravities had seen to that. But her computers were intact. It had taken three of Commander Harmon's LACs five hours to chase the hulk down and tow it back to *Wayfarer*, but Harold Tschu and Jennifer Hughes had crews tickling the system. Honor tried not to think about the human wreckage they were working amidst while they did it and turned away from the plot at last, hoping at least some answers would be forthcoming shortly.

Warner Caslet kept his shoulders straight as he followed the Marine lieutenant down the passage. It wasn't easy, and he raged at his own stupidity. He'd *lost his ship*, the most terrible sin any captain could commit, and he'd done it for *nothing*.

He clenched his teeth until his jaw muscles ached. It didn't do a bit of good to know he'd done the right thing—the *honorable* thing, his brain sneered—given the information he'd had. Intelligence hadn't warned him the Manties were using Q-ships. He'd had every reason to believe *Wayfarer* truly was a merchantman when he'd gone to her assistance. And even in his self-hatred, he remained convinced he'd made the right decision on the basis of everything he'd known. None of which could temper his self-contempt . . . or save him from the consequences.

At least it won't happen anytime soon, he thought mordantly. The People's Republic had refused to exchange POWs for the duration. There were precedents for and against prisoner exchange, but the Manties had a far smaller population than the Republic . . . which had no intention of returning trained personnel to the RMN.

Besides, he thought with a flash of bitter humor, *we'd have to trade them twenty to one just to hold even!*

Warner Caslet didn't look forward to spending the next few years in a POW camp, even if the Manties *were* supposed to treat their prisoners better than the Republic did. Still, it would be better for his health to remain a prisoner *permanently*. At least the Manties weren't going to shoot him for his stupidity.

He'd considered asking for asylum, but he just couldn't do it. He knew some PN personnel had—like Alfredo Yu, who was now an admiral in the Grayson Navy. Any one of them was a dead man if he ever fell back into Republican hands; that went without saying, but it wasn't the reason Caslet couldn't do it. For all the excesses of the Committee of Public Safety, for all the lunatic handicaps the Committee and its commissioners and StateSec had inflicted upon the People's Navy, Warner Caslet had sworn an oath when he accepted his commission. He could no more turn his back upon that oath than he could have let Warnecke's butchers rape and murder the civilian spacers he'd thought crewed this ship. It had come as a shock to him to realize that, yet it was true. Even if it did mean he was probably going to be shot by his own people.

He looked up as his escort came to a stop. A man in a green-on-green uniform which certainly wasn't Manticoran stood outside a closed hatch and raised an eyebrow at the lieutenant.

"Comman—Citizen Commander Caslet to see the Captain," the Marine said, and Caslet's lips quirked at the correction. It still sounded ridiculous, but it was also an oddly comforting link to who and what he'd been only a few hours before.

The green-uniformed man nodded and spoke into the intercom for a moment, then stood aside as the hatch opened. The lieutenant also stood aside with a respectful nod, and the citizen commander nodded back before he stepped through the hatch and stopped.

A long table covered in snow-white linen awaited him, set with glittering china and crystal. Delicious culinary aromas filled the air, and Denis Jourdain, Allison Mac-Murtree, Shannon Foraker, and Harold Sukowski were already seated, along with a half-dozen Manticoran officers, including Commander Cardones and the young lieutenant who'd commanded the pinnaces which had boarded *Vaubon*. Another green-uniformed man stood against a bulkhead, and a third—auburn-haired, with watchful gray eyes that whispered bodyguard—followed quietly at Captain Harrington's elbow as she crossed to him.

Caslet watched her warily. He'd been too shocked to form much of an impression of her in the boat bay gallery. That irritated him, though he'd certainly had ample excuse, but he was back on balance now, and he sized her up carefully. From her reputation, she should have breathed fire and been three meters tall, and something itched between his shoulder blades at finding himself in her presence. This woman was one of the PN's bogeymen, like Admiral White Haven or Admiral Kuzak, and he couldn't imagine what she was doing commanding a single Q-ship in this backwater. He supposed he should be grateful the Manties were misusing her abilities so thoroughly, but it was a bit hard at the moment.

She *was* a tall woman, and she moved like a dancer. The braided hair under her white beret was much longer than in the single picture in her intelligence dossier, and those almond eyes were far more . . . disconcerting in the flesh. He knew one of them was artificial, but the Manties built excellent prosthetics, and he couldn't tell which of them it was. It was odd. He knew about her hand-to-hand skills, and somehow he'd expected her to be . . . stockier? Heftier? He couldn't think of exactly the right world, but whatever it was, she wasn't. She had the sturdiness of her high-grav home world, and her long-fingered hands were strong and sinewy, yet she was slender and graceful—a gymnast, not a bruiser—without an excess gram of bulk anywhere.

"Citizen Commander." She extended her hand and smiled as he took it. That smile was warm but just a bit lopsided. The left side of her mouth moved with a fractional hesitation, and he heard a very faint slurring of the "r" in "commander." Were those legacies of the head wound she'd suffered on Grayson?

"Captain Harrington." In light of the aggressive egalitarianism of the People's Republic's new rulers, Caslet had already decided to take refuge behind her naval rank rather than use any of her various "elitist" titles.

"Please, join us," she invited, and walked him back to the table and seated him in the chair to the right of her place before sitting herself with a graceful economy of movement. Her treecat sat facing the citizen commander across the table, and Caslet felt a stir of surprise at the bright intelligence in those grass-green eyes. One look told him her dossier had been wrong to dismiss it as a dumb animal, but then, the Republic knew very little about treecats. Most of what they had were only rumors, and the rumors themselves were widely at variance with one another.

A sandy-haired steward poured wine, and Harrington sat back and regarded Caslet levelly.

"I've already said this to Commissioner Jourdain and Citizen Commander MacMurtree and Foraker," she said, "but I'd like to thank you once more for what you tried to do. We're both naval officers, Citizen Commander. You know what duty requires of me, but I deeply regret the necessity of obeying those requirements. I also regret the people you lost. I had to wait until the raiders were deep enough into my energy envelope to guarantee clean kills before engaging . . . and, of course, to be certain your own ship couldn't escape." She said it levelly, without flinching, and Caslet felt an unwilling respect for her steady eyes. "If I could have fired sooner, some of those people would still be alive, and I'm genuinely sorry that I couldn't."

Caslet nodded stiffly, unwilling to trust his voice. Or, for that matter, to respond openly in front of Jourdain.

The people's commissioner was in just as much trouble as Caslet, but he was still a commissioner, and just as stubbornly aware of his duty as Caslet himself. Was that, the citizen commander wondered wryly, one reason they'd gotten along so much better than he'd initially expected?

"I'd also like to thank you for the care you took of Captain Sukowski and Commander Hurlman," Harrington said after a moment. "I sent your Dr. Jankowski off with the rest of your crew to see to your wounded, but my own surgeon assures me that her care for Commander Hurlman was all anyone could have asked for, and for that you have my sincere thanks. I've had some experience of what animals can do to prisoners," her brown eyes turned momentarily into flint, "and I deeply appreciate the decency and consideration you showed."

Caslet nodded again, and Harrington picked up her wineglass. She looked down into it for a few seconds, then returned her gaze to her "guest's" face.

"I have every intention of notifying the People's Republic of your present status, but our own operational security requires us to delay that notification for a short time. For the present, I'm afraid I'll have to keep you and your senior officers aboard *Wayfarer*, but you'll be treated at all times with the courtesy your rank and your actions deserve. You will not be pressed for any sensitive information." Caslet's eyes narrowed a bit at that, and she smiled another of her crooked smiles. "Oh, if any of you let anything drop, I assure you we'll report it, but prisoner interrogation is properly ONI's function, not mine. Under the circumstances, I'm just as happy that's true."

"Thank you, Captain," he said, and she nodded.

"In the meantime," she went on, "I've had an opportunity to go over Captain Sukowski's stay aboard your vessel with him. I realize you didn't discuss any operational matters with him, but given what you did tell him and what we've pulled out of the privateers' computers, I suspect I know what you were doing in Schiller—and why you came to our assistance." Her eyes took on that flint-like cast once more, and Caslet was just as happy their cold fury wasn't directed at him. "I think," she continued in a calm voice that did nothing to hide its anger, "that the time has come to deal with Mr. Warnecke once and for all, and thanks to you, we should be able to."

"Thanks to us, Ma'am?" Surprise startled the question out of Caslet, and she nodded.

"We recovered the full database of the ship you disabled. We didn't get anything from the other two wrecks, but we got everything from her . . . including her astrogation data. We know where Warnecke is, Citizen Commander, and I intend to pay him a little visit."

"With just one ship, Captain?" Caslet glanced at Jourdain. Disregarding the fact that he himself was on board, it was clearly his duty to do anything he could to insure *Wayfarer's* destruction, but he couldn't shake off memories of what Warnecke's butchers had done to *Erewhon's* crew—or, for that matter, Sukowski and Hurlman. Jourdain held his eyes for a moment, then nodded ever so slightly, and Caslet looked back at Harrington. "Excuse me, Ma'am," he said carefully, "but our data indicates that they have several other ships. Even if you know where to find him, you might be biting off more than you can chew."

"*Wayfarer's* teeth are quite sharp, Citizen Commander," she returned with a slight, dangerous smile. "And we've got complete downloads on their fleet. They've taken over the planet Sidemore, in the Marsh System. Marsh is—or was—an independent republic just outside the Confederacy, which may explain why the Silesians never looked there for him, assuming they even know he got away. But it was a fairly marginal system even before they took it, and their sole logistic support seems to be a single repair ship they brought out of the Chalice with them. Their resources are limited, despite whatever contacts Warnecke may have maintained, and by our count, they have—had—a total of twelve ships. You've eliminated two, and we've eliminated another pair, which reduces them to eight, and some of them will be out on operations. From the prize's data, their orbital defenses are negligible, and they have only a few thousand troops on the planet. Trust me, Citizen Commander. We can take them . . . and we're going to."

"I can't say I'm sorry to hear that, Captain," Caslet said after a moment.

"I thought you wouldn't be. And while it may not be much compensation for the loss of your ship, I can at least offer you a grandstand seat for what happens to Warnecke's psychopaths. In fact, I'd like to invite you and Commissioner Jourdain to share the bridge with me for the attack."

Caslet twitched in surprise. Allowing an enemy officer, even a POW, on your bridge in time of war was unheard of. Trained eyes were bound to pick up at least a little about things your own admiralty wouldn't want them to know, after all. Of course, he thought a moment later, it wasn't as if he'd be able to tell anyone back home about it, now was it?

"Thank you, Captain," he said. "I appreciate that very much."

"It's the least I can do, Citizen Commander," Harrington said with another of those sadly gentle smiles. She twitched her glass at him, and he picked his own up in automatic response. "I propose a toast we can all share, ladies and gentlemen," she told the table, and now her chill smile was neither sad nor gentle. "To Andre Warnecke. May he receive everything he deserves."

She raised her glass as a rumble of approval came back, and Warner Caslet heard his own voice—and Denis Jourdain's—in that response.

• CHAPTER TWENTY-EIGHT

Aubrey Wanderman trotted into the gym. A dozen Marines who'd gone from incomprehensible strangers to friends over the last few weeks nodded in welcome, and he heard a handful of cheerfully insulting greetings to the "vacuum-sucker" in their midst. He'd gotten used to that, and—rank permitting—gave as good as he got. It was odd, but he felt more at home here than he did anywhere else in the ship, and he suspected he was never going to be able to share the proper naval disdain for the "jarheads."

He was looking forward to his scheduled session, and that, too, was odd for someone who'd only considered such training out of desperation. But the fact was that he'd come to enjoy it, despite the bruises. His slender frame was filling out with muscle, and the discipline—and confidence—was almost more enjoyable than the sense of physical competence which came with it. Besides, he admitted, the gym was his refuge. The people here actually *liked* him . . . and he didn't have to worry about Steilman turning up. He grinned. If there was one place where Randy Steilman would never dare show his face, Marine Country was certainly it!

But he came to a surprised halt, smile vanishing, as he saw the two people in the center of the gym. Sergeant Major Hallowell wasn't in his usual, well-worn sweats. Today he was in a formal *gi*, belted with the black sash of his rank, and Lady Harrington stood facing him.

The Captain, too, wore a *gi*, and Aubrey blinked as he saw the seven braided rank knots on her belt. He'd known she held a black belt in *coup de vitesse*, but he'd never realized she ranked quite that high. There were only two formally awarded ranks above seventh; the handful of people who ever hit ninth were referred to simply as "Master Grade," and only a particularly foolish individual asked for a demonstration of why.

Sergeant Major Hallowell's belt, however, had *eight* knots, and Aubrey swallowed. He'd known the Gunny was holding back in their sessions, but he hadn't guessed Hallowell was holding back quite *that* much, and he suddenly felt much better about his inability to score on his mentor. Yet the thought was almost lost in his surprise at seeing the Captain here. So far as he knew, she never came to the Marine's gym, and he felt a surge of ambiguous emotion over her presence.

He hadn't exactly been *avoiding* her—acting third-class petty officers seldom found it necessary to "avoid" the demigod who commanded a Queen's ship—but he'd been acutely uncomfortable in her presence ever since Steilman had beaten him up. Which, he admitted, was entirely because he knew Ginger and Senior Chief Harkness had been right; he *should* have told the truth about what had happened and trusted the Captain to handle things. But he was still worried about what a nasty customer like Steilman might do to his friends—or have *his* friends do to them. Besides, he admitted, he'd gone from total disbelief that he could do anything to square accounts with Steilman on his own to a burning desire to do just that. It was personal, and while he knew that was in many ways a stupid attitude, it was the way he felt.

He'd been afraid the Captain herself would ask him what had happened, and he'd dreaded the possibility. He didn't think he could have lied to *her*, and he *knew* he couldn't have held back if she'd explicitly ordered him to come clean. But though she'd given him a few searching looks the next time he'd reported for duty, she hadn't pressed him. Yet she was here now, and if she saw him, would she guess why *he* was? And if she did, would she put a stop to it? That she could was a given—Aubrey couldn't conceive of *anything* the Captain couldn't do if she put her mind to it—and he wondered if that was why she'd come.

At the moment, however, her attention was entirely focused on Hallowell. They both wore heavier protective gear than the Marines usually did, and they bowed formally before they fell into their set positions.

All other activity had ceased as the rest of the Marines gathered silently around the central mat, and Aubrey joined them. The Captain's treecat lay stretched out along the uneven parallel bars, ears cocked as he watched, and Aubrey felt himself holding his breath as the Captain and Hallowell faced one another in absolute motionlessness. Tall as the Captain was, the Marine was ten centimeters taller, and Aubrey knew from painful experience just how fast he could be. But seconds ticked past with neither so much as twitching. They simply watched one another, with an intensity so focused Aubrey felt he could almost have reached out and touched it.

And then they moved. Despite the concentration with which he'd watched, Aubrey was never certain who initiated the movement. It was as if they'd moved absolutely simultaneously, their muscles controlled by a single brain, and their hands and feet struck with a speed and power he'd never imagined possible. He'd thought Major Hibson was greased lightning, and she was, but the Captain and the Sergeant Major were at least as fast, and both of them were far larger.

Coup de vitesse lacked the elegance of *judo* or *akido*. It was an offensive hard style which borrowed shamelessly from every source—from *savate* to *t'ai chi*—and distilled them all down into sheer ferocity. Aubrey knew some people regarded the *coup* as crude or pointed out that its offensive emphasis was far more wasteful of energy than *akido*, that most perfect of defensive arts. But as he watched the Captain and the Sergeant Major, he knew he was in the presence of two killers. . . and why Honor Harrington preferred the *coup* over all other forms. It

was a moment of strange insight into his captain, an
instant in which he realized she would never be content
with the defense if she could possibly take the offense—
and that no one had ever taught her how to back up. She
moved directly into Hallowell, and despite his greater
reach and strength and his higher rating, it was *she* who
pushed the attack.

Mittened hands and padded feet thudded on their
protective gear, and he watched them execute combi-
nations he couldn't even have described, much less—
laughable thought!—executed himself. Their faces were
blank with concentration, and then he winced as
Hallowell's left foot slammed its sole into the Captain's
midriff.

But she'd seen it coming. She couldn't evade it, so she
moved into it, striking down with her right elbow an
instant before his foot made contact. Aubrey heard the
sharp *crack!* as her padded elbow hammered the Sergeant Major's thinly fleshed shin, and Hallowell grunted
as the blow negated much of his kick's force. Enough got
through to make the Captain grunt in turn, but her
expression didn't even flicker as her striking arm
rebounded and straightened. Her fist struck straight for
Hallowell's solar plexus, but his own arm came down to
block. It deflected her strike, but while he was block-
ing that hand, her *left* hand came up in a vicious chop
to the back of his still-extended leg's knee. The knee bent
sharply in reflexive response, and she spun to his right
on one foot while the other swept for his right ankle and
her right arm flailed around in what *looked* like an
uncontrolled windmill but was nothing of the kind.
Hallowell moved his head, snapping it out of the path
of her blow even as an arm flew up to block, but her fist
dropped instantly under the block and hammered his rib
cage just as her scything foot found his ankle. He went
down, deliberately throwing his weight towards her legs
in a bid to take her down with him, and he almost succeeded. He did bring her down, but she folded in a move
so controlled it looked as if she'd *wanted* him to. Her

left arm shot out, snaking through his left armpit from behind, then down to catch his wrist. She half-turned away from him and jerked up on his wrist, straining his elbow backward and leaning hard to her left to force him over onto his right side—which pinned that arm beneath him—and her own right hand flashed down in a chop that stopped dead the instant it touched the side of his exposed neck.

"Point," Hallowell acknowledged in unruffled tones, and they rolled apart and came back to their feet. The Marine worked his left arm, flexing the fingers of that hand, and smiled. "Iris Babcock taught you that one, didn't she, Ma'am?"

"As a matter of fact, she did," the Captain agreed with an answering smile.

"She always was a sneaky one," Hallowell observed. He finished working his arm and bowed again. "On the other hand," he added, "so am I," and the two of them came set once more.

Twenty minutes later, Aubrey Wanderman knew he never—and he meant *never*—wanted to get the Captain or Sergeant Major Hallowell pissed at him. The Sergeant Major had out-pointed the Captain by seven to six, but even Aubrey knew it could have gone the other way just as easily. She'd also managed something else Aubrey never had; Gunny Hallowell was actually sweating and out of breath when they exchanged bows at the end of the session. Of course, the Captain was, too, and she had an interesting bruise developing on her right cheek.

"Thank you, Gunny," she said quietly as they stepped off the mat and the rest of the gym came back to life. "I haven't had a bout that good since the last time Iris and I sparred."

"You're welcome, My Lady," Hallowell rumbled back, massaging an ache in the back of his neck. "Not too shabby for a Navy officer, either, if the Captain will permit."

"The Captain will permit," she agreed with a dimpled smile. "We'll have to try it again."

"As the Captain says," Hallowell agreed with a grin. She nodded, then glanced at Aubrey.

"Hello, Wanderman. I understand you've been working out with the Sergeant Major and Senior Chief Harkness."

"Uh, yes, Ma'am" Aubrey felt his face flaming, but she only cocked her head and regarded him thoughtfully for a moment, then looked back to Hallowell.

"How's he shaping up, Gunny?"

"Fair to middling, Milady. Fair to middling. He was a little hesitant when we started, but he's coming in like he means business now." Aubrey felt his blush deepen, but Hallowell gave him a wink as he smiled at the Captain. "We're still working on basic moves, but he's quick and I don't think he makes the same mistake twice very often."

"Good." The Captain mopped her face with a towel, then draped it around her neck and bent to pick up her treecat as he scampered across to her. She held him in her arms and smiled at Aubrey. "I'd say you're putting on some muscle, too, Wanderman. I like that. I always like to see my people stay in shape . . . and I like to think they can take care of themselves if they have to."

Her 'cat cocked his head at Aubrey, and the young man felt his pulse stop. She knew, he thought. She knew the real reason he was here, what he was trying to get into shape for. And then the second part of it hit him. She not only knew, she *approved*. No captain could come right out and *tell* a member of her crew she wanted him to kick the shit out of another member of her crew, but she'd just told him so anyway, and he felt his shoulders straighten.

"Thank you, Milady," he said quietly. "I'd like to think I could do that—if I had to. Of course, I still have an awful lot to learn from the Gunny and Senior Chief Harkness."

"Well, they're both good teachers," the Captain said lightly, and slapped him smartly on the shoulder, brown eyes bright with a curiously serious twinkle. "On the other hand, I've done all I can for you by trying to wear the Gunny out. From here on, you're on your own."

"I understand, Milady." Aubrey eyed the smiling Hallowell and felt a crooked grin on his own face. "Just as long as you didn't make him decide to take it out on me, Ma'am!" he added.

"Oh, I wouldn't worry about that, Wanderman," Hallowell said. "After all," he added, and gave the Captain a huge smile as he and Aubrey ended in unison, "this ship has a *fine* doctor!"

"Have a seat, Rafe." Honor tipped her own chair back and pointed to the one on the far side of her desk. Nimitz and Samantha sat side by side on the perch above it, and Cardones smiled wryly at them as he sat. Honor followed his glance and shrugged. Samantha was just as capable of operating lifts as Nimitz was, and the 'cats appeared to be trying to split their time so that neither had to abandon his or her person for too extended a period.

"You said you had something new, Ma'am?" the exec said, and she nodded.

"We didn't realize it right away, but we hit a minor gold mine aboard *Vaubon* after all. You know Carol's been working her way through everything we took off her?" Cardones nodded. Lieutenant Wolcott had wound up filling the slot of Honor's intelligence officer, and she'd shown a gratifying flair for the position. "Well, last night she and Scotty were going over some of the personal memo pads we recovered, and they turned up something very interesting."

"Carol and Scotty, hm?" Cardones glanced back up at the treecats, then cocked an eyebrow at his captain, who shrugged. Regulations forbade liaisons between officers in the same chain of command, but Tremaine and Wolcott held the same rank, though Scotty was senior, and they were in different departments. "So what did they find?" Cardones asked.

"This." Honor laid a pad on the desk. "It seems Lieutenant Houghton keeps a diary."

"A diary?" Cardones eyes narrowed. "Does Caslet know?"

"I don't know—and I don't intend to tell him," Honor replied. "Obviously we'd just as soon not let him know how much we know, but I don't want him coming down on Houghton for it, either. For one thing, he likes the man, and, in fairness to Houghton, I don't think he put any classified elements into writing. But a little reading between the lines tells us a lot."

"Such as?" Cardones leaned forward, face intent.

"Most of it's as personal as you'd expect, but there are several references in here to 'the squadron,' though he was careful never to give its strength. There's also a rather pungent comment on orders to assist Andy merchies— which suggests an effort at diplomatic spin control in the event their activities get blown—and a reference to a Citizen Admiral Giscard. I didn't really expect to find anything, but I checked our database anyway, and we do have a little on Giscard. He was only a commander before the coup attempt, but we've got excerpts from the package ONI put together on him because he'd served as a naval attaché on Manticore . . . and because he'd served as an instructor at their war college."

"A commander?" Cardones blinked, and Honor nodded.

"I suspect he'd have held higher rank if he'd been a Legislaturalist. You know how hard it was for anyone else to break into flag rank—they only made Alfredo Yu a captain, for goodness sake! But it seems Javier Giscard was one of the PN's foremost advocates of commerce warfare."

"That *would* make him a logical choice to send out here then, wouldn't it?" Cardones murmured.

"Indeed it would. I wish we had more details on him, though I suppose we're lucky to have even this much on someone who was so junior under the old regime. I also wish we'd known about this before we sent *Vaubon* off. There's a note in our file on him that ONI has a good bit more information than we do"—Cardones nodded; even with modern data-storing technology, there was no way everything from ONI's massive files on enemy officers could have been crammed into a single ship's memory—"but what we do have suggests that he advocated deploying heavy forces for systematic operations. He also insisted on the necessity of a proper scouting element for the main force. Apparently, he believes in monitoring target systems in some detail before moving in, which is probably what *Vaubon* was up to when Caslet stumbled across Sukowski and found out about Warnecke."

"I don't like the sound of that." Cardones rubbed an eyebrow. "If they picked him to put his theories into practice, then they probably let him build the kind of force he wanted."

"Exactly. I'd say we've got an excellent chance of being up against at least a squadron of CAs, possibly even battlecruisers, with light cruiser scouting elements. CLs would be bad enough, but heavy cruisers or battlecruisers could blow away almost any of our convoy escorts, given our general drawdown of forces."

"And then there's us," Cardones said quietly.

"And then there's us." Honor toyed with the memo pad while she frowned down at it. "If Giscard is out here," she said at last in the tone of one thinking aloud, "and if he's got all those Peep legations and trade missions for an intelligence net, then he's bound to have gotten a feel for local shipping patterns, right?"

"Yes, Ma'am." Cardones nodded, wondering where she was headed, and she grimaced.

"All right, let's go further and assume he already has—or shortly will have—picked up on the fact that we have Q-ships in the area. From our existing loss patterns, allowing for the Peeps' involvement in them, he must have been operating spread out in detachments. He may have been operating his heavy ships solo, but it's more likely he's kept them in at least two-ship divisions—his war college lectures were fairly emphatic about the necessity of never taking your security for granted and keeping your assets concentrated. But if you were Giscard and someone told you there was a squadron of Manticoran Q-ships in the area, would you change your ops pattern?"

"Yes, Ma'am," Cardones replied after several moments of thought. "If he stressed concentration of force for routine raiding, then he'd pull into larger forces. He couldn't cover as much ground, but he'd be better placed to deal with one or two of us. And, of course, he couldn't count on *us* operating solo, which would increase his own need to concentrate."

"Agreed, but I was thinking of something a bit more extreme than that."

"More extreme?" Cardones frowned. "How, Ma'am?"

"Let's grant that Giscard is at least as smart as we are, but that he doesn't know we've taken one of his ships or that we have any reason to suspect his presence. Given that, in his place I'd assume my Manticoran counterpart would do precisely what we *have* been doing: move into the area of maximum threat and patrol it."

She glanced at Cardones, who nodded, then went on.

"All right. Now, if I were he and operating from those assumptions, I think I might just decide to look somewhere else. Somewhere where I could swat a *lot* of ships, for relatively little risk, while all the Q-ships were busily looking elsewhere for me."

"I suppose that makes sense," Cardones agreed, studying his CO's face. "The question would be where you could find a target like that."

"Right here," Honor said quietly, and lit a holo chart. It showed the approaches to the Confederacy's southwestern quadrant, and she threw a light dot into it about twenty light-years short of Sachsen. Cardones looked at it for a moment, and then his eyes narrowed in understanding, for the light dot was in the area known as the Selker Rift.

"Rifts" were volumes of hyper-space between gravity waves. They weren't uncommon; in fact, most of h-space

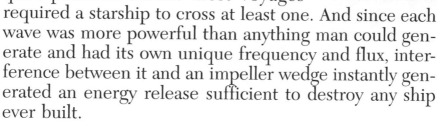

was one huge rift, since grav waves tended to be quite narrow in interstellar terms. Unfortunately, the waves' crazy-quilt patterns meant most voyages required a starship to cross at least one. And since each wave was more powerful than anything man could generate and had its own unique frequency and flux, interference between it and an impeller wedge instantly generated an energy release sufficient to destroy any ship ever built.

That was the reason colonizing expeditions had continued to use cryo-equipped sublight, normal-space vessels, despite voyages which might last centuries, before the invention of the Warshawski sail and gravitic anomaly detector. Survey ships crewed by daredevil specialists had used hyper to *explore* the universe, yet the death toll had been heavy. Crews had continued to come forward—drawn by a combination of wanderlust, adrenaline addiction, and incredible salaries—but people taking their families to the stars had settled for n-space and cryo.

In 1273 P.D., however, hyper-physicist Adrienne Warshawski had mounted radically redesigned and *much* more powerful drive nodes—which she'd dubbed "alpha nodes"—on the test ship *Fleetwing* and produced the very first Warshawski sails. On the gross scale, they were simply the two stressed-space bands of a normal impeller wedge, but *Fleetwing* had projected them as enormous disks, perpendicular to her central axis, not as a wedge. The real sorcery had lain in what Warshawski had managed to *do* with those sails, for what she'd done was to give them a "tuning" ability that allowed them to adjust phase and merge with a naturally occurring grav wave. They stabilized *Fleetwing* relative to the grav wave, and by making subtle adjustments to their strength and frequency, they generated a "grab factor" which allowed her to use the wave itself, in conjunction with her inertial compensator, to generate stupendous rates of acceleration. And just as a side benefit, the interface between sail and wave produced eddies of preposterously high energy levels which could be tapped by a ship underway, allowing her to enjoy enormous savings in reactor mass.

Needless to say, the Warshawski sail revolutionized interstellar travel. Rather than avoid grav waves like the plague, captains began seeking them out, aided by the gravitic detectors she'd already produced (and which were still known as "Warshawskis" in her honor), for they had changed from death traps to the most efficient means of transportation known to man. A ship could generate the same sustained velocities under impeller drive, but the evasive routing required to avoid waves added enormously to voyage times, and the consequences of encountering an unexpected wave remained fatal. By *riding* the waves, however, a starship accelerated faster, cost less to operate, and eliminated the danger of *running into* one of them.

At the same time, it was almost always necessary for a ship to make at least one transition (and usually more) *between* grav waves on any extended voyage, and those transitions were made—very cautiously—under impeller drive.

Especially, Cardones thought, in the Selker Rift.

The major interstellar routes had been worked out to avoid the wider rifts. It added a bit of length to several such routes, but that was considered well worthwhile in terms of safety and cost efficiency. The Selker Rift, however, was impossible to avoid. There simply was no way around it for vessels bound from the Empire to Silesia. And just to make things worse, it was also home to the rogue grav wave known as the Selker Shear.

Most grav waves were "locked," part of a web of mutually anchored and anchoring stress patterns which forced its strands to retain fixed relationships to one another. They moved over the years, but slowly and gradually, as a whole and in predictable fashion.

Rogue waves didn't. Rogue waves were spurs or flares thrown off by locked waves; they weren't part of the web. They could appear and disappear without warning or shift position with incredible speed, and while most hyper-physicists believed rogue waves were, in fact, cyclical phenomena whose timing could be predicted once enough data had been accumulated, accumulating data on them was exactly what merchant skippers were most eager to avoid.

But the Selker Rift *couldn't* be avoided, and so ships moving between the Empire and Confederacy crossed it under impeller drive at extremely low velocities—on the order of .16 *c*—in order to be sure they could dodge if the Selker Shear suddenly appeared on their detectors. It meant they took over five days just to cross the Rift, but it also meant they made it alive.

"You think the Peeps might hit a convoy in the Rift?" Cardones' question was a statement, and Honor nodded.

"Why not?" she asked quietly. "By now, everyone in the Confederacy knows we're using only destroyers to escort our convoys. That's enough to deter regular raiders, but not heavy cruisers or battlecruisers. And the particle density's abnormally low in the Rift. That gives greater sensor reach if you want to establish a picket line, and the low speed of your targets would make it a lot easier to intercept any you picked up. Not only that, you can go after them under impeller drive, with sidewalls up and without losing your missile capability. Heavy ships could slaughter the escorts . . . and then run down the merchies at leisure."

"And take out as many as forty or fifty freighters at once," Cardones said softly.

"Exactly. Of course," Honor crossed her legs and laced her hands together over her right knee, "this is all speculation. We can't afford to overlook the possibility that he might choose to go right on working his present hunting grounds—or even try both ops at once, though that doesn't feel right, somehow. It's too foreign to his insistence on concentration of force."

"I don't think we can afford to dismiss it out of hand, though, Ma'am."

"No, we can't do that." Honor frowned at the holo, then sighed. "Well, I only see one way to proceed. We'll pass Sachsen the day after tomorrow. I was going to do a simple fly-by and continue straight to Marsh, but now I think we'll have to stop. It's possible the Andies or Confeds have something in-system that might want to come along to Marsh."

"Unlikely, Ma'am," Cardones pointed out. "The Confed Detachment was about ready to ship out against the Psyche secessionists when we came through, and unless there's actually a convoy in-system, the biggest thing the Andies'll have available will be a tin can or two."

"I know. That's why I was going to bypass until this new information came to light. Now we might as well check, since we'll have to stop long enough to drop fresh dispatches for the squadron with our embassy. I'll send Alice orders to continue her operations but to switch to Andy or Confed transponder codes and be darned sure she stays covert on any interception until she's positive what she's dealing with.

"At the same time," she went on, leaning back once more, "I'll send dispatches to Gregor and the Admiralty. If Giscard *is* operating out here, we need more than Q-ships, and we need it fast. I don't know where Admiral Caparelli will find the extra units, but he's simply going to have to come up with them from somewhere."

"And the attack on Warnecke?"

"We'll carry through on that with or without Andy support," Honor said crisply. "Going after raiders at the source is the best way to cut down on their operations, and this is the first base we've been able to ID. More to the point, Warnecke's a lot more dangerous than the average freelancer. We need to take him out—hard—as quickly as possible."

"And afterward, Ma'am?"

"Afterward, I think we'll have a look at the Rift. We can look after ourselves better than any merchant ship, if we have to, but what I'd like to do is just cruise through the area—using an Andy transponder setting, I think—

while we see if we can pick up any sign of a picket line. They won't expect military-grade sensors aboard a merchie, and if they have orders to *assist* Andy shipping, they should leave us alone if they think that's what we are. We should be able to cross the area fairly safely, and if we get a sniff of lurking warships, it should confirm our hypothesis for higher command authority."

"What do we do in the short term if we pick them up, Ma'am?"

"One thing we *don't* do is engage them," Honor said firmly. "If they're operating with battlecruisers, they'll be a lot faster than us. And they can take us out eventually even in the Rift where we can use our pods and even if we get lucky against the first one or two ships. And if they've put together a picket line, somebody's going to notice if we start punching out their neighbors." She shook her head. "The Admiralty never intended us to take on capital ships, and I don't have any desire to rewrite our orders in that regard. Maybe with *Fearless* or *Nike* I'd feel more aggressive; with *Wayfarer*, I feel a very strong desire to be as inoffensive as possible where a Peep squadron is concerned."

"Um." Cardones considered that for all of two seconds, then grinned. "I can live with that approach, Ma'am," he said cheerfully.

• CHAPTER TWENTY-NINE

"All right, people." Honor looked levelly around her bridge, then at the split-screen com which held the faces of Harold Tschu and Jacquelyn Harmon, and wished the IAN's Sachsen commander *had* had someone to send along. But the best Commodore Blohm could promise was to organize a proper squadron with a ground combat echelon within three months, which left the situation squarely up to her in the meantime.

"Let's do this right the first time, shall we?" she went on. "Is Engineering ready, Harry?"

"Yes, Ma'am. I guarantee it'll be spectacular, Skipper."

"Just so long as it's *only* spectacular. Let's not lose an alpha node for real."

"No sweat, Ma'am."

"Good. Your people are fully briefed, Jackie?"

"Yes, Ma'am," Commander Harmon said from *Peter's* command deck, and her dark eyes glittered.

"Good." Honor turned in her chair and glanced at her irregular guests. Warner Caslet and Denis Jourdain lacked proper chairs with shock frames, but they wore their skinsuits as they stood beside the main plot. *Wayfarer's* green bead tracked steadily across that plot, coming up on the Marsh System's alpha wall, and she nodded to Caslet as the Peep glanced over his shoulder at her. Then she drew a deep breath. "In that case, let's be about it," she said calmly.

Admiral Rayna Sherman, who'd once been something approaching a real admiral in something which could almost be mistaken for a navy, braced against her ongoing despair as the lift stopped. By the time it opened and she stepped out onto her command deck, her face was utterly expressionless. The watch acknowledged her arrival respectfully but without the spit and polish of a regular navy crew, and she hid a familiar flash of sourness as she nodded back.

She crossed to the plot and glanced into it, but nothing had changed—of course—and she continued to her command chair while her flagship continued its slow, monotonous sweep. It was ridiculous. Her own *President Warnecke* (and wasn't *that* a modest name), *Willis*, *Hendrickson*, and *Jarmon* (named for the three systems of the Chalice, which anyone but an idiot knew they'd never see again) represented a full third of Andre Warnecke's "navy." They were also its most powerful units, and keeping them here was a complete misuse of their potential. Sherman had long since realized just how stupid she'd been to sign on with Warnecke in the first place. But if she was stuck here—and she was; people Warnecke suspected of planning to desert died messily, and the Confederacy's government had already condemned her to death, which left her nowhere to run anyway—she would have preferred to at least operate effectively. The squadron had been designed to cruise as a *squadron*, and with the heavy cruisers' support to take out convoy escorts, the lighter units could have cut a swath through Silesian space. Especially now that the Manties had cut their local forces to the bone. And the whole point in coming to Marsh had been that no one *else* ever came here. Their base's primary defense was its isolation, and if anyone ever did figure out where they were and came calling, her four cruisers were unlikely to stop them.

Besides, if Sherman had been there to ride herd on him, "Commodore" Arner and his pigs would have been denied their favorite form of entertainment. Most of Andre Warnecke's original female followers had bailed out once he showed his true colors, and Sherman understood exactly why she and the majority of his remaining female personnel had been transferred to the ships which never left Marsh.

She grimaced internally, careful to keep it from reaching her face. *At least being stuck here is better than watching someone like Arner at work,* she thought grimly. Arner's squadron should already have hit the convoy to Posnan, and knowing how he would have allowed his crews to *amuse* themselves sickened Sherman. *How did it come to this?* she wondered yet again. *I actually believed in this once, thought it would actually make a change for the better in the Chalice. Now I just don't see any way out of it . . . and "the Leader" is getting crazier every day. It was bad enough before they chased us out of the Chalice, but now—* She shivered. *He may actually believe he'll go back someday, but I doubt it. I think he's just pissed off with the universe. He wants to get even by hurting as many people as he can . . . and I'm stuck right in the middle of it.*

She closed her eyes. *You can't think about that,* she told herself sternly. *He may be crazy, but that only makes him more dangerous. If he even* thinks *you're going "unreliable" on him . . .*

She opened her eyes with another shudder and cocked her chair back. At least she wasn't forced to spend much time dirtside. That was something. "The Leader" had managed to cram over four thousand of his "Elite Guard" aboard the ships which had fled the Chalice, and every one of them was on Sidemore. God only knew what *they* did for amusement, and Sherman had no desire to find out. Her nightmares were bad enough already. Not that there was—

"Hyper footprint!"

Sherman snapped upright in astonishment. *Warnecke's* tac officer was already bending closer to his console, and Sherman closed her mouth firmly. He'd tell her what he knew as soon as he knew something, and she made herself wait, but Tracking spoke up again before he did.

"Jesus!" Lieutenant Changa gasped. "We've got a Warshawski flare, Admiral—a big one! Looks like somebody lost an entire alpha node—maybe two—crossing the wall."

"A flare?" Sherman stood and crossed to Changa, and the lieutenant tapped a waterfall display.

"See, Ma'am? Output jumped at least four thousand percent just as the last transit energy bled off. Whoever this is, he's damned lucky that sail held through translation."

"Is it one of ours?" Sherman asked, swiveling her gaze to Tactical.

"No way," Commander Truitt said. "We don't have any scheduled returns for the next nine days local. Besides, this guy's a hell of a lot bigger than any of ours. I'd say it's a merchie."

"Tracking concurs," Changa reported. "I've got his impellers now, and I make him at least six or seven m-tons. Could be a little more if he's lost more than one alpha node."

"Range and bearing?"

"He made a sloppy translation," Truitt replied. "Not surprising if he was losing a sail, I suppose. He's thirty light-minutes out, just above the ecliptic at zero-eight-two true. Present velocity . . . call it nine hundred KPS. Acceleration looks like about eighty gees—I'd say he *has* lost a chunk of one of his impeller rooms, if that's the best he can turn out."

"Heading?"

"Looks like he's headed for Sidemore," her astrogator said. "Unless he can get some more accel, though, its going to take him better than thirteen hours."

Sherman nodded and walked slowly back to her chair. The stranger was over eleven light-minutes from her own ships. Even if he knew they where here, it would be a while before any com transmission from him reached them, but she wondered who the hell he was. This could be a prize sent in by one of the ships out on ops, but that was strictly against SOP. "The Leader's" contacts in Silesia were an inconvenient distance from Marsh— seclusion had its drawbacks—and his captains normally sent prizes straight to one of the fences. It made getting prize crews back a pain, but that was why Warnecke had kept *Silas*. The captured liner-cum-freighter had a decent turn of speed and stayed busy on shuttle runs between Marsh and . . . elsewhere.

Yet if this *wasn't* a prize, what was it doing here? No one ever came to Marsh. That was why they'd chosen the system in the first place. And if anyone *was* going to come this way, it would certainly have been a smaller tramp freighter, not something this size.

The Warshawski flare. That has to be it. They knew their sail was about to fail, and we're not far off the least-time route between the Empire and Sachsen. They needed a system in a hurry, and we were the closest "safe port" they could reach . . . poor bastards.

She sat back down and rubbed her temple. If they were in trouble, they'd start screaming for help as soon as they saw someone to scream to, and what did she do then? Losing a sail didn't make it impossible for a ship to get into hyper; it only meant that if it got there and then hit a grav wave, it would be destroyed. But it could still maneuver there, and it could still attain an apparent velocity a thousand times greater than light. So if these people jumped back into hyper, they could eventually get *somewhere* else, as long as they were careful to avoid all grav waves en route. Sailing that kind of course would be inconvenient as hell, but it could be done.

Which meant that if they picked up anything suspicious and ran for it, she'd have no choice but to chase them down in hyper. In theory, that shouldn't have been a problem, since both their acceleration and their top speed would be far lower than hers, but one reason Marsh was so seldom visited was that only a single grav wave, and that a fairly weak one, served the system. That had probably been a factor in the stranger's decision to come here, since the weaker wave would have put less strain on a failing sail. But it also meant the freighter could run in almost any direction under impellers, and local h-space sensor conditions were lousy. If one of her people wasn't right on top of them when they made translation, they'd have an excellent chance to evade her. In which case the *next* people to call would be a Confed squadron.

No, she had to get close enough to be certain they couldn't evade. The best solution would be to intercept inside the Marsh hyper limit, where they couldn't get back into h-space at all, which meant less than nineteen light-minutes from the G6 primary. But it would take them a long time to get there—certainly long enough to change their minds and run if anything did make them suspicious—so the first order of business was to keep them from suspecting anything.

All right. If that was a merchant ship, it presumably had civilian-grade sensors, which were unlikely to see *her* ships at anything much above eight light-minutes, and it wouldn't send a message to her unless it could see her. So her first priority had to be to hold the range open until they were where she wanted them. It would also give her a chance to see if their sensors were better than she assumed, since they'd certainly send a message to her if they saw her. Ergo, no message meant they didn't know she was here. But if they didn't, they were bound to transmit straight to Sidemore, which meant. . . .

She rubbed her temple harder, then nodded and turned her chair to face her astrogator.

"New squadron course, Sue. We've should have a good three light-minutes to play with before we enter their sensor range. I want a vector to take us out and around in a dogleg that will bring us up from astern of them *after* they've made turnover for Sidemore, but we'll maintain our heading for—" she checked the plot's time display "—another ten minutes."

"No sweat," the astrogator replied. "We've got six times their accel to play with."

"Good." Sherman turned to her com officer. "Raise Sidemore. Tell them I'm going to maneuver to stay outside the target's sensor envelope until we get it inside the hyper limit, and send them our course once Sue works it out. If these people send them a message, I want dirtside to tell them there's a visiting Confed antipiracy patrol out-system of them, that their message is being relayed, and for them to maintain their present profile. Tell them the 'naval units' will make rendezvous with them at the point Sue's calculating. Got it?"

"Yes, Ma'am," the com officer said, and Sherman leaned back in her chair again.

"Sidemore should be receiving our message now, Ma'am," Fred Cousins said, and Honor nodded.

The privateers' maneuvers made it clear they had *Wayfarer* on gravitics, but very few "merchantmen" would be able to pick *them* up at this range, and they evidently figured *Wayfarer* hadn't. Their ships were swinging out to skirt Wayfarer's theoretical sensor envelope, then loop back in behind her in an obvious—and logical—attempt to head off any possibility of flight. All four of them were staying together, as well. That was nice. If she could suck them all in for the initial exchange, she wouldn't have to worry about any of them getting away.

She made herself sit back, radiating serene confidence while a skinsuited Nimitz curled in her lap. Tschu's "Warshawski flare" had been just as convincing as promised, and as he'd also promised, he'd managed it without actually damaging anything. Which was not to say he hadn't stressed the system right to the limit, and things like that always had *some* consequences. It had taken all eight forward alpha nodes to project a suitable power pulse, and Honor expected BuShips to speak to her firmly for taking a good thousand hours off their projected service life, but it had been worth it. Or, she corrected herself, it seemed to have been worth it *so* far.

Caslet had moved over to stand beside her, and their

eyes met as she looked up. He and his senior officers had dined with her each night, and a sense of mutual respect and even wary liking had grown up between her and the Peep commander. She remembered Thomas Theisman, the Peep destroyer skipper—and now admiral—she'd captured at the Battle of Blackbird, and smiled slightly. Theisman and Caslet had a lot in common. For that matter, so did Allison MacMurtree, Shannon Foraker, and—reluctant though she'd initially been to admit it about any "people's commissioner"—Denis Jourdain. All of them were too darned good at their jobs for her comfort, and all of them were people of integrity.

"Four heavy cruisers make for pretty stiff odds, Captain," Caslet observed quietly.

"I told you our teeth are sharp," she replied calmly. "I'm less worried by the numbers than I am by how slow we are. If they detach anyone, the detachee is going to get away from us."

Caslet blinked. She was worried that a *heavy cruiser* might "get away" from a converted merchantman? He was willing to admit her ship mounted powerful energy weapons, but he'd had ample opportunity to realize *Wayfarer* truly was a civilian design, with all the vulnerabilities that implied, and there couldn't be many places to put missile tubes. Her long-range armament had to be weak, especially given the space those god-awful grasers must eat up, and she couldn't take much damage. All of which meant a properly handled CA would cut her slow, unarmored, ungainly hull to pieces in any sort of sustained engagement. Granted she did carry those LACs, but LACs were fragile and weakly armed themselves. No matter how Warner Caslet looked at it, he expected *Wayfarer* to be severely damaged before she could take out that many opponents.

"Well, they seem to be sticking together for now," he said dryly. "So if that's your main concern, Captain, I'd say things are looking pretty good so far."

        *   *   *

"Message coming in from dirtside," *Warnecke's* com officer reported. She listened intently for a minute or two, then looked over her shoulder at Sherman. "Base says they're the Andermani freighter *Sternenlicht*. They've suffered a double node failure in their forward sail, and they took some nasty casualties when the nodes blew. They request engineering and medical assistance."

"Truitt?" Sherman asked.

"Checking database now." The tac officer watched his display for a few seconds, then shrugged. "We don't have her listed, but our Andermani lists've never been very complete. The message header's definitely Andy merchant service, though, and the transponder matches."

"I see." Sherman crossed her legs and considered, then looked back up at the com officer. "How did dirtside respond?"

"I'll play it back," the com officer said, and a moment later, Andre Warnecke's strong, mellow voice came from the speakers.

"*Sternenlicht*, this is Sidemore. Your message has been received, and we're making arrangements to render assistance. I'm afraid we lack the facilities to repair your nodes locally, but we've got a little good news to go with the bad. Two divisions of Silesian cruisers on antipiracy patrol out of Sachsen dropped by on a courtesy visit earlier this week, and they're still in-system. They probably can't help with your nodes, either, but they do have surgeons aboard, and they can at least let someone know you're here. I'm requesting their immediate assistance for you, but they've been conducting maneuvers in our outer asteroid belt, and it's going to take them a while to reach you. Maintain your present flight profile. I estimate they'll rendezvous with you in about five hours and escort you the rest of the way in. Sidemore, out."

"Not bad," Sherman murmured. *He sounds like he actually means it. I wonder how someone that crazy can sound so reasonable and helpful?* She shook herself and checked her plot once more. The range had fallen to ten

light-minutes as her squadron skirted around *Sternenlicht* to reach its ambush position, but that was still well beyond reach of a merchie's sensors.

". . . way in. Sidemore, out."

Honor looked at Rafe Cardones with a raised eyebrow.

"'Oh what a tangled web we weave,'" he said with a grim smile. "At least it confirms that we're in the right place. If those are Confed cruisers, I'll eat our main sensor array."

"I agree, Milady," Jennifer Hughes put in. "Carol has their emissions dialed in across the board. They're a dead match for the profiles we pulled out of that tin can's computers, and they sure as hell aren't anywhere near any asteroid belts."

"Good." Honor nodded in satisfaction. There'd never been much doubt, but it was nice to be certain they'd be killing the right people.

She gazed into her plot, watching *Wayfarer's* bead move steadily towards the planet while the cruisers sidestepped the "oblivious freighter." They were maintaining a tight-interval formation, too. That was nice. It would put them all in range simultaneously when the time came.

"Reply, Fred," she said. "Thank them for their assistance, and tell them we'll maintain profile. Be sure you include Dr. Ryder's description of our crew casualties for their 'surgeons.'"

Sherman stifled a sense of guilt as she watched the hapless freighter sail straight into her trap. Replacing that vessel's alpha nodes would be a gargantuan task for their repair ship—they'd have to build the damned things from scratch, since none of their ships used nodes that powerful—but it could be done. And Andre would be delighted to add her to his list of prizes. Better yet, there was a whole crew of trained spacers over there, people who could be "convinced" to provide some of the additional technical support they needed.

It'd be more merciful just to blow them apart, she thought grimly, *but I can't. Andre would take his time killing me if I blew away a prize.* She watched the light dot of the freighter, less than ten minutes from rendezvous now, and her eyes were haunted. *I'm sorry,* she told the blip, and turned her chair to face her tac officer once more.

"Nine-and-a-half minutes to intercept, Ma'am," Jennifer Hughes said. "They're folding in from starboard, rate of closure just under two thousand KPS, decelerating at two hundred gees. Present range to Bogey One just over three-one-one-thousand klicks; range to Bogey Four is four-zero-niner thousand. We're picking up fire control emissions from Bogey Two, but the others aren't even pulsing us. We've got 'em where we want 'em, Milady."

Honor nodded. The "Confederacy cruisers" had made com contact hours ago, and the woman who'd introduced herself as "Admiral Sherman" was actually in Silesian uniform. Or her com image was, anyway. Honor's own image had gone out in Andermani merchant uniform, courtesy of a little computer alteration. But unlike "Admiral Sherman," Honor knew the face on her screen was lying, for Tactical had tracked Warnecke's cruisers' entire maneuver, and it bore no resemblance at all to the one "Sherman" had described.

"All right, people." She glanced up at Caslet, and the Peep nodded back. "Begin your attack, Commander Hughes," she said formally.

"Aye, aye, Ma'am. Carol, roll the pods."

"That's funny."

Sherman turned to look at Commander Truitt, and the tac officer shrugged.

"I just picked up something separating from the target," he said. "Not sure what it is. It looks like debris of some sort, but it must be pretty small—the radar return's mighty weak. It's falling astern of her now, and—" He frowned. "There goes another batch of it."

"What sort of debris?"

"I don't know," Truitt admitted. "Looks like they could be jettisoning cargo or— There goes another batch." He grinned suddenly. "You don't suppose they were running contraband into the Confederacy, do you?"

"Maybe," Sherman said, but her tone was doubtful. If *Sternenlicht* was, in fact, carrying contraband—and most captains did in Silesia—she'd want to get rid of it before a Confed squadron sent people aboard her. But if she was going to dump cargo, why wait this long? Surely she had to know Sherman's ships were close enough to see it on radar. Of course, from their medical reports, they had some pretty seriously hurt personnel over there. What with a major engineering failure and casualties, it might just have slipped her captain's mind until now.

A fourth wave of debris had kicked out the rear of the freighter's wedge while Sherman pondered. Now a fifth followed . . . and then the freighter suddenly rolled ship, turning the belly of her wedge towards the cruisers, and Rayna Sherman discovered what that "jettisoned cargo" truly was.

In light of any missile pod's complete vulnerability to any weapon, BuWeaps was still trying to come up with a design made out of sufficiently low-signature materials to defeat enemy fire control. They hadn't quite managed that yet, but they *had* come up with one whose radar return was far weaker than something its size ought to have been, and their new optical coating was much more effective against both visual detection and the laser pulses of the lidar most navies favored for short-range fire control, as well. Which meant they didn't look big enough to be any particular threat . . . a fact upon which Honor had counted when she, Cardones, and Hughes planned their initial tactics.

Five complete salvos spilled astern, ejecting cleanly

from the outsized cargo doors, and the pods' onboard fire control was programmed for delayed activation. The first salvo waited forty-eight seconds, the second thirty-six, the third twenty-four, and the fourth twelve. . . .

The last fired on launch, and three hundred capital missiles streaked straight into the privateers' teeth.

The range was under a half-million kilometers, and the RMN's latest capital missiles accelerated at 92,000 KPS^2. Flight time to the closest enemy ship was twenty-four seconds; time to the most distant was only four seconds longer, and *Hendrickson*, *Jarmon*, and *Willis* never had a chance.

Seventy-five immensely powerful laser heads screamed in on each of them, and they didn't even have their fire control on-line, far less their point defense. There was no need for it. *They* were the hunters, and their prey was only a huge, slow, totally defenseless freighter. They'd known that—or thought they had. Now captains shouted frantic helm orders, trying to roll ship and interpose their wedges, and *Jarmon* actually managed it . . . not that it did her any good. Jennifer Hughes' exquisitely timed missile storm slashed down on them, and her birds had plenty of time left on their drives for terminal attack maneuvers. Bomb-pumped lasers smashed through their targets' sidewalls as if they were tissue, detonating at ranges as short as a thousand kilometers, and no heavy cruiser ever built could survive that sort of fire.

Warner Caslet stared at the plot in disbelief as the missile traces spawned like hideous serpents of light. He whirled to the visual display, and then staggered back a step as the laser heads detonated. The range was little more than a light-second and a half, and the savage white glare of nuclear fire stabbed at his eyes despite the optical filters.

God, he thought numbly. *Dear sweet God, this is only a Q-ship! What the hell happens if they fit a warship with . . . with whatever the hell that was?!*

*   *   *

Rayna Sherman went paper-white as the missiles tore down on *President Warnecke*. Her flagship had been about to demand the "freighter's" surrender, and her fire control was on-line for the task. *Warnecke's* merely human crew was taken totally by surprise, but her point defense computers observed the sudden eruption of threat sources and engaged automatically, salvoing countermissiles and snapping the laser clusters around to engage the leakers.

Unfortunately, her defenses were too weak to stop that much fire even if they'd known in advance that it was coming. She was only a heavy cruiser, and not even a superdreadnought could have thrown seventy-five missiles at her in a single broadside. She stopped a lot of them, but most got through, and Sherman clung to her command chair as lasers slashed into her ship. Plating shattered under the kinetic transfer, air belched out in huge, obscene bubbles, damage alarms screamed, and there was nothing—nothing at all—Sherman could do about it.

Warnecke's wedge fluctuated madly as alpha and beta nodes were blasted away. Half her radar and all her gravitics were blown to bits, and a raging wall of blast and fragments crashed through her communications section. Both sidewalls flickered and died, then came back up at less than half strength, and two thirds of her armament was totally destroyed. She reeled sideways, alive but dying, and her half-crippled plot showed the unmistakable radar returns of LACs exploding from the flanks of the huge "freighter."

"Com! Tell them we surrender!" Sherman shouted.

"I can't!" the panicked com officer shouted back. "They're gone—they're all gone in Com One and Two!"

Sherman felt her heart stop. The "freighter" was already rolling back down, presenting her broadside to *Warnecke*, and there could be only one reason for that. But without a com, she couldn't even tell them she surrendered! Unless—

"Strike the wedge!"

Warnecke's astrogator stared at her for an instant before she understood. It was the universal, last-ditch signal of surrender, and her hands flashed for her panel.

"Coming on target," Jennifer Hughes said coldly as *Wayfarer* completed her roll. Eight massive grasers came to bear on their target, and she punched the button.

Grasers, like lasers, are light-speed weapons. Rayna Sherman didn't even have a chance to realize she'd found an escape from Andre Warnecke's madness at last, for the deadly streams of focused gamma radiation arrived before she knew they'd fired.

"And that," Honor Harrington said quietly, staring into the visual display at the boil of light and expanding wreckage which had once been Bogey Two, "is that."

• CHAPTER THIRTY

"Message coming in from Sidemore, Skipper." Honor held up a hand, halting her conversation with Rafe Cardones, and raised an eyebrow at Fred Cousins. "Same guy as before, but we're getting a visual to go with it this time,"the com officer said.

"Really?" Honor smiled thinly. "Put him through."

Her small com screen blinked alive with the face of a man in the immaculate uniform of a commodore in the Silesian Navy. He was dark-haired, with a neatly trimmed beard, and without the uniform, he could easily have been mistaken for a college professor or a banker. But Honor recognized him from her intelligence file imagery despite the beard.

"My God, woman!" he gasped, his face twisted with horror. "What in God's name d'you think you're *doing?* You just killed three thousand Silesian military personnel!"

"No," Honor replied in a cold soprano. "I just exterminated three thousand vermin."

It took over four minutes for her light-speed transmission to reach the planet, and then Warnecke's eyes narrowed. His furious expression went absolutely blank as he gazed into his own pickup for several seconds, and when he spoke again, his voice was completely calm.

"Who are you?" he asked flatly.

"Captain Honor Harrington, Royal Manticoran Navy, at your service. I've already destroyed four of your vessels in Sharon's Star and Schiller"—she felt guilty at taking credit for Caslet's kills, but this was no time to introduce distracting elements—"and now I've taken out all four of your heavy cruisers. You're running out of ships, Mr. Warnecke, but that doesn't really matter, does it?" She smiled, her almond eyes colder than liquid helium. "After all, you've just run out of *time*, as well."

She sat back, waiting out the inevitable com lag, but Warnecke didn't even flinch when her transmission reached him. He only leaned back in his own chair and bared his teeth at her.

"Perhaps I am, Captain Harrington," he said. "On the other hand, I may have more time than you think. After all, I've got a garrison and an entire planetary population down here. Digging my people out could get . . . messy, don't you think? And, of course, I've also taken the precaution of planting a few nuclear charges here and there in various towns and cities. We wouldn't want anything *unfortunate* to happen to those charges, now would we?"

Honor's nostrils flared. It wasn't unexpected, but that didn't make it any better. Assuming the threat was real. Unfortunately, it probably was. As far as Andrew Warnecke was concerned, the universe ended when he died, and he knew exactly what the Confederacy government would do if it ever got its hands on him. If he had to die anyway, he wouldn't hesitate to take hundreds of thousands of others with him. In fact, he'd probably enjoy it.

"Let me explain something to you, Mr. Warnecke," she said quietly. "I now control this star system. Nothing will move in or out of it without my permission; anything which attempts to do so will be destroyed. I'm sure you have sufficient sensor capability to confirm my ability to make good on those promises.

"I also have a full battalion of Manticoran Marines, with battle armor and heavy weapons, and I will shortly control your planet's high orbitals. I can drop precision kinetic strikes anywhere I want to support my personnel. You, on the other hand, have four thousand men who aren't worth the pulser darts to blow them to hell as combat soldiers, and I will personally guarantee that your combat equipment is obsolescent, second-line garbage by Manticoran standards.

"Moreover, I've notified Commodore Blohm of the Andermani Navy of your location, and heavy units of the IAN and Imperial Army will be arriving soon. In short, Mr. Warnecke, we can—and will—take that planet away from you any time we want. And, as I'm certain you're quite aware, if we don't, the Confederacy *will*."

She paused to let that register, then continued.

"It's quite possible you have, in fact, emplaced the nuclear charges you've just threatened to detonate. If you do detonate them, you die. If we send in the troops, you also die—either in the fighting, or on the end of a Silesian rope; it doesn't matter to me. *But*, Mr. Warnecke, if you surrender yourself, your men, and the planet, I will personally guarantee that you will be turned over to the Andermani, and not the Silesians. At the moment, none of you have been charged with any capital crime by the Empire, and Commodore Blohm has empowered me to promise you that the Empire will not execute you all as you so manifestly deserve. Prison, yes; executions, no. I regret that, but I'm willing to offer you your lives in return for a peaceful surrender of the planet."

She smiled again, colder even than before, and crossed her legs.

"The choice is yours, Mr. Warnecke. We'll speak again when my ships are in orbit around Sidemore. Harrington, out."

Warnecke's face disappeared from her screen, and Honor looked at Cousins.

"Ignore any additional hails until I tell you otherwise, Fred."

"Yes, Ma'am."

"You pushed him pretty hard there, Captain," Caslet said quietly, and she turned her chair to face him. The Peep had recovered from the shock of what *Wayfarer* had done to Warnecke's cruisers, and his hazel eyes were intent.

"I know." She stood, cradling Nimitz in her arms, and crossed to the main plot. Commander Harmon's LACs moved across it—three of them speeding ahead to planetary orbit while the other nine collected *Wayfarer's* missile pods and towed them in for reuse—and she watched Sidemore drawing closer. She stood brooding down at the planet for long, silent seconds, with Caslet by her side, then shrugged.

"I don't have much choice, Warner." It was the first time she'd called him anything other than "Citizen Commander," but neither of them really noticed. "I have to assume he really does have the place mined, and I also have to assume he really will press the button. But if we— or the Andies—don't take him out, the Confeds certainly will. They have to, and frankly, I don't think I could stomach seeing him walk away, either. That means that unless someone convinces him to surrender, that button will get pushed and an awful lot of people will die."

She looked up at him, and Caslet nodded soberly.

"The man's an egomaniacal psychopath," she said flatly. "The only hope I see is to rub his nose in the fact that he's helpless and that the Confederacy *will* come in to get him, regardless of his threats. I've got to push him hard enough to break through his megalomania, then offer him a way out that lets him live. It's the only way to avoid enormous civilian casualties, but he's *got* to have that way out. If he figures he doesn't—" She shrugged, and Caslet nodded again.

"I understand your logic," he said after a moment, "but do you really think it will work?"

"With Warnecke?" Honor shook her head. "Possibly not. I have to try, but I can't count on anything where he's concerned. But he's not alone down there, either. He's got four thousand troops on the planet. They may be scum, but they may also be a bit closer to sane than he is. If I keep him talking long enough, sooner or later word of the options I've given him will get out. When that happens, somebody who doesn't want to die may just take Warnecke out for us."

Caslet looked at her silently and tried to hide a mental shiver as she gazed back. Her expression was calm and composed, but her eyes . . . He saw the doubt in them, the anguish . . . the fear. She sounded so dispassionate, so reasonable, projecting the aura of certainty which was one of a naval officer's essential weapons, yet deep inside she knew exactly what stakes she was playing for, and they terrified her.

But she'd seen this coming from the outset, he realized. She'd considered the options she'd just offered Warnecke long since, for she'd *known* she was going to face this decision, require those options. That was why she'd discussed them with Commodore Blohm ahead of time. Yet even knowing, she'd decided to attack herself rather than pass the responsibility off to someone else. The Silesians or the Andermani would have moved if she hadn't; she had to know that as well as Caslet did, but she'd refused to evade the job. He'd come to know her during his time aboard *Wayfarer*—not well, but well enough to realize how the deaths on Sidemore would haunt her if Warnecke pressed the button. And, he thought, well enough to know *she'd* recognized that, too. That she'd considered it the same way she'd considered every other aspect of the operation. If it happened, everyone in the galaxy would be ready to second-guess her, to blame her for the disaster, to argue that she'd been clumsy—that there *had* to have been a way to have avoided so many deaths. And *she* would, too. She would always believe she could have avoided it if she'd been smarter, cleverer, faster, and she knew she would, and *still* she'd come here to place herself on the line for a planet full of people she'd never met.

How did she do that? How did she make herself assume such a crushing responsibility when she could so easily have handed it off to someone else? Warner Caslet was also a naval officer, also accustomed to the burden of command, yet he didn't know the answer to that question. He knew only that she had . . . and that he could not have.

She was his enemy, and he was hers. Her kingdom was fighting for its life against the Republic, and the men and women who ran the Republic were fighting for *their* lives against her kingdom. There could be no other outcome. Either the Star Kingdom must be conquered, or the Committee of Public Safety would be destroyed by the mob its promises had mobilized to support the war. Caslet had no love for the Committee or its members, but if it came down in its turn, God only knew where the resultant paroxysms of bloodshed would leave his star nation. And because they were both naval officers, because the consequences of defeat were too terrible for either of them to contemplate, they could be only enemies. Yet at this moment, he wished it could be otherwise. He felt the magnetism which made her crews worship her, made them willing to follow her straight into the fire, and he understood it at last.

She cared. It was really that simple. She *cared*, and she could neither offer her people less than her very best nor settle for less than the complete discharge of whatever responsibilities duty required of her, however grim. He'd just seen the dreadful efficiency with which she'd annihilated four heavy cruisers, and he recognized the wolf in her. Yet she was a wolf who'd dedicated her life to facing other wolves to protect those who couldn't, and he understood that, for an echo of what she was lived within him, as well. He knew her now, recognized what she truly was and knew that what she was made her a terrible danger to the Republic, to his Navy—ultimately to Warner Caslet himself—yet for just this moment, it didn't matter.

He gazed at her a moment longer, then startled both of them by laying a hand lightly on her arm.

"I hope it works, Captain," he said quietly, and turned back to the plot before them.

*   *   *

"Entering orbit, Ma'am," John Kanehama said. Nimitz lay on his back in Honor's lap, true-hands and hand-feet wrestling with her, but she looked up at the astrogator's announcement and nodded. She gave Nimitz a last caress, savoring the surge of love and assurance he sent back to her, then rose, set him on the back of her chair, and folded her hands behind her.

"Hail Warnecke, Fred."

"Aye, aye, Ma'am." Cousins punched a command into his panel, then nodded to her, and she faced the pickup, her eyes cold, as Warnecke's face appeared on the main screen. He looked almost as calm as before, but not quite, and she wished they were close enough for Nimitz to give her a read on his emotions. Not that she was certain it would have helped. She was convinced the man was insane, and a madman's emotions might have been the most dangerous guide of all upon which to rely.

"I said we'd speak again, Mr. Warnecke," she said.

"So you did," he replied, and the com lag now was barely noticeable. "You seem to have an uncommonly capable 'freighter' up there, Captain. My compliments." Honor bobbed her head in cold acknowledgment, and he smiled thinly. "Nonetheless, I'm still down here with my button, and I assure you I *will* push it if you force me to. In which case, of course, the deaths of all these innocent civilians will be entirely *your* fault."

"I don't think we'll play that game," Honor replied. "You have an alternative. If you detonate your charges, you'll do it because *you* chose to do that rather than accept the unreasonably generous offer I've already made you."

"My, my! And I thought *I* was the villain of the piece!" Warnecke raised his hand, bringing a small, hand-held transmitter into the pickup's field, and bared his teeth. "Are you really so blasé about the possibility of my pressing this button? I have very little to lose, you know. I've heard about Andermani prisons. I'm not at all sure I'd prefer life in one of them to, well—"

He flipped his wrist to emphasize the transmitter he held, and his eyes burned with a dangerous light. Honor felt an icy breeze blow down her spine, but no trace of it touched her face.

"Perhaps not, Mr. Warnecke, but death is so *permanent*, don't you think?"

"Where there's life, there's hope, you mean?" The man on her com screen laughed and leaned back in his chair. "You intrigue me, Captain Harrington. Truly you do. Are you really so sanctimonious that you'd prefer to see hundreds of thousands of people killed rather than allow a single pirate and his henchmen to just sail away in their unarmed repair ship?"

"Oh?" Honor cocked an eyebrow. "You intend to put four thousand extra people into your repair ship's life support?" She shook her head. "I'm afraid you'd find the air getting rather thick before you made another planet."

"Well, sacrifices must be made, of course," Warnecke acknowledged, "and I suppose it would only be courteous of me to leave you *some* prisoners as a trophy. Actually, I was thinking in terms of myself and perhaps a hundred close associates." He leaned towards the pickup. "Think about it, Captain. I'm sure my privateers must have taken at least a few Manticoran ships—there are so *many* of them, after all—but the Confederacy isn't your kingdom. What do you care about its rebels and revolutionaries? You can have Sidemore, rescue Marsh, send the ragtag 'pirate' leaders packing in a single ship, and collect thousands of prisoners, all without risking a single town or city. Quite an accomplishment, don't you think?"

"Your loyalty to your people overwhelms me," Honor observed, and he laughed again.

"*Loyalty*, Captain? To *these* fools? They've already failed me twice—they and their incompetent shipboard counterparts. They cost me my own nation, my place in history. Why ever should I feel 'loyalty' to them?" He shook his head. "A pox upon all of them, Captain Harrington. You can have them with my compliments."

"While *you* scurry off to try it all over again? I think not, Mr. Warnecke."

"Come now, Captain! You know it's the best deal you're going to get. Death or glory, victory or magnificent destruction—those are a naval officer's choices, aren't they? What makes you think mine are any different?"

Honor gazed at him for a long, silent moment while her mind ticked away. His mellow voice was so cultured, so powerful, made anything he said seem so rational and reasoned. It must have been a potent weapon when he first began his career in the Chalice. Even now, he exuded a twisted charm, like the seduction of an incubus. It was the emptiness within him, she thought. The void where a normal person kept his soul. The blood on his hands meant nothing—less than nothing—to him, and that was his armor. Since he felt no guilt, he projected none.

"Do you really think," she said finally, "that I can let you go? That it's as simple as that?"

"Why not? Who was it back on Old Earth who said, 'Kill one man and you're a murderer; kill a million and you're a statesman'? I may not have that quite correct, but I'm sure the paraphrase is close. And navies and armies and even monarchs negotiate with 'statesmen' all the time, Captain. Come, now! *Negotiate* with me . . . or I may just press the button anyway, to show you how seriously you should take me. For example—"

His other hand came up into the pickup's field, and his index finger pressed a button on the transmitter number pad.

"There!" he said with a brilliant smile, and Honor heard someone suck in air behind her. She turned her head and saw Jennifer Hughes staring at her display in horror. The tac officer's head whipped up, and Honor's left hand made a quick, chopping motion outside her own pickup's field of view. Cousins was watching her intently, and he cut the sound in the instant before Hughes opened her mouth.

"My God, Ma'am!" the tac officer gasped. "We've got

a nuclear detonation on the planet! Tracking makes it about five hundred k-tons . . . right in the middle of a town!"

Honor felt a fist punch her in the belly, and her face paled. She couldn't control that, but her expression didn't even flicker while the horror of it rolled through her.

"Casualty estimate?" she asked flatly.

"I-I can't be certain, Ma'am." The tough-as-nails tac officer was visibly shaken. "From the size of the town, maybe ten or fifteen thousand."

"I see." Honor inhaled deeply, then turned back to the com and flicked her hand at Cousins. The sound came back up, and Warnecke's smile had vanished.

"Did I fail to mention that I can detonate any one of the charges separately?" he purred. "Dear me, how careless of me! And there you were, thinking it was an all or nothing proposition. Of course, you don't know how many charges there *are*, do you now? I wonder how many more towns I can wipe off the face of the planet—just as a bargaining ploy, you understand—before I set off the big one?"

"Very impressive," Honor heard herself say. "And just what sort of negotiations did you have in mind?"

"I thought it was quite simple, Captain. My friends and I get aboard our repair ship and leave. Your ships stay in orbit around Sidemore until my ship reaches the hyper limit, and then you come down and clean up the riffraff I'll be leaving behind."

"And how can I be certain you won't send the detonation command from your ship anyway?"

"Why in the world should I want to do that?" Warnecke asked with a lazy smile. "Still, it *is* a thought, isn't it? I suppose I might consider it a proper way to, ah, *chastise* you for crippling my operations here . . . but that *would* be vindictive of me, wouldn't it?"

"I don't think we'll take that chance," Honor said flatly. "If—and I say *if*, Mr. Warnecke—I were to agree to allow you to leave, I'd need proof that it would be impossible for you to detonate your charges."

"And as soon as you knew it was impossible, you'd blow me out of space. Come, Captain! I expected better from you! Obviously I have to retain my Sword of Damocles until I'm safely out of your reach!"

"Wait." Honor rubbed an eyebrow for a moment, then let her shoulders sag ever so slightly. "You've made your point," she said in a quieter voice, "but I've made mine, as well. You can kill the people of Sidemore, and I can kill you. The very thought of letting you go turns my stomach, but . . ." She drew a deep breath. "There's no need to do anything irreversible at this point. You can't leave the system without my permission, and I can't land Marines without your seeing it and pressing your button. Let me consider this for a little while. Perhaps I can come up with a solution we can both accept."

"Caving in so soon, Captain?" Warnecke studied her suspiciously. "Somehow that doesn't ring quite true. You wouldn't be thinking of trying anything clever, would you?"

"Such as?" Honor asked bleakly. "I haven't said I *would* let you go. All I said is that there's no point in either of us acting hastily. At the moment we're both in position to trump the other's cards, Mr. Warnecke. Let's leave it at that while I consider my options, shall we?"

"Why, of course, Captain. I always like to oblige a lady. I'll be here when you decide to com again. Good day."

The image died, and Honor Harrington felt her mouth twist in a snarl of hate as the ready light above the pickup went dead.

• CHAPTER THIRTY-ONE

The atmosphere in the briefing room could have been chipped with a knife. Honor's senior officers—and Warner Caslet and Denis Jourdain—sat around the long table, and more than one face was ashen.

"My God, Ma'am," Jennifer Hughes said. "He just went ahead and did it—killed all those people—and *smiled* about it!"

"I know, Jenny." Honor closed her eyes and pinched the bridge of her nose, and inside she shivered. She no longer doubted it; Warnecke *was* insane. Not in the legal sense of being unable to recognize right or wrong, but in a far deeper, more fundamental sense. He simply didn't *care* about right or wrong, and his casual mass murder only reconfirmed her earlier decision. Whatever happened, he could not be permitted to escape to do this again. Because that was the real crux of it. He *would* do it again, or something just as terrible. Again and again . . . because he *enjoyed* it.

"We can't—*I* can't—let him go," she said. "He has to be stopped, right here, right now."

"But if he's ready to kill everyone on the planet—" Harold Tschu began slowly, and Honor shook her head sharply.

"He's not. Not yet, anyway. He's still playing with us—and he still thinks he can win. Think about his record, what he tried in the Chalice and what he's done since. Whatever else he may be, this man is convinced he can beat the entire universe because he's hungrier and more ruthless than anyone else in it. He's counting on that. He

400

expects us to be the good guys and back away rather than accept the blame for the cost of stopping him."

"But if we don't back away and he presses his button, we *will* be to blame, Ma'am," Cardones said quietly. Honor's eyes flashed, and he waved a hand quickly. "I don't mean it that way, Skipper. You were right; the decision will be his. But by the same token, we'll always know we could have let him walk and avoided it."

He'd said "we," Honor thought, but he'd meant "you." He was trying to make it a group decision, to give her an out—to protect her.

"We're not going to consider that, Rafe," she replied softly. "Particularly not since we can't be sure he won't do it anyway." She rubbed her temple and shook her head. "However relaxed he may be trying to appear, he *has* to hate us for blowing away his fleet and his private little kingdom. He's already demonstrated how casually he's willing to kill an entire town, and he knows exactly how to punish us by using our own principles against us. The moral side of it wouldn't even occur to him, and what he's already done will earn him the death penalty from anyone who ever captures him. I offered him an option there, but he prefers to go for complete victory rather than accept prison as an alternative, so the threat of ultimate retribution won't deter him either. As he sees it, he's got nothing to lose, so why not do whatever he wants?"

She sat back, hugging Nimitz to her breasts, and silence ruled the compartment as the others realized she was right.

"If there were only some way to separate him from his transmitter," she murmured. "Some way to get him away from it so we could deal with him once and for all. Some—"

She paused, and her eyes narrowed. Cardones straightened in his own chair, gazing at her anxiously as he felt her mind begin to race, then looked around the other faces. Her other officers looked as anxious as he felt, but Warner Caslet's expression was almost as intent as hers.

"Separate him from the transmitter," the Peep murmured. Honor's eyes swiveled to him, and he nodded slowly. "We can't do that, can we? But what if we separated him *and* his transmitter from the *planet*?"

"Exactly," Honor said. "Get him out of range of the charges, *then* deal with him."

"He could still leave a timer," Caslet mused, and it was as if he and Honor were alone. The others could hear their words, but the two of them were communicating on a far deeper level than anyone else could follow.

"Timers we can deal with," Honor replied. "We know where he's transmitting from, and he wouldn't trust his detonator where anyone else could get to it. That means it has to be in his HQ, and we can take that out from orbit if we have to."

"It's in a town," Caslet objected.

"Granted, but if he did use a timer, he'd set it to hold the detonation until he was too far away from Sidemore for us to overtake him short of hyper, and his repair ship's probably even slower than *Wayfarer*. Even if he could pull two hundred gees—which he can't—he'd still need over four hours to reach the hyper limit, and our LACs can pull almost six hundred. That gives us three hours in which they could overhaul him from a standing start."

"Three hours to find a timer that could be anywhere in his HQ?" Caslet objected.

"We don't have to," Honor said, her voice cold as space. "That's a fairly big town down there, but his HQ's close to one edge. If we have to, we can probably evacuate that end of town, then take out the HQ with a kinetic strike. Blast and thermal bloom would still tear up the local real estate, but the explosion would be clean, and we wouldn't have to kill anyone. For that matter, he'll be leaving a lot of people behind. Suppose we tell *them* the charges are down there? Then we offer them life in prison if they find his timer, deactivate it, and turn it over to us . . .

and tell them that if it goes off, we'll execute anyone who survives the explosions. With their 'fearless leader' already having sold them out, I think we can count on them to find it for us."

"Risky either way, but you're probably right," Caslet agreed. "But how do we work it so that he's willing to leave the planet in the first place? He may be crazy, but he's too smart to go for anything that doesn't at least look feasible."

"The com systems," Honor said softly. "The repair ship's com systems. That's the weak spot in the thread he's hung his 'Sword of Damocles' from."

"Of course!" Caslet's eyes blazed. "His hand unit couldn't possibly have the range. Once he's more than a few light-seconds from the planet, he'd *have* to use the ship's com to transmit the detonation command!"

"Exactly." Honor's chocolate eyes burned as bright as Caslet's, and she smiled. "Not only that, but I think I may see a way to take the timer out of the equation, as well—or at least give us at least another hour to work on finding it."

"You do?" Caslet rubbed his jaw.

"I think so. Harry," she turned to her chief engineer, "I'm going to need you to whip up some specialized hardware fast to pull this off. First—"

"All right, Mr. Warnecke," Honor told the face on her com screen some hours later. "I've considered my options, just as I said I would, and I have an offer for you."

"Indeed?" Warnecke smiled like a benign uncle and raised his hands in eloquent invitation. "Talk to me, Captain Harrington. Amaze me with your wisdom."

"You want to leave the system, and *I* want to be certain you don't blow up the planet as you depart, correct?" Honor spoke calmly, trying to ignore the furnace of Andrew LaFollet's emotions. They beat at her through her link to Nimitz, for her chief armsman was aghast at what she proposed to do, but she couldn't let herself worry about that just now. Her personal participation was the one bait which might lure a man who saw the universe only as an extension of himself—and would expect others to do the same—into her trap, and she concentrated all her attention on her enemy.

"That seems to sum up our positions quite nicely," Warnecke agreed.

"Very well. I propose to allow you and your people aboard your repair ship—but only after I've sent a boarding party aboard to disable all of her communication systems." Warnecke cocked his head, expression arrested, and she smiled. "Without a shipboard system to transmit your detonation order, you can't double-cross me at the last minute, now can you?"

"You must be joking, Captain!" This time Warnecke's tone was testy, and he frowned. "If you take away my ability to transmit, you also take the gun out of my hand. I don't think I'm very interested in going aboard ship only to be blown out of space once I get there!"

"Patience, Mr. Warnecke. Patience!" Honor smiled. "After my people have disabled your vessel's coms, you'll send your designated 'henchmen' aboard her. You yourself, however, and no more than three others of your choice, will be aboard a single unarmed shuttle docked to the *exterior* of your ship, where I and three of my officers will join you. Your shuttle transmitter will, of course, be able to send the detonation command at any time during this process. My people will then disable all transmitters aboard all small craft docked in your boat bays. Once they report to me that all your long-range com systems—except the one aboard your shuttle—are inoperable, I'll allow it to depart orbit. You will also have aboard your shuttle a short-range radio—no more than five hundred klicks' maximum range, as determined by *my* people, not yours—with which to maintain communication with your shipboard personnel. Once you've satisfied yourself that all my boarders have left your vessel, you, myself, and my three officers will remain aboard the shuttle while you head for the hyper limit. Assuming nothing, ah, untoward happens before reaching the limit, you'll then go aboard your ship, and my officers and I will undock the shuttle and return to *my* ship, taking with us the only means by which you could detonate the charges. Since the shuttle will be unarmed, we will, of course, be unable to hamper your departure in any way."

She raised one hand, palm uppermost, and arched both eyebrows, and Warnecke stared at her for several seconds.

"An interesting proposal, Captain," he murmured finally, "but while it would never do to accuse a gentlewoman and an officer of duplicity, what's to prevent your boarding party from planting an explosive device of your own while destroying my transmitters? I would really be most unhappy to translate into hyper only to have my ship blow up."

"Your own people will be free to oversee their operations. My boarders will be armed, of course, and any attempt actually to interfere with them will be met with deadly force. But your people don't really have to interfere, do they? All they have to do is tell you such a device has been placed, and you press the button."

"True." Warnecke scratched his beard gently. "But then there'd be the situation aboard the shuttle, Captain. I appreciate your willingness to offer yourself as a hostage for the honesty of your intentions, but you wish to bring three of your officers with you, as well. Now, if you put four armed military people, including yourself, in a situation like that, they might just decide to do something heroic, and I wouldn't like that, either."

"Perhaps not, but I have to have some means of making certain you don't send the order over the shuttle com."

"True," Warnecke said again, then smiled lazily. "However, Captain, I think I'm going to have to insist that your personnel be unarmed."

"Impossible," Honor snapped, and prayed he wouldn't guess she'd already considered this very point. "I have no intention of providing you with additional hostages, Mr. Warnecke."

"I'm afraid you don't have a choice," he said. "Come, Captain! Where's that warrior's courage, that willingness to die for your beliefs?"

"Dying for my beliefs isn't the issue," Honor shot back. "Dying *and* allowing you to blow up the planet *is*."

"Then I think we have an impasse. A pity. It seemed like such a *nice* idea,."

"Wait." Honor folded her hands behind her and began to pace back and forth, frowning in obvious thought. Warnecke sat back, toying with his hand-held transmitter, and whistled a cheerful tune while the seconds oozed past. Then she stopped and faced the pickup once more.

"All right, you can check us for arms when we come aboard," she said, carefully hiding the fact that she'd intended to make that offer from the outset, "but my people will still be aboard your ship when you do so, so I advise you to be very careful about how you go about it. We'll board your shuttle before the transmitters on your other small craft are disabled, and one of my engineers will place a demolition charge on the exterior of your shuttle—one sufficiently powerful to destroy your entire ship."

"A *demolition* charge?" Warnecke blinked, and she hid a smile at the evidence that she'd finally managed to startle him.

"It seems only fair to me," she countered, "given the charges you've already placed on the planet. Our charge will be rigged to detonate upon command from my ship, and I will be in communication with it at all times. If communications are interrupted, my executive officer will blow the charge and your ship—and both of us—with it."

He frowned, and she commanded her own face to remain impassive. There was one glaring flaw in her offer, and she knew it. More, she expected Warnecke to see it. Assuming she'd read his personality aright, he'd almost have to plan on taking advantage of it . . . and the surprise when he found he couldn't should help distract him from what she *actually* intended to do.

"My, that *is* elegant, isn't it?" the man on her com screen said at last, then chuckled. "I wonder if we'll have time to play a hand or two of poker, Captain. It might be interesting to see if your gambler's streak translates to the cards."

"I'm not gambling, Mr. Warnecke. You can kill the planet, and you can kill me, but only if you're willing to die yourself. If nothing . . . untoward happens, however, and you board your ship at the agreed upon point—say ten minutes short of the limit—my officers and I will be able take the shuttle, your transmitter, *and* the demolition charge away from your ship."

"My, my, my," Warnecke murmured. He considered for several seconds of silence, then nodded. "Very well, Captain Harrington. You have a deal."

• CHAPTER THIRTY-TWO

The actual mechanics took hours to haggle out, but the basic format was the one Honor had proposed. It was galling to listen to Warnecke's mocking urbanity as he drove her to submit to his demand for freedom, but she could accept that, for in all the complicated negotiations, there was one thing he never seemed to realize. It was a minor point, perhaps, but a vital one.

She'd never once said she actually intended to let him go.

At every stage, she couched her own comments in conditionals. If Warnecke accepted her terms and *if* every point went as agreed, *then* he would be free to leave. But she'd already chosen the point at which she would make certain they were *not* carried out . . . and she'd never given her word that she wouldn't.

Putting boarders aboard Warnecke's ship was the first step, and it went more smoothly than Honor had anticipated. Scotty Tremaine's pinnaces delivered Susan Hibson and an entire company of battle-armored Marines to the repair ship while two of Jacquelyn Harmon's LACs hovered watchfully alongside. The repair ship's crew was obviously frightened at having those grim, heavily armed and armored troopers aboard their ship, but there was nothing they could have done to prevent them from boarding. The most cursory examination showed the ship was even slower than Honor had anticipated—a big, lumbering mobile repair yard, capable of a maximum acceleration of no more than 1.37 KPS². Nor was it armed in any way. It didn't even mount point defense, which

408

turned it into a target waiting to be killed whenever one of Harmon's skippers decided to press his firing key, and its crew knew it.

Some of those crewmen were *delighted* to see Hibson's Marines, for almost a third of them were captured merchant spacers, many Manticoran nationals, from the prizes Warnecke's squadron had taken, who'd been given the choice of working for their captors or dying. Very few of them were women, and Hibson's green eyes took on the cast of sea ice as Warnecke's liberated slaves told her what had happened to their female crewmates. She longed to turn her Marines loose on the repair ship's sweating crew, but she throttled her anger. She could wait, because she already knew what Captain Harrington intended to happen.

Once Hibson had secured the ship—and transferred the freed slaves to *Wayfarer*—the destruction of its communications systems began. Parties of Harold Tschu's personnel, shepherded by Hibson's watchful troopers and accompanied by dry-mouthed "privateer" technicians, made a clean sweep of the com sections, removing some components and simply smashing others. Instead of a single radio, Warnecke had insisted he and his three companions in the shuttle must be in skinsuits with their built-in coms. Those were somewhat more powerful than Honor had had in mind, but the change was acceptable, and the ship's receivers were left intact, as was one short-ranged transmitter, so that Warnecke could communicate with his crew from the shuttle. But every other transmitter was reduced to scrap. The crew could fix the damage eventually, of course—it *was* a repair ship—but that would take at least two days, which was ample for the purposes of what almost everyone involved thought was going to happen.

With the com systems disabled, Hibson withdrew all but one platoon of her Marines. The remaining platoon took station in the boat bay, where it both served as hostages against any attempt by Honor to destroy the ship and watched each shuttle as it arrived from Sidemore's surface. The major wondered just how the garrison still on the planet was reacting to all this, but they probably didn't even know what was happening. Indeed, she thought, that was inevitable. If they *had* known, a free-for-all battle for space on the repair ship would have erupted instantly.

Getting Warnecke himself from Sidemore to the ship was particularly tricky. It would have been simplicity itself for the LACs' lasers to annihilate his shuttle during transit, and the light-speed weapons would have given him no warning to press the button before he died. Honor had been afraid he'd respond by setting up a deadman switch to set off the charges if his transmitter *stopped* broadcasting, but she'd been ready for the possibility. After all, the whole object of their negotiations was to set up a situation in which there was only a single transmitter which would be taken away from Warnecke just before he hypered out of Marsh, and she'd been prepared to argue that those considerations made a deadman switch unacceptable.

Fortunately, however, the point never arose, since Warnecke accepted her proposal for dealing with the problem of getting him safely to his ship. The total transfer would require fifteen shuttle flights, and she offered to move her LACs beyond laser range and use only unarmed cutters to withdraw her Marines once all other arrangements had been successfully concluded. Since she couldn't know which shuttle Warnecke was aboard until it actually arrived and could no longer engage them with anything but sublight missiles, she couldn't attack them at all without giving him time to press the button.

In the event, Warnecke arrived in the fourth shuttle, which immediately locked itself to the outer hull of the repair ship with its belly tractors ninety meters from the nearest personnel lock. With no docking tube, there would be no way for any of the ship's crew to rush the shuttle—or reach the demolition charge Tschu's engineers rigged on its hull—without going extra-vehicular, and the shuttle's view ports would allow Honor to maintain a visual watch over the charge.

Once again, personnel from the repair ship watched as Tschu's people emplaced the charge, and then it was time.

"You're mad, My Lady." Major LaFollet's voice was low but intense as the cutter approached Warnecke's shuttle. "This is the most insane thing you've ever done—and that takes some doing!"

"Just humor me, Andrew," Honor replied, watching through a view port as her pilot maneuvered for a lock-to-lock mating with the shuttle. Her chief armsman clamped his mouth shut with an almost audible grinding of teeth, and she smiled faintly at her reflection in the port. Poor Andrew. He really hated this, but it was the only option that offered a chance of success, and she turned from the view port to inspect her "officers" as the locks came together.

There'd never been any question who would accompany her; she'd have had to brig her armsmen to make any other choice. That was why LaFollet, James Candless, and Simon Mattingly had exchanged their Harrington Guard uniforms for Manticoran ones, and she was pleased at how well ship's stores had managed to fit them. Candless wore the uniform of a commander, Mattingly that of a senior-grade lieutenant, and LaFollet that of a lowly Marine second lieutenant. That should tend to divert attention from the true commander of her bodyguard, but the main reason for the choices was that, of all her armsmen, LaFollet had the most pronounced Grayson accent. Candless had learned to mimic Honor's crisp, Sphinx accent almost perfectly, and Mattingly could pass for a native of Gryphon at need, but LaFollet simply could not shake the soft, slow speech of his birth world. It was unlikely Warnecke would be sufficiently familiar with Manticoran dialects to spot an imposter, but there was no point taking any chances, and no one would expect so junior an officer to say much.

The green light blinked, the hatch slid open, and Honor drew a deep breath.

"All right, people," she told her armsmen quietly. "Let's be about it."

LaFollet grunted like an irate bear, then stepped in front of her as she lifted Nimitz to her shoulder. She'd thought long and hard about leaving the 'cat behind, but he'd made his opinion of that option abundantly clear. That wouldn't have been enough to stop her from doing it anyway, but Nimitz had proved himself far too useful in the past. He was so small few strangers realized how lethal he could be, and his ability to read the emotions of Warnecke and his henchmen might literally be the difference between life or death this time. She felt his taut, coiled-spring readiness as she settled him in position and took the time to send him one last admonition to wait. She sensed his agreement, but she also knew it was conditional, and despite her own nervousness, she was content with that. In sudden threat situations, 'cats were prone to revert to instinct-level response, but she'd made certain Nimitz understood what she intended to happen, and she trusted his judgment. Besides, if things went utterly wrong, the empathic 'cat was far more likely than she or her armsmen to have sufficient warning to react in time.

Four skinsuited men were waiting in the shuttle when she followed LaFollet through the hatch. Warnecke sat at the extreme front of the passenger compartment, a transmitter in his lap. It was bigger than the one he'd had on the planet, more than sufficiently powerful to set the charges off from orbit, but Honor expected that, for the change had been discussed. All the pirates wore pulsers, and the two who flanked Warnecke carried flechette guns, as well. The fourth, whose skinsuit bore the stylized silver wings of a command pilot, stood just inside the hatch to search each of them for weapons. LaFollet already stood to one side, his face flushed and angry from the humiliation of submitting to a search, and the pilot smiled nastily as he reached for Honor.

"Keep your hands to yourself unless you want me to break them," she said. She didn't raise her voice, but it struck like an icy lash and Nimitz bared his fangs. The man froze, and her lip curled as she turned her head to meet Warnecke's eyes. "I agreed to be checked for weapons—not to be pawed by one of your animals."

"You've got a big mouth, lady," one of Warnecke's bodyguards snarled. "How about I splatter your ass all over the bulkhead?"

"Go ahead," she said coldly. "Your 'Leader' knows what will happen if you do."

"Calmly, Allen. Calmly," Warnecke said. "Captain Harrington is our guest." He smiled and cocked his head. "Nonetheless, Captain, you do need to convince me you're unarmed."

"But I'm not." Honor's answering smile was thin, and Warnecke's eyes narrowed in sudden alarm as she raised the rectangular case hanging from her left wrist. It was twenty-two centimeters long, fifteen wide, and ten deep, and its upper surface bore three switches, a small number pad, and two unlit power lights.

"And just what might that be?" He tried to make his voice light, but an edge of tension crackled in it and his bodyguards' weapons came up instantly.

"Something far more potent than a flechette gun, Mr. Warnecke," Honor said coolly. "This is a remote detonator. When it's activated, the charge out there is armed. It will detonate if I fail to input the proper code on the number pad at least once every five minutes."

"You never said anything about that!" This time his voice was almost a snarl, and Nimitz hissed as Honor laughed. It was a chill sound, like the snapping of a frozen sword blade, and her brown eyes were colder still.

"No, I didn't. But you don't have any choice but to accept it, do you? You're up here now, Mr. Warnecke.

You can kill me and all three of my officers. You can even blow up the planet. But that charge will still be out there where my ship can detonate it, and you'll be dead ten seconds after we are." His mouth twisted, and she smiled mockingly. "Come now, Mr. Warnecke! You have your flechette guns, and, as agreed, my people aren't even in skinsuits. You can shoot us or depressurize the shuttle any time you care to. All I can do is kill us myself . . . and, of course, take you with us. It seems like a reasonable balance of force to me."

Warnecke's eyes glittered, but then he forced his expression to smooth out.

"You're cleverer than I thought, Captain," he observed in something like his normal smooth tones.

"You didn't really think I'd forgotten the light-speed limit when I set this up, did you?" Honor countered. "We agreed to separate the shuttle ten minutes' flight time from the hyper limit . . . which would just happen to place the demolition charge *twelve* light-minutes from my ship's transmitters. But that won't matter if the transmitter's right here in the shuttle, will it?"

"But how can I be certain there's not a weapon hidden inside it?" Warnecke inquired lightly. "There's ample room in there for a small pulser, I believe."

"I'm sure you have a power sensor around somewhere. Run a check."

"An excellent suggestion. Harrison?"

The pilot glowered at Honor, then opened an equipment locker. He pulled out a hand scanner and ran it over the case when she held it out.

"Well?" Warnecke asked.

"Nothing," the pilot grunted. "I'm picking up a single ten-volt power source. That's plenty for a short-range transmitter, but it's too little juice for a pulser."

"Please excuse my suspicious nature, Captain," Warnecke murmured, nodding acceptance of the report. "I trust, however, that it's the *only* weapon you brought aboard?"

"All I brought is what you see," Honor said with total

honesty. "As for other weapons—" She handed her case to LaFollet, set Nimitz down in a seat, unsealed her tunic, shrugged it off, and turned in place in her white turtleneck blouse. "You see? Nothing up my sleeves."

"Would you mind removing your boots, as well?" Warnecke asked politely. "I've seen quite a few nasty surprises hidden in boot tops over the years."

"If you insist." Honor toed her boots off and handed them to the pilot, who examined them with surly competence, then threw them back to her with a glare.

"Clean," he grunted, and she returned his glare with a mocking smile as she sat beside Nimitz and pulled them back on. She slipped back into her tunic and sealed it, then gathered the 'cat back up, reclaimed the case from her armsman, and moved to the extreme rear of the passenger compartment. She settled into one of the comfortable seats and laid the case in her lap, then pressed the top button. One of the power lights blinked to life, glowing a steady amber, and the two bodyguards regarded her uneasily.

She waited while Candless and Mattingly followed her into the shuttle and submitted to the pilot's search, then cleared her throat.

"One more thing, Mr. Warnecke. Before my cutter undocks and my Marines leave your boat bay, Commander Candless will take a look at the flight deck. We wouldn't want anyone extra to be hiding up there, now would we?"

"Of course not," Warnecke said. "Allen, go with the Commander—and make sure he doesn't touch anything."

The bodyguard jerked his head, and the two men disappeared into the nose of the shuttle while Honor and Warnecke regarded one another down the ten-meter length of the passenger compartment. They were back in seconds, and Candless nodded.

"Clear, Captain," he said in his best Sphinx accent, and Honor nodded.

"And now, I think we should all have seats right here where I can keep an eye on you," she said pleasantly. "I realize your little transmitter has ample power to send the detonation command from here, but once we get beyond its range, I wouldn't want anyone having an accident with your com when I couldn't see it happen."

"As you wish." Warnecke nodded to his henchmen, and they took seats alongside him. All of them were between Honor and her armsmen and the flight deck, and they turned their chairs to face her just as her case beeped and the second light began to flash red. All four of the privateers tensed, and Honor smiled.

"Excuse me," she murmured, and punched a nine-digit code into the number pad. The red light went out instantly, and she leaned back comfortably.

"Everything green, Captain?" the cutter's flight engineer called through the open hatches.

"That's affirmative, Chief. Instruct Commander Cardones and Major Hibson to proceed."

"Aye, aye, Ma'am."

The hatches slid shut, and the cutter undocked. It drifted away on a puff of thrusters and turned for *Wayfarer*. Five minutes—and another beep from Honor's case—later, another trio of cutters left the boat bay carrying Susan Hibson and her Marines.

"Check to be certain they're all off, Harrison," Warnecke ordered. The pilot activated his skinsuit's com and murmured into it, then listened to his earbug for several seconds.

"Confirmed. They're all off, and we're breaking orbit now."

"Good." Warnecke leaned back in his seat. "And now, Captain, I suggest we all get comfortable. We still have several hours to spend in one another's company, after all."

The next three hours passed with glacial slowness. The seconds limped into eternity, and tension hung in the shuttle like smoke. Every five minutes, the audible alarm on the case in Honor's lap beeped and the red light flashed, and every five minutes she input the code to still them both. Mattingly and LaFollet each sat at a view port, Mattingly watching the demolition charge while LaFollet made certain no skinsuited crewmen were creeping up on the shuttle hatch. Warnecke had laid his heavy little transmitter in the seat beside him, but his bodyguards watched Honor and her armsmen as intently as Mattingly and LaFollet watched the charge and the hatch. One of them kept his weapon at instant readiness at all times, but flechette guns are heavy, and they changed off every fifteen minutes so that one of them could put his down and rest his arms. One flechette gun was more than adequate, however. Manifestly, no one could possibly get to Warnecke or his henchmen alive.

There was no conversation. Warnecke was content to sit in silence, smiling slightly, and Honor had no desire to speak to him or his men. She could feel their stress through Nimitz, but she could also feel their growing triumph as the repair ship left her warships further and further astern. They were actually going to get away with it, and their gloating exhilaration was hard on the 'cat. He curled in the seat beside Honor's, kneading his claws in and out of the upholstery, and her hand caressed his spine slowly and comfortingly as the minutes dragged away.

Her case beeped once more, and she took her hand unhurriedly from the 'cat and punched numbers into the keypad yet again. But this time it was a slightly different code. The red light went out, and she glanced casually at the bulkhead chrono.

Three hours and fifteen minutes. She and Fred Cousins had considered the maximum range of Warnecke's hand-held transmitter carefully before she allowed the privateer to exchange it for the original. It was remotely possible, assuming a sufficiently sensitive receiving array, that a unit that small might have a range of as much as two light-minutes. With that in mind, Honor had decided

Warnecke had to be at least *five* light-minutes from the planet before she dared take any action against him, and that time had now come.

She waited another few seconds, then pressed the third button on the case—the one the new number code had armed—and two things happened. First, the small but efficient jamming pod hidden in the demolition charge on the outside of the shuttle came to life, putting out a strong enough field to trash any radio signal. The shuttle's com lasers could still get the detonation order through, but even as the jammer went into action, the end of the case opened and the familiar weight of a cocked and locked .45 automatic slid out into her hand.

None of Warnecke's men realized anything had happened, for the seat in front of Honor hid the case from them. Besides, they *knew* she was unarmed, for they'd checked the case without finding the giveaway power source of a pulser or any other modern hand weapon. The possibility of a something so primitive it used chemical explosives had never even occurred to them.

Honor's expression didn't even flicker as she brought the pistol up in a smooth, flowing motion, and its sudden, deafening roar filled the passenger compartment like the hammer of God. The bodyguard named Allen had his flechette gun ready, but he never even realized he was dead as fifteen grams of hollow-nosed lead exploded through his forehead, and the stunning, totally unexpected concussion shocked every one of the privateers into a fatal fractional second of absolute immobility. The second bodyguard was just as shocked as anyone else, and he hadn't even begun to move when the gun roared again in the same sliver of time.

The bodyguard was hurled back out of his seat, spraying the bulkhead—and Andre Warnecke—with a gray-flecked bucket of red, and Honor was on her feet, holding the pistol in a two-handed grip.

"The party is over, Mr. Warnecke," she said, and her eyes were carved of frozen brown flint. She had to speak loudly to hear herself through the ringing in her ears, and she smiled as the privateer stared at her in disbelief. "Stand up and move away from the transmitter."

Warnecke swallowed, eyes wide as he realized he'd finally met a killer even more deadly than he, then nodded shakenly and started to push himself up. That was the instant the pilot made a dive for a fallen flechette gun, and the terrible, ear-shattering concussion of the .45 hammered the compartment twice more. The double tap wasn't a head shot this time, and the pilot had over fifteen seconds to scream, writhing on the deck while aspirated blood gushed from his mouth, before he died. But Honor didn't even blink, and the pistol was trained once more on Warnecke's forehead before he could even think about going for his own sidearm..

"Stand up," she repeated, and he obeyed. He moved away from the transmitter, and Honor nodded to LaFollet.

Her chief armsman wasn't gentle. He moved up the starboard passenger aisle, staying well clear of his steadholder's field of fire until he could reach Warnecke, then threw the privateer brutally to the deck. He drove a knee into his captive's spine and twisted both arms so harshly up behind him that Warnecke cried out in pain.

Mattingly was there in a moment, scooping up both blood and brain-spattered flechette guns and tossing them to Candless before he and LaFollet jerked Warnecke to his feet once more. A hand removed the pulser from Warnecke's holster and tucked it inside Mattingly's tunic, and then the two armsmen frogmarched him to the rear of the compartment and shoved him into a seat. Mattingly sat three seats away, leveling the liberated pulser at Warnecke's chest, and Honor carefully lowered the .45's hammer and shoved the heavy weapon into her tunic pocket.

"I made you an offer which would have left you alive," she told her prisoner. "I would have honored that offer. Thanks to you, I no longer have to." Her smile could have frozen a star's heart. "Thank you, Mr. Warnecke. I appreciate it."

She collected her case once more and punched a third combination into the number pad. The jamming pod shut down obediently, and the tractor pads holding the demolition charge to the shuttle disengaged. The device Warnecke had blithely assumed was *only* a demolition charge clanged to the repair ship's hull, and the amber telltale flashed confirmation as a second set of pads locked it in place.

Honor scooped Nimitz up, feeling the 'cat's fierce exultation as she held him close, and stepped over the bodies of the men she'd killed into the flight deck. The controls were standard, but she set the 'cat in the copilot's seat and took two full minutes to familiarize herself with them before she slipped the pilot's headset on and flipped up the plastic shield over the belly tractor power switch. Separating from a vessel underway under impeller drive was tricky, but at least the repair ship had no sidewalls, and she lit the acceleration warning in the passenger cabin and keyed the intercom.

"Acceleration in thirty seconds," she announced. "Strap in; it's going to be rough."

She waited, watching the chrono tick down, then killed the tractors holding the shuttle to the repair ship's hull and drove the belly and main thruster levers clear to the stop.

They were conventional thrusters, but they were also powerful, and just over one hundred gravities of acceleration hurled the shuttle away from the ship. The small craft's artificial gravity did its best, but its inertial compensator had no impeller wedge to work with. Twenty gravities got through, and Honor grunted as a giant's fist slammed down. But the shuttle blasted straight for the perimeter of the repair ship's wedge at an acceleration of one kilometer per second squared. It was more than enough to clear the wedge before its narrowing after aspect could destroy the tiny craft, and she gasped with relief as she hurtled free and killed the belly thrusters.

She burned the main thrusters for another thirty seconds, using her attitude thrusters to slew away from the repair ship at a more tolerable fifty gravities, then brought the shuttle's transmitter on-line.

"Pirate vessel, this is Captain Honor Harrington," she said coldly. "Your leader is my prisoner. The charges on the planet are now inoperable, but *you* have a two hundred k-ton charge in skin contact with your hull, and I have the transmitter which controls it. Reverse course immediately, or I will detonate it. You have one minute to comply."

The shuttle was far enough out to bring up its own impellers now, and Honor engaged the wedge and shot ahead at four hundred gravities. She watched the big vessel falling away from her with one eye and the chrono with another and keyed her mike once more.

"You now have thirty seconds," she said flatly, circling back around to maintain visual observation on the repair ship. Still it continued to run for the hyper limit, and she wondered if its crew thought she was bluffing or simply figured they had nothing left to lose.

"Fifteen seconds," she said emotionlessly, hand hovering over the case. "Ten seconds"

Still the ship maintained its course, and she slewed the nose of the shuttle away, taking it out of her cockpit's line of sight even as she polarized the passenger compartment view ports.

"Five seconds," she told the ship, her voice an executioner's as she watched it now on radar. "Four . . . three . . . two . . . one."

She pressed the second button on her case once, and the repair ship and its entire crew disappeared in a terrible flash.

• CHAPTER THIRTY-THREE

Ginger Lewis watched her work section help the crew of Rail Number Three maneuver the pod back into Cargo One. The pod was smaller than a LAC, but it was much larger than a pinnace, and its designers had been far less concerned with ease of handling than with combat effectiveness. Nor was the situation helped by the fact that *Wayfarer,* as one of the first four ships to be fitted with the new, rail-launched version, had been forced to work out handling procedures more or less as she went. But each pod cost over three million dollars, which put their reuse high on BuShip's list of desirable achievements. And, Ginger admitted, having them available to shoot at another enemy made sense all on its own.

None of which made the task any less of a pain.

Commander Harmon's LACs had tracked down all but three of the pods used in the short, savage destruction of Andre Warnecke's cruisers, which was outstanding, given how difficult the system's low signature features made finding them. *Be a good idea to put a homing beacon on them*, Ginger thought, making a mental note to suggest just that. *Wonder why no one at BuWeaps thought of that?*

In the meantime, all twenty-seven of the (beaconless) relocated pods had been towed to *Wayfarer*, where skinsuited Engineering and Tactical crews had worked their butts off recertifying their launch cells. Two had been down-checked—they were repairable, but not out of *Wayfarer's* onboard resources—and the Captain had ordered them destroyed.

That left twenty-five, all of which had to have their cells reloaded. That could have been done on the launch rails, but *Wayfarer* was equipped with the latest Mark 27, Mod C missile, which weighed in at just over one hundred and twenty tons in one standard gravity. Even in free-fall, that was a lot of mass and inertia, and the damned things were the next best thing to fifteen meters long. All in all, Ginger had to agree that reloading them outside the ship, where there was plenty of room to work, and *then* remounting them on the rails made far more sense.

It was also backbreaking and exhausting, and the combined teams from Engineering and Tactical had been at it for eighteen hours straight. This was Ginger's third shift, and she was starting to worry about personnel fatigue. Tired people could do dangerous things, and it was her job to be certain none of *her* people did.

She walked further up the side of Cargo One, standing straight out from the bulkhead to get a better view as the rail crew—wearing hardsuits and equipped with tractor-pressor cargo-handling units—babied the current pod into mating with the rail. The handling units looked like hand-held missile launchers, only bigger, and each end mounted a paired presser and tractor with a rated lift of one thousand tons. The rail crew was using the pressers like giant, invisible screw jacks to align the pod's mag shoe precisely with the rail, and despite their fatigue, they moved with a certain bounce. Ginger smiled tiredly at that. Morale aboard *Wayfarer* had soared since Schiller. First they'd taken out two raider destroyers—well, all right, *one* destroyer—and a light cruiser and captured a Peep CL for good measure. Then they'd sailed straight into Marsh and zapped four *heavy* cruisers, and *then* they'd captured one of the most wanted mass murderers in Silesian history in a personal shoot-out with the Old Lady, blown a thousand more straight to hell, and saved an entire planet from nuclear devastation. *Not too shabby*, she thought with another grin, remembering a long ago discussion with a bitterly disappointed Aubrey Wanderman. *Not a ship of the wall, no, Wonder Boy. But somehow I doubt you'd have wanted to be anywhere but on the Old Lady's command deck when* this *one went down!*

As always, thoughts of Aubrey woke a reflexive pang of worry, but there was something going on there, as well. Ginger hadn't managed to figure out exactly what it was. She was still new enough in her grade to be a bit slow tapping into the senior petty officer's information net—one couldn't call it *gossip*, after all—but she knew Horace Harkness and Gunny Hallowell were involved, and she had immense respect for both those gentlemen. Knowing they'd taken a hand was a huge relief, and so were the changes she was seeing in Aubrey. He was still wary, but he wasn't scared to death anymore, and unless she was seriously mistaken, the kid was starting to fill out. One of the side effects of prolong was to slow the physical maturation process. At twenty, Aubrey looked a lot like a pre-prolong civilization's sixteen or seventeen, yet he was turning into a solid, well-muscled seventeen-year-old, and his confidence was growing right in step. There was a new maturity there, too. The kid she'd teased—and taken unobtrusively under her wing—during training was growing up, and she liked the man he was turning into.

"All *right!*" Chief Weintraub's exclamation of triumph came over the com as the pod finally mated properly. The work crew stood back, clearing the rail safety perimeter, while Weintraub signaled Lieutenant Wolcott to run the pod in, and Ginger heard a chorus of tired cheers as it cycled smoothly back to its place in the launch queue.

"Only eight more to go, troops, and only two of 'em are ours." Weintraub used his suit thrusters to turn himself until he faced Ginger and waved a manipulator arm at her. "We've got our next baby coming along in about five minutes, Ging. Leave your people here to take a breather and go see how they're coming on the loading for Number Twenty-Four, would you?"

"No sweat, Chief." Ginger was technically senior to

Weintraub, but he was the missile specialist BuWeaps had trained specifically
to straw boss Rail Three, and this was
his show. Besides, it gave her a chance
to play with her SUT pack for the first time this shift.
She waved back, walked to the lip of the cargo doors,
and consulted the HUD projected on the inside of her
helmet. Ah! There Number Twenty-Four was. Nine klicks
out at zero-three-niner.

Ginger disengaged her boots from the hull and floated
free for a moment, gazing down at the huge, blue-and-
white marble of Sidemore. *It sure is a pretty planet. Glad
we could get it back for the people it belongs to.* Then
she looked out at the stars, and a familiar sense of awe
filled her. Unlike some people, Ginger loved EVAs. The
immensity of the universe didn't bother her; she found
it cleansing and oddly soothing—a special feeling of
privacy mixed with a wondering joy that God would allow
her to glimpse His creation from His own magnificent
vantage point.

But she wasn't here to admire the view. She centered
the HUD reticle on Pod Twenty-Four's beacon, locking
her vector into the automated guidance systems of the
outsized Sustained Use Thruster pack strapped over her
skinsuit. The SUT packs were designed for extended EVA
use, with much greater endurance and power than the
standard skinsuit thrusters, and Ginger loved her rare
opportunities to play with them. Now she double-checked
her vector, grinned in anticipation, and tapped the go
button.

That was when it happened.

The second she enabled the thrusters, the entire system went mad. Instead of the gentle pressure she'd
expected, the SUT went instantly to maximum power. It
slammed her away from the ship under an acceleration
intended only for emergency use, and she grunted in
anguish, unable to cry out properly under the massive
thrust. Her thumb reached frantically for the manual
override, finding the button with the blind, unerring speed

of relentless training, and jabbed sharply . . . and nothing happened at all.

Nor was that the worst of it. Her attitude thrusters were equally berserk, whipsawing her wildly and sending her pinwheeling insanely off into space. She lost all spatial reference in the first two seconds, and her inner ear went mad as she whirled crazily away from the ship. It was only God's good grace that she was headed *away* from the ship; her malfunctioning SUT could just as easily have turned her straight into the hull, with instantly lethal consequences.

But the consequences she had were bad enough. For the first time in her life, Ginger Lewis was hammered by the motion sickness which had always evoked amused sympathy when she saw it in others. She vomited helplessly, coughing and choking as the instinct-level responses her instructors had beaten into her fought to keep her airways clear. She'd never expected to need that training—*she* wasn't the sort to whoop her cookies over a little vacuum work!—but only the legacy of her merciless DIs kept her alive long enough to hit the vomit-slimed chin switch that dropped her com into Flight Ops' EVA guard frequency.

"Mayday! Mayday! Suit malfunction!" she gasped while her thrusters continued to bellow like maddened animals. "This—" She retched again, choking as dry heaves wracked her. "This is Blue Sixteen! I'm—God, I don't know *where* I am!" She heard the panic in her own voice, but she couldn't even see. The contents of her stomach coated the inside of her helmet, wiping away the stars, compounding her disorientation, and *still* the thrusters thundered without rhyme or reason! "*Mayday!*" she screamed into the com.

And no one answered at all.

"What the—?" Scotty Tremaine had just relieved Lieutenant Justice, LAC Two's ops officer, and settled into his chair in Flight Ops when he noticed the radar trace spearing away from the ship on an impossible vector.

He punched a query into the computers, but they didn't know what it was either, and he frowned. The guard frequency was silent, so it couldn't be somebody in trouble, but he couldn't think of what *else* it might be, either. He tapped a stylus to his display, painting the trace and dropping it onto the master plot in CIC, and then hit the all-hands transmit key.

"Flight Ops," he said crisply into his boom mike. "I have an unidentified bogey heading out at—" he checked the numbers "—thirty-five gees. All section leaders, check your sections. I want a headcount soonest!"

He sat back in his chair, gnawing his lip as reports started coming in. They rattled from the com with reassuring speed, and he checked each section leader off on his master list as he or she reported in. But then they stopped, and there was one section still unchecked.

"Blue Sixteen, Blue Sixteen!" he said into the mike. "Blue Sixteen, I need your count!" Only silence came back, and then someone else spoke.

"Flight, this is Yellow Three. I sent Blue Sixteen to check out Pod Two-Four three or four minutes ago."

Tremaine's blood froze, and he shifted instantly to his link to Boat Bay One.

"Dutchman! Dutchman!" he barked. "Flight Ops is declaring a Dutchman! Get the ready pinnace out now!"

A startled acknowledgment came back, and he plugged into CIC.

"Ullerman, CIC," a voice said.

"Tremaine, Flight Ops," Scotty said urgently. "Listen up! I've got a Dutchman headed away from the ship at thirty-five gees. I painted the trace on your plot three minutes ago. Tie into the ready pinnace and guide them in on it—and for God's sake don't lose it!"

"Acknowledged," the voice snapped, and Tremaine turned back to his own radar. It was short-ranged and much less powerful than the main arrays, and the trace was already fading from his display. He saw the much larger radar signature of the ready pinnace, driving hard on reaction thrusters to clear the ship, and his lips moved as he whispered a silent prayer for whoever that disappearing trace was.

If the pinnace didn't get to him before Tracking lost him, the poor bastard would become a Flying Dutchman in truth.

"Are you positive, Harry?" Honor asked quietly.

"Absolutely," Lieutenant Commander Tschu grated. "Some sick son-of-a-bitch rigged her SUT, Skipper. He tried to make it look like a general system failure, but he got too cute when he set her com up to 'fail.' The com's not part of the SUT, and he had to interface her SUT computers with her skinny. That's not hard, but it *doesn't* happen by accident; someone has to make it, and someone damned well did. The SUT computer's totally fried, and all his execution files were supposed to crash and burn with the rest of the system, but my data recovery people found a single line of code directing output to her com buried in the garbage. It's only a fragment, but it's also completely outside normal programming parameters, because there's not supposed to *be* a link from the SUT to her com. This wasn't a hardware failure, and it wasn't corrupted files. It took specifically *planted* files to make it all happen."

Honor locked her hands behind her. She didn't say a word for at least one full minute, but her eyes blazed. Morale—and performance—aboard *Wayfarer* had gone up by leaps and bounds. Her people had come together, fused into a single living, breathing whole by their shared accomplishments. They'd only had to look around to see how well they'd done, and she'd made certain they knew *she* was proud of them, as well. Even Sally MacBride and Master-at-Arms Thomas had commented to her on it, and Tschu's Engineering department had shown the greatest improvements of all.

Now someone had attempted to murder one of her crew, and the *way* whoever it was had done it was almost worse than the attempt itself. Few spacers would admit it, but the terror of being lost, of drifting helplessly in space until your suit air and heat ran out, was one of the darkest nightmares of their profession.

That was what someone had done to Ginger Lewis, and Honor's rage burned even hotter because it was *her* fault. She never doubted who was responsible for this, and *she* was responsible for the fact that Steilman was still at large. She should have forgotten about Tatsumi's career and Wanderman's sense of self-respect and smashed Steilman the first time he stepped out of line. She'd let herself be distracted—let herself actually look forward to Wanderman's giving Steilman his comeuppance—and forgotten that he might have marked *Lewis* down for a victim.

The right corner of her mouth began to tic, and Rafe Cardones, who knew the signs of old, felt himself tighten at the telltale sign of fury. Then he realized she was even more enraged than he'd thought, for her voice was calm, almost conversational when she spoke to him at last.

"Is Lewis all right?"

"Angie says she will be, but I'd say she's used up about two lifetimes of luck," he replied carefully. "Her attitude thrusters could just as easily have slammed her straight into the hull, and she inhaled enough stomach acid to cause major lung damage. Angie's on top of that, but she pulled thirty-five gees for twenty minutes, with no warning, and her vector looks like a near-weasel chasing a rabbit. That didn't do her a bit of good, and she was pretty far gone in anoxia—from the lung damage, not suit failure—before the pinnace got to her. By the way," he added, "Tatsumi was the ready section SBA. Angie says he's the only reason she's still alive."

"I see." Honor paced once around her day cabin while Nimitz crouched on his perch, tail lashing and coat bristled as he shared her searing wrath. Tschu had brought Samantha with him, and she quivered with her own echo of the emotions radiating from Honor and Nimitz . . . and her own person. The engineer reached up to stroke her spine soothingly, and she pressed back against his touch—but she also bared her fangs with a sibilant hiss.

"Who worked suit maintenance?" Honor asked finally, turning back to the others.

"I've pulled the duty roster, but we're working extra shifts with the pod reloading, and there were some extra hands involved," Tschu said. "I've got the check-off on Lewis's SUT—it was Avram Hiroshio, one of my best techs—but there've been so many people in and out of the suit morgue that anyone could have done it. It was all software, Ma'am. All the bastard needed was five seconds when no one was watching to overwrite his chip onto the SUT computer."

"You mean to tell me," Honor pronounced each word with deadly precision, "that someone in *my* ship tried to murder one of *my* crewmen, and we don't have the slightest idea who it was?"

"I can narrow it down some, Skipper, but not enough," Tschu admitted. "It could've been any one of two or three dozen people. I'm sorry, but that's the truth."

"Is Randy Steilman on the list?" she asked flatly.

"No, Ma'am, but—" Tschu paused and drew a deep breath. "Steilman isn't, but Jackson Coulter and Elizabeth Showforth both are, and they're part of Steilman's circle. I can't prove it was either of them, though."

"I don't care what you can prove. Not now." Honor turned to Cardones. "Screen the Master-at-Arms. I want Coulter and Showforth brigged, and I want them sweated."

"I understand, Ma'am," Cardones started, "but with no evi—"

"My authority," she said in that same flat, calm voice. "You tell them that. And you remind them a serving member of the military does *not* have the right to remain silent. One of those two people just attempted to commit murder, and I want them *hammered* until I know which it was."

Cardones met her gaze levelly, but his own was troubled.

"Skipper, I'll do it, but you *know* they're going to claim

they never actually meant to kill her—that it was only a prank that got out of hand—even if we break them down."

"I don't care." Honor Harrington stood very tall and straight, hands still locked together behind her, and her eyes were brown, blazing ice. "This is the second 'accident' to one of my people. Understand me. *There will not be a third.* I will have these two in the brig, and I will have them hammered, and I *will* find out who did it. And when I do, I will by God make whoever it was the sorriest piece of scum ever to wear Manticoran uniform. Do you read me on this, Rafe?"

"Yes, Ma'am." Cardones nodded sharply, fighting an urge to spring to attention, and she nodded back.

"Good."

Aubrey Wanderman sat in sickbay once more, this time holding Ginger's hand. She lay very still, mouth and nose covered by a transparent oxygen mask. Commander Ryder had promised Aubrey she'd be all right, that she only needed the oxygen until the quick heal repaired her acid-seared lungs, but she looked so still. So broken.

It's only the quick heal, idiot! he told himself sharply, and knew it was true. They'd put her under a general while they flushed the acid out of her lungs, and then they'd had to hit her with a massive dose of the quick heal compounds. That always put the recipient out like a light. But knowing it didn't make her look one bit less terrible, and he looked up as Yoshiro Tatsumi paused at the foot of the bed.

"Thanks," Aubrey said simply, and the SBA shrugged uncomfortably.

"Hey, it's my job, okay?"

"Yeah, I know. Thanks anyway. She's a friend."

"I know." Tatsumi nodded, eyes dark with compassion as he gazed down at her. "You know she's likely to have some problems when she comes out of the quicky, don't you?" he asked quietly. "I mean, she went for a wild one, man. Odds are real good she's gonna have some post traumatic from it." He shook his head. "I knew a tech once—an electronics guy, like you—went for a Dutchman. He was working on a gravitic array and some asshole in CIC didn't check the warning board. Threw power to the array while he was on it and blew him clear off the hull. Power surge fried his com and half his suit electronics. It took us almost twelve hours to find him. That man never went extra vehicular again. Just couldn't to it."

"Ginger's tougher than that," Aubrey said more confidently than he felt. "She's always loved EVA, too, and she was only out there about thirty minutes. She can kick it. No way she's going to let a stupid accident get to her that way."

"Accident?" Tatsumi blinked, then looked around carefully and shook his head. "It wasn't any damned *accident*, man," he said much more softly. "Haven't you heard?"

"Heard *what*? Lieutenant Wolcott gave me permission to come right down here, and I've been here ever since."

"Shit, Wanderman—the Old Lady's brigged Coulter and Showforth. Word is, somebody sabotaged her SUT, and the Skipper's pretty damned sure it was one of those two. She's gonna turn whoever it was into reactor mass when she figures out which one to hang, too. I mean, that lady is *pissed*, man!"

"Coulter and Showforth?" Aubrey repeated, and he didn't recognize his own voice. Tatsumi nodded, and Aubrey stood smoothly. He patted Ginger's hand gently, then glanced back at Tatsumi. "Keep an eye on her for me, okay? I want somebody to be here if she wakes up."

"Where are you going?" the SBA asked uneasily.

"I've got to see someone about a lesson," Aubrey said quietly, and walked away without another word.

• CHAPTER THIRTY-FOUR

"*Christ*, Randy! Are you outa your friggin' mind?" Ed Illyushin leaned close, voice low enough no one else in the big, half-empty mess compartment could hear.

"Me?" Randy Steilman smiled lazily. "I don't have the least idea what you're talking about."

"I'm talking about what happened to Lewis!" Illyushin hissed. "Damn it, they've already grabbed Showforth and Coulter—you think one of them isn't gonna roll over on us?"

Al Stennis nodded nervously, eyes flitting about to be certain no one was close enough to overhear. Not that anyone was likely to be. Steilman and his cronies weren't exactly popular with their fellows.

"Showforth doesn't know shit about it," Steilman said. "All she's gotta do is say so. As for Jackson—hell, it was *his* suggestion." That, wasn't precisely true, but it was close. Steilman had simply decided the general euphoria over *Wayfarer*'s recent victories had brought everyone's guard down, which made it the time to deal with Lewis. It was Coulter who'd suggested the perfect way to do it and planted the necessary files in Lewis' SUT. "And unlike *you* maggots, Jackson's got guts. Even if he didn't, you think he could turn us in without confessing to attempted murder?"

"But if they sweat them hard enough, they might tell 'em about—" Stennis began anxiously, only to shut his mouth with a click as Steilman glared at him.

"We don't talk about that outside the compartment," the burly power tech said softly. "And no one's gonna ask them about it, because no one *knows* about it. And as far as 'sweating' them goes, they've both been around the block. They've seen the inside of the brig before, and they ain't gonna cave in just because someone locked the door on 'em. And how the hell is anyone gonna sweat them when they haven't got any evidence?"

"What makes you so sure they don't?" Illyushin asked in a marginally calmer voice. "Why grab them—and only them—if there's no evidence?"

"Hell, the fact they hauled both of 'em in is the best proof they haven't *got* any evidence!" Steilman snorted. "Look, they know the two of 'em berth with us, right? And they know I had words with Lewis, right?" The other two men nodded, and he shrugged. "All right, that's why they're being questioned, you assholes. All they've got is a possible *motive*. If they had enough evidence to prove who did it, it would've told 'em *which* of them to grab, right? Which means all Showforth and Jackson have to do is hang tough and they can't do squat to us."

"I don't know," Stennis began dubiously. "It looks to me like—"

The environmental tech broke off in astonishment as someone slid a tray onto the table beside Steilman. The power tech turned his head, mouth already twisting up in a snarl to order the interloper away, but then his eyes widened. He stared for one incredulous second, and then his face flushed dark as Aubrey Wanderman smiled mockingly at him.

"What the fuck d'*you* want, Snotnose?" he grated, and Aubrey smiled more mockingly still. It was hard, but not as hard as he'd expected it to be.

"I just thought I'd grab a bite to eat," he said. "My watch schedule's sort of up in the air—they gave me a couple of days off to spend some time in sickbay with a friend—so I've got to eat whenever I can squeeze it in."

Steilman's eyes narrowed. There was something wrong here. The irony in Wanderman's voice cut like a knife, and his eyes were too steady. There might have been a flicker of nervousness deep inside them, but there was no fear, and there should have been. It took the power tech a moment longer to realize there was something *else* in those eyes, something he was accustomed to seeing only in his own, and a wave of pure disbelief washed over him. Why, the little prick was actually *looking* for a confrontation!

"Yeah?" he sneered. "Well why don't you go feed your miserable face somewhere else? I may puke if I hafta look at you too long."

"Go ahead," Aubrey said, picking up his fork. "Just try not to splash any on my tray."

Steilman quivered in rage at the derisive contempt in the younger man's voice, and his fist clenched on the tabletop. Stennis looked confused, but Illyushin was watching intently. He'd managed to avoid official action far more effectively than Steilman and frequently sided with the more cautious Stennis in discussions, but—like Coulter—he shared Steilman's vicious streak. He and Coulter were more hyenas to the other's rogue elephant, but his lip curled in an ugly smile. He didn't know what Wanderman thought he was doing, but he knew the stupid kid was about to get his butt kicked royally. He looked forward to watching . . . and his concentration on Aubrey meant neither he nor either of his fellows noticed when Horace Harkness and Sally MacBride walked quietly into the compartment.

"You want your ass kicked up between your sorry ears, Snotnose?" Steilman growled.

"Nope." Aubrey speared some green beans and chewed slowly, then swallowed. "I'm just sitting here eating. Besides, I thought you might like to hear how Ginger Lewis is doing."

"Why should I give a fart in a vac suit about that jumped up bitch?" Steilman smiled thinly as fire flashed in Aubrey's eyes at last. "So she jumped my ass for something I didn't do—so what? Happens all the time. Sounds like the smartass fucked up her own SUT. Not but what

I'd expect something that stupid from a 'senior chief' like *her.*"

"Actually," Aubrey's voice was a shade less calm, but he kept it even and locked gazes with his enemy, "she's going to be just fine. Doc Ryder says she'll be out of sickbay in a week or so, once the quick heal takes hold."

"So fucking what?"

"So I thought you'd like to know you didn't manage to kill her after all," Aubrey said in a conversational tone loud enough to carry to every table, and heads turned incredulously towards him. Most of the men and women in that compartment had reached the same conclusion, but none of them had dreamed that anyone—especially Aubrey Wanderman!—would actually say it.

Steilman went pale. Not with fear, but with fury, and exploded to his feet. Aubrey dropped his fork and spun erect himself, stepping back from the older man but never breaking eye contact, and his smile was no longer cool and mocking. It was ugly and filled with hate, and Steilman shook himself like an enraged bull.

"You got a big goddamned mouth," he grated. "Maybe someone should shut it for you!"

"Only saying what I think, Steilman." Aubrey made himself speak coolly, watching the bigger man alertly. "Of course, it's what everyone *else* thinks, too, isn't it? And when Showforth or Coulter cracks—and they *will* crack, Steilman—everyone in this crew will know it was true. Just like they're going to know big, bad Randy Steilman didn't have the guts to go after a *woman* on his own. What's the matter, Steilman? Afraid she'd kick your ass like the Bosun did?"

Steilman was no longer pale. He was paper-white with rage, consumed with the need to smash this insufferable little bastard. He was too enraged to think, to realize there were dozens of witnesses. But even if he had realized, it might not have mattered. His fury was too deep, too explosive to remember how he'd planned to catch Aubrey alone once more. How he'd intended to take his time, make the little prick whimper and beg. Now all he wanted was to grind him into powder, and it never even occurred to him that he'd been deliberately goaded into it.

Al Stennis watched with horror. Unlike Steilman, he could still think, and he knew what would happen if Steilman took the first swing. Aubrey hadn't made a single threatening move, hadn't even uttered a threat. If Steilman attacked him in front of all these witnesses and after the warnings he'd already received, he'd go to the brig and stay there until deployment's end, and that could all too easily lead to the discovery of the entire plan to desert, especially with Showforth and Coulter already under suspicion. Stennis knew it, but there was nothing he could do about it. He could only sit there, jaw hanging, and see it all come apart.

Randy Steilman bellowed his fury and lunged with murder in his eyes. He reached for Aubrey's throat, fingers curled to rend and throttle—then whooped in agony as a perfectly timed snap kick exploded into his belly. He flew backward, crashing down over two empty chairs, and heaved himself back to his knees on the deck. He fought for breath, glaring at the slender acting petty officer, unable to believe what had just happened. And then he swung his arms, smashing the chairs away from him, and lunged again, this time from his knees.

Aubrey's flashing spin kick took Steilman square in the face before he was half-erect. The power tech went down again, with a scream of pain as his nose broke and two incisors snapped. He spat out broken teeth and blood, staring down at them in shock and fury, and Illyushin stepped towards Aubrey with a snarl of his own. But his movement stopped as suddenly as it had begun—stopped in a gasp of agony as a steel clamp closed on the back of his neck. One of his arms was snatched behind him and twisted till the back of his hand pressed his shoulder blades, a knee drove into his spine, and a deep, cold voice rumbled in his ear.

"You stay out of it, sweetheart," Horace Harkness told

him softly, almost lovingly, "or I'll break your fucking back myself."

Illyushin went pasty white, arched with the pain in his elbow and shoulder. Like Steilman, he was a bully and a sadist, but he wasn't a total fool . . . and he knew Harkness' reputation.

No one else paid any attention to Illyushin or Harkness. All eyes were on Steilman and Aubrey as the power tech staggered to his feet once more. He shook himself, face slimed with blood from his nose and pulped mouth, and dragged the back of one hand across his chin.

"You're gonna *die*, Snotnose!" he raged. "I'm gonna rip your head off and piss down your neck!"

"Sure you are," Aubrey said. He felt his heart pound madly, felt the sweat at his own hairline. He was frightened, for he knew how badly this could still end, but he was in command of his fear. He was *using* his fear, as Harkness and Gunny Hallowell had taught him. Letting it sharpen his reflexes, but not letting it drive him. He was focused, in a way Randy Steilman could never even begin to understand, and he watched the other man come.

Steilman came in more cautiously this time, right fist clenched low by his side, left arm spread to grab and drag Aubrey in close. But despite what had already happened, his caution was only a thin veneer over his rage. He didn't understand, had no concept of how much Aubrey had changed, and his intellect hadn't caught up with his emotions. He'd taken damage, but he was almost as tough physically as he thought he was, and he couldn't even conceive of the possibility that he might lose. It simply wasn't possible. The snotnose had gotten lucky, that was all, and Steilman remembered how he'd terrified Aubrey the first time they'd met, then beaten him savagely the only time he'd ever laid hands on him. He knew—didn't think; *knew*—he could tear this little bastard apart, and he growled deep in his throat as he prepared to do just that.

Aubrey let him come, no longer afraid, no longer uncertain. He remembered everything Gunny Hallowell had taught him, knew Steilman could still take him, despite what had already happened, if Aubrey let him. But he also remembered what Hallowell had told him to do about it, and his eyes were cold as he stepped right into the other man. His right arm brushed Steilman's grappling left arm wide like a parrying rapier even as the power tech's fist came up in a smashing blow. There was immense power in that punch, but Aubrey's left hand slapped his wrist, diverting the blow into empty air, and then his right hand continued forward from the parry of the older man's arm. His fingers cupped the back of Steilman's head and jerked, and the power tech's own forward momentum helped bring his face down just in time to meet Aubrey's driving kneecap.

Steilman staggered back with another scream of pain, both hands going to his face. Feet pounded as two Marines in the black brassards of the ship's police burst into the compartment, but Sally MacBride's raised hand stopped them. Neither Marine said a word, but they came to a complete halt, eyes dark with satisfaction, as they realized what was happening.

Steilman's hands were still covering his face, leaving him blind and vulnerable, when a rock-hard right fist slammed a vicious uppercut into his crotch. The punch started somewhere down around Aubrey's right calf, and the sound Steilman made wasn't a scream this time. It was an animal sound of agony, and he jackknifed forward. His hands dropped instantly from his face to his groin, and the edge of a bladed left hand broke his right cheekbone like a hammer. His head snapped sideways, his eyes stunned, wide with disbelief and terrible pain, and then he shrieked as a precisely placed kick exploded into his right knee.

The kneecap shattered instantly, and he went to the deck, his screams high and shrill as his leg bent impossibly backward. He'd never even *touched* the bastard. Even through his agony, that thought burned in his brain like poison. The snotnose hadn't just beaten him; he'd *destroyed* him, and he'd made it look so *easy*.

"That's for me and Ginger Lewis," Aubrey Wanderman said, stepping back from the man he'd once feared as MacBride waved the Marines forward at last. "I hope you enjoyed it, asshole," he finished coldly through the other man's sobbing pain. "*I* certainly did."

• CHAPTER THIRTY-FIVE

Aubrey Wanderman waited for his trip to the Captain's quarters, and a Marine corporal stood beside him, her face blank. Aubrey knew her well—he and Corporal Slattery had sparred often—but her official expression told him nothing at all about his fate. The only good news, aside from the fact that Ginger was coming back extremely well from her ordeal, was that what awaited him was "only" a Captain's Mast, not a formal court-martial. The worst Captain's Mast could do to him was stick him in the brig for up to forty-five days per offense and bust him a maximum of three grades. Of course, that didn't count taking his acting petty officer's status away. The Captain could do that whenever she chose and start the busting process from his permanent rate.

She might just do it, too, Aubrey thought. Fighting aboard ship was a serious offense, but one the Navy had long since learned to handle "in house" without bringing up the heavy artillery. Crippling a fellow crewman was something else, and Randy Steilman's knee was going to require surgical reconstruction. That could very easily have turned it into a court-martial offense, with heavy time in the stockade or even a dishonorable discharge attending a guilty verdict.

He was going to lose his petty officer's stripe, he thought gloomily. That was the very best he could hope for . . . but it had been worth it. Now that the charged emotions of the fight had passed, the remembered *crunch!* of Steilman's knee made Aubrey more than a little queasy. It shocked him, too. Despite all Senior Chief

Harkness and Gunny Hallowell had taught him, his forebrain hadn't really caught up with the fact that he could *do* something like that. Yet shock and queasiness could do nothing to quell the cold satisfaction he also felt. He'd owed Steilman, and not just for what the rogue power tech had done to *him*.

But he still didn't look forward to facing the Skipper.

Honor Harrington sat square and straight behind her desk as the master-at-arms marched Randy Steilman up to face her. The power tech was in undress uniform, not his normal workaday shipsuit, but he looked terrible. His crippled leg was locked in a tractor cast, swinging wide from the hip with every awkward stride, and his eyes peered out through narrow, purple slits on either side of the blob of swollen flesh which had been his nose. Broken-off teeth showed between his equally swollen lips, and his broken cheek was a mass of livid, rainbow-hued bruises. Honor had seen the results of physical violence more than once, but she could seldom remember seeing someone who'd been as viciously beaten as this man, and she reminded her stony eyes not to show her satisfaction.

"Off caps!" Thomas barked, and Steilman reached up, dragged his beret off his head, and shuffled to what might have been called attention. He tried to look defiant, but Honor saw the fear in his face and the sag of his shoulders. He'd been beaten in more than one way, she thought, and swiveled her eyes to Sally MacBride.

"Charges?" she asked, and MacBride made a great show of consulting her memo pad.

"Prisoner is charged with violation of Article Thirty-Four," she said crisply, "violent, abusive, and threatening language to a fellow crewman; Article Thirty-Five, assaulting a fellow crewman; Article Nineteen," her voice turned colder, "conspiracy to desert in time of war; and Article Ninety, conspiracy to commit murder."

Steilman's eyes flickered at the third charge and turned suddenly very dark at the fourth, and Honor looked at Rafe Cardones.

"Have you investigated the charges, Mr. Cardones?"

"I have, Captain," the exec replied formally. "I've examined each witness to the incident in the mess compartment, and all the testimony supports the first two charges. Based on further testimony from Electronics Tech Showforth and Environmental Tech Stennis and corroborating evidence located in the prisoner's quarters and in Life Pod One-Eight-Four, I believe there is convincing evidence to support the latter two charges, as well."

"Recommendations?"

"Shipboard punishment for the first two, and return to the first available naval station for formal court-martial on the last two," Cardones said, and Honor watched Steilman pale. He could be shot under Article Nineteen or Ninety, and he knew it. Honor judged it was unlikely, since he hadn't actually managed to desert or kill Ginger Lewis, but at the very least, Randy Steilman was going to be a very old man before he ever got out of prison.

It was customary to permit the accused to speak in his own defense, but there wasn't much point this time, and everyone in her day cabin knew it. Besides, she thought coldly, she didn't want this man's words polluting air she had to breathe.

"Very well," she said, and nodded to Thomas.

"Prisoner, 'ten-*shun!*" the warrant officer snapped, and Steilman tried to square his shoulders.

"For violation of Article Thirty-Four, forty-five days close confinement on basic rations," she said coldly. "For violation of Article Thirty-Five, forty-five days close confinement on basic rations, sentences to run consecutively. On the charges of violation of Articles Nineteen and Ninety, prisoner will be kept in close confinement until remanded into the custody of the first available naval station for formal court-martial. See to it, Master-at-Arms."

"Aye, aye, Ma'am!"

Steilman sagged and started to open his mouth, but he never got the chance to speak.

"Prisoner, *on* caps!" Thomas barked. Steilman jerked, then placed his beret back on his head with hands that shook visibly. "About *face!*" Thomas snapped, and the power tech turned and shuffled awkwardly out of the cabin without a word.

The hatch slid open, and Aubrey looked up anxiously as Master-at-Arms Thomas appeared in the opening. His face was as expressionless as Corporal Slattery's, but he twitched his head commandingly, and Aubrey rose. He followed Thomas out into the passage and drew a deep breath as the hatch to the Captain's quarters came into sight. The green-uniformed armsman guarding it turned his head to regard them levelly, then pressed the switch to open the hatch, and Aubrey marched up to stand before the Captain's desk.

"Caps off!" Thomas commanded, and Aubrey removed his beret, tucked it under his left arm, and snapped to parade ground attention.

"Charges?" Lady Harrington asked the Bosun in crisp, official tones.

"Prisoner is charged with violation of Article Thirty-Six, fighting with a fellow crewman, with aggravated circumstances," the Bosun said, equally crisply.

"I see." The Captain regarded Aubrey with cold brown eyes. "That's a very serious offense," she said, and turned to look at Commander Cardones.

"Have you investigated the charge, Mr. Cardones?"

"I have, Captain. I've examined all witnesses to the incident. All of them agree that the prisoner intentionally sought a confrontation with Power Tech Third Steilman, in the course of which they had words and the prisoner accused him of attempting to murder Senior Chief Petty Officer Lewis. A fight then ensued, in which Steilman attempted to strike the first blow. Acting Petty Officer Wanderman defended himself, and in the fight which followed, systematically beat Power Tech Steilman, breaking his nose, cheekbone, several teeth—snapped at the gum line—and his kneecap, requiring reconstructive surgery."

"I take it those are the 'aggravated circumstances'?" the Captain asked.

"Yes, Ma'am. Particularly the knee. All witnesses agree Power Tech Steilman had already been effectively incapacitated, and that the kick to the knee was deliberately intended to have the effect it did."

"I see." The Captain returned that basilisk gaze to Aubrey and leaned back in her chair. The treecat on the perch above her desk also examined him, green eyes very intent and ears pricked, and the Captain lifted a finger at Aubrey.

"Did you in fact seek a confrontation with Power Tech Steilman?"

"Yes, Ma'am, I did," Aubrey replied as clearly as he could.

"Did you at any time use abusive or threatening language to him?"

"No, Ma'am," Aubrey said, then paused. "Uh, except at the end, Ma'am. I did call him an 'asshole' then," he admitted, flushing darkly. The Captain's lips seemed to quiver for just a moment, but he told himself that had to have been his imagination.

"I see. And did you intentionally break his nose, cheek, teeth, and knee?"

"Most of it just happened, Ma'am. Except the knee." Aubrey stood very straight, gazing at a point five centimeters above her head. "I guess I did do that on purpose, Ma'am," he said quietly.

"I see," she said again, then glanced at the Exec. "Recommendations, Mr. Cardones?"

"That's a very serious admission, Captain," the Commander said. "We can't have our people going around breaking one another's bones deliberately. On the other hand, this is the first time the prisoner has ever been in trouble, so I suppose *some* leniency might be in order."

The Captain nodded thoughtfully and gazed at Aubrey for sixty awful seconds of silence. He made himself stand very still, waiting for her to pronounce his fate.

"The Exec is correct, Wanderman," she said finally. "Defending yourself against attack is one thing; deliberately seeking a confrontation with a crewmate and then shattering his knee is something else again. Do you agree?"

"Yes, Ma'am," Aubrey said manfully.

"I'm glad you do, Wanderman. I hope this will be a lesson to you, and that you never again appear before me or any other captain on similar charges." She let that sink in, then fixed him with an unflinching gaze. "Are you prepared to accept the consequences?"

"Yes, Ma'am," Aubrey said again, and she nodded.

"Very well. For violation of Article Thirty-Five, with aggravated circumstances, the prisoner is confined to quarters for one day and fined one week's pay. Dismissed."

Aubrey blinked, and his eyes dropped to the Captain's face in disbelief. Her face didn't even move a muscle as she returned his goggle-eyed stare, but there was the ghost of a twinkle in the eyes which had been so cold. He wondered if he was supposed to say something, but the Master-at-Arms came to his rescue.

"Prisoner, *on* caps!" he barked, and Aubrey's spine stiffened automatically as he replaced his beret. "About, *face!*" Thomas snapped, and Aubrey turned and marched obediently out of the cabin to begin his confinement to quarters.

"Did you see the look on Wanderman's face?" Cardones asked when the bosun had departed, and Honor smiled.

"I think he expected a planet to fall on him," she replied.

"Well, one could have," Cardones pointed out, then grinned. "I'd say you put the fear of God—or someone—into him first, Skipper!"

"He had that much coming for not stepping forward

in the first place. And that knee thing probably was a bit much. On the other hand, Steilman *more* than had it coming, and I'm glad Wanderman gave it to him. He needed to learn to stand up for himself."

"Indeed he did. Not that I expect him to have any more trouble after the way he took Steilman apart."

"True. And if he hadn't landed Steilman in the brig, Showforth and Stennis might not have cracked about the desertion thing—or about Coulter and Lewis' SUT," Honor said much more seriously. "All in all, I think he did quite well by us."

"Absolutely," Cardones said. "I just wish it hadn't taken as long as it did—and that Lewis hadn't almost gotten killed in the process."

Honor nodded slowly and tipped her chair far back, resting her heels on her desk while Nimitz swarmed down to curl in her lap. The 'cat's approval of the way she'd treated Steilman—and Aubrey—radiated into her, and she laughed softly as she brushed his ears.

"Well, with that out of the way, I suppose it's time to decide what to do next."

"Yes, Ma'am."

Honor rubbed the tip of her nose thoughtfully. There had not, in fact, been a timer on the nuclear demolitions, and the ground troops had crumbled when they learned of their leader's desertion—and of what had happened to all their erstwhile associates aboard the repair ship. When *Wayfarer's* pinnaces disembarked a full battalion of battle-armored Marines and then went back upstairs to provide air support, they'd fallen all over themselves to surrender.

Not, she thought grimly, that it was going to do them a great deal of good in the long run. Sidemore's planetary government—or what was left of it after the long, savage months of Warnecke's occupation—had come out of hiding when it realized the nightmare was over. The planetary president had been among the first hostages shot by Warnecke's troops, but the vice president and two members of her cabinet had eluded capture. There'd still been a haunted, hunted look in their eyes when Honor went dirtside to greet them, but they constituted a functional government. Best of all, Sidemore had a death penalty.

She was still a bit shocked by the cold satisfaction she'd felt when she informed the ex-privateer leader he would be handed over to Sidemore for trial. Vice President Gutierrez had promised Honor his trial would be scrupulously fair, but Honor could accept that. There was more than sufficient evidence, and she was certain he'd have an equally fair hanging. A lot of his men would be joining him, and the idea didn't bother her in the least.

What *did* bother her was that four of Warnecke's ships were still at large. One was a light cruiser, and the other three were only destroyers, but the Marsh System had nothing with which to defend itself against them. And since the privateers didn't know their base had been destroyed, they were certain to return eventually. According to records captured on the planet, they were cruising individually, so they could be expected to return in singletons, but any one of them could destroy every town and city on the planet if its captain chose to take vengeance on Sidemore, and it would be some weeks yet before Commodore Blohm's promised IAN squadron could get here.

"I think we're going to have to detach some of the LACs," she said finally.

"For system security?"

"Yes." She rubbed her nose some more. "We'll detach Jackie Harmon as senior officer and give her LAC One. Six LACs should be able to deal with all of Warnecke's remaining ships, especially taking them by surprise and with Jackie in command."

"That's half our parasite complement, Skip," Cardones pointed out. "And they're not hyper-capable. They'll be stuck here until we can get back and collect them."

"I know, but we'll only be gone long enough for the

hop back to New Berlin, and we can't leave Marsh unprotected." She considered some more, then nodded. "I think we'll leave them a few dozen missile pods, as well. We can modify the fire control to let each LAC handle a couple of them at a time and then put them in Sidemore orbit. If any of Warnecke's orphans want to tangle with that kind of firepower, they won't be leaving again."

"I like it," Cardones said after a moment, then grinned. "Of course, the people we had reloading all those pods may be just a bit put out when we turn right around and *off*load them."

"They'll get over it," Honor replied with a matching smile. "Besides, I'll explain it's all in a good cause." She gave her nose a final rub, then nodded. "Another thing. I think I'll leave Jackie written orders to turn their ships over to Vice President Gutierrez if she can take them intact. They're not much, but these people are totally on their own, and they ought to be enough to scare off any normal pirate."

"Do they have the people to crew them?" Cardones asked dubiously, and Honor shrugged.

"They've got a few hundred experienced spacers of their own, and the ones Warnecke was using for slave labor will still be here until someone with enough life support can arrange to repatriate them. Jackie and her people can give them a quicky course on weapon systems. Besides, I'm going to recommend that the Admiralty put a fleet station in here."

"You are?" Cardones eyebrows rose, and she shrugged again.

"It makes sense, actually. The Confederacy's always hated giving us basing rights in their space. It's stupid, since we're the ones who've traditionally kept piracy in check, but I think part of it's resentment at having to admit they need us for that in the first place. Then, too, some of their governors hate having us around because we're bad for their business arrangements. But

Marsh has every reason in the world to be grateful to us, and they've just had a pretty gruesome experience with the consequences of not being able to defend themselves. They're also only fifteen light-years from Sachsen. We don't have a station there, but the Andies do, and if we put in a base here and kept a few cruisers or battlecruisers on station, we'd have a place to turn convoy escorts around . . . and to keep an eye on the Andies in Sachsen."

"The IAN's being very helpful to us at the moment, Skip."

"Yes, they are. And I hope it stays that way. But it may not, and neither they nor the Confeds can object to our signing a basing agreement with an independent system outside their borders. It'd also be something we could upgrade in a hurry if we had to, and if it ever does hit the fan between us and the Andies, having a fleet base between them and Silesia might not be such a bad thing."

"Hm." Cardones rubbed his own nose for a moment. She sounded more like an admiral than a captain, he reflected. But then, she'd been an admiral for the last two years, hadn't she? And even before that, she'd never been shy about accepting additional responsibilities. "You may have a point," he said finally. "Is that one of the things they teach in the Senior Officer's Course?"

"Sure. It's listed as Constructive Paranoia One-Oh-One in the catalog," Honor said deadpan, and Cardones chuckled. Then she took her feet from her desk and let her chair come back upright. "Okay. I'll float the basing idea by Gutierrez before we leave—no commitment, just sounding her out. Assuming we detach LAC One and the pods, how soon can we pull out?"

"Take about a day, I guess," Cardones replied thoughtfully. "We'll need to provide Jackie with at least some spares, and we've still got Marines scattered all over the planet."

"A day's fine; we're not in that big a rush."

"You know we're going to lose a fair piece of prize

money if Jackie does manage to take those ships intact and hand them over, Skipper," Cardones said.

"A point. On the other hand, if the Admiralty signs off on the idea of a station out here, they may decide to go ahead and pay up anyway. I don't need the money, but I certainly intend to recommend they do right by the rest of our people. They deserve it."

"Yes, they do," Cardones agreed.

"All right, then!" Honor rose, carrying Nimitz in her arms, and headed for the hatch. "Let's go see about getting all this in motion."

• CHAPTER THIRTY-SIX

Commander Usher was in a moderately foul mood. He'd been unhappy about his assignment from the beginning, and it had only gotten worse once *Hawkwing* and *Artemis* reached New Berlin.

He would have liked to blame Captain Fuchien, but the woman was exactly the sort of consummate professional one might expect to find commanding one of the Star Kingdom's crack liners. Captains for ships like that weren't picked out of a hat, and Fuchien knew all the moves to stroke irritated and irascible naval officers detailed to escort her ship. No one could have been more courteous, and she'd made it clear she intended to defer to his judgment, despite his younger age and junior rank, in the event anything untoward happened. Both of which only made Usher's foul mood fouler, since they prevented him from taking his ire out on *her*.

The problem, he thought as he walked to his command chair, was that he also couldn't take his ire out on the person who deserved it. The notion that Klaus and Stacey Hauptman were sufficiently important to drag a Queen's ship away from her proper duties had grated on his nerves from the start. Worse, the fiction that *Hawkwing* had just "happened" to be heading for Silesia when the Admiralty realized *Artemis* was bound there had worn transparently thin in the Sligo System.

Like every wartime passenger ticket, the tickets of *Artemis'* current passengers specifically included the proviso that her captain, at her discretion, could make such changes in scheduling en route to their ticketed

452

destinations as she deemed appropriate. That proviso was *intended* to allow a skipper to protect his vessel by avoiding danger spots without fear of legal action from an irate passenger, but that wasn't what it was being used for this time.

Klaus Hauptman had decided he needed three extra days with his primary Andermani factor in Sligo. It was typical of the man's arrogance that he'd directed Fuchien to hold the ship there while he dealt with his business affairs. Usher doubted he'd even considered the extent to which it might inconvenience others, though he *had* gone out of his way to provide free shuttle service to and from the planet Erin's renowned ski resorts.

That "generosity" might have defused the frustration of *Artemis'* passengers, but it hadn't done a thing for Gene Usher's. Nor had it helped him maintain the appearance that his ship was only coincidentally dogging *Artemis'* coattails. Sligo was the Empire's second most populous system, and there'd been plenty of IAN vessels around to look after the liner while she was there. Which meant Usher could have proceeded on his way with a clear conscience . . . if he'd actually been ordered to a duty station in Silesia. Unfortunately, his *real* mission was to escort *Artemis*, which meant he couldn't leave until *she* did, which, in turn, meant he'd had to spend the same three days in Erin orbit with her.

Wasting his time that way would have been bad enough, but Hauptman was no fool. Watching *Hawkwing* sit there in parking orbit had confirmed what he'd undoubtedly suspected from the outset, and he'd decided to take advantage of it when they reached New Berlin. He hadn't extended their layover there; instead, he'd found something *worse* to do.

There were three Hauptman Line freighters in New Berlin when *Artemis* and *Hawkwing* arrived, all waiting to join the next scheduled convoy. But ships didn't earn any money sitting still. Despite their huge size, interstellar freighters were cheaper to operate on a ton-for-ton cargo basis than most forms of purely planetary transport. A single freighter could easily stow four or five *million* tons of cargo, and counter-grav and impellers made it easy enough to lift freight out of a gravity well to make even interstellar transport of foodstuffs a paying proposition. But she also cost her owners almost as much to operate sitting in a parking orbit as she did earning revenue between stars, and no shipowner liked to see his vessels waiting around.

Of course, given ship losses in Silesia, only an idiot wanted them to proceed independently when they didn't have to, either. Swinging around a planet while they waited for the next convoy might shrink profit margins, but not as much as losing the entire ship would. Unfortunately, Hauptman had seen no reason not to make use of the destroyer which "just happened" to be going his way, and he'd instructed his freighters to join *Artemis* for the trip to Sachsen.

Which, Usher reflected, reminding himself not to gnash his teeth audibly, was no more than he should have expected from the old bastard. Left to their own devices, *Hawkwing* and *Artemis* could easily have translated clear up to the zeta bands and maintained a steady .7 *c*, for an apparent velocity of well over twenty-five hundred times light-speed, completing the passage from New Berlin to Sachsen in three T-weeks, or fifteen days subjective. Lumbered by Hauptman's freighters, however, they were limited to the delta bands and a maximum speed of only .5 *c* . . . which meant the same trip would take almost forty-eight T-days and that dilation would shave only five days subjective off that wearisome total.

That three-fold extension of the passage was bad enough, but what absolutely infuriated Usher was knowing Hauptman had manipulated a Queen's ship—*Usher's* ship.

The old bastard must just love *this,* Usher thought moodily, watching his repeater plot. *Hawkwing* held station on the port quarter of the improvised convoy, where she would be best placed to intercept any threat, as it trekked steadily down its current grav wave. *Artemis* was the third ship in the column, with the freighter *Markham* following directly astern of her, and it all looked maddeningly complacent. *He's feuded with the Admiralty over one thing or another for decades,* the commander told himself, *and he's lost more often than he's won. Now he's sitting in his stateroom gloating over the way he's "forced" the Fleet to increase its escort efforts just this once. And the cast-iron bitch of it is, he's never even had to say a single* word *about it. He didn't ask, didn't plead, didn't bluster. He simply abused the discretionary clause of the standard ticket form, and I can't even protest, because I'm not officially escorting him at all!*

He glowered at the repeater for a few more moments, and then his expression changed. His glower turned into a wicked grin, and he punched a code into his com.

"Exec," Lieutenant Commander Alicia Marcos' voice responded almost instantly, and Usher tipped his chair back to turn his wicked smile up at the deckhead.

"Sorry to disturb you when you're off watch, Alicia, but I've just had a thought."

"A thought, Skipper?" Marcos had served with him long enough to recognize that tone, and her own was suddenly wary.

"Yes, indeed," Usher said, fairly beaming at the deckhead. "Since we've got all this, ah, *unanticipated* time on our hands, don't you think we should put it to best use?"

"In what way, Captain?" Marcos inquired even more warily.

"I'm glad you asked that," Usher said expansively. "Why don't you and Ed come on up to my briefing room so we can discuss it?"

"Captain to the bridge! Captain to the bridge!"

Margaret Fuchien's head jerked up so suddenly her

second cup of coffee sloshed over her second-best uniform trousers. The brown tide was scorching hot, but she hardly noticed as she vaulted out of her chair at the head of the breakfast table and ran for the lift.

"Captain to the bridge!" the urgent voice repeated, and she swore as she skidded into the lift, for her standing orders were crystal clear. Unless it was a true emergency—and a time-critical one, at that—the passengers were not to be panicked by broadcast messages, and there'd been plenty of stewards available to murmur discreetly in her ear.

She hit the emergency override to slam the lift doors shut and whirled to the intercom pad.

"Captain to th—"

"This is the Captain! Shut down that goddamned message!" she snarled, and the recorded voice died in midword. "Better! Now what the *hell* is so damned urgent?"

"We're under attack, Ma'am!" her second officer replied with an edge of panic.

"Under at—?" Fuchien stared at the com panel, then shook herself. "By who and how many?" she demanded.

"We don't know yet." Lieutenant Donevski sounded marginally calmer, and she pictured him inhaling deeply and getting a grip on himself. "All we know is *Hawkwing* broadcast an attack alert, ordered us onto a new heading, and then peeled off to starboard."

"Damn." Fuchien's mind raced. It would have been nice of Usher to tell her what the problem was! *Artemis* did have the missile armament of a heavy cruiser, after all, and the trained personnel to use it. Those missiles would have been a hell of a lot more useful if Fuchien had some idea of the parameters of the threat.

But Usher was Navy, and the law was clear. In any case of attack, the decisions of the senior Navy officer present took absolute precedence.

"Come to the heading ordered. I'll be on the bridge in two minutes."

"Aye, Ma'am!"

Fuchien released the "send" button, stood back with a sour expression, and tried to tell herself she wasn't afraid.

The lift slid to a halt almost precisely two minutes later, and Fuchien stormed onto her bridge. The relief on Donevski's face was painfully obvious, and she waved him off as she strode briskly across to the plot.

Artemis' bridge was a peculiar hybrid. Civilian vessels required fewer watch officers, yet civilian bridges were usually larger than those aboard warships, where internal space was always at a premium. That normally made a merchant ship's bridge seem almost ostentatiously spacious to a naval officer, but *Artemis'* command deck was more crowded than most. A naval-style tactical plotned by Lieutenant Annabelle Ward and her tactical crews, was placed right beside it.

Fuchien came to a halt at Ward's shoulder and glared at the plot. All she could see were the freighters and her own ship, all accelerating at their best speed—close to two thousand gravities, thanks to the grav wave—at right angles to their previous heading. *Hawkwing* was also visible, on an exactly reciprocal heading at over fifty-two hundred gravities. The range between them was opening at over fifty-one KPS^2, and the destroyer was already 3.75 light-seconds—over a million kilometers—astern of the merchantmen.

"What the hell is she going after?" Fuchien wondered aloud.

"Damned if I know, Skipper," Ward replied in a strong Sphinx accent. "She just took the hell off like a wet treecat and ordered us to run for it. I can't see a damned thing on that bearing."

Fuchien studied the blandly uninformative plot for another handful of seconds, then spared a single fulminating glance at the visual display. Particle densities were higher than normal, even for h-space, along this particular wave, and the glorious frozen lightning of hyper-space was more beautiful than usual. But that same beauty also cut her sensor range considerably, and Margaret Fuchien didn't like the thought of what might be headed her way from just over her sensor horizon. But, damn it to hell, what *could* be out there? Her sensors were as good as *Hawkwing*'s, so how could anything *she* couldn't see have picked them up?

"Anything further from *Hawkwing*?" she demanded, turning to Donevski.

"No, Ma'am."

"Play back the original message," she directed. Donevski nodded to the com officer, and five seconds later, Commander Usher's voice crackled over the bridge speakers.

"All ships, this is *Hawkwing!* Condition Red! Come to two-seven-zero immediately, maximum convoy acceleration! Maintain heading until further notice! *Hawkwing* out!"

"That's *all?*" Fuchien demanded incredulously.

"Yes, Ma'am," Donevski said. "We copied his message, but before we could respond he took off like a bat out of hell, and Anna caught his sidewalls and fire control coming up."

Fuchien turned to crook an eyebrow at Lieutenant Ward, who nodded.

"I don't know what Usher's picked up, Skipper, but he's not fooling around with it," the tactical officer said. "His combat systems came on-line in less than twelve seconds from the moment he started transmitting, and he was on his new heading before he finished talking."

Fuchien nodded and turned her attention back to Ward's plot. The destroyer was a full thirty light-seconds astern now, with a relative velocity of over thirty thousand KPS, and she was already deploying missile decoys. That was an ominous sign, and Fuchien swallowed a sudden lump of fear. Why was Usher doing that? Nothing could be in missile range without showing up on *Artemis'* scanners, whatever local conditions were like!

"Why deploy decoys so soon?" she asked Ward tautly.

"I don't know, Skipper." The tac officer had herself well

under control, but an edge of uncertainty burned in her crisp reply.

"Could somebody be out there under stealth?"

"Possible, but if they're already in missile range, we should have a sniff of them on gravitics by now however good their systems are." Ward tapped a sequence of commands into her console, then sat back with an unhappy sound and shook her head. "Nothing, Skipper. I don't see a single damned thing out there for—"

Her voice chopped off abruptly as Usher threw *Hawkwing* into a violent turn to port. The destroyer screamed around, and even as she turned, she was spinning on her axis. Missiles spat from both broadsides, drives programmed to bring the double salvos in together on *whatever* she was shooting at, and Ward paled. *Hawkwing*'s launchers were at maximum rate fire, each launcher spitting out a missile every seventeen seconds. What in God's name was *out* there to draw that kind of fire from the opening broadside?

"Skipper, Mr. Hauptman's on the com," Donevski announced. Fuchien started to snarl a command not to bother her, but then she drew a deep breath and gestured sharply.

"Yes, Mr. Hauptman?" She couldn't quite keep her anger at his timing out of her voice. "I'm just a bit busy up here right now, Sir!"

"What's happening, Captain?" Hauptman demanded.

"We appear to be under attack, Sir," Fuchien said as calmly as she could.

"*Under attack?* By what?!"

"I don't have an answer to that question just yet, Sir. But whatever it is, *Hawkwing*'s engaging it now, so it must be close."

"My God." The quiet words were squeezed out of the magnate almost against his will, and he closed his eyes at the far end of the com link. "Keep me informed, please," he said, and signed off. Which, Fuchien reflected, showed more common sense than she'd expected from him.

"What the *hell* is she *shooting* at?" Ward fumed. "I *still* can't see a damned thing!" The ready lights of her own batteries glowed a steady red, but without a target, they were useless.

"I don't know," Fuchien said quietly, "but whatever it is, it's—"

Hawkwing's first double salvo detonated, bomb-pumped lasers slashing at something no one on *Artemis'* bridge could even see. There was absolutely nothing *there* according to their sensors, yet five full double broadsides tore down on exactly the same spot and detonated with savage fury. And then, suddenly, *Hawkwing* ceased fire, turned another ninety degrees to port, and came loping after the merchantmen.

Fuchien stared at the plot in total confusion, then turned to meet Ward's gaze. The tac officer looked just as confused as Fuchien was and raised her hands in baffled ignorance.

"Beats the hell out of me, Skipper. Never saw anything like it in my life."

"I—"

"Burst transmission from *Hawkwing*, Captain," the com officer announced.

"On speaker," Fuchien said tautly.

"All ships resume original heading," Gene Usher's voice said pleasantly. "Thank you for your cooperation and excellent response time, but this concludes our unscheduled exercise."

• CHAPTER THIRTY-SEVEN

Honor leaned back on the couch in her day cabin with her legs curled comfortably under her and a book viewer in her lap. Her right hand held a long-stemmed glass of her prized Delacourt, an open box of chocolates sat beside her, and she smiled as she pressed the page advance with her left forefinger.

Like the wine, the novel in her lap was a gift from her father. She hadn't had much time to read over the past arduous months, and she'd decided to save it for a special treat—a reward to herself, which she would know she'd earned when she actually had time to read it anyway.

It was a very, very old book, and despite the way printed and audio recordings had frozen the language, its prespace English was hard to follow, especially when characters used period slang. It had also been written using the old English system of measurement. Math had never been Honor's strong suit, and all she knew about English measurement was that a "yard" was a little shorter than a meter and that a "mile" was a little less than two kilometers. She had no idea how many grams there were in a "pound," which was of considerable importance for this particular novel, and the situation was complicated by the fact that "pounds" (and also "guineas" and "shillings") seemed to be monetary units, as well. She remembered pounds (and "francs") from her study of the Napoleonic Wars, but her texts had converted most monetary amounts into present-day dollars, which left her only a vague notion of how much a pound had been worth, and she'd never

461

heard of "guineas" or "shillings" in her life. It was all very confusing, though she was fairly confident she was catching most of it from context, and she considered—again—querying her desk computer for English measurement equivalents and a table of pre-space currencies.

For the moment, however, she was entirely content to sit exactly where she was. Not only was her father's gift proving an extraordinarily good read in spite of its archaisms, but she was also aware of a rare and complete sense of satisfaction. *Wayfarer* might not be a ship of the wall, but she'd cut quite a swath, and after the better part of six months, her crew had come together as well as any Honor had ever seen. The newbies had their feet under them, the best of the experienced hands had been given time to pass along their own skills, the bad apples were in the brig, reformed, or keeping a very low profile, and department efficiency ratings were closing in on a uniform 4.0. She felt certain the rest of TG 1037 was doing equally well—though it would be nice to have confirmation when they checked in at Sachsen on their way back from New Berlin—and, best of all, she was back in Manticoran uniform. *And,* she thought, turning another page, *what we've accomplished so far should go a long way to completing my "rehabilitation."*

Even the fact that she'd ever needed "rehabilitating" no longer had the power to disturb her, and, she admitted, she actually preferred *Wayfarer* to the battle squadron she'd commanded in Grayson service. She'd been born to be a captain, she thought wistfully, commander of a starship, mistress after God and all alone on her own responsibility. It was, without a doubt, the loneliest job in the universe, but it was also the proper task—the proper challenge—for her . . . and one she would have to give up all too soon.

She thought about that last point fairly often. She was a captain of the list with almost nine years' seniority. Even if the Opposition managed to block any Admiralty plans to promote her out of the zone, time in grade would make her a commodore within another four or five years—probably less; wars gave ample opportunity to step into a dead man's shoes. And from what Earl White Haven had said on Grayson, she'd probably be dropped into an *acting* commodore's slot much sooner.

When that happened, her days as a captain would be over. A part of her looked forward to it as she always looked forward to the next challenge—with anticipation and an eagerness to be about it—and for once she didn't feel the nagging uncertainty that *this* time she might not be equal to the task. She'd proven she could command a squadron of the wall—or, for that matter, an entire heavy task force—in Yeltsin. More than that, she knew she'd done it well. Her abilities as a strategist had not yet been tested, but she knew she could hack the tactical side of it.

But for all the satisfaction that brought her, and for all her awareness that without flag rank she could never play a role on the larger stage of actually shaping the war's direction, she hated the thought of giving up the white beret of a starship's commander. She knew she'd been lucky to command as many ships as she had, and to have had two of them straight from the builders as a keel plate owner, but she also knew she would always hunger for just one more.

She smiled wryly and sipped more wine, wondering why the thought didn't hurt more than it did. Why it was a thing of bittersweet regret mingled with pleasure rather than total unhappiness. *Maybe I'm just a* bit *more ambitious than I'd like to admit?*

Her smile grew, and she glanced at the gently snoring ball of treecat on the couch beside her. Nimitz, at least, had no second thoughts at all. He understood her love for starship command, but he was also smugly confident of her ability to handle any task which came her way . . . and not at all shy about making it clear *he* thought she deserved to command the Queen's entire Navy.

Well, that was for the future—which had a pronounced gift for taking care of itself in its own good time, however much humans dithered in the process. Meanwhile, she had an excellent glass of wine and a novel which was thoroughly enjoyable. *This Forester guy writes a darned good book!*

She'd just turned another page when the admittance chime sounded softly. She started to set her novel aside, but MacGuiness padded into the compartment, and she settled back as he crossed to her desk and pressed the com key.

"Yes?" he said.

"The Chief Engineer to see the Steadholder," Eddy Howard announced, and MacGuiness glanced at his captain with a raised eyebrow.

"Harry?" Honor glanced at the chrono. It was late in *Wayfarer's* day, and she wondered why Tschu hadn't simply screened her. But he probably had his reasons, and she nodded to MacGuiness, who punched the hatch button.

Tschu stepped into the compartment with Samantha on his shoulder. The female 'cat looked unbearably smug—Honor blinked, wondering why that particular adjective had occurred to her—and Nimitz gave a soft snort and roused instantly. He sat up, then stretched with a long lazy yawn that stopped abruptly. He cocked his head, gazing very intently at Samantha, and Honor blinked again as she felt a deep, complex stir of emotion from him. She couldn't sort it all out, but the strongest component of it could only be described as delight.

"Sorry to disturb you, Skipper," Tschu said wryly, "but there's something you should know."

"There is?" Honor laid her novel aside as Samantha hopped down from the engineer's shoulder. The 'cat scampered across the deck to jump up on the couch beside Nimitz, and the two of them sat so close together their bodies touched. As Honor watched in bemusement, Nimitz curled his prehensile tail around the smaller 'cat in an oddly protective gesture and rubbed his cheek against the top of her head with a deep, softly buzzing purr.

"Yes, Ma'am," Tschu said with that same wry smile. "I'm afraid I'm going to have to put in for maternity leave."

Honor blinked a third time, and then her eyes narrowed.

"Yes, Ma'am," the engineer said again. "I'm afraid Sam is pregnant."

Honor sat up very straight, jaw dropping, then whipped around to stare at the 'cats. Nimitz looked back with an absurdly complacent—and proud—expression, and his sense of delight soared. He held her gaze for several seconds, and then she shook her head with a slow smile of her own. Nimitz? A *father?* Somehow she'd never really believed that could happen, despite all the time he'd spent with Samantha. She'd considered the possibility intellectually, but it had been just the two of them for so long—aside from her brief, happy months with Paul Tankersley—that her emotions had assumed it would *always* be just the two of them.

"Well," she said finally, "this *is* a surprise, Harry. I assume you're certain about it?"

"Sam is," Tschu half-chuckled, "and that's good enough for me. 'Cats don't often make mistakes about things like that."

"No, no, they don't." Honor glanced at MacGuiness, whose surprise seemed just as great as hers but who also stood there with a huge smile on his face. "I think we need another glass, Mac," she told him dryly. "In fact, make it two glasses—you're about to become an uncle. And, under the circumstances, a few stalks of celery probably aren't out of order, either."

"Yes, Ma'am!" MacGuiness gave her another smile, then hurried out of the cabin, and she returned her attention to Tschu.

"This is going to leave me with a bit of a problem. I'm going to need a darned good replacement for you, Harry. You've done an outstanding job."

"I'm sorry, Skipper. I hate to run out on you, but—"
The engineer shrugged, and Honor nodded. It probably
hadn't happened more than twice before in the entire
history of the Royal Navy, but the precedents were clear.
The Admiralty didn't like them much, but seven of the
last nine Manticoran monarchs, including the present
Queen Elizabeth, had been adopted by treecats, and
they'd been very firm with the Navy. 'Cats were people;
they would be treated as any other people in the company of a Queen's ship, and that meant pregnant females
were barred from shipboard duty or anyplace else where
they might encounter a radiation hazard. Nor would they
be separated from their adopted humans, even if that did
make problems for BuPers, which meant Harold Tschu
was entirely serious about requesting "maternity leave."
He and Samantha would have to be returned to Sphinx
by the earliest available transport, and he'd probably be
stuck there for at least three years. It would be that long
before Samantha's (and Nimitz's) offspring—of which
there would probably be at least three—were old enough
for her to foster with another female 'cat.

Which brought up another point, and Honor turned
to look at the two 'cats on her couch.

"You two do realize what this means, don't you?" she
asked gently. Nimitz cocked his head at her while
Samantha leaned her cheek against his shoulder. "The
regs are the same for you as they are for us two-foots,"
Honor told him. "We're going to have to send Sam back
to Sphinx as soon as we can so she and her babies will
be safe."

Nimitz made a soft sound and tucked a strong, wiry
arm around Samantha. He looked down at her, and their
eyes met and held. Once again, Honor felt that deep,
subtle flow of communication—and their unhappiness
at the prospect of separation. They truly were mated, she
thought, wondering where *that* was going to end, and the
idea of being parted caused both of them pain. But even
if they hadn't had to be separated for *this*, Honor thought,
sooner or later she and Tschu were certain to be assigned

to different ships. Had Nimitz and Samantha even considered that?

Then Nimitz turned his eyes back to her. They were grave and dark, without their usual mischievousness, and she knew the answer. They *had* considered it. And, like any Navy personnel who chose to wed, they'd accepted that they would be parted both often and for extended periods. Honor knew how the prospect felt, for *she'd* faced it before Paul's death, and she could tell they didn't like it any more than she had. But neither of them could any more have ended their relationships with their adopted people just to be together than they could have renounced their feelings for one another, and that was simply the way it was..

Honor felt their unhappiness, and their love—not just for one another, but for her and Harold Tschu—like an extension of her own psyche, and it hit her hard. There was so much joy with the sorrow, such intense pleasure at the thought of the children to come and such regret that Nimitz would not be there when they were born, that she felt tears in her own eyes. She blinked them away and reached out, running her hand over both of them, then looked up at Tschu.

He lacked her own link to Nimitz, but the emotions being generated in Honor's cabin were too intense for him not to feel them, and she saw them echoed in his face.

"Have a seat, Harry," she said softly, patting the couch on the other side of the 'cats. He hesitated for a moment, then nodded and sank down, with the 'cats between them, and the soft, sad rejoicing of the 'cats' harmonized purring reached out to them both.

"Never thought the little minx would decide to settle down." Tschu's deep voice was suspiciously husky, and his hand was gentle as he stroked Samantha.

"And I never expected this to happen to Nimitz," Honor agreed with a smile. "Looks like we're going to be seeing quite a bit of each other over the next several years. We'll have to try to juggle our leave schedules so they can have time together."

"Won't be that big a problem for *me* for at least a few years, Skipper," Tschu pointed out with a grin. "I'll be stuck on Sphinx till they're old enough to foster, so you should know right where to find us."

"True. And it's a good thing the 'cat clans are such extended family arrangements, or you might be stuck there for at least *ten* years. Think what *that* would do to your career!"

"Hey, everyone has to make adjustments for his family, doesn't he? I wish they'd given us a little more warning, but—"

He shrugged, and Honor nodded. No doubt if more female 'cats adopted Navy personnel the Admiralty would have extended the contraceptive program to them, as well. But it hadn't, and Nimitz and Samantha had a right to make their own decisions. Which they'd undoubtedly done, she reflected, recalling how uncommon pregnancies were among unmated 'cats.

"Will you be able to locate Sam's clan?" she asked after a moment. It wouldn't be at all unusual for the answer to that to be no. Her own visit to Nimitz's clan was highly unusual; about the only adoptees who regularly knew both the identity and location of their companions' home clans were Forestry Service rangers.

"As a matter of fact, I'm not sure I will," Tschu admitted. "I was vacationing in Djebel Hassa over on Jefferies Land when she adopted me. I know she's from somewhere up in the Al Hijaz Mountains, but as to exactly where . . ."

"Um." Honor rubbed an eyebrow, then glanced down at the 'cats before she looked back at the engineer. "As it happens, I *do* know where Nimitz's clan hangs out in the Copper Walls."

"Oh?" Tschu considered for a moment, then turned to Samantha. "How about it, Sam? You want to be introduced to Nimitz's family? I'm sure they'd be delighted to see you."

The two 'cats looked into one another's eyes for a moment, then each turned to his—or her—person and flipped his—or her—ears in agreement, and Tschu chuckled.

"Glad that's decided," he said wryly. "I had this picture of spending all my free time for the next six months wandering around Djebel Hassa until Sam said 'We're home!'" He looked at Honor, and his expression turned much more serious. "It must be nice to be able to communicate as clearly as you and Nimitz do, Skipper."

Honor raised an eyebrow at him, and he laughed.

"Skip, people who haven't been adopted might not notice, but anyone who has would know damned well you've found an extra wavelength we don't know about. Is it something you could teach me and Sam? I know *she* understands *me*, but I'd give just about anything to be able to hear her back."

"I don't think it's something anyone can teach," Honor said with genuine regret. "It just sort of happened. I don't think either of us knows exactly why or how, and it's taken years to get to the point of exchanging emotions in a clear two-way link."

"I think it's more than just emotions, Skipper," Tschu said quietly. "You may not realize it, but the two of you are an awful lot more in tune than anyone else I've ever seen. When you ask him a question, you get a much clearer—or less ambiguous, at least—answer than any other pair I know. It's like you each know what the other's actually thinking."

"Really?" Honor considered that for a moment, then nodded slowly. "You may have something there." She'd never actually discussed her specialized link with another human, but if she couldn't talk about it with her fellow "grandparent," then who *could* she discuss it with? "I can't actually hear what he's thinking—it's not like full telepathy—but I *do* seem to get . . . well, a more complete impression of the *direction* of his thoughts than I do just emotions. And we *can* send one another visual images—most of the time, anyway. That's a lot tougher, but it's been darned useful a time or two."

"I imagine," Tschu said wistfully, then stroked Samantha again, radiating love for her as if to reassure her that his inability to feel her emotions in return made her no less precious to him.

"I'd appreciate it if you didn't mention this to anyone else, though," Honor said after a moment. Tschu looked a question at her, and she shrugged. "I can sense *human* emotions through Nimitz, too. That can be very useful—it saved my buns when the Maccabeans tried to assassinate the Protector's family on Grayson—and I'd prefer to hold it in reserve as my secret weapon."

"Makes sense to me," Tschu replied very seriously after a moment's consideration. "And I'm glad you can. In all honesty, there's no way in the universe that I'd want to have to wear all the hats *you* do, Skipper. I've got enough troubles just being a lieutenant commander."

Honor smiled, but MacGuiness returned with the extra glasses and a small bowl of celery before she could reply. The steward set the bowl in front of the 'cats and started to reach for the wine bottle, but Honor waved him off and pointed at a chair.

"Drag that up and have a seat, 'Uncle Mac,'" she told him, picking up the bottle herself, then poured for all of them. "A toast, gentlemen," she said then, and raised her own glass to Samantha, who sat in the protective curl of Nimitz's tail nibbling delicately on a celery stalk. She lowered it and regarded Honor gravely, and Honor smiled. "To Samantha," she said, "may your children be happy and healthy, and may you and Nimitz have years and years together."

"Hear, hear!" Tschu said, raising his own glass, and MacGuiness joined them both.

• CHAPTER THIRTY-EIGHT

Citizen Captain Marie Stellingetti swore as another laser head slashed at her battlecruiser's sidewall and fresh damage alarms shrilled. *Kerebin* had taken nine hits so far, and if none were vital, all were serious, for it would take the task force's repair ships weeks—more probably months—to handle them without proper base support.

"He's altering course again, Skipper," her tac officer reported tersely. "I don't— *Jesus!*" Another double broadside spat from the Manticoran destroyer, and at least half the incoming birds carried jammers and penetration aids, not warheads. They played merry hell with *Kerebin*'s point defense, and Stellingetti swore again as yet another laser smashed into her ship's hull.

"Graser Nine's down!" her chief engineer reported from Damage Control. "We've got heavy casualties on the mount, Citizen Captain!" There was a pause, then. "Collateral damage to Sidewall Generators Fifteen and Seventeen. We may lose Seventeen completely."

"This son-of-a-bitch is good, Skipper," the tac officer said.

"Yeah, and it's my fault for screwing around with him this way!" Stellingetti snarled. She could make that admission, since People's Commissioner Reidel—who, in Stellingetti's considered opinion, was an unmitigated asshole—was away on *Achmed* for a conference with Citizen Commodore Jurgens. Which meant she could at least fight her ship without worrying about being second-guessed . . . and that she could be honest with her officers.

Citizen Commander Edwards only grunted from his

471

station at Tactical, but they both knew she was right. Their much heavier laser heads had scored at least three times on the enemy destroyer, despite her preposterously efficient point defense, and her falling acceleration indicated serious impeller damage. But missile duels with Manticorans usually worked out in the Manties' favor. Stellingetti knew that, yet she'd hoped to pick this one off without closing to energy range where a single lucky hit could have catastrophic consequences.

It wasn't working out that way. *Kerebin* was still winning—she was so much bigger and tougher that any other outcome was inconceivable—but while she crushed the Manty, the Manty was shooting big, nasty holes in *her*. And, Stellingetti conceded angrily, the damned merchies were running like hell. It wouldn't save them in the end— probably—but they were scattering in all directions while their tiny escort fought its desperate, hopeless battle to cover their flight. Against a single raider, their rapidly diverging vectors would have given at least three of them an excellent chance of escaping.

But *Kerebin* wasn't alone. Her two nearest neighbors were already closing in, summoned by Stellingetti's initial sighting report, and they'd undoubtedly passed the word to *their* neighbors, as well. The pickets were spread so wide it would take even the closest another hour to get here, but particle densities were low (for hyper-space) in the Selker Rift, and that wouldn't be long enough for the merchies to disappear from *Kerebin's* gravitics before help arrived.

Or that was true for *three* of them, anyway. The one Tactical had originally assumed was a battlecruiser might just pull it off. She was generating delta vee at an amazing rate for a merchie, and Stellingetti wondered what the hell she was. She certainly *wasn't* the warship CIC had initially called her. No Manty battlecruiser would run away, leaving a single destroyer to cover her flight.

No, that had to be a merchant ship, and Stellingetti felt a cold chill as a thought occurred to her. Whatever it was, it mounted excellent point defense as well as a military-grade drive, and she was abruptly glad it did. The entire picket line had been coasting towards Silesia under total EmCon at barely 40,000 KPS to allow other traffic—traveling at the maximum 44,000 KPS local conditions imposed—to overtake, when the small convoy strayed into *Kerebin*'s sights, and Stellingetti had thrown her entire opening salvo at the "battlecruiser" on the assumption that it was her most dangerous foe. Its defenses had stopped a lot of her birds, despite its surprise, yet she'd scored at least three direct hits. If it *hadn't* mounted point defense, she would have blown it right out of space, and if it was what she suddenly suspected it was . . .

"All right, John," she told Edwards grimly. "No more screwing around. Rapid fire on all tubes." She hated burning through ammunition that way with the task force so far from resupply, but unless she swamped the destroyer's active defenses, this would take all damned day.

"Aye, Skipper. Going to rapid fire now."

"Helm, come to two-six-oh, maximum accel. Close the range."

"Coming to two-six-oh, maximum accel, aye."

Kerebin swerved towards her maddeningly effective opponent, and Stellingetti watched her plot for a moment, then commed the Combat Information Center direct.

"CIC, Citizen Commander Herrick."

"Jake, this is the skipper. Have someone compare Target One's emission signature to our data on the Manties' *Atlas*-class passenger liners."

"Pass—" Herrick broke off. "Christ, Skipper! If that's an *Atlas*, she could have up to five thousand passengers on board, and we hit her clean at least three times!"

"Tell me about it," Stellingetti said grimly, watching her intensifying fire tear at the destroyer even as another pair of bomb-pumped lasers chewed into her own ship. "I'll be back to you, Jake. Things are getting a little hectic up here."

*   *   *

Margaret Fuchien slammed her fists together, eyes burning with shame as she glared down at Annabelle Ward's tactical display. *Artemis'* missiles might have made the difference between death and survival for *Hawkwing* . . . if she'd been allowed to fire them. But Commander Usher's harsh orders had been unequivocal, and he'd been right. If *Artemis* fired on the Peep, the Peep would certainly—and justifiably—return fire, and the unarmored liner's weapons were intended to deal with pirates of cruiser size or smaller. No one in her worst nightmares had ever anticipated her going toe-to-toe with a Peep *battlecruiser.* Even if *Artemis* and *Hawkwing* won, the liner would be hammered to scrap, and she had almost three thousand passengers on board. Fuchien couldn't endanger those passengers by trying to help *Hawkwing,* and so she was running at her best acceleration while the destroyer died to cover her flight.

Her earbug buzzed with a priority message. She punched to accept it, and her engineer's harsh voice burned in her ear.

"I've reached Main Hyper, Skipper," he said grimly. "It's a mess down here. Half the power runs are out, we've lost pressure, and we've got fourteen dead."

Fuchien closed her eyes in anguish. The Peep's initial broadside had taken all of them by surprise. She couldn't imagine what an enemy battlecruiser had been doing lying absolutely doggo here in the middle of the Rift, but it had paid off for the bastards. With their impellers and active sensors down, there'd been no emissions signature to warn *Hawkwing*—or *Artemis*—until they launched, and they'd obviously misread *Artemis* for a battlecruiser. That was all that had prevented *Hawkwing*'s instant destruction, and Ward had done almost impossibly well to stop seventy-five percent of the incoming fire. Fuchien knew that, but the five bomb-pumped lasers which had gotten through had done grievous damage. By God's mercy none of her passengers had been killed, but thirty of her crew were confirmed dead, she'd lost three beta nodes and two of her outsized lifeboats, and one of the hits had burned straight into Main Hyper.

"The generator?" Fuchien asked harshly, refusing to let herself think about her dead.

"Not good, Skip." Commander Cheney's voice was flat. "We lost both upper-stage governors; their molycircs fried when the power runs went. The basic system's intact, but if we try to go higher than the delta bands, the harmonics'll rip us apart."

"Damn," Fuchien whispered. She opened her eyes and stabbed another look at Ward's plot. The Peep was charging the destroyer now, bearing down on her at maximum acceleration, and *Hawkwing* was too lamed to hold the range open. She might last another fifteen minutes; every second beyond that would require a special miracle. When she was gone, the Peeps would be coming after *Artemis*, and if Fuchien couldn't climb higher than the delta bands, there was no way in hell she could outrun them. She could match them kilometer for kilometer in actual velocity, but she'd been caught in the delta bands because the accompanying freighters could go no higher. From Cheney's report, *she* couldn't either, now, and that was going to be fatal. Unlike her, the Peeps could still pop up into the epsilon or zeta bands, overfly her easily, then drop back down into the deltas right on top of her.

The captain made herself look away from the plot as more missiles tore down on the destroyer in her wake. She couldn't let herself think about Usher and his people. It was her job to save her passengers and her ship, to make *Hawkwing*'s sacrifice *mean* something, but how—?

"Helm, take us to maximum military power," she said, and felt her officers' shock, despite their desperate circumstances, for *Artemis* had never maxed her drive since her trials. At maximum military power, the failsafes were off-line, leaving zero tolerance for compensator fluctuation, and if the compensator failed, every human being aboard *Artemis*, including Fuchien's passengers, would die. But—

"Aye, aye, Skipper. Coming to maximum military power."

Fuchien held her breath as her helmsman redlined his impellers, but *Artemis* took the load like a champion. Fuchien could feel her beautiful ship strain, stretching every sinew to meet her harsh demands, and wanted to weep, for she already knew it would be too little. Yet it was the only chance she had. She couldn't climb to evade the Peeps, but if she could open the range enough, put enough distance between her and the enemy's sensors while *Hawkwing* delayed them, she might be able to *dive* far enough. If she dropped a couple of bands—or even clear back into n-space—then cut her drive and all active emissions, she might avoid the bastards yet.

Might.

"There go *Hawkwing*'s forward impellers!" someone groaned, and Fuchien clenched her jaw as she tried to think of something—*anything!*—more she might do.

"Skipper, I'm showing another bogey!" Ward announced, and Fuchien shook herself.

"Another Peep?" she asked harshly.

"I don't think—" Ward broke off, then shook her head. "It's not a warship at all, Skipper. It's a merchantman."

"A *merchantman?* Where?" Ward highlighted the bogey on her plot, and Fuchien's eyes widened. It *was* a merchantman, closing from starboard, and it was headed straight for *Artemis*. Closing velocity was already over thirty thousand KPS, and the bogey was accelerating at a full two hundred gravities. But that was crazy! Even civilian sensors had to be able to pick up the detonation of laser heads at this range, and any sane merchant skipper should be running the other way as fast as her ship would go.

"Com, warn her off!" Fuchien ordered. There was no point at all in adding another ship to the Peeps' bag. The unknown freighter was still light-minutes away, and Fuchien turned to her own ship's survival rather than wait out the com delay. She punched for Cheney again.

"Sid, what's your best estimate for repairs?"

"Repairs?" Cheney laughed bitterly. "Forget it. We don't begin to have the spares for this kind of damage. It'd take a fully equipped repair ship a week just to run them up."

"All right. You say it's just the upper-stage governors?"

"I *think* that's all," Cheney corrected. "That and the power runs. But we're still tearing things apart down here, and working in skinnies—" Fuchien could almost see his shrug.

"I need to know soonest, Sid. If we can't go up, we'll have to go down, and I need to know if the generator'll stand a crash translation."

"A *crash* translation?" Cheney sounded doubtful. "Skip, I can't guarantee she'll hold together through that even if I don't *see* anything else wrong. We took an awful spike through the control systems, and if they're not a hundred percent when you try that, we're all dead."

"We may all be dead if I *don't* try it," Fuchien said grimly. "Just get me the best info you can as quick as you can."

"Yes, Ma'am."

"Oh, Jesus." Annabelle Ward's whisper was a prayer, and Fuchien looked up just in time to see HMS *Hawkwing* vanish from the display with sickening suddenness. She stared at the empty spot for a long, terrible moment, then licked her lips.

"Would we see life pod transponders at this range, Anna?" she asked very quietly.

"No, Ma'am," the tac officer replied, equally quietly. "But I doubt there are any. She went off the display too fast, and I read an awful sharp energy bloom. I think it was her fusion bottle, Skipper."

"God have mercy on them," Margaret Fuchien whispered. *And now it's our turn,* a small, still voice said in her brain. "All right, Anna. Do your best with point defense if they get close enough to fire on us, but for God's sake, don't shoot back at them!"

"Skipper, I can't stop a battlecruiser from blowing us

apart eventually. We *might* last a while against just her chaser tubes, but we'll never stand more than a half-dozen full broadsides."

"I know. But their accel isn't that much higher than ours. They'll need the better part of an hour just to catch up—*Hawkwing* bought us that much—and as soon as Sid tells me it's safe, I'm going for a crash translation down to the beta bands. I'll risk a couple of chaser salvos first if it takes him that long to tell me go or no-go on the maneuver."

"All right, Skipper. I'll do what I can." Ward punched commands into her console, deploying missile decoys, and then kicked three EW drones over the side. The drones were each programmed to duplicate *Artemis'* current, wounded impeller signature, and she sent them racing off on widely divergent courses. Their power wouldn't last long, and they were unlikely to fool the Peeps even that long, but the delay while the enemy sorted out which were which might buy Engineering a few more precious minutes.

"Skipper, that merchie's still coming on," she reported. She picked up a faint transmission and put her computers on-line to enhance it, then shook her head. "It's an Andy, Ma'am."

"What is this—a wormhole junction?" Stellingetti growled, glaring at her repeater plot. Its reduced size made things appear closer together than they actually were, and she glared at the new bogey closing on her fleeing prey. The plot was further confused by the Manty's EW drones, but *Kerebin* had been close enough to see them launch and CIC had managed to keep track of them as they came on-line. Knowing which were false targets allowed her to ignore them to concentrate on the real one, and the battlecruiser plunged after it. Battle damage had reduced her own acceleration by five percent, but she was smaller than her prey, and she could still pull a higher accel than the Manty could.

"Who's that coming up behind us?"

"I think that's *Durandel* in front, Skipper," Edwards replied. "The bearing's about right, and her accel is cranked too high for a battlecruiser. That's probably *Achmed* astern of her."

"Is *Durandel* in com range?"

"Barely, under these conditions," Stellingetti's com officer said.

"Order her to slow down and recover our search and rescue pinnaces."

"Aye, Citizen Captain."

Stellingetti didn't expect her pinnaces to recover very many Manties, but at least some life pods had blasted clear before the destroyer blew up. Those people were no longer enemies; they were only a handful of human beings lost in the middle of unthinkable immensity. If they weren't picked up right now, they never would be, and Marie Stellingetti refused to abandon anyone to that sort of death.

"Who the hell is this newcomer, John?"

"From her impeller strength, she's another merchie," Edwards replied, "and I'm picking up an Andermani transponder."

"An *Andy?*" Stellingetti shook her head. "Wonderful. Just wonderful! Why would an Andy be maneuvering to match vectors with a Manticoran with a battlecruiser on its ass?"

"I don't know, Skip." The tactical officer punched a query into his system and shook his head. "It's a horse race. Whoever's driving that ship is good, and she's running some heavy-duty risks with a civilian drive. Target One's outaccelerating her, but she's got the angle on his track. It looks like she'll match vectors with him about the time we come into extreme missile range."

"Damn!" The citizen captain gnawed on a thumbnail and, for the first time, wished Commissioner Reidel were aboard. It wasn't like Stellingetti to evade responsibility, but if the Committee of Public Safety was going to saddle her with its damned spy, the son-of-a-bitch could at least make himself useful by telling her how to clean this mess

up! Her orders required her to "use any means necessary" to prevent any Manticoran-flag vessel from escaping
with word of the task force's presence, but when Citizen Admiral Giscard and People's Commissioner Pritchart
wrote that order, they'd never contemplated having a
passenger liner on their hands. Stellingetti's conscience
would never forgive her if she killed several thousand
civilians, yet her orders left no option. If the liner wouldn't
stop, she had to destroy it, and her soul shriveled at the
thought. No doubt Public Information would claim the
ship had been armed—which it was—and that its armament and refusal to stop had made it a legitimate target. Public Information was good at blaming victims for
their fate. But Stellingetti would still have to look into
her mirror every day.

And what was the damned Andermani up to? Her
orders also required her to steer clear of Andies, and even
to assist them against other raiders. But if that freighter
insisted on poking its nose into this, it would be sitting
right there, witness to the entire incident if she blew away
the liner. And what did she do then? Did she kill the
Andy, too, just to finish off any witnesses who might dispute Public Information's version of what had happened
out here?

"Com, warn the Andy off! Tell her to stand clear, or
I can't be responsible for the consequences."

"Aye, Skipper."

"Forget about any crash translations, Skipper," Sid
Cheney said flatly. "We've got two bad sectors in the
primary data line, the main computer's fried, and the
auxiliary took its own hit from that spike. You throw a
crash translation at it, and the odds are at least seventy-
thirty that either the backup computer or the control runs
will blow half way through."

"How long to replace the bad control sectors?" Fuchien
demanded.

"Even if I replace them, we've still got the computer
damage to worry about."

"I know." Fuchien was grasping at straws, because straws were all she had left. "But if we can take at least part of the uncertainty out of the equation—"

"I've got crews on it now, but it's a twelve-hour job by the manual. I'm cutting every corner I can, and I think I can make it in six, but that's not gonna be good enough, is it?"

"No, Sid," Margaret Fuchien said softly.

"Sorry, Maggie." The engineer's voice was even softer than hers. "I'll do my best."

"I know."

Fuchien forced her shoulders to straighten and drew a deep breath. Ward's EW drones hadn't fooled the pursuing Peep. They'd be into missile range in another eighteen minutes, and with an unreliable hyper generator, there was no way *Artemis* could translate down quickly enough to drop off the Peep's sensors.

She looked back at Ward's plot, and her brow furrowed. The Andermani was closing on her ship quickly, coming in at an angle that would match vectors in just under fifteen minutes. She wouldn't be able to pace the liner long—even with damaged beta nodes, *Artemis* could out accelerate any bulk carrier ever built—but at the moment their courses merged, they'd be moving at almost the same velocity. She had to admire the ship handling of whoever had pulled that off, but for the life of her, she still couldn't see any reason to do it in the first place.

"Anything from the Peeps yet?" she asked Com.

"No. Ma'am."

The reply sounded as tense as Fuchien felt, and she smiled raggedly and made herself take a turn around the command deck. There really wasn't any choice, was there? When the Peep got into missile range, all she could do was heave-to and surrender. Anything else would be madness.

"Skipper!" It was her com officer. "We're being hailed by the Andy!"

"Well, they've made rendezvous," Edwards observed. "Now what?"

"I don't know. Did she respond to our warn-off at all?"

"No, Skipper," Com replied. "Not a word."

"What the *hell* is she playing at?" Stellingetti fumed. She shoved herself angrily back in her command chair and glared at her plot. Whatever the Andermani vessel's ultimate intentions, she'd just screwed *Kerebin*'s attack options all to hell. She was too close to the Manty. Edwards' missiles were as likely to home in on her as on the Manty at this range, and the Manty skipper knew it. He'd cut his own accel to match the Andy's, riding just ahead of her to use her for a shield, and Stellingetti gritted her teeth.

"The Andies won't like our raiding commerce this close to the Empire, Skipper," Edwards pointed out quietly. "You don't suppose this joker's trying to warn us off, do you?"

"He's in for a hell of a surprise if he is," Stellingetti grated.

The battlecruiser continued to race closer, eating up the distance between herself and the other two ships. Far astern of her, the cruiser *Durandel* launched her own pinnaces to assist *Kerebin*'s SAR efforts. They'd already picked up over eighty members of *Hawkwing*'s crew, an amazingly high number which spoke volumes for the determination of the searching pinnaces, yet the cruiser's rescue operations had effectively taken her out of the hunt. The battlecruiser *Achmed*, however, had come rumbling past *Durandel* over forty minutes ago, with her velocity building steadily, and she still had an excellent chance to overtake *Kerebin* and *Artemis*.

Other ships of the People's Navy were also closing in, and one of them had already locked onto the Manticoran freighter *Voyager* and begun closing rapidly while another peeled off to pursue RMMS *Palimpsest*. The entire situation was wildly confused, but the Peep warships were clearly in control of it, and the distance between *Kerebin* and *Artemis* sped downward.

*   *   *

"Coming up on eight hundred thousand klicks," Edwards announced, and Stellingetti grunted. Another light-second and a half, and she could bring the Manty under fire with her energy weapons. The Andy's interference wouldn't save the liner from *that*, and when the Manty captain realized he couldn't possibly get away, he'd have no choice but to—

"*Missile trace!*" Edwards screamed, and Marie Stellingetti half-rose from her command chair in disbelief. *It wasn't possible!* That titanic salvo couldn't be from the Manty, or she would never have abandoned the destroyer! They had to be from the *Andy*, but how—?

"Hard skew port!" she shouted. "Return fire on the Andy!"

Kerebin snapped around to her left, rolling frantically to interpose her wedge against the incoming holocaust, but there was no escape—not from that many missiles. She got a single broadside of her own into space before her writhing evasion maneuvers threw her tubes off target, but no one aboard had time to see what—if anything—her fire accomplished. The missiles roaring down on her would arrive a full twenty seconds before her own did. They streaked in, spreading out to englobe the battlecruiser, and there was nothing she could do to escape. ECM fought to confuse them, countermissiles roared out, laser clusters trained onto the incoming laser heads and fired with desperate intensity, and almost a hundred missiles lost track or vanished in the fireballs of successful intercepts. But five hundred others kept coming, and as they reached attack position and detonated, their X-ray lasers engulfed *Kerebin* like a dragon's breath.

They didn't all reach attack position at once. They came in in sequence, and it took almost nine seconds for all of them to detonate, but the trailers were simply wasted effort. Five seconds after the first laser head detonated, PNS *Kerebin* and every man and woman aboard her had become an expanding ball of plasma.

• CHAPTER THIRTY-NINE

Honor Harrington made herself sit motionless as the damage reports washed over her. A part of her was horrified at what she'd just done, but a *Sultan*-class battlecruiser was simply too dangerous to fool around with. She'd *had* to take it out with her first salvo, even knowing that so much overkill virtually guaranteed there would be no survivors from her target, and so she'd just blown over two thousand people to plasma without giving them any chance at all.

But the Peep hadn't gone without striking back. Her single broadside had sent twenty missiles slashing towards *Wayfarer* and *Artemis*, and the liner's proximity had forced Honor to make her own ship an even easier target. If any of those missiles had gone after *Artemis* and gotten through, they could easily have destroyed her, and with her the very civilians Honor was fighting to protect. And so she'd turned *Wayfarer* directly across the liner's stern, deliberately sucking *Kerebin's* dying vengeance in upon her. Her missile defense crews had done well, but she'd never had a proper warship's point defense, and eight laser heads had gotten through.

"We've got ninety-two confirmed dead so far, Skipper," Rafe Cardones said harshly. "Sickbay reports over sixty additional casualties, and they're still bringing them in."

"Material damage?"

"We've lost Grasers One, Three, and Five out of the port broadside," Tschu replied from Damage Control Central. "Missiles One and Seven are gone, as well, and Five and Nine are available only in local control. LAC

484

One's launch bays are totaled, but at least they were empty. Gravitic Two is gone, I've lost three sidewall generators, also from the port sidewall, and Impeller Two's lost a beta node."

"Skipper, I'm reporting negative function from Cargo One," Jennifer Hughes added urgently, and Honor felt her belly knot.

"Harry?"

"I'm checking now. We don't show a rail malfunction, but—" The engineer broke off and mouthed a silent curse. "Correction. We *do* show a malfunction—it's just not with the launch system." He studied his monitors, then shook his head. "The rails are still up, Skipper; it's the cargo doors. That hit in the after impeller ring must've sent a surge through their power train. The port door's cycled halfway shut, and the starboard door's almost as far in."

"Can we reopen them?"

"Not soon," Tschu said grimly. He tapped a command into his console, then tried a second and grimaced. "Looks like they only stopped where they did because their motors burned out. It *could* be just the control systems on the port door—I can't be certain from the remotes—but the starboard door's definitely burned. If it *is* the controls for the port one, we might be able to rig new runs and get it back open. That would give you two clear launch rails, but that hit ripped hell out of the hull, and I don't have any surviving visuals in the area to tell me how much wreckage is in the way. Repairs are going to take at least an hour—assuming they're possible at all." He met her eyes squarely from her small com screen. "Sorry, Skipper. That's the best I can do."

"Understood." Honor's mind raced. Her ship was pathetically slow compared to the Peep warship still charging towards her, the brutal damage to her port broadside reduced her close-range firepower by a quarter, and the jammed cargo doors amputated her ability to deploy pods. Even if Tschu had time to get the port door open again, she'd lost two-thirds of her long-range punch. Her chance to survive against a regular warship which got inside her missile envelope was virtually nil, and as the first Peep battlecruiser had just demonstrated, even a ship she managed to kill with missiles could still take *Wayfarer* with it.

She still had her second LAC squadron—that was why she'd exposed her port side, rather than the starboard launch bays—and she could use them here in the Selker. With them to support her, she'd be willing to take on a heavy cruiser even without her missile pods, but they wouldn't be enough against a battlecruiser. Even if she managed to destroy something that size, it would smash *Wayfarer* up so badly any of the other Peep warships could take her with ease.

"I've got Captain Fuchien, Skipper," Fred Cousins reported, and Honor shook herself. She held up one hand at Cousins long enough to look Jennifer Hughes in the eye.

"How long before the Peeps come in on us?"

"We can probably stay away from them for another three hours," Hughes replied. "I don't know what happened to that heavy cruiser—she slowed down and dropped clear off the plot twenty-six minutes ago—but that second *Sultan's* coming up fast. It's a cinch she's got us on passive, and her sustained velocity advantage will run us down eventually."

Honor drew a deep breath as her options clarified with brutal simplicity. It wouldn't be a heavy cruiser when the attack came in, she thought grimly, then waved at Cousins. "Put Captain Fuchien through," she said, and Margaret Fuchien's face replaced Tschu's on her com screen.

"Thank you, Captain—?" the civilian skipper said, and Honor smiled crookedly. There hadn't really been time for introductions before.

"Harrington, of Her Majesty's Armed Merchant Cruiser *Wayfarer*."

The other woman's eyes widened, but then she shook her head, like someone shrugging aside an irritating fly.

"What's your situation, Lady Harrington?" she asked.

Her own sensors had shown her the halo of atmosphere and water vapor which indicated massive hull breaching, and her optics showed her the gaping holes smashed in *Wayfarer's* flank and port quarter.

"We've got at least a hundred and fifty casualties," Honor told her flatly. "I've lost a third of my port broadside and most of my missile capability. We're trying to get the missiles back, but it doesn't look good. If you're thinking we can fight them off, I'm afraid you're wrong."

She felt the silence ripple out across her bridge as she said it. They'd all known already, but the finality of hearing their captain admit it aloud echoed in every mind. Fuchien's mouth tightened on the com screen, and she closed her eyes for a moment.

"Then I'm very much afraid we're in deep trouble, Milady," she said quietly. "My hyper generator's seriously damaged. I can't climb any higher, and my downward translation rate's been cut by something like eighty percent. Anything more than that, and the entire system is likely to pack in on us. Which means we can't run away from them, either."

"I see." Honor leaned back, ordering her face to remain calm while a skinsuited Nimitz crouched on the back of her chair. Her link to him carried her bridge crew's fear—and the discipline which held it at bay—to her, and she rubbed an eyebrow, making herself think. "In that case—" she began, when another voice cut suddenly into the circuit.

"This is Klaus Hauptman!" it snapped. "*Your* hyper generator's not damaged; why can't you take our passengers aboard *your* ship?"

Honor's lips thinned, and her eyes hardened. Hauptman's presence aboard *Artemis* came as a complete surprise, but the abrupt intrusion was so *typical* of him that she wanted to hit him.

"I'm speaking to Captain Fuchien," she said coldly. "Clear this channel immediately!"

"The hell you say!" Hauptman shot back, but then he

paused. She could almost see him throttling back his own temper, and his voice was marginally calmer when he went on. "My presence on this channel doesn't prevent you from speaking to Captain Fuchien," he said, "and my question remains. Why can't you take us off?"

"Because," Honor said with icy precision, "our nominal life-support capacity is three thousand individuals. We still have nineteen hundred crew aboard, and our enviro systems have also been damaged. I doubt I have sufficient long-term capacity for my own people, far less the entire company of your vessel. Now either clear this channel or keep your mouth *shut*, Sir!"

Klaus Hauptman's face suffused with fury, but he clamped his jaw, then raised his eyes from his com's blank screen to look at his daughter. No one else would have recognized the fear behind Stacey's controlled expression, but he knew her too well. He could almost *feel* that fear, and everything within him shouted to scream at Harrington, to threaten her, bully her—*bribe* her, if that was what it took!—to get his daughter to safety. But something in Stacey's own eyes froze the threats and bribes on his lips, and a dull, burning sense of shame he didn't really understand mingled with his rage when he looked back down at the com.

"Now, Captain," Honor went on more calmly. "What does *your* life support look like?"

"Undamaged," Fuchien said, only her slight, humorless smile betraying her reaction to the way Honor had slapped her employer down. "We've lost three beta nodes, some of our lifeboats, and ten percent of our point defense, but aside from that—and the hyper generator—we're in decent shape. So far."

"What's your passenger list?"

"We're running light. I've got about twenty-seven hundred, plus the crew."

"Understood." Honor rubbed the tip of her nose, feeling Nimitz's whiskers brush gently against the back of her neck while his support poured into her, then nodded.

"All right, Captain, here's what we're going to do. I'm going to transfer all nonessential personnel to your ship, since you've got the life support to handle them. Then—"

"Wait a minute!" the interruption exploded out of Klaus Hauptman almost against his will. "What d'you mean, transfer people *to* this ship?! Why—"

"*Mr. Hauptman, be silent!*" Honor snapped. "I have neither the time nor the patience for your interruptions, Sir!"

Silence crackled for a brief eternity, and she returned her attention to Fuchien, whose face already showed the beginnings of understanding. In his stateroom, Klaus Hauptman swore with silent, bitter venom, furious at her tone. But then he looked up at Stacey again, and this time he saw something besides fear in her eyes. He saw . . . disappointment, and then she looked away from him without a word.

"As I say, I intend to transfer all nonessential personnel to your vessel," Honor went on. "I will also be detaching six LACs to support and cover you. As soon as the transfer is complete, you and the LACs will shut down all emissions. *All* of them, Captain Fuchien. I want you to turn your ship into a hole in space, do you understand me?"

"Yes." The word came out of Fuchien in a near-whisper, and Honor made herself smile.

"Before you shut down, I'll deploy an EW drone programmed to match your emissions. *Wayfarer* will break away from you, taking that drone with her. With any luck, the Peeps will think we're remaining in company and leave you alone. As soon as you're certain they have, I want you to begin a gradual downward translation. Drop into n-space and stay there for at least ten days. Ten days, Captain! Repair your generator and put as much space between you and this volume of h-space as you can before you go back into hyper."

"You *coward!*" Klaus Hauptman hissed. He was out of control, and he knew it, and it shamed him, but he couldn't help himself. It wasn't fear for himself; it was fear for his daughter which drove him. "You're not even going to *try* to defend this ship! You're just going to run away and *hope* no one spots us! You're abandoning us to save your own gutless—"

"Daddy, shut up!" Hauptman whirled from the com, for the icy voice wasn't Honor Harrington's. It was Stacey's, and her eyes flamed with a fury he'd never seen in them before.

"But she's—"

"She's about to *die* for you, Daddy," Stacey Hauptman said in a voice of iron. "Surely that should be enough even for you!"

Hauptman staggered, wounded as no one had ever wounded him, and his soul shriveled at the look in his daughter's eyes.

"But—" He swallowed. "But it's *you* I'm worried ab—" he began again, but Stacey only reached past him and slammed her hand down on the com disconnect. And then she turned her back and walked out of his stateroom without another word.

"He's off the link, Milady," Fuchien said quietly. "I'm sorry. You don't need that kind—"

"Don't worry about it." Honor shook her head, then glanced at Rafe Cardones. "Start the transfers. I want all our wounded and every nonessential member of this crew aboard that ship in thirty minutes. Be sure Dr. Holmes and all our POWs go with them."

"Yes, Ma'am." Cardones nodded sharply, and she turned back to Fuchien.

"We'll do our best to draw them after us. How good are your sensors?"

"We've got the same electronic suite the *Homer*-class battlecruisers started the war with, and we've received most of the Phase One and Two upgrades, including the decoys and EW drones—everything but the stealth systems and FTL com. Those were too highly classified."

"That good?" Honor was impressed, and she rubbed the tip of her nose again. "That's better than I'd hoped for. You should have a significant advantage over the Peeps, then."

"I know," Fuchien said. "They must've been lying doggo under tight EmCon when we blundered right into them. If they weren't, *Hawkwing* should've seen them even if we—"

"What did you say?" Fuchien frowned in surprise, for Honor's face had suddenly gone paper-white. "Did you say *Hawkwing*?" she demanded harshly.

"Yes, Milady. *Hawkwing*, Commander Usher. Did . . . did you know the Commander?"

"No." Honor closed her eyes, and her nostrils flared. Then she shook her head. "No," she repeated in a low voice, "but I knew *Hawkwing*. She was my first hyper-capable command."

"I'm sorry, Milady," Fuchien said softly. "I don't know what to—" It was her turn to shake her head. "I know it's not much, Milady, but she and Commander Usher are the only reason we even had a chance to run. My tac officer . . . doesn't think there were any survivors."

"I see." Honor had commanded five starships. Now the second had been scrapped, the first had been destroyed, and the last was about to die with her. She allowed herself one more moment to grieve for the ship which had once meant all the universe to her, then opened her eyes once more, and her soprano voice was calm and even. "All right, Captain. I'll be transferring at least one of my surgeons, as many SBAs as I can spare, and all our wounded to you. Do you have the facilities to handle them?"

"We'll damned well *make* the facilities, Milady."

"Thank you. Now, about the LACs. They're a new model, and the six of them can probably stand up to a heavy cruiser for you if they have to. They don't have hyper generators or Warshawski sails, however. They can't enter a grav wave, and you'll have to take their crews off and destroy them when you begin translating."

"Then you should take them with you," Fuchien said. "If we're going to run for n-space anyway and they're powerful enough to be that much use—"

"They aren't powerful enough to make the difference

against a battlecruiser," Honor said, the words a tacit admission of the truth both women knew. "They'd be destroyed either way, and at least this way you'll have some cover if another Peeps stumbles over you." *And I can at least get* their *people out alive.*

"I—" Fuchien began, then stopped herself. "You're right, of course," she said quietly.

"I'm glad you agree." Honor allowed herself a brief smile. "I think that's about everything, then, and I have things to attend to here. I'll make only one final request of you, if I may."

"Anything, Milady."

"Please stand by to receive a data transfer for the Admiralty. I'd like the First Lord to know what we accomplished before—" She shrugged.

"Of course, Milady. I'll deliver it in person. You have my word."

"Thank you." Honor's plot showed the LACs launching from her undamaged starboard side and the first pinnaces and cutters moving towards *Artemis*. The liner's shuttles were launching as well, to aid in the transfer, and she nodded.

"In that case, Captain Fuchien, let's be about it," she said quietly, and cut the link.

The frantic flow of personnel from *Wayfarer* to *Artemis* went with breakneck speed, for time was critically short. Despite the pressure, Rafael Cardones and Scotty Tremaine managed to impose a draconian order on the transfers, and the list of evacuees Cardones had drawn up at Honor's order was inflexible.

All three of John Kanehama's assistants went, for *Artemis*' stealthy escape maneuvers would require as much astrogation assistance as she could get. Fred Cousins and his entire department went, for there would be no one for *Wayfarer* to communicate with once she separated from *Artemis*. Harold Sukowski and Chris Hurlman went, as did every one of *Vaubon*'s surrendered officers. Hydroponics specialists, extra sick berth attendants, and Marines who would not be needed for boarding parties went. Logistics officers and storekeepers, signal yeomen and quartermasters, personnel officers and cooks—every human being not essential to fight the ship or repair her damages went, and if they were relieved to be spared, every one of them was also consumed with guilt for leaving their shipmates behind.

But not all of those on the list went.

Master-at-Arms Thomas was dead, as was his senior assistant, and none of *Wayfarer*'s surviving police force thought to check the brig. Randy Steilman, Jackson Coulter, Elizabeth Showforth, Ed Illyushin, and Al Stennis had been given skinsuits when the ship went to battle stations. But they were still confined in their cells—which were located at the core of the ship and safer than almost any other place aboard her, anyway—and brig skinnies didn't have coms . . . which meant no one heard their screams for release.

Scotty Tremaine was supposed to go, along with Horace Harkness. There would be no need for a Flight Ops department with all but two of their pinnaces and all their LACs away. But neither Tremaine nor Harkness had any intention of leaving their ship, and Tremaine sent two of his regular pinnace pilots and their flight engineer in their place.

Ginger Lewis was supposed to go, too. She was still on the restricted-duty list, but she knew Harold Tschu would need every available hand to try to clear the jammed cargo doors. And so she ignored the order to board a pinnace, passing her place to a twenty-two-year-old computer tech on his first deployment, and made her way with white-faced calm to Damage Control Central.

Yoshiro Tatsumi was another who turned down the chance of escape. He'd been detailed to accompany Dr. Holmes, but he quietly swapped places with another SBA. Dr. Ryder had stood by him when he needed her; now she would need him.

Other men and women made the same decisions,

turning their backs on the way home. In some cases it was courage, in others defiance, but for all of them, it was also loyalty. Loyalty to their ship, to their fellow crewmen, to individual officers and duty, and—above all—to their captain. Honor Harrington needed them, and they refused to leave her.

Klaus Hauptman sat in his stateroom, hunched in a deeply cushioned chair while he held his face in his hands, and shame filled him. Not the anger which so often drove him: *shame*. Raw, biting shame. The kind that crawled up inside a man and destroyed him. A part of him knew it was his terrible fear for his daughter which had driven him to defy Honor Harrington, to rail and curse at her, yet that offered no comfort, no shield against the hurt shock, the disbelief that he could do such a thing, he'd seen in Stacey's eyes. The one person in the universe whose good opinion truly mattered to him had looked into his soul and turned away from what she saw there, and he felt his eyes burn with the tears he somehow refused to shed.

Yet behind the look in Stacey's eyes was the cold contempt he'd heard in Harrington's voice. It wasn't the first time he'd heard it, but this time he'd *deserved* it. He knew that, with no ability to tell himself differently. And in facing that poison-bitter truth, he was forced to face his memories of their earlier encounter, as well. Forced to admit, possibly for the first time in his adult life, that he'd lied to himself. He, who'd always thought he could face himself unflinchingly, knew better now. Harrington had been right the first time, too, he thought wretchedly. Right to reject the pressure he'd tried to bring to bear, right to feel contempt for him—even right to threaten a man who could stoop so low as to use her parents against her out of nothing more than choler and pique and offended pride. A man who could do that without even *realizing* how contemptible it was, because such considerations meant nothing beside his anger of the moment.

He sat there, alone with the acid reality of what he was, and all his wealth and power and position and accomplishments were no armor at all against himself.

Harold Sukowski trotted down the passenger ship's grav-generator-equipped boarding tube with one arm protectively around Chris Hurlman. The commander had fully recovered from her physical injuries in her time aboard *Wayfarer*, and she'd come far further back from her psychological wounds than he would have believed possible. But she was still fragile, without the tough, devil-may-care humor he'd known for so many years, and he kept her close, shielding her from any casual contact in the chaos about them.

Margaret Fuchien had detailed stewards and any other crewman she could find to act as guides for the influx of refugees. It was essential to clear the boat bay galleries as quickly as possible, and *Artemis'* personnel did their best to keep the evacuees moving without pause. But there was a knot in the flow as Sukowski and Hurlman emerged from the tube on Shannon Foraker's heels. All of *Wayfarer*'s POWs had been sent over together, with a single Marine to ride herd on them, and Sukowski's head came up quickly as he saw the instant anger on the faces of their waiting guides. Anger turned almost as quickly to hate—hate for the people who wore the uniform of the Navy which had just destroyed *Hawkwing* and killed thirty of their own— and the senior steward in charge of their group opened his mouth, face curdled with rage. But Sukowski stepped quickly forward, moving between Warner Caslet and Denis Jourdain at the head of the prisoners, and his eyes were hard.

"Shut your face," he told the steward in cold, biting tones. The man twitched in confusion as the scar-faced, mutilated man in a plain shipsuit spoke in an icy command voice, and Sukowski drove ahead before he could continue. "I'm Captain Harold Sukowski," he said in that same cold voice, and recognition of his own shipping line's fourth ranking captain sparked in the steward's eyes. "These people saved my life—and my exec's—from the butchers who took *Bonaventure* in Telmach. They also executed every one of the pigs who had us in custody, then lost their own ship trying to save another Manticoran vessel." He didn't mention exactly which vessel that had been. It didn't matter—and Caslet and Jourdain hadn't known when they went to *Wayfarer*'s rescue, anyway. "You will treat them with *respect*, Senior Steward. *Is that clear?*"

"Uh, yessir!" the steward blurted. "As you say, Sir!"

"Good. Now get us out of here to clear this gallery."

"Yes, Sir. If the Captain and . . . and his friends would follow me, please?"

The man led them off, and Sukowski felt a hand on his shoulder. He turned to see Caslet gazing at him, and their eyes met with a shared, bleak smile of understanding . . . and sorrow.

"Last boat, Skipper," Cardones announced. The exec was hoarse from passing orders, and Honor looked up with a nod from her conference with Jennifer Hughes. She spared time for one anguished glance at the back of her command chair, wishing desperately that she'd sent Nimitz across, as well. But he would no more leave her than Samantha would leave Harold Tschu—or than Honor would leave *him*. She might have had him forcibly removed, but she couldn't do it. She simply couldn't, and at least he was better off than Samantha. He had his skinsuit; Tschu hadn't been able to afford one, and he'd had to settle for a standard life-support module. But that much Honor had been able to improve upon. She still had the deluxe module she'd bought Nimitz before Paul designed his suit—the one with the built in antiradiation armor and the extended life support—and she'd insisted that Tschu take Samantha to her quarters and put her inside its greater protection.

Not, she thought grimly, that it would make that much difference in the end.

"How soon can we break away?" she asked.

"Any time, Skip." Cardones' smile was as grim as she felt. "That boat's not scheduled to come back. We're down to two pinnaces . . . and, of course, our life pods."

"Of course," Honor agreed with a ghost of true humor, then punched back into Damage Control Central.

"DCC, Senior Chief Lewis."

"Lewis? What are you doing down there?" Honor demanded in surprise.

"Commander Tschu has every warm body he can spare down in Cargo One, Ma'am, including Lieutenant Silvetti. I'm minding the store for them," Ginger said, deliberately misunderstanding her question, and Honor's lips quirked in a small, sad smile.

"All right, Senior Chief. Tell me how they're coming."

"The starboard motors are definitely frozen, Ma'am," Lewis said crisply. "They're completely shot; they'll need total replacement. Two of the port motors are still operable, and the third *may* be, but the entire control run's blown away between Frame Seven-Niner-Two and the stern plate. They're rigging new cable now, but they've got to clear wreckage to get it in, and two pods have come adrift from Number Four Rail. They'll have to get them tied down before they can even get at that portion of the problem."

"Time estimate?"

"Chief Engineer estimates a minimum of ninety minutes, Ma'am."

"Understood. Tell him to keep on it."

"Aye, aye, Ma'am."

Honor cut the circuit and looked at Jennifer Hughes. "Time to enemy intercept?"

"Missile range in two hours, five minutes."

"But she still has us only on gravitics?"

"At this range and under these conditions, that's all she can possibly have us on, Ma'am," Hughes said confidently.

"Very well." Honor turned to Cardones, who'd taken

over Communications after Cousins' departure. "Rafe, get me Captain Fuchien on the main screen."

"Yes, Ma'am."

The two-meter com screen on the command deck's forward bulkhead lit. Fuchien's face was grim, her eyes haunted, but she nodded courteously.

"It's time, Captain," Honor told her in a voice whose calm surprised even her. Perhaps it surprised *especially* her. "Move your ship ahead of us. I want you in our impeller shadow when your drive goes down."

"Yes, Milady," Fuchien said quietly, and Honor looked over her shoulder. "Deploy the EW drone, Jenny."

"Aye, aye, Ma'am."

Artemis slid in front of *Wayfarer* once more, riding directly ahead of her, and Honor turned to Senior Chief Coxswain O'Halley.

"This is going to have to be smartly done, Chief," she told him quietly, and her helmsman nodded his understanding. *Artemis* was so close the safety perimeter of her impeller wedge cleared *Wayfarer's* by barely sixty kilometers. She had to be, if she was going to hide her own impellers from the Peep battlecruiser behind the Q-ship's, but *Wayfarer* was still accelerating at over a hundred gravities. The tiniest helm error on her part when *Artemis'* wedge went down and Honor executed her breakaway maneuver could bring her own wedge into direct contact with the liner's hull, which would tear the other ship apart instantly.

"Understood, Ma'am," O'Halley said far more calmly than he could possibly feel, and Honor raised her eyes to the main plot, watching as *Artemis* settled exactly into the agreed upon position, then drew a deep breath and looked at Fuchien.

"Good luck, Captain," she said.

"God bless, Milady," Fuchien said softly, and the two captains, each with eyes filled by the pain of what duty required of them, nodded to one another.

"Very well," Honor Harrington said crisply, turning back to her own bridge. "*Execute!*"

• CHAPTER FORTY

Citizen Commodore Abraham Jurgens glared at the two light beads in his flag bridge plot. He'd known Marie Stellingetti and John Edwards well, known how good they'd been, and *Achmed* had had *Kerebin* on gravitics when the battlecruiser vanished. As far as Jurgens had been able to tell, she'd done everything right . . . yet she'd been destroyed, and he had no idea what the *hell* had happened. Nothing weaker than a starship's impeller signature would have been detectable at that range, and all he knew was that *Kerebin* had suddenly gone to evasive maneuvering, then vanished.

It wasn't supposed to be *like this!* he thought savagely. Like many of the PN's officers, he hated the Royal Manticoran Navy for what it had done to them. He wasn't like that idiot Waters, who saw butchering even merchant spacers as his holy duty in the Republic's cause, but he would shed no tears over them, either, and he'd seen the value of raiding Manty merchant shipping. He'd also expected it to be a relatively safe operation, yet half his battlecruiser division had just been wiped from the face of the universe, and he didn't even know how it had been done!

But you do *know, don't you?* he told himself. *Or, at least, you know* who *must have done it. That extra "merchantman" has to be a Manty Q-ship. God only knows what it's doing here—and He's also the only one who knows what the* hell *it could be armed with to punch* Kerebin *out that way—but you know that's what it is.*

He'd picked up enough information from *Durandel* as

he passed to know Stellingetti's "Target One" hadn't done the job; if it had that kind of firepower, it would have used it before *Kerebin* snuffed its destroyer consort. No, it had to have been the second ship, and that ship had a civilian-grade compensator, or it would have been running a hell of a lot faster than it was. So it had to be one of the Manties' "merchant cruisers," which meant it was far more fragile than his flagship. But it obviously carried something extraordinary in the way of armament, and the range had been eight hundred thousand kilometers when *Kerebin* died, well beyond energy range.

More of their damned missile pods? he wondered. *It could be, but how could a* merchie *put enough of them on tow? Even their SDs are limited to ten or so, and that shouldn't have been enough to just wipe* Kerebin *out that way. But even if that was what they did to her, they never slowed down enough to deploy more of them, so they can't do it to* me.

That was not his estimate, alone. Citizen Captain Holtz, *Achmed's* CO, and his own ops officer shared it. Yet Jurgens had no intention of walking into anything. He would approach carefully, with every missile defense system on-line. He would treat this ship as cautiously as if it were another battlecruiser—even a battleship—until he knew for *certain* that it couldn't do to him whatever it had done to *Kerebin*. But once he *was* certain—

"Target One shouldn't have slowed down," People's Commissioner Aston said quietly.

Jurgens turned his head to look at the chubby man in the uniform with no rank insignia. By and large, the task force had been fortunate in its people's commissioners. Eloise Pritchart had been allowed a remarkably free hand in their selection, and aside from one or two fools who'd been forced on her by their own sponsors—like Frank Reidel, the sole survivor from *Kerebin's* entire company—most of them were surprisingly competent and unusually human. Kenneth Aston was both of those things, and Jurgens nodded.

"You're right. The Q-ship's got a civilian compensator,

so she's pulling close to her max accel, and she's probably only got civilian-grade particle shielding, too. But Target One—" He shook his head. "She has to be a liner to produce the kind of accel we've already seen out of her, and they should have let her run for it. She's probably got the legs to get away, especially if the Q-ship can slow us down, and we're the only ship close enough to have either of them on sensors now. If they'd split up, we'd never have caught her."

"Unless they *couldn't* split up for some reason," Aston suggested.

"Unless they couldn't," Jurgens acknowledged. "I suppose it's possible *Kerebin* got a piece of her drive, but her acceleration was much higher before the Q-ship joined up. No," he shook his head. "Whoever's in command of the Q-ship has screwed up. He's trying to keep her close enough to 'protect' her."

"I agree." Aston nodded, but he also rubbed his double chin thoughtfully. "At the same time, he *did* destroy Citizen Captain Stellingetti's ship with remarkable speed, and if he has military-grade sensors, he may know we're the only ship which still has them on its plot. Could he be expecting to do the same thing to us?"

"He may," Jurgens said grimly. "If he took us out, then both of them could break contact, and we'd never find them again in all this garbage." He waved a hand at the flickering energy flux of hyper-space on the flag bridge's view screens. "We've even lost *Durandel* now, and the rest of the pickets who were close enough to respond are off chasing freighters. But if he thinks he's going to take *my* flagship without losing his ass in the process, he's sadly mistaken!"

"He's found another few gees of acceleration somewhere, Skipper," Jennifer Hughes said. "Revised time to missile range is now one hour, seventeen minutes."

Honor simply nodded acknowledgment. She'd done all she could. Tschu was laboring frantically in Cargo One, but the damage was worse than he'd initially thought, and he'd already lost six of his people: two crushed to death and four "merely" injured by one of the dismounted pods before it could be tied down. His original time estimate had been revised upward twice, and badly as she wanted to com him to urge him on, she knew it would have achieved nothing except to distract and delay him further. He'd tell her the moment he had anything to report.

Other damage control people had managed to put Missile Seven back into the central fire control net, and Ginger Lewis was doing an outstanding job in Damage Control Central. DCC was no job for any petty officer, however experienced she was, but Tschu needed every man and woman he could get for other jobs, and Lewis' voice was confident whenever she buzzed the bridge with another report. *Harry was certainly right about her ability*, Honor thought with a slight smile, and glanced at her repeater plot once more.

They were on their second EW drone now, and they'd need number three shortly. The drone's transponders required a fearsome amount of power to simulate the drive strength of an *Atlas*-class liner, and no drone could keep it up forever. But that was one reason Honor was holding the drones in so tight. It was also why she had Carolyn Wolcott maneuvering them in and out of *Wayfarer*'s grav shadow at random intervals. It must look like sloppy station keeping to the Peeps, but it also let Honor bring "*Artemis*" squarely back in front of her for each drone changeover. It probably wasn't necessary—by now, the Peeps must have it firmly fixed in their brains that they were chasing *two* ships—but there was no point being clumsy.

Especially now. *Artemis* had cut her drive, but she was still plunging ahead at the .39 *c* velocity she'd attained first, and her *side* vector was almost directly towards *Wayfarer* at well over thirty thousand KPS. The Peeps had passed her position less than ten minutes previously, and if they realized what had happened and decelerated for a search pattern, they might just find her after all. The odds were against it, but it was possible, and Honor would not permit that to happen. Not when she'd already decided to sacrifice her own ship to save Captain Fuchien's.

She made herself face that, accept that she'd deliberately sentenced her own crew to death *knowing* they couldn't defeat their enemy. The Peep CO astern of her had to know she'd killed his consort with missiles. He wouldn't want to get in any closer than he had to, so he'd turn to open his broadside at maximum range and fire his own birds in to see how she responded. And when she didn't return a matching fire, he'd stay right there and pound *Wayfarer* to death without ever closing into the reach of her energy weapons.

She was going to die. She knew it, but if she could cripple the enemy too badly to catch *Artemis* even if they detected her, the sacrifice would be worth it. She accepted that, as well . . . but behind her calm face her heart bled at condemning so many others to die with her. People like Nimitz and Samantha. Like Rafe Cardones, Ginger Lewis, and James MacGuiness, who had flatly refused to evacuate the ship. Aubrey Wanderman, Carol Wolcott, Horace Harkness, Lewis Hallowell . . . *All* those people—people she'd come to know and treasure as individuals, many as friends—were going to die right beside her. She could no more save them than she could save herself, and guilt pressed down upon her. Those others would die because she'd ordered them to, because it was her duty to take them all to death with her and it was their duty to follow her. But unlike them, *she* would die knowing it was her orders which had killed them.

Yet there was no other way. She'd gotten another eight hundred people off *Wayfarer*, reducing the death toll to just over a thousand. One thousand men and women—and two treecats—who would die to save four thousand others. By any measure, that had to be a worthwhile bargain, but, oh, how it *hurt*.

She hid her pain behind serene eyes, feeling her bridge officers about her, knowing how they would focus on her—take their lead and their inspiration and their determination from her—when it began, and pride in them and grief *for* them warred in her soul.

Margaret Fuchien, Harold Sukowski, and Stacey Hauptman stood and watched Annabelle Ward's plot with haunted eyes. The battlecruiser had burned past them twelve minutes ago, never even noticing the liner or its protecting LACs. And why should it have? They were only seven inert pieces of alloy, radiating no energy and lost in h-space's immensity as *Wayfarer* deliberately sucked their enemy after her.

"Seventy-five minutes," Ward murmured.

"Will they still be in sensor range, Captain Harry?" Stacey asked softly.

"We should still have their impellers, but it won't be very clear." Sukowski closed his eyes for a moment, then shook his head. "In a way, I'm just as glad. I don't *want* to see it. It's going to—" He met Stacey's gaze squarely. "It's going to be ugly, Stace. Her ship's already badly damaged, and if the bastards just stand off and pound her—" He shook his head again.

"Will she surrender?" Fuchien asked out of the silence, and Sukowski looked at her. "When they open fire on her, will she surrender?"

"No," Sukowski said simply.

"Why not?" Stacey demanded, her voice suddenly sharp. "Why *not*? She's already saved us—why won't she surrender and save her *own* people?"

"Because she's still protecting us," Sukowski told her as gently as he could. "When they get close enough to engage her, they'll also be close enough to spot the drone. They'll know *we* aren't there, but they'll also know within an hour or two when we must have shut down our drive—and our vector when we did. That means they'll have a good idea of where we *could* be if they come back and look for us. The odds are against their finding us, but Lady Harrington intends to make certain they don't. She'll hammer them as long as she has a weapon left, Stace, to cripple their sensors and slow them down." He saw the tears in Stacey's eyes and put his arm about her as he had about Chris Hurlman. "It's her job, Stace," he said softly. "Her duty. And that woman knows about duty. I spent enough time aboard her ship to know that."

"I envy you that, Harry," Margaret Fuchien said softly.

"Missile range in twenty-one minutes," Jennifer Hughes announced. "Assuming constant accelerations, we'll enter energy range thirteen-point-five minutes after that."

Honor nodded once more and keyed her com.

"DCC, Lewis," the woman on her screen said, and Honor smiled crookedly.

"I don't want to joggle Commander Tschu's elbow, but I'd like to confirm his latest estimate on the cargo doors."

"Current estimate is—" Ginger glanced at the chrono and did some mental math "—thirty-nine minutes, Ma'am."

"Thank you," Honor said quietly, and killed the circuit. So there it was. The pods would come back on-line just as the Peeps closed to energy range anyway. But there was nothing Honor could do about that. All she could do was continue to run as long as possible, drawing the Peeps after her, buying *Artemis* time, and she prepared to play the game out to its final, hopeless throw.

"We'll go with Alpha-One," she said. "Rafe, tell all hands—seal helmets in ten minutes."

A curiously shrunken Klaus Hauptman stepped onto *Artemis'* bridge. The people clustered around the plot looked up at him, and his face clenched as he saw Sukowski's arm around Stacey. *He* should have been the one to comfort his daughter. But he'd forfeited that right, he thought drearily, when he proved himself so much less than she'd always thought he was in her eyes.

And in his own.

He crossed to the plot, making his gaze meet theirs. It was almost an act of penance, an ordeal deliberately inflicted upon himself and embraced. Fuchien and

Sukowski nodded to him, their expressions neutral, but neither spoke, and Stacey never even looked at him.

"How soon?" he asked, and his normally powerful, confident voice was frayed and rough.

"Sixteen minutes to missile range, Sir," Annabelle Ward replied.

"All right, Steve," Abraham Jurgens told his flagship captain. "I don't want to get in close until we're sure their teeth have been pulled."

"Aye, Citizen Commodore." Citizen Captain Stephen Holtz looked at his repeater plot and frowned. The Q-ship was putting out some damned effective decoys. Her EW was starting to play games with his sensors, too, and hyper's natural sensor degradation made her efforts even more effective than usual, but he was five thousand kilometers inside the powered missile envelope.

Under normal conditions, he would have turned to open his broadside, but these weren't normal conditions. He had his own EW systems fully on-line, and the same conditions which hurt his fire control had to be hurting the Q-ship's, as well. Under the circumstances, it actually made sense to keep the vulnerable throat of his wedge towards the enemy, for it gave the Manty a weaker, fuzzier target than his sidewalls and the full length of his wedge would have.

Of course, it also restricted him only to the three tubes of his bow chasers, but that was all right. He wanted to sting the bastard, goad him. If he could get the Q-ship to fire off any pods it might have at extreme range, his point defense would be far more effective . . . and the Manty's target would be far harder to hit.

"Missile separation!" Jennifer Hughes announced. "I have two—no, three inbound. Time of flight one-seven-zero seconds. Stand by point defense."

"Standing by," Lieutenant Jansen replied.

"Spread Decoys Four and Five a little wider, Carol,"

Hughes said. "Let's see if we can pull these birds off high."

"Aye, aye, Ma'am." Wolcott made an adjustment on her panel, and Honor reached up to check Nimitz. Like her, the 'cat had his helmet sealed, and he'd secured the safety straps mounted on her chair to the snap rings on his suit. It wasn't as good as a shock frame, but no one made treecat-sized shock frames.

"Impact in niner-zero seconds," Jansen announced, and pressed the key that sent his countermissiles out to meet the incoming fire.

"They've killed the birds, Skipper," Holtz's tac officer reported as the third missile tore apart. None of them had even gotten as deep as the Q-ship's inner boundary laser defenses, Holtz noted in disgust. Well, it wasn't all that surprising, and at least their damned pod-launched missiles hadn't come back to kill his ship.

"Any sign at all of missile pods?"

"None, Citizen Captain. No return fire at all." Holtz knew Citizen Commander Pacelot was irritated with him for asking the obvious whenever she called him "Citizen Captain" instead of "Skipper." He grimaced, but he couldn't really blame her. He considered a moment longer, then nodded.

"All right. Let's go to sequenced fire, Helen."

"Aye, Skipper," she said, much more cheerfully, and punched the new commands into her console.

Honor's eyes narrowed as the Peeps' firing patterns changed. The battlecruiser was using her three bow-mounted tubes to fire the equivalent of a double broadside. It doubled the interval between incoming salvos and gave point defense longer to track, but it also increased the threat sources and allowed the battlecruiser to seed her fire with jammers and other penetration aids. Honor understood the logic behind that; what she didn't understand was why the Peeps were restricting themselves solely to their chasers. They had twenty tubes in each

broadside and far higher acceleration. They could sla-
lom back and forth across *Wayfarer's* wake, hammering
her with salvos from each broadside in turn, and send
in six times as many missiles in each wave.

She frowned, then dropped her suit com into Cardones'
private channel.

"Why do you think he's sticking to his chasers?" she
asked, and Cardones rubbed the top of his helmet.

"He's probing," he said. "This reduces the target he's
offering to *us*, and he's trying to get a feel for what we
can shoot back at him with."

"Which is nothing at all," Honor observed quietly, and
Cardones gave her a lopsided grin.

"Hey, you can't have everything, Skipper."

"True," she said with an affectionate smile. "But I think
it might be a little more than that." Cardones raised his
eyebrows, and she shrugged. "More than just probing.
He had us on gravitics when we killed his consort, but
he was too far out to see how we did it. He's probably
deduced we had to have used missile pods, and he may
be trying to goad us into firing off any we have left at
extreme range."

"Makes sense," Cardones agreed after a moment, even
as Lieutenant Jansen's point defense dealt with the last
missile of the most recent salvo. "Of course, he's going
to be figuring out pretty soon that we don't *have* any pods,
or we *would* be shooting back."

Missiles continued to bore in on *Wayfarer*, racing up
from astern in groups of six. Carolyn Wolcott's decoys
and jammers played merry hell with their onboard seekers
once they went into final acquisition, and Jansen's
countermissiles and laser clusters picked them off with
methodical precision. But the laws of chance are inexo-
rable. Sooner or later, one of those missiles was bound
to ignore the decoys, burn through the jammers, and
evade the active defenses.

Honor's earbug buzzed, and she looked down to see
Ginger Lewis' face on her small com screen.

"Message from Commander Tschu, Ma'am! He did it! He's got power to the port door and its opening! *It's opening, Ma'am!*"

Honor's heart leapt. They could only launch two pods at a time, even if the port door functioned perfectly, but that might be enough. With the enemy still coming up astern, running directly into their fire when he hadn't seen even a single shot coming back at him, they might—

That was when a missile finally slithered past the countermissiles and slipped like a dagger through the desperate lattice of the last-ditch laser clusters. The single missile shrieked in to twenty-four thousand kilometers before it detonated, directly astern of *Wayfarer*, and sent five centimeter-wide X-ray lasers ripping straight up the wide open after aspect of her impeller wedge.

Wayfarer's megaton bulk bucked as energy seared through her unarmored plating with contemptuous ease. Beta Node Eight of her after impeller ring took a direct hit, and Nodes Five, Six, Seven, and Nine blew in a frenzy of energy which took Alpha Five with them. Generators exploded in Impeller Two, killing nineteen men and women and sending mad surges of power crashing across the compartment like caged lightning bolts. Point Defense Nineteen, Twenty, and Twenty-Two were blasted away, along with Radar Six, Missile Sixteen, and all the men and women who'd manned those stations.

But none of those were the cruelest thing that missile did.

A single laser slashed through Cargo One's port door. It blew the motors which had just begun to whine, blasted two complete missile pods into deadly, man-killing splinters, and smashed the control runs Honor's engineers had fought so desperately to repair. And along the way, it killed seventy-one people, including Lieutenant Joseph Silvetti, Lieutenant Adele Klontz . . . and Lieutenant Commander Harold Tschu.

Honor *felt* Tschu's death. Felt it crash in on Samantha like a thunderbolt, felt it blast through her to her mate

and from Nimitz into Honor herself. Rafael Cardones'
head whipped around as his suit com carried him her
animal sound of pain even over the wail of alarms, and
he went white as he saw the loss and agony, the terrible,
wrenching desolation, in her eyes. He didn't know what
had happened; he only knew the woman upon whom
every individual in *Wayfarer* relied had just taken a blow
as shattering as her ship's, and he started to his feet in
terror for her.

But Honor clenched her teeth and fought the agony
down. She had to. Every strand of her being cried out
to yield to it, to keen her grief as Samantha and Nimitz
did, to reach out to her beloved friends in their moment
of terrible loss. But she was a starship captain. She was
a Queen's officer, and the bone-deep responsibility of
thirty-two years in uniform and twenty years of command
had her by the throat. She could not afford to be human, and so she was not, and her voice was inhumanly
calm even as agony burned in her eyes.

"Bring her bow up, Chief O'Halley. Straight up—stand
her on her toes!"

"Aye, Ma'am!" Senior Chief Coxswain O'Halley
snapped, and *Wayfarer* drove straight upwards, rear-
ing like a wounded horse to snatch her stern away from
the enemy.

"We got a piece of her, Skipper!" Pacelot exulted.
"Drive power just dropped significantly, and look at her
run!"

"I see it, Helen." Holtz punched a query into his own
plot, checking the spectrography, and gnawed the inside
of his lower lip. They'd obviously gotten a good, solid hit
on the Q-ship, but the atmosphere loss was low. He didn't
know Cargo One had been depressurized; all he knew
was that despite the Manty's antics, she was spilling far
too little air.

His brain raced as he tried to guess why that was. The
Manty's new course had robbed *Achmed* of a good missile target, but it also stole her forward acceleration from

her. She was building delta vee perpendicular to *Achmed's* base course, but she was starting from scratch, which would let Holtz close on her rapidly if he chose to. But—

He thought a moment longer, then looked at the com screen tied to Jurgens' flag bridge.

"We're getting very little atmospheric loss from her, Citizen Commodore, and she hasn't fired a single shot at us, much less flushed any pods. I think—" He drew a deep breath, then committed himself. "I think she's not firing because she *can't*. I can't conceive of any captain who *could* shoot back not doing it. She may not be trailing more air because *Kerebin* already got a much bigger piece of her than we thought and depressurized a lot of her spaces."

Jurgens grunted, and his eyes narrowed. Holtz could be right. His theory fit the observed data, at any rate. And if he *was* right, they might be able to forget this long-range pussyfooting and get down to it. But if she was that badly hurt, then why—?

"Skipper!" It was Helen Pacelot, her voice sharpened by discovery and chagrin. *"That isn't Target One in front of her!"*

"What?" Holtz whipped back around to her, and she shook her head savagely.

"I just got a good read on it. It's a drone—a goddamned *drone!"*

Jurgens heard Pacelot's report, and his eyes met People's Commissioner Aston's in sudden understanding. *Oh, those bastards,* he thought. *Those poor, gutsy, damned* bastards!

"It's a decoy," he whispered. "They *deliberately* sucked us away from the liner because they *knew* they couldn't stop us . . . and because we were the only ship with a chance to catch it!"

"Agreed," Aston said flatly. "But what do we do about it?"

Jurgens rubbed his chin, brain racing, then shrugged.

"I only see one option, Sir," he said flatly. "From their maneuvers and Tactical's observations, we can only assume

Kerebin hurt them far worse than we'd estimated. That makes sense; if they can't fight us, all they could do was run to draw us off the liner. But every minute we spend chasing them is another minute we're not decelerating to go after Target One."

He punched rapid commands into his own display, projecting the Q-ship's track—and *Achmed*'s—across it. Another command produced a shaded cone that crossed *Achmed*'s track port to starboard almost ten light-minutes back and stretched far out to its left, as well.

"The liner's got to be in that area. Our chance of finding it is slight if they're careful, but the sooner we start looking, the better the odds. Only we've got to finish the Q-ship, too; if she gets away, the covert side of the operation is blown just as wide as if we let the liner get away."

"Agreed," Aston said again.

"I think we have to assume the Manty *is* hurt worse than we believed. We have to go in, close with her, finish her off, and then come back after the liner."

Aston gazed at the citizen commodore's plot for perhaps ten seconds, then nodded.

"Go get her, Citizen Commodore," he said.

Ginger Lewis' soul cringed as the tidal wave of damage reports spilled across DCC's displays. Half-hysterical shouts from the remnants of the Cargo One work party had already told her what had happened to three-quarters of Engineering's officers. Only Lieutenant Hansen, in Fusion One, and two ensigns were left. That dropped total responsibility for DCC squarely onto Ginger's shoulders, and she swallowed hard.

"All right, people," she said flatly to her shocked personnel. "Wilson, get on the link to Impeller Two. I need casualties and damage. Do what you can to assist through your telemetry." Wilson nodded curtly, and she turned to another petty officer. "Durkey, you're on SAR. Tie into sickbay and try to steer their rescue and medical parties around the worst wreckage. Hammond, you've got Radar

Six. It looks like it's the array, but it may just be the data feed. Find out which it is, soonest. If it's the array, see if you can reconfigure Radar Four to cover some of the gap. Eisley, check Mag Four. I'm reading pressure loss in the compartment; that hit on Missile One-Six may have damaged the feed queue to Missile One-Four, too. If it has, reroute through—"

She went on snapping commands, reacting with the trained instinct for which Harold Tschu had picked her for this post, and her orders came with an unerring precision which would have filled the dead chief engineer with pride.

"He's coming in, Skipper!" Jennifer Hughes cried in astonishment. "He's gone back to max accel, and he's boring in like a bandit!"

Honor shook herself, still shuddering with the echoes of Tschu's death, and looked at the plot. Jennifer was right. The Peep couldn't know he'd just gutted *Wayfarer*'s most potent weapon system, yet he'd obviously decided she was badly hurt, and he was coming in to finish her off. But from his profile, he was coming in to kill her with *energy* weapons.

It didn't make sense. He'd hammered her for almost forty minutes without drawing a single missile in reply. He *had* to know he could hang on her stern and keep on battering without any realistic risk to his own command, so why—?

The drone! He'd IDed the drone, and he wanted to finish *Wayfarer* before *Artemis* slipped totally away from him. It was the only thing which made sense, and it would have made sense to Honor in his place. But just as she would have been wrong, *he* was wrong.

"All right," she said, and her soprano voice was a cold wind, smothering the sparks of panic that single devastating hit had ignited. "He's coming in, and we're going to get hurt—but he doesn't *begin* to guess what kind of energy armament we've got. Jenny, it looks like we're going to have a chance for Fire Plan Hawkwing after all."

"Aye, Skipper," Jennifer Hughes said, and her own fear had vanished in a hungry snarl of anticipation. She knew *Wayfarer* wasn't going to "get hurt"; the Q-ship would never survive a pointblank energy engagement with a *Sultan*-class battlecruiser. The Peep had sixteen energy mounts—eighteen, counting the flank chasers—and twenty missile tubes in each broadside, while *Wayfarer* had only eight grasers and nine tubes left in her *stronger* broadside. But the converted freighter mounted *superdreadnought* weapons, and the Peep didn't know it.

"He's coming in to cross our stern if we maintain heading," Honor went on, speaking now as much to Cardones and Senior Chief O'Halley as to Hughes. "Rafe, tie the helm into your station; I want you on backup if we lose primary control. We *will* maintain heading until he's committed, then I want a hard skew-turn to starboard. As hard as you can make it, Chief. I want our starboard broadside on him as he passes below us, and then I want to cut down across his stern and stick it right up his kilt. Clear?"

Cardones and O'Halley nodded, and Honor looked back at Hughes.

"Lock it in, Jenny," she said quietly. "We only get one pass."

"She's maintaining profile," Pacelot said, and Holtz nodded. It was another sign of the Q-ship's desperate straits; if she'd had anything left in either broadside, she would have rolled to present that broadside to the bow of *Achmed*'s wedge as Holtz came in on her. No doubt her captain was hoping to continue up and over in a loop, holding the roof of his wedge towards *Achmed* as the battlecruiser passed below him, and he might even manage to pull it off. It was unlikely, given the mass differential, but even if the Q-ship managed to evade the first pass, the sort of twisting, dodging dogfight which would follow could only favor the more maneuverable battlecruiser. Sooner or later—and probably sooner—*Achmed* would find the single opening she needed to reduce a merchant hull to scrap.

"We'll go in as planned, Helen," he said grimly, and his eyes burned with the need to avenge *Kerebin*.

"Here they come," Honor said in a soft, almost soothing voice. She watched the range speed downward, watched the battlecruiser begin the roll to bring her own starboard broadside to bear. Then she looked up at Chief O'Halley and Rafe Cardones, and she knew the final maneuver of her career was going to be perfect . . . even if there would be no one left to remember it.

On either side.

"All right," she crooned. "Steady . . . Steeeady . . . *Now!*"

Achmed came roaring in just as Kendrick O'Halley hauled back on his joystick and slammed it to the right. *Wayfarer* heaved like a maddened beast, as if the ship herself was fighting to escape her destruction. But she answered the helm, heeling over, rolling, pointing her starboard side at her foe even as *Achmed*'s weapons came to bear upon her.

For a frozen sliver of eternity, both ships had clear shots at the other, and in that instant, the firing plans locked into two different computers activated.

No human sense could have coped with what happened next; no human brain could have sorted it out. The range was barely twelve thousand kilometers, and missiles and lasers and grasers sleeted destruction across that tiny chasm of vacuum like enraged demons.

Achmed staggered as the first massive graser blew effortlessly through her sidewall. Her flanks carried over a meter of armor, the toughest alloy of ceramic and composites man had yet learned to forge, and the graser tore through it with contemptuous ease. Huge splinters blew out of the dreadful wound, and her relative motion turned what should have been a single puncture into a huge, gaping slash. It opened her side like a gutting knife opening a shark, and air and wreckage and human beings erupted in a howling cyclone.

But that was only one of *eight* such grasers. Every one of them scored direct hits, and no one on the battlecruiser had dreamed a converted merchantman could mount such weapons. Her communication circuits were a cacophony of screams—of agony, of shock, of terror— as *Wayfarer*'s fury rent her like a toy, and then the Q-ship's missiles came blasting in, stabbing her again and again with bomb-pumped lasers to complete the grasers' dreadful work. Weapon bays blew apart, power surges ran mad, control runs sizzled and popped and exploded. Her forward impeller room blew up as a graser stabbed straight into its generators, and the blast tore a hundred meters of armored hull into shredded wreckage. All three fusion plants went into automatic shutdown, and blast doors slammed throughout the ship. But in all too many instances, there was nothing for those blast doors to seal air *into*, for *Wayfarer*'s grasers had blown clear through her hull and out the other side, and she spun away, a dying, helpless hulk.

Yet she did not die alone.

Wayfarer had fired a fraction of a second before *Achmed*—but only a faction of a second, and unlike *Achmed*, she had no armor, no tightly compartmentalized spaces. She was a merchant ship, a thin skin around a vast, cargo-carrying void, and no refit could change that. The weapons which survived to tear into her hull were far lighter than the ones which had disemboweled *Achmed*, but they were hideously effective against so vulnerable a target.

Her entire starboard side was shattered from Frame Thirty-One aft to Frame Six-Fifty. The empty LAC bays blew open like so many glasses shattering under an enraged heel. Magazines Two and Four were torn apart, along with every tube except Missile Two. Six of her eight graser mounts exploded in ruin, taking virtually their entire crews with them. A laser slashed deep into the heart of her hull, destroying Fusion One and stabbing through the brig, where Randy Steilman and his fellows would never come to trial, and another blew straight into the command deck itself. Shock and concussion whipsawed the bridge madly, bulkheads and hull members tore like tissue, and a raging hurricane plucked Jennifer Hughes from her bridge chair despite her shock frame and whipped her into space. No one would ever find her body, but it scarcely mattered, for the tidal bore of atmosphere slammed her against the edge of the hull breach and shattered her helmet instantly. John Kanehama screamed over his com as a flying alloy spear impaled him; Senior Chief O'Halley was cut in half by a splinter as long as he was tall; and Aubrey Wanderman retched into his helmet as the same splinter slashed through his own control party and tore Carolyn Wolcott and Lieutenant Jansen apart.

That pocket of hell was repeated again and again, throughout *Wayfarer*'s vast hull. Bits and pieces of the ship exploded into the people *Achmed*'s fire had missed, as if the dying ship were wreaking vengeance on the crew who had brought her to this, and HMS *Wayfarer* went tumbling away, her drive dead, her hyper generator destroyed, and with eight hundred dead and dying people in her shattered compartments.

• CHAPTER FORTY-ONE

Honor fought her way out of her buckled shock frame and whirled. Nimitz's safety straps had snapped, and he floated limply away from her in the sudden zero-gravity. But he was alive; she knew he was, and she gasped in relief as a shaky Andrew LaFollet snagged the unconscious 'cat and dragged him close. She took him from her armsman and used one of the broken straps to lash him to the shoulder grab ring on her own suit, then turned to her ship and her crew.

Or what was left of them.

Two-thirds of her bridge crew were dead, and others were wounded. She saw Aubrey Wanderman and Rafe Cardones bent over a Tracking yeoman, hands flashing as they slapped emergency seals onto her skinsuit, and her eyes flinched away from the mangled ruin which had once been Carolyn Wolcott and Kendrick O'Halley and Eddy Howard's drifting corpse. Then she was throwing aside pieces of wreckage herself, dragging bodies out and searching desperately for signs of life.

She found all too few of them, and even as she fought to save *someone* and her heart raged at the universe, she knew the same scene was being repeated all over her ship.

DCC survived, but all the central links were down, and its computers were on backup power. Ginger Lewis dragged herself up off the deck and flung herself back into her chair, and somehow her mind still worked. The internal com net was gone, but her gloved fingers flashed over her keyboard. She called up the watch bill which identified the men and women at each duty station by name and keyed her suit com.

"Lieutenant Hansen," she said, reading the first name off her display, "this is DCC. Report status on Fusion One." There was no answer, and she inhaled sharply. "Any person in Fusion One, this is DCC. Report status!"

Still there was no answer, and she dropped to the next name. "Ensign Weir, this is DCC. Report status on Fusion Two."

An endless moment dragged out, and then a hoarse voice replied.

"DCC, this is PO Harris, Fusion Two. We—" The petty officer coughed, but his voice was stronger when he resumed. "The plant's on-line. Ms. Weir's dead, and we've got four or five more casualties, but we're still on-line."

"DCC copies," Ginger said, and waved urgently at Chief Wilson. She hit a key, throwing a segment of her list onto his display, and he nodded. Ginger took one moment to paint Fusion Two as operable on her schematic—the single green compartment looked pathetically tiny on the board—and went to her next priority.

"Commander Ryder, this is DCC. Report status on sickbay and wounded."

Scotty Tremaine groaned and shook his head. He wished instantly that he hadn't, but his brain cleared slowly. He wondered for a moment what he was doing on the deck with half his Flight Ops console blasted over him, then looked up into Horace Harkness' worried face.

"You with me now, Sir?" he asked, and Scotty nodded. "What's our situation?"

"Dunno yet, but it ain't good." Harkness pried the last wreckage off his lieutenant's ankles and lifted him effortlessly. "No grav," he pointed out. "Means Engineering took a heavy hit, and the com links're down."

"What about us?" Scotty asked hoarsely.

"Mr. Bailes and Chief Ross are still with us; I haven't heard from anyone else," Harkness said grimly, and Scotty winced. There'd been twenty-one people left in his skeletal Flight Ops. "Both birds look intact," Harkness went on, "and we've got a clear bay. We can get 'em out, Sir . . . if we've got somewhere to send 'em."

"I—" Scotty broke off as another voice sounded over his suit com.

"Lieutenant Tremaine, this is Chief Wilson, DCC. Report status on Flight Ops," it said.

Angela Ryder looked up as another rescue party staggered into sickbay. She and her sole remaining assistant had just amputated Susan Hibson's right leg and had no time to spare from their desperate, losing fight to save Sergeant Major Hallowell's life, but Yoshiro Tatsumi was there in an instant, bending over the writhing, skinsuited woman the party carried.

It was a miracle sickbay had retained pressure. The surgeons were working on backup power only, and Ryder refused to let herself think about what happened when that power ran out. Anyone she saved would only die later. She knew that, but she was a physician. Her enemy wore no uniform, and she would fight him to the last ditch.

"Well, whatever they did to us, we must've hit them just as hard," Cardones said wearily, and Honor nodded. They'd done what they could for their wounded, and she and Rafe had tried every sensor in an effort to find the Peep battlecruiser. None of the systems they'd tried still worked, but Rafe was right. If the Peeps weren't at least as badly hurt as *Wayfarer*, they would already have finished her off.

Not that she needed much "finishing."

Honor shook herself, then reached up as Nimitz stirred on her shoulder. The 'cat twisted, and she felt his pain and confusion. But she also felt him reaching out to her—and to Samantha. She sensed his terrible surge of relief as he realized both of them were still alive, and he clung more firmly to the grab ring as he poured that relief into her.

But for now, she had to determine the condition of her shattered command, and how—?

"Captain Harrington, this is Lewis in DCC," a voice said over her suit com. "Captain Harrington, please reply."

"Lewis?" Honor shook herself. "Captain here, DCC. Go."

"Aye, Ma'am." The relief in Ginger's voice was as vast as Nimitz's, and she paused just a moment before she continued. "Ma'am, I've been contacting each station by suit com," she said, and her tone was flat now. "So far, less than twenty percent have responded. What we know so far is that Fusion One's gone, but Fusion Two is still on-line. Environmental's a total write-off. Main Hyper took a direct hit, and we've lost the generator. Both Warshawski sails are down, and Impeller One and Impeller Two are both badly damaged. We may be able to get a few beta nodes back in each ring, if we can find anyone for repair parties, but not the sails. Artificial gravity's also out—the Bosun's trying to get down there for a look. I won't know if we can get it back until I hear from her, but it doesn't look good. As nearly as I can tell, all sensors are out. We've got one operational graser in the port broadside, and a single tube to starboard, but no sidewalls, no radiation fields, and no particle shielding. The hull's a mess. Without a survey, I'm not sure we've got enough frame integrity left to stand up to the drive even if we can get the impellers back. Sickbay still has pressure and backup power, and I've got some people trying to restore main power to it. Flight Ops is totaled, but both pinnaces are intact, and we've got a pilot for both of them—one'll need a replacement flight engineer, though."

The voice on Honor's com paused, hesitated, and then resumed quietly. "The head count from the people reporting in is under a hundred and fifty, Ma'am. I think that's pessimistic, but it's the only hard number I have now." Ginger cleared her throat. "That's my report so far, Captain. Sorry it's not complete, but we're working on it."

Honor's eyes were wide with astonishment. It was incredible. A senior chief—and one who'd been jumped from a mere second-class tech less than six months before—had somehow managed to pull together all that information entirely on her own initiative. Anguish for the death toll Ginger had reported twisted deep within her, but it only confirmed what she'd already guessed, and she couldn't let it paralyze her.

"Don't apologize, Ginger," she said, unable to see the other's flush of pleasure as she used her first name. "I can hardly believe you've already managed so much. Stay with it, and keep Commander Cardones informed in parallel with me. First priority is getting sickbay's power restored and making sure nothing happens to its atmospheric integrity."

"Aye, aye, Ma'am. We're on it."

Honor turned to Cardones, and the exec shook his head grimly, then leaned forward until their helmets touched.

"We've had it, Skipper," he said quietly, letting the contact of their helmets carry his voice to keep it off the com. "With no generator *and* no sails, we're dead, even assuming we could get enough life support back to take us anywhere."

"Agreed." Honor spoke softly, her face wrung with pain. "On the other hand, we may as well keep our people busy." He nodded, and she went on. "See what you can do to organize a repair party from up here. Try to get into the central lift trunks. They don't have power, but they're the only way we're going to be able to get people into contact with one another. Check for compartments that are still pressure-tight, then I want you and MacBride to take over on the rescue parties. I want everyone who's still alive found. It may not matter in the long run, but I won't have any of my people trapped alone and dying in some compartment somewhere."

"Yes, Ma'am." Cardones nodded again and pulled their helmets apart, and Honor switched com channels to one she hadn't yet had the courage to try.

"Mac?" she said hesitantly, and some of the anguish leached out of her face as a voice replied.

"I'm here, Ma'am. I'm afraid your quarters are a mess, but I've checked the life-support module. Samantha seems to be all right, but I can't be sure. She's curled up on the floor and won't look up when I tap the view port."

"Harry Tschu's dead, Mac," she said softly. "All we can do for now is leave her in peace, but I want you to stay with her. I want her to know *someone's* there."

"Understood, Ma'am," he said quietly.

"I'll get back to you," Honor promised, then changed channels once more, this time to the all-hands frequency, and her voice was strong and calm when she spoke again. "All right, people, this is the Captain," she told the shattered remnants of her crew. "We're in bad shape, but we're still here. Work your way towards Deck Zero-Zero. We'll assemble there and work back out on SAR and damage survey. Anyone wounded or trapped in a compartment, report by com to Senior Chief Lewis in DCC or to Search and Rescue. Don't worry. We'll get you out. Captain, clear."

She switched her transmitter off and looked around her command deck once more, wondering what she could do once she did get them all out.

But nothing came to her.

"That's it, Skipper." Annabelle Ward's voice was hushed. "I don't know what happened, but both impeller signatures went off the plot almost simultaneously."

"We didn't just lose the range?"

"No, Ma'am. They just . . . vanished."

Fuchien looked at Sukowski. It was possible one or both of the other ships had survived, but both had clearly lost their drives, and that was a bad sign.

"Skipper, we don't have anything at all on sensors," her exec pointed out in the low voice, of a man who hated what he heard himself saying, and Fuchien nodded. Lady Harrington's orders had been clear, and she and *Wayfarer* had bought *Artemis* the chance to escape. But

Artemis was also the only ship which knew what had happened to *Wayfarer* and the Peep battlecruiser—or, at least, *where* it had happened.

"We can't leave," someone said, and Fuchien turned in shock, for it was Klaus Hauptman. Her employer faced her, his face gaunt and his eyes haunted, but there was something behind the shame in them now. He shook his head, then looked at the other officers on her bridge— and at his daughter—and went on in a quiet, almost humble tone none of them had ever heard.

"I . . . haven't handled this well. If I hadn't held *Artemis* in New Berlin for the freighters, we would've crossed the rift up in the epsilon bands, and the Peeps never would have seen us. As for the way I spoke to Lady Harrington—"

He paused and shook his head again, and his voice was a bit stronger when he resumed.

"But that's beside the point now. We know where *Wayfarer* went off the plot, and we know what her vector was. If there's anyone left alive aboard her—or aboard the Peep, I suppose—we're the only people who can help them."

"I can't possibly justify taking *Artemis* over there," Fuchien said flatly. "First, the Peep may have survived, and her damage may be repairable. We could sail right into her broadside, and I cannot risk all the people aboard this ship. Secondly, it would take hours for us to make the flight, whatever happened, and every minute we spend under power increases the chances *another* Peep will come along and spot us."

"I realize that, but we can't simply *abandon* them."

"We don't have a choice, Sir!" Fuchien's voice was harsh, and her eyes flickered with anger. Anger directed irrationally at Hauptman for making her say what she knew was true. "And, Sir, you may be this ship's owner, but *I* am her captain."

"*Please*, Captain." More than one eye widened in disbelief at the pleading in Hauptman's voice. "There has to be *something* we can do!"

Fuchien started to snap back, then closed her mouth and settled for a grim headshake. Hauptman's shoulders slumped, and the stricken look in his eyes hit Harold Sukowski like a hammer. *He* has *to do something,* the captain thought. *He's hard, arrogant—a copper-plated son-of-a-bitch, but he understands responsibility, and Lady Harrington rubbed his nose in it. And so—* Sukowski glanced at Stacey Hauptman *—did making a fool of himself in front of his daughter. But Maggie's right. We can't risk the ship, however much we* all *wish we—*

His thoughts chopped off, and he frowned. He heard Fuchien and Hauptman continuing to speak, but they sounded distant and far away as his brain worked at frantic speed.

"I'm sorry, Sir," Fuchien said at last, her voice much gentler than it had been. "I truly am. But there's nothing we can do."

"Maybe there *is,*" Sukowski murmured, and every person on the bridge swung to stare at him. "We can't take *Artemis* out on SAR, no," he went on, "but there may be another way."

"I've got a visual on the Peep, Skipper," Scotty Tremaine said.

He and Harkness had taken a pinnace out for an inspection of the hull, and one look had told them there was no hope. *Wayfarer* was broken and buckled, her impeller rings shattered. That meant none of them would survive, and Honor had sent Tremaine and Harkness to search for the Peep. Perhaps her damages were less serious than *Wayfarer's.* If they were, and if the survivors of both crews worked together, perhaps they could get *her* to a port . . . and at the moment, even a Peep POW camp would be heaven.

Now Honor listened over her suit com as Scotty described *Achmed's* damages, and her heart sank. She was in one of the enlisted mess compartments which had somehow retained pressure, with her helmet off, and aside from a few small parties MacBride still had probing wreckage where someone might be trapped alive, all of her surviving personnel were either here, in sickbay, in DCC, or down in Fusion Two.

There were few enough of them that no one felt crowded, she told herself grimly, and waited until Scotty finished his report.

"All right," she said then. "She's not going anywhere with that bow damage, and we're drifting steadily apart. See if you can contact anyone on board. It sounds like they're in even worse shape than we are. If so, offer to take them off and bring them aboard *Wayfarer*. Tell them"—she smiled bleakly—"we can figure out later who's whose prisoner."

"Aye, Ma'am," Tremaine replied, and sent his pinnace moving closer to *Achmed*.

"Is that wise, Skipper?" Cardones asked too quietly for anyone else to here. "We're on canned life support, and Environmental looks bad."

"There can't be many left, Rafe," she replied, equally quietly, "and for all we know, they don't have *any* life support over there. We, on the other hand, may be able to get some of ours back. Our only hope is that we can and that one of their consorts has some idea where we both are and comes looking for us, but they may not have even that much hope. We have to give them the best chance we can. It's the only decent thing to do."

Cardones nodded slowly, then moved off to his own duties, and Honor looked back up and beckoned to the petty officer she'd been speaking to when Tremaine's report came in.

"All right, Haverty," she said briskly. "Once you've got that leak in Seven-Seventeen patched, I want pressure back in there. Commander Ryder needs to move people out of sickbay to relieve crowding, and that's the best place to put them. So as soon as we've got pressure, inform Senior Chief Lewis so we can organize a working party to move them. Once you're through in Seven-Seventeen,

I want you and your people to do an eyeball on Main Environmental. Then—"

She went on speaking, passing her orders in the confident tones of a captain, and wondered how much longer she could keep the pretense up.

Stephen Holtz followed the Manty lieutenant into the mess compartment, and his face was numb, still frozen with the shock of loss. His casualties were far worse than the Q-ship's, in both absolute and relative terms. There'd been twenty-two hundred men and women on his ship; the forty-six survivors had all been able to fit into the single pinnace which had come to pick them up.

The Manty pilot—Lieutenant Tremaine—had invited him to take the copilot's seat aboard the shuttle, and he'd watched the Q-ship's mangled hull grow through the view port. He'd found a bitter satisfaction in knowing he'd destroyed it just as certainly as it had destroyed his beautiful *Achmed*, yet he'd known it was foolish. These people were his enemies, but the only reason *any* of his people were still alive was because those enemies had taken them off the airless, powerless hulk which had once been a battlecruiser. And they, as he, had simply been doing their duty.

Duty, he thought bitterly. *Oh, yes. We did our* duty, *didn't we? And look where it's brought us all.*

A tall woman in a captain's skinsuit turned to face him, almond eyes dark with matching grief, and he nodded to her. Somehow the formality of a salute would have been out of place.

"Stephen Holtz, PNS *Achmed*," he said in a rusty-sounding voice.

"Honor Harrington, HMS *Wayfarer*—or what's left of her," she replied, and Holtz felt his eyes widen. So this was Honor Harrington. Just as dangerous as the intelligence reports suggested . . . and as good. *Well, I suppose I've managed* one *thing no one else seemed able to do. She won't be pounding any more of our ships into wreckage.*

"I'm sorry your losses were so high," Harrington said. "As you can see, my own—" She shrugged, and Holtz nodded. There was no point in either of them hating the other. "We may be in a little better position than I'd thought," she went on more briskly. "It looks like we can get at least some backup Environmental on line. It'll be canned life support, but one of our main scrubber plants is still intact, and we've got one operable fusion plant. If we can duct to the scrubber, we'll have enough life support for four hundred or so. Which," she added with quiet bitterness, "will be more than enough." She inhaled deeply, then went on. "Unfortunately, we've only got six or seven environmental techs left, and all our engineering officers were casualties, so it's going to take a while."

"My assistant engineer's still alive," Holtz offered. "He may be able to help."

"Thank you," Harrington said simply, then looked him straight in the eye. "Our vector's carrying us lengthwise down the Rift, Captain, but we're angling towards the Silesian side. My best guess is that we've got about nine days before we drift into the Sachsen Wave and break up. That, of course, assumes the Selker Shear doesn't get us first. As I see it, our only real chance is to use the pinnaces to mount a sensor watch and hope one of your people comes looking for you so we can get a com message to them. If they get here in time," she drew a deep breath, "I will surrender myself and my people to you. For now, however, what's left of this ship is still a Queen's ship, and I am in command."

"Should we consider ourselves *your* prisoners in the meantime?" Holtz asked with a ghost of a smile. Both of them knew the chance of rescue was effectively nonexistent, yet both of them continued to play their roles, and the thought amused him.

"I'd prefer for you to think of yourselves as our *guests*," Harrington said with a small, answering smile, and he nodded.

"I can live with that," he said, and offered her his

hand. She shook it firmly, and the skinsuited, six-limbed creature on her shoulder nodded gravely to him. Holtz amazed himself by nodding back, then waved at his small party of survivors. "And now, perhaps Citizen Commander Wicklow should get with your environmental techs, Captain," he said quietly.

"We've got the backups on-line down in Environmental, Ma'am," an exhausted Ginger Lewis reported from DCC three hours later. "Commander Wicklow's been a big help, and I think he's found a way to beat the temperature loss when we put in the ducting to the scrubber."

"Good, Ginger. Good. And my quarters?"

"We can't get pressure in there, Ma'am—there's just too much bulkhead damage. But the Bosun thinks she's found a way to get the module out."

"She has?" Honor was relieved to hear it. Samantha's module was intact, but the bulkhead niche in which it was mounted had deformed badly, locking it in place. Samantha couldn't survive outside it, yet there'd seemed to be no way to get it out of Honor's day cabin.

"Yes, Ma'am." Sally MacBride's voice came onto the circuit. "There's a serviceway behind the bulkhead. I can put in a crew with a torch and cut the entire bulkhead out, then take the module out through the serviceway. It'll be tight, but we can do it."

"Thank you, Sally," Honor sighed. "Thank you very much. Can we spare anyone for it?"

"Yes, Ma'am. After all," Honor heard the bosun's weary smile, "she's the only crewman still trapped. I've got your Candless with me; he and I can handle it ourselves."

"Thank you," Honor said again. "And thank Jamie for me, please."

"I will, Ma'am," MacBride assured her, and Honor looked up as Rafe Cardones paused beside her again.

"I think we've got the immediate situation under control, Skipper."

"Good. In that case, let's start getting the people fed." Honor waved at the tables, where volunteers had managed to assemble huge plates of sandwiches out of the mess compartment's galley supplies. "We're going to have enough trouble from fatigue without adding mistakes induced by hunger and low blood sugar."

"Agreed. And it should help morale some, too. God knows *I* could eat a kodiak max!"

"Me, too," Honor said with a smile. "And once—"

"Skipper! *Skipper!*"

Honor jerked, jumping half out of her skin as the urgent voice blurted from her skinsuit com. It was Scotty Tremaine, mounting sensor watch in his pinnace with Horace Harkness, and she'd never heard such urgency in his voice.

"Yes, Scotty?"

"Skipper, I've got the most beautiful sight in the goddamned universe out here!" Scotty half-shouted, swearing in her hearing for the first time in her memory. "It's *gorgeous*, Skipper"

"*What's* 'gorgeous'?" she demanded.

"Here, Skipper! Let me relay to you," he said instead of answering directly. Honor looked at Cardones in bafflement, and then another voice came over her suit com.

"*Wayfarer*, this is Harold Sukowski, approaching from your zero-two-five, three-one-niner," it said. "I am aboard LAC *Andrew* with your Lieutenant Hunter, with *John*, *Paul*, *Thomas*, and three shuttles in company. *James* and *Thaddæus* are keeping an eye on *Artemis*, but we thought you might like a ride home."

• CHAPTER FORTY-TWO

Citizen Commander Warner Caslet and his officers followed the Manticoran Marine down the hall. A familiar man in a green uniform gave them a quick once over, then knocked on the frame of the opened door at the corridor's end.

"Citizen Commander Caslet and his officers, My Lady," Simon Mattingly said, and a clear soprano replied from the room beyond.

"Send them in, please," it said, and Mattingly smiled and waved the Republican officers on. Somewhat to Caslet's surprise, the Marine peeled off at the door, and Mattingly closed it quietly behind them, leaving them alone with Honor Harrington and Andrew LaFollet.

Well, not *quite* alone. Two treecats sat on the back of her chair, the smaller, dapple-coated female pressed tight against the back of her neck while her mate hovered protectively. Caslet knew what had happened to Samantha's person, and he saw her loss in her body language, but he also sensed the loving support flowing to her from Nimitz and *his* person.

"Please, be seated," Honor invited, waving to the chairs before her desk. The half-dozen Peeps sat at her gesture, and MacGuiness appeared to pour each of them a glass of wine.

Honor leaned back to gaze at them, and Samantha slipped down from the chair back to huddle in her lap. Honor gathered the 'cat in her arms, hugging her as she would have hugged Nimitz, and felt Nimitz channeling her own support to Samantha. But even as she held the grieving treecat, her mind was flickering back over the last month's hectic events.

She hadn't been able to believe it when Sukowski turned up. For all the brave front she'd projected, she'd known—not thought; *known*—they were all going to die. Changing her mind had been hard, even with the proof right in front of her, and then her elated relief had been replaced by a deep, terrible anger that Sukowski and Fuchien and her own detached LAC skippers could have run such an insane risk after *Wayfarer* had paid such a terrible price to buy *Artemis'* escape.

She'd known at the time that her fury was born of her own whipsawed emotions, but the knowledge hadn't been enough to keep her from *feeling* it, and the haste with which Sukowski and Lieutenant Commander Hunter had begun explaining that they weren't *really* running a risk would have been hilarious had she been even one or two centimeters closer to rational.

And, in fact, they *had* been careful. *Artemis* had dropped the LACs and her shuttles and then translated very cautiously down to the alpha bands without using her impellers at all—possible for such a slow translation, though only the best ship handler and engineer could have pulled it off—and hidden in the lower bands while Sukowski led the search mission towards *Wayfarer's* last known position. The LACs' sensors were inferior to those of a battlecruiser, but their impeller signatures were far weaker, as well; they would have seen any Peep long before the Peep could detect them in return, and all of them had been prepared to shut their own wedges down instantly.

It was Sukowski who'd plotted their search pattern, and he'd done a good job. But they would probably have missed *Wayfarer's* inert hulk if Scotty Tremaine and Horace Harkness hadn't picked them up on passive and guided them in, and Honor still woke shivering when she considered the odds against their success. Yet they'd done it. Somehow, they'd done it, and the four LACs and three long-range shuttles had lifted

every surviving crewman—Manticoran and Peep alike—
off *Wayfarer*.

The chance that anyone would stumble across her
before she blundered into a grav wave and broke up was
less than minute, but Honor had made sure no one would.
She'd set the nuclear demolition charge herself, with a
twelve-hour delay, before she went aboard *Andrew* with
Sukowski and Hunter.

Space had been tight enough she'd ordered all bag-
gage abandoned, but MacGuiness and her surviving
armsmen had somehow smuggled the Harrington Sword
and Key, her .45, and the golden plaque commemorat-
ing her record-setting sailplane flight at the Academy
aboard *Andrew*. She'd picked up her holocube of Paul
personally, but that was all she had left of everything she'd
taken aboard—that, and her life, and Nimitz . . . and
Samantha.

The return flight to *Artemis* had been nerve-racking
for everyone. Linking back up with something as small
as a flight of LACs and shuttles after twice translating
through two distinct sets of hyper bands was the sort of
navigational feat legends were made of, but Margaret
Fuchien had pulled it off. *Artemis* had risen slowly back
into the delta bands, like a submarine surfacing from deep
water, and she'd hit within less than two hundred thousand kilometers of Fuchien's estimated position. After
that, it had been a straightforward if anxious proposition
to drop back down into normal-space and spend ten days
making repairs before creeping stealthily back up to the
gamma bands and heading back for New Berlin. There'd
been plenty to do, and Honor had thrown herself into
assisting Fuchien in every way she could. *Artemis'* captain had been grateful, but Honor had known the real
reason for her own industry. Miraculous as Sukowski's rescue had been, exhausting activity had been her only
refuge from her dead.

It had been the afternoon of the fourteenth day when
Klaus Hauptman had asked quietly to be admitted to the
cabin Fuchien had assigned Honor. Five of her twelve

armsmen had died with the rest of her crew, but Jamie
Candless had been her sentry when Hauptman arrived.
Honor could still hear the cool contempt in Jamie's voice
as he announced her visitor, and she'd seen the matching contempt in Andrew LaFollet's eyes as the magnate
walked through the hatch. But neither armsman had been
prepared for the reason behind his visit.

"Lady Harrington," he'd said, "I've come to apologize."
The words had come low and slow, but his tone had been
firm, and Honor had felt his sincerity through Nimitz.

"Apologize, Mr. Hauptman?" she'd replied in the most
neutral voice she could manage.

"Yes." He'd cleared his throat, then looked her squarely
in the eye. "I don't like you, Milady. That makes me feel
smaller than I'd like to feel, but whether I like you or
not, I know I've treated you . . . badly. I won't go into
all of it. I'll only say that I deeply regret it, and that it
stops here. I owe you my life. More importantly, I owe
you my *daughter's* life, and I believe in keeping my
accounts squared, for better or worse—maybe that's part
of what makes me such a son-of-a-bitch from time to
time. But the debt I owe you is one that *can't* be repaid,
and I know it. I can only say thank you and apologize
for the way I've spoken to you—and of you—over the
years. I was wrong in Basilisk, too, and I want you to know
I realize that, as well."

She'd looked back at him levelly, feeling his strain and
recognizing how monumentally difficult it had been for
him to say what he just had. She didn't like *him*, either,
and she doubted she ever would, but in that moment,
she'd come far closer to respecting him than she'd ever
believed she might, and she'd nodded slowly.

"I won't disagree with you, Sir," she'd said quietly, and
if his eyes had flared, he'd taken it without protest. "As
far as debts are concerned, my crew and I were simply
doing our duty, and no repayment is necessary. But I will
accept your apology, Mr. Hauptman."

"Thank you," he replied, then surprised her with a
small, wry smile. "And whether you see it that way or

not, *I* know I still owe you more than I can ever hope to repay. If I or my cartel can ever serve you in any way, Lady Harrington, we're at your service."

She'd simply nodded, and his smile had grown.

"And now, My Lady, I have one request, which is that you and your treecat—or 'cats," he'd added, looking at Samantha "—will join me for dinner tonight."

"Dinner?" She'd started to refuse politely, but he'd raised one hand almost pleadingly.

"Please, Milady," he'd said, a proud and arrogant man asking a favor he knew he had no right to. "I would truly appreciate it. It's . . . important to me."

"May I ask why, Sir?"

"Because if you *don't* dine with me, my daughter will never believe I actually apologized to you," he'd admitted. "And if she doesn't, she may never speak to me again."

He'd gazed at her with a raw appeal too strong to refuse, and she'd nodded.

"Very well, Mr. Hauptman. We'll be there," she'd said, and, to her surprise, she'd actually enjoyed the meal. She and Stacey Hauptman had turned out to have a great deal in common, which had amazed her . . . and made her suspect there must be more to the man who could raise such a daughter than she'd ever believed Klaus Hauptman could have inside.

Now she shook herself, brushing aside the memories, and looked at the prisoners of war she'd invited to the room Herzog Rabenstrange had assigned her at the IAN's main fleet base on Potsdam. The Andermani had not been pleased to learn the Peeps were operating raiders in their vicinity, and they were making their displeasure known through diplomatic channels. The decision to offer Honor's crew—and prisoners—the IAN's hospitality until the RMN could retrieve them was another way to make the same point, and it hadn't been lost on the Havenite ambassador when he tried—unsuccessfully—to demand those prisoners be released to him.

"Thank you for coming," she told those same prisoners now.

"You're welcome, of course," Caslet replied with a wry smile. "Equally of course, we would have found it somewhat difficult to decline the invitation."

"True." Honor smiled, then shrugged. "Herzog Rabenstrange is waiting to join us all for dinner. He'd like to meet you all, but the reason I asked you to stop here first was to tell you something Citizen Captain Holtz has already been informed of. At my recommendation, and with the approval of the Andermani and our ambassador to the Empire, you and all survivors from *Achmed* will be released to *your* ambassador in three days. We're attaching no conditions to your release."

Caslet's smile froze, and she felt his alarm—and his fellows'. She paused a moment, knowing she shouldn't but unable to resist the temptation, then cleared her throat and continued calmly.

"Despite Citizen Commander Foraker's efforts to wheedle technical information out of my people," she said, watching Foraker blush under her level gaze, "none of you have observed anything which isn't already or won't very soon become available to your Navy through other sources. For example, you're aware our Q-ships mount heavy energy weapons and are able to deploy powerful salvos of missile pods, but by now other sources within the Confederacy have undoubtedly already sold that information to one of your many spies there. Accordingly, we can return you to the Republic without jeopardizing our own security, and given your services to Captain Sukowski and Commander Hurlman, not to mention Captain Holtz's people's efforts aboard *Wayfarer*, it would be churlish not to release you."

And, she thought, *letting you go home to tell your admiralty that our "mere" Q-ships destroyed two of your heavy cruisers and a pair of* battlecruisers—*not to mention Warnecke's entire base—for the loss of only one of our ships may just cause it to rethink the value of commerce raiding in general.*

"Thank you." Caslet couldn't quite keep the flatness out of his voice as he visualized what StateSec would do to him for losing his ship trying to save a Manticoran-flag vessel, and she smiled at him.

"You're quite welcome, Citizen Commander," she said gravely. "I do have one small favor to ask of you before you depart, however."

"Favor?"

"Yes. You see, I'll be returning to Manticore for reassignment shortly, and I've been trying to tidy up my paperwork. Unfortunately, we lost many of our records when *Wayfarer* was destroyed, and I'm having some trouble reconstructing my after-action reports." Caslet blinked at her, wondering where she could possibly be headed, and she frowned. "In particular," she went on evenly, "I can't seem to remember the name of the Andermani ship whose transponder code I was using when you came to our assistance in Schiller."

For just a moment, it totally failed to register, and then Caslet stiffened. *She knows*, he thought. *She* knows *about our orders to assist Andy merchantmen! But how can she possibly—?*

He shook that question off. It didn't matter. What mattered was that she *did* know . . . and that the men and women in this quiet room were the only people who'd been on *Vaubon*'s bridge. They were the only ones who knew they'd deliberately gone to the assistance of a Manty vessel, and every one of them knew what would happen if their superiors found out they had.

Caslet looked around, seeing the same confusion and dawning comprehension in all of their faces. He looked at Allison MacMurtree, who nodded with a crooked grin, and then at Denis Jourdain. The people's commissioner sat very still, face expressionless, while seconds trickled past, and then his shoulders gave a small twitch and his lips curved in the shadow of a smile.

"Ah, I believe it was the Andermani ship *Sternenlicht*, My Lady," he said, addressing her with a nonmilitary title for the first time ever, and Honor smiled back at him.

"I *thought* that was it," she murmured. "Thank you. I'll see to it that my report—and those of my other officers—reflect that information."

"I'm happy to have been of service, My Lady." Jourdain's voice said far more than his words, and he and Honor nodded to one another as their eyes met. Then she rose, with Nimitz on her shoulder and Samantha in her arms, and Andrew LaFollet fell in on her heels as she led the Peep officers towards the door.

"I'll miss you all," she said with a small, wicked chuckle, "but I'm sure you'll be glad to get home. For now, however, Admiral Rabenstrange—and Citizen Captain Holtz and Citizen Commander Wicklow, of course—are waiting for us."